The Bellamy Blues

Tony Beatty

This novel is dedicated to everyone who has ever been in love
To God, family and friends

Thank you

Table of Contents

PRELUDE

"I should say, I was looking forward to this for some time now."
Jack clinked his glass against Jennifer's, a soft ring piercing through the cool ambience of the restaurant. A grandeur interior, embellished with refined brick walls, ivory cresting, sophisticated dining spreads, raised seating, and seemingly endless reverberation of harmonious strings echoing throughout; not to mention the abundance of indistinct conversations invitingly steeped in sensualism. It was the perfect location for a first date. Just what he needed to prove his worth, paying no mind to the superficiality of his efforts.
He examined his fellow males in the restaurant as he sipped his drink, observing their tense demeanor as they stumbled through conversations with their respective dates. Jack knew he was not the only uneasy one here tonight. After all, it is probable to assume most single guys share a like objective on Valentine's Day.
A valentine, conceptually, could be a bit overwhelming for a first timer to understand. As it should, considering it is a celebration of continuous love between partners. Partners, some of whom come together by taking a shot in the dark, hopeful it may gradually shroud itself from any ray of doubt. The partners should not be formidable, but fetching; not equivocating, but engaging. Their connection should be binding and challenging to break. It is a shame, however that humanity dedicates an entire day to love, basing its significance on a twisted definition of what it truly is: underneath the flash and admiration, is simply a thick cloud of delusion and infatuation. Guess it makes sense when they say how love is blind. And in this case, Jack was no different.
"It's so beautiful in here," Jennifer trilled, aweing at the diamond chandeliers. "What did you say this place was called?"
"*Crepuscolo,*" Jack pronounced, "It's Italian, I believe the English translation meaning, 'twilight.'"
"So you're cute *and* smart. That's good to know."
Jack returned a smirk, proud of how rehearsed his response was. Truth is, it was. This was not his first time there, let alone with a girl he brought to woo. It was his signature approach to seducing women, and at this rate, it would not be a surprise if he had the entire menu memorized.
The waiter breezed past, placing menus on the table before stopping at another table nearby. Jennifer's eyes widened upon reading the triple digit prices.

"The food here is…*really* expensive."

"Yes it is. Good thing I've been saving up."

Jennifer rested her hand on Jack's and tried to meet his eyes. "We can always go somewhere else if it is too—"

"Not at all! "I've never been here and always wanted to try it. Trust me, it won't be a problem."

A petty lie. But warranted, given his biggest secret.

Jack was rich – okay, it could not hurt to rephrase that: Jack was born, raised, and currently profits off of his tremendously wealthy parents. They used money as a buffer from dredging up insecurities that made up their reality shortly into their relationship, including a collective recklessness that resulted in his mother's surprise when her frequent cramps and vomiting were not, in fact, from food poisoning. Denial can be a powerful influence, as it had evidently passed on to Jack, who from a young age, had since convinced himself that the only way to thrive in this reality was through escaping it at all costs. Who said it was wrong to belie one's identity out of love? Granted, honestly was the best policy, but for Jack, the only way to ensure the purity of his partner's motive was through fabricating who he was. No matter how much time he spent brooding over his choices afterwards, it never hindered the justification that it was for the best.

"I bet I could serve tables for a straight week and still not be able to afford a bottle of champagne here." Jennifer said.

"Well, it depends on the kind of champagne."

"You think so?" she giggled, sipping from her glass when her eyes lit up.

"Hey, you still never told me what you do."

"Right," Jack choked. "I work for my dad. He uh, is a manager for a small business out in Bellevue."

"That's cool! What's the business?"

Jack's forehead warmed up when the waiter returned.

"Have you both decided what to order?" he pulled out a notepad. "Were either of you interested in our specials tonight?"

"Actually yes," Jack replied, gracious for the interruption. "The sirloin sounds perfect, don't care the temperature. A small plate of calamari with butter would also be sublime." he tilted his head up to the waiter. "The smoked salmon – is it any good? I haven't seen it on the menu before so I'm assuming it's new. I'd like to sample that, please."

The waiter nodded and focused on Jennifer. "And you, ma'am?"

She smiled hesitantly. "I'll just have the fettucine."

The waiter nodded again and retrieved the menus before pacing away.

Jennifer waited until he was out of earshot before she spoke.

"You haven't seen the smoked salmon on the menu *before*?"

Jack lifted his head, oblivious to his mistake. "Sorry?"

"When you ordered," Jennifer repeated. "You said that you haven't seen the smoked salmon on the menu before. Isn't this your first time eating here?"

Jack, catching his mistake, pretended to laugh. He studied her eyes and saw that they were filled with confusion rather than frustration. At this moment, anyway.

"That's my bad," he added, shifting in his chair. "I am mistaken with another place not far from here."

"Oh," Jennifer paused. "Do you come to eat in this neighborhood a lot?"

"Yeah, but there are a lot of places that are much more affordable. You know how every town has that one restaurant no one goes to because it's way too expensive."

"I guess, but this is also Mercer. You have to be like a millionaire to live here."

Jack chuckled at her comment and returned to his menu, immediately relieved to be done with the brief, but tense moment.

The waiter returned with a bottle of red wine and two glasses. He began to pour when Jack raised his hand.

"Excuse me, we didn't order this."

The waiter grinned. "Yes sir. This is a gift from the gentleman behind you."

Flummoxed, Jack followed the waiter's gaze, where sure enough, four tables down, he locked eyes with an older gentleman and a woman. He raised his glass to Jack, to which Jack reciprocated.

The bottle was half-empty when the waiter finished pouring for Jennifer and placed it at the table's center.

"Who are they?" Jennifer asked Jack once the waiter left.

"I'm not sure Jen," he admitted. It was true that he did not know who these people were, but not that he could take an accurate guess. He looked back at Jennifer and watched as she sipped her wine. He smiled at her, still thinking about the couple behind him, wondering if they were still looking, wondering if they were talking about him, wondering if and when they would visit their table and pay tribute.

Jennifer's voice penetrated through his cloud of thought. He had not the slightest clue how long he was in his head.

"Do you think we should go over?" Jennifer asked him.

Before Jack could respond, he felt a hand on his right shoulder. He turned to see the older gentleman, peering down at him.

"Jack Douglas, is it?" he bellowed. "I am Steven Dumphreys. I must say, you look exactly like your father Wayne!"

"Yes. Yes right, my dad," Jack stammered.

Steven laughed and motioned to the woman beside him. "This is my wife, Natalia. I tell her all about how much I love working at the D-Group. Everyone there is so brilliant, that I feel out of place myself. Is that right, sweetheart?"

Natalia nodded. "Absolutely. Funny enough, my firm recently collaborated with them on a joint account with a potential distributor overseas. Your father and his team were incredible. He managed to close the deal a week before the deadline with an offer thirty percent higher than our original estimates!"

Jack's voice dwindled to a mumble. "Yeah…my dad is pretty stellar."

Steven focused on Jennifer. "And who is this doll with you tonight?"

"This is Jennifer Parlor. We're uh, on a date."

"A date at the *Crepuscolo*," Steven chuckled. "Wayne must have given you his card for tonight, huh?"

Jack gave a nervous smile.

Steven looked at his wife. "Well, it seems we should get back to our table. Don't want anyone thinking we dine and dashed!" he went in to shake Jack's hand. "It was nice to finally meet you, son."

The couple left, and Jennifer maintained a hard glare at Jack.

"The D-Group?"

"I'm sorry?"

"What is the D-Group?"

"…Douglas Group," Jack murmured. "My dad works there."

"Wait, Douglas Group as in *the Douglas Group*?"

Jack sighed. "Look, I —"

"Can you please just answer my question?"

Jack lowered his eyes. This was it. It always started off fairly smooth, then got sort of bumpy – and bam, bang, bash – before he knew it, the girl catches along, gets upset, and leaves.

"Yes Jen, Wayne is my dad." Jack clarified.

"I don't understand…why did you lie to me?"

"Listen, can we just –"

"No!" Jennifer snapped and reached for her bag. "This is ridiculous." She rose from her chair and turned away.

"Jen, I just thought that if I didn't tell you who I was that you would like me more. I'm sorry."

Jennifer faced him. "So you think that it was okay keeping this a secret for the last two weeks? Honestly, this is more my fault than it is yours. I should have seen the signs."

"Signs?"

"For God's sake, Jack," she insisted, gesturing to his outfit. "You're wearing a Burberry!"

Jack glanced down at his perky white long-sleeve. "It's just a polo," he paused. "Sorry, I guess I see how this may look."

Jennifer rolled her eyes. "You're lucky I am not the kind of girl to make a scene," she said. "I'll see you around, Jack." And with that, she was gone.

Jack did not call for her. Instead, he slouched in his seat, staring at the pair of merlot before him. He had grown adept at concealing his feelings. His current emotion, specifically, was all too familiar. Not joy, no, but maybe the opposite, if one could find the term for it. The low tones from the string bass seemed fitting enough to complement.

He noticed his waiter slowly approaching the table.

"Sir," he began. "I'm sorry for the wait, we have been very busy this evening. Your food will be out in a few minutes."

"There's no need. Thank you for tonight," Jack said as he reached for his wallet, pulling out three crisp hundreds and setting them down on the table. He stood up, remembering to grab his coat draped behind the chair.

"Sir, the money," the waiter stuttered. "The cost –"

"Thank you." Jack repeated and continued out of the restaurant. Did not even make it to seeing his meal. A personal record.

The air was fragrant in heavy mist, progressing swiftly to a light pour, its droplets generously moistening the already dampened soil Jack trudged through. He paid no mind with his jacket still in hand, maintaining a moderate stroll to his car.

For most people, this would be the pit of their day: an embarrassing engagement shortly following what was intended to be an elegant evening at the most expensive restaurant in town. In Jennifer's defense, no one likes being lied to, and storming out in frustration is more than an appropriate reaction.

But Jack is not like most people. He is a son of one of the wealthiest families in the state, perhaps in the entire northwest, perhaps in the country. Assuming the economy improves over the next few centuries, he, his kids, nor their kids...and maybe not even their kids, will have to work a single day in their lives. He can achieve virtually everything he sets his mind to, all through the casual signage of a check. Money does not buy happiness – most would tend to agree with that statement. Ironically, those same people will realistically never come close to obtaining enough wealth to verify if the famous adage is true or false.

Not Jack though. Jack was already there and had been his entire life. If someone asked whether money brought him happiness, he would say – well, it does not matter what he would say.

Happiness is interpretive. There is no true definition, and any attempt to try would be foolish. True intelligence does not come from formulating an opinion, but the *right* opinion. What is right or wrong, is based strictly on the eyes of the beholder.

Jack found himself contemplating in his car, taking a deep breath before driving off. He took his time, as he was in no rush. Regardless of the pace, he knew he would eventually end up in the same place. He rolled down his window and reached his hand out, feeling the rain roll down his fingers as he quietly recited the lyrics to his favorite song, Midnight Rider.

*****

Sleep was never Jack's friend. They got along and had some great nights together over the years. Perhaps *frenemy* is the better term to describe their relationship: nothing more than a single thread being pulled on opposite ends by forces of same strength. Occasionally, one side may naturally have the upper hand and grow stronger, but they almost always fall static. As long as the string is intact, so is the relationship – burned, but never incinerated; strained, but never broken. If the string would ever snap, however, the relationship is lost, and if put back together, would be too impaired to return to its original perfection.

Sleep was a tad disgruntled with Jack that night, as he laid in his bed, gazing at the moon's rays seeping through the blinds. He forced his eyes shut but was distracted from the muted traffic sirens and sequences of remote voices beyond the thin drywall. He peeked outside his bedroom, where across the hall he could visualize the silhouette that was his best friend, in his bed resting. Snoring, actually.

I should call Jen, Jack thought. *I should call her again and apologize.*

He reached for his phone on the nightstand beside him and searched for her contact but hesitated when he saw her name. How would calling her make the situation any better? What was he to say? Perhaps it would make things better…

"Don't," mumbled a voice. "It's not worth it."

Jack jumped at the motionless silhouette at the doorway. "Jesus Christ, Tommy, you scared me."

Only his shaggy head was visible, underneath a wool blanket he was tightly wrapped in.

"I don't know why you do this."

"I haven't the slightest idea what you are talking about. I'm just on my phone."

"You know you are going to call her again. What's her name? Linda?"

"Jennifer," Jack corrected. "You really thought her name was Linda?"

Tommy went back to his room momentarily and returned with a small can of pills. He struggled to open it due to his blanket restricting his ability to move normally.

"You want another? I'm getting a refill tomorrow afternoon so we may as well waste them now."

"I don't know," Jack sighed. "I think the pills make me feel worse."

"Trust me, a lot of people have trouble getting a lick of sleep," Tommy picked two tablets out and resealed the bottle. "This shit isn't supposed to cure you, but it does the trick for the short term. Rich people always take this stuff, so in a sense we're practically programmed for it."

Tommy handed Jack a tablet, prompting them both to exchange a cheesy smile before dosing down.

"Thanks Tom. And I'm sorry for waking you," Jack patted his friend's shoulder. "I guess I'm just waiting for something. I don't know what exactly, though."

"Like, a change of scene?" Tommy suggested, making his way back to bed.

"Maybe. I've been in the same mood…kind of like a funk, but I just cannot seem to get out of it. Every time –"

"Stop, you know I'm always here for you and love these 'talks' but it's four in the morning and I don't have time for this right now, okay?" Tommy interjected. "I'm more tired than a hooker after a three-hour gangbang."

"Totally unnecessary man," Jack shook his head in disgust.

"Noted." Tommy mumbled, not long before his snores were once again audible.

Jack laid back down, breathing deeply as he faced back at the ceiling.

It was almost comforting, feeling the pill take effect. He embraced the feeling, trying to recount the last time he could reach it on his own, without any help from a substance. He remained still as he felt his own low hum transcend through his body, imagining himself being closed off from the rest of the world, lonely in his thoughts. He did not need anyone to soothe the despair. His misery was his, and his alone. If he was unable to change, then no one else could. He admittedly loved the feeling. Solitude. Isolation. It never bothered him. It was when he was most fearful, but most fearless; when he was most vulnerable, but most confident; when he was most alone, but most content.

And amid the growing silence, Jack smiled, awaiting Sleep to reaccompany him.

Welcome to the Bellamy Blues.

Part I: Merge

i

Jack knew something was off that morning. He never pegged himself for being highly intuitive, and Mondays tend to have a poor reputation for being the worst day for *everyone*. He never thought of himself to be overly superstitious, but if one walks under enough ladders, sees enough black cats, or has an umbrella open indoors for *too long,* it may not be a coincidence. It was a gut feeling…which also happened play a literal role in Jack's mystery, groaning at the sensation of his stomach tightening. Audibly loud. In class. During an exam.

Several pairs of eyes fell on him, including Dr. Hagen's peering up from his book to detect the source of the commotion.

"Everything all right, Douglas?" he asked.

"I'm sorry…just not feeling the best."

"If that is the case, please excuse yourself," Dr. Hagen insisted rather condescendingly.

Jack thanked him, snatching his bag and stepping out of his chair to approach the front, placing his paper on his professor's desk. He minded the snickers from the students on his way out, many of whom lacked any pity due to their presumption that it was expected of people like him. Not that Jack cared, as his reputation was already one to spur unwanted controversy amongst his peers. He did not have much regard for his eventual glowing test score, because it was also expected. As was his transparently apparent guaranteed success in everything that he sets his mind to. That said, it had little to do with his intelligence, and more to do with his paycheck.

Jack pulled his hood on as he raced out of the building. Per his habitual routine, he took note of the picturesque campus: modern edifices walled with contemporary illustrations stretched before him, tree-lined with lush shrubbery, projecting its significant vibrance from the sun beaming directly overhead. It was around midday, usually the time that the campus blossomed from its bleak surroundings. He kept his eyes glued to the footpath, passing through frantic exchanges from other students that gradually surged into boisterous enthusiasm. University District is usually lively, but such connotation would be taken to a higher degree on this particular day; reasonably not the most ideal scenario for Jack, who momentarily imagining himself crumbling onto the pavement from the intensified burn resonating in his stomach. Despite the mild, temperate climate, he was totally parched, clinging to the little saliva that was left in his throat with the risk of regurgitating his last meal for the public to relish.

He stopped walking to catch his breath, when he was distracted by a familiar face.

"Jack, I thought that was you."

"Hi Amanda," he grinned while awkwardly wiping the sweat off his forehead. "It's only allergies, don't worry. Not serious enough to cancel our date tonight."

"Is that so?" she replied condescendingly. "It's funny you mentioned our date."

"How so?"

"Next time you think about fucking someone, how about first taking the time to know more about the person, okay?"

"Wow," Jack stammered, taken aback by her bluntness. "I'm completely lost here."

"Your date last night with Jen?"

"How did you know about that?"

"Like I said, you should have taken more time to get to know me," she reiterated, rolling her eyes. "She's my best friend. What, you don't think we tell each other everything?"

Jack gave her the blankest of stares.

"So now you're just going to sit there like a little bitch and not say anything?"

"I had no idea," he finally muttered.

"She also told me something that I found to be very interesting," she folded her arms. "Apparently you *lied* about who you were? Giving her a fake last name...what's the matter with you?"

"I get how that sounds—"

"Do you?" she snapped back. "Because to me, it sounds like you're a sociopath trying to take advantage of my friend."

"Okay, while I think your way of thinking is, dare I say 'crazy,' I can assure you that I am not a sociopath, nor was I trying to take advantage of Jen," he sighed. "If you could please give me the chance to explain why I lied?"

"Right," she sighed tartly. "I don't think that will be necessary."

She marched off, not even reaching her tenth step before turning back to Jack.

"And as for our date—"

"Yeah, yeah," Jack cut in dismissively. "Not happening, I get it."
Amanda grunted and continued off, angrier now for not getting in the final word.

Three blocks later, Jack arrived at his apartment and went straight to the bathroom. He kneeled before the toilet, bringing two fingers to his mouth and letting his throat do the rest. Taking drugs is never a good decision, especially if that decision was backed by Tommy. Damn that kid.

He was head deep in the bowl when, coincidentally, overheard a mild clatter from nearby.

"How're ya feeling?" Tommy smirked, sitting beside Jack on the hardwood and sliding his water bottle to him. "You don't seem to be at your usual one hundred percent."

Jack graciously accepted the water and pulled a swig. "When have I ever been one hundred percent?"

"Sense the tone! I was being sarcastic. What's wrong with you?"

"In addition to being verbally attacked and dumped by who would have been my date tonight," he cited. "My stomach is also on fire…your pills are blatantly ineffective."

"'Blatantly ineffective,'" Tommy echoed. "You're starting to sound like me. That's hilarious."

Hilarious. The word spurs a sliver of amusement even for those that are unable to comprehend the 'hilarity' of the situation itself. And for Tommy Beech, it is not only said but overused to a point where it may lose its suggestive intent. Not that the situational jokes are not funny, but its contextual usage exudes blandness. Sort of like a world-class chef ranting about the fantastical taste of his own food.

But Jack treasured his friendship with Tommy. They have been in each other's lives for as long as he could remember; a shockingly strong bond despite their considerable differences. Jack was more justified, preferring routine and security over Tommy's progressive desire to seek all things new. Both valued their respective freedom, but with Tommy, it was to an arguable fault, subsequently leading to his increased skepticism and resistance to compromise. He was a true nonconformist, always drumming offbeat, and it was demonstrated through his actions and philosophies. Inherency was his enemy, as his ambitions were governed from a larger scale: one that did not delve into the interpersonal visions of those he surrounded himself with, but on the undiscovered nature of the visions themselves. His intense conviction was enough to turn his peers on – or off – and for Jack, it was subliminally exhilarating, as it presented a fundamentally new channel of understanding a greater reality.

Platonically, Tommy was also Jack's emotional counterpart. Their dynamic was rare, where inexplicable self-revolutions deepened into a sounder awareness and understanding of themselves, and ultimately, each other. Jack was indeed grounded, but Tommy was his rock. Tommy was free, but Jack the door to reaching freedom's infiniteness. Such elements are difficult to prevail on their own, and it was at a younger age that the two acknowledged the strengths each brought to the table, as well as how to capitalize on them. Their dynamic also influences their differing perceptions of a relationship. While Jack understood the need for romanticism, Tommy found little value, especially if it was at the expense of another's feelings. He had always been unprecedented, unattached, unpredictable. Yet, he respected Jack's insight, seeing the emotion complement his practical outlook. An optimist and a pessimist. Patient and impatient. Unnaturally open, and naturally locked in. Opposites are said to attract, after all.

Jack arched back and pushed himself away from the toilet.

"Feeling better?" Tommy probed.

"How do you do it?"

"Do what?"

"Go crazy with all these drugs and still function normally? I mean, you know I smoke, but I know that it's not the best thing to do *all* the time."

"Hey now, don't refer to them as 'drugs.' It implies that I'm an addict, which I refuse to accept. It's all about moderation. Overindulgence is the key to self-ruin."

Jack rolled his eyes as he lightly sipped the water. "Whatever you say man."

Tommy went on. "Are you hungry? The boys should just be getting done with their last class of the day. I said that we would meet up with them for lunch."

"I don't think I can eat right now," Jack fretted, noticing a change in Tommy's expression. "What is it?"

"Actually, it's probably best that you get something in your system," Tommy jumped to his feet and pulled Jack up. "Go change, you smell awful."

"Gee, thanks."

"I'll meet you downstairs in ten. I got to hit the ATM for drinks tonight."

"How do you know that we're going out tonight?" Jacked called, following Tommy out to see him already halfway out the door.

He returned a menacing grin, announcing, "It's Friday baby!" and shut the door behind him.

Jack continued into his bedroom, sliding open his closet to observe his massive collection of designer apparel. He had an eye for fashion and expressed it liberally. He preferred a style's simplicity and had no regard for the price tag. That said, he still struggled to find the perfect outfit according to the occasion, and the weekend typically prompted an urge to dress more presentable, compared to stringing in comfort just to make it to class.

Much of the university's buildings were evidently aged due to the administration's willingness to maintain historical preservation, however the HUB posed a special story. The nucleus of interaction on campus, it was a contemporary setting to study, play, and dine.

Despite his frequent visits, Jack never managed to not be astonished, admiring the decorative, colorful canvasses showcased amidst lavender and cream plasters across the walls. Tall, arched ceilings stretched throughout the center, contrasted with earthy tones and dangling matte light fixtures. Just nearby were an array of rooms serving various purposes, clean-lined with modern amenities, cozy furniture, and fun for all to enjoy. There was always something going at the expense of at least one of the multitude of clubs and organizations that called the university home, some of Jack's most interesting encounters including an extravagant silent auction prepared by the arts faculty, a lively debate club showdown, profound poetry slams, independent film showings, political demonstrations, and musical concerts. Indeed, there was never a moment not being roused at the HUB.

For Jack and company, it was the ideal spot for recurrent overspending on already pricey foods to match their unnaturally progressive appetites.

They strolled through the sliding doors and slipped past hordes of fellow students sharing their determination to kick back and break away from their diligent schedules. Jack spotted the rest of the gang sitting at their designated table in the mess hall. There was Kevin Johnston, the most mild-mannered of the group until he had a taste of tequila; Isaac Benson, the epitome of wit if there was one deserving of the title; Bennett Nash, the soft-natured ambivert with a side of haughtiness (usually triggered by the last guy); and of course,

Tommy Beech, the contentious wisecrack who sneaks aged wisdom in his social ineptitude.

They all grew up together and have since been inseparable. For childhood buddies living in the same neighborhood, it was never a mystery to Jack that all their families excelled financially. Life as a kid was simpler, having been sheltered and rarely put into public light. Unlike his friends, who were literally years ahead in assimilation: in expression, comfortability, the whole nine yards. Jack never went out of his way to meet someone new. Even his boys were a result of a grand orchestration on behalf of their parents, all of whom were very close for years and saw more benefits to raising their children together. It begs the question if Jack could have formulated such strong bonds or even met his guys, had it not been for them.

"There they are," Bennett announced. "I heard you had a rough night there, Jacky."

"Rough morning too," he cracked, joining his friends.

"What was her name? Ken?" Isaac trilled.

"Jen," Jack corrected. "Everything was going fine until she found out who I was."

"*Found* out? Did you not tell her?"

"Goes back to what I've been saying this whole time man," Kevin chimed in. "You need to be honest with these girls. No one likes being lied to."

"Chill out there buddy," Bennett scolded. "Let Jack treat these women however he wants. He has the right."

"Do you hear yourself?"

"I do," Bennett confirmed. "It's not Jack's fault that she wasn't attracted to him because he's rich. It's actually a bit hypocritical if you think about it."

"How do you figure?"

"Not gonna lie boys," Jack interrupted. "I would appreciate if we didn't talk about it." He focused on Kevin. "And you're right. But put yourself in my shoes. It's different with you guys, because you all *know* me and don't care. Honestly, do you think that Lebron likes bragging about who he is?"

Isaac laughed. "So you're comparing yourself to Lebron now?"

"If I may," Tommy entered, his hand rested on Jack's shoulder. "I think that what Jack is trying to say is that he wants the relationship to be real. And if that's the case, then it only makes sense that the impression is unbiased, which could be compromised if he told girls who he was right off the bat."

"Maybe, but telling the truth is important," Kevin countered. "If you go in lying about your name, or identity, or anything along those lines, all you're really doing is putting yourself in a weird predicament. And what's worse, is you are the only person to blame for it. Doesn't matter how good your intentions are."

"Am I in a therapy session right now?" Jack sighed. "Guys please, I know, okay? I won't do it anymore."

"You hear that, everyone? Jack won't do it anymore!" Kevin cackled. "Let's give him some space and talk about what's really important here. Peep this."

He sprung out of his chair and reached inside his pack. The boys watched attentively as he pulled out a handful of shooters and tossed them on the table before them. Tequila. Classic Kevin.

"Who's ready to have a *night*?" he grinned.

Jack was nauseous at the sight of the shooters, regrettably shrugging it off due to his friends' eagerness.

"Starting this early, eh Kev? I dig it," Tommy uttered. "Although, Jacky and I may need to fade for now. We'll be having some fun of our own in about an hour. If you catch my drift."

Jack caught them exchange a sneaky grin.

"What was that?" he faced Tommy, perplexed. "What are we doing?"

"Do you not feel it yet?"

"Feel what?" and at that moment, Jack blinked hard. He looked at his hands, noting the particularly detailed shape of his hair and pores, following with a diminutive, unidentifiable presence in his belly that steadily climbed into his brain. It was a feeling he knew all too well.

His eyes beaded at Tommy, whose initial smirk was now a wide grin.

"You didn't…" Jack trailed off, already expecting Tommy's response.

"Yeah baby!"

"The water bottle?"

"Yep."

"Why didn't you tell me?"

"I thought it would be more enjoyable this way."

The rest of the boys burst into laughter, obviously in on the joke.

"You can't just drug me, Tommy. That's some criminal shit."

"Hey! What did I say earlier? Don't refer to it as a drug, it's not fun when you do that."

Jack brought his hands to his face, sulking for what was to come.

"While we are on this topic, "Tommy added. "I should probably mention these are from Ricky."

Jack slowly lifted his head. "*Ricky's?*"

LSD, commonly referred on the street as "acid," is a complex drug. There are many tales of the substance, particularly known for its indescribable effects told by those brave enough to endure the experience. The market certainly varies depending on location and overall societal acceptance, which was great for Seattleites, as it was rich in demand.

Ricky's, however, were a beast of their own and highly acclaimed for their extreme potency. In layman's terms, one of Ricky's tabs was equivalent to three of your average joe's.

"I guess that's why you told me to eat something," Jack said to Tommy, his concern quickly fleeting.

"You should have hopped on the lover's speed," Kevin suggested.

"That *definitely* would have been better," Jack concurred, grabbing one of the shooters, the other boys following his example. "Care to give a toast, Tommy B?"

As if he anticipated the request, Tommy hopped onto his chair, causing nearby commotion to seize and direct their attention to him.

"We find ourselves here once again boys. Another week, welcoming the opportunity for us to chase our secondary ambitions. We're still young, still alive, and most importantly, still with each other. Let's make the most of our time now and get fucking silly."

The boys joined him in harmony, cheersing and downing the shooters.

Tommy's right, Jack thought as he forcibly swallowed the tequila. *These may be some of the best times of my life. Only makes sense to make it last as long as possible.*

It would be a memorable night for Jack. He was determined to make it so.

*****

Usually following some mild heartbreak, Jack would expect being spoiled by his boys on a night out on the town. Not to say it was unordinary for Jack and his friends to enjoy an evening of drinks and reckless decisions for the sake of preserving their youthful side that would ultimately translate into goofy memories; however, the intention was different on nights like these, as they collectively agreed it would be more beneficial to set aside their own interests in helping Jack's own riddling pain as he tried to get over his most recent attempt for love. Accompanied by the abundance of alcohol, music, and delightfully overcrowded streets brewing through downtown was also the subtle prospect of boundless opportunity in meeting someone worthwhile. Interactions are more certain to be bleak, but what mattered was the result, and not necessarily the journey.

Nightclubs were a great scene for such an instance. Especially the Den, otherwise referred to by the boys as the breeding ground for their future wives. Centrally located between campus and the heart and downtown Seattle, it never failed to charm the younger scene in search of an inexpensive location for their festivities, while also guaranteeing a nondescript choice for partying in style. Its ambiguous façade was complemented with a surprisingly ornate interior: sprawling lights trickling from reflective ceilings, coupled with a vast dancefloor adjacent to a lavish bar, stocked with assorted drinks illuminated from the glowing fluorescence installed at the base of the oaken shelves. The floors were paneled with glossy hardwood, which was visible about half the time due to the thick haze generated by the smoke machines hidden throughout the bar. Atop the dancefloor was a rooftop courtyard, patterned in an arabesque montage of foliage and evergreen alike, sheltered tables for casual seating, flatscreens, and backyard games, completed with a stimulating scenic view of the vibrant cityscape.

Jack was still dumbfounded by Ricky's tabs despite how much time had passed since he dropped. It is almost like the full effects do not kick in until they are least expected.

He studied the drink in his hands, reflecting on what compelled him to continue washing down his starch throat with alcohol when he was just face-deep in a toilet that same morning. He leaned on the bar and watched obnoxious crowds intermingling amid the deafening music, sensing the pretentious moods middling between ultra-alpha males and surface-level females. He never took interest in this type of scene, but reluctantly accepted that it was one of his best options to fit in, not only with the rest of his schoolmates, but his own friends.

Tommy appeared to share his contempt, timidly pocketing his change from the bartender and joining Jack to people-watch.

"You all right?" he asked at the sight of Jack's wavering stance, almost like he was about to retch right there for everyone to see.

"I'm good," Jack replied and cleared his throat. He had to pace himself if he was to make it through the night. "Why are we here, man? Can't we just go home and get high?"

"While that sounds amazing, there's a reason why we are here."

"Yeah I know. I get it," he sighed, managing a sip from his drink. "And although I obviously appreciate it, you guys don't have to do this for me." Tommy faced the bar, his back to the crowd in hopes that what he said would be more discrete.

"Look Jacky, you've had your head in the dirt for too long. This entire game you keep playing – taking girls on dates and pretending to be someone you're not – it's so cliché. Kevin was right, you know. It doesn't make sense to think that you will find someone worth it in the long run if you're not honest with them in the first place."

"Where are you going with this?"

"I'm making it my personal mission that you find your wife tonight. And when it happens, I advise that you just be honest with her." Tommy shrugged. "What's the worst that could happen?"

Jack pondered any plausible consequences to Tommy's proposal. People with money are frequently taken advantage of, and he ironically thought money was the only thing that could keep a girl by his side, which logically defeats the purpose of lying to them about his wealth to begin with. He could not remember the last time he rejected the desire to find his 'wife,' and no matter how it happened – including being bored in the idle of a club – he was hopeful for an ideal companion to introduce herself soon. Chasing dreams can be like flipping a coin, specifically if the dream itself was realistic. He did not think he was asking for too much. Nevertheless, he knew how he had been going about it was wrong, and that it would not hurt to try a new approach.

"You're right," Jack concluded, signaling the bartender to replenish his drink. Gladdened by his friend's approval, Tommy relayed a smile.

"I'll check back with you in a bit, all right?" and with that, he tootled to a group of strangers nearby, proceeding to shake hands and befriend them. Classic Tommy B.

Jack retrieved a fresh drink from the bartender and turned around, when he suddenly collided with the person behind him. He jerked to his right, losing control of his drink as it toppled over his shirt. Thank heavens no one could notice in the bar's dim lighting, otherwise he could have been met with embarrassment for the spillage in addition to already having to replace his costly apparel. He faced the source of the push with mild aggression, but stopped himself when he saw a girl staring back at him. She was clearly appalled by her party foul, covering her mouth and taking a step back.

"Oh my god, I am so sorry!" she screamed.

Jack adjusted his demeanor accordingly, opening his arms and managing a smile in hopes of defusing the situation.

"It's fine." he replied coolly.

"Hey, I know that logo," she added, quick to disregard the spill as she pressed her finger on his chest. "Davidson Prep, right?"

"Uh yeah, it was custom embroidered."

"All logos are man," she mocked. "Do you know HG by chance?"

"Yeah, she's a few years younger than me though," he muttered, still focused on his shirt.

"I know! I went there too, I'm in her grade."

"Oh. That's cool," he said, realizing how passive he was coming off. Either this girl was oblivious, or simply did not care enough to mention it. He raised his head to look at her.

She was dressed down in a turquoise tank top, black denim, and white sneakers, yet she was dazzling, becoming, and perfect. Like no one he had ever seen before. Her dark maroon hair straightened down behind her round ears and slightly over her arched eyebrows, forming slight curls as it reached just past her modest shoulders. Her silvery ring stood out on her upturned nose, as it sat just above her dimpled cheeks and soft, provocative lips. And her eyes: startingly grey, with distinct slivers of hazel; enough to shut down ones' confidence and sense of thought. Subtle, but piercing. Intimidating, but beautiful. He was stunned by her exuberant smile, transcending through the already lively mood of the bar. What was this infatuation? It would not be the first time with any man. Especially Jack.

But no, this was different. He already knew.

"Wow," Jack uttered, seemingly speechless.

She giggled and tilted her head to scope the dancefloor beyond them before leaning in close and whispering in his ear.

"You're my fake boyfriend tonight."

Jack was taken aback by how direct she was.

"Sounds good," he indicated, playing along. "Can your fake boyfriend buy you a drink?"

"Nah, I don't come here for the drinks. I like dancing though."

"I see."
She took Jack's hand and dragged him to the dancefloor. He took one last glimpse at his friends at the table, all of whom had witnessed the entire interaction. Notably Tommy, who nodded vigorously in approval. It was all Jack needed to settle into the situation. He was good to go.
Jack let the girl lead, the pair slipping between the increasingly dense crowd of drunkards. He could not stop checking her out, admiring her confident stroll and complete disregard from the reactions of everyone she pushed through.
He knew he would need to do things differently, relying on nothing more than his innate impulsiveness from here on out. While it was normal for others to succumb to instinct, it was unnatural for Jack, since under like circumstances he would be irking into the situation. With her, however, it was different. *She* was different. There was no need to worry, for he knew he just had to trust the process.
They reached the center of the dancefloor, the girl turning to Jack and wrapping her arms around him. They matched each other's gaze, swaying to the music.
"I'm Emma Keva, by the way. I'm sure you were waiting to ask."
"Jack Douglas," he said, still awed by her beauty. "You're a freshman, then?"
"Yeah, every time I come here, I'm always scared that they'll be able to tell from my horrible fake."
"What state did you get it from?"
"Michigan. I figured anywhere too close was expected, and too far away be suspicious, but a state where most of the kids stay in-state? That's a hard one to guess being real or not."
"That's smart thinking there."
She smiled at his awkwardness. "What are you studying?"
"Business. I'll probably end up working for my dad once I graduate."
"Oh yeah? What does your dad do?"
This was it. Truth time.
"He runs his own small business in Bellevue."
Yes, he lied. He thought he could tell the truth, even after being inspired by his friends. But he figured this route would be better. If she was actually worth it – and he believed she was – then everything would work out regardless of whether he lied or not.
"I understand why you're a business major then," she sneered. "Sounds like you're set for a pretty nice gig."
"Yeah, he's a great guy. Really solid." *Okay,* he thought. *That wasn't so bad.* Then, Jack felt his stomach tighten. He recognized the feeling: the undesirable effects from Ricky's acid were kicking in.

"Are you okay?" Emma asked.

Jack shot upward and forced a grin. "Yeah, I'm great."

"Are you sure? Because it looks like you're dying right now."

"It's nothing," he lied. *Be a little honest.*

"My friend and I dropped acid earlier today and I'm still tripping pretty hard." *Wow,* he thought. *That was way too honest.*

Emma snorted, doing her best to hold back a laugh.

"Come on, let's go sit down. You can meet my friends!"

Jack dismissed his outburst and let Emma guide him off the dancefloor and up to the rooftop, where he saw a large group huddled at the other end of the floor.

"Jack!" Tommy shouted, popping his head atop the cluster and motioning them to draw nearer. The rest of the boys were there, all of whom acknowledged Emma instantly.

"Hey guys!" Emma greeted, mimicking a similar sense of familiarity toward them

"What a small world we live in!" Isaac cheered.

"Emma Keva, long time no see," Tommy mused. "Smart girl there, Jacky. We had Calc together back at Davison."

"That's good to know," he cracked. "I'll make sure to see you for my homework."

"Amongst other things," she flirted, close enough that only he heard.

"Come sit with us," Kevin invited. "We're having a TIME."

It stunned Jack to learn how they all knew of each other. At the same time, it did not surprise him given his shyness and parents' effort to shielding him from the world.

The rest of the night was filled with joy and amusement, surpassing Jack's expectations. What's best, was that he finally found someone who just happened to hail from his own alma mater. He was certain the opportunity to mull the coincidence was close; for the time being, however, he decided to treasure its serendipitous progression.

The acid was still in full effect. An incredible rush or euphoria filled Jack's mind, body, and soul. He felt an immediate urgency to project his radiance on everyone, engaging in openhearted discussion about anything that materialized in thought. A wondrous collection of emotions, and Emma beside him was the icing on the cake. He struggled to control his arousal, deliriously wrapping his arms around her while she reciprocated eagerly. She fit in well with the boys' dynamic, goofily slamming them through frequent chirps that always followed with an intoxicating giggle. Even her mannerisms were attractive, particularly her need to point at people when she asserted one of her many bold opinions.

For the first time in a long time, Jack welcomed the universe to play out before him, not once falling anxious because of his inability to control it. Then something happened.

Jack gazed into the mirror, his pupils dilated, cavernous, ever-deepening with a rush of feelings dubious to his own logic. *Get it together, you're fine,* he assured himself before lunging back to the toilet, doing everything in his power to not regurgitate his last meal. He refused to permit such indigestion to meddle in this affair with his potential wife waiting beyond the bathroom door. If he were to puke, he knew he must follow it with a rally of the century. Jack blinked hard.

When his eyes opened, Tommy was standing next to him speaking to a group of randoms on the roof. Based on their captivated expressions, he inferred it was likely due to one of his friend's compelling stories.

Wasn't I just in the bathroom? What's happening here?

He watched Tommy frantically wave his hands, unable to hear what he was saying, but trying to match his demeanor in an attempt to pretend he was consciously present. In truth, he thought he was losing his mind. Jack blinked hard.

When he opened his eyes this time, he was sitting beside Emma and her girlfriends in a booth on the ground floor. He just met them tonight but was blanking on their names. Yet, he vividly remembered a period of awkwardness earlier when he had to ask all of them for their names again. *My God, what are their names? How could I have forgotten their fucking names?*

He could not hear a word they were saying – not because of the loud music – he could not hear that either. It was total muteness, until seemingly out of nowhere, Tommy appeared and slapped his palm on Jack's shoulder.

"How's it going here?" came Tommy's voice, and with it every sound resuming in real time around him. Jack lightly slapped his ears in hopes that the temporary deafness was over.

"More drinks are on the way," Tommy added, pointing at one of the girls. "Morgan, I made sure to ask for more olives this time."

Morgan Rogers, a fellow local and aspiring nurse, smiled at Tommy, who promptly squeezed next to Jack, as if he had been sitting there all along. *Okay, we have been here for a while,* Jack concluded, relieved at the gradual return of his memory. He felt his eyelids become heavy. *No, don't close them. Not again.*

He begged his brain to obey, but quickly realizing the inevitable, tilted his head back and waited for his sight to blur once more.

Jack opened his eyes. He was outside, apparently, wincing at the sharp wind brisking through his bare skin. He was walking, albeit clumsily, one jelly leg

after the next as he imagined collapsing into the concrete sidewalk below. Surely he would have been in a worse state, had it not been for Emma's pronounced grip around his arm as she steered him along. He identified her girlfriends a ways ahead, and from the vulgar fragments and Tommy's distinct drunken laughter, guessed that his boys were not far behind.
"You are something else," Emma panted, her tone more humorous than condescending. "What's going on?"
"What's going on, is that I am taking you back home," she teased. "All your friends could use a helping hand, but sadly I could only carry one of you."
She was slow to release him when they reached his apartment.
"Can you stand?"
"Yep," Jack managed to say, his weak legs miraculously holding his uneven teetering when she let go of his arm. "You're the best Em. I owe you one."
"Oh I know," she mused. "And in case you were curious, I'm already thinking of how you can repay me."
One of Emma's friends called out from the end of the block, signaling for her to join.
"I should get back," Emma sighed. "We all have an early morning."
Jack straightened up, now more composed. "Of course, yeah, I totally understand…" his voice faltered, nervously averting his gaze in hopes of preserving an already embarrassing night.
Emma, sensing his discomfort, grabbed his stained shirt and pulled him close. She kissed him. Jack, initially taken aback, cupped his hand on her cheek. In that moment, all his former doubts dissipated. He slowly pulled away, staring into her eyes.
"Text me tomorrow," she said, and turned to her friends patiently waiting for her at the end of the block.
"I don't have your number," Jack called to her.
"Already taken care of!" she shouted back without pause.
Jack observed their shadows disappear into the distance, promptly producing his phone where, sure enough, highlighted one notification. A text from Emma.
You're welcome ;)
He was about to reply but stopped himself, thankful that the receding acid was sluggishly replaced with the return of rational thought.
Emma inspired the introduction of a new feeling for Jack. She had just left, yet he desired to see her again. Hear her. Touch her.
But what was the source of this foreign emotion? Desire? Infatuation? Lust? He knew she was not like any other girl. In fact, he could feel it. This was not like his previous trials, when he superseded a crush in longing for more than a

fling. It was more than that. And after spending a single night with her, Jack confirmed it.

He did not consider himself obsessive, yet the image of Emma was imprinted on his psyche. Just when he decided to abandon all hope of companionship, she presented herself as a viable prospect.

Perhaps Emma was the one capable of shattering his shield. Perhaps she could transform him into the man he sought to become. Or perhaps, it was all in his head…but if so, just maybe it was in hers too.

She was the oasis to his desert; the light to his shadow; the cure for his cancer; the blessing to his curse. Perfection, in its most imperfect state. She was her, and he was him.

And he loved her.

ii

There is much to experience for one under the influence. Perceptions vary, as do opinions and takeaways. Whether it be strange, euphoric, deleterious, intoxicating, frightening, fantastical – it is safe assuming they all share a rather unpleasant aftermath typically occurring the next morning.
The comedown.
With a more potent substance, it is comparable to an unfit person's state after finishing a grueling marathon. Jack also erred by not keeping himself hydrated last night, enhancing the hangover to an intensity he would not wish on his worst enemy. His brain was mangled that morning, promptly choking a series of coughs as he emerged from the bedroom to see Tommy tending to the espresso machine in the kitchen. A usual sight on any given morning in the Douglas-Beech household.
"What time is it?" Jack asked him, rubbing his neck from the little moisture in his parched throat.
Tommy pointed to the clock displayed on the oven. "It's a quarter past two. Which according to your schedule, puts you about an hour past your last class for the day."
"Well shit."
"It happens to all of us, believe me," Tommy consoled. "Maybe more expected when we were freshman, but still…"
Jack ignored him and checked his phone to see Emma's name pop up on his screen.
"No way!" he cheered, lofting his phone to Tommy.
Tommy flinched at the phone hurtling at him and caught it without a second to spare.
"What the hell?"
"Read it!"
Tommy rolled his eyes and peered down at the phone.
"Congratulations. Emma wants to hang out with you," he noted and tossed the phone back. "This is good news."
"Better than good news!" Jack rejoiced and sprinted into the bathroom. He hated making plans because he felt it constricted his ability to act freely and according to his own will. But with love on the line, dismissing the distaste was easier than tying shoes. He got dressed in ten minutes and returned to the kitchen, pleased to see Tommy right where he left him.
"How do I look?" he asked, gesturing to his outfit.
Tommy blinked hard as he inspected Jack's choice of luxurious apparel.
"Are you *posing?*"
"Come on Tom, be serious."

"I am."
Jack rolled his eyes and proceeded to the front door.
"What do you have planned on your date?"
"The usual."
 "Not surprised…are you going to tell her tonight?"
"Absolutely not," Jack shook his head. "She's different than every girl I've met. I need to make this one work."
"So, you say she's different and you want to make it work, yet you're still pulling the same method on her as you did with all your past gals?" He observed Jack's blank stare for a long moment before giving in and adding, "You *do* see the irrationality there, yeah?"
"I got this, don't worry," Jack relented, opening the door.
"Wait!"
Jack reluctantly obeyed and glanced back. "Yes?"
"Lose the polo," Tommy advised. "The Jack Douglas *I* know would wear that."
"Good point," he agreed, stripping off his shirt as he darted back to his bedroom to change.
"And put on a jacket, it might rain tonight."
Jack came out of his room after a couple minutes and posed again for Tommy to evaluate.
"Much better."
"What would I do without you Tom?"
"Probably kill yourself."
"Very funny," Jack cackled, bidding him farewell and racing out the door. There was a heightened degree of eagerness tied to the first date. The cliché dynamic fascinated Jack, and he looked forward to sharing the experience with Emma.
She was waiting for him outside the dorms, sporting leggings and a grey top that matched the hue of her eyes. Strapped around her neck was a camera nestled beside her torso, to which she removed momentarily while she slouched in the passenger seat. Her nonchalant demeanor was slightly off-putting for Jack, but he disregarded it quickly by the sight of her naturally stunning beauty.
Emma casually pulled up her shades when she noticed the car's fine interior. "Is this yours?"
"It's my dad's. I asked to borrow it for today," Jack lied. "Figured it would make a solid impression for our date."
"Cheesy, yet charming. Someone's already off to a good start."
She held up her camera for Jack to see.

"I thought it would be fun if we drove around the city so I could shoot some pics for my catalog?"
"Absolutely, where do you want to go?" he asked, resting his foot on the brake before shifting the car in drive.
"Surprise me."
Jack capitalized on the opportunity to show off, speedily shifting between traffic. He stole the occasional glance at Emma, who appeared more than delighted to marvel at the city from inside the convertible.
"Do you photograph for fun?"
"Kind of, I'm an Art major, with an emphasis in Photography and Graphic Design. The latter is not as interesting to me, but my mom thought I should get it if I ever wanted to get a job that paid well."
"That makes sense…that's why I'm taking Business. My parents want me to get my MBA after I graduate. And I gotta say, the idea of a two more years of this does not sound nice in the slightest."
"Is it hard?"
"I mean, it's not easy," Jack chuckled. "Every subject is different, but I think we'd all agree the coursework gets harder by the year," he turned to her. "I assume you're still in your generals?"
"Not really. I tested out of most of my entry courses after I graduated from high school, so I was able to jump right into the curriculum."
"So if I'm hearing you correctly, you're telling me that you're smart?"
Emma blushed. "You're sweet."
So far, so good, Jack thought, pressing harder on the gas.
They took the bridge, where Jack recorded glimpses of Emma snapping photos of the moving boats on Lake Washington, before continuing through Bellevue and moving south until they reached Cougar Mountain Park. It was only twenty minutes from the city, yet the landscape reflected otherwise. Replacing the densely populated urban environment, was instead one of many areas in the region that projected the inhabitants' appreciation of the natural wilderness. Even with the abundance of suburbs spreading throughout the forest, the effort dedicated to preserving the surrounding greenery was beyond impressive. Jack reduced his speed as they trailed the swirling lanes, listening intently to Emma's alluring narratives detailing her upbringing. He noted the vagueness in her language as she rattled presumably exaggerated visions of her future, the likeness of which could compare to a child proclaiming their dreams of becoming an astronaut. Jack did not mind, because he was aware such goals were embedded for the purpose of preserving one's sanity. Since his wealth played a large role in never formulating his own, it was reasonable to suggest how he managed his judgement could subsequently lead to his own demise.

Jack pulled over at a break in the road, when Emma left the car and paced to the opposite end of the street.

"Are you coming?" she called to him.

Jack juggled his keys and followed her into the brush. Before long, they were deep within the verdurous terrene, drastically unfurling whelms of shrubbery. Ancient bark erected from the soil, towering overhead as they emanated a raspy hiss articulated from the million leaves rustling against one another.

It was difficult for Jack to keep up with Emma's steadfast pace. He studied her, admiring her animated conduct with the undulated territory. The element foreign, yet she looked perfectly comfortable. Almost vested in tranquility. Jack wondered about her capability of prevailing in disparate environments and concluded her preferred ties to be genuinely unrigid. Everywhere she went was instantly hers, regardless of whether she chose to ultimately keep it. It was intriguing, and attractive.

Emma was directly in front of Jack when she finally drew to a halt, tilting her head back and squinting at the sun casting its ray across her face.

"It's beautiful," she gasped.

"Yeah," Jack uttered, refusing to take his eyes off her. She truly was.

"There is so much life here," she continued, motioning to the surrounding forest. "We go about our days trying to find something that makes us more meaningful than ourselves, that we forget about one of the most obvious reasons for our existence."

"You sounded like Tommy B there."

"He sounds like a smart guy."

"When he wants to be, anyway," Jack joked, changing the subject. "What is your catalog for?"

"Two reasons. For one, I recently applied for this art internship-program thing at the Ember House in New York, and part of the selection process is to submit a portfolio of my work."

"That's cool," he commented, privately acknowledging the need to revisit the point at a later time. "What's the second reason?"

It's more of a digital scrapbook of my experiences," she explained. "When I was younger, I realized that there were so many things that I would do, but I was worried that I would not be able to remember it all..." her eyes glossed over her camera. "This helps me keep track of everything that matters to me."

"Okay, now you *really* sound like Tommy," Jack chortled. "I'm honored to witness your art in action."

"Me too," Emma smiled. Just then, she held her stomach and revealed a strained look.

"Are you hungry?" Jack guessed.

Her eyes lit up at his question.

"I'm *starving.*"
"There's a really nice spot we can stop at on the way back to campus."
"Resourceful," Emma remarked. "I'll be sure to check that off, too."

*****

Emma was impressed with Jack's choice for dining, gaping at the glittering lights stringing from the vaulted ceilings.
"This is the nicest place I've eaten at. What's it called?"
"*Crepuscolo,*" Jack replied as he guided her deeper into the restaurant. "It's Italian, the English translation meaning, 'twilight.'"
Per Jack's request, their table had been fabulously prepared, the top donned in a silky overlay, and a collation of tantalizing appetizers encircling a skinny candle with a flame bright enough to cast its glow to the edge of the chairs.
He even preordered a bottle of wine, for obvious reasons.
Jack found his seat, and without skipping a beat, reached for his glass and lifted it to cheers Emma. She giggled and followed his example before picking up a menu, letting out a delicate gasp.
"Wow, you didn't tell me how pricey the food is."
"Right," Jack started, easing into the ever so predictable dialogue. "Good thing I've been saving up."
They sat in modest silence, taking in the environment.
"I like your shirt," Emma pointed out.
He could not help but smirk at the compliment. *Thanks again, Tommy.*
"Are you originally from Seattle?"
Jack shot her a confused expression. "We went to the same school, remember?"
"I know, I know, but since I knew your friends who were all on the opposite end of their high school careers…I don't know, I figured you must have moved here late in the game like I did."
"That's understandable," Jack grinned. "But yeah, I'm from here. Born and raised in Mercer. You?"
"Originally north Seattle, but I moved to Mercer shortly before high school because my parents thought it'd be easier since I went to Davidson."
"What do your parents do?"
"My dad was a cop and my mom's a nurse—" she paused. "It was their choice to enroll me at Davidson."
"You didn't want to go?"
"I mean, I did. It's a long story, probably best for another time. I was really happy with my life before moving, but you know how life has a way of throwing a lot of curveballs."

"I definitely understand that."
 Emma trilled, her curiosity not seeming to diminish. "I still can't believe that I never met you…not even via social media…"
Jack nodded subtly, unsurprised. Anyone whose tried peering into his background would be quick to realize its impossibility. Between his private lifestyle and nearly nonexistent digital presence, he may as well have been involved in WITSEC. He would be lying if he said it was entirely a personal choice, although he was less resistant to reinforce his parents' idea given their reputation, and the idea that too much projection as an open book to the world may jeopardize their empire. Needless to say, it was difficult for Jack to mask his identity from the girls he entertained.
"Do you ever feel like leaving?" she asked.
"What do you mean?"
"You know, taking a break from home, and going somewhere else?"
Jack pondered her question, eventually shrugging.
"I would travel a lot with my parents, but I haven't given much thought on permanently relocating. I love Seattle."
"Tell me about your family."
Jack choked on his drink, recovering quickly and managing a calm smile.
Damn, she wants to get right into it.
"My family," he stammered. "Um, well let's see. I am an only child, which I know usually has a negative connotation, but I like to think that I turned out okay. Let's see, what else…"
He grew slightly more relaxed after hearing her faint chuckle.
"As for my parents, my dad manages a small company—"
"In Bellevue, right?"
"Yes, in Bellevue," he echoed delicately. "And my mom is a teacher in the city."
"A teacher! You know, they say that the children of teachers are usually the most considerate."
Usually, Jack thought. *If only she knew.*
They were briefly interrupted by the waiter.
"Good evening Mr. Douglas, it's good to see you again," the waiter greeted. "Are you thinking the usual?"
Jack pretended to ignore the waiter's question as he perused the menu. If he kept it casual, perhaps Emma would not have picked up on the context.
"I think I will take the fettucine," he looked up. "What about you Em?"
Emma grazed the menu sightlessly before closing the menu and turning to the waiter.
"Sorry, this is my first time here," Emma said, closing the menu. "I'll have the same."

Jack waited for the server to leave before shooting her a playful wink.

"I've had it before. You'll love it, trust me," he said.

"Do you come here a lot?"

Choosing his words carefully was a must. Luckily, he had plenty of time to prepare for all the "what-ifs". He knew the only way to get over this hump was by being honest. Or, what he made her believe to be the truth.

"My parents take me here sometimes. We've always have the same guy serving us too."

"I love that."

Jack relaxed again, pleased to avert another potential failed date. At that thought, he furtively looked past Emma to see that they were alone in their section.

Perfect. No need to worry about another Dumphreys debacle.

Even with a firmer grasp on controlling how the night would progress, Jack still felt nervous engaging with Emma. Sure, the conversation had a radiant flow thanks to her inquisitive nature. Where his anxiety lingered however, was in how much he was willing to reveal about himself, knowing well that it would be strictly based off the questions she asked. Winning her heart would be more challenging than his ventures with other women. Nevertheless, Jack had only one goal for the evening: to keep Emma interested. It was a task he struggled with, admittedly, but for the sake of winning her over, he was determined to make it work.

Emma interlinked her fingers and leaned forward. "Tell me a secret."

"What kind of secret?"

"The kind you would tell someone without risking the shame that may come with it."

"Isn't that the definition of a *secret*?"

"Yes Jack, that's the joke."

"Right, of course," Jack said, his mind immediately resorting to the glowing elephant in the room that was the concealment of his true identity.

Before he could answer, the waiter returned to their table with their meals and a bottle of wine.

Oh no, not again.

"Excuse me, I didn't order more wine."

"It's on the house," the server noted. "We try our very best to demonstrate our appreciation for our most favorable patrons."

Jack leaned back in his chair, his attention fixating on the pair of identical dishes in front of them.

He watched Emma carefully twirl her fork in the pasta and bring it to her mouth.

"This is incredible."

For as many times as Jack had eaten at the *Crepuscolo*, he never recalled a time when the food tasted as exquisite as it did that evening. It could have been a result of the remarkable efforts from the staff. Then again, it also may have been the fact that he was enjoying it with exceptional company.
They finished their dinner just in time for the waiter to return with the check. Jack automatically snatched it from the table, sliding a couple folded bills in the pocket and handing it back.
"Keep the change."
The waiter answered with a respectful nod before focusing on Emma.
"This is a great young man you are here with." he soothed.
The waiter left the table, prompting Emma to give him a puzzling smirk.
"Let me help pay."
"Don't worry about it," Jack said, politely waving off her request. "It's not a date if the guy doesn't pay."
"I think a *lot* of people would disagree with that statement, especially in this town."
"My friend Tommy once told me that the values each of us hold is the only inherent method of defining our true purposes."
"What does that mean?"
"Honestly, I have no idea," he laughed. "But I like to think its meaning is relative to your point."
"You talk about Tommy a lot. I have the feeling that he is a very…*eccentric* person."
"I prefer 'unusual specimen.' For real, sometimes I have to convince myself that he's not from this world, and that's not always a compliment either."
A sudden chirp came from Emma's phone.
"Sorry," she apologized as she glanced at the illuminated screen. "It's Morgan. I promised her I'd help with this project she is working on for her marketing class.
"I understand," Jack kindly noted as he peeked at his watch. "It's getting pretty late anyway. We can head out."
Jack rose from his chair and took Emma's hand. Ending the dinner on a positive note. A personal record.
It had started to rain when they left the restaurant, prompting him to strip off his jacket and wrap it around her shoulders.
"Sweet *and* chivalrous," Emma mused as they strolled to the car. Jack carried the role well, jolting in front of her to open the passenger door.
"I hope you had a good time."
"I did, thank you so much," she assured, pinching her lips as she peered up to him.
"Are you sure?" he asked, studying her crinkled expression.

A long moment passed without Emma acknowledging his question.
"Sorry, I was just thinking about something."
"What's on your mind?"
She smiled faintly, almost like she was holding back on the truth behind her lips.
"You're starting to grow on me, Jack Douglas."
At that, Jack's admiration for Emma overwhelmed him. He leaned toward her, feeling his lips press against hers. quickly recalculated, pulling away to see Emma's puzzled expression staring back at him. He watched as she bit her lip – almost hesitantly – before suddenly bringing herself back to him.
Jack wallowed in the sensation, reveling in the tender, sweet taste of her lips. The essence of time seemingly diminished for what was only a short minute seemed to be an eternity for Jack. It was all too perfect. Even the oncoming drizzle enhanced his overall pleasure, paying no mind to the drops percolating over his face and around their conjoined mouths before tricking across his hands that he used to caress her delicate cheeks.
They amicably pulled away from each other, sharing a moment of silence and meeting each other's eyes.
Emma turned away and entered the car, leaving Jack to circle around to his side. He opened the door, taking a brief moment to surveil the lack of stars beyond the misty heavens. Even amid the supposedly gloomy weather fanned atop the skyscrapers in the distance, Jack could not have asked for a better ending to the night. At long last, he had received confirmation of a desire yearned for by many. Today marked a monumental step toward the outcome that would surely be a fruitful relationship with Emma Keva.
His satisfaction was short-lived upon his choice to revisit the single reservation that he had been keeping from her.
Tell me a secret.
The words thrummed again and again in is line of thought. The lie was weighing heavier now, thickening like moss on river rock. But he figured any degree of guilt was worth coping if it meant that he would end up with her. Emma deserved the truth, and he was fully prepared to tell her.
Eventually.

iii

Tommy skipped hastily into Padelford for his first course of the morning. He was conscious of keeping his pace light as he breezed through the empty hall, overhearing muted lectures echoing from beyond the closed doors.

A guidebook explaining the requirements for guaranteed success does not exist. There are accepted theories however, all of which depict a handful of likable qualities one may need to further their path to fortune. Of those qualities, Tommy believed punctuality to reign supreme. Tardiness was not to be taken lightly, and such intolerance was emphasized whenever it was within his control.

Had it not been for Jack's endless rant about Emma last night, he would have arrived on time. In Jack's defense, Tommy's duty nurturing his glaringly obvious symptoms of frequent heartbreak was self-nominated. Then years passed, and as tribulating as it became, he remained interested in evaluating Jack's incessant need to dismiss his own ambitions at the expense of his 'gal' of the week. He did not share his friend's yearn for romance, yet sympathized with the notion of how it affected him. Tommy was committed to do whatever it took for Jack to be happy, and accepted that with every choice comes a price. Because if it was important to a friend, then it was important to him too. Sometimes loyalty can be a bitch.

He stalled outside the classroom until Dr. Skinner turned his back before sneaking in, casually slipping into an open seat beside Bennett.

"You're late," he whispered.

"That's a good observation, Benny. What did I miss?"

Bennett motioned the packet on his desk. "Chapter review."

Just then, Dr. Skinner spun around, noticing Tommy immediately.

"Good morning, Thomas," he addressed. "We are going over the study guide if you would like to tell us the answer to number sixteen?"

Tommy froze when he heard his name, realizing he had not completed the assignment.

"I gotta be honest with ya, Professor Skins,...I didn't get it done."

Dr. Skinner was widely known across campus as one of the more uncompromising instructors. His knowledge was vast, and methods steadfastly rigid. In addition to his tenured rank as the chairman of the department, he was rarely met with resistance from his frequent proclamations

on the university's respective curriculum. Unofficially, he also had the
reputation of being a schmuck sometimes. As a result, every student who had
taken one of his courses were smart enough to never upset him.
Except Tommy Beech.
He was a mere freshman when he first experienced one of Dr. Skinner's
lectures. It had since developed into a mentor-apprentice dynamic, which
prior to Tommy, was an unreachable prospect given Dr. Skinner's
benevolence, especially in the face of staunch tenacity.
A series of musing mutters from the other students followed Tommy's
remark. To their surprise, Dr. Skinner managed a casual shrug and shifted his
focus to Bennett.
"Mr. Nash, care to help your friend out?"
Bennett straightened in his chair.
"C!" he shrieked nervously.
"'C' is correct, good work."
Bennett sighed and glared at Tommy once Dr. Skinner continued off with his
lecture.
"You're welcome," Tommy shrugged.
Behind them, a student spoke up.
"With all the money your daddy makes, you would think he can afford a tutor
for you."
Bennett gave Tommy a skittish stare, for he knew him well enough to expect
a rather dramatic reaction from him. Instead, Tommy swiveled in his seat and
stared blankly at the student.
"Since you mentioned it, my 'daddy' actually thought it would be a humbling
experience if I went to college with normal people before inevitably giving
me the keys to his empire," he sneered. "Don't worry about it, though. I
wouldn't expect a poorer observation from someone like you."
He spun around and smirked at Bennett.
It was not uncommon for Tommy to be a target for mockery, notably because
of his frequent tendency to behave, well, silly. He rarely let it get the best of
him and actually welcomed the persecution, finding it better to portray
himself as a fool so he can better disguise his true motives. The desire to
demonstrate his true intellect was nonexistent, unless of course it was
challenged, to which he faced with delusional confidence.
"Want to get some food?" Bennett asked on their way out of class.

Tommy's stomach whirred at the question, remembering he skipped breakfast. "Does entropy increase in a closed system?"
Bennett nodded in bewilderment. "Bro, just say yes, it's not that deep."
The campus was livelier by the late morning: hundreds of kids strolling along the widely paved sidewalk, shouldered against one another like a herd of cattle blazing through a narrow field. Winter may have removed the leaves from lining the path, but there was still a subtle beauty to its presentation. They reached the HUB, where Tommy spotted Morgan alone on a bench, peacefully engrossed in a book amid the astir from the passing students.
"I'll see you in there," Tommy said to Bennett and started toward her.
Shortly after Jack and Emma's meet, Tommy developed his own attraction for Morgan. Like Jack, he was still in the merge, but unlike Jack, he minded the difficulty weighing its eventual result with goals he considered more important than companionship.
"What are you reading?" he probed.
"Tommy!" she acknowledged, holding up the book for him to see.
"Elizabeth Bowen," he read. "Never thought you'd like the literary classics."
"Are you calling me dumb?"
"No, not at all! I've just found it rare to see anyone our age into this sort of stuff."
"I know what you meant, I was just messing around," Morgan giggled. "Do you like to read?"
"I did a lot when I was younger…now not so much," he bit his lip. "I'd use the excuse of never having time, but the truth is I grow more illiterate by the day."
Morgan laughed and playfully slapped his leg.
"I haven't seen you around," he added. "Why don't we grab dinner tomorrow evening?"
"Tomorrow evening…" Morgan began, pursing her lips. "I can't. I'm going to this fundraiser that the Student Government Association is hosting."
"The Semester Splendor!" Tommy remarked, his eyes widening. "I totally forgot about that."
"You know about it?"
"I'm actually a part of the SGA leadership," he admitted sheepishly. "Guess it doesn't look good on my part that I wasn't aware of my own organization's event."
"I'm sure you have a lot on your plate."
"Are you interested in getting involved?"
"Maybe, I don't know a lot about politics."
"That's a common misconception that people have about most of these clubs on campus. As long as you care about the mission, you won't have to know

much else. After you get your first taste of it, everything should come naturally."
"You make it sound so easy."
"Describing a task as 'easy' or 'hard' are simply a result of our cognitive biases…I think it's better if we skipped our concern over the probability of success, and just do it anyways."
"Wow," she mused, enamored at his bold, yet nonchalant demeanor. "Has anyone ever told you that you have an unconventional way of thinking?"
Tommy heard the intrigue in her tone, smirking slightly.
"Many times. Although they often phrase it as 'individualistic.'"
Morgan giggled. "So I take it you'll be going?" she asked.
"Apparently so. What do you say we still get dinner tomorrow like I proposed and swing by afterwards?"
"I'd love that, but won't we get there late?"
"You read my mind. Even better if you ask me," Tommy chuckled, leaving her to join his friends for lunch.
Earning the date. Check.

*****

Tommy twiddled his fingers as Morgan retouched her makeup in the passenger seat. Having to wait on a task so menial would typically annoy him, but having dominated their dinner with an assortment of philosophical topics (which may or may not have bored her to death), he chose to set aside his instinct.
"How do I look?" Morgan asked him as they approached the chamber.
Tommy glanced at her charcoal dress, admiring its simple elegance as it wrapped tightly around her slender body and rested above her knees.
"You know what I'm going to say," he casually replied.
Morgan stopped and grabbed his arm, pulling him back to meet her eyes.
"Tell me anyways."
Tommy took a moment to settle into her alluring gaze. He studied every detail of her radiant beauty.
"Well?" she pressed, her tone growing more seductive.
He grinned. "You're breathtaking. Sorry, had to take a minute to get mine back."
Morgan rolled her eyes. "You can do better than that," she snickered.
"I've had too much to drink. I'll come up with something better later."
They neared the doors when they were suddenly obtruded by the SGA president, Hannah Sheridan.

"Hey there, Hannah! Tommy greeted. "It's a lovely day for a gathering, wouldn't you agree?"
He was met with a disheartening scowl.
"It's eight o'clock," she corrected, tapping her watch. "You were supposed to be here three hours ago. Where have you been?"
Tommy held on to his sarcastic tone as he scratched his head.
"I was a little busy."
"A little *busy*?" Hannah reiterated. "Tommy, you're the Vice President of the club. You can't always be running off and doing what you want and not check in!"
"Give me a break, Han," Tommy said, motioning to Morgan. "As you can see, I am here with a lady, who I should also add is very interested in joining the SGA. Personally, I think she has more than enough promise to be our next leader after we graduate."
Hannah exchanged a genuine smile with Morgan and returned to Tommy.
"Thomas Michaels Beech, you find pleasure in pissing me off."
"Oh come on, you love me," Tommy retorted, kissing her on the cheek.
"Don't push it," she warned.
"You're my favorite, don't you forget it," he winked before taking Morgan's hand and continuing into the building. While he and Hannah were close friends, he knew he was guaranteed a good smacking from her by night's end. Tommy had a reputation on campus for bending the rules by his own accord. It all started freshman year, when he launched his own ghostwriting service for other students. In addition to creating an outlet where he could flaunt his exceptional writing skills, it also served as a sufficient money-making scheme. Word spread quickly of his venture, however, reaching all the way to the university's disciplinary committee – specifically, the dean – who ironically was also the first faculty member to have met Tommy after he slipped off his longboard and watched it roll into her shin on the first day of class. Coupled with his annoying ability to charm nearly anyone who crossed his path, it was not a surprise when he learned that she had buried the incident altogether, on the condition that he would not violate it again.
Since then, Tommy found it beneficial to involve himself on campus. He would spend countless hours networking and campaigning on behalf of various organizations, with the ultimate goal of creating a wider space of free-will for him to act on without any administrative intervention.
Regardless of how hard he crafted his image, Tommy had little interest in succumbing to the glowing recognition associated with it. Sure, there had been times when he fantasized eminence, but it never served as the primary motive. Rather, it was his own pride: believing that the only thing holding him back from his dreams was his own doubt telling him he was incapable of

achieving them. A vigorously grueling cycle he had designed solely for the purpose of his own continuous improvement.

In his opinion, it seemed to have been steadily paying off, as he awed at the elegant chamber packed with hundreds of students and faculty, all of whom were dressed in some of their finest apparel.

"This happens every year?"

"Yeah, it's definitely our biggest event."

Tommy scanned the room, gasping suddenly at the sight of his father onstage. He averted his gaze, instantly thinking his mind was playing a trick on him. But upon examining closer, he confirmed it was true.

Harrison Beech.

He gently took Morgan's hand and started walking toward him.

"Where are we going?" she asked.

"Well, I am taking you to meet one of the greatest men of our generation."

Tommy viewed Harrison as the epitome of success. Even if he were to come up short of his personal feats, it would be more than enough if his father was proud of him.

"Dad" he blurted.

Harrison was conversing with faculty when he noticed his son. He hurried off the stage and embraced him.

"Tom!" he bubbled, glancing over to Morgan. "And this lovely lady is…?"

"Morgan Rogers," she introduced, shaking his hand.

"It's nice to meet you," Harrison replied, turning back to Tommy. "This is quite something that Hannah put together."

"Yeah, it's great. What brings you here?"

"As alumni, it does not hurt to remain up to date with everything going on here," he explained, leaning in closer to them. "Between us, I was also curious to see if my contributions were being put to good use."

"Contributions?" Morgan queried, perplexed.

"My dad sits on the Board of Regents."

"Wow, that's impressive!"

Harrison gave a hearty chuckle. "Trust me, Morgan, it is more boring than impressive."

Tommy checked his watch and looked at his father. "Did we miss the presentation?"

"You did, as a matter of fact. I was wondering why you were not here earlier. Your name was even mentioned."

"I thought it would be a better use of my time to be with Morgan," Tommy said flatly.

Harrison's apathetic grin may have been subtle, but it was glaringly obvious for Tommy, who chose to cut the encounter short.

"We're going make another round and head out of here," he said, hugging his father. "I'll find you before we leave."

"Your dad is awesome," Morgan said when they were out of earshot.

"He really is," Tommy agreed, doing his best to conceal the concern he had over his father.

Tommy did not waste time intermingling with the different social circles. He never looked forward to saving face from the narrow-minded that he had to interact with. Public events like these were the worst, as it forced him to reluctantly dip into his extroverted side. His efforts were short-lived, and called it quits after thirty minutes jollying with his professors. Morgan joined him as they bidded farewell before continuing out of the chamber. He was mentally exhausted, deeply inhaling of the crisp air swelling his nostrils once the doors swung open.

Harrison was already outside, waving patiently from the bottom of the steps.

"Give me a minute," Tommy whispered to Morgan and rushed down the steps to meet his father. "I hope you weren't leaving without saying goodbye."

"Of course not," Harrison replied. "I had to get out though. Too crowded in there for me."

"Yeah same," Tommy agreed, glancing back up to see his date waiting at the entrance. "So, what did you think about Morgan?"

"She seems like a wonderful girl. It does not surprise me that you also have a keen eye for such things."

"Like father, like son."

Harrison chuckled. "How has this semester been? Are you enjoying your classes?"

"I'm passing all of them, if that's what you are asking."

"Not necessarily, but that is also great to know, since you mentioned it."

Tommy felt uneasy, reluctant to shift the tone of their conversation.

"You have nothing to worry about her Dad," he said.

Harrison frowned in confusion. "What do you mean?"

"I haven't forgotten about why I am here…what all of this is for. I know how much time and money you and Mom invested in me, and I will do whatever I can to make you both proud."

Tommy was dumbfounded at the sound of Harrison's horselaugh.

"Let me tell you something Tom: you are not here for me or your mother, nor should you feel the pressure to perform on our behalf. Yes, we worked our hardest to give you a good life, but we also know that you are a kid with your own dreams. Do not confuse our love with false suppositions we expect from you. Do you understand?"

"…Yes," Tommy muttered.

Harrison placed his hand firmly on his son's shoulder.

"I know I do not tell you a lot, but I am very proud of you. I have no doubt that you will grow into a better man than myself."
Tommy shrugged. "I don't know about that."
"The fact that you are so worried about it not being so is more than enough evidence of it," Harrison reinforced. "Always remember who you are and be unapologetically yourself."
Tommy hugged his father one last time and watched as he walked off.
He felt indebted to his parents, crediting them for everything he attained at this point in his life. College, sports, internships: although he had much to benefit, he always viewed them as the source of his drive. Coming up short on anything, naturally, was not an option. Seeing his father again was refreshing, and just what he needed to reconsider his concerns. He treasured the moment, hoping it would continue to serve as a reminder for himself to always be the best he could be, for *him*.
Morgan approached slowly behind.
"Did you have fun tonight?" she asked.
Tommy turned and grasped her waist, pulling her close.
"I did."
He walked Morgan back to his car, refusing to let go of her hand the entire way there. He had no desire to seek affirmation for his choices. He knew exactly who he was. And he loved that for himself.

iv

An impatient Jack kicked his feet atop the shoulder of the creaky armchair, resisting the urge to scan the dim corridor and occasionally jolting upward in his seat at even the slightest sound. With the exception of the low buzz of the fluorescent above, which ironically was comforting for him from the fear of complete silence. Like most students, he joined the shadowy, self-devouring abyss of anxiety reintroduced with finals around the corner, and he was determined to finish the semester with a glowing rapport from his professors. In his experience nothing proved more effective than paying a last-minute visit during office hours.

 His last appointment was with Dr. Hagen, his International Business instructor. A major requirement, but not one he dedicated much effort into. Jack watched a fellow student leave the office. His eyes were glued to the patterned ceramic, presumably from the sensibly traumatic encounter he just underwent with their intimidating superior. Shouldering up courage, Jack proceeded inside, where his professor scribbled away diligently on a stack of assignments.

"Dr. Hagen," Jack greeted, taking a seat. There was a prolonged silence, and it made Jack grow uneasy while he observed the vigor in his professor's crinkled olive hands jotting across the papers.

"Douglas," he finally spoke, cobbling the papers to set aside and linking his hands on the desk. "You wanted to speak about the recent exam."

"Yes," Jack cleared his throat. "I'm sorry again for leaving early that day, I wasn't feeling well. I was wondering how I could make up for the lost points."

"What were you thinking?" he implored, Jack detecting what seemed to be a patronizing tone in his voice.

"Well, if I don't get an A on the final, I won't pass this course."

"It appears so."

"I've had you since I was a freshman, so you know that I work hard and—"

"So speculative," Dr. Hagen interjected, shaking his head despondently. "If there is one thing you should have learned from my lectures, is that assertiveness is the key to getting exactly what you want."

Jack nodded to play along. He regretted doing this. It would have been smarter to escape with the other guy when he had the chance.

Please don't make me have to do Plan B, he thought to himself. He hated Plan B.

"Is there any way I can retake the test? Or even finish what I had already done and take a late penalty, or something?"

Dr. Hagen reclined, his temperament stern.

"Unfortunately, I cannot do that."
"Why?"
 "Although to you, it may seem like a simple request, what you may not realize is the burden that it will have on myself, and the message that it sends to other students who share your concerns, to whom I had already denied my help."
"Professor, I will fail this class if you don't give me another chance."
"You were very much aware of that possibility the moment you reviewed the syllabus at the beginning of the semester. You assumed the terms and you will have to abide by them, just like every student."
All of Jack's unease dissipated after that. He felt his chest warming up, and his face tightened. As much as he resented special treatment, he secretly hated the idea of being equal to everyone. The sulking approach was not effective, contrary to his presumption. It was time for Plan B.
Jack rose and pulled out his wallet, flinging some hundreds on the desk without skipping a beat and matching Dr. Hagen's inscrutable glare.
The room went silent, and sharply tense.
Dr. Hagen propped up in his seat laggardly and glanced at the money.
"What is this?"
"A compromise," Jack folded his arms. "If there is one thing you should have learned by now, it's that I am not like every other student…but I'm sure you knew that already."
"Have you ever heard of academic dishonesty? You're risking expulsion."
"Only if you tell anyone. Which we both know you won't."
Jack flouted Dr. Hagen's scowl, and even smirked slightly when he saw his professor slap his hand on the cash and drag it under the desk. *Mission accomplished.*
In truth, Jack was disgusted with himself once he left the office. Not because of the stunt he pulled to get his way, but rather because of the fact that he was always privileged with the ability to pull the stunt with very little risk. He hated the idea of cheating his way through a situation, and remained mindful when he had to demonstrate that he was, clearly, not like everyone else. It is crazy what five hundred dollars can buy. In this case, it was an automatic A, and unconditional discretion from his professor.
Now that he was done with such triviality, it was time for pleasure: specifically Emma, who was awaiting him for yet another study session.
Jack had become increasingly drawn to her. They were inseparable since their drunk encounter. Not necessarily the most unusual meet for fool's love, but instead of fizzling, it prospered into an established fling, only strengthening by the day. Their friends were fully supportive and equally adamant in sharing time together, forming a consensus that Jack and Emma were, factually,

meant to be. And with the semester drawing to a close, Time and its common urgencies were suspended briefly, which meant more verses he could dedicate to her.

Jack jogged to the library and skipped upstairs to find Emma on one of the tables. She did not care to look appealing that afternoon, her greasy hair tucked in her oversized pullover and scrubby sweatpants that drooped just above her sneakers. Even in her blemished state, Jack was enchanted by her beauty.

"Sorry I'm late, I had a meeting with my professor," he muttered, finding a chair.

"Don't worry about it! How did it go?"

"Not bad. I'll be passing his class with flying colors, as they say."

"That's great! I guess the studying has been paying off, huh?"

"Amongst other things," Jack leaned forward to kiss her. As little as it mattered to him, he had noticed how much more he valued his academics since he met Emma, who was a strong advocate for exemplary work ethic. He originally agreed to these study dates solely for the purpose of spending more time with her. It was not until he was nose deep in his textbook, however, when he would reevaluate additional benefits. Finals week was always a pain in his ass, but being with Emma made it tolerable.

It did not take long before she was plugged into an online lecture, sweeping through her notes, occasionally pausing and highlighting orange lines across her notebook. He would wait for her intermittent head lifts, each time exchanging a flirtatious smile.

Time had passed when Jack was distracted by a sudden, lengthy applause thundering from downstairs. He looked up at Emma, who matched his confused expression. "What's going on?" she murmured.

"Beats me," Jack shrugged, nestling his pencil in his textbook and rising from his chair. "I'm gonna check it out."

Emma nodded and returned to her lecture, leaving Jack to saunter downstairs to the lobby, where he was greeted by a massive crowd. Their backs were to him, forming a semicircle that blocked off the aisle. The applause eventually died down, and a commanding voice followed.

"I want to thank you all for being here. I know that most of you are very busy with your finals. I remember being in your place – and yes, while it was centuries ago – I can only imagine that the level of stress is unchanged." Muted chuckles. Jack peered over the crowd and saw a line of faculty standing shoulder-to-shoulder, all of whom focused on the invisible voice. "With the help of your university's president, Dr. Radford, and the rest of her administration, we have agreed to introduce a new scholarship fund for students to pursue internship opportunities with our firm, the Douglas Group." Jack froze. *No way. Could it be?*

Excitement took over as he politely advanced his way to the front of the crowd. It had been months since he had seen his father. What were the chances he would be here? His anticipation was shortly lived, however, when the voice was in fact not Wayne's. It was the firm's Vice President, Ian Thorne, whose eyes lit up in familiarity when he noticed Jack gaping back at him.

"Our firm is an ideal option for anyone willing to apply themselves and learn crucial skills that will assist in their professional development, regardless of their chosen career path. While we only offer opportunities this summer for graduating seniors, we expect to open up more roles as soon as next fall."

Applause.

"With that, I will turn it over to Monique."

Ian nodded at Dr. Radford to approach. Jack shifted back amongst the crowd, embarrassed for mistaking him for his father. He started back for the stairs, where Ian intercepted him unexpectedly.

"Jack!" he exclaimed, shaking his hand. "It's good to see you. How are your finals?"

"They're going great…so, is this like some exclusive college recruiting?"

"Of the sorts. It was your dad's idea. He was supposed to be here to deliver the news but couldn't make it. I'm sure he told you all about it."

"He didn't actually."

"Well," Ian slowed. "I'll let you get back to your studies. Stop by the office over the summer, we'd love to put you to work."

Jack watched Ian rejoin the crowd and made his way upstairs. He paused at the top, seeing that Emma was still deep in her lecture.

"Did you find out what was going on?"

"Some presentation," he said, changing the subject. "Hey, let's do something today."

"Oh yeah? What did you have in mind?"

"Anything, I just want to be with you."

"We could go check out Pike's," she suggested. "I haven't been there in forever."

"It's a date."

"I have to go to my parents' to grab a few things first."

"That's totally fine, I could pick you up if you'd like."

"That'd be great! What are you going to do in the meantime?"

"Most likely chill with the boys…" Jack replied, checking the time on his phone. "They should be grabbing lunch about now."

"Oh, see if they want to come! I can ask my girls too. We can make it a group date."

More people was not what he envisioned, but Jack agreed anyway and begun gathering his things. The lobby was already clear by the time they made their exit.

"I'll see you at your place in a bit?"

"Pretty perfect. Just text me." She kissed him and proceeded into a herd of fellow students washing through campus.

Jack checked the time on his Rolex, noting the shadow from his arm was the only one he visibly as the sun roasted the earth below. He strode eagerly through an empty hallway leading to the HUB when he stopped in his tracks upon the sound of a familiar voice.

"Jack Douglas! Holy shit, I don't believe it!"

Jack turned to meet the voice, immediately recognizing the dark, piercing eyes of the man approaching him.

Logan Berg. Hands down the biggest prick to ever walk the earth. Sure, he was not a murderer, or rapist, or terrorist. Those titles are earned for people of greater evil. But in Jack's opinion, he was pretty darn close. They were neighbors growing up, and inseparable before aging and drifting apart. The reason why was faint after so many years, but he remembered Tommy had a lot to do with it. Jack considered the two – ironically his best friends – to be like-minded individuals who saw themselves uniquely from the world. They were eerily similar, which made him question how they did not get along. Jack did not always resent Logan. His vindictive manner did not bother him as much as his means in obliviating their peers in seeing him as a gentle soul. The perfect cover-up, indeed, and meticulously calculated to his benefit. He was too young at the time to understand who Logan really was, but he knew Tommy never had a problem with anyone. So, for him to sever a friendship, and convince Jack to do the same? It was very telling of Tommy's character – as well as Logan's.

"I see you've been preying on the freshman," Logan joked. "Emma is quite a catch."

"It's not like that," Jack defended. "Plus, we went to the same high school, if you remember."

"Come on, you think I'm stupid? Of course I remember her."

"Why do you care so much anyway?"

Logan matched Jack's pace, wrapping his arm around him.

"You know, I have been waiting for the perfect opportunity to apologize to you, Jack."

"What for?"

"Oh I don't even know where to begin," Logan paused. "Let's just say that I've changed since we were younger."

"Bullshit, you haven't changed."

"That's not fair to not give me a chance to prove it at least."
"I'm not interested."
"Don't you want to hear what I have to say first?"
"Not really," Jack admitted, driving away from his arm. "I don't have time for your shit."
"My, you've become more self-assured since the last time we spoke," Logan chided, overlooking Jack's annoyance. "Look its off topic, but just so you're aware, Emma and I had something of a history in high school."
"What *history*?"
"We talked for a bit my senior year…it didn't really work out."
"Wait, lemme guess: she didn't let you fuck?"
"That's a good one!" Logan's eyes lit up. "She did happen to have a strict-ass mom, which probably had something to do with her 'good girl' vibes, if you know what I mean."
"What do you want, dude?" Jack snapped impatiently. "Is it money? If so, just say it."
"You don't have to remind me how rich you are," he seethed. "But no, it's not money I want. Just a simple request."
"Why would I ever do anything for someone like you? You're a piece of shit."
"Hey hey, no need for insults here," he playfully scorned. "Look, all I'm saying is that before you fall head over heels for this chick, you should let me have another shot."
"You're not serious?" What is this man, some sort of fucked up power move? Do you actually think I'd say yes to that?"
"I figured that you would be more open to it, given everything I've been through," he shrugged. "We both have Tommy to thank for that."
Jack gave him a perplexed expression at his mention of Tommy.
"I still can't tell if you're being serious or if you just enjoy messing with me," Jack scowled. "Just fuck off, will ya?"
"Come on, learn to take a joke sometimes," Logan chuckled. "You know I use to love joshing with you back in the day. I honestly don't give a shit about you being with Emma. Sure, she was a bit of a tease, but to each their own, right?" he became more serious. "I just wanted to see how you were doing. And again, if you wanted to catch up soon."
"I have nothing to say to you," Jack retorted dismissively. "Now please, just leave me alone okay?"
Logan frowned.
"You know, you say that I haven't changed, but I can see that you haven't either, Jacky."
"You don't know anything about me."

Logan shook his head in disappointment and watched Jack storm off. "Guess that makes two of us," he muttered to himself.

*****

Jack found the boys at the usual table, their collective attention focused on Kevin's phone. He drew closer to see them slack-jawed at a lustrous image of a woman, which was apparently enough to spur a conversation captivating enough to not notice his presence.
"What are you guys doing?"
"Jack!" Kevin blubbered, retracting his phone under the table. The boys imitated Kevin's impulse, situating themselves in what they figured were their most normal postures, hoping they were not caught in mutual drool.
"So…" Jack continued, changing the topic. "Emma and I were planning on kicking it to Pike's. You guys down to join?"
The boys relaxed, and Isaac initiating their response.
"I see you two have completely disregarded the 'friends first' tactic. I like it."
"I didn't realize that was the best method," Jack pondered. "I think we've been pretty casual, if I had to say so myself."
"You haven't always been the best observer my friend," Bennett chided.
"Sounds like our Jacky is in *love*."
The boys exchanged mocks.
"Whoa whoa whoa, you guys are pushing it a bit," Jack stammered. "Like I said, we're keeping it casual."
Tommy smirked. "That's not what your heart says."
"You can read my heart now?"
"It's just a figure of speech," Kevin added.
"Is it though?"
"Absolutely."
Jack shifted to Bennett.
"Back me up here, Benny. Didn't you keep it casual before you started dating Naylah?"
"Not really. We were friends first but we definitely liked each other from the beginning," Bennett shrugged, shooting the boys a passive glare. "Kinda disappointed how rarely you guys mention her, given she's my girlfriend. She's doing great, by the way. Thanks for asking."
Unanimous groans.
"She's amazing," Tommy assured.
"Whatever, I'm over it," Bennett said flatly.
"Don't be a little bitch," Kevin teased. "You know we love her."
"All I'm saying is that it wouldn't hurt to hear it a little more."

The boys rolled over in hysteria, their subtle mocks growing more prominent as they rattled a variety of colorful jokes at Bennett's expense.

Jack patiently waited again for their hubbub to die down before continuing. "We're leaving here in about an hour, so let me know before then if you want to join."

"Does Em know that you're inviting us?" Tommy asked.

"Yeah. Actually…it was her idea."

"I see!" Kevin cheeked, nudging Isaac him. "Seems like she's not yet ready for just the two of them alone."

"What are you talking about? We've been alone together a lot."

"Yeah but this is different. This is your first time leaving campus together. It's a different world out there."

"We've also been off-campus already, Kev."

"It was different then, is all I'm saying."

"I think you're putting too much thought into this."

"I think you're putting too *little* thought into this."

"God, I love our repartee," Bennett gleamed, wrapping his arm around a calm Tommy.

"But seriously," Kevin went on, straightening up. "I won't be able to join. I have to study tonight for my next final."

"Same," Bennett chimed in, raising his hand. "Saac also said he would help me study since he claims that he doesn't have to for himself."

"I'm a genius," Isaac clarified. "It's not a secret. We all know it."

Alas, Tommy came in.

"I'll tag along. Sounds fun."

"Great, Jack resumed, relieved to be done with his friends' specially rowdy nature. "I'm gonna grab a coffee."

"I could use the caffeine," Tommy said and followed him to the Bistro bar.

"Guess who I ran into today?" Jack began.

Tommy cupped his mouth, astonished.

"Bill Gates?"

"What?" Jack retorted. "Why did you immediately think I met Bill Gates?"

"You asked me to guess blindly," Tommy reasoned. "It's not like I had any context, nor a frame of reference. Besides, not the craziest guess in our case."

"I saw Logan."

"Logan Berg?"

"Crazy, right? What do you think of him?"

"You know damn well how I feel about him."

"I know, but it's been years. Figured I'd ask again."

"He's always annoyed me."

"Not sure if it's fair to hate him then."

"Eh, it's not worth my time getting into it," Tommy said, quickly changing the subject. "It's nice that you and Emma are taking time to get away from all the stressful shit going on here…you know, with finals and all. How are you two?

Jack nodded silently, moving past how suddenly they were onto another topic. "It's good. We hang out all the time."

"Well yeah, but you know what I'm getting at," Tommy insisted, handing his friend a lid. "Are there any reservations you have at this moment that could lead to you acting differently?"

"Hm, not sure what you mean."

"I just want to make sure that you and she are on the same page?"

"And that page is…?"

Tommy glanced away, throwing away his initial intent to keep their conversation light.

"Have you told her yet about who you are?"

Jack chuckled. "You asked that like I'm a spy or something."

"It's nice that you think it's funny," Tommy scolded, repeating the question. "Have you?"

"Not yet…why, did you tell Morgan anything?"

"Of course not. But you *do* realize the situation you've put me in?"

"I'll tell her eventually. Things are so good right now. I'd be an idiot to risk it because of something so minor."

"I understand, I really do. But that 'something' is a pretty big deal, one that affects all of us."

"By all of us, you mean it affects just you, right?"

"Partially," Tommy mumbled.

"You have nothing to worry about. I got it all planned out."

"I see, you little schemer," Tommy entreated. "I can't tell if I should be proud or nervous."

They rejoined the boys at the table. With Emma siphoning off more of his time, Jack was grateful for however much he could spend with his friends. They were distracting enough to keep him from overanalyzing the several situationships he endured with women. It may have been the first time he had a desirable routine; and yet, he understood even the most ideal dynamics were bound to change. If not now, then soon.

*****

Jack minded the GPS navigating them to Emma's. It was odd for him to drive on a road he had never driven on in a town he believed to know better than the back of his hand. Though the familiarity, nor its proximity ever bothered him.

When he was in high school, the idea of attending a college so close to his roots brought a lurking angst, but it was a disguised blessing. Having all those he cared most for within a twenty-minute radius coupled with the ability to practice an independent lifestyle? Sometimes he would forget that he lived in the same city his whole life.

"I bet it's because we have to take the bridge," Tommy said from the passenger seat.

"What?"

"Why it feels like we are so far away from home," he clarified. "It's probably because we have to take this bridge to get there."

"Oh," Jack paused, momentarily suspecting his best friend of possessing the gift of telepathy as he steered off a main road and onto a private gravel driveway.

"Have you been here before?" Tommy asked.

"No, you?"

"When would I ever be at her place?"

"I don't know, you apparently knew her long before I did."

"I know a lot of people," Tommy replied. "And while that's true, you definitely know her better than I ever had."

Emma's home was gorgeous, albeit modest compared to the neighboring mansions. Only speckles of the brick exterior were visible, as the front was draped in alfresco vinery. Jack slowed behind the single vehicle in the driveway before parking.

"A Porsche," Tommy observed. "I like this family already."

A middle-aged woman awaited them with the door ajar. Her look was all too familiar to Jack, who privately noted the demure, dubious smirk below her dazzling grey eyes.

"Jack Douglas?"

"Yes, ma'am," Jack affirmed, shaking her hand.

"I'm Emma's mother, Julia."

Tommy choked incredulously. "You're a *mom*?"

Julia blushed and snagged onto Tommy's cheeks.

"And who is this handsome boy you brought with you?"

"This is my buddy, Tommy."

"It is nice to meet you both."

She released her grasp from a dreamy Tommy and entered the house, leaving Jack to slap him back into reality as they followed her inside.

"Emma, your friends are here!" Julia called up the stairs as she guided the boys past the stairwell.

The main floor was a split-level, blanketed entirely in sienna hardwood, which boasted a gleam reflecting from the sunlight pouring through from the

French doors directly ahead that led to the solarium. They veered left toward the kitchen, where leading up Jack glossed over an assortment of multi-sized frames of the Keva family housed in a massive shrunk. In addition to Emma and Julia, was a man he noted as the father, and presumably out of the picture given the few instances Emma mentioned him.

The kitchen stood out from the rest of the home, with marble tiles and dimmable recessed lights that gave a new-world feel unlike the earthier tone he compared closer to Tommy's.

"You have a lovely home Julia," Tommy glazed.

She thanked him and retrieved a pair of water bottles from the fridge. "Emma told me that you all go to school together."

"That's right."

"Douglas," Julia pondered. "You know, there is a family that lives in the neighborhood with the same last name—"

"Wayne and Anita Douglas," Jack chimed in before she could finish. "No relation, just a big coincidence. I get it a lot."

"That's funny. I don't know them well, but I also don't think they have any children," she noted, changing the subject. "It seems the girls are taking their sweet time. I'm sure you both are in a hurry. I'll go get them."

Jack watched her pace daintily upstairs. It was oddly surprising how quickly she dismissed his namesake, until he remembered who his parents were; specifically, their need to keep personal affairs private from everyone outside their inner circle of friends. Affairs including (but not limited to) the existence of their son.

He caught sight of Tommy inspecting him.

"What?"

"Nothing," he whispered as they trailed back to the hallway. "Just blows my mind how you're not an antisocial psychopath by how much your parents shielded you from the world."

"I told you, I'm waiting for the right time to tell her."

"Hey, I hear you, but tell me again what the objective is by holding the truth out for as long as you are doing?"

"I'm not like you, Tommy. I don't like going about flexing about who I am, especially to girls. People like to take advantage."

"You're such a cliché. We're young, brother. Now is the perfect time to indulge the youthful spirits of these beautiful women."

He noticed Jack's attention diverted to the picture of Emma's father as they walked past.

"What do you figure happened there?"

"Huh—" Jack paused, realizing Tommy was watching him. "Oh, I'm not sure. Emma doesn't talk about him a lot…maybe a bad divorce."

Tommy shook his head. "No shot. Did you *see* Emma's mom? I bet he's just no longer around."

"What do you mean?"

They were interrupted by commotion at the top of the stairs before Tommy could respond, causing them to look up. There she was again. Emma Keva. She and Morgan were both dressed down in t-shirts and yoga pants – not the most surprising attire for a Seattleite. Even so, he was dumbstricken by her radiance.

"Are you okay?" Emma asked.

She was directly in front of them when Jack realized he had checked out the last ten seconds.

"Yeah, I'm great," he stammered, swallowing the little saliva left that had not yet dried from his mouth and twirling his keys in hand. "Should we get going?"

Julia intercepted them at the front door.

"Now Jack, I'm sure you are good person, but I just want to make sure she is in the best hands—"

"Mom please," Emma cut in, grabbing Jack's arm. "We'll be fine, it's not a big deal."

"I think it is."

"Let's go," she said to Jack before looking back at her mother. "I'll call you when we're on our way home."

"I understand, ma'am. I'll make sure she's safe," Jack assured her and continued outside, oblivious to her signaling.

He's perfect for you, she mouthed, to which Emma returned a glare.

Julia was most of what a child would want in a mother. Including her incessant support, which unfortunately, was not for Emma's freedom, but rather ensuring she would have a secure future.

Emma understood how different life was when her mother was young. Julia rarely needed to rely on herself, because that was man's duty. She eventually left her family for her late husband, Bruce, who provided a comparable dynamic.

It was difficult for Emma not to resent her for it. Emma's outlook on life was more ambitious, contrasting Julia's parenting style and advice. She was not a delinquent, but a rebel – which Julia believed to be worse.

Morgan circled around Jack's beamer and jumped in the backseat.

"This car is awesome!"

Jack acknowledged her comment and adjusted the rearview mirror. The naïve enthusiasm. It reminded him of the girls he entertained.

Emma was grounded, and intuitively curious about seeking the devil in the details. There was no question she, too, had considered how nice his ride was when she mentioned it on their first date. A slight overlook on Jack's part, but then again, he figured a solid alibi that could be used indefinitely.
"It's my dad's," he explained, winking at Emma.
"It *is* really nice," Emma added, fastening her seatbelt.
Jack sent a look of concern to Tommy in the passenger seat as he started down the driveway and back onto the highway.
He was in the clear. For now.

*****

Thunderclouds loomed across the inlet, with rumbles of an imminent storm just beyond the bay. Jack peeked at Emma, who seemed blissed by the sweeping waters as she inhaled the cool air. Before reaching legal age, Jack rarely felt compelled to venture into the city, especially if the sole purpose was to sightsee. Had it not been for Emma, he would have suggested calling off the excursion early. But she did not appear bothered by eventual spillage, and as such, it did not bother him either.
"It's amazing," Emma observed when they were within sight of the market.
"True. A *lot* of folks out too," Tommy added. "Do they not have anything better to do?"
Jack patted Tommy's back. "We're here too, buddy."
"What are you implying?"
Jack shrugged. "Just following your lead."
Tommy rolled his eyes disapprovingly and guided them into the crowd.
For those that have never been, Pike Place Market is a historically modern wonder. Steeped on a hill overlooking the inlet, it was a modern marvel for its respective residents, and all who used it for their source of foods and entertainment alike.
The market was a narrowing maze, bordered with boisterous, flickering colors and a distinguishably potent aroma that made Jack question whether having a sense of smell was truly a blessing. That said, even he could not deny the lively atmosphere, strolling amidst the hundreds, if not thousands, of Seattleites pouring through the open-aired walkway.
Morgan stopped at a table displaying an assortment of charming, handmade jewelry.
"Guys, look at this!" she implored, holding up a beaded necklace.
Emma joined, leaving the boys to spectate. From the corner of Jack's eye, he could see Tommy's paranoia come to life, watching him scan the market almost deliriously.

"Not a big fan of people, are ya Tom?"
"People, I have no problem with," he clarified. "It's when there are *many* people. You ever watched movies? Something always happens when you least expect it."
"What kind of movies are you watching?"
Tommy ignored his question, distracted by the people surrounding them.
"You're making me nervous. Could you relax?"
Tommy took a deep breath.
 "Sorry, you know I've always been ambivalent when it comes to crowds."
"Right, I should have considered that when I asked you to come. Sorry about that."
"No need to apologize. This is important to you. I'm here 'til the end." They found produce situated deeper in the hall. Tommy followed his lead, watching him pick up squash from the stack.
"I don't think I've ever actually seen on these," Jack laughed.
"I don't remember the last time I've eaten a vegetable."
"I thought it was a fruit?"
"Is it?"
"I don't know."
"Wait, what did I say?"
"I think you said it was a vegetable."
"Oh right, yeah it is," Jack confirmed, howbeit confused. "Right?"
It is clear they were at their most inane when they were together.
Emma and Morgan regrouped with them shortly after. Together, they proceeded to the end of the hall, the scent of seafood replaced with a salty breeze from the ocean. The path took them downhill and out to the city avenue, Emma and Morgan pacing in front of the boys. They were in no rush, and the destination wherever their feet took them.
The boys lagged close behind, busied in their own conversation. Although he did not intend to, Jack had inadvertently began to eavesdrop on the girls' chatter.
"I'm not at all prepared for this summer," he caught from Morgan. "I'm taking online classes on top of my job. I'll literally have no social life."
"I feel that," Emma concurred. "I'm still waiting to hear back from that internship I told you about a couple months ago. And if I get it, I'll have to be in New York City for the whole summer. I won't even be able to go to Lolla and I already bought my ticket."
Jack pressed his lips together, connecting the dots of a glowering truth he was reluctant to address.
Emma's internship.

It was only the second time she had mentioned it around him since their first date, which caused him to wonder why she had not discussed the topic with him directly. What could be the reason for not being upfront about something that could jeopardize their relationship? Unless, perhaps she did not imagine it would.

No, Jack caught himself, ignoring his inner thoughts. Now was not the time to overthink about something that could be nothing.

"The semester is almost over, and you still haven't heard from…"

"Ember House," Emma finished.

"What are you going to do if you don't get it?"

"Don't worry, I have a couple options in the city just in case. Between you and me, I've accepted that it probably won't happen."

"You're going to get it. I know it for a fact."

Jack knew better than to take Morgan's insight as law. But just hearing her say it with so much certainty…he began to panic again.

He promptly slowed his pace, taking hold of Tommy's wrist and pulling him back as the girls obliviously walked on.

Tommy faced Jack, glancing down at his tightened grip on his arm.

"What's up man?" he asked. "Why do you look like you're about to throw up?"

"Did you hear what Emma said?"

"No, sorry," Tommy replied blankly. "If you can believe it, I was totally focused on the conversation that *we* were having."

"Summer break," Jack went on. "Everything is going to be different once the semester is over."

"This semester is essentially over," Tommy corrected, immediately catching himself and tending to Jack's apparent distress. "Sorry, as you were saying?"

"What happens when we go home for the summer?"

"Are you being rhetorical?"

"Sort of. Play along anyway."

"Okay," Tommy nodded. "Let's see…we go home. We work *a lot* – at least I do – that's about it."

"Exactly, do you see my point now?"

"I think so…you don't want to work?"

"No Tom, well yes I guess that's true, but no, that's not what I'm getting at."

"What then?"

"Emma," Jack finally revealed, subtly gesturing in her direction. "I overheard her talking about the internship again. She still doesn't know if she has gotten it yet."

"And that matters because…?"

"If she gets it, she will have to go to New York," Jack explained. "I won't see her all summer! What do I do?"
"I'm not sure, but I don't think it hurts to talk to her about it."
It was indeed a discussion he needed to have with Emma, but Jack feared he would come off too strong if he decided to be the one to initiate it.
"I really like her Tommy."
"That's great, you should tell her that too."
"She already knows that. Besides, that isn't the point," Jack pouted. "If she ends up leaving for the internship before we even have the chance to grow closer…"
"You already accomplished getting Emma to agree to date you," Tommy reasoned. "So she leaves for the summer. Who cares? You two will still be together."
"I just had a certain plan as to when to tell her some things."
"Oh, you mean lying to her about being rich and not the son of a mechanic from Bellevue?"
"I didn't say my dad was a mechanic."
"Regardless, I don't see how I can help with this one."
"Don't give me that," Jack scolded. "A few months ago, you promised to help me find my wife."
"I agreed to help you *find* her, yes. And look – you have! 'Mission accomplished, Tommy, you're welcome' – that's what you should be saying."
"I know you, Tom. There is no way you could live with yourself if you thought you had anything to do with me and Emma breaking up."
Tommy rolled his eyes, privately acknowledging truth in Jack's statement. It would be a lie if he was not thrilled upon being informed of Jack and Emma's continued infatuation with each other. In fact, the primary reason he agreed to these double dates was to ensure they thrive. Not to say he did not desire a closer relationship with Morgan, but simultaneously, he was rational enough to not let emotions persuade his actions. He struggled with obligations, or commitment of any kind – not for the sake of trust – rather his own self-reliance and doubt in his own improvement on behalf of associating with another person. Like Jack, though, he yearned for companionship, and forced himself into unnecessary sacrifices at the expense of his own ego.
At the end of the day, as long as Jack was happy, he was determined to roll with the punches. He considered Jack and Emma to still in the 'merge' of their relationship; and since its future was blurry, Tommy recognized the importance of utilizing his gift of influence in helping steer it on the right course.
"Okay, give me time to think of something."

The sun had begun to sink below the horizon when they returned to Emma's house. Jack was anxious to get off his feet after walking all day, and more anxious that Tommy had yet to propose an idea to the group. For someone who touted his creative solutions to problems, Jack feared if he would be able to pull through this time around.

"Today was exactly what I needed to get my mind off of everything," Morgan started. Thanks, boys."

"Of course," Jack replied, grinning at Emma. "There's never anything wrong with a spontaneous adventure every now and then."

"You know," Tommy began. "It may be a while before we are all going to be here again, making memories like these. I think we should have one final send off to commemorate our time together this semester."

Yes Tommy, Jack thought, anticipating what was to follow. *Right at the eleventh hour, I love it.*

"What do you have in mind?" Emma asked.

"A vacation, of sorts," he motioned at Jack, who was now beginning to dread the scheme his friend brewed up.

"Vacation, eh? Where do you suggest?"

"It just so happens that our friend here has an impressive network of connections, one person in particular who would most likely open his home for us for a nice getaway," Tommy turned to Jack. "Isn't that right?"

Jack was lost. He searched for any clues in Tommy's words but failed to understand.

Then he got it. Tommy was referring to his parents' private cabin. He and his boys would stay there on occasion, but he was hesitant to comply given the false backstory he told Emma.

"I don't know," Jack cautioned, choosing his words carefully. "I'll have to check. There is a big chance that we won't be able to."

He felt guilty when he saw the girls' changed expressions, and glared at Tommy, who gave him a puzzled look.

"But you know what? Let's do it anyway," Jack announced. "I should be able to make it work."

They all cheered, Emma embracing him.

"I'm so excited!" she said happily. "Let's shoot for next weekend?"

"It's a date," Jack concluded, kissing her waving as she and Morgan headed inside the house.

Jack waited until they were inside and out of sight before he turned to Tommy.

"Really man?"

"What?"

"If I knew your brilliant idea involved us taking Emma to my cabin, I would have said no."

"It was a last-minute call. You put me in a quite the predicament." "You put me in a bigger one!" Jack spat when they were back inside the car. "What's going to happen when we get there, and she finds out that it's my cabin? She'll know I lied to her. What if the tables were turned and you were in my shoes?"

Tommy shrugged dismissively.

"Morgan isn't the one for me. I know that for a fact."

It astounded Jack at how careless Tommy projected his feelings toward Morgan. Of course, one would assume such behavior to be a result of his insecurity of being vulnerable. But Jack knew Tommy well, and how he could be characterized under a structure, however rigid or flexible, of social comprehension. Tommy was different. An enigma, if it had to be labeled. That said, Jack believed Tommy secretly longed for a real relationship. He recalled how often he flinged with many girls growing up and would even share snippets with said girls with his friends, Jack happening to be his main confidant and wingman.

Above all, Tommy had the reputation of being very outgoing and transparent, but because Jack was so close to him, he was also aware of how secretive he could be. Tommy chose his words carefully, and after years of absorbing his personality, Jack knew when he would intentionally withhold details in his endless narratives. The objective may still remain unknown to him, but Jack suspected Tommy's motive behind why he did it: a fear of being judged. Tommy was not perfect by any means. But he was oddly brilliant in delivering even the most unbelievable tales. It was a quality that most found envious. At the same time, it made Jack question the most extreme hypotheticals. Why, someone who was capable of making the most unfathomable ideas seem sensible…it could make one ponder just how far that person would be willing to go for something they rationalized to be true, however good-natured the intentions are.

There was one girl that Tommy entertained. One that some would say, he even loved. Jack first got the hint of her from Isaac, but it was swiftly discredited after he began rattling off about the hottest celebrities of the 21st century.

The origin of their relationship is largely unknown, and more so their eventual end. Even her identity was a mystery to Jack, who occasionally attempted to riddle off into the abundance of names once mentioned by Tommy over the years. It reached a point where Jack would mentally sort their names in alphabetical order.

Abby, Alexis, Avery, Ashtyn.

Bailey, Baylee, Brooke, Brooklynn.
Caitlin, Carlie, Carly, Cherish, Cheyenne, Chloe, Crystal.
Girl after girl. There was at least one for every letter.
Samantha, Sarah, Savanna, Shannon, Shelby, Sidney, Skylar, Sydney.
Tatiana, Tatum, Taylin, Taya, Taylor, Tori, Torrie.
No, none of those.
He would eventually give up, wondering if she ever even existed. If it was all a distant, fragmented piece of his friend's memory. Perhaps it was real, but a blend of experiences with multiple girls mistakenly believed by Tommy to be rooted in a single candidate.
Regardless, Jack knew there was one thing about the girl that Tommy Beech loved: she was a queen, inside and out. Inordinately perfect.
"Maybe this is meant to be," Tommy reasoned. "After all, if what you told me about your feelings for her are true, then it is better to come clean sooner than later."
Jack tried to stay upset, but now found it hard hearing Tommy's argument. It may not be the most ideal scenario, but he also never expected for his relationship with Emma to progress this far.
"You're right."
"I know."
"That said, I still think we have to play it safe."
"What does that mean?"
"It means that you and I have a lot of work to do."
"I see," Tommy beamed. "Jacky D scheming up another plan. I gotta say this recent behavior is very unlike you."
He was right: plans were not in his wheel of talents. But if it meant securing Emma's love, Jack was willing to do whatever it took.

V

Flurries raced through swaying evergreens, causing a cluster of leaves to stir across the windshield before sliding off in a hurried sail back to the damp roadway. Jack pressed his hand on the window and, using his finger, etched his initials through the condensation. He pushed the creeping anxiety out of his mind, keeping his focus on everything but the road as they drove deeper into the northern Washington woodlands.

The gloomy environment was not the source of Jack's unease, however. This was his first weekend away with Emma, or any girl, for that matter. It helped that Tommy was with him. But Morgan was also in the car, suggesting that there would be minimal time for his wingmanship. While the opportunity to be with Emma delighted Jack, he was nervous to find himself in a situation similar to Jen. She still did not know of Jack's wealthy upbringing, and a weekend at his cabin could bring questions he was not yet ready to answer.

Tommy leaned forward and peered out the windshield, fantasized by the Cascades resting atop the trees.

"I am so pumped for this!" he announced, swerving into the oncoming lane temporarily before correcting the wheel.

"Could you *please* keep your eyes on the road man?" Jack uttered from the backseat.

"Don't worry buddy, I'll be on my best behavior when we get to your friend's house," Tommy met Jack's eyes in the mirror. At least he had not forgotten their alibi to explain how two college kids could manage an intimate, luxurious weekend getaway.

As humble as Jack believed his parents were, it was certainly not reflected through their cabin away from home. Perhaps *cabin* was not the best term to accurately describe it.

The property was an oasis, perched on a hillside adjacent to the ivory mountains. The exterior was impressively pristine, its three stories nearly reaching the forest canopy, and a massive structure appearing to float if it were not for the cylindric pillars that braced it deep into the rigid earth.

Its backyard was an outdoor experience on another level, stacked with a brick fireplace, basketball court, and heated pool, with lights stringing from the pines circulating the property. The interior was just as splendid, with amenities anyone would dream for, including a game room, two private offices, gym, and theater room. Surrounding the property was a ten-foot fence, lined with a plethora of exotic shrubbery dancing at the million raindrops meeting the earth.

Emma took a moment to admire the cabin once they parked.

"This place is incredible. Your friend lives here?"

"My dad's friend," Jack corrected. "I don't come here often. They usually invite us over the holidays."

"I'm ready to get wild," Tommy lifted the trunk door. "You girls head inside and get settled; the door's unlocked. Jack and I got your stuff."

Emma and Morgan skipped up the steps excitedly and entered the house.

"Not gonna lie, I was curious how we were going to pull this off, but so far it seems to be working out."

"We just got here," Jack tensed. "Also, did you remember to take down all the family pictures?"

"Come on dude, you're insulting my intelligence here. Of course I did," he handed him Emma's bag. "You can have the *master* bedroom."

"Gross man, my parents sleep there."

Tommy closed the trunk and snatched his and Morgan's bags before starting up the stairs.

"They won't be tonight!"

Prior to their arrival, Jack and Tommy spent a full day ridding the cabin of anything that could imply who exactly owned it, which yes, included a multitude of pictures that hung aside the stairwell connecting the three floors. They even went as far as clearing Jack's bedroom, stashing his clothes and belongings in the shed just down the hill from the backyard. As long as they exercised caution, Jack figured there was nothing to worry about.

But Emma was a smart girl. No one ever mentions the negatives that come with that.

Jack grew nostalgic when he entered the master bedroom. The California king was neatly decorated with silk banners wrapped around steel poles, spanning across both ends as they tapered along the walls layered with an assortment of expensive art. He was telling the truth when he told Emma he was rarely here. Wayne and Anita saw it as a private retreat during special occasions, and it was the only time Jack was guaranteed to be with them outside their busy schedules. Certainly, there is sadness that comes at the price of happiness.

Emma emerged from the bathroom. She had changed her outfit, dressed down in a hoodie and yoga pants – Jack's personal favorite.

"You look nice," he marveled.

"Thanks," she replied coolly.

Jack was perplexed by her tone, raising a brow and shouldering their bags on the bed. *Did something happen within the last fifteen minutes?*

Before he could ask, Tommy and Morgan entered the room.

"Okay! I'm all settled," Morgan said, her profound eagerness splitting through the previous awkward tension. "What should we do?"

Jack tabled his concern with Emma. "Whatever we want," he mused.

Tommy focused on the girls.

"Looks like the rain is letting up. I say we take our talents outside while we still have the sunlight."
"There's a nice lookout not far from here," Jack proposed. "It'll probably be dark by the time we get there, but it's one of my favorite places to go."
"Look at this guy!" Tommy jested, giving Jack a friendly nudge. "First the cabin, and now this. You're killing it with the brilliant ideas, I love it."
 Jack peeked at Emma for approval, who reciprocated with a halfhearted nod. "Sure. Sounds fun."
Jack frowned. Something *definitely* happened in the short time between their arrival to their moment. He reckoned it would be in his best interest to pretend as if he did not notice.
"Okay," Jack started, taking initiative. "Let's get to it."
Dusk neared its course as Jack strayed them out of the cabin and to the other end of the property, where sure enough was the beginning of a pathless trail extending deeper in the woods. The trail was narrow, forcing them to file in a single line. Jack led, keeping his eyes forward. He had the path memorized over the years, and it did not take long before he became lost in thought, highlighting the picturesque landscape that grew more familiar with every step. The lush scenery pulled him away from the indistinct conversation held by his friends close behind. Not that it bothered him. He was used to doing this on his own. If anything, he assumed the dynamic would remain unchanged with them, only discovering how much more he treasured it; having the opportunity to share his own hidden piece of the vast wilderness. While he had hoped that Emma would be more involved – rather than confusing him with her strange behavior back at the cabin – he tried to not let it affect any pleasure of enjoying himself. Perhaps there was a good excuse for her tension. After all, he had his share of uncertainly on the ride up here. They reached the end of the trail, seating themselves just a few feet from the daunting cliff. A full moon gleamed before them, illuminating a crystalline lake that rippled with the wind's breath. An ethereal scene, indeed, coupled with series of amplified howls and screeches echoing from the cresting mountains resting below the darkening horizon. Jack had never been out here this late in the night, which under normal circumstances would be discomforting. That said, it was virtually impossible for him to regard his brooding anxiety with his friends by his side, not to mention the stunning view.
Tommy reached into his pocket, producing an unlit joint. The girls giggled as he cupped one hand over the joint and lit the end with the other. After a couple attempts, an orange glow sparked, prompting the group to cheer as he took a hit and passed it along.

Jack followed his lead, pressing his lips to the joint and drawing a deep breath. His eyes closed upon exhaling the potent smoke, the high hitting him immediately and causing him to sit down.

Emma joined him, reluctantly pushing up beside him for warmth and resting her head on his shoulder.

"You keep that one," Tommy insisted, retrieving another joint from his pocket and smirking at Morgan. "This is for us."

They situated themselves just out of earshot from Jack and Emma, leaving the pair alone in silence.

After a few long moments, Jack turned to Emma, motioning for her to take the joint. She pinched it, listlessly bringing it to her lips.

"Is everything okay?" he asked.

"Yeah," she replied dismissively.

"Hey," Jack poked, leaning forward to meet her eyes. "You can tell me."

Emma was clearly unwilling to get into whatever was on her mind, averting her gaze on the glowing lake.

"This just reminds me of my dad," she finally revealed.

Jack nearly choked in amusement as he took a pronounced hit.

"Getting high reminds you of your dad?"

"No silly. I meant being here like this," she smiled faintly. "My dad would always take me camping when I was little." Another pause. "He loved exploring the most random, far-off places. A campsite wouldn't be enough for him, there had to be views like this."

"Your dad sounds awesome," Jack commented, privately regretting his choice to smoke as much as he did now that he feared entering an intimate conversation. Better if he had her do most of the talking. "Tell me more."

"His name's Bruce. You would have loved him, he was the goofiest guy ever," she continued. "There was one time we had to go to my grandmother's funeral, and my dad went up to speak. I swear that guy thought he was the star of his own standup. He went *on* about her, telling so many stories about when she would get mad at him for all the stupid things he used to do when he was a kid. My mom was so embarrassed," she took another hit before intermittently breaking out in laughter. "He waited on the alter after his speech like he expected a standing ovation, and my mom had to go up and drag him back to our seats."

"You're kidding?"

"I wish I was. Another time he thought it would be a good idea to prank me at our high school dance. He showed up telling all the kids that he was a cop and threatening to take them to jail if they didn't give him the drugs they had on them," she paused again, glancing at Jack. "A joke, obviously," she confirmed, before fixating back on the lake and continuing. "When our

principal found out what he was doing, my dad ended up joking with him and took him out for a beer afterwards. He had a way of making someone's bad day amazing…" she trailed off. "Before he died, I promised him that I would do the same. Because there is nothing more important in life than showing how much you care about everyone in your life."
Jack listened intently, absorbing her words, her voice, her mood. He was unsure what to say, piecing together an appropriate response before speaking. "I didn't know that your dad passed. I'm sorry."
Emma shrugged it off. "Thanks. Cancer isn't prejudice, you know? It happens to everyone. Maybe not their dad, but someone they love. All part of life, right?"
"Right," Jack agreed, biting at his curiosity in asking how he died. Another time. "I can see Gus laughing along with your dad, though. That guy was crazy."
"First name basis with our former principal, huh?"
"My parents were good friends with him. He got me out of a lot of jams, no thanks to Tommy over there."
"Tell me about your 'jams,'" Emma teased, evidently shifting the conversation to a lighter tone.
Jack still sensed her sadness and took the chance to cheer her up. He delved into a series of tales from high school – from freshman year when they started a food fight in the lunchroom, to paying off the announcer at graduation to mispronounce his buddies' names as they walked across the stage to receive their diploma. Story after story, he watched as Emma's tight frown gradually expanded into a beautiful, beaming smile, accompanied by her endearing snorts. He loved it. He loved her.
The hike back was euphoric, the foursome swapping glowing remarks and hugging each other when one began to teeter off the invisible path. Nothing could have made the night better.
"I'm starving," Tommy spoke up when they made it back to the cabin. "Did anyone bring anything too eat?"
"There should be some frozen pizzas inside."
"*Frozen pizza?*" Tommy snickered. "I've said this before and I'll say it again: you know the way to my heart brother."
Jack chuckled and peered down at Emma, noticing her piercing stare from earlier that afternoon. He joined Tommy in the kitchen, doing his best not to overthink it.
"We're going to change," Morgan called to them while she pulled Emma upstairs, leaving the boys alone once again.
"So," Tommy started once he heard the door close the top floor. "Seemed like you and Emma were in a pretty serious conversation back at the lake."

"Yeah, she was telling me about her dad. He died a few years ago."

"Oh," Tommy mumbled while he preheated the oven. "Hey, it's good that she told you though. Probably means she's starting to take you two more seriously."

"Are you saying she hasn't before?"

"No, not at all. But you know how relationships tend to get more real once you get past all the things we prefer to be left unsaid."

"I guess…" Jack uttered, looked up to see Tommy still eyeing him. "What?"

"Do you not know what I'm going to say next?"

"…No?"

"Dude, I know you have your reasons not to, but if you want to make this work, you need to tell Emma the truth."

Jack moaned begrudgingly. "You want me to come clean *now?* We literally based this weekend on a lie. How do you think that would look?"

Tommy raised his hands almost jokingly. "Hey man, my mom always told me that lying is like digging a hole."

Jack rolled his eyes. "Your point?"

Tommy rested his hand on Jack's shoulder. "The more lies you tell, the deeper the hole gets, and the harder it is to get yourself out once you start telling the truth. Get out of the hole now while you still have the chance."

Jack never liked his analogies; particularly because they were always too accurate to his situation.

Not to say that Emma's past was secretive, but he reasoned it was not information she shared with just anyone. It required a qualified confidant, and as that confidant, Jack reluctantly agreed with Tommy's notion of revealing the truth to her in hopes that it breaches through a renewed standing of their relationship. Precisely the kind of relationship he originally envisioned: one without secrets.

Tommy pointed to the oven. "I'll bake them slowly so they're ready for you lovebirds when you're done."

"Ugh, fine," he whined and left upstairs.

Emma was sitting at the foot of the bed when Jack entered. He closed the door behind him, seeing her peer up at him without saying a word. Even when she was clearly upset, Jack was taken away by her beauty. He slowly approached the bed and sat beside her, his hands clasped together.

"I know I asked you already…but are you okay?"

She turned away, barring any further assessment.

"Do you remember our first date Jack?"

"Of course I do. It was amazing."

"Yeah," she said curtly. "I never got around to telling you, but after that night I did a lot of thinking about us…about some things that I found really weird that day."
Jack gave a puzzled frown. "What do you mean?"
"Well, first with the car – which you said was your dad's – but anyone with a 'small business' as you put it, could realistically never afford the type of car that you were driving that day. But I ignored it because, hey, there's a world where it could happen."
"Okay…"
"Also," Emma continued, Jack sensing that she was just getting started. "When we were at the restaurant, you and the waiter were a little *too* familiar with each other. Which, after hearing your excuse, I chose to accept it at the time. But going back to your parents and their jobs, it still confused me that they were able to afford you all going there so frequently, as you mentioned. And now *this*," she paused, gesturing to the room. "Which I know, is not any of my business as to how your family does financially. At least, not until it comes between us, which I think is the situation we find ourselves in now."
Jack remained silent.
"Is there anything you would like to say to me Jack?"
"Emma—"
"This is the only time I will ask you," she warned. "I like you, and I want this to work. For that to happen, I need you to be honest with me."
"I want this to work too."
"Good, then tell me Jack: what are we doing here?"
Jack dragged his words. "Do you mean like, here in this room? Or are we still talking about our first date—"
Emma suddenly arose and faced him. "Why did you lie to me?"
"About what?"
She brought her hands to her temple, maintaining her composure.
"You know, I forced myself to believe that all my concerns from that night was just my imagination. But then it came back when I noticed how you were acting on the drive up here. You were so quiet in the car, and then when we got here, I kept putting it out of my mind. But now as I'm talking about it, I know I have to do the healthy thing, and that is get this all off my chest."
"…Okay?" he muttered, trying not to come off as apprehensive.
"The first thing was as soon as we got here: the door was just *unlocked*. I know Tommy said that it should be, but I mean, it's such a nice place, and I personally would never leave it open for anyone to just walk in. But I figured that your dad's friend knew that we were coming, so I let it slide. Then the house – amazing, by the way – was perfect…*perfect*, Jack. Better than any rental I've stayed in. So, I thought that whoever this man was, he was the

OCD type. Which, totally understandable, because we all have those tendencies from time to time. But whatever, I thought, and didn't let it affect me. But then when I checked out the basement, I noticed the door to a closet was open. I figured I'd be a polite guest and close it for him."

Shit, Jack thought. *How could I forget to close the door?*

"As I was going to close it, I got a peek of what was inside: clothes, papers, pictures, a bunch stuff that looked pretty personal, and again, none of my business. But then something caught my eye…" she took a brief pause, producing a small envelope from her back pocket.

Jack squinted at the envelope she waved in his face, only able to make out two words: *birthday,* and *son.*

"Finally, I'm able to learn more about this guy," Emma added, unfolding the card inside. "He has a son! And he was willing to give him this beautifully written card for his birthday. So naturally, I'd love to know more about this guy, right? And then that had me thinking: what does this dude even look like? And if he has a son, that means he would have a family too, all of whom I have absolutely no idea what any of them look like. Why would he throw all these pictures in a closet, hidden from the world?"

Jack understood what she was doing. This was her way of telling him that she knew; she knew everything, and she found out on her own using her insane FBI-esque probing skills. Should have dated a dumber girl, pal.

"Okay, I get it Em," Jack stepped in.

"Do you want to know the name of his son?" she asked.

Jack lifted his head, meeting her stern glare. "Is it Jack?"

"It *is* Jack," she confirmed, her already steel expression hardening. "Do you understand what is on my mind now?"

"So you knew I was lying since we got here, and after tonight – everything we talked about at the lookout – why did you wait to call me out?"

"Because I wanted to see if you were going to tell me the truth on your own," Emma explained, tossing the envelope on the bed and folding her arms. "When you didn't say anything to me back at the lake, I knew that you were planning on keeping this a secret indefinitely, and I wasn't going to let you think that I was stupid enough to keep talking to you without first letting you know that you weren't as clever as you thought. That's why I gave you that nasty look before you went to the kitchen. I'm glad it was enough for you to realize that something was *indeed* on my mind, and I expected that Tommy would sway you into coming up here to tell me the truth. Am I correct?"

Jack was stunned by her analysis. Was he in some alternate universe? Did he actually know this girl as well as he originally thought?

"I'm sorry."

"You lied to me."

"Yes, I did," he admitted. "I can explain myself though."
"Please do."
Jack tried to relax, his fingers numbing from an uncontrollable twiddling
failing to cease. He paled, upset for putting himself in this blundering mess. A
personal nightmare of his, having to reveal his deepest vulnerability to
someone he cared so much for. Honesty in the best policy, and he chose to
neglect it out of protection for his own prudence.
"My entire life, everyone – even my friends – think that being me is the best
thing ever, but it's not. My parents are so successful, but I'm just me. I was
always taught growing up to live as normally as I could…I know it's easy for
people with money to say that it doesn't mean anything to them, and I know
how hypocritical it is for me to say it to you now…but I mean it," he paused,
studying her eyes. "I never cared about any of it, and I want everyone to know
that. Including you, but I was scared to tell you because I was afraid you
wouldn't look at me the same. I love everything about you, and I wanted you
to see me as Jack Douglas, the regular guy…not Jack Douglas, the billionaire.
I know I sound a little silly, but it's true."
"You *do* sound a bit silly right now," she taunted, bringing her hand to his
cheek. "But I understand. I probably would have done the same thing. I can't
imagine what it would be to be in constant fear about something that isn't
even negative, but is still big enough that it shapes how you present yourself
to others."
"Tommy refers to it as the 'Ironic Tragedy.'"
"Tommy's very interesting," she smiled. "I think you are, too."
Emma leaned in close and brought her lips to Jack's. He rested his hands on
her hips, moving them around her waist and pulled her to him. His eyes shut,
he kissed her back, tilting her body on his as he fell back on the bed. She
rolled on top of him, stripping off her clothes and pushing up against his
pelvis. They both opened their eyes. The moment was clear. She took over,
easing herself in him and rising to complement his upward push. Jack caught
his breath, inhaling the burning air as they shared the same pulse, thrusting
back and forth, slowly, moderately, quickly. She laid her hand on his chest,
matching his gaze as she crept her fingers closer to his neck, lightly pressing
into his collar. He spun her to her back and kissed her again, driving deeper
and breaking through the established rhythm, his tongue drawing across her
chest. She gripped his right hand and planted it on her thigh, clutching his
wrist as he tasted every piece of flesh that met his mouth. Her moan was
intoxicating, the two of them holding, shifting, tangling, stirring together in a
spirited clash of passion. He leaned forward where their heads touched,
catching a glimpse of the side of her face, her beaming grin widening the
harder he thrusted. He was immersed in her scent, the lustrous look in her

glassy eyes, her silvery ring pierced through her charming nose, her maroon hair darkened from the beading sweat across her forehead, her reassuring sound amplifying over his own. He felt her embrace tighten again, her trembling becoming more evident as he raised his face and focused on her eyes as she reciprocated. His concentration was solely on her, and hers for him, coupled with a growing, and sudden urgency of electric sensualism. She was wet, excess moisture rolling down and seeping between his legs. He gripped her torso, sensing her subtle quivers reverberating through him. Alas, they fall, their naked bodies pressed beside each other as they both grasped for a steady breath.

"You weren't quick," she chuckled. "That's a good sign."

"Yeah, I actually rubbed a quickie right before all this for continued stimulation."

"Oh my gosh, that's so gross," she giggled. "Keep that in mind for next time, would ya?"

"Oh yeah absolutely." Repartee was always appreciative, and Jack was thankful she was willing to partake.

After a few moments to catch their breaths, Emma mumbled, "So, you should know…I'm not on anything…"

Jack jolted upwards, turning towards her. "As in…"

"Yeah."

Jack paled, fear rushing down his spine. He noticed Emma's mouth twitch, causing him to raise an eyebrow.

"Wait, are you joking?"

Emma laughed hysterically. "Yes I'm joking. What, did you think I wouldn't tell you that before having sex?"

Jack cooled down, slumping back to his original placement beside Emma. "Sorry I freaked out there for a minute."

"Scared of having a child this early in the game?"

"I wouldn't say I would be scared, just *really* unsure of how to adjust," he said, staring blankly at the ceiling. "I don't even know what kind of food it needs to eat."

Emma rotated to face him. "Okay, one: 'baby,' not 'it'."

Jack let out a hearty laugh. "You're right, I'm sorry."

"You apologize too much."

"Is that a bad thing?"

Emma held his face and brought it to hers. "Apologizing for nothing defeats the purpose of apologizing at all. If there is no blame to give, why take it for yourself?"

"You should hang out more with Tom," Jack grinned. "I think you two would get along."

"I know Tommy," she assured. "I remembered always seeing him hanging around with the rest of your friends in the parking lot after school."
Jack laughed, recounting hilarious memories of his time with his friends. "We were a goofy group of guys forsure."
"Doesn't surprise me," she whispered, giving him an affectionate forehead kiss and proceeding to gather her clothes from the foot of the bed.
Even after sexually exhausting himself, Jack was mesmerized by Emma, contently watching as she pulled her pants over her legs. He was thrilled to see the steps toward an enlightened prospect of being with her finally fall into place. This summer was destined to be one he would never forget.
Emma's internship.
He was so distracted that he had forgotten about the one thing that would be between them. To his knowledge, the status of Emma's acceptance in the program was still in the air. Summer break was right around the corner; surely, she must have heard back from them.
Jack shrugged it off. Tonight was perfect. He felt no need to dredge it up now. Besides, assuming Emma *did* know, she would have her reasons for telling him when it was appropriate.
He took Emma's arm and waited for her to look back at him.
"I think I'm falling in love with you."
Emma smiled.
"Good. I think I'm falling in love with you too."
Jack smiled back, reeling her in for one last kiss.
"Come on," he jeered. "We have pizza downstairs."
Emma laughed, holding on to him as long as she could before eventually breaking away to dress herself. They sauntered out of the room and down the stairs, where they were greeted by Tommy and Morgan.
Jack was relieved. At last, he found someone willing to overlook his own insecurities; someone who chose to see him for who he was. Even better was he finally got the clarity he had long awaited from the moment he met her: she loved him. The coming days were sure to be better than they have ever been, because now, his drive to make it so was confirmed. Given the prior circumstances that he foolishly set up, this was surely the best way their relationship could have played out. There was no need to worry, because she was his, and he was hers.
He had made it this far. Now all that was required was making sure it would stay this way.

vi

There are four seasons in the year. Tommy preferred autumn, with its darkling murkiness and period of depression prior to its eventual resurrection. The satisfaction from observing a myriad of natural shifts following summer's end; almost welcoming his urge to reflect on life in preparation for the upcoming year. He was not a moody person, but he appreciated the symbolic undertones that God passed along to His underlings. It served as a reminder for Tommy, that there is no definite thing in this world. Like time, it will continue, with or without him.

He strongly disliked the summer for this reason – prolonged, with very little change. It had been only an hour after dawn, yet the sun marked its presence on Tommy, singing his forehead and the dirt speckled on his bare legs.

"Tommy boy, there you are!"

He remained still at Jack's voice carrying through the forest. Years of meditation demanded tolerance from noticeable sounds, particularly those intended to break his focus.

Jack stopped a few feet before his friend, seeing that his eyes were closed.

"Sorry, I forgot you do this every morning. Am I disturbing you?"

"No," Tommy lied, opening his eyes. "Good morning."

Jack peered up at the sun.

"How can you sit here like this? It's hot as shit."

"Beats coming out here in a couple hours. It's only going to get worse as the day goes on."

"True…anyways, I have good news."

"Oh yeah?"

"Emma and I did the deed last night."

"That's great man. Did you remember to stretch?"

"Um, no? Why does that matter?"

"It's a vigorous activity. I wouldn't want you cramping up in the middle of it."

"I didn't cramp up Tom, look can I continue?"

Tommy sighed, sensing Jack's eagerness to spill the details. Looks like the meditation would have to wait for later.

Jack resumed his recount of last evening, and while his intentions were good, Tommy was privately exasperated from having to listen to what he could only describe as unnecessary drama that Jack was compelled to entertain. He was pleased to see him enthralled by this girl, noticing the jaunt in his step as he circled around. Five minutes later Jack eventually squatted near Tommy, consciously shielding himself under a tree to avoid direct sunlight.

"Did you have fun with Morgan last night?"

"We didn't have sex, if that's what you're asking," Tommy clarified. "I'm in no rush."

"You never are," Jack chuckled, lying back in the grass. "Can you imagine if we ended up marrying each other? We could have matching houses, cars, the whole thing – what if we also planned it so that our kids would be the same age, and then they grow up and start dating?"

"Chill out man. How are you thinking about marriage already?"

"Come on, don't tell you haven't once thought about it."

"I live one day at a time. You know that."

"*Sure* Tommy, I'll convince you later."

If something warranted change, Tommy would do it then and there. The integrity surrounding change, in his mind, was not determined strictly with time – the main reason why he refuses to ever make New Years resolutions. Tommy sighed again, changing the subject.

"What are the girls doing? I want to do something fun."

"Still sleeping...what did you have in mind?"

"Let them sleep. Let's go for a hike."

"Sounds good to me, and I know a spot we can check out."

"The same as last night?"

"Even better," Jack shot to his feet and extended a hand. "Hopefully the girls are up by the time we get back."

Tommy followed him to the other end of the yard, hopping over the fence and proceeding on the verdant trail. They trekked on a decline, sweeping over crackling leaves and mossy clumps. Nature seized their desire for dialogue, overhearing the churrs of a nearby stream, accompanied by various chatters coming from the trees overhead. It all reminded him of the countless adventures he and his boys would take growing up, as there was never a shortage of sights to marvel in the sprawling forest. Particularly in his environment, the mountains were the closest Tommy could get to the unspoiled primitiveness that once dominated the earth. As much as he enjoyed taking his current life for granted, he wondered what would have been like back then – wandering through an untouched land, abundant in peaceful, pathless serenity.

They reached the opening of a valley, where they emerged from the shade and into the swelling heat.

Jack cleared the sweat above his brows and glanced over to acknowledge Tommy's shared appreciation of the beauty before them.

"Look at this," he awed.

They stood in silence, listening intently to the natural symphony playing for their enjoyment; the birds' sequential flitters and chirps; the noticeable gust through the glade, its fluttering breeze encircling ancient bark and splitting through the tingling buzz from the multitude of insects that flew carelessly around their ears.

"I haven't been here before."

"I usually take the other path to the lake. But one day…I don't know, something made me go exploring –" he glanced at Tommy. "You remember how we used to do that growing up?"

"I don't know how I could forget. We always thought that we would come up at a fire lookout, and then end up getting lost half the time."

"I didn't mind getting lost," Jack mumbled, lowering his head. "Not like I have much direction in my life to begin with."

Tommy studied Jack's face.

"Did you and Emma talk about…you know…?"

"Let's just say that Em is a smart girl."

"What do you mean?"

"She figured everything out before I could even tell her last night. Like, *everything,* Tom. She's like a walking bullshit detector."

"Are you serious?"

"We can talk about it later. It doesn't matter anymore though, we cleared the air and she's still into me, so I'd say that we dodged a bullet."

"*You* dodged a bullet," Tommy corrected. "I have no affiliation in your relationship."

"Are we really getting into this again?"

Tommy rolled his eyes and turned back to the field when he was distracted by the sight of a buck appearing in the meadow. Jack joined as they watched it prod out of the trees, closely followed by its doe and child. It was not long before the threesome was accompanied by an entire herd, their snailing trudge quickly transcending into a lively dance across the field. The fawn remained close to their respective mothers while they swirled in the grass, leaving the bucks lounge on the outer ring of the herd. A spectacularly peaceful, enchanting sight.

"What are the odds," Tommy nudged Jack, who too, was amazed at how close they were to the lively activity occurring before their eyes.

This is amazing, Jack concurred, his mind returning to Emma. How he wished she was here to share this moment with them.

And a moment, was all it was.

"Look," he heard Tommy say, pointing to the other end of the field. Jack followed his direction, detecting the shaking brush just a few hundred feet from the deer. He watched a shadowy creature come forth, with massive paws and a dense coat of brown fur. Its incredible size was frightening enough, as it pointed its prominent snout and sauntered closer toward the herd.

Jack's heart dropped. He never figured he would see one in the wild, let alone so close to where he stood. He noted its slowed pace, as if it was intentionally dragging its legs through the thickening brush.

"Is that…"

The bear came to a sudden halt, before instantly charging its hinds pulling out the grass as it harrowed deeper into the meadow.

The deer scattered, scurrying in every direction as the bear trampled on. The once calm grass had evaporated into a thick cloud of dust, briefly blinding Jack's vision. He considered looking away, for he had already foreseen the tragic result. Even from their distance, it was clear there would be no return for the unluckiest of the rangale.

As the dust settled, Jack kept his eyes glued ahead of him, where sure enough, the bear stood alone, hunched over what remained of a lifeless fawn in the wrecked pasture.

"Oh my God," Jack muttered. "We gotta get out of here."

He glanced over at Tommy, who was busy zooming in on his phone to snap a picture.

"Just a second," he said.

"*Now,* Tommy."

Just then, a raucous huff came from the field. Jack turned toward the sound to see the bear now staring directly back.

"Oh fuck!" Tommy screamed, gripping Jack's wrist and pulling him back into the trees.

He took the lead, tearing through the forest, trying to retrace their steps up the hill. He felt the adrenaline spiking in his chest, wincing at his flailing arms scratching against branches. He assumed Jack was behind him, awaiting to hear his assistance in guiding them back to the cabin. It was not until he shot a glimpse over his shoulder, however, that he realized Jack was no longer with him.

Tommy panicked, questioning his sense of direction and panning around as he tramped over the uneven ground. He called for Jack's name over his heavy pant, finding it hard to keep his eyes fixated on the disappearing path below his feet.

He was too distracted to see the ingrown root catching his right foot, fear instantly trickling up his spine as he fell forward and tumbled off the trail. He instinctively shot his hands out to brace his fall, only managing a subtle groan as he smacked his side on the ground before skidding down the slick hillside. He tried digging his fingernails into the dirt to slow himself up, the jagged rock scraping his skin as he promptly moved on to drawing what power was left in his legs to wildly kick against the oncoming trees as he clumsily maneuvered between thickening underwood. His face was overpowered by a cloud of debris, blinding his sight as he screamed for the terrorizing ride to stop.

The slope eventually let up, braking Tommy's roll until he came to a gradual stop. He laid still, keeping his face buried in the riddled filth before lifting his head. The forest was quiet at last, the deafening silence pulsating in his eardrums as he rose to his feet and brushed off what he could from his grimy clothes. Then pain began to settle, Tommy wincing from the intense throbbing in his thighs. He skimmed around and did not recognize his surroundings, leaving him to swivel back to the hill he came from and try to make out a possible way back. He pulled out his phone, cursing at the deep crack stretched across the black screen. He was on his own from here on out. "Jack!" he called, immediately feeling stupid for thinking that his cries would be heard.

This is fucked, he thought, reluctantly hobbling up the hill. He ignored the throbbing soreness in his thighs, pushing forward as he endured to the top before stooping over to vomit.

"Fucking a," he boomed, straightening up and scanning the ground once again for a familiar trace.

Tommy had no idea how much time had passed, trying to measure his best guess by the position of the sun overhead. He regretted not eating that morning, groaning as he clenched his empty stomach. If anything, he was grateful that his overall demeanor was still calmer than he expected. It was possibly thanks to his tendency to over-rationalize the situation rather than resorting to panic.

He marched on, growing weary at the sight of the sun slowly dipping closer to the horizon. The mountains were no longer visible, and the clouds elevated over the light, creating a shroud of haze that blurred the trees' shadows. His feet finally drew to a stop, prompting him to reconsider an approach to the cabin that was more strategic than the aimless wander he had initially chosen. "This isn't working," he muttered, figuring that it would not hurt to audibly coach himself into formulating a plan. "You can do this."

This was not the first time that Tommy found himself lost in the woods. As a teenager, he and the boys would frequently explore the wilderness. They drove out at the break of dawn, and after considerable time driving out on a random road, would intentionally pull off on its side and enter with only the contents stored in their packs. They paced without purpose, no specific destination in mind other than the shared desire to be alone in contemplation with the natural scene to comfort them. Tommy cherished those memories. It was not just an enjoyable pastime spent with friends, but also an opportunity for him to leave the constructive routine forced on him by society. He did not recall a time in his life when he resented the notion of losing any sense of individualism, and believed quality time in nature would bring greater understanding of the more important things in his middling life. And during their quality time spent, the boys would become so enthralled in wanderlust, that they would ultimately find themselves lost in the forest, with no recollection as to how they arrived in the first place. It was oddly comforting for Tommy, who, despite his inability to recognize his surroundings, was supported by his boys to take the lead in safely guiding them back to the car. Only this time, his boys were not with him, nor the calming reassurance that everything would be okay. Tommy was alone, and – pun unintended – the burden resulting from this trial would only be his to bear.

In that moment, where urgency was required, his only resolve was to return to what he knew he was best at. Tommy dropped to the ground, crossing his legs, and carefully resting his mottled hands over his raw knees. He drew a deepening sigh, waiting for his body to relax.

His eyes were tautly sealed, ignoring the musty stench stifling at his nostrils. Attaining a state of tranquility did not always come easy for Tommy. It required years of disciplined repetition, and of course, the acceptance that even the most theoretical things are somehow, someway, capable of being materialized. Imagine his surprise, when he realized one particular day alone in the woods that it was actually achievable. He treasured the feeling the first time it happened, fascinated by the evergreens in a synchronized dance, flitting aside the frolicking wildlife jollying around him. In modern society, nature is likely marked as a foreign territory, and rejecting the idea of assimilation. And yet, Tommy viewed it to be the ideal setting when trying to understand the purpose behind his existence. At the end of the day, he believed all one had to do was ask.

As if God heard his plea, the echo of a distinct ring caught his ear. He sprouted up and followed the sound, his breath matching his feet's speedier pace. The sun was no longer above him, receding back to the crest of the mountains he made out beyond the brush.

Wait a minute, he thought. *I can see the mountains.*

Tommy immediately grew hopeful, realizing that the sight of the range also meant he was close to a clearing of some sort. Coupled with the ringing, he was confident to finally be heading in the right direction. The overwhelming green soon tapered off, his head tightening due to the ring growing louder with every step.

He finally reached a dried ravine, concentrating on the direction from where the ring emitted. He lumbered onward, where a couple hundred yards ahead, he made out the familiar gates that marked the edge of Jack's property.

"Fucking Douglases," Tommy jeered, tilting his head to the sky. "I owe you one for this, Big Guy."

Tommy sprinted to the gates and hurtled over the fence, losing traction and crumbling to the ground as he called for Jack's name again. The ringing stopped shortly after, and he laid on the grass for what seemed like an eternity, until alas, Jack appeared and rushed over.

"Holy shit, Tommy!" he shrieked, helping him up. "Are you okay?"

"Peachy," Tommy managed, catching his breath. He wrapped his arm around Jack and was carried back to the house, where Jack laid Tommy by the pool, reveling the water's cool breath wafting over his warm face.

"Oh my God," came Emma's voice.

"Get some water!" Jack shouted.

Tommy tried sitting up, only to have Jack push him back down.

"Easy man, just relax."

"What the *fuck* happened back there?" Tommy exhaled.

"I don't know. One minute you were in front of me, and the next you just disappeared."

"Damn, I didn't know I was that fast."

Emma and Morgan hustled over to his side.

"Are you okay?" Morgan asked.

"Totally," Tommy replied lightheartedly. "Just outran a bear. No biggie."

They all shared a laugh as he sipped tediously from the water glass.

"I don't think I'll be hiking for a while after this," Jack stated. "It'll just be going to class and bars from this point out."

"Shit!" Tommy slapped his forehead. "You just reminded me that I a final paper due first thing Monday."

"Since we're on the topic," Morgan chimed in. "Should we just call it a weekend? I don't think any of us are still in the mood to stay here any longer after what you've been through, Tommy."

"Nonsense!" he sat up, his head spinning. "We're just getting started." Jack glanced at Emma, who gave him a subtle nod.

"I think Morgan has a point," Jack agreed. "You'll need your rest, especially if you have stuff to get done this weekend."

"I see," Tommy pouted, embarrassed. "Sorry I ruined our vacation."

"You didn't!" Emma defended. "I think going back is a good idea. I'm actually a bit tired."

Tommy reluctantly accepted. He hated being the reason for their early departure.

"Okay," he said, facing Jack. "You're driving. I'm still a little cooked over here."
"Are you hungry? There's a cool diner we passed that's on the way into town. We can stop there for a bite."
"I love that idea!" Morgan grinned, grabbing Emma's hand. "Come on Em, let's go pack. I'm starving."
Jack sighed in relief as he watched the girls head into the house.
"Thanks," Tommy uttered to Jack.
"Of course, brother. Let's get out of here."
Tommy sat shotgun on the quiet drive back, still in shock as Jack occasionally eyed over from the driver's seat.
"What are you feeling?" he asked him after twenty minutes of silence.
"Huh?"
"For food," Jack continued, his eyes glued to the road. "I'm thinking eggs…maybe some bacon."
"That sounds nice."
Jack's head swiveled back to the girls, both fast asleep.
"You would think they'd be wide awake," Jack commented. "They were both still in bed after I got back."
"Yeah," Tommy mumbled.
Jack glanced at him, noticing him fidgeting in his seat.
"Are you sure everything's okay?"
"I dunno," Tommy admitted. "I still can't get over what happened back there. I would've died if it wasn't for your ring."
"My *what*?"
"The ring," Tommy repeated. "That's how I knew my way back. I must have ran a few miles."
Jack shot him a perplexed expression.
"I don't know what you're talking about."
"Come on, seriously?"
"Seriously," Jack affirmed, his eyes returning to the road. "What did the ring sound like?"
"It sounded like a ring!"
"But was it like a droning sound or—"
"More like a dog whistle."
"A dog whistle?"
"Have you never heard a dog whistle before?"
"No, no I have," Jack paused in thought. "A *dog* whistle?"
"A dog whistle."
"That's so weird. Sounds like an act of God to me."

Tommy was about to dismiss his comment, but then recalled the peace swimming through him during his urgent break of meditation. He viewed himself as religious, yet still found it difficult to accept that his miraculous return to the house was an act of any higher power.

"Perhaps," Tommy sighed, pivoting to observe the trees speeding past them. "Maybe He was trying to teach us a lesson of sorts."

"What do you think the lesson was?"

Tommy shrugged.

"Things can be going great, and then just like that –" he snapped his fingers.

Jack maintained a confused expression, leading Tommy to elaborate.

"It can all change," he continued. "It can be so unpredictable…so unprecedented…"

"Everything happens for a reason. The same way in nature, also in our own lives."

Tommy tilted his head, resisting his indifference to Jack's statement.

"I hope I never have to experience anything like that again."

"Me neither," Tommy agreed. "It sucks that's all we can do, at the end of the day."

Jack turned to him again, waiting for some clarification.

"Hope," Tommy added. "In a world where we are always challenged with the worst, it's fascinating that our only method of overcoming it is through wishing for it to happen differently."

Jack let out a hearty chuckle.

"If law school doesn't work out, might I suggest becoming a philosopher?"

Tommy smirked, leaning back and slowly closing his eyes. He did not believe things happened for a reason, but that it came down to a person's decisions. And with those decisions, there were consequences. He found himself praying to God, thanking him for the opportunity to live another day. If His reasons were intended to be unexplainable, then Tommy was prepared to not delve any deeper into wondering why he was spared. After all, who was he to dictate why things are the way they are? A purpose can be pursued all it wants, but it first must be revealed; and no one who has ever existed was capable of revealing it on their own. Maybe it was all actually random. Maybe not.

Tommy consciously stopped himself from trying to figure it out. He had done enough thinking for today. Now it was time to rest.

vii

It did not matter the subject, nor how much time given to complete: test-taking was not a forte of Logan's. Studying was no use for him either, as the knowledge retained would vanish the moment he needed it. It was the same thing, every time: itching at the clock tediously ticking, piercing through his already shaky line of focus; dampening the paper between his sweaty palms as he clutched tighter, hoping it would spur any recall of information. He refused to cheat, yet felt the temptation with so many students around him, the pressure at a gradual increase by the forceful scratching of pencils against parchment. No way could he have been the only clueless one in here. These other kids had to be faking it, assuming that frantically bubbling in a pattern of circles on a Scantron would magically result in a glowing A. It was a dilemma he expected. And at this point, he did not care. Sulking would not change the result, and according to his repeated error after so many trials, neither would trying harder the next time.

Now, he was always the first to submit his test, as well as the first to leave the class, pulling over his hood and he stormed back to his locker for his only chance to relieve himself from the unlikable environment that was Davison Prep.

There was a single stall in the third floor bathroom, where directly above was an industrial-sized ventilator. It was a popular choice for those needing to take a number two without any shame. For Logan, however, it was the prime location to smoke undetected.

He sat on the toilet and lifted his right leg to bar the stall door while simultaneously pinching at the nugget inside his baggie until it broke apart into the bowl on his lap. A sudden drumming on the stall door came, causing Logan to fumble the pipe and spill the remnants on the floor.

"Busy," he muttered.

"It's me, open up."

Logan sighed and reluctantly kicked the door open, unsurprised to see Jack Douglas glowering back at him.

"What the hell man? You said you would wait for me!"

"Keep your voice down."

Jack threw off his backpack and shared the narrow seat with his friend.

"I hope you understand that I wasn't going to wait for you," Logan added. "Besides, it didn't take long for you to finish that test."

"You finished it before I did."

"Yeah, I *sure* did," Logan affirmed, his tone steeped in sarcasm as he proceeded to reload the bowl.

"I spent this entire week studying for it," Jack said, edging closer to inspect Logan. "I might lose it if I got anything below an A."
"Quit bragging, I don't want to hear it."
"I wasn't bragging."
"Not everyone is as smart as you. Know your audience Jack," he sneered.
"You're bragging."
"Whatever," Jack dismissed, rolling his eyes, before noticing the near empty baggie sitting on the tank. "Wasn't that full yesterday?"
"I don't know. Maybe."
"It was," Jack confirmed. "How did you go through it so quickly?"
"God, you can be a little shit. Why do you have to read into every little thing?"
Jack pursed his lips, taken aback.
"Sorry," Logan apologized, regretting his outburst. "I've been going through a lot lately. You're right, I should chill a bit."
Jack nodded, watching as Logan sparked the bowl before passing it to him. Jack fiddled with the pipe, letting out a slight chuckle as he sharply choked on the smoke after taking a foolishly menial hit.
"I'm not good at this," he admitted sheepishly.
Logan took the pipe back and finished what was left. "No, you're not."
"I was going to ask Tommy B if he wanted to join, but he wasn't even close to done with the test."
"Cool," Logan scoffed. Although he lacked in intellect, Logan could detect one's emotions rather exceptionally. Something was off with Tommy in recent weeks. Logan assumed it was a phase at first, as he could not figure a reason that could prompt his longtime friend to resent him. Stuff like this happens with friends, growing more intolerant of one another's presence after so much time spent together. It may be a personal grudge, or maybe not. It was never easy to tell with Tommy.
Logan stuffed the pipe and baggie and left the stall.
"Maybe you should talk to him," Jack blurted, almost as if he could read Logan's mind.
"Tommy?"
"Yeah, I can feel the tension when I'm with both of you."
"He's just being a pussy," Logan said flatly. "He'll get over it."
"I don't know. I know Tommy. *You* know him, too. If something is bothering him, he doesn't get over it."
Logan shook his head. "I'm gonna dip."
"Where are you going?"
"Home."

"The day is almost over, why don't you wait and we can caravan back? We're basically going to the same place."

"Yeah, I know Jack. It's not like we do it every day," he scorned. "I'll see you later."

Logan stopped at his locker. He kept his stash concealed behind a block of textbooks on the top shelf. He was usually particular to his drug usage during school hours, but test days were his only exception, as they demanded the opportunity for a fix to get his mind off of the bad grade he would ultimately get. He inconspicuously panned down the hall to make sure no one was around before retrieving the baggie from his backpack and shoving it into the locker.

"Hi Logan," Emma greeted, startling him as he accidentally pulled out one of the books in the process and jumping back as it slapped the tile, just missing his feet.

"Emma!" Logan was alarmed at how she appeared so suddenly without making the slightest sound.

She giggled at the sight of his timid expression before glancing down at the book between them. "Did I scare you?"

"Yeah – I mean no!" Logan tittered, taking a deep breath and snapping back to his senses. He bent over to retrieve his book, easing up. "I forgot this for my class."

"I do that all the time. It happens to the best of us."

"Right," he gulped, forgetting how to act normal. In addition to pretending not to have enough weed in his locker to subdue a gorilla, he was not exactly the most comfortable talking to attractive girls. And Emma was undoubtedly a looker.

"Anyways," Emma went on. "I was talking to Kenz, and she told me that you still didn't have a date to prom next weekend. Is that true?"

"Uh, yeah."

"Are you going?"

"I haven't given it a lot of thought," Logan admitted. "What about you?"

"I really want to, but since I'm an underclassman it's not really my choice unless someone asks me to go."

Logan nodded slowly. *Does she want me to ask her to prom?* He doubted it initially, but noticing the flicker in Emma's eyes seemed apparent enough for just about anyone to understand what she hinted at.

He never asked a girl out before. Not that he was scared of rejection; he was certainly used to that. He stared at Emma, taken aback by her vivid grey eyes, freezing up as they pierced through his ability to focus.

"Do you…would you –" he choked, taking another deep breath. "I mean, I could—"

"Yes," Emma smiled. "I would love to go."

"Great," he uttered though his nervous smile, closing his locker. "I should get going."

"Oh, okay!" Emma said. "We'll talk about it more then?"

"Looking forward to it," he agreed, bidding her farewell and watching until she was down the hall and out of sight.

Thinking of Emma excited him. Never in his life would he imagine the exchange that transpired moments ago. He had a skip in his step on the way out of school and to the parking lot.

His car was in sight when he was intercepted by his associates, Baker and Dunn, waiting until he was middled between cars before sliding in front of him.

"Baker!" Logan greeted, surprised to see him outside of his typical element. He may have only known their last names, but Baker and Dunn's notoriety was known well around the city.

Their appearance was a stereotypical reflection of their profession, dressed down in oversized thrifts, each balancing a cigarette in their mouths. They were entrepreneurs. Well, *gangbangers* a more accurate term. But to Logan, they were business partners. He was in a time of desperation when they crossed paths some odd years ago, their shady meet eventually leading to him becoming one of their most trusted lieutenants amidst one of the largest drug rings in the Pacific Northwest. Wrong place at the wrong time, sure – but one that Logan had shaped into a profiting career.

At the same time, Baker's presence usually did not come with positive circumstances. And one so sudden and far away from his base territory, Logan figured it was due to his recently poor performance in selling their product.

"Logan," Baker acknowledged. "It's been a bit."

"Yes it has, how have you been?"

"Do you actually want to know?"

Logan sensed Baker's intense tone, quickly realizing his initial suspicion for his visit was likely correct. Regardless, he figured it would be in his favor to remain calm for the sake of preventing any escalation.

"Well sure," Logan replied, giving him a blank stare.

Baker leaned on the minivan beside him, shifting his gaze to the school beyond Logan.

"I hate Mercer," he groaned. "The people here reek of pretension, and entitlement. Most of these kids will only experience the bubble they were born in. It's sad to think about, don't you think?"

Logan did not respond, glancing at Dunn's stone expression.

"I'm not originally from this area," Baker continued. "My parents moved up here from SoCal when I was a kid. They wanted to keep me away from all the violence." He scoffed, shaking his head before continuing. "Bless their hearts for thinking something so inherent to our human nature was escapable, you know? No, they came here, only to find a culture worse than the one that scared them out of leaving everyone we ever loved back home.

"I'm sorry," Logan mumbled.

"I hated being a kid here…didn't make a lot of friends. School was even worse. My God, I'm happy I was smart enough to get myself out of that shithole when I had the chance. You see, Logan: I was one of the lucky ones, to see the horrible product of this place that I would have become if I decided to ignore my gut. I realized at a young age, that you can't trust anyone, no matter how kind they pretended to be; no matter how much they claimed to care about you. Because the end of the day, all they care about is themselves."

Logan grew more anxious, giving a subtle nod.

Baker shrugged. "I don't usually share much about myself, but I found it to be applicable to my reason for taking you in," he paused. "Because I trusted you."

Logan's eyes widened. "Is this when you tell me what's wrong?"

Suddenly, Dunn lunged at Logan, seizing his arms and throwing him against the minivan. Logan fell to the cement, groaning in pain.

"Where is my money, Logan?"

"What the hell are you talking about?" Logan winced, believing he was faking it well enough for Baker to back off.

"I get you're stupid, but it still really pisses me off when you think playing dumb is the smart move."

Worth a shot, Logan thought.

"You promised me that I would get my money from the last month's batch," Baker added. "I gave you an extra week to figure it out, remember? Well, here we are, three days past the deadline, and you have nothing to show for it."

"I've been busy with shit. It's just a lull, I promise."

"You know, you use that word a lot," Baker scoffed. "*Promise.* It's almost like you think it helps your case."

"I don't know what else to tell you," Logan pleaded, rolling over until his back was fleshed against the pavement. "You want your money. I said I will get it for you."

Baker pivoted to Dunn.

"Get the truck ready."

Dunn trotted off, leaving them alone. Baker threw his hand up, signaling Logan to stand.

He was slow to his feet, doing his best to mask the ache living in his side as he straightened his back.

"You want to know what I think Logan?"

"Okay…"

"I think you're full of shit. I think that you sold the batch, spent the money, and think that you can lie your way out of this as you come up with a way to pay me back."

Jackpot.

"I promise that is not the case," Logan lied.

"There's that word again," Baker grudgingly nodded before striding away to the pickup. "Next week at our usual spot, or it's your ass." he called back to Logan before hopping in the passenger seat and smacking the door.

This was not the worse interaction he had with Baker. However, it was the first time that it occurred this close to home. It did not take a genius to see Baker's true frustration, considering he was willing to make a point with Logan in the middle of the day at a high school parking lot – arguably the most jeopardizing scenario for a felon with a temper.

Logan watched until the truck was out of sight before hurrying to his car, twisting around to make sure no one witnessed what had happened. He had already brewed up a plan on how he would get the money. That said, he kept his foot planted on the accelerator all the way home, recognizing the need for urgency.

He pulled up to his house, relieved to see his parents were not home.

Logan bolted through the front door and into his father's office, detecting the safe situated in the corner of the room. He entered the code and opened the vault, his gaze settling on more money than he had ever seen in his life.

Only for emergencies, Logan thought, recalling the words that his mother hammered in his psyche. His dad would certainly explode if he learned his son memorized the combination to the safe. If he discovered that some was deliberately *taken* – it was a hypothetical that Logan preferred not to entertain. He sifted through the cash, counting how much he owed Baker before stuffing it in his backpack. He reeled back at the sound of a door slamming from downstairs, immediately followed by commotion.

Guess they're home.

Logan shut the safe and scurried out of the office, and to the top of the stairs. He dragged his feet down the steps and poked into the living room, where sure enough, he saw his mother facing away from him, wildly throwing her hands above her head.

There was no one Logan loved more than his mother, Adriana. She hailed from South America, forced to emigrate to the States when her family sold their farm to make ends meet. Once she reached the New World, she committed her time to her career in education, eventually becoming a professor and saving up for the family she hoped to create in later days.

It was not long until she met her husband Wesleyan, who, at the time, was a young professional from the Northwest. She had no warning about Wes's drug addiction, and following the birth of their son, she knew it was too late. A young woman – desperate for the need of companionship and support for her newborn – it was difficult for her to weigh the advantages if she left Wes. She chose to stay with him, understanding that she would spend the rest of her life paying the price. Both metaphorically, and literally.

Her savings were largely spent on their home in Mercer, the rest she consciously hid away for Logan's future. It was not much and having to dedicate more time away from the classroom, she feared the lack of steady income would be an issue worth revisiting down the line.

Wes was a capable contributor, financially, having founding a firm based in the city. But he was riddled in greed. Regardless of how the trait originated, it caused him to resent his own son, feeling entitled that the money he earned should not be freely bestowed upon his offspring, which personally, he had always regretted having to begin with. As one would expect, it is not the biggest surprise that Logan endured a strained relationship with his father for as long as he could remember. He did not consider him family, but a threat, who under the right circumstances would be willing to risk he and his mother's well-being at the cost of his own achievements.

Logan suffered through his childhood, fearing his existence was at any time capable of prompting Wes to act dangerously toward the one person he loved most. He did not ask for this life, and yet, he was forced to stomach its reality. As much as he knew his episodes of delinquency attributed to his parent's estranged relationship, he also saw partial blame from Wes, believing he would not be the person he is today if it was not for the poor dynamic established by his father. His yearn for amiability was pointless at this point, especially since he was the frequent target for the source of the disorder.

Logan emerged from the stairwell, coming to his mother's aid.

"What's going on, Mom?"

"Get out of here Logan," Wes glared at him from across the room. He was fidgeting in his recliner, visibly agitated.

The sight of his father filled Logan with sheer rage. He hated himself for picking up all of Wes's negative traits, and was punished in response to the resentment he frequently demonstrated.

"Don't listen to him," Adriana whispered. "I'm sorry for shouting. I didn't notice your car when we pulled up."

"Decided to come back early. I had to rest my eyes for a little bit," Logan replied, kissing her cheek and breaking away to face his father. "I see you couldn't go one day without starting something with Mom, huh?"
Wes sat up in his chair, glaring at Adriana.
"Mind your tone," he warned. "You should be thankful to be given a second chance in your miserable life."
"A second chance?" Logan tested. "Mind telling me when you gave me my first?"
"Not now Logan," Adriana cautioned, fearing escalation.
"I blame you, you know," Wes scolded, pointing at Adriana. "I told you that having him would be a mistake."
Logan could feel his jaw tightening, grasping for every sliver of patience.
Wes noticed his son's flushed expression, choosing to escalate.
"What's wrong, Logan?" Look at you, trying to act like a man," he mocked.
"Ever checked yourself in the mirror?" Logan shot back. "What kind of man treats their family like this?"
Wes casually waved him off.
"Get out of here. You're pissing me off."
There are tell-tale signs that distinguish the feeble from the fearless. Some common traits include passiveness, perception, and a sharp, analytical outlook on social situations. At the same time, there are those who are simply too afraid of a quarrel, choosing to retreat at the sight of danger.
As one would expect, Logan did not identify with either of those types of people. And God forbid issuing a threat in hopes that it would prevent any further aggravation from him – doing so is likely to only worsen the situation. Wes learned the hard way, because in a matter of moments, Logan threw off his backpack and was hovering directly above him, straddling the chair as he proceeded to mercilessly pound at his father. His first hit struck Wes square in the nose, followed by a swift series of punches across the rest of his face.
"Fuck you!" Logan raged, ramming his knee into Wes' stomach.
Adriana's temporary freeze was quickly shattered by her maternal instincts, darting to Logan and wrapping her arms around his waist as she tried to pull him off Wes. But Logan was stronger, gently breaking her hold so that he would not hurt her as he continued to attack his father.
Wes was completely defenseless, thrashing his arms until he was knocked out from what ended up being Logan's final blow.
"Stop Logan!" Adriana shrieked.
Her scream rippled through Logan, prompting him to spring off the chair and stumble back on the floor. Wes leaned over in his seat, horrified at his palms that were bloodied from his broken nose.

Adriana circled past Logan to her husband, crouching beside him and muttering indistinct cries.

Logan watched his parents in dismay, glowering at his calloused knuckles. He had exhausted himself, catching his breath as he snatched his backpack and stormed out of the house. He stopped at the porch steps, head cowered in his hands.

He hated Wes almost as much as he hated himself. It was already a struggle for him to find a sense of belonging, such instances of coming close in moments like this, when he mulled over his own darkening thoughts, embracing a mood that seemed to bring him comfort.

He did not ask for this life, but he did not have a choice. It had to be enough for him.

"You all right?" came a soothing voice.

"Tommy," Logan addressed, watching his friend inch up the driveway. "Are you watching me now or something?"

"Don't flatter yourself," Tommy said. "I live across the street. It's not unusual for neighbors to be, well, neighborly."

"It is when your neighbor has been acting like a prick over the last month."

Tommy shrugged off Logan's insult.

"May I sit?"

Logan grudgingly slid aside to give Tommy room, refusing to meet his eyes. Tommy's gaze fixed on Logan's blood-stained hands, finding it difficult to choose his words.

"Is it Wes again?"

"Yeah."

"Fuck that guy, he's a prick."

"Couldn't have said it any better."

They shared a light chuckle.

"How do you think you did on the test?"

Logan gave Tommy a strangled expression.

"You know I don't like talking about that kind of shit."

"You don't like talking about anything."

"It's none of your business, Tom."

"Okay, okay," Tommy relayed.

Despite his distaste for Logan, Tommy pitied him. He did not have to know the full scope of the issue that lied in his conscience. His face told the whole story.

"You know, it's always good to talk through your problems."

"Why do you care so much?"

"Frankly, I don't. Which is why I think that I would be an ideal person to listen – no worries about being judged, "Tommy managed a reassuring smile. "Not that I would anyway."
Logan shifted on the steps, facing Tommy.
"You are a professional bullshitter."
"I'll take that as a compliment."
"I have shit to do," Logan announced, rising to his feet and walking away before reluctantly stopping and turning back to Tommy.
"Thanks," he uttered.
Tommy gave a pleased look as he watched Logan proceed to his car, his expression changing at a green paper poking out of his backpack.
"What's that?" Tommy gasped, pointing at what appeared to be a hundred-dollar bill.
Logan followed Tommy's finger, his spine stiffening.
"It's nothing," he said, forcing the bill back inside before speeding his pace to the car. He could hear Tommy's footsteps growing louder behind him.
"What is the *shit* that you have to do, Logan?"
"It's best if you don't know."
Tommy crossed in front of Logan, standing between him and the car.
"I know you man…whatever you are planning to do, please don't."
Logan controlled his temper, noticing the concern in Tommy's eyes.
"Get out of my way."
"Not until you tell me what's going on."
"Fuck!" Logan shouted. "I owe these guys some money, okay?"
"Who?"
"Why does it matter?"
"Logan…"
Logan threw his head back, annoyed by Tommy's usual persistence.
"They're drug dealers, all right? Are you happy? Is that enough for you?"
Tommy's jaw dropped.
"I thought you were done with that. What are you doing?"
Logan did not want to force Tommy away, but he had enough of him. He took hold of Tommy's collar and jerked him aside. It caught him by surprise, tumbling on the driveway and immediately scrambling back to his feet.
"You're no better than any of those fucks we go to school with!" Logan yelled. "You pretend to act like you care about me when it suits you, when you really don't give a shit!"
"This is not just about you," Tommy defended. "What you are getting into is a bad idea. I would say the same thing to anyone in your situation."

"You don't know anyone else in my situation! My entire life I've had to survive. You and the rest of the guys go about your lives, never having to worry about anything. I can't even trust my own fucking parents!"
"I get it—"
"No you don't! Quit saying that you do because you don't!" Logan continued. "I need to do whatever I can to get through this fucked shit and if that means dealing, then I'm going to do it. So fuck off."
Tommy took in Logan's words. He knew of his drug use. After all, Tommy was guilty of frequently partaking in such activities with him over their time together. But this was different. *Selling drugs?* It seemed too reckless to imagine any of his friends being capable of it. Now that he was thinking about it, Tommy did occasionally wonder how someone who wore the same three pairs of jeans to school to afford such a nice car. He assumed the funds were sourced from his parents, which clearly could not have been the case given their strained relationship that he had grown used to hearing about since they were children.
He pictured the hundred-dollar bill that sat in Logan's bag. He was curious, to say the least. There had to be more where that came from. Tommy had no interest in hustling for survival. He knew such a scenario could escalate beyond one's control. Having a less dramatic motive, however? The notion sparked Tommy's curiosity.
"Do you make a lot of money?" Tommy asked.
"What?"
"From dealing," he repeated. "Do you make a lot of money?"
"I guess," Logan shrugged, calming down.
"I see."
Logan noted Tommy's sudden smirk. The look was too familiar.
"The answer is no."
"You don't even know what I –"
"Yes I do, because I also know you too well," Logan countered. "You're interested in being a part of it and I'm telling you no."
Tommy tilted his head and shrugged.
"A little extra money never hurt."
Logan broke out in sarcastic laughter.
"Are you being serious?"
Tommy skirted to the passenger side and opened the door.
Logan raised his brow, stunned at Tommy's change of demeanor.
"What are you doing?" he asked.
"I'm coming with you," Tommy stated confidently.
"Are you out of your mind?"
"If I am, then we both are."

Logan rolled his eyes, considering Tommy's request. He would never admit it, but Logan had always respected him. He considered them to be like-minded individuals, both who saw themselves in a way unique to the rest of the world. There was no way only he saw it, either.

As unique as Logan may have considered himself to be, however, he would be forced to face the daunting prospect of how drastic an outcome may be based on the poor degree of measurement of one's actions.

He did not ask for this life. Yet, it was his to live.

viii

Emma thoroughly enjoyed the single life. In addition to relentlessly pursuing her personal ambitions, the idea of a relationship never seemed worth entertaining. She had very little patience for boys and was always quick to dismiss their amateurish solicitations. The attention she received was surely appreciative, but not when it came at the expense of her independence. Even on the occasion when she dawdled the prospect of having a boyfriend, she acknowledged her tendency to grow bored, and how it could factor in the inevitable erosion of its probability to prevail.

Then came Jack Douglas.

She was slightly troubled upon discovering her unwavering infatuation following their initial encounter. She recalled how unexpectedly the night unfolded through her blurred, drunken memory: his picturesque, sullen expression as he peered down at his stained shirt, struggling to bibulously formulate a single sentence. Yet, he was soft-spoken, and considerate. Goofy, but also charming. Most of all, he was genuine.

Well, partly genuine, anyway.

Emma knew her perception of Jack was too good to be true, which laid grounds for her to investigate for red flags. They had good times together. However, there ended up being truth to her speculation, and she was unsurprised when she learned Jack lied about his wealthy background. But even during a crucial moment, she chose to give him the benefit of the doubt. He told her he was falling in love with her. He said it. She heard the words, audibly leaving his lips. It was not the first time a guy shared his affection for her, let alone as prematurely as Jack. She was used to the phrase, but not used to feeling so happy after hearing it. And despite her intention to disregard it, something else came over. She said it *back*.

Now at the time, she did not know if what she had said was true or not. She wondered if she was truly falling in love with him, or if it was an impulsive utter.

Emma believed falling in love only introduced more complications. Complications that she was not ready to face. She trusted her head over her heart. Maybe she wanted him, maybe she did not. The real question for her to answer was whether she was willing to endure the tumultuous journey in making a potential relationship thrive above all else. Sure, it could likely jeopardize her goals, as Jack had the effect of molding himself into everything she also considered important, gnawing through her own fear of a relationship and rebranding it as a notion worth chasing.

Tommy's dramatic endeavor in the forest took up much concern for most of the day, and now in its end, Emma was finally given the chance to reflect on the weekend, specifically her conversation with Jack the prior night. She sensed her mood shifting as they returned to civilization, a heap of realism surging back into her psyche. It was her first time away with a guy, and as enjoyable as it played out, there still lingered uncertainty of such commitment. She pretended to ignore it that morning, believing it to be imaginary, but her intentional disregard only grew more profound as the day progressed.

She was relieved when they pulled up to the dorms, leaving the car quickly and refusing politely when Jack offered to grab her bags. Morgan joined her after bidding farewell to the boys, joining her inside the building. Her heart pulsed rapidly as she lumbered up the stairs and into their room, shrugging off her bags and proceeding to plop on her bed before wrapping her body under a swaddle of throws strewn over the mattress.

Morgan let out a friendly chuckle upon seeing Emma already situated.

"How are you still tired? You slept the entire ride back."

"I just need to catch my breath."

"Oh right, I'm sure you did a lot of that last night with Jack, huh?"

"What are you saying?" Emma spluttered, embarrassed.

"Relax," Morgan assured. "I'm team Jack. I think he means well."

"I guess so."

"Do you disagree?"

Emma shrugged. "He's interesting, I'll give you that."

Morgan examined Emma's blank expression.

"Have you told your mom yet?"

"No, why would that matter?"

"Because that's the only reason I could think of as to why you are trying not to like him."

Morgan had a good point. Had her mom found out that she was talking to the son of the Douglas dynasty, she would likely put a gun to her head and force her to love him for the money.

No, it was not the traits of a gold-digger, but simply an over-caring mother committed to ensuring her daughter and her future were taken care of. And as a recent widow, her concern for having the ability to do it on her own only grew.

"What happened at the cabin?"

"Nothing."

"Emma, I know something is bothering you. It's not like you can keep it from me."
Emma rolled back into bed, smothering a pillow over her face.
"I caught him in a lie."
"About what?"
"Everything. The only thing that was true was his name, and even that wasn't completely accurate."
"Give me an example."
"The cabin didn't belong to his 'family friend.' It's his."
"I'm confused…you're talking about the cabin we stayed at?"
"What other one would I be talking about?"
"Sorry, you're right. Stupid question," Morgan said, pausing. "Continue."
"He's Jack Douglas. *Douglas,* Morgan, as in the Douglas Group."
Morgan let out a bellowing gasp. "He's a richie?"
"The richest of the richies."
Morgan froze, gripping her wrinkled clothes shortly before resuming to unpack.
"Wow, that's crazy," she added. "Why did he lie about who he was?"
"We went into it. Like, I *really* let him have it, Mo. I can't imagine how he felt after I yelled at him. Even I feel terrible about it. I must have sounded like a bitch…but you of all people could understand why I did it, right?"
"I do," Morgan snickered, her brow raised. "He was wrong for lying."
"I understood his reasoning, though. I mean, imagine if your whole life, people only see you as something you don't want to be known as."
"So everyone sees him as rich – who cares? He *is* rich. I don't see the big deal."
"That's what I told him. But I don't know, I guess he's been hurt a lot from it."
"So what happened?"
"Nothing. We just talked about it."
"That's it?"
"What else was I supposed to do?"
"I don't like liars, Em. It doesn't matter what about, there should never be a reason for that. Maybe he isn't the guy we thought he was."
"I wouldn't go that far."
"Now you're defending him? Are you upset or not?"
Emma gave another deep sigh. It was not that she was not upset, as Morgan suggested. Rather, she was compelled to assume the best in his intentions.
"I think he's different," she finally said after a long pause. She turned over to see Morgan inspecting her.
"What?"

"Something else happened that you're not telling me."
"What are you talking about?" Emma choked, straightening up.
"Oh my god," Morgan gasped. "You told him you loved him, didn't you?"
Checkmate, Emma thought.
"I *may* have said something along the lines—"
"Oh no Em, this is bad."
"I said I was *falling* in love with him."
"Why would you do something so stupid?"
"It was post-sex, Morgan. The words just slipped out," she defended. "Plus, he said it first."
"Just because he says it doesn't mean you have to say it back! Not unless you actually mean it. Boys are idiots, they don't understand the meaning behind words."
"I know, I know! Shit, I'm in trouble, aren't I?"
Morgan sat beside Emma to console her.
"You'll be okay. Who knows, maybe he forgot."
"Has Tommy told you that he loved you yet?"
"Let's be real, I don't think Tommy is capable of loving anyone other than himself."
Emma burst into laughter and hugged her friend.
"Thank you, Morgan. I don't know what I would do without you."
"You do you, Em," Morgan said flatly. "Whoever you end up with, I only ask that you don't make him distract you from what is important. I know you would say the same to me if I were in your shoes."
A boy was a distraction, and nothing more. And rich boys were typically regarded as the worst, who swam in so much privilege that it was rare for them to not project their self-justifications in light of problems that were ultimately a fault of their own. They tended to be righteous, viewing themselves as untouchable from the world below them.
Emma knew such a person could potentially divert her from her dreams. And as a college freshman dedicated to making a name for herself, there should be no time for even entertaining such an irrelevant proposition.
"Speaking of which," Emma mumbled, grabbing her backpack before starting for the door.
"Where are you going?"
Emma swiveled back to Morgan.
"The boys are not the only ones who have homework," Emma sighed gloomily. "I'm going to the library to finish my paper."
"We just got back!" Morgan tried, quickly realizing it would be impossible to persuade Emma's stubbornness.

Just then, there came a knock at their door. It was their RA, in his typically flat-toned demeanor.
"Hey Willy."
"I waited by your door for three hours yesterday. I was supposed to give you this," he glowered, shoving an envelope in her face. "You owe me one for having to come here on my day off."
He stormed off begrudgingly.
"Sorry Willy!" she shouted before shutting the door and returning to the envelope now in her hands.
"It's from the Ember House," she muttered to Morgan, who gasped skittishly and rushed up to see for herself.
"Open it, open it!"
Emma took a deep breath, absorbing the suspense as she tore open the envelope and pulled out the folded paper.
"Wait," she hesitated. "I can't, Morgan. You do it."
Morgan snatched the paper and strolled to the other end of the room, reading the letter.
Emma trembled impatiently, watching her friend read on.
"What does it say?"
She tried reading Morgan's face, her friend's lack of expression causing her to grow more nervous.
After the longest minute she ever endured, she watched Morgan raise her head from the letter.
"…Well?"
"Congratulations," Morgan cheered, revealing a heartwarming grin.
Emma lost it, embracing Morgan as the two gave out a scream that surely carried through the floor.
"I'm so happy for you!" Morgan said when they calmed down. "That said, I am a little sad I won't be able to room with you next fall."
Emma's joy suddenly dissipated.
"Next fall?"
"Yeah, says here that the program starts in late August."
Emma followed Morgan's finger on the paper.
"That doesn't make any sense," she said tartly. "I thought it was supposed to be for the summer?"
"Did it say it would be for the summer?"
Emma grew silent, pondering Morgan's question.
"Now that I think about it, I don't remember ever reading about the start date…I guess I just assumed…" Her voice trailed off.
"What are you thinking?"
Emma's eyes darted back and forth across the paper.

"I can't do it."

"Are you serious?"

"Come on Morgan, I would have to miss a semester. I can't do that to you."

"It's an internship, Em. People do it all the time. Plus you're still getting credit for it. Come on, this is what you have been working for!"

Emma frowned behind her nod in agreement with Morgan's comment, thinking about the other factor that drew concern.

Jack Douglas.

She regretted not being communicative with him, intentionally keeping any mention of the internship brief whenever the topic arose. In her defense, she had no idea if she would be accepted, nor the state of their relationship progressing so quickly. Particularly after his deceitful debacle, Emma wondered if accounting for Jack's opinion was even worth it.

"I need to think about it," she mumbled, grabbing her backpack and heading for the door. "I'll be back tonight...I have to study."

Emma debated calling her mom to give the news of her internship, but was distracted when she scrolled over her father's contact. It had been years since they spoke, but his voice remained clear as day in her memories of him. She knew he would have been overly ecstatic about the news, just like when she was accepted to Davison several years prior. She may have been too young to fully understand the feat, but his reaction made up for everything.

"I'm proud of you sweetheart," he had said, boasting the widest grin despite his fatigue from lugging boxes back and forth from the U-Haul. "I think you're going to really enjoy it. I've heard a lot of great things about that school."

"Bruce!" came Julia from the entryway. "I told you not to overwork yourself. That's why we have the movers!"

One of the movers gave her a bemused look as he passed.

"Oh relax Cody, you know what I mean. We love your family for helping us." Bruce chuckled at his wife's usual bluntness. "It's okay honey, I know my limits. Besides, the more hands on deck, the faster we can be done with it. Isn't that right Cody?"

"Don't bring me into this," Cody quipped. "Besides, it's not like I could say no to my boss."

"Marshall promised each of you a couple days of PTO, and don't forget all the free beer for afterward."

"Oh yeah, so you can prank me into drinking and driving like you did at the K-9 demonstration when I was a first year associate?"

The other movers overheard and busted out laughing in acknowledgement of the incident.

"Hey, blame that all on Marshall. He just wanted to see how you would defend yourself to see if you were up for the job. It's not like we were actually going to press charges,"
Bruce turned to his daughter. "Marshall has since stopped his initiation antics."
"Is it normal for cops and defense attorneys to be as buddy-buddy as you and Marshall?"
"I'm sure it's not, but you know Marshy. He's one of my best friends ever since we roomed together in law school."
One of the movers passed them going up the driveway.
"Your dad made the mistake of choosing the dark side," he joked.
"That's funny Andre, because we say the same for you lawyers."
"Oh come on, I'm a prosecutor!"
Julia's patience was tried hearing the guys being, well guys.
"I'm going back inside to order pizzas."
"Sounds great honey!"
Emma rolled her eyes in amusement. She was all too used to her father and his jovial banter with his colleagues.
"Mom's never been a fan of your bro-time, huh?"
"Only at times," he replied casually. "She's just been dealing with a lot of stuff recently. Don't be too hard on her, you two are more alike than you may think."
Emma's gave a faint shrug and scrunched her nose at that. She loved her mom, but she silently rejected the idea that they were that similar. She was always more drawn to her father's bubbly personality versus her mother's cool demeanor.
"Why don't you go inside and help your mom and with unpacking? We'll finish up here soon."
Emma obeyed and made her way up to the house, taking one final glance at the driveway where her father and friends cackled on.
Even with the tragic revelations that were to follow, at that moment, she had remembered the peace in life and its simplicity then. If only she had another chance to re-live it—

Reality returned when she distractedly ran into someone, fumbling her phone and watching helplessly as it smacked the cement below her feet.
"Oh crap," Emma muttered as she reached for her phone, averting her eyes to avoid further embarrassment.
"Emma?"
She peered up.
"Logan?"

It was astonishing how different he looked since she last saw him: his once shaggy blonde hair now clipped short just above his brows; his former lanky stature, replaced with a stockier build; the only feature unchanged – also her only way of knowing it was him – were his icy blue eyes. Vibrant in color, but forever solemn in nature.

"It's really you," Logan affirmed. "I heard that you were a student here, but it's still crazy seeing you after so long."

"Likewise, how've you been?"

"I'm good. Being here took some getting used to, but it's growing on me. How are you managing your first year?"

Emma took a deep breath.

"It's been a lot, honestly. Sometimes I forget what it's like to have a social life."

"I feel that—" he started, shaking his head. "Actually, I never had much of a social life to begin with, so never mind…but to that point, I heard about you and Jack. How is he doing?"

"He's good," Emma said hesitantly, "We're just hanging out, but it's been fun. We just got back from spending the night at his cabin."

"Well that's cool. He's a good guy."

"Yeah, he is."

A few seconds of awkward silence. Then Emma spoke up.

"I should get going…I have to study."

"Yeah, of course…well hey, I hope to see you around more."

There was something about his tone that intrigued Emma. He started off, but in that instant, her constrained apprehension shattered.

"We're actually planning on going to the Locks next weekend, if you are interested?"

Logan stopped and turned, lowering his head.

"Yeah, I don't know. I'm not on the best terms with those guys…not sure how much Jack would like that, thinking I'm a piece of shit and all…"

"You two used to be close, though! Who knows, maybe it will be different this time."

"Maybe," Logan said, giving a dismissive chuckle. "We'll see."

"I won't take no for an answer," Emma winked.

Logan straightened his posture, now more attracted to Emma's request.

"Okay, I'll text you," he agreed, his gaze averting to his watch. "I'll let you get to your studying."

Emma nodded and waved him goodbye.

A sense of allurement breezed through Emma as she watched him continue down the footpath. She ignored her heart beating out of her chest when she entered the library. It was simply an attraction. Nothing more. She shook her head, forcing it out of her mind. Jack would surely be upset if he ever learned about what just happened. Good thing that he did not have to know. Emma hated meddling over the thought. Why should she feel anxious about something that she deemed to not be big deal? That is, unless it was not as insignificant as she pretended it to be.

Emma would end up being distracted for the rest of the evening, her notebook open before her as she glossed over the sun slipping away, and waiting for nightfall to take course.

What was it about this boy, Jack, who was riddled in so much desperation for companionship that he was willing to lie about his own identity just to have her? She did not know him well. While he pretended to be someone he was not, he at least humbled up to admit the truth. He played his cards unlike most would in his given situation because he did not want to be treated differently. She had little compassion for liars. He may have been a couple years older than her, but she still viewed him a boy at heart – one incapable of understanding what it meant to love, wholeheartedly. There was a likable quality about him, nevertheless; one that she could not help but figure to be inherently true, nor a figure of her imagination.

She did not know him well. And yet, here she was, tempted to entrust a false promise to a hopeless romantic, who was more than determined to shape a skewed vision into a potentially inescapable reality. What was she to do? Was she already in too deep? She did not know him well. Breaking away could have repercussions she would be unwilling to accept. And if she forced herself to accept it – at least for the time being – when would she know the appropriate time to end it? She did not know him well, but at least for the time being, she was prepared to. At this point, all she could do was hope.

ix

Tommy sprawled across the bed, nearly blinded by the morning glare as he squinted at his phone displaying the stacked agenda of meetings over the next eleven hours of his life.

His eyes drifted to today's date at the top of the screen.

August 11th.

About two months ago, Tommy was cooped up at the Seattle airport, awaiting a red eye to take him east. His friends threw him a farewell party the night before, which unfortunately for him, ended only ninety minutes prior to his departure. He regretted being so ripped when he booked a last-minute flight to Washington D.C. The only reason one should not fly first class is unless they are flying private, and Tommy was given the third, abhorrently unheard of, option.

Economy: Corporate America's gilded term to convince the poor that they can regularly afford aerial travel.

He hated being sardined between the Idahoan grousing about last season's harvest, and the Californian venting about his girlfriend's dietary changes as advised by her attractive, recently divorced therapist.

And now, two months later, he was caught somewhere between completely relaxed and utterly stressed. Tentatively lingering in bed, understandably, as procrastination stems directly from his personal devaluation of work over, well, everything else he viewed to be important. He did not reject the notion of a successful career, but such a feat comes with implications. And the fear of failure driving one to waste incessant decades working toward an egoistic, imaginatively meaningless end goal strictly deemed off the society's approval? *No thank you.* But also, *yes please.*

An astringent odor floated about Tommy's breath of scent, causing him to lurch forward in disgust. He would be brushing his teeth, had he not remembered the impossibility of being the first to the bathroom in the morning. That is, every morning spent with her.

He moved to the edge of the bed when she emerged from the bathroom.

"Look who's finally awake," she acknowledged without looking at him as she proceeded to get dressed.

He still stared at her. It was all he could ever do when she came into his view.

"I am fairly hungover," Tommy managed, gently rubbing his aching forehead. "My brain needs water and fresh air."

"Have you ever thought about not drinking so much?"

"I would if someone was gracious enough to dictate an algorithm explaining the appropriate amount of liquor one *should* drink to enjoy the fleeting intoxication without feeling like shit afterwards."

"Hmm, I feel like something along the sorts exists already," she cajoled. "That said, you could always take the initiative on developing it yourself."

"Algebra, golf, finance," Tommy sighed. "If it involves numbers, I wouldn't consider myself a subject matter expert."

"Is that *humility* I detect from Tommy Beech?"

Tommy reached out and took hold of Zoe's waist, pulling her back to the bed where they laid beside each other.

"I prefer to view it as an acknowledgement of my strengths and weaknesses." Zoe snickered and straddled atop him, her head perked up to meet his eyes as she rested her chin on his chest.

"What do you have planned for today?"

"Today…" Tommy began, gathering his thoughts. "'Saac and I need to go in early to meet with potential vendors for the convention."

Yes, Isaac – the same Isaac who poked fun at Tommy for taking his freshman summer too seriously – succumbed to his contagious persuasion to accompany him across the country for three months of work for one of the most prestigious political internships. He had no knowledge or interest in the industry, frankly, but who would turn down a funded summer of nice suits and tantalizing post-work cocktails?

"Since when are interns given such a responsible task?"

"Since the staffers realized that we're more competent than them," Tommy chirped, rolling his eyes. "That, or our bosses simply don't want to go into the office on a Saturday."

"Sounds like a good time," she said sarcastically. "I'm going up to the ranch today. I can't wait to see Ash but it's a bitch of a drive to get there."

"If 'Saac and I get done early, we can head up after. Maybe even grab a bite on our way back."

She laughed. "There's not much up there, you know."

"I grew up in a city," Tommy reminded. "Soaking in the natural beauty of our country sounds like the perfect vacation for me."

"As if we're not treating this internship like a vacation already."

Touche, Zoe. Their work was crucially important, although its interns refused to acknowledge the reality of prioritizing its value over their desire to splurge their existence on mind-altering substances.

They exited the elevator into the lobby, where they met with Isaac standing beside the swiveling doors.

"Good morning lovebirds," he greeted, embracing Zoe before treating himself to a swig of water from his bottle. "Wherever you're headed today, I hope you remembered to bring a hat. It's already roasting out there."

"I did, in fact," Zoe said, patting on her backpack.

Isaac faced Tommy. "You've chosen well brother."

Tommy smiled and focused back on Zoe, placing a kiss on her forehead and hugging her.

"Enjoy your day. I'll let you know if we end up having time to join you later."

"Sounds good," she agreed. She was halfway through the door when she turned back to the boys.

"I hope you two absolutely kill it today."

Isaac wrapped his arm around Tommy.

"Oh we *absolutely* will!"

Saac was right: the heat was dreadful that morning. The nation's capital was not known as the "swamp" for nothing. Even keeping a normal pace, his body was nearing its onset of gratuitous perspiration, causing him curse and shake the droplets of sweat forming under his button up.

Walking to the office was the most boring sequence of Tommy's workday. Even that was an overstatement, however, with Isaac striding along, listening intently as he would humorously analyze his observations.

The general scope of their responsibilities varied, yet their time spent on foolish antics was nearly endless.

They were approaching the building when Tommy saw one of the interns, Karen, waiting for them at the door.

"Wow, you're actually here on time," she sneered, obviously directed at Tommy.

Under normal lens, Tommy figured that with a negative, there is also a positive. Prejudice is different, apparently to some, likely because it is perceived as being blind to reason. And regardless of how much effort is applied to dissect its broad definition (as a result of its susceptibility to heightened subjectiveness), there was no way he could hold a respectful debate in an attempt to opening one's mind.

Karen could have changed her name to Prejudice, and it would have no effect on how she formulates conclusions from her twisted method of reading the lines.

All Tommy had to do was say he was from Seattle before she attacked him with a range of baseless stereotypes, much of which were skewed to an extraordinary degree when she met Isaac just minutes after. And because Tommy was not one to take criticism lightly, he certainly had a lot to say back; much of it, admittedly, may be received as insulting, harsh, and intolerable. There may have also been a moment when he snarked on her brother for his mental disorder. As a result, their working relationship has been short of pleasurable. It was entertaining for the other interns, however, who took every opportunity to gas even the calmest situations until they had to shield their eyes from the blazing fires they intentionally caused. For Tommy and Karen, the wildfire never subsided on its own.

Isaac subtly tapped Tommy's arm and cut in front of him in hopes that speaking to her first would diminish any chance of a confrontation. After all, it was impossible to rain on the sunniest of personalities.

"Good morning, Karen."

"Hi Isaac," she smiled. "I cannot understand why you hang out with this guy. Ditch him, before you find yourself looped into some stupid shit he caused."

"Ooh, so cynical," Tommy mocked. "You do know I'm standing right here?"

"I'm aware," she hissed as she rolled her eyes and went inside.

"Looking forward to our meeting in an hour!" Isaac called back to her. They continued upstairs to their shared office.

"God, she can be such a bitch," Tommy said after closing the door behind them.

"You can't take it personally," Isaac consoled, tilting his head. "Well, actually you absolutely should, given what you said about her brother."

"She started it."

"And now you sound like a child," Isaac tittered. "So you're not used to people hating you – what's the harm in that?"

"The harm 'Saac, is that she has no reason to hate me. What am I supposed to do, apologize for having a better comeback?"

"Sometimes you have to be the bigger person. You know that."

"We're past that," Tommy dismissed, settling in and opening his laptop. "I have no use for her anyway."

"Damn, so much tension," Isaac taunted jokingly. "How are you going to be if you and Zoe ever get into a fight?"

"That will never happen, because she's actually intelligent," Tommy answered. "Also, I don't like describing disagreements as 'fights.' I prefer 'discussions.'"

Isaac was unsurprised by his friend's stubbornness. Growing up with him, he had frequently witnessed Tommy being called every psychological term in the book. Most of the altercations were simple misunderstandings, and in Tommy's defense, he believed him to be a sympathetic, caring person.

The disconnect came when he was in a 'discussion' with a stranger, and those rarely ended well. He sometimes wondered how Tommy was able to maintain healthy relationships in general, but always reasoned it was because the people Tommy respected were, personality-wise, more like him.

Not that Isaac viewed himself as stubborn. Unless, of course, it was to his reluctance of reevaluating the argument against why he still chose Tommy as a best friend, per Karen's remark.

Midday was near when the boys begun constructive work. Then another hour went, and it concerned Tommy since he expected to be on their way to Zoe instead of rummaging through complex spreadsheets. He was sure a witty text from her was imminent.

And sure enough, it came.

Ya'll putting on your makeup?

Tommy chuckled and tossed his phone to 'Saac so he could read.

"Damn, she's more demanding than you."

"I know. Is it bad that I don't consider it a red flag?"

"Tommy, my friend, you are literally a walking red flag."

"Should we finish up before heading out?"

Isaac sniffed the sarcasm and joined Tommy's lead in gathering their belongings before slipping out of the office.

"Where do you two think you're going?"

The boys swiveled to their boss glaring back at them as she cradled several bottles of vodka.

"Hey Lane…" Saac began, slow to assist. "Do you need help with those?"

"I always knew you were the most intuitive of the bunch."

Tommy raised his hand. "I would like to argue that statement."

"I don't want to hear it Tom. Listen, before you go—" she handed him a bottle. "Nice job on the security report for the Service. *Take it home with you. I don't want to catch you two drinking here again.*"

"But everyone does it."

"Not like you two. The cleaners spent an extra hour last weekend because you were too stupid to aim at the toilet."

"Damn, I love you too Lane."

He could hear Lane's teeth grit when she shook her head and guided them in her office.

"I didn't puke last weekend," Isaac said.

"As his friend, you are complicit in everything he does."

"I never agreed to those terms."

"Then you shouldn't have agreed to work for me."

"I didn't even know what I was getting myself into!"

"Join the party," Tommy relayed.

Lane rolled her eyes and sighed. "Boys. Sometimes I forget how young you two are."

For someone as stern and demanding as Lane Miller, it surprised Tommy that she took a liking to them. Through their frequent interactions, he could count on one hand the number of times he had seen her happy, let alone smile. It was different for Isaac, whose wittiness was impossible to not enjoy.

"Where's Nicole?" Isaac asked.

Lane raised a brow. "Why are you asking about my daughter?"

"No reason!" he blabbered quickly, causing Tommy to step in.

"She's been very helpful with our work. There's an authoritative quality about her, in the way she orders us around. It's very respectable. I wonder where she gets it from—" he winked at Lane. "That, and her good looks, of course."

"Sucking up to your boss. You're perfect for this line of work," she turned to Isaac. "Nicole wasn't feeling well today. She'll be back Monday."

"Incidentally, 'Saac and I are taking off. We'll come in early next week to make up for the time missed."

Lane sat behind her desk and waved them off. A common signal that she was finished talking.

Tommy pulled Isaac out of her office and continued to the stairwell.

"Good rule of thumb," he began. "Don't give hints to your boss that you love her daughter."

"Oh please, she loved it."

"Would you?"

"Absolutely!"

They hailed a ride to take them across the Potomac into Virginia. Zoe's ranch was an hour south of the Capitol, which would have been a boring drive, had it not been for the exuberant brush of greenery encircling the highway.

She was standing outside of the stables when they arrived. Tommy started to admire her prior to leaving the car. Other than her mid-rise, outseam jeans, the rest of her outfit sported an equestrian vibe: the black, spurred boots, white button up under the hunt coat, and an ever-so endearing helmet, which she took off to adjust her hair.

It left him speechless. Her grace could suffice a hundred songs, and the best part was how little effort she put in to make it so.

"Tommy?" he heard Isaac say, seeing that the driver was still waiting for payment.

"Shit, right yeah—" Tommy pulled out his wallet and handing the driver a few hundreds.

"This is too much," the driver said.

"Don't worry about it," he replied, keeping his eyes ahead and he started for Zoe.

Isaac shrugged at the driver and waved him off before skipping up to Tommy.

"I have to say: you are the only person I enjoy third-wheeling with."

"Why's that?"

"Because unlike the other guys, you get so sappy. It's very unlike you."

"Dude, we're thirty feet from Zoe, she might hear you."

Isaac smirked. "Does that bother you?"

"A little bit, I don't want her to think I'm obsessed or anything."

"But you are—"

"Shh!"

They fell silent when they reached Zoe.

"Fun ride?" she asked.

"As fun as long drives can be with this fella," Isaac playfully nudged Tommy.

"Oh, I can imagine," she giggled. "Come on, I'll give you a tour of the place." Tommy had visited the farm once before, during his second weekend. He was accompanied with a couple other interns then, who had all accepted an invite from Zoe, as her way of treating the foreigners to the east's country scene. For Tommy, though, it was an opportunity to grow closer with Zoe, who at the time, had hinted mutual feelings of affection. And while nothing happened on the trip, it certainly did the moment they returned to the Capitol. They entered the stables, where Zoe's prize steed, Ash, stood in stoic posture on the opposite end of the aisle.

"Do you have other horses?" Isaac asked upon noticing the vacant stalls.

"Yeah we have a couple more. I think our trainer is with them."

"You have a trainer?"

"We sort of need one. Knowing how to ride is one thing, but drilling a horse is another challenge entirely," she laughed. "I'll be the first to admit that I haven't the slightest clue how they do it. But I will toot my horn when I say I am a great rider."

Isaac nudged Tommy again as Zoe paced on, whispering in his ear, "Would you agree with that?"

"Bro, why even take it there?"

They continued to the end of the stable, where a single horse stood motionless.

"And this is my black beauty, Ash," Zoe announced, resting her hand gently on Ash's forehead before sliding it down to his muzzle. "How are you, my guy?"

After placing a kiss on Ash's cheek, she turned back to the boys. "These are our friends, Tommy and Isaac."

She extended her hand toward the boys. "Who wants to go first?"

Tommy has been around Ash before, but never this close, watching it drop its head and flick its ears.

"Are you sure?" he asked hesitantly.

Zoe smiled. "He would really appreciate it."

Tommy exchanged a sheepish frown at Isaac and approached the horse, doing his best to mimic Zoe's relaxed demeanor. He was ten feet out when Ash begun whickering and stomping its hooves.

"You're fine," she said softly.

"Does he understand that?" Tommy asked.

"I was talking to you silly," she chuckled. "Ash is a big sweetheart. You have nothing to worry about."

Tommy ambled closer until Ash's snout was directly in front of him.

"Your turn Saac," Zoe invited, waiting for him to get close before taking his hand and pulling him beside Tommy.

Tommy started with his hand on Ash's crest and gingerly ran it over his neck to his muzzle. Isaac gently patted, peering over Ash's neck to meet Zoe.

"What should we say to him?"

"Whatever you want."

Tommy waited for Isaac to go first, exchanging a goofy smirk as Isaac leaned into Ash's ear.

"You think you're so fast, but I bet I could take you."

Tommy and Zoe laughed, causing Ash to bobble his head.

"Whoa, hey now Ash, they're just a bunch of jokers. It's how they show their love."

Ash gave a sonorous snort at the boys, his muzzle now inches from Isaac's nose.

"I *do* love making jokes," Isaac pleaded, now caressing Ash's snout.

"I have a couple more things to do before we head out," Zoe began. "Are you two good to wait for another twenty minutes or so?"

"No worries. Come on, 'Saac."

The boys found a bench outside of the stables to rest, where a massive oak shaded them from the sun's heat. Isaac buried his attention with a game on his phone while Tommy's gaze floated off to the surrounding nature. Several minutes passed when he looked back at Zoe, curious to now see her staring down at her phone.

"Everything okay?" he called out to her.

"No," Isaac muttered, showing his phone to Tommy. "This was just sent to all the interns."

Tommy leaned over to read:

"Good afternoon team,
Due to the ongoing events from earlier today, we are deciding to indefinitely
suspend the duration of your internship. Your team manager will be reaching
out directly with instructions on your current projects and final day of
employment. We will also coordinate your respective travel out of the District
of Columbia (if applicable).
Thank you all for your tremendous work and public service. We hope that you
consider joining the team again during the next election cycle."

He hated reading each word. The unpredictability in this line of work was
preached to him since he entered the industry years ago, but he figured it was
a myth given it never happened to him.
"This is a joke, right?" he scoffed, checking his phone. "Are we sure it's not
April 1st?"
They looked up from to see Zoe now standing in front of them, her eyes
watering from the disappointing news.
"Can you believe this?" she moped grumpily as she clenched her phone.
"It's fucked, but it is what it is, I guess," Tommy remarked, echoing her tone.
"What do we do now?"
"Head back to the city…get fucked up until we have to leave," Isaac
suggested. "I reckon we have at least to the end of the week."
"Why do you think they would do this though? Why not keep us until the end
of the election like they originally promised us?"
"It has to be a budgetary reason," Tommy assumed.
"Why wouldn't they clarify that in the text then?"
"She has a point," Isaac added. "I mean, we're not even getting paid to begin
with. This is the closest we can get to slave labor, and they're still getting rid
of us."
"Maybe we were just bad slaves," Tommy joked.
"Bro…"
"Oh please, I'm the only one who should be offended at that, and I said it!"
"Thank you for that," Zoe shook her head. "This sucks." Hearing her say it
got to Tommy, who despite his effort in lightening the mood, was also torn
by the news. On one end, going home early did not bother him – he felt to
have gotten enough experience from the job. But on the other end, he would
be saying goodbye to everyone he was recently acquainted with.

Specifically Zoe, who he now feared would be the last person he could ever love.

"I'll still drive us all back to the city," Zoe said. "Just let me finish up with Ash."

Tommy frowned helplessly at Isaac. It was easy to accept forces out of his control. But the lines were blurred now that Zoe was a factor in the formula. Isaac placed a hand on his shoulder.

"Let's try to be positive," he nodded towards Zoe. "If not for you, then for her."

Tommy forced a grin and settled on the bench.

For her, he will quit sulking and be positive. Because for her, he would do anything.

*****

They laid there in silence, sharing a comforting warmth pulsating through their still bodies.

"I can't believe it's almost over," Zoe finally said. "It sounds stupid, but I imagined this would last forever."

"A dream that never ends…if only there was a way to live in our imagination."

"Maybe it's fate that we met…is there a word for that?"

Tommy shrugged. "Kismet?"

"Kismet!" she repeated. "Smart boy."

"If you consider knowing the definition of that word to determine one's degree of smartness, then this is probably not going to work out."

"Oh please, you say that, but now in your head you're definitely running through the percentage of chance that it still could."

Tommy hummed thoughtfully to himself.

"Please don't tell me that you are actually trying to come up with algorithm for that."

"Hey now, I'm trying to explore a way that we can stay together, like this," Tommy contested. "Once you get your J.D., feel free to commemorate the accomplishment by filing your first lawsuit in my name."

Zoe rolled over to face him.

"To that point," she started. "I intend on staying here for the foreseeable future. I made sure my parents were aware of my long-term plans."
"Neither of us planned for this though."
"Is *this* bad?"
"No, that's not what I'm getting at," Tommy paused, rephrasing. "It's just that I didn't consider the possibility of never going back to Seattle. I mean, I still have to graduate before I can think about my future."
"We both know your future was set in stone before you were even born," Zoe countered. "You mean a future with someone else."
She was right. A future with someone else. Tommy did not want to commit so early in his life, and he was frankly surprised by Zoe, who appeared to be more inclined than he was. She never came off as a romantic.
"Nevertheless, here we are, staring in the face of our end; one that I hope is short-lived."
"Oh Tommy, don't be so poetic."
He kissed her, acknowledging it may be the last time he would have the chance.
Breakups are unanimously frowned upon. The pain and confusion are an experience so belittling for anyone unfortunate to have endured. For Tommy, however, it was the opposite; not only to understand the feeling of loss, but that it gave him a chance to learn from it in future endeavors. There comes a time when such emotions warrant growth, and coming to realization, ironically, was to prevail through the dilemma more than once.
Their time together was relatively short, but he was certain that Zoe was the one. No one else could ever come close. They had more chemistry than the periodic table, and her aura was everything he yearned for in a partner. Someone he would, one day, willingly commit to spending the rest of his days and dedicate all effort on her behalf. Imperfection is inevitable, but she was imperfectly perfect. Incapable of being acquired, nor inherited. A true definition, that according to Tommy, was specially created for only her.
It would be a difficult readjustment for Tommy on his journey west. It was unlike him to fall hard, which reinforced his assumption about her. That she was unlike anyone he had, and will ever meet.
He will see her again. It was fate. If only there was someone in his life that mirrored the same predicament.

Part II: Doubt

X

"As you all know, there are a lot of treats to savor in a Washington summer. Personally, I find the Locks to be the most enjoyable."
Jack raised an eyebrow at Tommy. "The Locks?"
"At Ballard."
"Right…I just didn't know anyone referred to it as that."
"Did anyone remember to bring sunscreen?" Morgan asked.
"Don't panic babe, I got you," Tommy assured, patting his backpack before swinging it around his back. "I'm glad I never have to worry about stuff like this."
"It doesn't matter if you have darker skin," Jack pointed out. "The rays can hurt anyone."
"That's what the government *wants* you to think."
"I don't even understand what you're saying right now," Jack tested. "And on the topic of thinking, what were *you* thinking bringing us here when Discovery is literally a mile away?"
"There's always too many people on the loop. Besides, there's supposed to be a concert today right at the water's edge. Not to mention food trucks – food trucks, Jack!"
Jack decided against asking further. After all, it was already a reach for Tommy to consider a ship canal as a seasonal highlight to check out without lending some praise to the neighboring botanical gardens. Blame it on the possible autism or unassuming bad taste, but Tommy's interests were fairly not everyone's cup of tea.

Emma was busy in her thoughts during their exchange, glimpsing periodically at her phone. She hoped to hear from Logan. He always preferred to follow the beat of his own drum, which fascinated her, as it contrasted her high attentiveness for things most people·would consider "important." She panned around for a bit longer, miraculously spotting him staring back at her at the foot of the bridge across the street. She watched him lift his phone, and at that moment, she felt the vibration from his incoming text.
Come here.
She lifted her head, finding an excuse to leave the group.
"I'm going to grab a lemonade," she announced. "Do you want anything?"
"That's a good idea," Jack replied. "I'll come with you –"
"No worries!" she interrupted.
"Oh," Jack frowned, surprised by her response. "Are you sure?"

She nodded calmly, hoping he would not pry. "I'll be quick," she promised, reassuring him by tightening her hold on his hand before breaking away. She was intentional to detour down the sidewalk until she disappeared into the lively crowd before crossing the street, where she saw Logan waiting for her on the other side.

"I thought it would be harder to find you with all these people," Emma greeted. "How long have you been here?"

"Just now," he lied, knowing full well he was there an hour prior to their agreed-upon time.

"I still can't believe I'm talking to you again," he stammered. "I honestly didn't think I would ever see you after high school."

"Oh come on, there's no way I could drift that far away from my *prom* date."

"Right, prom..." Logan faltered, hesitant to revisit his high school memories. "I was kind of a piece of shit back then."

"According to Jack, you still are."

"When did he say that?"

"He didn't. You told me that, remember?"

"Oh yeah, of course," he muttered. "I don't talk to him that much anymore – has he changed a lot since?"

"I'm sure you know that answer better than me, considering he was one of your best friends and all," Emma said. "You know, I can actually see it."

"What makes you say that?"

"Well, Tommy is his best friend," she reasoned. "And you two are more alike than different, I would say."

Logan concealed his disgust, hating the fact that she just compared him to Tommy B.

"So, how are things?" Logan mused, changing the subject.

"They're good," Emma began. "I actually just got accepted for an art internship in New York..." she faltered, questioning her impulse to share it with him even before telling Jack.

"No way? That's amazing!" Logan cheered as he suddenly embraced her. Emma eased into his arms, noting how much he had grown since grade school. She tried to hide her blushed cheeks as he pulled away.

"I'm very excited about it."

"When do you leave?"

"Next semester. It's three months, but there's a chance that it gets extended into the spring...so we'll see."

"What's so bad about that?" Logan asked, noticing the contempt in her tone.

"I don't know," Emma shrugged. "I think it's going to be hard to be away from home for that long. In a way, my life is established here, so having to pack up and leave—"

"—You want closure with things before moving," Logan finished. "Because even though the internship is temporary, it is still long enough for you to find new opportunities there. And if that's the case, you want to make sure you don't keep any open here, back home."

"Yes, exactly!" Emma exclaimed. "How did you know that?"

Logan gave her a friendly wink.

"I was in a similar situation a few years ago."

"How did you figure it out?"

"I didn't," Logan replied flatly. "I tried to, but after a couple months, I accepted that no matter how hard I pushed away the things that bothered me, it would always be there. You think you are able to get over it…to get that closure…but at the end of the day, it isn't always done by how much you try. Sometimes, you just have to wait for it to happen."

Emma pursed her lips, wondering if it would be wise to ask him to delve more into his past. She liked to think she had changed. Whether it was good or bad did not matter as much. She did not know Logan intimately back then, but from what she knew, Emma considered it safe to assume that whatever "bothered" him was highly distinctive to hers.

"I assume you still don't want to join us?" Emma suggested.

"Still probably not a good idea. You should get back though – don't want to have them worrying."

"Yeah," she mumbled, realizing the interaction had reached its end. "I'd love to see you again before I leave for New York, if that's okay?"

"That's something you should be asking yourself," he smirked. "But for the record, I would love to whenever you have time."

Emma was usually anxious in unfamiliar situations. She first became aware of her extreme introversion, ironically, when she met Logan Berg. In many ways, he was her first crush, and while their friendship never promoted romantically, it managed to stick with her over the years. She remembered every detail of that initial interaction: his sullen, charming gaze change to a shocked gape as his textbook plopped on the floor between their feet; the astonishment in his eyes when she asked him to prom, almost like it was the first and only time having a genuine conversation with someone of the opposite sex.

She expected to speak to that same Logan, but to her surprise, he had grown into a new, arguably better, version of himself. At least in how he projected it, anyway.

Emma awkwardly stood there, wondering how she was to say goodbye. Luckily for her, Logan proceeded to make the first move, leaning in and embracing her again. She hugged him back, the two of them meeting each other's eyes one more time before Logan ultimately broke away from her and started down the path.

Emma could not deny the butterflies circulating in her stomach as she watched him disappear in the crowd. Her feelings for him were undoubtedly real, and from how he looked at her, she could tell that he felt the same. Who knows, if things happened differently, perhaps they would be more than what they are now…

It may not have been strong enough to disregard her current relations with Jack. Its glowing prominence was worth questioning, nevertheless. She retraced the last few months of her life, bewildered at how a range of unpredictable events have brought her to this moment.

Simultaneously, Jack had difficulty concentrating shortly after Emma walked off, sulking as he treaded close behind Tommy and Morgan, distracted in his own thoughts to partake in the ongoing discussion. He had expected a follow-up from Emma about what happened at the cabin. Not only had she failed to mention it, but to his surprise, seemed happier than usual. Even so, he noticed something was off with her. Something that she was apparently unwilling to share with him.

He let his feet carry him aimlessly through the crowd, instinctively reacting to the red traffic light across the street. His gaze continued to drift in every direction, where just beyond the bridge, he spotted Emma.

"There she is," he said to Tommy and Morgan and begun to walk toward her. Emma's back was turned to him, and judging from her body language, Jack presumed she was speaking to someone. As he drew closer, however, he caught a glimpse of who she was talking to, causing him to come to an abrupt stop.

No, it couldn't be…

Logan Berg.

Jack stood there, slack jawed. He hoped that he was mistaken. He prayed what he saw was wrong. How could this have happened? What were the odds that Logan would be here, of all places, at this particular time and place? Was he following them? Did he approach Emma? Could this be his twisted way of sending a message? And if so, what could that message possibly be?

His memory traced back to her words: *I'm going to grab a lemonade.* Was she lying?

No, there was no way she'd do that, he thought, pushing away the truth of not knowing for sure.

"There you are, you were quick to walk off from us," Tommy said.

"Where's Emma?"

Jack nudged his head in Emma's direction, Tommy and Morgan following his gaze.

"Is that who I think it is?" Tommy asked.

"Yeah," Jack sighed. "He just doesn't know when to stop."

"How do you mean?"

"Nothing. Nevermind," Jack shook his head, unwilling to dredge up his last encounter with Logan.

"Do he and Emma know each other?"

"No…well yes, but I don't know how well…let's change the subject."

"Do you think he's trying to steal her from you?"

"Now why do you have to go there with it, Tommy? I told you to change the subject."

"Aren't you just a little bit curious though?"

Jack gave a dismissive shrug. The truth was, he was *too* curious. He had not gotten over what Logan said about her: not only that they talked in high school, but that she was a *tease*.

"Who is Emma talking to? One of your friends?"

"Sure," Tommy chuckled sarcastically. "If you would consider Peter Parker and Harry Osborn to be friends."

Jack gave a discerning squint. "*Who*?"

"Spiderman!"

"I know that, but who's Peter and who's Harry in this case?"

"Logan is Harry, and I'm Peter. I figured that would be obvious.

"Why can't I be Peter?" Jack contested.

"Two people can't be Peter. You have to be someone else."

"So, if you're Peter, than I'm Mary-Jane, right?" Morgan chimed in.

"It seems that way," Tommy flirted back.

Jack rubbed his eyes in annoyance.

"This is ridiculous," he said dryly, "I'm going for a walk."

Jack stormed off and joined the endless train of tourists on the walkway before retreating to the water's edge, circling around the food stands and trucks until he was amongst the serious fans glued to the floating boats entering and exiting the locks. So many people had their phones out taking photos. It was mind-blowing, to think just how risky some were being, thinking that an extra two feet closer to the boat was worth the risk of dropping their phones in the bay. Or falling in, which would not only be the worst-case scenario, in Jack's opinion, a deserving outcome for few of these ornery hags shoving aside for the best view. This close to the water, it felt like he was in an entirely different place. There was a reeky scent coming from the water below, but it only aided what became a suitable distraction from Emma, who chose to abandon him on their date for his greatest rival. He wanted to confront Logan right there and then, but knew showcasing his jealousy would worsen the situation. When in doubt, withdraw and process it clearly. It was typically then when one is presented with enough clarity to empathize with the reasons for another's actions, as well as receive a sign on how to move forward.

Then he saw her.

He was stunned by her willingness to disobey commonly accepted seasonal norms, as she was dressed in a crinkly red flannel with sky blue jeans. She was not like most girls he had come across, with her remarkable amber complexion that seemingly glowed even in the absence of sunlight; her honey-tinted hair stretching clear past her elbows; and the appealing curiosity in her intense blue eyes as she inspected the glittering ocean.

She was alone and appeared perfectly content. Could it be possible that seeing her here, at that time, was coincidental? Coming here with one girl, only to squander time for himself in a place of no importance to him – just to come across her – it piqued Jack's curiosity.

He collected himself before approaching her, trying to think of an acceptable icebreaker. What could he possibly say to a girl like *her*?

"You know, the city fishes nearly all of its seafood right here," he said.

The girl turned to him, her eyes penetrating through his shroud of anxiety. "Really?"

"Well…no," Jack replied nervously. "I don't actually know if that's true, but I thought it would be a nice attempt in trying to talk to you."

Jesus, that was horrible, he thought.

"I see," she said coolly. "Well look, if you're going to flirt with me, you'll have to try harder than that."

Jack immediately regretted doing this. He already had Emma, so why did he feel compelled to talk to her?

"Lighten up babe, I'm messing with you."

"Oh," Jack stuttered, taken aback. "Yeah, of course. I knew that."

"Sure you did. And for the sake of being completely transparent, I was waiting for you to come talk to me."

"Wait what? Y-you saw me?"

"You were literally staring at me for five minutes."

Is that how long it was?

"Don't worry," she continued. "Although it would normally creep me out, you seem more nervous than predatory, so I'll let it slide."

"That's my bad. I don't get nervous often—"

"I totally understand."

Jack sighed deeply in relief.

"So, are you going to ask for my name or are we just going to stand here in silence?"

Get it together man.

"I'm Jack," he said, shaking her hand.

"Molly Brown."

"Molly," he repeated. "I happen to know a lot of Mollys."

"I doubt any of them are as pretty as me."

"Wow."

She cracked a smile. "I take it you're not one for sarcasm, huh?".

"No, sorry, that's not it," he stammered. "I guess I'm just a little surprised at how…direct you are."

"I get that a lot. If it makes you feel any better, I am naturally shy and hate talking to people."

Jack examined her expressionless face.

"You're being sarcastic again, right?"

"Someone is a quick learner," she winked. "Are you from here?"

"Mercer, but I study at UDub."

"Me too! Well, for the latter, anyway. I don't know where Mercer is," she said. "I transferred up here from Montana, so I'm still pretty unfamiliar with the city," she looked around them. "Actually, this is my first time here too."

Jack grinned at the acknowledgement of her invitation but held himself back from engaging further.

Emma, he remembered. *Do not get yourself deeper into this. You have a girlfriend.*

"That is great to know," Jack beamed, ignoring his thoughts. "If you're not busy, I would be honored to give you a quick tour."

She smiled.

"The honor would be all mine."

They started down the walkway. Even just minutes into meeting Molly, he noticed the uncanny similarities between her and Emma. They were both incredibly confident, naturally assertive, and wildly intelligent. Speaking to her was effortless, and interesting enough to keep him captivated, and longing for more.

They reached the end of the path, where greeting them was a scenic view of the inlet.

"It's beautiful," she awed.

"I've lived here all my life, and still can't get over how amazing it is either."

Molly pulled out her phone, and before he could object, inched closer to him and brought the phone to his face, snapping a picture of them.

"I'll have to tell my friends all about this," she said, tapping away on her phone.

"About what?"

"About how a handsome gentleman took time out of his day to give me on a personal tour."

"I'm happy to do it."
"By the way," she paused, raising her head. "You never told me your last name?"
Jack's heart sank. He had forgotten about his everlasting fear of revealing his identity. Emma was the only girl who took it well, and even that trial was difficult to overcome.
"It's Douglas," he mumbled, his voice faltering.
"Douglas," she pondered. "Why does that name sound familiar?"
"My dad is Wayne Douglas."
Her eyes widened.
"I know. Believe me, I don't enjoy talking about it as much as people do hearing it."
"Oh, don't be so pretentious. Your daddy's rich. You can just say it."
"I mean, I don't refer to him as my 'daddy,' but…"
"Do a lot of people ask about it?"
"Yeah, I don't think it should matter, but you know how some people can be…"
"Right," she nodded. "I'm sure you get tired of always having to talk about getting rich when you'd much rather kick your feet up and smoke a bowl."
Jack blinked. "What?"
"You look like a stoner. Take it as a compliment."
"Are you into stoners?"
"Not historically."
"Um…okay." *This girl is weird.*
"Are you spending your summer in town?" she continued, pocketing her phone.
"Yeah, I'll most likely just be chilling everyday with my friends," he said, recalling his reason for being there. "I actually came here with them…they're probably waiting for me to get back."
"I understand," she said, turning away from him.
Jack hesitated, contemplating how he should go about an appropriate farewell, when she spoke up.
"Are you dating someone?"
"Excuse me?"
"I figured you weren't, considering you went out of your way to talk to me, but I have a fairly negative history with boys, and I don't want to revisit a similar situation."
Jack froze. Was she testing him?
"It's complicated," Jack admitted. "I'm sorry, you probably think I'm a piece of shit right now. That wasn't my intention…"
He felt guilty when she frowned.

"I just saw you, and I couldn't help myself," he continued. "I can't explain it, but I just had a feeling when I saw you."
Molly's eyes flickered. She grabbed his hand.
"It's not my business to ask, so I won't. I hope everything works out with whoever you are with."
Jack nodded, refusing to make eye contact.
"I will say this though," she resumed. "I also think that you are unlike anyone I have ever met. And just because we can't be together like 'that,' doesn't mean that we can't be friends."
"Definitely, I mean, we both go to Udub! I'm sure I'll see you this fall."
"Totally!"
They both paused, standing in an awkward silence.
"I should get going," Jack relented. He did not want to leave. He wished he could stay with her. However, reality was rushing back to him, and he knew that this newfound infatuation he found in Molly was meant to be nothing more than a short-lived fantasy he would be foolish to entertain.
"Go on then," she smiled, her eyes flickering. "It was nice meeting you, Jack Douglas."
Jack left her at the dock, retracing his steps back to the other end of the park. He found his friends huddled around the corner of a congested block. Tommy was first to see Jack, intercepting him in the street where they were just out of earshot of the girls.
"Where have you been?"
"I'll tell you later," Jack replied hesitantly.
"I see. Emma was asking for you. We didn't know what to tell her."
"That's interesting, since she didn't seem so concerned while she was talking to Logan."
"I seriously doubt that's something you should worry about."
"Like I said," Jack repeated. "We'll talk later."
Tommy agreed and led him back to the girls.
"There he is," Emma acknowledged. "The Prince of Seattle returns."
"Sorry girls, I just went for a walk."
Emma's stare made Jack nervous, almost as if she could taste the dishonesty seeping through his teeth.
The drive back did not help Jack's case either, as he sensed Emma's despondence in the car. He continued pretending like everything was normal when they made it back to the dorms.
"I had a great time," he said to her when they exited the car.
"Yeah, me too."
Jack peered back at Tommy and Morgan exchanging goodbyes, realizing he was running out time before their privacy would be intruded.

"Have you heard back from your internship?" he asked, noticing her paled expression at the question.
"Not yet," she lied. "I'm sure I'll hear about it soon."
Jack nodded silently, sensing her reluctance to keep the conversation going.
"When can I see you again?"
"I'm not sure yet. Since the semester is finally over, I have a lot of stuff to take care of before I can do anything."
"Of course! Yeah I completely understand," Jack babbled, uneasy from Emma's lack of enthusiasm. "Okay well…I'll be around. Just let me know?"
"Sounds like a plan."
Jack anxiously leaned in to kiss her, growing more worried when he noticed her hesitation to kiss him back. He knew something was on her mind, slowly pacing backward as he felt Tommy's hand pressed against his back. Morgan strolled past them and joined Emma as they proceeded to the dorms, giving the boys one last wave before they entered the building.
"What a day," Tommy said glowingly on the drive back home. "Morgan is really taking a liking to me."
"That's great man," Jack droned.
Tommy tilted his head, trying to observe Jack's expression.
"You good?"
Jack nodded, faking a smile to relieve Tommy's concern. He hoped Emma was only annoyed from not knowing his whereabouts earlier. He thought back to seeing her with Logan. Was he a player in a twisted game, seeing the two of them together? If he had even a sliver of doubt in Emma's love for him, he knew it was likely caused by something Logan had said.
At least he was smart enough to not mention it to Emma right there and then. Knowing her detective-like qualities, spilling his feelings about Logan was sure to have an adverse effect on what already seemed to be the beginning of a strained rapport with the girl he loved more than anything else.
He would keep it private, and let Time unfold the truth.

xi

The Fourth of July: a historic day stiffed in nostalgia and unforgettable memories alike. Celebration methods differed among the masses, but the purpose was the same: to commemorate America's independence. For the boys, it was no better time to get absolutely trashed.
Jack, however, and per usual, was deep in his feelings.
Emma never hit him up after the Locks. No dates, calls, or texts. It was almost as if she had vanished. Jack was grateful for his friends, as they were the only reason for him to bear Emma's absence over the last month. Summer reached its peak, but he secretly wished for its end. Despite straining through the typical college routine, it comforted Jack to know he would be reunited with Emma upon their return to campus.
"I fucking love this country!" Kevin rejoiced, finishing his beer and tossing it in the ocean.
"Jesus Kev," Jack scowled. "I've said it a thousand times: we have a trashcan bottom deck. Stop throwing shit in the water."
"Oh come on Jack, the fish will love it," Isaac snorted.
"That's not funny."
Tommy joined Jack at the wheel, handing him a beer.
"Lighten up," he said. "There's no time for fussiness on the Fourth."
Jack rolled his eyes. "Just trying to make sure we don't get ourselves in a pinch like the last time."
"Oh yeah," Tommy chucked, recalling their awkward run in with the cops the last year. It is crazy how upset people get with someone who disrespects the environment.
"I think I'm seasick," Bennett moaned, spread-eagled on the bed of the boat.
"You say that like it's an actual thing," Kevin said.
"It is!"
"It's not though."
"What?" Bennett wailed, turning to Tommy. "Tom, can you help me out here?"
"I've never been seasick," Tommy shrugged.
"You're both just being soft," Kevin dismissed, cracking open another beer.
"I think we should hit the beach for a bit," Bennett suggested. "We've been out here all morning."
Jack reeled closer to shore, just within earshot of the lively vibes on land. There he saw a massive group of faces closest to them, many of whom he recognized from their high school days.
Then he saw her.

They were only a month into the season, yet she looked like she had weathered under the sun for a century, her once clear skin peppered in browned freckles, complemented with tan lines tattooed across her shoulders that stretched down to her thighs. Stunned by her beauty, and watching as she squeezed her stomach in imperceptible glee.

Jack parked the boat and signaled Tommy B sitting near him.

"You're the captain now," he relayed, hurling himself into the water and paddling off.

"Emma!" he exclaimed when he reached the shore, rushing up through the crowd and embracing her.

"Jack," she baffled, reluctantly hugging him back.

"It feels like forever since I've seen you! How have you been?"

"I've been okay."

"That's it? Okay?" Jack jested. "Hey, what ever happened to the internship? I take it you didn't get it since you're here, right?"

Emma frowned, regretting her initial decision to keep the truth from him. She hoped that by ignoring his calls, their relationship would eventually fizzle just in time for her departure. But Jack was more relentless than she had suspected. For whatever reason she used, breaking it off with him would only be harder.

"It's still up in the air," Emma lied, changing course. "What about you? How has your summer been so far?"

"Not bad. This sort of sums up all I've been up to," he said, gesturing to the raging beach.

"Do you not have a job?"

"It's not really necessary in my condition. You know, me being rich and all."

Emma's face tightened, slightly annoyed at his arrogance.

"I know," she said flatly. "But still, it wouldn't hurt to have a little bit of work experience just in case…"

"In case of what?"

It could have been her imagination, but she was taken aback by Jack's unusual, curt demeanor.

"Well you know," she hesitated, choosing her words. "There is always a chance that things don't work out in the way that we plan – take my internship for example."

"That's a little different," he countered, his tone partially defensive. "I already have my future planned out for me. If anything, working would be a waste of my time if I know that the outcome is guaranteed."

"Right," she replied, trying her best not to roll her eyes and changing the subject again. "Where are the boys?"

Jack pointed toward his boat sitting just beyond the shore. Emma squinted to make out Tommy and Isaac deep in laughter as Kevin and Bennett wrestled for the wheel.

"Do you trust them out there with your boat?" she asked.

"Not really," Jack admitted, facing her. "But I really wanted to see you."

Emma faked a smile. She was troubled, to say the least. One minute, Jack was boasting about his wealth, and the next, he was back on his charm; the latter a driving reason she fell for him in the first place.

She pondered the sudden change in his behavior, and if her ghosting was the cause. To her knowledge, Jack was not always this way. Unless he actually was, and simply hid it well.

"Come on, let's go for a walk," Jack invited.

Emma unwillingly agreed, taking his hand as he guided her along the beach. They leisured along the water's edge, relaxing on a bench away from the noise to exchange stories about their notable summer moments. Despite growing up fifteen minutes from each other, Emma was astounded at how remotely different Jack's life was compared to hers. What surprised her more, was that he did not have to explicitly illustrate it for her comprehension. It was riddled between the lines of his self-assured attitude. She respected his occasional effort to conceal it, however no matter how well it worked, the truth was still transparently obvious, throning her conscience and prompting her to judge him for it.

As if she needed further confirmation, they were suddenly interrupted by a group of girls who circled around the bench. Emma glared at them, clearly noticing they were all intently focused on Jack.

"Sorry," one of the girls muttered, peeking a nervous glance at Emma before looking away. "You're Jack Douglas, right?"

Jack tensed at the girl's ability to identify him. He had never seen her before. "Uh, yeah," he relented.

"We were all there the night you bought drinks for everyone at the bar."

Jack gave her a friendly nod of recognition, his memory racing through his already blurry recollection of his times being out on the town.

"You're welcome," he uttered.

"What are you doing later?" another girl asked.

At that, Emma interceded.

"He'll be with me," she said cheekily, sliding closer to Jack.

The girls shared a dumbfounded stare at Emma, all of whom weaved back except for the girl under Emma's scrutiny.

"Right," the girl retorted, matching Emma's hardened glare before returning
to Jack. "We just saw you over here and thought we'd stop over and say hi
and thanks again."

Jack blinked inscrutably, intentionally keeping his eyes on the girl and not
daring to look at Emma.

"I appreciate it," he mumbled as he averted his eyes beyond them, hoping that
it would signal the end of the awkward encounter.

To his success, the girls carried on. He could feel Emma's disdain and he
consciously waited until the girls' chatter was reduced to nothing before
speaking again.

"That was something," he said to an irritated Emma.

"Do you know those girls?"

"No," he replied quickly.

"Okay," Emma said, noting the edge in his voice.

To make matters worse for Jack, they were interrupted again by the sound of
another voice.

"Hey Jack!"

"Jennifer," he muttered, spinning around to face her. "Hi, how have you
been?"

"I've been great!" Jennifer averted her gaze to Emma. "Who's this?"

"Right," Jack stammered, acknowledging Emma. "This is Emma Keva."

"Nice to meet you," Jennifer beamed, shaking her hand before turning back
to Jack.

"I'm actually glad to see you right now."

"Really?"

"Yeah," she paused. "I've been wanting to apologize about Amanda grilling
you last semester. In my defense, I had no idea that she was going to be that
crazy."

"Don't sweat it," Jack uttered, hoping Jennifer wouldn't delve any deeper
with Emma there. She clearly didn't detect his tone.

"It was also wrong for me to get so worked up with you that night," she
added. "As mad as I was at the time, I totally understand where you were
coming from."

"I appreciate it, but honestly, it's all in the past now so nothing to worry
about," he rambled, becoming more uneasy. "You have a good time today, all
right?"

"Oh," she uttered, hearing the impatience in his tone. "Yeah of course. Nice
meeting you Emma."

She walked away from them, causing Jack to sigh in relief.

"She seemed nice," Emma started.

"Yeah, she is."

"How did you two meet?"

"We've had a couple classes together over the years."

"She goes to college with us?"

"Yeah, she's in my grade."

"I see," Emma said, studying Jack. "She's very pretty, don't you think?"

"What?"

"She's very pretty."

"I guess so…"

Emma was aware of how uncomfortable Jack was with her questions. She figured after the night at the cabin that there would no longer be any secrets. And although she acknowledged the hypocrisy according to her line of thinking, it still bothered her that Jack was adamant in his practice of selective honesty.

"She said that her friend Amanda 'grilled' you…" she continued. "What about?"

Jack, too, remembered their conversation at the cabin. He paused, fully aware that her tenacious search for the truth was unbearable.

"You're clearly taking this conversation somewhere," he accused. "Why don't you just tell me what's on your mind?"

"I think I should be the one telling *you* that."

"You want to know if we were ever together, right?" Jack presumed. "The answer is yes. It was short-lived, though, and nothing came from it."

"Why did you two stop talking?"

"It's complicated."

"Every relationship is," she pressed. "Doesn't hurt to talk about it."

"Why do you want to know so badly?"

Emma folded her arms.

"I think the reason why you don't want to tell me is because you did the same thing to her that you did to me," she revealed. "Maybe knowing more about your past relationships would also help me not follow in their footsteps…did you ever think about that?"

"Christ!" Jack shouted. "I thought we were over that, why are you bringing it up?"

Emma withdrew, startled. It was her first time seeing him upset.

At that moment, Morgan came up. She was wasted, stumbling around the loose sand as she clung on to Jack's shoulder for support.

"Hey Jack!" she bellowed, swinging her arms around Emma.

"Morgan, good to see you," Jack said, calming down. "What are your girls' plans later?"

"We didn't put a lot of thought into what we are doing tonight," Emma cut in, still not over Jack's outburst. "I'm sure we'll head back into town."

"We rented a place at the end of the beach," Jack suggested. "Why don't you stay with us?"

Morgan's eyes lit up.

"That would be fun!" she looked at Emma, suddenly thinking she was competent enough to call the shots.

"*You* need to sober up," Emma advised, rubbing Morgan's head.

"Jacky!" Kevin called out, now standing on the beach before the boat docked onshore.

"I should head back," Jack muttered, taking one last glance at the girls. "The offer still stands if you need a place to stay."

Emma watched him rejoin his friends before turning to Morgan.

"How are you feeling?"

"I am *fucked* up."

"Yes you are," Emma assented, not finding any amusement to her situation. They both had been drinking all day. There was no way either of them could drive if it meant not risking a DUI.

"Let's go to Jack's tonight," Morgan pleaded.

"I don't think that's a good idea Morgan. I'm starting to think he isn't the guy I thought he was."

"Why? What did he do?"

"I'll tell you when you can actually comprehend what I'm saying."

Morgan was unable to stand on her own, proceeding to crouch on the sand at Emma's feet.

"Whatever," she slurred. "All I'm saying is that you should give him another chance—" she peered up to Emma glowering down on her. "I have never seen you this happy about a guy. We all have bad days. Maybe he's just pent up for not seeing you all summer and he is mixing it with his love for you."

Emma gasped at her friend's sudden coherence.

"Wow Morgan, for someone who can't stand straight, that made a lot of sense," she chortled, helping Morgan back to her feet and starting back toward the crowd.

Meanwhile, Jack reached his friends, all of whom displayed perplexed looks.

"Was that Emma?" Bennett asked.

"It was," Jack confirmed, drying himself off from the water. "I asked them to come over tonight."
"Well would you look at that! Looks like nothing can stop you two from being together," Isaac cheered.
"I didn't know we could invite pieces back," Kevin babbled.
"She's not a piece, Kev."
"Still, it's not fair."
"I never said you couldn't invite people over. We have the place for the night. Bring whoever you want."
"*Really?*"
Jack regretted saying it as soon as it left his mouth.
"No party," he clarified. "Just a kickback."
"I see. You hear that, boys? We're in for a night."
"Don't say it like that Tom," Jack said. "You're making it sounds like we're throwing a rager, and we're not."
"Sure Jack," Kevin taunted. "Whatever you say, buddy."
"Would've been nice to know we were having a party. I would have invited my girlfriend," Bennett monotoned, glaring at his friends before continuing his own dialogue. "'How is Naylah, Bennett?' 'She's terrific, thanks for asking guys.'"
Jack rolled his eyes, moving past Bennett's self-directed dialogue.
"Guys, come on. The last thing we need are cops up our asses again."
To the boys, Jack's adamance was nothing more than a friendly precaution. He had already spoken the idea into existence, which meant it would happen no matter the cost.
Jack sighed nervously, knowing that there was little he could do to retract what was to come, especially if it was at the expense of the boys' reckless fun.

*****

Emma wished she had not gone over to Jack's that night. Her prediction of the unfolding events was so clear.
First, the party: it was, in a word, overwhelming. Hundreds of sun-burned kids thinking it was better to puke and rally than call it a night. Tommy was naturally elected to command the event, directing the massive horde of drunkards in a line to hit the seemingly bottomless keg stands situated around the living area. There was a larger crowd in the backyard, consisting of Kevin and Bennett inconsiderately blasting their favorite playlist as a swarm of unknowns prattled across the sand.

As for Emma, she found herself wrapped in Jack's charm – and his arms – her eyes on the ceiling while she laid beside him, indifferent at her choice to sleep with someone she imagined would soon be an ex.

Jack, however, could not have contrasted Emma's internal feelings more. Sex was indeed a drug, and before tonight, Jack had been deep in withdrawal. He had frequently pieced his memory of their time together, alluring over her voice and touch. Vivid as it was, it was nothing like the real thing. And yet, he wanted more. He needed more – enough to reminisce the enchanting fantasies that brought the thrill in exploring her. Perhaps it was lust. After all, there is nothing more physically intimate than two individuals sharing each other's bodies for pleasure. But after being with her again, he reaffirmed this was different. Incomparable to previous trials with other women. Here he was, a man who emotionally struggled with commitment, partially for the sake of his own fear in becoming too vulnerable down the line. He was also never too fond of sex to begin with, as he would cite from Tommy: "In the grand scheme of things, sex is nothing more than a period of temporary gratification,"– an ironic outlook for someone who supplements his own impulses with recreational drugs. Jack was mature enough to know that sex was not everything, but with Emma, the giddiness was sure to never leave, as it tended to lay out a more defined course toward fading away from emotional awareness.

Emma had her hand on his stomach. They had spent several minutes catching their respective breaths, growing more accustomed to the muted party rumbling from outside their room.

"I love being with you," Jack finally said.

"Oh *do* you now?"

"Yes."

"Care to elaborate?"

Jack paused, recounting his memory.

"Do you remember when I finally told you who I was? At my family's cabin?"

"Right," Emma recalled. "I think you mean the moment I caught you in your lies and forced you to come clean?"

"Hey in all fairness, I was planning on telling you before you beat me to it."

Emma sat up.

"Anyways…" she invited.

"I can't tell you how happy I was after that night," Jack continued. "For the first time in my life, you were the only girl who could understand why I did it."

"As weird as I think it was, I can see how you would resort to doing something like that," Emma added. "All said, you aren't the best at being sneaky."
"I'll take that as a compliment," he joked.
Emma examined Jack's expression. Humility. She saw it.
"What about your friends?" she asked him. "Did you ever hide you were when you first met them?"
"I never had to. Those guys have been a part of my life for as long as I can remember. Money didn't play a factor in our friendship, because none of us knew what it meant to have money until we got older…" he trailed off. "It also helps that all our parents were close friends growing up. They knew me before I came to know myself. We're all essentially just kids of a larger family, if that makes sense."
"They liked you for *you.*"
"Yeah, they did."
Emma bit her lip.
"Would you say that you finally know who *you* are?"
"I like to think so."
Emma gave him a quizzical expression.
"What?" he uttered, blinking hard.
"Who are you then?"
"Not sure I follow…"
"You said you know who you are," Emma reiterated. "I'm curious as to who you think that is."
"Well, for the sake of not sounding like an asshole: I'm rich," he declared. "Obviously, I don't like having to say it, but I know it is important for me to accept that about myself."
"Why?"
"Because for so long, I thought I would be happier if I denied it," he explained, sitting up. "Growing up, my mom would tell me stories about people who are so wrapped up in themselves that their they care less about how they treat others. They think they are better than everyone else, in every aspect. I may not have realized it when I was a kid, but I learned that in many cases, I was not accepted because I was nice, or funny, or kind. It was because of who my family was.
"Everyone tells me how lucky I am, and I get where they were coming from, but I still hated hearing it, because it only made me think about how they saw me, and not how it was something I couldn't control. I was born into it and now that I'm thinking about it, I don't think anyone except for my best friends cared to try to understand me on a deeper level. They only saw me as the rich kid with no real personality. And yes, I know that I can act that way

sometimes. I get so worked up thinking about what other people think of me, that it just happens. Even when I try to be myself – like, *genuinely me* – that I would finally be seen as someone different than how society labels me. And it never seemed to work until…"
He fell silent.
"…until?" she pressed.
Jack looked at her.
"Until I met you."
Emma managed a heartfelt smile. This was the Jack she fell for. After the beach, it was reassuring for her to know that this side of him still existed.
"I appreciate you telling me all this Jack," Emma said. "But I don't think that I am the reason for your clarity. I'm not saying that I am ungrateful for how you see me, but if we're being real, I'm not so different from anyone else. And I think you should come around to accepting that."
Jack's face tightened at her response.
"I'm telling you that you are though."
"I know."
"So how can you be so sure about that?"
"Because Jack, you still have the impression that everyone only gives you attention because of your wealth, which just isn't true. You don't think life is all about how much money you have – which I think is amazing, and I'm happy that you value it less than others – but do you honestly think that you would have that same belief if you weren't 'born into it' like you said?"
"I'm having a hard time seeing why that matters."
"And that's why I don't think that you know who you are yet," she concluded, shaking her head. "You're too invested in how others judge you, that you are unable to figure it out on your own. Until you first do that, you'll keep looking for closure in anyone who values money as little as you do."
Jack turned away from Emma, slightly irritated at her input.
"How much money you have doesn't define you," Emma added. "I hope you like me for other reasons, but I think the biggest reason why you do is because I simply agree with that notion, which also explains why I see you as *you*."
"But I don't know where to start in figuring out who I am."
"I don't know either…but I know the first step is to not care about what anyone thinks and be yourself."
"Be myself?"
"Yes," she confirmed. "That means no longer hiding anything about you. Accept all of it. Embrace it. Don't see it as a weakness, but a strength."
"Using my wealth as a strength," Jack noted. "Won't that make me just like every other rich asshole who thinks the world of themselves?"

"Maybe, but that's when you'll find out who you really are in here," she brought her hand to his heart. "My dad used to tell me that our biggest insecurities are our ultimate resolve to prosperity."
Jack watched Emma grow despondent, lowering her eyes to avoid eye contact.
"Go on."
Emma let out a deep sigh.
"I kind of know what you're going through. I like to think that I had a good childhood. It was normal: nothing flashy or unique about it. But growing up, I always had a hard time loving who I was. It's a common thing for us girls, as I'm sure you know. Loving yourself is one of the hardest things to do."
Jack leaned in closer, studying her dismal expression.
"I loved art growing up," she continued. "Painting, music, literature. Everything about it. I would spend hours drawing whatever image popped in my head. I can't tell you how many times I got sent to the office because my teacher would catch me doodling or humming my favorite song instead of paying attention. It also bothered my parents for a bit, especially my mom.
"Freshman year, our teacher entered all of her students in this 'creativity competition'…I think you may remember."
"Yeah, with Mrs. Lewis, right? I made a snake out of paper mâché," Jack recounted, giggling to himself. "It was fucking horrible."
"I'm sure it was awesome," she soothed. "Anyways, I decided to paint a canvas. I vividly remember it being one of the most stressful week of my life. I would cry to sleep worrying that I wouldn't be able to think of what I could draw; I would even skip my other classes and go to the art room and work on it. It meant so much to me, because for the first time I had a school assignment was something I was so passionate about. It's kind of funny now to think about now, but I even dumped my boyfriend at the time because he was upset that I was choosing the painting over spending time with him."
"Breaking up with your boyfriend for a good grade. That's something else."
"Truly tragic, but I don't regret it," she retorted. "I ended up winning the *entire* contest. There were thousands of entries from people all around the country, and I came in first place. There was a cash prize and feature on some big newsletter and stuff, but I didn't care about any of that. I was happy for the chance to do something I felt defined me.
"I found out when I was on the bus going home. I was so excited to tell my parents. My dad wasn't home yet because he had a late shift, but I was so pumped to let him know. I told my mom first…"
"What did your mom say?"
Emma took a deep breath.

"She said, and I quote: 'You're wasting your time with this crap.' She then suggested that if I want to stick with art, then I should pursue something that I have a better chance in making it, like modeling.
"What?" Jack exclaimed, stunned. "Modeling?"
"My mom saw it as a compromise. But I hate modeling…it's literally the most degrading profession. Only being recognized for a pretty face? It's all substance. It was one thing to be complimented for my looks. But to base your entire identity on something so superficial? I didn't want that. To this day, I can't get over thinking of my mom's face when I showed her my painting. She was so…disappointed."
"I'm sorry, I can't imagine having to hear that from a parent…what about your dad?"
"He picked it out of the trash after I threw it away. I was so sad after my mom's reaction that I was embarrassed for getting so pumped about it. I was in bed when he came in my room holding my painting, and I watched him hang it right on the ceiling, above my head… it was funny how long it took him to do it, too.
"He then sat next to me and hugged me, and said: 'Em, this is the most beautiful thing I have ever seen. And before you go to bed every night, and open your eyes in the morning, I ask that you take the time to look at it for as long as you need, to remind you of who you are, and why I will always be proud of you."
She wiped the tears filling in her eyes.
"Thank you for telling me," Jack started, slow to respond. He was grateful for the chance to be with her again. They were more relatable than he thought. That said, he found himself moping over what prompted her to open up at this time without considering to address their awkward fallout a month before. Was she intentionally trying to ignore the obvious? Surely, it would be a mistake to mention it now, when she was clearly distraught over her late father. But he could not help himself.
"I need to get something off my chest," he began.
"Okay…?"
"I've been thinking about the last time we were together, at the Locks."
"Yeah…"
"I hoped that we could address it…"
"Address what?"
"Well you know," Jack hesitated. "You seemed a little off. And this is the first time we've spoken since."
"Right," she took a deep breath. "That was a weird day all together; can we just move past it?"

"Yeah, but I figured it would be a good idea if we talked about *why* it was weird?"
She gave him a blank stare, dumbfounded at his curiosity. All the opportunities Jack had through the night to bring this up, and he chose *now?* "What do you want me to say?"
Jack anticipated her reluctance. He knew she was smart enough to know where he was trying to get at, yet she was firm in not taking it there. Little did she know that Jack was not in the mood to cower at the expense of her gratification. He needed to hear Emma say it herself.
"I saw you talking to Logan," he revealed. "And I know that we've talked about how you two were never serious or anything, and it was years ago and shouldn't matter – and it totally doesn't – but I can't help but think that it had something to do with that."
"I see, you want to talk about *him* again," she murmured.
"I'm not trying to come across as jealous or anything, and frankly I'm cool with whoever you want to hang out with. But after you two talked—"
"You think I like him, is that it?"
"I just think it would be healthy if we cleared the air," he said, keeping a cool head.
Morgan burst into the bedroom.
"Emma, we have to go!" she said, hastily waving her phone in hand.
Jack glanced back at Emma. "What's wrong?"
Emma sighed again, breaking away from Jack and reaching for her clothes. "Morgan has some drama with her sister. It's a long story," she casually dismissed, throwing on her shirt.
"So, you're not spending the night?"
Emma shot him a glare.
"How do you think I'm going to reply to that Jack?"
Jack shook his head, fearful of further escalating the already existing tension. "Right," he said grudgingly, pulling away. "When can I see you again?"
"Please Jack," Emma pleaded, raising her hand at him. "Not now, okay?"
Jack nodded partly confused at Emma's quick shift in behavior. He watched as she left abruptly with Morgan, leaving him alone in the room.
Jack was upset with how she left his question dangling. She did not confirm any feelings for Logan, but she did not deny it, either. Regardless of whether Jack chose to believe her, he affirmed that he did not have a reason to distrust her, by any means. If anything, he viewed himself to still be in the hot seat after lying to her about who he was in the first place. In a situation where the tables were turned, he knew it would not be easy for him to forgive someone for what he had put her through.

He let out a tired sigh, leaving his worries in the room as he returned to the party.

A lot more people arrived during his absence. An undesirable stench accommodated the already dense humidity in the living area, where he spotted Tommy on the opposite end, commanding a queue of drunkards to the keg stand.

"There you are!" Tommy exclaimed as Jack approached him. "Where's Em?"

"She left. Where did all these people come from?"

"Beats me. Apparently word spread about our party back at the beach."

Bennett appeared, clutching a bundle of shooters.

"Where did you get those?" Jack asked.

"The fridge in the garage."

"You realize that this house belongs to another family, right? We shouldn't be going around taking things that don't belong to us."

"Wow," Tommy chimed. "You're being a bit of a pooper right now."

"We rented this home," Bennett defended. "Which means that we also rent everything in it."

"That's not exactly true," Jack sighed, rubbing his eyes. "Whatever. Just keep track of everything that we take."

The boys jumped at an overwhelming crash behind him. Jack turned to the source of the sound to see a couple guys on the floor covered in glass. He peered up to the top of the stairs, where Isaac and Kevin accepted cash to have randoms jump from the second floor onto the sofa.

"Holy shit!" Isaac cheered. "We have a new record for buoyancy! Who's next?"

The room boomed, piercing through Jack's tightened face at the sight of the broken sculpture strewn across the carpet.

"What the hell man?" Jack shouted at them. Isaac turned to Kevin for backup, who was distracted with the oncoming line up the stairs.

"Let's get some air, eh?" Tommy suggested, taking a couple of shooters from Bennett's arms and guiding Jack out of the house.

He folded his arms as he watched Jack pace in the front lawn, riddled in his thoughts. Beyond him, Tommy could make out a throng of juveniles resetting for the lot of remaining fireworks stashed opposite the water's edge. He waited patiently for Jack to calm down, seemingly distracted by the tiny rocket shooting up into the atmosphere before painting the sky with a colorful illustration of bright sparks.

"We should have bought some," he relayed to Jack, nodding to the fireworks overhead.

Jack stopped and faced him, astonished.

"Really, Tom?" he grimaced.

"You're being a bit uptight dude. Was the sex bad this time?"

"Emma was confusing, as always."

"Confusing?"

"It's hard to explain," Jack added. "She's hasn't been acting like herself lately. It's impossible to make plans with her, for one; and tonight we just had an amazing, deep conversation, yet it feels like it didn't change much… am I making any sense here?"

"Not really," Tommy admitted, scratching his head. "Have you two not been hanging out all summer?"

"Are you kidding? Today was my first time talking to her since the Locks. I don't know of any couple that goes that long without speaking to each other."

"Maybe it's not intentional. You know how busy people can be during the summer."

"I feel like that is just an excuse people use when they don't want to see you, ya know? Like, if you want to be with someone, you will make time for them."

Tommy tilted his head.

"It's possible, but I don't think you running into her today was a coincidence —" he paused. "—in fact, watch her hit you up tomorrow asking to catch up."

"Come on, Tommy."

"It'll happen, trust me."

Jack trusted Tommy. And if his justification on Emma's behalf was indeed true, he agreed that waiting for it to come to fruition was the best course of action.

xii

The elemental shift from summer to fall is beautiful: the sun cools on the earth, slowing its tides, dampening the natural moisture that coats shrubbery on usual chilly mornings, with the coloring transition the leaves undergo as they inevitably fall and drift away with the breeze from the heavens above. Washington is rather unique, however, in that maintains steady temperatures, and even in the dead of the night, has exceptional heat with low humidity. Its breeze is also saltier, scattering its scent from the vast Pacific, when even in its slumber, tosses and turns as if it tries to remain awake.

It mirrored Jack's daily routine, who – personally indifferent to the respective mobilization – would struggle to keep his eyes closed as he observed the darkness drag on. Night after night, he would notice the glimmer from the moon gradually crawling down the walls of his room, plastered with outdated frames of memories from his childhood.

The season drawled on for him. As did his anxiety, which gradually crippled over the last few weeks as a result of Emma's prolonged absence in his life. He would spend much of the day riddling over the validity of Tommy's prediction, finding it difficult to concentrate on anything else. Fortunately, his friend's earned reputation of foresight followed through again. And while he may have been slightly off on the timing – an entire month off, to be exact – it did not matter for Jack, who was naturally elated upon receiving a text from Emma asking him to come over, claiming to have good news.

Tommy was juggling his phone while also in the middle of cheffing up a spectacular breakfast when Jack scurried out of his room. He noted the negligence in Jack's haste, appearing to have no regard for the stained hoodie he threw on as he proceeded to slip on his shoes.

"Were you talking to Morgan again?" Jack scolded, seeing Tommy rapidly pocket his phone and return to cooking.

"That was my dad," he replied. "Apparently he got a huge epiphany after watching some documentary last night and is going to start investing in real estate around the city."

"I see! Has he decided where he will lay claim?"

"Not sure yet," he paused when he noticed Jack's haste. "Are you going somewhere?

Jack shot Tommy an excited grin.

"Emma wants to see me!"

Tommy lightly chuckled at Jack, comparing his demeanor to that of a wild pup eager to be let out of its cage.

"You're still down to hit the bars later, right?"

"Why do you ask?"

"Well, considering that you are going to be with Emma, I figured your plans could change."

"Come on, this is our last weekend before classes start," Jack assured as he shot him a playful wink. "Bros before hoes, right?"

"You and I both know that you would never say that if Emma was here."

"That's why it's only said by guys, to guys. What idiot would have the audacity to say it in front of a girl?"

"You apparently haven't been around Kevin when he gets drunk."

Jack was halfway out the door when he glanced back and posed at Tommy.

"How do I look?" he asked.

Tommy stared at him in disbelief.

"Seriously?"

"Deadly."

Tommy grinned at his friend's ebullience.

"You look great, brother."

Jack returned a thoughtful smile before parading out of the apartment.

He was inexplicably pleased by the change of scenery in his neighborhood. Autumn's impatience to return was evident, as the once jaded trees have begun to lose their bloomed shape, the stagnant leaves now hued golden as they rustled against one another before breaking away and strewing across the suburban streets.

He pulled up to Emma's house, instantly noticing a moving van parked in her driveway. It was not the most uncommon sight this time of year, yet Jack still managed to feel oddly vexed as he trailed past it on the way to the front door.

He walked in to see her sitting among a messy pile of clothes, noting the dresser and closet nearly emptied out. Even the majority of her pictures that once hung on the walls – vanished, presumably packed in one of the several boxes in the corner of the room.

"Jack!" she ran up and hugged him.

He was taken aback by her embrace, anticipating her demeanor to reflect how they had left things. Her unpronounced enthusiasm could have possibly been the result of the good news she was adamant in sharing with him.

Nevertheless, Jack had suddenly found himself turned off at her elation. It was too lighthearted to assume that it was a total result of his presence. Someone was off.

"I see you've been busy," he observed, motioning to the room. "Are you moving off-campus like me and Tom?"

Emma pulled away and turned to the boxes. "Yeah, um...this is actually why I wanted you to come over."

He sensed the immediate change in Emma's demeanor, noticing her grow more hesitant.

"What's going on?"

"Do you remember at the start of the summer, when I told you I still didn't know if I got that internship?"

"Yeah, sorry again about that," he consoled, assuming she would inform him of her rejection. "I know how much you really wanted it."

Emma frowned.

"I actually got accepted."

"Oh shit, congratulations!" he blurted, exploding in enthusiasm. "But the summer is essentially over. Are they pushing it back to next year?"

"Right," Emma hesitated, pacing to the opposite end of the room.

"What's wrong?"

"The internship isn't for next summer," she mumbled. "It's actually in a week..."

"...what?" Jack tested. "The one in New York?"

Emma silently nodded.

"I don't understand," he stammered, beginning to piece it together. "I thought this was supposed to be a summer internship." At that moment, he realized she never gave him an official answer on the Fourth.

"Me too," Emma affirmed. "But after Morgan and I read the letter—"

"Morgan?" Jack cut in. "Wait, *when* did you find out about this?"

Emma froze, staring back at the quizzical look on Jack's face. She knew she did not have to respond. Deep down, he knew the answer.

"I'm sorry I didn't tell you when I found out," she lowered her head. "I was going to, but I was scared about how you would react..."

Jack's gaze drifted off from her and to the boxes surrounding her feet.

"You're going to do it," he muttered, his chest sunk. "That's why you are packing. It's not to go back to school..."

His mind was racing, unsure how to proceed with the conversation. It was good news, but he did not expect the reveal to directly affect their relationship. And negatively, on that note. He did not know what to feel. How could he?

"That's amazing," Jack finally said as he managed a halfhearted smile.

Emma lifted her head, surprised by his reaction.

"You think so?"

"Absolutely," he lied, doing his best to control his feelings.

"So you're saying that I should do it?"

"I mean," Jack tilted his head at the boxes, hoping his tone wasn't too condescending. "It appears that you have already made up your mind."

Emma hugged him again, but Jack could feel her guilt through her unusually affectionate embrace.

"Thank you," she said. "I was so nervous to tell you."

"Why?"

"I guess I thought you would feel betrayed," she replied, her clench around his waist tightening. "We never really talked about what we are or where we're going with…whatever *this* is…" she faltered for a moment. "I didn't want to ruin what we had here, but this is just a huge opportunity for me to do what I love. I don't know why I thought you would be upset about it." She rested her chin on his chest, peering up at him. "And hey, I'll visit during Thanksgiving, and be back for good for Christmas! I know how important that is to you."

"Right," Jack frowned, no longer finding it necessary to mask his apathetic feelings for her news. Emma could not have been more correct; he *did* feel betrayed. He did not believe she waited to tell him for his sake, but for the purpose of biding time and entertaining him as she focused on what really mattered to her.

It was all happening too fast. One minute, Emma was snuggled in his arms; and the next, she was leaving him. What was worse, is that she felt it was appropriate to activate the next steps without his consent, nor his knowledge. He hated it. He wanted to yell and shout; do anything to make it clear to Emma that he was fervently against her choice to leave. He gazed into her eyes, trying his hardest to empathize with her situation. He did not want to be the obstacle preventing her from achieving her dreams. While he was a hypocrite of his own expectations, he hoped that she would be capable of overlooking his mistakes and try to be better. Be more communicative. More transparent. It was not until now, however, when he had realized that she was incapable of doing so, for which he ultimately blamed himself.

"I'm sorry," he said. "I have to go…I need to process all of this."

"Oh," Emma mumbled, releasing him. "Are you sure you don't want to stay until I leave?"

"No."

Jack ignored Emma's calls to him as he stormed out the room and down the stairs. He was halfway out the house when Emma caught up to him, grabbing his hand.

"Hey, let's talk about this."

"We already did," Jack shot back, pulling his hand away.

"Whoa, would you chill a bit? What's wrong?"

"What do you think, Em?" he flared. "You're leaving for New York and you didn't tell me until the last minute. I mean, I don't mean to sound irrational, but do you not see how shitty seems to me? Not even a quick text or anything!"

"I'm telling you now," she reasoned. "I apologized that I didn't tell you when I found out, but I just explained why I chose not to. Even now, I feel like I haven't given this whole thing a lot of thought."

"You clearly did, Em! You're literally packing up to go! Shit, I just wish you would have told me."

"As I said, I'm telling you now," she repeated sternly. "Look, let's not start something, okay? I'm on a deadline here."

Jack watched as Emma started back for the stairs, enraged at her dismissiveness.

"Is it Berg?"

Emma stopped in her tracks, turning back to him.

"What did you just say?"

"Logan," Jack reiterated. "You still never gave me a clear answer when I asked you. Is it him?"

"Are you serious?"

"You're not denying it!"

"I can't believe you right now. Nothing happened between us. *Ever.*"

"I don't know if I can believe that," Jack fired back. "Who knows what kind of person you were back then."

Emma stormed up to Jack, getting right in his face.

"What are you saying, Jack? That I used to be a slut? You really think that low of me?"

"I just want to know the truth."

"The truth," Emma mocked. "You don't even know what that word means, do you?"

"You're turning this on me now?"

"For God's sake Jack, you lied about who you were when we first met!"

"That has nothing to do with this," Jack defended. "Besides, I thought we were over all of that."

"Oh I see, so when you do something wrong, it's okay, but you don't even think twice about accusing others based on your own suspicions that aren't even true?"

"So just that we're on the same page: it's *not* true?"

"*Nothing* happened between us. I'm not leaving because of him, and I'm not leaving because of you. I'm doing this for *myself...*"

She rested her hand on the side of his face. "I like you, and for you to think any different…I don't know how else I can make it apparent."

"You can stay," Jack pleaded, clutching her hand. "Stay here with me. Or let me come with you."

"I'm going to pretend you didn't say that," she smirked passively, pulling her hand away. "I'll see you later, Jack."

Jack cupped his hands over his head, helpless as he watched her pace into the house.

He got to his car and peeled off, forcing himself to relax his trembling palms on the steering wheel. It was uncommon for Jack not to get his way with something he wanted. He braked to a halt at edge of the block and slapped his hands on the dash in frustration while letting out an ear-splitting scream. He was not going to let it end this way.

Impulse took over at that moment.

He rejected self-control of his actions, mentally anchored in stillness as he watched his hand reach into his pocket and pull out his phone. He browsed for the Ember House website, dialed the number, and put the phone to his ear, breathing loudly through his bared teeth and succumbing to his selfish spirit as the line trilled.

"This is Clarene," the voice on the other line spoke.

"Clarene, I am calling on behalf of Emma Keva," Jack heard himself say.

"She was accepted for an art internship this fall."

"Okay. Was there an issue with the admission letter we sent out a few months ago?

A few months, he noted. *Figures.*

"Yes, in fact there was," Jack stated. "I think you made a mistake and would like for you to take back the offer."

"Excuse me, I don't understand. Are you asking for us to rescind Ms. Keva's offer?"

"Seems like you got the message just perfectly."

There was a momentary pause on the other line.

"May I ask who I am speaking to?"

"My name is Jack Douglas. I am only looking out for what is best for Emma. She never wanted to leave and has changed her mind and would like to stay here in Seattle."

"Mr. Douglas, I am unfortunately not in charge of admitting students, and I am uncomfortable having this conversation with you, given I do not know anything about this student, nor you for that matter."

"How much will it take?"

"I'm sorry?"

"You're a human being, so I take it that you will do anything for the right price," Jack started. "So how much do you want?"

"Mr. Douglas, I have had enough," Clarene said, her tone cold. "You have been disrespectful for the entirety of this conversation, and I will not tolerate it anymore. For your sake, I will not share your name or the nature of this call with anyone, but I strongly advise you do not call us again. Do you understand?"

"Oh, fuck off," Jack muttered and hung up the phone.

Setting aside his resentment toward Emma, Jack wanted to understand her decision to leave him. He really wanted to, as he found the necessity in accepting what was true in order to move on.

Unfortunately for Jack, it was not that simple a task, especially with how short notice he was given to process it. There was no rationale in impulsivity, yet if he could return to the moment when she told him – silently watching her lips speak the words into existence – he would not have reacted differently.

Jack felt no base, foundation, or central code. Prescribing to a religion was not a desirable option for him, because he rejected the notion of believing.

It all changed when he met Emma, however, for she was the one person in his life that made him faithful. And now, he was challenged with finding faith without her.

He returned to his apartment to see all the boys engaged in one of their typical discussions. They were on the sofa, their backs to him as they watched TV, allowing him to slink inside unnoticed.

"This is bullshit," Kevin wept as he kicked his feet up on the ottoman. "I interviewed for a job at the bank downtown, and they told me that they were looking for people with previous work experience."

Tommy exchanged a confused look with the boys. "So?"

"It's an entry-level job," Kevin explained. "Like, how do they expect us to get a job right out of college if half of them require previous experience, which we obviously won't have?"

"Quite the catch-22 you got there."

"What?"

"Never mind," Tommy dismissed, glancing behind to see Jack. "Hey! You're back early."

"Why do you look like shit?" Bennett asked.

Jack replied with a disgruntled groan.

"I see the bad day blues are going around," Bennett added jokingly, nudging Isaac.

"Emma is leaving," Jack spoke up.

At once, the boys bobbed up in their seats.

"Leaving where?"

"New York City. She got an internship."

"Good for her!" Isaac sang, oblivious to Jack's disappointment. "That's good, right?"

"No. I mean, yes, it's good, and I'm happy for her. But…"

"I don't see the issue here."

"She'll be gone for the semester," Jack reiterated. "We'll have to breakup."

"Did she say that?"

"Well no, but—"

"Then I don't understand why you are so worked up."

"How many relationships do you know that have worked out when they go long distance?"

"Correct me if I'm wrong," Isaac cut in. "But isn't that a normal scenario? The movies make it seem so."

"Right," Jack mocked. "You're getting your take from the *movies*. Do you hear yourself?"

"Regardless, I think Isaac has a point," Tommy said flatly. "I think you're letting your worries get the best of you."

"Okay," Jack said, tugging on his hair as he gathered his thoughts. "Maybe you're right. It wouldn't help to take a step back think about this for a second."

"Solid plan."

"So first, we were great. We were—"

"Whoa hold on," Tommy interjected. "You want to do this now?"

"Yeah," Jack replied blankly. "Isn't that what you were getting at?"

The boys let out a collective groan.

"What's wrong with you all?"

"Please don't do this to us," Kevin wailed. "At least let me get high first."

"I cannot believe you guys don't want to help me with this."

"You're not serious," Bennett jumped in. "We've helped you since the day you met her!"

"You *have* been constantly talking about Emma," Kevin concurred, reaching for his stash hidden under the table. "Also, I got to say I'm a little bugged that you all jump to help Jack when he's going through his shit, but none of you care about what I'm going through."

"The job at the bank?" Jack clarified.

"Yes!"

"I don't want to hear this again," Bennett muttered. "Hurry up and load that bowl, Kev. I want a hit."

"Sorry to hear that, Kevin," Isaac continued. "Let's talk about your situation first."

"Or we could agree to let you two deal with it on your own," Bennett chimed. "After all, it's not like we can do anything about both your problems."

"You don't mean that," Jack snapped, turning to Tommy. "You always say that we are in control of our futures."

"Well yeah, but to an extent," Tommy defended. "I also always advise to take what I say with a grain of salt."

"He's got you there, Jacky," Isaac shrugged.

"Whatever," Jack dismissed. "I need to get my mind off this. What do you all say we hit the town later and have a couple sips like we planned?"

More groans.

"Really? The one time I propose going out, you all aren't feeling it?"

"We talked about it before you got here," Bennett fretted. "We've been going hard for a month straight, and classes start in a couple days. I need a break."

"I'm with Benny on this one," Tommy concurred. "I'm burning a hole in my checking account."

"Dip into your savings then," Jack suggested.

"Sorry we're not as rich as you, Jack," Kevin chided before ripping a prolonged hit from the bong.

Jack rolled his eyes.

"Okay, let's reach a compromise here: I will buy you all a round of shots if you come out with me tonight."

Bennett's eyes widened. "*Now* we're talking."

"Hold on, you said Emma was leaving, right?" Isaac recounted. "Why don't you invite her out with us as a farewell gesture?"

"Absolutely not," Jack said. "She's the reason why I want to get hammered. Having her there would defeat the purpose. What were you thinking, coming up with a suggestion like that?"

Jack stuck to his word when they went out, not only buying his boys the first round, but the entire shelf that they ultimately found themselves chugging through the evening. Good times with the boys. It was exactly what he needed.

After his fifth shot, Jack realized the pointlessness in sulking about it for the rest of the night.

*****

Class resumed on Monday, and Logan was not looking forward to it. He had enjoyed his time free of routine, and the ability to light a joint in public without judgmental stares.

He took another hit, savoring the solitude while he overlooked the barren campus.

"Logan."

Hearing his name was enough to trigger his already short fuse. He stood and turned around, calming himself immediately as Emma peered back at him.

"Emma! What are you doing here?"

"I'm leaving for New York today," she began, averting her eyes. "I guess I couldn't forgive myself if I left without telling you before I go."

"Oh, I had no idea…thanks for that," he said, hesitantly offering her the joint.

"No thanks, I don't really do that stuff."

"Right, of course," he stammered. "How do you feel?"

"I've been better."

He examined the frown plastered on her face.

"Jack didn't take the news well, huh?"

"He did not," she affirmed, managing a disheartened shrug. "…Not totally sure how to deal with that at this moment."

Logan paused, debating whether it would be wise to delve further in his personal view of Jack.

"Well, I'm on my way to grab some lunch. You want to join?"

"I can't," she sniffled, glancing at her phone. "I'm already on a tight window to make my flight. I stopped here to see all my friends before I left—" she paused. "—honestly perfect timing seeing you here on that matter."

"No worries. I get it, you have a lot on your plate," he consoled. "No pun intended."

"Thanks for understanding," she smiled, turning away from him.

"You'll be amazing at everything you choose to do, Emma," he blurted. "I'm proud of you."

Logan was taken aback when she rushed up to hug him.

It was only for a few moments, yet Logan perceived it as an eternity. Her arms wrapped around his torso aroused him slightly, feeling her fingers clinging into his back.

He pretended not to notice the tears swelling in her eyes as she broke away and paced down the sidewalk, leaving him to watch until she had left the courtyard. He was sure that Emma knew how he felt about her. And he hoped that even a small part of her felt the same.

Logan continued to the HUB, his concern over Emma diminishing steadily at the sight of the same food he would be eating in a couple days as he chose an empty booth.

At least this time, he was not bothered with any classmates who would frequently approach him. Small talk sickened him, and after multiple instances when he would turn down their invitations, Logan quickly discovered that despite his choice of being a loner, other students still, for some reason, wanted to engage. He wondered if it was due to his nonthreatening appearance, as he boasted a boyish complexion even when he tried growing out his scrubby hair in hopes that it would make him look older. He was aware of his genuine attractiveness, which, coupled with his exceptional personable skills, made him presume the simplicity in formulating friendships with these people. If only he ever recognized the advantages of networking, perhaps he would not be so prone to rejecting others.

He lost his appetite thinking about it, poking disdainfully at his eggs like he expected them to jump off the plate.

"Good morning, Berg!"

Logan lifted his head.

"Isaac?"

Isaac helped himself to the empty seat across from him.

"I saw you here and thought that I'd come say hi."

Logan was slightly on-edge, tilting his head out of the booth.

"What are you doing?"

"Nothing. Like I said, I just figured I would see how you are doing," Isaac shrugged. "Why are you here alone?"

"I prefer it."

"Oh, I'm *sure* you do."

"What is this, man? Are the boys hiding somewhere to see if you can get a reaction out of me or something?"

Isaac shot him a quizzical expression.

"I don't know what you're talking about," he revealed, bringing out his phone. "Last time I checked, they're all still sleeping. They got pretty wasted last night."

"So you mean to tell me that you are here out of your own will, with no ulterior motive?"

"Geez, I don't remember you being this paranoid," Isaac chuckled, raising his hand as if he were reciting an oath. "But to answer your question: yes, Logan, I am here on my own will, without a malicious motive.'"

Logan folded his arms and examined Isaac's friendly expression. He may have been a childhood friend, yet Logan justified his skepticism given they had not held an actual conversation in years. From what he remembered, Isaac was always different than the other guys. His ability to project sheer happiness, and humorous anecdotes he would randomly insert in serious, or glum moments. Logan never had an issue with him; after all, it was Tommy who was solely to blame for his strained relationship with the group.

Isaac reached across the table and gave Logan a friendly pat on his shoulder. "What have you been up to, man? How are you enjoying your classes? Are you pumped for this upcoming semester?"

"They're okay," Logan muttered, adamant to keep the interaction short. "I should get going."

"Are you in a rush?"

"A little bit."

"Would you mind if I tagged along?"

Logan could not help but reveal a bewildered look.

"Why?"

"Why not?"

"All right," he sighed, concluding there was nothing he could do to get rid of him.

Isaac followed Logan out the HUB, chipping away at Logan's patience with his unintentional persistence to make small talk.

Intolerance. Logan was aware of how it influenced his treatment of others. Was it helpful in most situations? Not necessarily. But he was comforted knowing that he could acknowledge its impact on his personality, which at this point, appeared engrained as a natural reaction to the abundance of things that bothered him.

They reached Logan's place on the outskirts of campus. It was a typical abode for a college student: a studio with four walls, all lined with an assortment of tapestries and graphic art, strictly for the purpose of covering up the discolored blemishes that were placed there from the previous tenant. There was an upkept bed, a pair of sofas parted by a splintered coffee table, a lamp, a desk, and a tall shelf cluttered with various textbooks he never opened.

"Sorry for the mess," Logan remarked, realizing it had been a while since he last had company.

Isaac did not shy away from his excitement, taking the liberty to peruse through the room, picking up and setting down every object that his eyes laid on.

"This place is insane!"
Logan sat on the couch before reaching for his bong and drugs stashed behind the cushion.
Isaac stopped in the middle of his scavenger hunt and glowered at the bong in Logan's hands.
"What are you doing?"
Logan stared at him, baffled.
"What does it look like, 'Saac?"
"It looks like you're going to get high."
"Pretty self-explanatory, huh?"
Isaac sat across from Logan and watched him prepare the bowl.
"Do you smoke a lot?"
Logan nodded dismissively, focusing on the puny nuggets in his hands as he delicately broke them apart and flattened them in the bowl. He proceeded to grab his lighter and spark a light, bringing the bong to his mouth and inhaling until he could feel the smoke reach the back of his throat. He waited a few moments before pulling away from the bong, blowing out the potent fumes that escaped his lips.
Isaac extended his hand.
"May I?"
"You know how to do it?"
"Totally," Isaac gloated, taking the bong from Logan's hands and inhaling deeply. He held the smoke in his mouth for a few seconds before choking it out, causing Logan to chuckle.
"Okay, so I'm still an amateur," Isaac admitted.
"You're good man," Logan assured. "It's better than most people I know."
They sat there in silence as their respective highs plateaued.
"I'm baked," Isaac eventually hummed.
Logan ignored him, believing the unresponsiveness would imply his reluctance to engage.
Unfortunately for Logan, Isaac was a talker.
"This is nice," he continued. "We should all get high together."
"*We?*"
"The rest of the boys," Isaac clarified. "Kevin smokes more than the rest of us, but we could all still partake and vibe as a group."
"Forsure."
Logan was surprised at Isaac's sudden muteness, peeking over to see him blinking hard at him.

"Are you good?" Logan asked.

"I sensed the passiveness in your tone."

Logan was astonished by Isaac's remark.

"Sorry," he apologized, sitting upright. "It's just that I don't talk to any of your friends anymore. I guess I still find it awkward whenever they get brought up around me."

"Why is it awkward?"

Logan took a deep breath. Isaac had put him on the spot. There was no way of getting out of this one.

"Sometimes I wonder how different my life would be if I didn't do some things," Logan paused, glancing at Isaac. "You know, if I kept hanging with you guys."

"I think about that too," Isaac concurred. "It was weird to me: one day, you were there, and the next, you were gone…almost like you vanished."

"What have you heard?"

"Not much. Tommy told us that you dipped from town, but that was it. We all sort of accepted it when he told us…and I'm just now realizing that I never reached out to you to see how you were doing," Isaac shamefully lowered his head. "I'm sorry about that, by the way."

"No need to apologize," Logan sighed, choosing not to elaborate on the validity of Tommy's story. "It's not like I went out of my way to let anyone know in the first place."

Isaac managed a sheepish smile and reached for the bong to take another hit.

"Tommy also mentioned that you and Jack had an argument," he added. "He didn't say what about, only that it was enough for you two to stop talking."

Logan let out a scoffing chuckle.

"You never asked Jack about what Tommy was talking about?"

"Nope, never did…but since we're on the topic: what ever happened between you guys all those years ago?"

Logan tensed, taking the bong from Isaac and placing it on the table before reclining on his futon.

"A lot of stuff happened, Saac…I wouldn't want to bother you with it."

Isaac sat up in his chair, clasping his hands together.

"A lot happens every day. That's not a good excuse."

"You're right," Logan agreed, dipping his head to meet Isaac's curious gaze. "But that said, I think it would be best for the both of us if we tabled this topic for now."

Logan correctly presumed that Isaac had no knowledge behind his estranged relationship with Tommy, or what had transpired on that unforgettable night. He studied Isaac's naivety – not out of judgement, but envy – as he yearned for the opportunity to be free of the ills corrupting his own psyche.

He was relieved when Isaac obeyed his wish, slouching back into the sofa. "You know, you're good shit, Berg," Isaac remarked. "I don't know what went down with you and Jack, but I don't think you should keep letting it bother you."

"It doesn't," Logan lied.

"Why don't you try talking to him about it?"

"Come on, man—"

"I mean it. You're clearly not an asshole like Tommy says, and I think deep down, Jack also knows that. Maybe he's just too afraid to go against Tommy," Isaac noted, smirking. "I love those guys, but sometimes I wonder if they're butt buddies, or something."

Logan gave Isaac a heartfelt smile before averting his gaze.

"Okay, I can take a hint," Isaac said, rising to his feet and stumbling for the door. He was halfway out the door when he turned back.

"Do it for me," he pleaded. "Sure, you'll get salty with each other – maybe throw a couple punches – but at the end of the day, it will be worth it…what's the worst that could happen, right?"

"I appreciate the advice man."

Logan watched Isaac leave before staring down at the bong on the table. He found himself middling in his thoughts again. Isaac's advice sounded wild at first, but perhaps he was right. The situation with Jack was nothing more than a dramatic example of miscommunication between friends. He thought – and even attempted – to single him out for a potential conversation about it, but would always coward out due to his fear of its repercussions. Maybe it was time to bring the truth to light.

There was still Tommy, however, who happened to be Logan's driving excuse in not confronting Jack. He had no doubt that Tommy would do whatever it took to prevent any course of reconciliation between them.

Logan picked up his bong from the table and proceeded to load another bowl. He would consider Isaac's input. Until then, he would smoke his conscience away.

xiii

Isaac never got around to checking in on the boys following his encounter
with Logan. He figured they may have well been dead after their night
drinking at the expense of Jack's sorrows.

Tommy likely would have agreed with Isaac if he was alive that morning.
Okay, he was alive, but not necessarily conscious enough to know for sure.
While the truth surrounding dreams remained a mystery, Tommy liked to
think they served a deeper purpose than a series of random, unexplainable
visualizations that occurred under closed eyes. Specifically, he believed them
to be an outlet to reliving lives from alternate realities of himself. He was
extremely observant and able to notice even the most insignificant aspects of
his dreams that paralleled his reality. Drunk slumbers were his favorite,
because they were his most vivid.

He maintained a journal to document his experiences, making sure he
recorded them the moment he would wake up, when the recollection was
fresh. It was mildly therapeutic for him, for even when he could not see any
theme to the dream, a summary of what he recalled was enough to assure
himself of his sanity in respect to his perception of what was real, and what
was not.

Unfortunately, Tommy's remembrance swept out of his mind as he was
abruptly woken up by a series of laughs.

He sauntered out of bed to find Kevin and Bennett rolling over in the living
room.

"What are you guys doing here?"

"We spend the night here after leaving the bars," Bennett replied. "I'm pretty
sure we all blacked out, right?"

"Apparently so," Tommy ridiculed, rubbing his eyes and glancing at the clock
in the kitchen. "Jesus, is that the right time?"

"*Apparently so,*" Bennett mocked.

"Well, that's just fucking fantastic."

Kevin peered over to Jack's closed bedroom door.

"Is he in there?" he whispered.

"If he is, I'm not waking him up," Tommy said. "He's the crabbiest son of a
bitch when he's hungover."

"Ain't that the truth," Bennett grimaced at his throttling stomach. "We should go eat. I'm dying over here."

Kevin perked up, signaling the imaginary light bulb going off above his head. "I know just the place."

Like any smart person, the boys agreed that breakfast was always an option, no matter the time of day. And per Kevin's suggestion, the Windmill was unofficially their favorite spot in the city. It was their last day before classes began, and Tommy wanted it to be a proper sendoff to summer. A recipe for chaos, which mattered less to Tommy than the chance to have a good time. He mentally outlined how he expected the day would unfold, making sure to grab the baggie from his bedroom prior to leaving and piecing a proposal convincing enough for his friends. It may seem a bit much to some, but Tommy acknowledged the groups' indifference to getting silly over consecutive days, unless the circumstances were overwhelmingly in their favor to believe there was no better option.

Just the thought of his friends' approval excited him, and despite his pounding headache from the lingering hangover, Tommy managed to keep his vibes high as they entered the diner and found an empty table.

The approach was simple and, if executed impeccably, would yield a successful result.

1. <u>Order a round of coffee for the boys.</u>

"I appreciate it man," Bennett thanked, pulling out his phone and glossing over the list of unopened notifications. Kevin did the same, only after Tommy poured sugar in his mug to better serve the chances of his childish scheme coming to fruition.

2. <u>State how nice it is to have a free day, rid of responsibility.</u>

"Imma be honest, I was feeling like doing nothing today and going back to bed after this," Tommy began, "But being here with you guys is more than I could ever ask for after such a fun night. Nice call to come here, Kev."

"Thanks, Tom. I agree!" Kevin boomed.

Positive response, that's a good sign, Tommy thought to himself. *This is going to be easier than I thought.*

He waited until the server returned with menus before making his next move.

3. <u>Hint the opportunity to get silly, with the expectation it be shut down.</u>

Tommy leaned awkwardly on his side of the booth, peering up at the ceiling. "What if I were to suggest something?"

Bennett and Kevin's eyes left their phones momentarily.

"Go ahead," Kevin permitted.

"I don't know," Tommy shrugged, intentionally coming across as reluctant with his own idea. "I was just thinking that since none of us have anything important to do, that we could just spend a day chilling."

"Depends on what your definition of 'chilling' is."

"Oh, I don't know," Tommy continued, interlocking his fingers and resting them on the table. "I was thinking that maybe we could get just a *tad* silly."

"I could get silly," Bennett agreed, turning to Kevin, who maintained a stone look.

"Damn, I'm not sure," he said begrudgingly. "I'm not really feeling—" "I know what you're going to say," Tommy cut in. "And I think I have something that could perhaps sway your response…if you'll allow me."

"Proceed."

    4.   <u>Bring out the treats.</u>

Tommy reached into his back pocket and slapped the baggie on the table for his friends to see, smiling when Bennett gasped.

Shrooms. Arguably the most magical substance for humanity blessed by God.

"I see," Kevin observed.

"Are you serious?" Bennett asked.

"Deadly." Tommy smirked, lifting his mug and lightly blowing on the coffee as he fixated on his friends' wavering expressions.

It did not take long for Bennett to entertain the offer.

"Let's get silly," he declared, glancing at Kevin. "Come on, let's do it."

"Jesus Christ…fine."

Tommy grinned. *Mission accomplished.*

He emptied the contents of the baggie into a napkin, pressing firmly and massaging over the mushrooms like one does when rolling dough. The ever so familiar stench from the shrooms gradually filled his nostrils with every subtle crunch, as he pictured the once bite-sized stems eventually deteriorating into dusty speckles of fungi.

Bennett and Kevin watched closely as Tommy unfolded the napkin and separated the mound into three separate piles and scooped them into their respective mugs. They sat silently as Tommy collected himself.

"To living."

The boys followed Tommy's lead, clinking mugs, and downing as much as they could before they broke away to cool their now scorched tongues.

"Damn, I don't think I'll ever get used to that," Bennett uttered repugnantly, taking a moment to swallow the last bit of coffee before chasing it with some water.

Tommy nodded without saying a word, also needing to readjust from the foul taste.

"I kinda like it," Kevin grinned sarcastically.

They all giggled and sat back in their seats, acknowledging their shared suspense for the effects to come. It would only be a matter of time.

Just then, Bennett motioned to a gentleman sitting at a table adjacent to them, perfectly minding his own business as he rambled on his phone.

"Look at him, just yelling away," Bennett scoffed. "The audacity for that man to not care what others feel about him talking so loud."

"I don't see the big deal," Tommy muttered.

"The big deal, Tom, is that we chose this fine establishment to eat in peace, without any distraction from annoying people who consider it to be their own private lounge."

Tommy gave Kevin a perplexing frown.

"Do you hear what you are saying?"

"Hundred percent."

"I think you're trying to find a reason for doing something silly, and it's not working in your favor," Kevin added.

Bennett comically threw his hands up.

"Whatever, I'm just trying to have a good time."

"We *are* having a good time," Tommy assured, gesturing to the food before them. "Look at us: having lunch together; it's just like old times."

"Oh please, what we are doing now is not even close to what we did back in the day," Bennett countered. "We would get into the funniest shit all the time…what happened to us? We're so boring now."

"We grew up," Kevin reasoned.

They sat quietly, each of them mulling over what to say next. Tommy was particularly enlightened by Bennett's insight. He agreed that the dynamic had changed in their college years. Their definition of fun was not the same. It undoubtedly had its positives, but the more he pondered, Tommy realized that the long-term result of his determination to not live life precariously could have more negatives. He figured it would not hurt to entertain Bennett's offer.

"You convinced me," Tommy finally said to Bennett, opening his hands.

Bennett's eyes widened.

"Are you for real?"

"I am," he affirmed, glancing over to Kevin. "What do you say we get even sillier today?"

Kevin nodded reluctantly.

"We just dropped shrooms. How much sillier can we get?"

Bennett was already past Kevin's question.

"That's what I like to hear!" he exclaimed, grabbing a waffle fry from his plate and hurtling it towards the phone man.

The boys instinctively turned away at the sight of the fry bouncing off the man's shoulder, prompting him to turn in their direction.

"Hey!" the man hollered, pulling his phone away from his cheek.

Bennett naively peered back at him, pretending to be surprised.

"Yes?"

The man's face reddened, glancing down at the fry by his feet and staring at Bennett.

"Did you do that?"

Bennett shook his head at Tommy and Kevin, who were trying their best not to laugh.

"Nah, that wasn't me dude."

"You're lying. I know it was you."

Kevin lowered head, gazing at Tommy.

"What do we do?"

Tommy slouched into his chair, praying the altercation did not escalate.

Bennett, on the other hand, was doing an excellent job keeping his composure, as he returned a fixed, cool grin at the man.

"I don't know how you know it was me," Bennett added, pointing at Tommy. "For all you know, it could have been this dude here."

Tommy shot a death glare at Bennett.

"Is that right?" the man growled, now directing his anger at Tommy. "Was it you, you little shit?"

Tommy did not mind arguing, but he considered it to be more of a pastime, if anything. That said, there was perhaps one thing that Tommy hated more than unnecessary confrontation, and that was being patronized. The degree of threat did not matter to him; he was willing to go as far as he needed to make his point. And in this case, his point was very clear: do not fuck with him.

"You're overreacting," Tommy started, swiveling in his seat to face the man. "Quit getting so worked up for a fry and leave us alone. I hate to state the obvious, but you're kind of being a prick right now."

Tommy could feel the man's bubbling rage from where he sat, watching as he bared his teeth, his jaw clenched and chest heaving.

"Stop what you're doing," Kevin warned, growing more uncomfortable by the second.

At that moment, the boys' server returned to their table. Tommy could tell from her confused frown that she was unsure how to mediate the commotion. He shoveled a hundred from his wallet and left the booth, awaiting his friends to join him.

"You guys ready?" he asked cautiously, relieved that Bennett and Kevin copied his example in a matter of seconds.

"Thank you for your service," Bennett said to the waitress, leaving a charming smile stretched across his face as Kevin pulled him toward Tommy leading them out of the restaurant.

"What's next on the agenda?" Bennett asked.

"Not sure," Tommy admitted, starting to feel the initial effects from the shrooms trickle into his fingertips. He clenched the wheel, savoring every millisecond of the uneasy, yet comforting sensation. A sudden chill ran up his spine and into his neck, prompting him to involuntarily shake his head as he slowly braked at the red light before them.

"It's hitting me right now too," Kevin said upon noticing Tommy's demeanor.

"How about a hike?" Bennett proposed, rubbing his hands together. "We could hit a something in town so we don't have to drive out too far."

"I would be down to not be around other people given your vibes right now."

"What do you mean? What's wrong with my vibes?"

"I think what Kev is saying is that he doesn't want to spend the rest of the afternoon having to babysit you in making sure you don't keep trolling random people."

"Fair enough. What do you guys want to do, then?"

"I don't know," Tommy admitted, thinking back to what Bennett was saying at the restaurant; specifically on the topic of them not getting to the antics they had enjoyed when they were kids.

"What are some things we can do, without fearing of getting arrested?"

"That's a hard one," Kevin looked at Bennett. "Aside from hiking, what else do you feel like doing, Benny?"

Bennett was quick to jump on Kevin's question.

"Ballooning?"

"I don't think you listened to what I just said."

"I actually like that idea," Kevin agreed.

"Seriously, Kev?"

"I mean, I'd rather do *something* than *nothing*, you feel?"

As if destiny supported Bennett's idea, Tommy's eyes hovered above the vast cityscape beyond the windshield and into the clear sky.

Or so he may have thought.

Because there, directly in his line of sight, was the largest hot air balloon he had ever seen. It was lined with neon hues so bright it nearly blinded him, as he watched it levitate higher into the atmosphere, seemingly avoiding the oncoming aircrafts. The view grew more captivating in that moment, however, as he inspected closer to see tiny white balls falling from the already unnoticeable basket suspended from the balloon. There were easily thousands of them, increasing speed as they rained toward the earth, many of which broke out into a wave of golden liquid before falling behind the buildings. He tried to make sense of what he was seeing, until his attention was shattered by Bennett's voice.

"Tom?"

"Huh? Are you talking to me?"

"Yeah," Bennett said humorously. "You spaced there for a hot minute."

"Did I? What were we talking about?"

Kevin shot him a concerning look.

"We were debating if we were going to get eggs or balloons."

Tommy lowered his eyes from the sky and realized that he was parked in a lot of a grocery store. He was confused, to say the least, not once concluding when he stopped driving, or how they ended up there. And when he glanced back at the sky, he saw that the balloon was no longer there. Nor the thousand golden balls.

He felt his mouth open without a sliver of thought in what words would leave his lips.

"Por qué no los dos?"

"Look at that!" Bennett exclaimed. "Someone is *definitely* down to get silly!"

Tommy took a moment to shake off the hallucination, seeing that his friends were halfway across the lot to the store.

That was weird, he thought, getting out of his car and going inside. He lost his friends immediately and spent a painfully long time searching for them in the maze of the market. And boy, did he wish that he had found them sooner. He did not even have to see *them* – the shopping cart full of eggs and balloons he ran into was more than enough evidence of his friends' reckless state of mind.

"Whoa, what is this?"

"Don't worry, it's on me," Bennett smirked.

"I don't care about how much it costs, but since when have we ever bought this many? We have more eggs to last a lifetime of breakfasts."

Kevin tossed several more bags of balloons in the cart.

"Good thing we won't be eating them," he winked.

"Fine. You'd have to be an idiot to not know what we're up to. But fine."

"Stop worrying," Bennett said calmly. "That's why self-checkout exists."

"You're not getting my point."

He regretted saying anything soon after though, as he observed just how easily it was to bypass through the checkout lane with not one person batting an eye.

They returned to the car. Bennett leaned forward from the backseat and flung the receipt in Tommy's lap.

"See, what did I say? Nothing to worry about."

"You must have spent a fortune on this," Tommy said, but fell silent when he read the astonishingly low sum.

"What—" he paused, turning to the backseat to see only three bags beside Bennett: four cartons of eggs, and two bags of balloons.

"This is all we bought?" Tommy asked.

Bennett snickered.

"Were you expecting more?"
Tommy then directed his attention to Kevin.
"Are you two pranking me right now? I could have sworn we had way more."
If Kevin could display a poker face, he did an exceptional job giving it.
"Never mind," Tommy dismissed, remembering he was on shrooms. He
rubbed his eyes, struggling to calibrate with the surprising potency of this
batch. "Where shall we take our talents?"
"Same place we used to," Kevin suggested.
Nothing more had to be said; Tommy understood perfectly as they made their
way to his family home.
Mercer was a large island, with only the interstate providing access to the
mainland. The historical prevalence was reflective in the various
neighborhoods: amidst the magnificent manors sprinkled across the rugged
landscape, were the occasional, modest abodes, all of which were nuanced in
eerily antiquated greenery that fortressed the inhabitants from the boisterous
cacophony of the city emitting from across Lake Washington.
None of that mattered to the boys then, however, as they were too busy trying
to prepare for night's arrival while simultaneously melting.
"This one isn't as full as the others," Kevin complained from the back seat,
handling one of the many balloons toppled in the bucket beside him.
"What was that?" Bennett addressed.
"Look at this," Kevin repeated, clumsily bringing the balloon up to Bennett's
eyes for him to see.
"Are you for real?"
"Absolutely, this is a shit job on your part!"
"Hey man, I did my best, all right?" Bennett snapped back. "There's only so
many balloons I could fill up…not like you offered to help."
"You said you could do it yourself!"
"Guys please, the balloons look great," Tommy said, keeping his eyes on the
road.
"I agree," Bennett scoffed, shifting back to Kevin. "I expect an apology."
"Eat my ass, buddy."
Bennett faced Tommy, shaking his head contemptuously.
"Can you believe this guy?"
"I can't believe either of you, if I'm being totally honest."
Tommy parked on the side of the dark road.

"Okay boys, we all know the drill," he began. "Let's keep it quick and to the point. Eggs on the houses, and balloons on the cars. Any questions?"
"No mom," Bennett mused.
"I don't see a scenario where a mother would ever say that."
Bennett rolled his eyes. "Sometimes I hate how literal you can be."
Tommy looked at Kevin.
"You ready with the eggs?"
Kevin held up one of the cartons for them to see, beaming the most mischievous of smirks.
"You already know it."
Tommy began the route, rolling down all the windows lightly pressing on the gas. He maintained a moderate speed, occasionally bursting in laughter at the hilarious comments his friends would scream as they volleyed eggs and balloons from every direction.
Kevin mistakenly undershot his first egg, cringing when it cracked on the pavement.
"Come on Kev, do better!" Bennett laughed as he propped atop his seat and out the moonroof. From there, he grabbed a fresh batch of balloons, peppering them at every piece of metal he could make out on the dim road.
Kevin followed his lead, lurching out of the rear window on the driver's side, and flicked a couple eggs at each house they passed. Tommy could not witness every impact, but he certainly heard each one, praising his friends for their masterful aim as he increased their speed.
"Watch this one, Tommy!" Kevin called, winding up as if he was pitching a fastball. He yeeted three eggs clear across the lawn to the next house, laughing playfully as the yolk splattered across the windows.
Tommy echoed his enthusiasm, naturally closing his eyes and clapping his hands in appreciation.
His attention was off the road for seconds – however many, he did not know – but by that time, it was almost too late.
"Look out!" Bennett shouted.
Tommy connected Bennett's warning to the alarmed expression of a cyclist on the curb as they drove directly at him. He instinctively clutched the steering wheel and pulled away from the cyclist, ignoring his friends' screams as they swerved into the other lane before ramming through a mailbox.
"Other way, other way!" Kevin shrieked.

Tommy corrected the wheel and veered them back to the middle of the road before slamming his foot on the brake.

"Fucking A," Tommy groaned, seeing his friends collecting their breaths.

"Is everyone good?" he asked.

"That was awesome!"

"I agree, I'm glad we did this. Brings me back to when we were kids," Tommy added, peeking into the carton between Bennett's legs.

"Are we out?"

"Looks like it," he confirmed.

"No more balloons either," Kevin noted.

"Well shit," Tommy sighed. "Should we call it a night, then?"

Long pause.

"I don't know about you guys," Bennett spoke up. "But I haven't gotten all of it out my system yet."

"*Really?*"

"Really, really."

"What are you thinking?"

Bennett tilted his head, pondering Kevin's question.

"What we always do when we have nothing left," he hinted.

Tommy instantly knew what he was talking about, grinning at Kevin before looking back at him.

"You don't mean…"

"Oh yeah."

Tommy exchanged a series of jitters with Kevin before looping around and out of the neighborhood.

Every community had the one old, lonely fart that hated his neighbors. Larry Greep was Mercer's. His family had resided on the island for generations – long before the boys were born – and after years of solitude, he grew distasteful at the growing number of new incomers. He tolerated few of his neighbors, many of whom were near his age.

But then came the nuclear families…

To be clear, Larry did not hate children. He had a few of his own, but they had since matured, moving out and starting their own families off the island. He did resent Tommy and his friends, who seized any opportunity to disturb his privacy and wellbeing. His contempt was shared with a couple other neighbors, notably Dr. Peter Beaufort (he is for another time), who had his own traumatic experiences with the kids. Coupled with how they would refer to him as "Creep" because its close sounding to his surname, Larry was overjoyed when they all left for college, believing it would translate to an end of their pranks.

If only he knew.

Tommy and his friends parked down the road, where they continued on foot for the remaining half mile up to Larry's home. It sat alone at the end of a cul-de-sac, encircled by a withered wooden fence. They were far enough from neighbors that any noise would have faded before reaching them. It was an ideal location for what they had planned.

They reached the front of the house, where Tommy straddled the fence and scope out any signs of movement from beyond the darkened windows.

"I don't see anything," he whispered, turning back to the boys. "He must have hit the hay early."

"That doesn't surprise me," Bennett chuckled. "The man must be like 90 now."

"Are we sure he still even lives here?" Kevin asked. "Who knows, maybe he died."

Tommy peeked back at the house, noting the familiar shed that Larry would house his dog.

"Nah, he's still here," Tommy assured, adjusting on the fence so that both his feet were directly in front of him. He drew a deep breath, relishing the adrenaline already bursting in his chest. "Who wants to start?"

Bennett and Kevin ducked below the fence behind Tommy, silently signaling their dissent to go first.

"Pussies," Tommy muttered, shaking his head at them and starting for the house; that was the easy part. There were no streetlights, and unless the moon was fully illuminated on a clear night, the boys could essentially come and go undetected.

Tommy pressed the doorbell, and instantly jumped off the steps before sprinting to the edge of the fence and laying on his stomach beside the boys. They waited patiently. Seconds later, the porchlight turned on and the door opened, where the old man teetered out.

Tommy was too far to make out Larry's expression, but he could tell from his physical gestures that he was confused to see nobody there.
"I don't think so!" Greep yelled out. "Go home or I'm calling the cops!"
He went back inside, leaving the porchlight on.
"You'd think that he'd have gotten used to this," Tommy commented. "All right, who's next?"
"I think you should go again," Kevin suggested. "You did it perfectly."
"Fuck no, I already went!"
"I think it's your turn, Kevin," Bennett teased.
Kevin reluctantly rose to his feet, keeping his knees bent as he crept toward the house.
Tommy turned to Bennett. "Are you sure you're cool with going after him?"
"Hey now, you're talking to a state champion in track. There's nothing that my legs can't do."
They watched Kevin reach the door and slap the bell before sprinting back. The door opened quickly this time, but not before Kevin managed to reach his crew on the grass.
Greep emerged, this time cradling a shotgun in his arms. He was more animated now, and although they could not comprehend what he was saying, they felt his anger as he slammed his fist on the porch railing. A large German Shephard strolled between Greep's feet, patrolling down the steps and disappearing behind the house.
The boys remained still as Greep simmered down and went back inside.
"I swear that man has officially lost his mind," Kevin said.
Tommy rolled on his side to face Bennett.
"Okay, Benny: your turn."
Bennett's eyes widened.
"No way. He left his dog out. What if it attacks me?"
"What the hell happened to 'state champion in track?'
"Sprinting against *humans,* not a dog. I'm not going to take the chance. One of you can go again if you want to keep this up. I'm out."
"Dude come on. Tommy and I both went; it's your turn now. That's only fair."
Bennett rolled his eyes and got to his feet.
"If I get bit, it's on both of you."
"Get in there, champ!" Kevin hollered.

Bennett was slow to approach the house, listening intently to any sound not caused by the light crunch of his shoes on the grass, or the heavy breath after each exhale. When he finally reached the steps, he glanced back at the boys, who both gave him a thumbs up.

"Assholes," Bennett mumbled to himself, inching closer to the door.

He stalled as he rested his finger on the doorbell. Just then, the door swung open, where he was met with Greep's wrathful glare staring back at him.

"Ope!" Bennett panicked, still ringing the doorbell and hurtling the porch rail behind him. He landed rather gracefully, sprinting across the lawn opposite the boys.

"Get back here, Nash!" Greep called after him, holding up and cocking the gun in Bennett's direction.

"He's not actually going to do it, right?" Kevin asked Tommy, trembling as Bennett vanished in the dark night.

Tommy was too in shock to reply.

"Tom—"

Kevin was abruptly interrupted by the booming howl from the shotgun, causing them to jump and scamper away.

Tommy was familiar with the fear that suddenly blended with his adrenaline, still thinking clearly as he guided his hysterical friend.

"This way!" he said to Kevin, leading him down the hill. They could not see anything in front of them, disregarding the occasional dips in the land that caused intermittent trips until they ultimately stopped to catch their breath.

"Boys!" Bennett appeared, stumbling up from behind them and falling into Tommy's arms.

"Holy shit, are you okay?" Kevin asked.

"No man, I'm not fucking okay!"

"Were you shot?"

"Of course not."

"But you said you weren't okay."

"Well yeah, that was terrifying!"

"Oh my god, man," Tommy muttered, releasing Bennett and shaking his head as he fell on the ground.

"Wow, we were idiots today," Kevin panted.

They all nodded slowly before bursting out in laughter.

"I miss this," Bennett added. "Why did we ever stop?"

"Maybe because it was time for us to grow up?"

"Growing up doesn't mean we have to be serious all the time," Tommy chimed in. "It's society's expectation of how we should act. Like, everyone agrees that they want to live a happy life, full of freedom and rid of any restriction. Yet, we all find ourselves leaning toward the opposite as we age."

"Damn, that was beautiful, man," Bennett said.

Tommy patted Bennett's leg in appreciation, checking his watch to estimate how much longer they had until the shrooms wore off. As if his curiosity was the resulting spark, he instantaneously felt the effects cease from his body, the last bit transuded into his hands and dripped off his fingertips.

He saw a similar reaction from the boys.

"And just like that, we're back in the real world."

"About time. I think I'm ready to call it a night," Kevin said.

"I agree," Bennett assented, propping up to his feet.

Tommy could have stayed all night if it were not for their impatience to return home. He anticipated the deep contemplation that would eventually follow his trips. It was a good day. And one he was sure to remember for a long time. If only Jack had been with them; surely, would have benefited the most from this with his troubling drama. The chance to release oneself from societal constructs was always a blessing, and one that he never took for granted. A lesson he hoped Jack to learn someday, soon.

xiv

Emma thought her first time flying would make for a more memorable ordeal. She used to imagine stepping off the plane in a place that she assumed unlike the one she called home in Washington. The flight was unbearably long, but any sort of hoopla was worth it if the destination was none other than New York City.

Her only frame of reference came from movies, and while stereotypes are generally unsafe to take as law, an opportunity to find out for herself sprung on her lap. Perhaps she would not have dropped everything to go there had she considered exactly what she would be getting herself into – after all, it is not like impulsivity has ever resulted poorly for anyone.

Nevertheless, she was finally making meaningful steps toward her dream, which for most of her life, she considered an outlandish fantasy. Not only did it come sooner than she expected, but at an oddly convenient timing with the drama she chose to leave behind in Seattle. This could be the chance for her to rebrand herself and prove to everyone that she was in fact capable of living up to her aspirations. It was time for her dreams to no longer be dreams, but her reality.

The internship came with perks, some more glowing than others: particularly, the free lodging in the heart of Manhattan. Emma was dumbfounded by her upscale apartment, from the glossy hardwoods to the elegant furnishings peppered around the flat. Its chic flair was complemented with a breathtaking view, to which she found it impossible to appreciate fully in a single glance. She was in literal awe at how the illumination from the expansive metropolis poured through her panoramic window, with profound, glittery lights matching the distinct commotion emitting from the avenue below. She was prepared to embrace this city as her own, and hoped the city would return the sentiment.

Emma arrived a week prior to the start of her internship, solely for the purpose of getting accustomed to a tolerable routine. Fortunately for her, it only took three days, as she took mental notes to survive the humdrum of the bustling city. For instance, she had resorted to purchasing her own coffeemaker, after concluding the impossibility of stopping at a café while *also* making it to class on time. She prepared to pack her own lunches most days, after learning the rarity in finding an affordable eatery in the area and reluctant to settle with the abundance of pizza joints that she admittedly could not tell much difference from the next.

The city never sleeps – Frank Sinatra could not have been more right. But Emma had observed that the streets were most passable in the late afternoon, precisely after people returned to work after lunch, but just before escaping from their jobs for the rush hour home. Even then, it was a nightmare using the subway, and she relied largely on her own two feet and rideshares to get around the neighborhood. She even picked up a serving job at a steakhouse only a block from her apartment, mindful that it could further sustain her financial needs in the wake of an increasingly expensive environment she had knowingly placed herself in.

The last couple afternoons leading up to her "first day of school," Emma would find herself in a bookstore, swept in vellichor upon glossing over the multi-colored books stacked away on the wooden shelves as she strolled in and out of the endless aisles. She loved the concept of a library, viewing it as underrated – and often undervalued – from a society so adamant in resorting to their own prudence, rather than literally taking a page from another's perspective that could likely assist their methodical approach in virtually any predicament they encounter. She was absorbed in the serene atmosphere this particular day, when she was interrupted by an unfamiliar voice.

"Is there anything specific you are looking for?"

Emma spun around to see a man curiously staring back at her. He could not have been more than a couple years older, comfortably sporting a tracksuit and sandals. He was conventionally handsome, with a defined facial structure that was partly covered underneath his well-kept stubble. His quirks were not at all subtle, as Emma noted the twitch in his umber eyes and how he bit his lip before speaking.

"I'm looking for Dorothea Lange, but I'm not having any luck."

"Right," he nodded. "You may have better luck in the fantasy section."

"Excuse me?"

"Wizard of Oz, right?" he questioned. "From what I remember in the movie, it has more of a mystical, otherworldly spin to classic American culture. It's also a literary classic, so I see why you chose this section," another lip bite. "Still, I think any type of fiction is your best bet."

"Who do you think I'm talking about?"

"Dorothy. That's the girl's name…right?"

Emma burst into laughter, especially amused by his willingness to come off sophisticated over such a naïve error.

"Did I say something funny?"

"Okay first: *Dorothea;* and second: do you seriously think I would be browsing the photography section of a library looking for a copy of the Wizard of Oz? You could get that at Wal-Mart for five bucks."
"Okay, you got me. I have no idea who that person is, nor where we are in this library."
Emma rolled her eyes, charmed by his cheesy demeanor.
"It's okay. In your defense, it isn't a name that most people know."
He nodded. "So, this Dorothea takes pictures?"
"Amongst other things," she replied. "She was one of the reasons why I got into photography."
"Photography, wow! I know a lot about that."
She studied his bright expression.
"Do you actually?"
"Totally," he stammered, panning the shelves before randomly picking one out and holding it up for her to see."
"What do you know about his work?" Emma pointed at the book. "He's one of my favorites. Hailing from the classical era, his art was really…symbolic to the methodology behind abstractionalism."
Emma raised an eyebrow.
It did not take long for the boy to fold, glowering cluelessly into the textbook before giving up.
"Okay, I actually don't know the first thing about photography."
"Believe me, I can tell," Emma teased, taking the book and swiping through the pages.
"Classical era? That was a good one," she remarked. "Also: *abstractionalism?*"
"Please tell me that's an actual word."
"I appreciate your effort."
"Thanks," he nodded, mildly embarrassed. "I take it you are from the city?"
"Why do you say that?"
"You're very…blunt."
"I'm actually from Seattle."
"Seattle?" his eyes widened. "I was a little off there."
"Only a little."
"What brings you to New York?"
"There's this art program that I am in," Emma revealed. "It's essentially an internship and with the occasional college courses all rolled into one."
"That sounds really cool! How long is the internship?"
"A few months."
"I'm sure it'll be one hell of an experience."

"I appreciate it," Emma thanked, her lingering skepticism beginning to evaporate. She was surprised at how long he kept the conversation going despite her rather dismissive tone. She did not detect creepy vibes from him. He seemed nice enough. But especially given the standoffish nature of the majority of the people in this city, she was hesitant to believe that this guy saw her as nothing more but a potential hookup. And at the *library* of all places? He was likely not the best at charming women for him to resort to this location for said motive.

"Sorry, I have to run," Emma said. "I have my first shift at my new job in fifteen minutes."

"Where do you work?" he asked, matching her haste. "I can give you a ride."

"That's okay," she said, stopping in her tracks at the sight of the downpour from outside of the library doors.

She turned around, giving him a blank stare.

"Is there something wrong?" he asked.

"It's raining…"

"Well yeah," he confirmed, slightly confused by her expression. "Doesn't it rain a lot in Seattle?"

"That's not—yes, it does. I've only been in here for an hour and wasn't expecting it to rain so suddenly."

"A lot can happen in an hour," he said, clearing his throat. "The offer still stands, by the way."

Emma sighed. "At least tell me your name so I can remember if you abduct me."

"That's a good idea," he laughed. "I'm Hunter Graham."

"Emma Keva."

"Nice to meet you, Emma."

Hunter guided her to the end of the block, where they were presented with a black stretch limo.

"Is this yours?" she asked him, her eyes widening.

"Sure is."

She buckled in, mesmerized by the buildings as she pressed her face to the window. It fascinated her, only the bristling salty chill posing a remote semblance to her hometown. The sheer number of people on the sidewalks were overwhelming, as they joined the congested traffic.

"For someone from Seattle, you act like you've never been to a city before."

"This is my first time leaving home actually."

Hunter raised his head to the driver.

"West fifty second," he said.

"How did you know?" Emma asked, stunned.

"You're a waitress, right?"

"Yeah, but I didn't tell you that…"

"This is my city," he revealed. "Plus, you give off that vibe."

"Care to elaborate?"

"You know, the 'small town girl in the city' vibe," he explained. "Have big dreams of stardom but waits tables on the side to pay the bills."

She gasped sarcastically. "That's a bit cliché. Believe me, my life is nothing close to a 90's romance."

"I'm a dreamer, what can I say?"

"Oh yeah? What do you dream about?"

Hunter glanced out the window, watching the droplets smack against the glass.

"That's a 'second date' discussion, wouldn't you say?"

"Second…"

"Yeah," he implored, focusing on her. "We're on our first right now. I'd say it's going pretty well, what about you?"

That made her giggle. She did not see any harm in entertaining his flirts; after all, it was the least she could do for the ride. Despite his blatantly apparent ego, he supplemented it with affectionate ingenuity, and quirky expressions that warmed her heart. It was uncanny to Jack.

Jack.

The limo slowed to a stop in front of the restaurant.

"I am *not* looking forward to this," she mumbled.

"Yeah, doesn't seem like fun."

"It isn't."

Hunter's eyes flickered.

"I don't want this date to end yet, so I'll tell you what: you skip work, and spend the rest of the afternoon with me."

"Are you serious?"

"Come on, you're in New York City! When is the next time you'll find yourself in a situation like this?"

"I'll get fired."

"No you won't. I'll take care of it."

"How?"

"Like I said, this is *my* city."

Emma hesitated. She was not one to make impulsive decisions, let alone with someone she had just met. Under normal circumstances, Hunter's offer would have been an easy no.

But this circumstance was anything but normal.

"I'll take you up on that," she smiled.

"Perfect, promise you won't regret it," Hunter cheered, signaling the driver.

Emma took one last glimpse at the restaurant as they pulled off down the avenue.

Hunter gave her a tour of the entire neighborhood, spending the rest of the afternoon trailing through every inch of Manhattan as he incorporated his own take of the area through delightfully narrated anecdotes. He had a way of blending charisma in his endless chatter, telling her about his time growing up in the city.

They made frequent stops at where he claimed to be his favorite places. She blushed every time he would help her out of the limo, observing the abundance of bystanders spectating their every movement. She could not justify her lack of sexual attraction toward him. He was the epitome of a pretty boy, with dazzling eyes and a calm, charming gaze eternally fixated on her whenever she spoke. Even though she did not know him well, he somehow felt like she had known everything about him. And judging from the shrewd expressions from every person passing them, it was clear that he was not just another person in this city.

It seemed like an eternity of driving. She did not realize how drained she was until they arrived at her apartment, taking a dep breath and wrestling with the buckle.

"Thank you so much for today," she said to Hunter.

"It's been a pleasure," he smiled, reaching his hand over her shoulders.

He leaned in close, prompting her to instinctively pull away.

"I'm sorry, but I kind of have a boyfriend," she revealed.

"Kind of?" Hunter smiled as he raised an eyebrow. "I find that hard to believe."

"Really?" she glared, her brows narrowing. "Do you think I would lie about something like that?"

"People lie about stuff all the time."

"Do they now? I'm sure that my *boyfriend* would tend to disagree with your statement."

"If you have a boyfriend like you say, then why did you spend all day with me?"

"Good question," she spluttered, trying to gather a suitable response.

"I'm messing with you, please don't answer that," Hunter said cheekily, pulling his arm out from behind her. "All said, I would love to see you again, if you are okay with that?"

She paused as the driver opened her door.

"I would like that," she grinned as she exited the car.

"Excellent! I'll text you with the details."

Emma's face scrunched in confusion.

"How do you have my number?"

"Like I said before," Hunter reiterated, smirking. "This is *my* city."

With that, the driver shut the door and continued into the limo, leaving Emma to watch it disappear into traffic.

Hunter really made an impression on Emma as she struggled to concentrate on anything other than him on her way to the apartment. She had just finished spilling the details to Morgan on the phone, going into the bathroom and drawing a bath.

Her impatience paid back immediately, letting out a muted scream by the searing water on her tender skin as she gripped the edge of the marble tub. She preferred showers, but she was also in New York City. What better time to bask in new things – even the menial ones?

Emma tried to remain still as the steam filled her nostrils, allowing her thoughts to float free. In that freedom, harbored another feeling – one that she had not felt since the worst day of her life.

One cannot reflect on an experience until after it has happened, but in Emma's case it was almost as if there came a preemptive indication as she curled up under her blanket, absently aware of everything except her mental imagery of which poster of her favorite movie or boy band would be lucky enough to earn a spot on her blank four walls. She was too excited to care about anything else, including why she was there in the first place.

No, that is not a segue into a deeper revelation. She literally did not know the true reason behind why her family packed up and moved so suddenly. The outcome would not have changed had she known, and arguably, neither would her outlook. Because even in the still quietness of the night, her own parents were uncertain in their reasoning, and like parents who came before them, had a habit of discussing private matters indiscreetly enough for children to eavesdrop.

It was moments after Emma concluded Styles would get the best spot when the feeling came. Moments after she tried shutting her eyes in hope that it would magically make her fall asleep and pretend nothing happened.

Moments after she ultimately rolled out of bed and lightly pressed her ear to the door as she overheard her parents out in the hall at the top of the stairwell.

"I trust you Bruce, but are you sure this is the right thing to do?"

"Baby, we've talked about this. You heard Marshall – he's got it taken care of."

"I know, but what we've done…we're talking so much more money in addition to the hospital bills that we already can't—"

"Please Julia, I know all this is happening fast, but it's not like I have a lot of choices. This is the best-case scenario for us…for Snappy."

When someone is cursed with a terminal illness, the dolour touches everyone, not at equal proportion but to a degree meaningful enough to often change the course of their collective action. Catalyzing such action is the idea that living life fully, and present in the finite time given to them is paramount; although for Emma, even in her youth mind, dreaded it beyond hope of repair.

She would return to bed, now fully aware of her surroundings and situation, dwelling over realizations so subtle like how different it felt to lie in the same bed only in a room that she had yet to accept as her own. How much longer could it be her own, before it was taken away from her, like the one person that she trusted would remain beside her no matter what.

The pain she felt when she learnt of Bruce's diagnosis was worse than when he inevitably passed. It is one thing to acknowledge life's finiteness and choose to live fully, but it is entirely different when finiteness is burdened further with improbable natural occurrences that establish a literal expiration date. Four years. That was all she had left with her favorite person, who she dreamed being there for all the great days in a person's life. From future birthdays and holidays to meaningful experiences like getting married and having children – doing it all without her father was a dread she shouldered since the beginning. Parents wish to never outlive their children, and for Emma, it too pained her that in a strange sense, he was already dead. She could have everything else she hoped for, including this internship, but as long as Bruce was not there, she felt truly alone.

And during periods of loneliness, is when the mind opens itself up to any effort in securing other outlets of intimacy, even when it comes at the cost of sacrificing one's own inner peace. Who was to say that distance was the leading factor, or the increased carelessness to consider those she missed dearly. Even Morgan, who despite just speaking with her only minutes ago about her time here, could never match quality had she been there personally to experience it together. Most of all, she thought of Jack, who aside their emotional dispute, remained at the core of Emma's prayer for his acceptance of her decision, and willingly await her return.

Just then, Emma heard a door close. Tedious footsteps followed, growing louder until they stopped right outside the bathroom door.

She peeked out of the tub as the door cracked open, seeing a startled girl standing at the entryway.

"Shit! I'm sorry," the girl exclaimed, quickly averting her stare.

"It's okay," Emma said calmly. "You must be my roommate."

The girl perked up. "That's right! My name's Baylee."

"I'm Emma."

"Nice to meet you," Baylee smiled, hesitating at the sight of Emma in the bath. "What do you say we formally meet each other once you're done? I'm not planning on sleeping much tonight."

"That sounds like a great idea, Baylee."

Emma giggled faintly at the awkward introduction long after she left. She already knew that they would get along swimmingly.
She eventually left the bathroom, where she saw Baylee's still image glued to the paneled window.
"Hello again!" she greeted, her eyes still intently overlooking the city.
Emma continued to the kitchen, noting the neatly arranged foods aligning the counter.
"I bought us groceries for the week," Baylee added, spinning around to face her. "Nothing too glamorous, since I didn't know what you prefer. There's more in the fridge."
"I appreciate it. And don't worry, I wouldn't consider myself to be a picky eater."
Baylee smiled and returned to the window.
"I still can't believe I'm here."
"Oh my god, I know. I don't think I will ever get over how nice this apartment is."
"Kudos to the designer," Baylee added, directing her attention to the panes.
"The attention to detail is spectacular. It's postmodern, yet you can see the obvious Brutalist themes all around."
Emma gave her a perplexed expression.
"*Obvious?* I don't even know what that means."
"I'm an architecture major," Baylee replied. "Also from Nebraska, so you can imagine the lack of structural diversity."
"I can understand that."
"How about you?"
"Seattle."
"I meant your type of art!"
"Oh, right of course," Emma paused, adjusting to Baylee's nerdiness. "I'm primarily into graphics and visuals, but I concentrate in photography."
"Fascinating! I'll keep note of that when you and I partner up on some projects in the future," Baylee bellowed, approaching her. "Are you ready?"
Emma squinted confusedly.
"For...?"
"To get some food, of course!" Baylee retorted. "What better way to celebrate our union than with some dinner?"
"But you bought so much—"
"Nonsense! We'll have all semester to stay in and cook meals. Let's go enjoy ourselves!"
Emma was tired, but Baylee's eagerness was too compelling to turn down the offer.

"Okay," Emma relented, doing her best to reciprocate Baylee's enthusiasm.

They journeyed around the neighborhood for an ideal spot when Emma received a notification on her phone from Jack. All the problems she intentionally dragged out of her mind immediately slipped back at the sight of his name.
All said, Emma could not resist a subtle grin. What was it about him that struck her admiration? It had nothing to do with his wealth – she had her share of *those* kind of men – arrogant, envious, and controlling – certainly not her ideal cup of tea.
Jack was different from them, because he viewed his upbringing as a weakness, as opposed to strength.
She ignored his missed call, shoving her phone back in her pocket before rejoining Baylee at the end of the block. Her reluctance to sever the distraction that was Jack Douglas did not appear to be necessary. Not at the moment, anyway.

*****

Jack knew the freedom to choose was ultimately his. He also knew Tommy's skills of persuasion were, in a word, superb. In his opinion, his friend's primary objective that day was simple: to get on his nerves.
He had little interest in shopping to begin with, trudging closely behind Tommy as they perused through the aisle.
"What are we doing here?"
"Getting something for Isaac's birthday," Tommy replied. "I've narrowed it down between a coloring book and a Pictionary."
"He's going to be twenty-two."
"And he loves drawing," Tommy reasoned, blinking hard. "It doesn't take a lot to impress the guy. You know that."
"Just get both. You can afford it."
"Just because I can afford something, doesn't mean I should get it. Besides, you're richer than me. With that logic, you should be buying it."
Jack shook his head and observed the products lining the shelves.
"Emma's birthday is coming up too," he added. "What do you suggest I get her?"
"How about a candle?"
"A candle?" Jack repeated, raising his brow. "What is it with you and these ideas?"
"They smell nice," he shrugged. "I'm actually going to get a couple for our place. Hopefully that helps get the stench out."

"She's not going to want a candle, Tom."

"Look, let's stop with the Emma talk," Tommy said as he shouldered past Jack to the other end of the aisle. "This is a day for the boys."

"Don't wave me off like that, man. I'm being serious."

"I am too," Tommy asserted, grabbing a coloring book from the shelf and signaling a store employee to come over.

"How can I help you?" the associate asked as he neared them.

"Hey there, I have a quick question. Does this come with colored pencils? I'm not trying to buy them separately."

"I believe it does."

"Thanks man, I appreciate you."

Jack waited until the associate walked off to speak up.

"Are you kidding?"

"What?"

"I can't believe you just asked that!" Jack exclaimed, trying not to laugh for Tommy's benefit. "Can you, for once, act your age?"

"'Act your age.' Such an ironically precocious thing to say – how does one even go about doing that?"

"You're doing it again."

"Doing *what*?"

"Acting like you don't know what I'm talking about."

Tommy tilted his head, still on the question.

"Hmm, maybe *that's* how to do it then..."

Jack groaned as Tommy went on.

"Look, I'm just trying to get your mind off Emma, which defeats the purpose of all of this if you keep bringing her up." He glanced back at the coloring book. "Yeah, I think I'm gonna get this."

Jack shot him a jaded stare as they continued to the checkout lane.

He typically enjoyed accompanying Tommy on his errand runs. The destination did not matter for him since he was with his best friend, whose presence was enough to keep the day interesting.

The primary goal was different this time around for Jack, though, as it served as an excuse to help get his mind off Emma.

It had been two weeks since she left, and he had grown more miserable when he learned she was deliberately ignoring his calls. Lovesickness only worsened, nevertheless, causing him to meddle over the time when he was with her and go with the motions.

"There it is!" Tommy shouted, causing him to break away from his thoughts.

They were on the road approaching the freeway when Tommy pointed to a
warehouse stretching beyond the ramp and toward the water's edge. He failed
to get a catch a good glimpse due to Tommy's need for speed.
"That's what your dad bought right?" he asked Tommy.
Tommy twisted his head at Jack, his eyes no longer on the road.
"Behold, he speaks!"
"Ha," Jack laughed mockingly, noting Tommy's reference to the one-sided
conversation he had been entertaining himself with since they left the store.
"What's it going to be used for again?"
"Not sure yet. I'm sure he'll make up his mind eventually."
They reached the bridge, where they sped between lanes amidst the
bombarded traffic. Lake Washington was particularly blinding that morning,
causing Jack to squint in order to make out the shimmering gleams bouncing
off the water and cars.
"A lot of people on the road," Jack commented.
"It's the weekend, and the weather is nice. We're just one of the many who
are taking advantage of the day."
Jack nodded, noticing a scar drawn across Tommy's elbow.
"When did that happen?" he asked him, reaching over to feel the reddened
scrape on his friend's arm.
"It's from when I hit the mind erasers with Bennett and Kevin."
"Mind erasers," Jack echoed. "Got a little crazy, from the looks of it."
"A bit. It was nice to get away from the hubbub of life, you know?"
Jack rested his head on the window. "Hubbub" may not have been his choice
of term, but pretending to share Tommy's outlook was better than being in his
own head. In a twisted way, he wondered if Emma had done the same to him
before she left.
"I'm just realizing I never asked where we're going," Jack said.
"You'll see."
"I don't like your surprises, they make me nervous. Can't you just tell me?"
"No, that's no fun."
They reached the other end of the bridge before exiting off on a narrow road
that whirled around a massive hillside. Jack's eyes lit up at the familiarity of
the area, turning back to Tommy.
"Are we going home?" he asked excitedly.
Tommy nodded, his tone with Jack's.

"We're going home."

Tommy rolled down the windows as they slowed into the suburbs, allowing Jack to breathe in the earthier tone than the unpreferred odor he had grown used to from the city.

They arrived at Tommy's house, where Jack noted the absence of cars in his own driveway next door.

"It must be nice to know you can come back home anytime and your parents will *actually* be here," he muttered.

"Believe me, it was not always the case with me, either. I made sure my mom was home so she could help me grab some things for our apartment."

Had he forgotten about the Beech's love for lush verdure, Jack could have believed that he had just entered a natural greenhouse. It was as if the home itself grew from a small forest, and the modern features that made up the actual home were merely undertones to the thematic energy emitting from the umbrage. The hallway was painted with countless pieces of art across periods of history from different origins around the world. They continued deeper, where the narrow path opened up into a vast living area, enclosed by a variety of vividly colorful houseplants.

Tommy's mother, Maria, was in the middle of her routine watering. Jack snickered upon overhearing her humming peacefully along to the classical music that filled the room, as he could genuinely not picture a sight more suitable and aligned with his understanding of her personality.

"Hey Mom, we're here," Tommy greeted. "Did you get the stuff I asked about?"

"It's in the garage," she replied, placing the canteen on the center table and hugging him before turning to Jack.

"Hey Maria," Jack greeted, exchanging a heartfelt embrace and proceeding to the living room. "I always liked your house over mine. Feels homier."

"We get that a *lot*," Maria assented, handing him a beer and sitting across from him. "I've told your mom many times to apply more earthy tones, but she just loves her pastels too much."

"Believe me, you're preaching to the choir on that one."

"How are your parents? Last I checked they were in Brazil, is that right?"

"Your guess is just as good as mine. My mom likes to join dad whenever he travels."

Tommy rolled his eyes, uninterested in where this was going.

"I'll leave you two to the talking," he said before going to the garage.

The Douglas-Beech bond could be traced back before Jack and Tommy were born. The boys' parents were old friends, first acquainted as teenagers. They were adamant in sharing their personal experiences, including efforts in keeping Jack and Tommy close since their infant years. Jack cherished Tommy's family. He had grown close to Harrison and Maria Beech as he aged, and at this point, he had considered them to be his second parents.

Maria waited until Tommy left the room before leaning forward in her chair.

"Tom told me that you were dating someone. What's her name, again?"

"Emma," Jack replied. "It's been weird the last few weeks. I haven't even told my parents about her yet, so if we could, you know—" Jack brought his finger to his mouth as a subtle gesture for Maria to respect the discreetness on the topic at hand.

"Oh please, you don't have to worry about me."

Jack believed her. He viewed his relationship with Maria as an extension to Tommy's. No matter how personal, he knew they were always worthy confidants.

"How has it been weird?" Maria pressed. "Is it because you two are getting more serious?"

"Quite the opposite," Jack admitted. "Things were great at first, but then she moved away, and things are…well, fizzling."

"Fizzling?"

"I think she's having doubts about us. I've reached out, and she just ignores me."

"Well, I'm sure my son has given his opinions on the matter."

"He tells me to keep trying."

"I agree."

"Why though?"

Maria folded her arms.

"I admire tenacious men. It's how I met my husband, and I was glad to see the trait pass to Tommy. I'm sure you're well aware of that side of him."

"Absolutely," Jack chuckled.

"He is very much like his dad, whether he believes it or not," Maria continued. "When I met Harry, I did not think he was the one for me. But he kept trying. I mean, he went *all in.* As you can see, it worked, but when I look back on it, I think that he knew it would not be easy for him to win me over.

And yet, it didn't stop him. I really respected him for it, and how much effort he put into showing how much he cared and respected me and every decision I made, whether it aligned with his intentions."

"You're saying that I should copy his example?"

"I'm simply sharing my two cents. I do not know what kind of person Emma is, but as a woman myself, I can confidently tell you that we want to feel *valued.* Love is not an emotion, nor is it a feeling. It belongs in its own category. There are so many languages, but love supersedes it all. You may be saying the right things in your mind, but it only works if she can understand it from her end."

Tommy emerged from the garage, breathing hard as he lugged a stack of boxes. He paused momentarily to examine Jack and Maria staring back at him.

"I didn't realize how much shit I left here," he muttered before proceeding out the front door.

"Looks like that's my cue," Jack relayed.

Maria stopped Tommy at the door and hugged him.

"Thanks again Mom. I love you."

"I know, Tom. You're my son. I know you better than you know yourself."

Tommy broke away to meet his mother's eyes, knowing full well she was going to speak the famous thread all mothers give their children.

"Don't you dare say it," he grinned.

Regardless, she said it.

"I brought you into this world; and I can take you out."

Jack's eyes widened as he watched them break out in laughter. *Such an odd family.*

"Okay Bill," Tommy chided, turning to Jack. "I'll be in the car."

"You'll figure it out, Jack," she consoled, hugging him. "Just know that we are always here to help you with everything you need."

"I appreciate it. See you on Thanksgiving."

"Thanks again for distracting my mom, I would have appreciated her help," Tommy said when they had reached the freeway.

"My bad, we kinda got into it."

"What did you talk about?"

"Emma."

"I see! Good things, I hope?"

"You could say that." Jack pulled out his phone and searching for Emma's name in his texts. He resonated with Maria's insight and wondered the reason for his efforts falling short of expectations. Maria's argument was fair. He remembered the world without Emma. How empty it was. The circumstances were already uncharted. Unprecedented. He feared that it could shape into a reality. If it did, what then? Jack was unsure if he was able to move on from something that he originally believed he would never have to.

Maria may have thought her advice was merely a suggestion, but Jack understood it to be imperative to any indication of a potential severance with Emma. He was not prepared to let that happen.

XV

"We're not going to find a seat. There's no way."
Baylee noticed Emma's frown tighten when she said it. She was clearly stressed by the hundreds of civilians closing in the dimly lit subway tunnel.
"That's why we should have gotten up at *my* alarm."
Emma nodded. She was quick to acknowledge her roommate's quirks. In particular, her obedience in following a proper sleep schedule.
"Let's just walk there," Baylee suggested, gently patting Emma's shoulder. "It's only few blocks."
"It's farther than that."
"Makes for a great exercise!"
Emma obeyed in relief and followed her friend back upstairs and out on the busying chaos that was a typical Monday morning in Manhattan. To her surprise, the ongoing horde did not hinder her ability to get anywhere. Unlike Seattleites, everyone here had skip in their pace, marching past one another in jumbled patterns that would appear incoherent to an aerial observer. Keeping up with their speed was still a challenge, but her sense of navigation had improved remarkably as a result.
Alas, the day was finally here.
The Ember House was a private agency that – in addition to serving as a leading benefactor and resource of the art scene in the city – also functioned as an education institution. It housed and trained a modest number of interns every semester, each of whom were individually responsible for capitalizing on the incredible opportunity given to them by an elite board of advisors that oversaw the program.
The girls met with other interns outside of the agency. They leisured past, overhearing snippets of sagacious discussion. So many personalities, with presentations more glaringly obvious than the next. Emma could accurately distinguish the actors from the artists; the photographers from the cinematographers; the crafters from the executives. Whether one sported a pair of leggings, or a polka-dot pocket square, it was clear that these young adults welcomed the idea of esoteric placement in a society riddled in normalcy. Self-confidence was their greatest ally, and they had no problem projecting it according to their specialty. They were the future leaders of the industry, no doubt, and no matter the outcome of this semester, it was

collectively understood that joining the most prestigious art school east of the Mississippi was more than a statement. Their names would forever be etched into a legacy that only few were fortunate to experience.

"I'm getting a little nervous," Emma whispered to Baylee as they maintained a safe distance from the interns.

An older woman suited in wooly blazer emerged from the doors. Her demeanor was formidable, to say the least, maintaining a solid posture and a glare hard as steel.

"Good morning, my name is Margaret Pellany," she greeted. "I wanted to personally welcome you all on your first day here. Please follow me."

The interns followed Dr. Pellany inside the lobby, its layout mirroring that of a symphonic hall. Emma listened intently to Dr. Pellany's explanation on the history of the building, including its distinct wings: Visual, Literary, Performing, and Multidisciplinary. They proceeded into the Visual wing, where they were met with another woman waiting in front of one of the classrooms.

"For some of you, this will be where you will spend the majority of the next couple weeks," Dr. Pellany addressed, standing beside the woman. "This is Dr. Alene Yuki. She oversees this wing's curriculum and will be the instructor and primary resource for all course activities," she addressed. "In addition to your respective wing director, you will each be assigned to a program advisor, who can assist in ensuring you have the most optimal experience over the duration of your time here at Ember."

"I am looking forward to testing your skills," Dr. Yuki added. "For today, you will all be with me. I will be giving a broad overview of your dedicated classifications and an introduction to the general studies we will be learning together."

Emma dismissed the derisive tone in her voice, as she accepted the sheer pretentiousness of this place was something she would need to get used to.

Dr. Pellany gave Dr. Yuki a nod and walked away without speaking, leaving blank exchanges from the interns.

"Shall we?" Dr. Yuki continued.

"We're having class now?" one of the interns asked.

Dr. Yuki darted a scornful look at him.

"Do you have another preference?"

The intern shriveled.

"No ma'am. I'm sorry."

Like Emma, Baylee had learned early in her life the importance of first impressions, electing herself to enter the classroom first and choosing a spot in the front row. Emma followed, growing self-conscious when the rest of the interns chose seats farther back.

Dr. Yuki carried on to the front of the room once they had all settled in, hovering over her desk and pulling up a document on the screen projected behind her.

"Before we get into anything, let us first go over the syllabus," she announced. "I strongly advise that you take notes, because we will cover all contents of this semester, which will better prepare you for the lectures."

Dr. Yuki did not skip a beat, maintaining an authoritative tone in her voice that split through the tense silence. She was already a quarter of the way through the syllabus when half the interns finally had her notebook and pen out of her bag.

Emma was no different, gripping the life out of her pen as she scribbled away. She never quite got used to simultaneously retaining the information she wrote. Dr. Yuki spoke so quickly that Emma had defaulted to listing broken phrases on the off chance it would be enough to fit together, like a puzzle missing a quarter of its pieces.

Emma's phone suddenly went off, its vibration causing it to judder on her desk.

Dr. Yuki paused and dropped her eyes on Emma, who nervously swept the phone in her lap and slouched in her chair.

"I'm sorry," Emma murmured, reluctant to make eye contact with the professor.

Dr. Yuki studied Emma's discomposed frown before shaking her head and continuing on.

Emma's nervousness changed into pure frustration when the phone rattled again between her legs. Feeling her patience fading quickly, she slyly tossed it into her backpack, hoping she could proceed without any further embarrassment.

She swallowed the agony for another half hour until they were finally dismissed. But before she should even leave her desk, Dr. Yuki spoke up.

"You," she addressed, pointing directly at Emma.

"I'll be outside," Baylee whispered to her before walking out with the other interns.

Dr. Yuki was waiting behind her desk when Emma slowly approached.

"Not exactly how you hoped your first day to go, would you agree?"

"I'm very sorry. It was a stupid mistake and it will never happen again."

"What is your name?"

"Emma Keva," she said nervously. "I'm from Washington, interning in photography. Being here is an absolute dream and I would never do anything to jeopardize that."

Dr. Yuki was slightly amused by how apologetic she was.

"A little more information than what I asked. Don't worry about it," she soothed, her eyes lowering to a line of papers on her desk. "Moving forward, I suggest you be more secretive when you want to be on your phone. Setting it to silent would be a good first step."

Emma nodded and stood there uncomfortably. Ten long seconds passed until Dr. Yuki lifted her head again to see Emma still standing there.

"Do you not have better things to do than watch me work?"

"Sorry," Emma stammered. "Thank you, professor. I'll see you tomorrow."

Emma stormed out of the classroom to find Baylee waiting for her as they made their way to the exit.

"Remind me to start recording those lectures," she said. "How did that go?"

"Horrible. That was *so* humiliating."

"Who called you anyway?"

Emma retrieved her phone, realizing she had never checked.

Jack Douglas.

She showed Baylee and shook her head.

"That's your boyfriend, right?"

"Yeah. He's been calling me nonstop since I left Seattle."

"Why don't you answer him?"

"I don't know, I just need a break from talking to him, or anyone for that matter," she said flatly. "I need to focus on everything going on here, you know?"

"I agree…but maybe telling him that would be better instead of screening his calls. It may not be sending the right message."

And then, as if Irony wished to prove its existence, Emma's phone went off for the third time.

Baylee gave an incredulous smirk.

"Either the kid is in love with you, or batshit crazy."

Or both, Emma thought, only to check and see that the missed call was from Hunter.

"To both our surprise, it's not him."

Baylee began to probe, jumping at the potential drama.

"Who? Someone else? Another boy?"

"I'll tell you about it later. What's next on the agenda?"

Bayle checked the schedule on her phone. "Looks like we are all meeting with our program advisors. After that, it seems like we're done for the day."

"Perfect," Emma droned, shielding her eyes from the sunlight's glare once they stepped outside.

"I'll see you back home?"

"Sounds good."

Emma waited until Baylee trotted across the street before calling Hunter back.

"Emma Keva, thanks for not ghosting me," he greeted. "How's your first day?"

"It's…going. What are you up to?"

"I happen to be in quite the conundrum, if you're willing to pitch some advice."

"A *conundrum,*" she giggled. "Sure, let's hear it."

"So there is this girl that I really want to ask to dinner tonight, but I am worried that she may hit me with an 'I'm too busy,' which would totally ruin me."

"Dinner huh? Sounds like you're asking this girl on a date, which could be problematic, given that she has a boyfriend."

"I thought about that," Hunter countered without breaking a pause. "And I think that this girl's boyfriend would actually be appreciative of me to be going out of my way to make sure that his girlfriend is enjoying her time in New York…platonically, of course."

She acknowledged the underlying motive in Hunter's invitation. At the same time, she secretly admired his lack of concern for Jack's opinion. He was daring, that was for sure.

"A *platonic* evening," Emma clarified.

"That's all I'm asking for."

Emma paused once she reached the closed door to her advisor's office.

"In that case, I'm down. I have a meeting right now, just text me where and when."

She hung up and knocked on the door.

"Come in," a voice said from inside.

Emma peeked in to see a middle-aged woman busying away on her computer. Her desk was lined with deep shelves, consisting of framed pictures with what she suspected were former students.

"You must be my 3:00," the woman commented, her eyes still on the monitor.

"Yes, um…" Emma began, uneasily choosing one of the available chairs before the desk. "My name is Emma Keva."

The rampant sequence of clicks on the keyboard suddenly seized, and the woman tilted her head away from the monitor.

"Ms. Keva," the woman said with a noticeable flicker in her eyes, extending her arm across the desk to shake Emma's hand. "My name is Clarene Hanzel."

"Nice to meet you," Emma greeted, hoping she did not notice her trembling palms.

"Relax, you have nothing to worry about. This is merely a formality that we do with all our incoming students," Dr. Hanzel said. "Think of this as a preliminary check-in. I am available as a resource for you to help enhance your overall experience during your time here at Ember."

Emma immediately relaxed as a result of Dr. Hanzel's warm introduction. She wished to have felt this same degree of ease the entire morning.

"I apologize for not having time to look at your file before meeting you. I'll be sure to read it right after this," Dr. Hanzel said as she folded her hands on the table. "How are you feeling so fa-?"

Emma drew a deepening sigh.

"Honestly, it was a little crazy," she began. "Just with all the other kids, and getting around campus…not to mention knowing my way around this city in general."

"It is a lot to digest."

"Yes, exactly."

"Is it very different from your experience going to school in Seattle? My niece transferred there after a couple years studying here, uptown."

"I never really thought about that," Emma started to say, dismissing Dr. Hanzel's knowledge of her origin without seeing her file, as she mentioned.

"It's likely because I am still riding the culture-shock train that I have been more focused on adjusting to…all of this."

"I understand. Speaking of which, it wouldn't hurt if I shed some light on the general aspects of the internship.

"For multiple reasons, we limit the enrollment to fifty interns per semester. As you may have already been able to tell, all of you will have the same schedule in the beginning, but as we progress, we will adjust the time you spend in class, versus in the environment that corresponds with your field of study. Our goal, ideally, is for you to not only build lasting relationships with every one of the other interns, but also learn how all of our programs interact with one another. You'd be surprised how extensive your network could be, if you play your cards right."

"Makes sense," Emma said. "My roommate specializes in architecture. So, while I won't be working directly with her everyday due to our different programs, we will still frequent each other every now and again, both in and out of class?"

Dr. Hanzel grinned.

"I am glad that you chose to come here. I can't tell you how many times I would have to further elaborate that point to former students," she said. "That said, we also pair roommates based on the compatibility of their majors. Which basically means that you will be spending more time with her than other interns. Once again, we want to give you the full scope of career paths that you can take with your specialty."

"I love that."

"I should get back to this," Dr. Hanzel said before shaking Emma's hand again. "It was nice to meet you, Emma. Let me know if you ever need anything during your time here. My door is always open."

They shook hands again when Dr. Hanzel added, "During office hours, I should say."

Emma left the office and headed back to her apartment, where she saw a twitchful Baylee skimming through the pages of one of her many textbooks stacked on the table.

"Hey Em," she acknowledged curtly. "How did your meeting go?"

"Really well. I might end up being one of my advisor's favorite students by the end of the semester."

Emma observed her roommates unchanging demeanor.

"Are you good?"

"Yes. Sorry," Baylee apologized, raising her head. "Before I left, I got into talking to someone from my department. He's now an employee at Ember, but he told me he interned here before being hired."

"…and?"

"Apparently, they rarely bring people in that aren't from the East Coast."

"Really?"

"'Slim to none,' he said. When he was an intern, there wasn't one person from the Midwest. Not only that, but a handful of the other interns in his class were people he knew from his high school upstate."

It could have been a coincidence. But given her predisposition, Emma concluded that there was a clear motive behind the Ember's reluctance to diversify their prestigious workforce.

Before she could respond, Emma noticed Baylee's widened grin. Clearly for her, the fact that she was a rare addition to the program gave her enough drive to overcome any adversity. It was not near the same for Emma, who momentarily spaced to recall the moody faces from the other interns earlier. She could not help but consider her acceptance into the program as a token addition to an elite, classist group. Merely an outcast, unworthy of the same opportunity and, more importantly, its reward.

She was ever one to defiantly stay somewhere she was unwanted.

"So is this your way of getting ahead of the curve?" Emma asked, motioning to the books between them.

"Pretty much," Baylee shot her a teasing smirk. "I take it you have other things on her plate?"

"Why do you say that?"

"Oh nothing, just figured that you would be busy with your mysterious lover."

"What?"

"Come on Em, don't pretend like I didn't see how awkward you got when he called you earlier."

"For the record: I wouldn't say that I got *awkward*," Emma defended before letting out a defeated sigh. "But yes okay, I'm having dinner with a friend tonight. *Just* a friend. Nothing mysterious about that."

She noticed Baylee closely examining her.

"What?"

"You're lying. You like him."

"Oh my gosh, no I do not."

"Mhm sure," Baylee teased. "You have a really bad poker face."

"Okay, he's a little cute, all right?"

"Emma! You got the hots for this boy, I love it. What's his name?"

"Hunter Graham."

Baylee's excitement suddenly disappeared.

"Wait, Graham?"

"Yeah…"

"You don't mean Hunter Graham from Graham Brands International?"

"I don't know what that is."

Baylee returned to her laptop, rapidly typing before sliding it across the table to Emma.

Emma panned the screen to see a recently published article, immediately recognizing Hunter's face amongst a group of other people in the picture plastered directly under the headline.

"That's Hunter," Emma confirmed. "How do you know him?"

"Everyone knows him," Baylee rattled. "His family is like the Warren Buffet of restaurants in the East Coast."

Emma froze.

"What restaurants do they own?"

"Too many to count," Baylee pondered. "They definitely have a foothold of most of the places in the city."

"Quinn's Steakhouse?"

Baylee gasped.

"That's where you work! You don't think…"

Speculation was not necessary. Hunter knew the exact street. It could not have been a coincidence.

"This is blowing my mind," Emma said. "He gave me a ride to work when we first met. That is, until I ended up not even going…"

Baylee gasped.

"You *skipped* work for him? That's it, you love him. It's official."

"Okay, whatever you say."

"What does your boyfriend think about all of this?"

Emma paused at the sound of her ringing phone.

"Speak of the devil," she sighed, seeing Jack's name illuminated on her phone.

"I'll give you the room."

"You don't have to do that," Emma set her phone face down on the table.

"You're not going to answer him?"

Emma shook her head. Ducking his calls was becoming habitual, and new priorities that came with a new city and school – in addition to her developing acquaintance with Hunter – well, it was safe to assume that her intolerance for Jack was growing.

"I better get ready," she sighed and left to her room.

Baylee cheered in excitement. Her contributions were a godsend – not only due to her logistical and relationship aide – but the ease Emma felt in the development of their unbroken friendship, which was supplemented through their like minds and similar interests in the arts. It brought closure to Emma's peace of mind, embracing her spontaneous decision to come here in the first place.

While she was secretly looking forward to seeing Hunter that evening, Emma grew more hesitant by the second to reveal her true emotions on the matter. She was too busy allowing the thought of Jack to dwell on her decision, as she wondered what he would be thinking if he ever found out that she would be doing this. It is not that she had completely moved on. In that regard, it is essentially impossible to say that anyone could definitively let go of someone that once meant so much to them.

*****

Hunter sent a car for Emma that evening. It would have struck her as odd if it were not for Baylee's exceptional skill in profiling him as a member of one of the wealthiest families in New York. A customary approach he used on all his dates? Likely so, but impressive either way. The initial infatuation was already shifting into a more meaningful adoration – which troubled Emma – for as long as she convinced herself to not fall for another guy, the adverse outcome seemed almost inevitable at this point, playing out of her control. Emma glanced down at her silvery dress, mesmerized at the shimmering from the diamond necklace around her neck as it reflected off the neons of the world outside, smearing a colorful mosaic across the tinted windows.

It was not long before she noticed they were already uptown and pulling up to the restaurant, where she saw Hunter waiting at the curb.

The driver promptly left the car and circled around to Emma's door, gently taking her out and settling her hand in Hunter's.

"I feel like a celebrity," Emma joked as Hunter guided her into the restaurant.

"You look fantastic."

"Thanks," she acknowledged uneasily.

They were met with a host who skipped them past the line and to a private table on the opposite end of the restaurant.

Emma had forgotten everything she once knew about fine dining at the sight of the marvelous spread on their table. She noticed how opposite her reaction to the presentation was to Hunter, who did not appear impressed in the slightest. He seated Emma and then circled to his side, where he thanked the host before joining her.

"What do you think? Isn't this great?"

Emma's mouth was already stuffed when he asked, prompting him to dismiss his question and follow her lead.

"Sorry, this is amazing," Emma finally said between chews.

"Don't apologize. I'm just happy that you like it," Hunter said as he placed a napkin on his lap. "How was the rest of your afternoon? Are you feeling good about your first day?"

"I thought it would be easier," she admitted. "I'm excited for the challenge though. It's nothing like what I am used to back home."

"You mean in Seattle?"

"Good memory," Emma noted, her eyes panning around the restaurant. She admitted how the posh furnishings complemented the swank vibe observable through the distinctive artifacts accessorized across the obsidian walls. The environment was strikingly close to the *Crepuscolo,* which he helplessly connected to Jack's choice of their first date.

Jack.

She regretted having her thoughts wander to him at such an inappropriate time. Here she was, having dinner with a great guy. The last thing she should think of is her ambivalence about Jack, whose image flashed in her mind faster than an electromagnetic wave in a wire. She wondered what he would say if he knew she was here, especially with a young man she had just begun to realize also possessed staggering similarities.

"Is there something wrong?" came Hunter's voice, bringing Emma's attention back to the table.

The question alone annoyed her, and upon examining Hunter's clueless frown, suspected he may have been playing a similar mind game. Unlike Jack, Hunter was not as subtle with how he demonstrated his exuberant wealth. Yet, he still kept the details of his identity a secret. Emma felt foolish to abandon her skepticism with Jack, who incorporated a higher degree of calculation in his intentional deceit. Understanding how a boy thinks is already frustrating, and although she had no logical reason to group Hunter with her negative connotation with richies, she could not help but wonder if it was an inherent trait they all shared.

She disregarded her instincts when she met Jack, and she was disinclined to do the same this time around.

"You own this restaurant, don't you?"

She immediately wished she could have reconsidered her phrasing. But Hunter did not react how she anticipated, watching as he casually sipped from his glass.

"Why do you ask?"

"Oh, um, nothing," she stammered. "I'm just a little surprised that you never got around to telling me yet."

"Would you feel better if I told I told you everything now?"
"I mean, yes…I guess so."
"Sure," he began, leaning back in his seat. "Yeah, my family owns this restaurant. We also own more around Manhattan, including Quinn's—" he winked at her, recognizing it was where she worked. "—But we own other properties other than restaurants. Let's see, there are a few hotels, apartments, a gym, a couple casinos upstate –"
"Okay, I get it," Emma giggled. "So you guys are rich?"
"We do pretty well," he replied modestly, flashing her a quizzical grin. "In case you happened to be a gold digger."
"I'm not," she assented, holding back her laugh. "But I feel a lot better now that we got it all out of the way."
"Glad to hear it. And if you have any more itching questions, please feel free to let me know," he grinned, opening his hands. "I'm an open book, baby."
Emma blushed.
"What about you?"
"What about me?"
"You value honesty, and I appreciate that," Hunter said. "That said, I think it is only fair if your returned the favor."
"I'm not sure where you're getting at," Emma shrugged, shifting in her chair.
Hunter tilted his head.
"Are there any 'secrets' that you would like to share with me?"
Emma studied Hunter's grin. The only revelation she could think of is her ongoing relationship with Jack, to which Hunter already knew about, to a certain degree.
"Is this about Jack?" she asked.
"Jack," Hunter repeated. "That's the first time you told me his name."
"Is it? I didn't notice."
"You two must not be happy."
"I don't know where you get off assuming that."
"Well, in addition to the fact that this is not the first time he's been brought up, I can also tell that he is on your mind right now."
"You're very confident for someone who could be wrong," she jeered.
"Am I wrong?"
Emma bit her lip.
"I'm sorry, I know you probably feel like I am interrogating you right now – I promise that's not my intention. I'm just curious as to where you head is at with all of this."
He was sincere and understood that it would not be in his best interest if he bidded more patience and returned to the topic of discussion at a later time.

"I have a surprise for you, if you are up for it," he changed the subject, checking the time on his watch.

"I thought the dinner was the surprise?"

Hunter grinned, relieved at the intrigue in Emma's voice.

They finished eating and left the restaurant, where their driver was waiting to take them to the cinema. She watched as the line of people outside turned their attention to them when they pulled up.

"If only we had a red carpet," Hunter joked, taking Emma's hand.

"I don't know the last time I went to the movies."

"You mean the theater?"

"Same difference."

Hunter laughed.

"What's so funny?"

"My friend is one of the actors in the play we are seeing," Hunter explained, once again guiding her past the line and into the venue. "He would have a fit if he heard you say that."

They strolled through the crowded aisle. Plausibly due to his wealth, Emma concluded that Hunter was not just another guy. She was astounded at how many people greeted him on their way to the front, watching as he flashed a genuine smile and engaged in delicate chatter with these strangers. His demeanor echoed similarities to her remembrance of Tommy Beech's, making her question if his emotional intelligence was more adept than she thought. It was a useful skill, mastering the craft of politicking.

"You're very popular," Emma teased when they finally reached the front row. Hunter leaned close to her so only she could hear him.

"If I'm being completely honest, I have no idea who half of those people were."

"Seemed like you did."

Hunter shrugged modestly.

"Years of practice, I guess. Sometimes you have to be someone else just for the sake of making others happy."

Emma giggled.

"I appreciate that you care that much about what I think. But trust me Hunter, you can know no one in this room and it wouldn't affect my happiness."

"Right, *your* happiness. That's what I meant," Hunter muttered hesitantly. His reaction slightly confused Emma, causing her to suspect if his motive to make "others" happy was not a reference to her. Whoever the people were that he tried so hard to impress, it was clear that he was not totally enthusiastic about doing it.

She had no time to delve further, however, as she noticed the lights dimming overhead, prompting Hunter to sit back in his seat and face the stage.

The thought left Emma's mind for the time being. In a strange way, she was relieved by Hunter's quavering reaction. He had been *too* perfect so far, that it was oddly comforting to know that even he could have flaws, even if she was not sure then what they exactly were.

The fifteen minutes driving home posed an appropriate time of reflection for Emma, who momentarily forgot that Hunter was sitting beside her. She revisited their conversation at the restaurant, sorting out a reasonable explanation behind Hunter's sudden questions. She now concluded he was smarter than he looked; there was no doubt about that, anymore. He was also not afraid to make a point, which she found enthralling, as it was a trait she considered uncommon in most boys she entertained.

Hunter rolled down the window and called out to Emma before she reached the door.

"I'd love to do this again."

"I'll make sure to save up for a new dress," she joked.

"Money isn't something you have to worry about when you're with me."

Emma gaped as he rolled up his window and signaled his driver to leave, leaving Emma to overhear the subtle screeches from the tires dragging off the pavement and into the desolate avenue.

A pleasant night for her, overall. To Hunter's point of being an open book, Emma had also perceived her progression of befriending him like a piece of literature: uneasy to read at first glance, but eventually comforted upon being convinced that there was more to him than she initially imagined.

Such an impression was never acknowledged during her time with Jack, whose intense benevolence frustrated Emma beyond words.

She was aware of her inclination to be cynical, and cynicism can only go so far before it potentially jeopardizes her chances of finding the right person.

She mulled over her time so far in New York. What was once a startling quandary had now transcended into an enticing opportunity to live a life she never imagined to be reachable.

This was her life now, and she was not prepared to give it up just yet.

xvi

Night has an ominous connotation. Even the sun's brightest blazes could become eclipsed behind tenebrific wickedness of the souls creeping the earth long after its setting. The shadows left the barren Seattle streets as Tommy scanned the starless sky, thirsting grace from even the narrowest sliver of light to join him. He gripped the bottom of his seat and glanced over to a relaxed Logan, toggling with the radio as they navigated further into the unfamiliar neighborhood.

"You know where we're going, right?" Tommy asked.

"Chill, you got nothing to worry about."

Logan's calmness was unsettling. Due to his natural skepticism, Tommy already found it difficult to trust anyone. Especially Logan Berg, someone he refused to embroil with, had not been for his nagging, curiosity usually getting the best of him.

Logan glowered at the backpack situated between Tommy's legs.

"Can you double-check to make sure I got everything?"

Tommy brought the backpack to his lap and sifted through the cash, shuddering at a handle of the gun. He pulled it out, now more anxious by the weight of it in his hand.

"Are we going to need this?"

"Geez, quit being a pussy. You've been hanging with Jack for too long."

Logan chuckled, taking the gun and stashing it under his jacket.

Tommy frowned and zipped up the backpack.

His disdain for Logan traces back to a field trip at the zoo with his elementary class. Tommy was nine, vividly observant, loved animals, and had a reclusive upbringing; the perfect combination for someone who once aspired to become a zoologist. Watching them sordidly bordered off in captivity was disappointing, but under practical circumstances, it was the best opportunity he could ask for.

It was then he met Logan. His mischievousness was the first thing he noticed, utterly speechless the first instance he witnessed Logan snap back at the guide and mock harmless questions from the rest of the classmates.

His judgement was replaced with joy when they reached the big cat exhibit, where they watched a Bengal tiger rummage through the remains of its meal. The children were in collective wonderstruck, exchanging delighted chitters as they lined the exhibit and tapped on the glass to get the tiger's attention. Tommy, too, was thrilled when the tiger finally lifted its head and peered back at them. Its enormous size was staggering, with a thick coat blazed in orange and black. Tommy pressed his hand on the glass as the tiger strode past him, pausing momentarily and setting its amber stare back at him. It was a memory he never forgot.

The dream suddenly turned nightmarish, however, when Logan jolted out of the throng and onto the ledge, proceeding to beat profoundly on the glass. The tiger tensed at the resounding vibration, letting out a whimper and folding its ears as it scuttled off into its den.

Some children began to cry, and the teacher pulled Logan off the ledge and scolded him. The fascination suddenly evaporated. And that beautiful moment for Tommy, was stolen.

His unhinged personality was unexpected at the time, but Tommy later concluded that personalities were not totally aligned with their upbringing. Or at least how he perceived it. The idea of Logan resorting to distasteful activity did not surprise Tommy, but drug dealing? He never imagined having a friend who did it willingly.

Even as the years went on, Tommy relived that experience, and the consequential resentment he felt for Logan. First impressions have a lasting impact on how a person's outlook is shaped, especially for children. And in Tommy's case, it was unflinchingly negative toward Logan.

He judged Logan for this lifestyle, yet he acknowledged its perks, including a change of scene from his usual routine. He could have stayed home. He did not have to come. But he rationalized having occasional glimpses into the other side was fine as long as he controlled his urges. Nothing wrong with just having a taste.

So he thought.

"How is Jack, by the way?"

"He's good. We missed you at his birthday party."

"A bunch of kids bragging about whose parents got them the nicest car? Not my type of scene."

A poor delinquent shitting on the privileged. Go figure.

"Speaking of parents: your dad's been killing it lately," Logan continued.

"Yeah," Tommy sighed. Everyone in the world knew the renowned data scientist Harrison Beech, and in connection, knew of Tommy: the prodigal child destined to carry the torch and revolutionize the industry.

They parked in an empty lot except for another car on the opposite end.

"They're early. That's a first," Logan observed. "Give me the bag. And just be cool, you got it?"

Tommy followed Logan out the car and started toward the center of the lot, where they were met with two other men, cloaked in black. One was holding a bag, the other opening his arms at Logan.

"Berg!" he greeted. "It is unlike you to not come alone."

"Nice to see you again, Baker," Logan said, embracing him before nodding at the bagman behind him.

"How are you doing, Dunn?"

Dunn nodded silently and exchanged bags with him.

They stood there awkwardly as Dunn inspected the bag's contents.

"It's all here," he confirmed.

"Always is," Logan added, shaking Baker's hand. "Until next time?"

He swung the new bag over his shoulder and rejoined Tommy.

"That was pretty quick," Tommy whispered to Logan.

"Told you. There's nothing to worry about."

"Hey," Dunn called out, pointing at Tommy. "Where do I know you from?"

Tommy returned a confused expression.

"I know your face from somewhere," he added. "What's your name man?"

"He's one of my friends," Logan clarified.

"Oh *shit*," Dunn's eyes widened. "You're Thomas Beech!"

"I don't know who that is," Logan cut in, stepping in front of Tommy. "Like I said, he's just one of my friends who wanted to tag along."

Dunn faced Baker. "That's Harrison Beech's son! I remember seeing a picture of them on the news last week."

"Is that so?" Baker raised a brow, glancing over at Tommy. "Is that right, boy? Your dad is Harry Beech?"

Tommy was unsure how to react. He was not a celebrity by any means, and generally went about unnoticed by virtually everyone, especially a couple gangbangers who he doubted could tell their left from right.

"Don't listen to your guy, Baker," Logan warned. "You'd be making a fool of yourself."

"You think so?" Baker ginned menacingly. "Because what I'm hearing is that your friend there has a zillionaire of a dad who would be willing to pay a pretty penny for his son's safety."

"Come on Baker, after everything we've been through…"

Baker lowered his head.

"You know what, Logan? You're right. You and I have always been able to see through our differences and come to an agreement. Let's make another deal—"

Dunn produced a gun from his cloak, resting it beside his leg.

"We will cut you in on however much Harry will pay us for pretty boy. We're not going to hurt him, just a classic ransom gig and we all get paid in the end," he pointed at Tommy. "And if you play along, we'll even give you a cut. Win-win."

"Stealing from my own dad is a wild offer. This is ridiculous, right Logan?" Logan turned hesitantly to Tommy.

Baker's offer was tempting. He was against including Tommy in his shady antics to begin with. It seemed that fate had dealt him a favorable hand, and at the expense of someone he was not at best terms with.

Nevertheless, Logan knew he would forever blame himself for willingly putting his friend in this predicament. As reluctant as he was to admit it, he did not want anything to happen to Tommy.

Logan mouthed his lips for only Tommy to read.

Run.

At that moment, Tommy's feet took over, scurrying back and sliding behind the car.

"Get back here!" Dunn shouted and discharged his gun in the air before pointing at them. Tommy covered his ears, holding back his screams at the bullets splintering into the car protecting him before scampering off the parking lot. He cut into a clearing across the street, his feet moving faster than he thought possible.

The wind was like a serrated edge slicing through his numbed skin, and he felt blood pulsated through his aching muscles. His vision blackened, occasionally tripping over his own feet as he overheard two final shots penetrate through the chilly air. The commotion behind him gradually fizzled, prompting him to slow his pace until he arrived at a playground. He took shelter under the slide, peering behind him as he shifted in the pebbles. The profound heartbeat steadily receded back in his chest, followed by the deafened mute in his ears. Before long, silence returned.

He collected his breath. Seconds seemed like minutes, and minutes like hours. Suddenly, he was startled at the sight of a police cruiser speeding into the park. Tommy jumped to his feet to run, but immediately lost all feeling in his body. His hands were the first to go. His arms came next. Then his legs and feet. He stared into the blinding headlamps as he fell to his knees. He kept his eyes glued to the asphalt when the sirens finally shut off. He heard a car door close. Footsteps. And then, two large palms wrapping around his wrists and pulling them behind his back and bringing him back to his feet. He winced at the subtle pinch of the weighted cuffs on his wrist. Another officer appeared in front of him, aiming a flashlight directly in his face.

"Don't move," the officer ordered. "Tell me what you are doing out here." Tommy was unaware that he had begun crying, shaking off the tears rolling down his numbed cheeks.

"Please don't hurt me. I didn't do anything wrong."
"Shut up! Answer my question: why are you out here?"
"Let's relax a minute," the other officer paused, looking at Tommy. "The cuffs are just a formality, kid. You're not under arrest."
They guided Tommy to their cruiser.
"Take them off," the same officer said, pointing at the cuffs.
"Are you sure?"
"The boy is more likely to piss himself than act up. Go on."
The officer did as instructed, releasing Tommy.
"Open your eyes, son. It's all right."
Tommy peeked at the two officers starting back at him, his back to the car. He squinted to read their badges, *Briar,* and *Gentry.*
"Let's start over, okay?" Briar spoke up. "What's your name?"
"T-Tommy."
"Okay Tommy," the officer continued, motioning his colleague to lower his flashlight. "We apologize for giving you a scare. We had reports of gunfire in the area. Do you know anything about that?"
"Um, I don't know."
"You don't know?" Gentry snapped. "What does that mean?"
"Gentry," the Briar scolded. "Look kid, we're just looking for some answers if you could help us out here."
"Yes," Tommy stammered. "Gunfire – yes, there was gunfire. I heard gunfire."
"Can you tell us more? Where was it coming from?"
Tommy panned around the dark, failing to recognize his surroundings.
"There were two men. They wanted to take me, and I was told to run; and I ended up here."
"So you were there? And with someone?" Gentry probed.
"Yes…my friend…"
"Does your friend have a name?"
"Logan…Logan Berg."
Gentry gave a heartless chuckle. "Of course he's involved."
"Logan Berg is your friend?" Briar interjected.
"Well yes," Tommy began, choosing his words. "We grew up together."
"What were you doing with him this late at night?"
"He asked if I wanted to come with him to…"
"Hold on," Briar stopped him, producing his notepad to take notes. "Before we go any deeper, I think we should get your information down: what's your full name?"
"I thought you said I wasn't in trouble—"

"Formalities, kid. You have nothing to worry about if you didn't do anything. Now, your name."
Thomas Beech," Tommy replied. "B-E-E-C-H."
Briar stopped writing, raising his eyes to Tommy.
"Your name is Thomas Beech?"
"Yes."
Briar put away his notepad and nudged Gentry.
"I need to talk to you," he muttered before turning to Tommy. "Wait here.."
Tommy remained still as the officers paced away from him, periodically glancing back at him as the exchanged indistinct whispers.
A couple minutes passed before they returned, all forms of tension seeming to have evaporated.
"Here's what is going to happen son," Briar started. "We will send word out and get to the bottom of all of this. In the meantime, how about you give your parents a call and let them know that we will be giving you a ride home, okay?"
Tommy was shocked at his welcoming tone.
"What about Logan?"
"You said that Logan Berg was there with you when the firing started?"
"Yeah."
"We understand," Gentry smirked, "Don't worry about your friend. We'll take care of everything."
Tommy texted his parents and was guided to the backseat of the cruiser, where he was escorted home.
His head was spinning, as he pictured the crestfallen frown on Logan's face, rehearing the single word he had spoken before leaving him.
Run.
Tommy trembled in his seat, forcing himself to analyze every detail from what transpired in the parking lot. He wondered how his friend became involved with those gangbangers. And his willingness to bring him – knowing the plausible chance of the encounter becoming dangerous – it troubled Tommy, who truly believed in giving people the benefit of the doubt. Was it possible that Logan had maliciously orchestrated the whole thing? Highly unlikely, but Tommy knew it was not something he would put past him. Logan's singular outlook was very much like his own.
Due to his natural distrust of others, the notion that Logan was capable of threatening Tommy's future was nothing new. What was new, however, was the inclination that he was brilliant enough to calculate its success. Tommy wondered if his thoughts simply resulted from his surging paranoia

after what he had just witnessed, or rather, the door to another revealing, sinister truth.

Regardless, Tommy hoped that Logan was okay; that nothing horrible happened to him. He wondered where he was…whether he was even still alive…

He remembered his parents, half asleep in robes when they greeted him at the driveway; he remembered his mother rushing up to hug him, kissing his forehead; he remembered his father speaking with the cops while the neighbors straggled out of their homes to witness the unnatural presence of a police car in their neighborhood; above all, he remembered an intriguing revelation.

The Universe has a twisted sense of humor in revealing one's perception of truth at the expense of another's demise. It was at that moment that Tommy came to realize who he was: his privilege, and the degree of influence he was capable of potentially achieving; that he would always seek the best scenario from any obstacles that dare cross him.

Tommy always respected Logan because of their like mindsets. He understood that Logan also saw things in a way different from the world. Fundamental, philosophical, moralistic, ways. Unfortunately for Logan, the key difference between him and Tommy was the quality of their upbringing. Tommy never had an initial intent on capitalizing off of Logan's misfortune, but with further contemplation, he would come to believe that this may be an ideal case for him to achieve everything he ever wanted.

And as for his best friend, Jack Douglas…oh Jack, the weak-minded soul; Tommy could smell his potent naivety from where he stood across the street amongst the spectators, standing before his parents. He was his brother. And as much as he loved him and wanted what was best for him, he would pity him from then on. Jack's value was heightened with the inclusion of his tremendous wealth. From his birth, he was offered so much promise, but was incapable of demonstrating it effectively due to riddling insecurities holding him back. Everyone should be strong-willed, and those who were not are to be treated accordingly. Jack needed guidance, and riddance from any and all distractions, specifically the toxicity that was Logan Berg.

The ball will always be in Tommy's court – literally, and figuratively. Nevertheless, it's an understatement to say that at only seventeen years old, he had much to learn. One lesson in particular: there will always be consequences for one's actions.

xvii

Hey Em :) just checking in. How are things?

good hbu

They're good! Suit shopping with the boys rn, we're supposed to look our best for next week.
Which reminds me: are you still planning on flying in this weekend? I can pick you up from the airport.

shoot i'm sorry. i haven't had the time to tell you.
i'm staying in NY for Thanksgiving.

What why?

i just don't think it's worth spending a lot of money on a plane ticket when I also have to be back for class first thing Monday...
also my friends here are staying, so we're just going to have a friendsgiving here

Makes sense. I wish you would have told me sooner. I told my parents that you would be joining.

i'm sorry, i had no idea until like yesterday

You said you would come though…how did you have no idea?

well i figured after how we left things that it would be off the table

I see.
What if I paid for your flight? And anything else you would need while you're here

lol

What?

it's like you didn't listen to anything i said jack.

How do you mean? I'm just offering to pay for your plane ticket.

it's not just about the money

I never said it was?
What's wrong? talk to me

nothing. i'm fine.

Are you sure?

yes why wouldn't i be sure of how i'm feeling

Idk you seemed okay last time I texted you, and you're clearly being short with me right now. Obviously something is wrong

so now you're saying something is wrong w me bc you think i'm being short with you? honestly jack where do you get off

I'm sorry, I don't mean to be escalating anything. Tbh I don't even know what's going on right now

i just have a lot of stuff to deal with here. Idk what you are asking of me.

Maybe be a little bit more communicative? I mean come on Em, I haven't seen you in months. And before you left we agreed that we would be back together for Thanksgiving. Like, we literally talked about this so many times even after you left.

and I told you why i can no longer make it. what more do you want me to say?

I don't know.
I guess I just don't understand why your friends staying has anything to do with you coming here.
And then you just hit me with this news like really last minute, like idk what to even say to my parents.

you're making this such a bigger deal than it is.

I think it's justified if I do, don't you? You're flaking on me.

lol flaking huh?

You know I don't like it when you say lol because it makes it seem like you're being dismissive with me.

idc jack. i already feel bad for not being able to come next week, and you're trying to make me feel worse for absolutely no reason.

Because you've been short with me this entire conversation

i don't think i am being short?

I feel like you know what you're doing.

and what is that jack?

It's like you want me to be the bad guy here. and if I did get mad it gives you a reason to stop talking to me.

jesus you can be so difficult to talk to sometimes. do you not see that you are doing all of this on your own?

That's not true and you know it. There is always another side to everything.

...
sorry jack. but I don't think this is working.

What do you mean?

things have just been happening here. I don't want to get into it right now

Um okay not sure what you're saying?

i am ending this conversation

**Wtf Em you can't seriously mean that
Tell me what's going on
What happened to full transparency?**

i have to go.

> *Look I'm sorry, okay? I just care about you. I want to know what's going on, that's all.*

...

> *Emma?*

...

> *So now you're just not going to reply? I know that you're ignoring me on purpose.*

"Hey Jack! Get off your phone, I need your advice."
Jack lifted his head to see Kevin holding a pair of suit jackets.
"Black or blue?"
"Black."
Kevin studied the suits in his hands, nodding at the black one.
"Yeah, I think you're right."
Tommy came up to Jack, glossing over his shoulder to read Emma's name in his phone.
"Judging from your demeanor, I take it that you and Emma are arguing again?"
"'Arguing' is an understatement."
"What are you two fighting about now?"
"No, we're not doing this," Kevin interjected. "Jack, you promised us that today is for the boys, and *only* the boys."
"I don't remember saying that."
"It was heavily implied."
From the corner of his eye, Jack spotted Tommy looking intently at his phone and bring it to his ear, stepping away from the group.
Isaac and Bennett joined them, each holding a suit.
"I'm good to go," Bennett said, beaming a wide smile. "Saac and I decided to go matching. We're going to pretend to be a couple."
"I'm telling Naylah," Kevin chirped.
"Please do. It's about time she knows the truth."
"You do realize that most of the people at the dinner will be our neighbors, right? People that have known us for years and have seen us with girlfriends."
"Screw you, I have the freedom to change my sexual orientation anytime I want," Isaac spat.
"I don't think that's how it works."
"How do you know how it works, Saac? Have you ever tried yourself?"
Issac glanced at Jack. "Want to help me out here?"
"I have no part in this," Jack murmured, raising his hands. "Let's just get our stuff and get the hell out of here."

Tommy was slow to rejoin the group. He pulled his phone away from his face, giving Jack a troubling expression.

"That was Morgan," he shared. "I don't know how to tell you this…"

Jack matched Tommy's nervous expression.

"What's going on?" he pressed.

Tommy pulled Jack away from the rest of the boys, whispering so that only he could hear.

"Don't quote me on this, but I think Emma may have met a guy in New York."

Jack immediately broke out in hysterical laughter.

"What are you talking about man?"

"Morgan didn't get into it, but I could tell that was what she was hinting at."

"Come on, Tom. Be serious."

"I am."

At that, Jack's smile disappeared. He studied Tommy's intense stare, his heart sinking upon acknowledging the possibility. He did not want to believe it. He refused to believe it.

Jack peered back at his phone to reread his messages with Emma.

Things have been happening here.

Things have been happening: was her hesitance to reveal the truth because of another guy? How could something like this occur so quickly? What compelled her to move on, when she was aware how it would affect him?

To Jack, there were two potential explanations: Emma had actually moved on, or she was so deep in denial of her feelings for him that she had chosen to rebound with another man; the latter of which Jack had hoped to be true.

"I was just texting her…I literally asked her about what was going on, and she didn't even mention it."

"Sounds about right," Tommy estimated, shrugging.

Jack's gaze drifted off his phone and back at his friend.

"I did this," he uttered.

"No you didn't."

"Yes, I did. I knew Emma was hurt by how angry I got when we last talked. I paved the way for her to end up with someone else."

"Hey, shit happens. You know that."

"You don't actually believe that."

"No, I don't," Tommy admitted. "But you do, and that's all that matters, right?"

Jack fell silent, still struggling to process the news.

Perhaps this was just a phase of Emma's. It would be foolish of him to not expect her to endure one every so often.

There was once a time when Jack believed he and Emma were soulmates. The perfect match, unsusceptible to weaken from the external forces operating around them. If the attraction of opposites happened to be true, then she was undoubtedly his antithesis. She was the harmony to his melody. Without her, the fusion of instrumentals would break, forcing him to improvise over what he once believed was already written. The rhapsody had ended, but Jack did not grow mute. He was sure that she would come back. She had to. Until then, he would change the tune, transitioning into a solo as he hummed along to the blues, exercising patience for Emma's return to the stage.

Perhaps it was Jack's delusion that drove him to try and make it work with Emma. Or perhaps, it was a clear motive. He did not care how long it would take, or how many obstacles that was sure to present itself. He knew that as long as he continued to love Emma, she would eventually return to him. That she would be his. Forever.

*****

Emma fixated on the marble tombstone recently placed where her father rests. The plot was still topped with fresh dirt, speckles brushing against her exposed ankles as she adjusted her dress swimming through the wind's gentle whips. In addition to Bruce's name, inscribed the phrase: Forever in Our Hearts.

Forever.

Such a classic word is used in theory, but rarely accepted in practice. What constitutes perpetuity when observed through the lens of beings only capable of temporal experiences? If it is only understood by conceptualizing its reality, was it ever intended to be real, or simply a guise for one's consciousness to alleviate pain from ultimate acceptance of its falsehood?

She was emotionless during the reception that took place immediately after, where she escaped to a corner away from the gathering. Every now and then, Emma could overhear fragments of the muted talks between Julia and the other adults, all of whom steeped in nervous sympathy to not smother the young daughter for her loss, and instead give condolences and filled promises to her equally devastated mother. There were many faces Emma recognized, many she did not, but most of whom unbeknownst to her held high roles in society, and higher admiration for Bruce Keva.

"Emma is a star student at Davidson, and you know of all her achievements that directly benefit our administration. We want to work with you in any way to ensure she continues to have the best possible experience leading up to her graduation," the academy's director shared with Julia, leaning in closer. "And

between us, I owe it to your husband to do whatever I can to make sure you get whatever you need."
There were several others who gave similar assurances to Julia, most of which even she was unsure of the detail behind what Bruce did to earn their debt. Eventually, she came over to Emma.
"I know it's hard, but you should try talking to the people here," she consoled. "It's good to hear more about the kind of person your father was."
Emma turned stiffly to her mother.
"I *know* who my dad was more than anyone else here. What could I possibly get from listening to them? It won't change the fact that he's gone."
Julia nodded off her daughter's contempt and inched closer.
"Don't be afraid that things may change from this. Everything will get better with time. We will get through it all together, okay?"
Emma shook her head.
"How can you say that when we both know you have no idea what is going to happen? I'm tired of being kept in the dark about things. I didn't even know he was sick until after the fact – do you think that was a good choice, to leave me in the dark like that?"
"I was respecting your dad's wish, he didn't want you to feel burdened by this. You're too young to understand—"
"That's the problem mom. You all see me as this defenseless girl who can't take care of herself."
"Emma, that's not true."
"It clearly is. Next you're going to tell me that I shouldn't go to college and start a family instead."
"You're bringing that up again," she sighed. "I didn't mean it like it was one or the other, I was just trying to explain that you are not expected to do anything you don't want to do. Your dad and I—"
"Please mom, not now okay?" Emma pled, tears returning to her eyes. "Just leave me alone right now."
Julia lowered her head, noting her daughter's like stubbornness.
"Okay, I'll come get you when it is time to go," she muttered before leaving to rejoin the gathering.
Emma did not care when they would leave. She did not care about anything. Her father was gone, and the blame could only be pointed at the invisible perpetrator that aggressively invaded his pancreas and left him with an expiration date too short to even consider the aftermath of its impact. At least the silver lining favored Bruce, who no longer was burdened with the idea of falling short of his hopes for the future. But for Emma, it was the opposite. Not only was she pressured to imagine her future without him; she was forced

to endure it with every waking day. Life is not permanent, so what benefit is there to believe that there is permanence in anything?

Man may live through moments that he and the rest of the world may claim unforgettable and etched in history, but what does it matter if all who remember will eventually cease to be remembered? A memory only lasts as long as its essence, but once what *is* becomes what *was,* then was it truly ever different from nothing at all?

Emma did not view her fate and legacy as only hers anymore. It had expanded, like a lie stretched so thin that it believes itself.

If that meant shouldering the weight of further etching Bruce's name in the stones of humanity, then who better prepared and most willing than the daughter who was shaped in his image?

It has to be me, she thought to herself, rising from her chair and storming out of the venue. Julia was right that everything will get better with time, for as long as Emma breathed on this earth, she will demonstrate the upside to never waiting for Time to mark its end.

xviii

Thanksgiving: renowned by calendrists as a historic event held on the fourth Thursday of November every year, when Americans commemorate their ancestors' shared harvests amidst the eventual establishment of a young nation. It signified a time for reunion, sharing stories, and engaging in traditional activities, all typically circulated around a usually glamorous palette of earthy foods and tasty desserts.

It was a unique occasion at the Douglas household, however, as it was not necessarily a family dinner, but rather an exquisite business party: a time when they could display their glowingly admirable societal achievements to fellow elites, largely with the goal of further solidifying their sphere of influence.

Jack was very much looking forward to it, only because it marked one of the few times a year he interacted with both his parents for longer than an hour.

"Wow, I haven't been here in *forever*," Tommy bellowed when they entered the house.

"Is my tie straight?" Isaac grogged. "I don't think Bennett did it right."

"Watch a tutorial on YouTube next time then!"

Jack ignored them.

"Okay boys, come here quick."

They huddled in the entryway, dipping their heads closer to Jack so he could speak softly.

"I know I probably don't need to say this since it's been the same message for years now, but I would like to remind everyone again to please know where we are tonight. This is *not* a party. It may look like it is, but it is *not*. Does everyone understand?"

"We're not idiots, Jack," Kevin said. "You can speak to us like human beings."

"You sure about that?"

"Jack's just nervous," Bennett eased. "He doesn't want to get a spanking from daddy Wayne."

"Please don't refer to him as my daddy."

"Daddy Wayne!" Tommy squealed. "That's *hilarious*."

"Okay, you have thirty seconds to get it all out of your system, but once we break, I ask that you all please be on your best behavior."

"Jesus man, quit worrying so much," Bennett assured. "We won't be assholes."

Jack nodded and guided them into the ballroom. He noticed the hushed conversations from the other guests when they entered. Many of the attendees knew Jack and his friends *very* well. Growing up, they were commonly referred to by the "ShenaniGang," – a combination of the words *shenanigan* and *gang,* respectively. Not to say that Jack and the boys ever engaged in gang-related activities, but they were, well, disruptive. Especially from the perspective of Dr. Peter Beaufort.

In addition to officially coining them as the ShenaniGang, Beaufort was adamant in stirring complications for Jack and his friends, never refraining to recall his frequent run-ins with the boys in the past. An infamous anecdote traces back to one particular Halloween, when following a graceful autumn evening of family trick-or-treating, the boys came out to engage in their usual antics. Beaufort singled out Tommy B, who upon successfully rallying a few dozen preteens, persuaded them to deliver a series of undesirable pranks on their neighbors, including but not limited to: tee-peeing, egging, ding-dong ditching, invisible roping, batting over mailboxes, and Tommy's personal favorite: the *porchshit,* which involved a brave soldier with an angry stomach to sneak up to a house and relieve oneself at the doorstep. There was something about this time of year that caused Tommy to reach peak menace status.

Dr. Beaufort saw Tommy first as the gaggle sifted through the crowd, prompting him to leave his group and intercept them.

"Happy Thanksgiving boys!" Dr. Beaufort huffed, glowering down at Tommy.

"Bowey!" Tommy scoffed, leaning in for a hug that Beaufort resisted. Their contempt for each other was obvious.

"It's good to see you all back home for the holiday," Beaufort scoffed. "I was hoping you would choose to stay on campus tonight."

"As much as we all would have enjoyed that, I have an obligation to be here for my parents," Jack politely reasoned. "I'm sure you understand."

"Of course, Mr. Douglas," Beaufort replied cordially, never having any disdain for his colleague's son. "Nevertheless, I will never know what you see in your friends here," he switched his focus to Tommy. "Especially this one."

"Lick me, Bowey." Tommy snapped back, causing Jack to slap his shoulder while the others erupted in laughter.

Jack shook Beaufort's hand and gave an apologetic nod before letting him rejoin the crowd. He turned back to Tommy, alarmed by his unneeded pugnaciousness. Tommy had a reputation for intentionally disrupting the peace, and while it usually sparked from friendly banter, it never failed to resort to a thunderous outrage. Jack knew his friend did not care about self-justification but playing devil's advocate out of pure intrigue and spite. It used to rile him up in the past, but he had since found it amusing.

"I know I know, I'll be on my best behavior, but Bowey is an exception."

"Fair enough," Jack chuckled, panning around the ballroom. "I'm going to find my parents. I'll be back in a bit."

Jack proceeded from the commonspace, slightly anxious about the unfamiliarity of the new additions integrated into the already opulent interior. It was eclectically decorated with a pair of roomy sectionals and lacquered nesting tables, adorned with multicolored throws that overlayed nearly every piece of furniture. The grand fireplace was ablaze, its light reflecting the showcase of family portraits that sat atop of the mantel. He observed the multitude of artwork framed across the walls, a few of which were protected in dusty plastic due to its noticeably aging condition. This impressive attention to detail had to be the work of his mother.

It was comforting ages ago, when he was a child coming home from school and kicking his shoes off and joining his parents as they gazed out the broadening, luscious landscape of the northern Cascades.

He especially treasured his memories during the winter when his parents spent more time at home. Numerous late evening discussions, entertained by his parents' playful handling over whatever topic they chose to delve into that night. It progressed like clockwork, basking in the still-warm sunset before night took course.

An inviting aroma drew him to the kitchen, where he was greeted with a platter of colorful foods neatly situated across the island bar. Meats, fruits, and rich commodities were of abundance, organized according to their respective course.

Sure enough, his mother appeared from the pantry cradling a fruit basket. Her pristine dress complemented her luxurious jewelry, partially blinding Jack as it twinkled under the recessed lighting.

Anita Douglas was credentialed as one of the most competent physicians on the West Coast. While her intelligence was already impressive – being the youngest valedictorian in her home state of Texas – her family is to thank for her success, who achieved all means in expediting her collegiate career and subsequent stronghold over the leadership at one of the top medical networks in the nation. Like her son, poverty never defined her. She grew up with a silver spoon in her mouth; maybe a gold spoon; actually, a gold spoon brimmed with caviar…yeah, that sounds about right.

"Jack!" she exclaimed, setting down the crate and speeding around the bar to embrace her son.

"Hi mom. You're really going all out this year, huh?"

Anita glowed over the eloquent platters.

"I got help from Romero and his family. It was a travesty having to get this all set up, you just missed the craziness."

"A lot more people this year, too. Are we crowdfunding for a yacht or something?"

"Very funny," Anita played along, maintaining her bright smile as she returned to behind the bar. "We were actually expecting *more*, but unfortunately the staffers at the French embassy couldn't make it." She tossed an assortment of produce into the scorching wok. "How are you though? I bet school is certainly taking a toll this time of year."

"'Toll' is an understatement," Jack replied, taking a seat at the bar to watch her. "I brought the boys again this year, I hope that was okay."

"Oh please, you know you don't have to even ask. They're family at this point."

Jack smiled. "Where's dad?"

"He's in his study," his mom recalled. "You know how he is, never been a fan of these functions."

Jack surely did. His father was a lot of things, but a socialite was not one of them.

He embraced his mother and left for the private study upstairs: an open, hazy room, with paneled walls crawling with countless plaques and pictures, transmitting an unsubtle projection of success. And sure enough, there he was: Wayne Douglas, contradicting his well-known perception of a man driven by progress, as he enjoyed his little time of leisure engrossed in his journal, exchanging his cigar on the eloquent ashtray for a self-stirred cocktail. Although he was a member of the elite, Wayne was often overlooked due to his loathe for participating in their needless extravagance. Unlike his wife, Wayne struggled to reach his prominence as the founder and president of the most powerful consulting firm that was the Douglas Group. He had to first face the horrors of life and its cynical game over questioning humanity's perception of happiness and fortune. Ethics was far more than a word to him, as it defined virtually every challenge he has every faced in his long life. Contrary to his cold demeanor, he was very sensitive as a child; flooded with naivety, with a willingness to comfort others at the expense of his own wellbeing. Emotion was his friend, as it never judged him, nor bound him to acting in his self-interest. It was not until losing his parents when he was inevitably forced to recognize the denial of reality, hardening himself for his own protection.

He never saw the world the same, and disallowed his heart to open up again in what he perceived as a living, hopeless hell. That is, until he met Anita.

For many, it remains a mystery as to how their love prevailed. Having a firsthand glimpse of the fruitful dynamic between them was probably what drove Jack's trivial endeavor to find his own love. Perhaps it was his own delusion, believing he could achieve a similar feat. But is it delusion if the feat could be realistically attained? Maybe, just maybe, he had no power to change his eventual fate. If it was true, then was it truly power he possessed, or the *idea* of power?

Thankfully in Jack's case, such extrapolation for the truth was not needed. His parents were successful in their relationship and individual careers. They made it work. And as for Jack? Well, he was primed to ultimately reap the rewards.

"Whatcha reading?" he asked, circling around his father and gandering at his paper.

The text was barely legible under the dim lights, however Jack could make out a faded picture of a building. He squinted closer to see that the picture was not faded, but the building itself, blanketed in a gray haze. The still shot of the scorched tower was encircled by helicopters, some of which were brimmed with people in dismay.

Wayne took another sip of his whisky, gesturing to the bottle on the desk.

"You want some?"

"Seriously?"

Wayne poured another glass and handed it to Jack, prompting him to take it as if it were a shot. The bitter taste hit him instantly, choking lightly from the burn in his throat as he managed to keep it down.

"Drinking whiskey is like living life son," Wayne started, refilling the glass. "It is more delightful if you take the time to savor it."

"I see why you and Tommy B get along so well," Jack replied, noting their shared use of analogies.

Wayne set aside the newspaper.

"How are you?"

Jack took a seat across from his father.

"I'm good."

Wayne heard the hesitant tone in his son's reply.

"Good? What's troubling you Jack?"

"Nothing important." Jack hesitated, his thoughts briefly landing on Emma. The room fell silent for a moment before Wayne spoke up.

"It's a girl, is it not?"

"How did you know?"

"I can see it in your face," Wayne said. "I started having the same look after I met your mother."

Jack wondered what his expression was telling but was then distracted from his father's leeway in another matter that peaked his intrigue.

"When did you realize that mom was the right person for you?"

Wayne straightened in his chair. "Here I was expecting you to tell me about your life."

"I have a lot to learn before I can formulate my own opinion," Jack admitted. "Hearing your story won't hurt."
Wayne chuckled.
"That is a good point. As for your mother, all I can say is there was not sliver of doubt that she was the one when I first met her."
"How though? I mean, I'm not trying to sound pessimistic, but how was she any different than other girls you talked to?"
"It is different for everybody. I do not think there is a right way to loving someone, nor is there an ideal, methodological approach to finding it. I guess you can say that it is all about how *you* feel in that moment. If it is not love, the instance will only be that – fleeting over time—" he finished his whiskey and poured another glass. "That never happened with your mom."
Jack's expression tightened, applying his father's wisdom to his respective predicament.
"So...what's her name?"
"Emma."
"Is she here?"
"No, she's in New York for an art internship. We're on a break, sort of."
"Ambitious. Good for her," Wayne jested. "Are you sure she is the one?"
Jack shrugged.
"I think so. She checked off all my conditions."
"Conditions? What do you mean, like looks, or—"
"Not really. I wanted to make sure that she was not interested in me because…you know…"
"Because you're rich?" Wayne retorted. "There is no shame in saying it, Jack."
Jack leaned back in his chair.
"Essentially yes. It's always hard to know when a girl likes me, or likes the money."
"I understand," Wayne lowered his head. "You are worried that your wealth will cause people to take advantage of you."
"In a sense."
"What are you doing, lying to these young women about who you are?"
Jack gave an embarrassed nod.
"Oh, I was just being affable there," Wayne exhaled. "Do you not see the problem in your approach?"
"I do," Jack agreed, taking a deep breath. "But it's my only way of making sure that I can find the right person."
"No Jack. You have to be honest, always."

"I mean, I plan to tell them eventually, but I don't see why it is a big deal if I can't filter out the gold diggers from the ones who aren't…" he paused. "Is it wrong to be skeptical of others?"

"Of course not," Wayne assured. "But you should understand that regardless of how hard you try to shape your own expectations, it may not translate to how they perceive it."

"Hmm…care you dumb that down for me?"

"What I am saying is that as long as you never stop being yourself, everything will work out."

"Okay, so what should I do with Emma? I told her everything about me, including 'this'—" he gestured to Wayne's office as he continued. "And to your point, none of it mattered to her. So yes, it was a bad call on my part to lie about it in the first place. But it all worked out."

"Did it, though?" Wayne pressed. "Because if I heard you correctly, you and Emma are currently on a 'break'."

"Well yeah, but that's for something entirely different."

"Is it?"

Jack concentrated on his father's words.

"I know there is an implication here, I just don't know what it is."

Wayne stared at Jack, more serious.

"How would you feel if someone who you trusted lied to you?"

Jack understood his father's point. Emma could have been relieved, or furious when Jack finally told her the truth. But that did not matter, because the deed was already done. Preserving a bond that was already splintered from the start, due to his foolishness. It would not be impossible for them to reach the end when they live happily ever after; but it would now be more difficult than if he told her the truth in the beginning.

Wayne rose from his chair, glass in hand. "Take everything we discussed with a grain of salt. You are in control of your future. And if you see Emma in that, then that is something you must act on and not wait for the opportunity to leave. Remember that."

"Thanks dad."

"Anytime," Wayne swigged the remaining whiskey from the bottle, letting out an amusing belch. "Now, I should head out there or else your mother will surely bend me over tonight. I'll see you out there, okay?"

Wayne Douglas. Here was a man who had everything in the world, yet he treasured love over all of it. Jack envied his father's clarity to distinguish what was most important in his life. If only he could do the same with Emma. He wished she was here. He wanted to speak to her; laugh with her; admire her for everything she was.

Jack eventually returned to the ballroom, taken away on his phone as he scrolled for Emma's contact. He wanted to call her, but after their last conversation, he reckoned texting was more appropriate. He thought of a message that could be perceived as both an icebreaker and apology.

Happy Thanksgiving, Emma. I really miss you.

He watched the message illuminate in a blue bubble before shutting off the screen.

"You seem stressed."

Jack jumped, casting his eyes over to Logan Berg.

"What are you doing here?" Jack scowled, unafraid to display his contempt.

"Your parents invited me."

Jack glared at him.

"Anyways, about the last time we talked," Logan continued. "I was being an ass and I'm sorry."

Jack was alarmed by his sincere tone.

"Thank you," he uttered. "It's no problem. Really."

"Good," Logan sighed. "We actually should talk if you got the time."

"About?"

Logan's voice dwindled to a whisper.

"I would prefer if we took this somewhere private."

"That may not be a simple request," Jack snickered, motioning to the party. "Why don't you tell me here?"

"I don't think *you* would want to have this discussion here," he reiterated, his stare hardening.

Jack studied Logan's expression, his curiosity getting the best of him. He guided him to the corner of the ballroom, away from the crowds.

"This will have to do," Jack relayed. "What is it?"

"It's about Tom."

"Tommy? What about him?"

"Did he ever tell you why I was sent away all those years ago?"

Jack maintained a perplexed gaze.

"I'll take that as a no," Logan assumed. "Given everything that has happened between us, I understand if you think what I am about to say may sound crazy, but you need to hear me out."

The rest of the boys suddenly appeared. Tommy's face steeled at the sight of Logan before turning to Jack.

"What is he doing here?"

"My parents invited him."

Logan stepped in front of Tommy, staring him down. "I was just going to tell Jack about our last night together…remember that, Tommy?"

Tommy's expression quickly changed, disguising his fear with a wry smile. "You shouldn't be here man," he cracked. "Last thing we would want is you starting your usual stupid shit, am I right guys?"

Logan shoved Tommy, prompting the rest of the boys to intercede. They discreetly pulled Logan away from Tommy, pushing him deeper into the corner.

"Fuck you, Tommy!" Logan spat.

"You love to cause unnecessary trouble. When are you going to realize that kind of toxicity isn't welcome?"

"Tommy's right, Berg," Isaac added sympathetically. "This is not the right time nor place."

Logan threw their hands off him, turning back to Jack.

"You should put more thought in who you choose to surround yourself with," he warned.

"Fuck off!" Tommy snarled, his imperious tone causing the rest of the huddle to fall silent.

Logan shot him a hateful glare before storming off.

"What was that about?" Bennett asked.

Just then, Isaac entered Jack's gaze, raising his finger.

"I may have had something to do about that," he frowned regrettably.

The boys gaped in bewilderment.

"*What?*" Tommy glowered.

"We hung out a while ago, and I guess I may have told him that it would have been a good idea if he tried to bury the axe with you guys."

"Okay, one: 'bury the *hatchet*'," Tommy corrected, shaking his head. "And two: what would make you to do something like that?"

"Chill out," Isaac soothed. "It's not easy having to deal with this drama. It's like you've forgotten about how good friends we were."

Tommy lowered his head.

"You're right…I'm sorry."

"What a gimmick." Kevin rasped, turning to Tommy. "Why do you love provocation so much?"

"Because it's hilarious."

"Tommy please, I asked if you could be on your best behavior," Jack pled.

"I'm not feeling myself right now."

"Jacky's not feeling himself?" Isaac chirped.

"I didn't mean it like that."

"Why are you so stressed?" Kevin asked.

"It's Emma," Bennett guessed. "I get it, man. She was your love. And now she's gone."

"Damn, thanks for that great reminder," Jack said sarcastically.

"Why did she have such a hold on you?" Kevin implored. "You two barely dated before she left. It's not like you two were that serious."

"It's not that she had a hold on me," Jack replied, shaking his head. "Look, it's probably best if we don't visit this topic right now given where we are."

"Who gives a shit what anyone here thinks?"

"This is my parents' night. They have their own stuff to worry about."

"Seems to me that this is what it has always been every year: a fundraising scheme."

"Well yeah."

"Your parents are sort of like politicians," Isaac prodded.

"Don't compare them to politicians," Bennett scolded. "Those are the worst type of people. No offense, Tommy."

"None taken, they can be bitches."

"When have you ever went out of your way to raise money for a cause?" Isaac asked."

"Last week," Bennett replied. "I asked my brother for cash to get this fire jacket."

"That's not even close to the same of what he's saying and you know it," Kevin chided, breathing hard. "When are we going to eat? I don't think my tummy can take it anymore."

"I'm losing it," Jack declared. "I'm convinced that I might lose it tonight."

"If it makes you feel any better," Isaac started, wrapping his arm around Jack. "We're here for ya…and I think Kev is right behind you on that because he loses it once he gets hangry."

Kevin rolled his eyes, shooting a finger at Jack.

"I swear I'm going to have a fit if your dad spends twenty more minutes going off-script like he did last year."

"Let's go get a drink," Jack declared, rubbing his eyes before peering down at his watch. "We should go find our seats afterwards, it's almost time to eat."

Jack waited as the boys continued to the bar before reaching for Tommy's arm, pulling him back.

"Hey," he murmured. "What was all that about with Berg?"

"Logan is delusional," he said coolly. "He'll say anything to make you distrust us. A real-life Wormtongue, if you ask me."

"He was going to tell me something about *you*," Jack specified. "You never actually told me the details about what happened that night?"

"What night is this?"

"You know what night, Tom," he insisted. "The night Logan got arrested. You were with him. What happened between you two?"

"Why do you care so much?"

"You convinced us to completely shun the guy afterwards without even telling us the whole story. He was one of our best friends. Looking back on it, I should have asked you to explain, but instead I just trusted that you knew what was best."

"Look, all you need to know is that all of our lives are definitively better without him in it. The details are irrelevant."

"If they are so irrelevant, why don't you tell me?"

"Because it's not worth my time," Tommy reassured, placing his hand on Jack's shoulder. "Or yours."

Jack was reluctant to let it go, but for the sake of preventing any further escalation, he managed a slight nod and carried on with his friends in the dining hall.

Kevin was in the middle of devouring his steak when he lifted his head, vigorously swallowing the food and clearing his throat.

"The porterhouse is simply *choice*, Mrs. Douglas," he praised.

"Thank you, Kevin," she opened the discussion to the rest of the boys. "How has this semester been for y'all?"

"If I'm being honest," Isaac started. "I think I'm ready to drop out and just start making music. The new age of hip hop is shameful. They really need to take a lesson out of the Book of 'Saac."

"You're an artist?"

"Of sorts," Isaac confirmed, downing his wine and lifting it above his head to signal one of the butlers to tend to his now empty glass.

Anita turned to Jack. "Speaking of artists, I noticed Emma didn't show up. Was she not able to make it."

It was a harrowing question for Jack. He loved his parents, but these public events could get overwhelming for him, and her presence would have certainly eased his anxiety.

"Yeah," Jack sighed, glimpsing at his father, who managed a supporting smile. "We're on a break; she moved to New York earlier this month to pursue her dreams."

"Not as dramatic as Edna Pontellier's arc, but just as admirable," Tommy interjected."

"*Nice,*" his father Harrison added.

"Oh, I'm sorry to hear that Jacky," Anita frowned. "I was looking forward to meeting her. From what you told me, she really seemed like the one."

Yes, she was, Jack thought. *She is.*

"We talked about it earlier, Anita," Wayne noted. "It seems like she is."
"Really?"
"*Really?*" Tommy mocked, whispering so only Jack could hear.
"They're great together," Bennett joined in.
"Oh please do tell," Anita pleaded.
"There's not much to it, Mom," Jack cut in. "I just said that we broke up."
"Nonsense!" Isaac chimed. "You should hear it when Jack talks about her: 'I think she's ducking my calls, guys. I miss her so much.'"
"Saac!" Jack tested.
"Oooo, the drama!" Anita heckled, rubbing her son's head. "My boy is such a hopeless romantic, isn't he?"
The topic at hand shifted at the sound of Isaac's fork clattering on his plate. Jack noticed his friend's wild eyes, nearly drooling when he saw the servers circling around with an array of desserts.
"I must be dreaming," Isaac said to himself when one of the servers laid a platter of cookies directly in front of him, impatiently filching for as many as his hand could hold.
"You boys must not have a lot of time to eat," Anita giggled.
"Well miss Douglas, between classes and the hundred dollars in my checking account, there isn't a lot of opportunity to satisfy my appetite," Isaac mumbled behind his noisy chews. "I will say, however, that my tolerance for ramen has peaked over the last few years."
Jack welcomed Isaac's ridiculous yapping, sighing in relief to no longer be the topic of discussion for the time being. The rest of the evening resumed in a typical manner, allowing him to retreat in an imaginary trance.
"Thank you for the food, Mrs. Douglas," Kevin cheered.
"Truly exquisite," Isaac added sincerely, although his natural tone came off more sarcastic.
"Thanks boys. What are you guys up to for the rest of the night."
"Not sure," Tommy stepped in. "Figured we could go grab a drink."
"It's Thanksgiving," Jack countered.
"No Jack, it's Thursday night. Bars are open."
"I'd be down." Kevin added.
"Me too." Bennett chimed.
Jack sighed and turned to his mother. "I guess we'll be going out for a nightcap. I'll be back later tonight."
"Sounds good," she kissed him farewell and watched them head out the door, before adding. "Be safe out there!"
Wayne joined his wife, squinting at his son and friends making their way outside.
"Where are they going?"

"'Grabbing a drink'," she remarked, quoting Tommy. "They have always surprised me watching them grow from children to now…never once having the desire to sit still."
"Oh come on, let's not act like we weren't exactly like that when we were their age," he chuckled. "Besides, it's better for them to exhaust this behavior now."
Harrison and Maria joined beside them.
"Speak for yourself Wayne," Harrison chortled and held up a sealed bottle of champagne. "I intend to finish this before midnight."
"Wrong holiday, Beech."
"Looks like we'll be spending the night *again,*" Maria sighed.
"You two are always welcome," Anita smiled.
Wayne and Harrison exchanged overly-merry grins. "Sleepover!"
Anita giggled. "And they say *women* are too much."
"Boys will be boys," Maria added, snatching the bottle from her husband. "Now come on, let's get this over with."

*****

It was only an hour past and Jack was already drunk, barely keeping his head up as he gurned down at his near-empty drink. He had been here, literally and figuratively, time and time again. He rested his back on the bar, spectating the unpleasant sight of his fellow collegemates stumbling over each other. Everyone seemed so happy, but Jack knew it could not have been true. He sensed the pretention in the air, knowing full well that all the men were there for the same thing. And it was not to 'bro out.'
Tommy came up and situated himself beside Jack to partake in the people-watching.
"This is a waste of time, Tommy," Jack complained.
"Maybe so," he agreed. "But there is a reason why we are here tonight."
"Why is that, so I can 'find my wife' like you always say? Have you ever considered that I may never find her?"
"I consider everything. And if what you say is true, then you would not have agreed to come out tonight."
"I don't see where you're getting at."
"You were on your phone all evening, dude. You're obviously not over her."
Jack sighed.
"I guess I'm just confused with what I should do. She has a boyfriend for God's sake."
"You don't know that forsure," Tommy reasoned. "The world's your oyster Jack. You're free to do what you wish. Drink your sorrows away; find some

random to fuck; hell, you can fly to New York right now if you really wanted to. Just explore your options."

"Those all seem…drastic."

"Well there you go, you're not so down in the dumps after all!" Tommy laughed, patting Jack's shoulder. "Just enjoy yourself now, in this moment. The more you worry about what you can't control, the worse you'll find yourself. Does that make sense?"

"Live in the moment," Jack reiterated, a wave of confidence rushing through him. "I think I understand."

Tommy's confidence was observably apparent, but for those who believe the trait can only be inherited, look in the mirror. Because confidence is not only the strength to spark a light in the darkest of rooms, but also the ability to endure any fear or doubt without shaking off the belief in oneself. Confidence is a muscle, not a gene, and can be exercised into a higher form strictly through consistent reaffirmation of one's true self, as opposed to one's *false* perception of who they are. Someone in the early stages of building this tolerance are met with this most challenging curve: distinguishing confidence from arrogance.

On that note, something happened to Jack.

Tommy watched him finish his drink and signal the bartender to return with another glass, before promptly climbing on the bar.

"What are you doing?" Tommy said, shocked. "Get down from there."

"Come on Tommy," Jack teased. "*You* of all people telling me to stop having a good time? Where's your spirit, buddy?"

"Nice pun, but for real, get down."

Jack ignored Tommy, raising his glass before the growing crowd.

"Attention, everyone! I'd like to make a toast!"

The bar went silent and all eyes fell on him. And just then, Jack was truly in his element. He could feel the ego taking over. It was inexplicably appealing to look past all the faces staring back at him. The yearn for this attention was always a part of him; instilled in his core, grateful to finally be released from captivity after being suppressed for so long. He could not determine whether it was the alcohol, or Tommy's advice, or even Emma. Maybe it was a combination of the sorts.

"My name is Jack Douglas, and I want you all to know how much I appreciate you. So much, in fact, that I will be buying all of your drinks for the rest of the night!"

He licked his lips at the eruption of cheers from the bar.

"You know what, fuck it!" he continued, his screaming even louder. "Where is the owner? Show your face!"

A small man appeared from behind the bar, peering up at Jack.
"I am the owner," he addressed.
"Sir, I would like to buy this fine establishment."
"What?" he stammered.
"*What?*" Tommy echoed, grabbing Jack's leg. "Dude, you're not thinking straight—"
"It's fine, Tom," Jack dismissed, producing his wallet from his pocket and pulling out a stack of cash, tossing it at the owner.
"Consider it a down payment," he grinned, turning back to the crowd. "Now let's get fucked up!"
The owner astonishingly eyed the money in his hands and shrugged at his employees.
"You heard him," he said, pointing to Jack. "Let's get back to work."
Jack hopped off the bar and faced Tommy.
"How was that for living in the moment?"
"What has gotten into you? Have you lost your mind?"
"Actually," Jack slurred. "I think I've finally found it."
Tommy left Jack on his power trip when the other boys approached him.
"What was that about?" Bennett asked.
"He may have officially lost it," Isaac suggested.
"Let's watch him tonight," Tommy uttered. "We need to make sure he doesn't do anything stupid."
Kevin laughed. "I think he's already there man."
Jack was indeed already there, tearing through the bar and soaking in the undivided attention given to him from the strangers who clapped at any chance to talk to him. He was too drunk to care about anything. Where he was, what he said, what he did.
At the opposite end of the nightclub, Logan stood with three acquaintances as he waited patiently for Jack to eventually return to the bar.
"Why are we still here, Logan? This place sucks." One of the guys said.
He debated following the boys here after dinner, but he anticipated Jack's appetite for alcohol would help his chances of finishing their conversation from earlier. He recruited his friends on the way to the bar because, as he learned, it was nearly impossible to pull Jack away without any of his friends trying to interfere. It did not hurt to have some backup if things got shifty, which in any situation involving Tommy, was almost expected.
He had witnessed the entirety of Jack's unraveling and chose to wait until he returned from the pit, figuring his drunken state would be preferred to offset the weight of his truth bomb. As the night drew on, however, his hopes of seeing him again started to dissipate.

"I can't leave until I talk to Jack," Logan replied to his friends, reaching for his wallet. "Sorry for dragging you all here, first drink's on me to make up for it."

They made their way to the bar, where he surprisingly spotted Jack leaning on the ledge like it was the only thing keeping him from falling over.

"It's kind of insane how many times we keep seeing each other," Logan teased, having to shout so his voice split through the heavy bass. "Here, I'll get you some water."

Jack glared at Logan and his friends, all of whom he judged immediately before facing away from them.

"I don't think it's a coincidence," he belched. "You're clearly obsessed with me."

"Relax man, I'm not here to start anything. I just wanted to see if you were okay," he glanced back at his friends before continuing. "And if you have time, I'd like to pick up with where we left off with what I wanted to tell you."

"Sorry, I'd rather talk to anyone else."

"Bro, you're standing here all by yourself," Logan tried before catching himself. "But whatever. Do you need anything? I can look for the other guys. Or Emma – is she here?"

Hearing her name leave Logan's mouth triggered Jack, flashing him back to when he saw them together at the Locks.

"You're such a fuck," Jack yelled.

"Calm down man," Logan took a step back. "I'm just trying to help. Like I said, I only wanted to talk to you about the other thing…"

But Jack was in no mood nor mindset to talk. He tightened the grip around his beer bottle, bringing it to his mouth and managing a sloppy sip. Logan took hold of the bottle to assist him from spilling, which startled Jack, pulling away and swinging his right fist into Logan's stomach.

Logan's friends reacted, grabbing Jack and restraining him on the bar.

"Hold on, guys, stop!" Logan cried as he tried intervening before being pulled back by a group of bystanders who folded him over the bar, leaving him to watch helplessly.

Jack flinched as a fist connected with his face. He fell over and smacked the hardwood below, his bottle flying out his hands and rolling beside his head. He tried hobbling over, wincing as he absorbed a series of kicks to his side. It took all his power to spring back up to his feet, taking hold of his empty bottle and swinging it at one of the attackers. The crack over his head was deafening, Jack gasping at his own action as he watched the man stagger back.

He then lunged toward the other two, tackling them into the beer-soaked floor. They started wrestling while bystanders joined, the initial altercation now transformed into a full-blown brawl.

"Get off of him!" he heard Tommy scream, seeing from the corner of his eye that he was accompanied by officers who took hold of Logan's friends.

The chaos ended as soon as it started, leaving Jack to only hear the bass of the music take over.

Jack sighed in relief, feeling someone roll him on his stomach and pull his wrists together and bringing him to his feet.

"What do you think you're doing?" Tommy shouted when the cops cuffed Jack.

"We're taking him in."

"Do you have any idea who he is? He's not going anywhere."

"Yes, he is."

Jack met Tommy's eyes.

"It's all right, Tom," he uttered, struggling to find his footing as the officer pulled him away from the crowd and out of the bar.

The cold air outside peeled through his body, burning his wounds as he was forced into the back of the patrol car. He sat there awkwardly as he dipped his head below his shoulders, his blood trickling down his face and falling to his dampened pants.

What a fucking mess, he thought, before eventually drifting off to sleep.

*****

Jack opened his eyes to find himself lying on a steel bed, alone in a dark room. He had no idea how long he had been out, quivering in pain as he brought his hands to his eyes, observing their scarred complexion.

The door opened abruptly, followed by an officer peering in.

"Let's go, Douglas," he announced, tossing a white bag to the bed.

Jack stared blankly at the officer, opening the bag to see all of his belongings.

"What's going on?" he asked.

"Your friend is here to get you—" the officer hesitated. "I apologize for the misunderstanding. Please forgive my men. I hope you understand that they were only doing their jobs."

Jack gave a subtle nod, picking up the bag and following the officer out of the cell.

Tommy was waiting for him in the lobby, fidgeting on his phone when Jack walked in.

"Here you are," the officer said. He glanced over at Tommy. "Sorry again. I think we are fine with pretending this didn't happen."

"You think?" Tommy snapped, returning a scowl to the officer.

The officer flinched uneasily, facing Jack. "Have a good night, sir."

Jack nodded again and thanked the officer before walking to Tommy, already by the exit.

"It's funny, never in my life would I have imagined bailing you out of jail," Tommy jeered, holding the door open for him. "If anything, I would have figured it would be *me* getting in a jam like this."

"I don't agree with that statement."

"Hey, it's a good thing that you are…you know, *you*," Tommy continued. "It didn't take much explaining to the lieutenant where their department's funds come from. They agreed to not put your name in the system." "Yeah, lucky me," Jack mumbled.

They leisured to the car, where they sat in an awkward silence. Tommy pushed his key in the ignition, observing Jack.

"I'm sure you have no intention of divulging," Tommy hesitated. "But if you want to talk about it…"

"No," Jack declined, facing the window.

Tommy nodded, starting the car pulling out of the lot.

It was a quiet drive home. Understandably for Jack, considering the heap of drama he had endured over the night. What could he say to Tommy? Not even he could understand why he did what he did.

Emma. It had to be her.

He pulled out his phone and brought it to his eyes, stunned by the coincidence as he read a message from her.

happy thanksgiving jack. i really miss you too

Reciprocation. Nothing more. Too little to confirm any validation, but just enough to get through the rest of the night. He imagined what she was doing at that moment, three hours ahead of him, in the big city. Was she alone? With others? Spending the night in, unattached from the world? Was she attending a raging social gathering that could have affected her ambiguous response? He tried to blend his anxiety with some droll, but nevertheless found himself once again sinking into his own thoughts, spiraling down a never-ending tunnel with no light at the other end.

Part III: Disillusionment

xix

The faint scent of chai had become an indication for Emma to assume Dr. Hanzel was in her office. Thanks to her anxiety, it took time and consistency to progress from a tedious knock and nervous handling of her program advisor's monotone, yet intimidating demeanor. Three months later however, such restraint diminished entirely, bursting through the door unannounced and riddling of a dialogue as if she were in mid-conversation.

"I'm *so* sorry for being late," Emma apologized when she entered, nearly slipping off the chair as she set a stack of textbooks on her advisor's desk that she would have argued having no time stash prior to her arrival. "Also – and it totally doesn't matter – but the door has always been closed whenever I come in here, even during your office hours."

Dr. Hanzel grinned amusingly while Emma settled in.

"Apologies are not necessary. Finals week tend to get the best of everyone, including our most impressive students," she kindly noted. "And *you*, Emma, just happen to be the best."

Emma gawked and shifted in her seat. "I appreciate that. And I want to thank you again for all the help you've given me."

"How do you feel?"

"A little weird. It sucks the semester is almost over, but I'm excited to go back home. I feel I learned so much in such short time."

"That's actually why I'm pleased that you came," Dr. Hanzel interlinked her fingers. "As you know, your internship is ending, but I spoke with your program director, and she expressed her thoughts to amend your contract."

Emma gulped. "You want me to stay?"

"Yes, it is simply an extension. We would like you to remain in New York through the spring semester. I also spoke with your academic advisor back in Washington, and we reached an agreement where you can split time between your studies online and work here with us. You would graduate on time, and potentially, be offered to join our team full-time upon graduation."

Emma slouched back in her seat and absorbed the news.

"Now Emma, I know you probably have a lot on your plate, but I would like to stress how rare of an opportunity this is," Dr. Hanzel added. "It is not common for us to welcome back interns, let alone be inclined to work an arrangement like this."

Emma clamped her hands and stared blankly at Dr. Hanzel, who sat patiently as she awaited her response.

"It's just…I don't know. I'm still having a hard time believing that this is actually happening," Emma stammered pensively. "What do you think I should do?"

"We can discuss the details when you are ready. But first, I want you to take a deep breath."

Emma obeyed and forced a smile.

"Good. Now, you have plenty of time to think about this. I suggest that you put it out of your mind for now. Go home, enjoy the holiday break and speak with your family," she leaned forward, keeping her tone at a sympathetic murmur. "I can't guarantee that this is the right choice for you. If you decide that it is, then let me know as soon as you can and we will take care of your return flights at the end of the year."

Had she expected the news, Emma would have set time aside for deep contemplation. But per one of life's many lessons, things can happen outside the control of one's imagination.

She waddled out of the building to find Hunter waiting at the foot of the steps. Based on his uncontrollable shiver, she reckoned he had been there for quite some time, doing his best to brave the blistering cold as his fingers curled into his wool overcoat.

His widening grin was pleasant to see, but taken aback from the enlightening news of her internship, she felt pressured to tell him immediately.

"Hey!" she hugged him. "What are you doing here?"

"I remember you saying what time you got done with your last final so I figured I'd stop by to take you out for lunch to celebrate," he replied, glancing at his watch. "I guess I came a bit too early huh?"

"No not at all, I had a last-minute meeting with my advisor. Sorry, I should have told you."

"No worries! I figured that was the case," he gleamed. "Besides, it gave me a chance to get my steps in for the day."

"Are you up for a little more cardio?"

He took her arm to keep her from slipping. "Truthfully no, but for you, why not?"

They strolled off campus and toward midtown. For someone who was infamous for keeping things bottled until the last minute, Emma was compelled to tell him about the extension right there and then. Hunter's excitement was apparent however, and she submitted to his lead in their dialogue on their way to the diner. He was eccentrically simple, with a charismatic quality that attracted her. So much in fact, that she momentarily forgot why she was so frazzled.

It was quick to return, though, when they settled into their table.

"How was the meeting with your advisor?" he asked.

Emma gave a vacant expression at the question, privately comparing the eerily similar circumstances to when she told Jack about leaving for New York earlier that year.

"We just talked about the future."

Hunter's eyes lit up. "That's a doozy. Anything specific?"

"What makes you think there is more?"

"Because you have refused to look at me since we came in here," he chuckled.

Emma had realized the truth in his observance, lifting her head and meeting his fixed, inquisitive stare.

"They offered me an extension on my internship."

"Congratulations! Are you going to take it?"

"I have no idea…what do you think I should do?"

"It's best if I don't share my input on the matter."

"Because…?"

"Because I would clearly want you to stay – not just for the internship, but for me too," he shrugged charmingly. "It's funny, I knew that this day would come, when you would have to go back. At the same time, I had no idea we would have gotten this close."

Emma blushed.

"Look Em, I hate to be so forward but this news only begs the question," he paused. "Where is this is going?"

Emma tilted her head. "How do you mean?"

"You know, 'this,'" Hunter gestured to the two of them.

"There is a lot going on in my life right now Hunter."

"I know, and I get it," he soothed. "You don't live here, and this whole internship was a temporary thing you had going on—"

"And Jack," Emma added.

"I know," Hunter lamented. "But there are times when we hang out when you don't even mention him. And when you *do* bring him up, it always seems to be about how you two are not in a good place, or about how he did something that upset you."

"That's fair."

"Maybe it's my fault for not specifically asking what is going on between you two, and I hope you understand that the reason why I ever did was because I figured it was something you felt that you needed to handle on your own."

"I appreciate you telling me all of this Hunter," Emma said. "But I didn't have any expectations when I came here."

"New York is a big city. There are millions of people who call it home, and although a large percentage of them were born and raised in the area, we all know it is not uncommon for others around the world to flock here. Some of them simply pass through, but there are others who stay. I've heard every excuse in the book as to why they do. Whether it is for their career, preferred lifestyle, family, etcetera – I discovered there is one major aspect that distinguishes a wanderer from a settler…"

"And what is that?"

"Curiosity. It is fundamental in our experiences. Where the distinction lies, however, is when your curiosity becomes obsessive. There is a reason why we call New York the City of Dreams—" he leaned in closer to Emma and motioned to the other tables. "Look at these people. They sit here, eating, drinking, talking about their joys and pains, seeking reassurances for their thoughts and actions. Some are happy. Others are sad. But they all have aspirations, whether they want to admit it or not. And by the time they finish paying their checks and go back to their homes, they fall asleep without realizing that all these emotions are part of understanding what it means to be alive…what it means to be human. They'll wake up tomorrow and go about their days, wishing, hoping everything will get better, because their curiosity of how their fate unfolds will keep them going. For some of us, it can become so grueling to the point that we choose to give up. And if that happens, we leave. Sure, in their minds they may think of this city still being a part of them, but in their hearts, they know that it never was. Because if it was not the case, then they would not have left in the first place.

"You may not be originally from New York, but it was your curiosity that brought you here. I think there is a reason why I met you. And no matter what

you go through during your time here, I think you should stay. After everything you have been through, you owe yourself that much."
Emma remained silent.
"Sorry, I know that was a lot," he snickered. "No matter what you choose, I'll always try to make it work. If we end up together – and I get from your side that is a big *if* - then I would want the decision to be mutual, and when you are ready for it." Emma tensed and lowered her head to the table.
"I promise to let you know what I decide," was all she could say.
He smiled. "Sounds like a plan."
Hunter escorted Emma back to her apartment after lunch. Gladdened that she had already gotten through one of the more difficult talks, Emma drew up a mental list of who else should be aware of the news. Baylee was logically next, given that she would see her as soon as she walked through the door. She was relieved to find her roommate not there, leaving her to escape to her bedroom and throw herself on the bed.
Part of Emma wondered if Hunter knew how bold it was to be so direct in his intentions, yet another part secretly loved it. He was superb in articulating his feelings, no matter if it may be marked as premature. But it was honest, and that was appreciable nevertheless.
The idea of Hunter as romantic partner lingered in her thoughts since she met him, and while she did her best to put if off for as long as she could, it did not mean the idea was not worth indulging.
She felt her hand skim across her chest and down to her waist, before falling further beneath underwear. It was not just his physical appearance that incited pleasure. He was a good man, arguably one she had dreamed of waiting for. Her initially slow breath escalated as she recalled each tense moment between them, fantasizing how great the outcome may have been had either of them made a move then. It did not take long before thoughts synced with her body, fingering herself to the rapidly glowing idea of being in Hunter's arms, and he inside her. She could not help Jack momentarily popping in, causing her to suppress any subliminal guilt for thinking of another man. At the same time, it was not like she should feel guilty for acknowledging a piece of her heart still clung onto Jack. She knew it was not fair to either of them for her to drag out her decision as long as she had so far, especially given the permanent end of her relationship with Jack becoming even more real to her.

Still, she fancied the passion too much to stop, driving her finger deeper and moaning indistinctly, figuring at this point it mattered less who she thought of and mattered more just getting off.

A series of sudden rapping from the door stopped Emma cold in her tracks from finishing, pulling her hand out and pretending to look as normal as possible when she saw Baylee storm in and jump on the bed.

"I heard the news!" she screamed, hugging Emma tight enough to make her nearly pass out from lack of oxygen. Emma extended her hand away when the embrace came, dreading the thought of her soiled fingers touching anything other than soapy water.

"How do you know already?"

"Advisors talk. Apparently there were only a shortlist of students selected."

Emma gasped for air, having been released from Baylee's bear hug.

"So does that mean…"

"Yep, I got an offer too. We get to still live together!"

"I don't know if I'll be coming back yet Bay."

"You'll come back. There's no way you won't. You and I both know this is where you belong."

Emma's phone buzzed before she could respond.

"Give me a minute?"

"Take it outside, I'm gonna start packing for you," Baylee initiated, moving to Emma's closet. "I'm a great folder."

Emma went out onto the balcony, taking a moment to overlook the active streets below as she cradled the phone in her palms. For the first time since she arrived, she recognized how noisy the city was. It overwhelmed her thoughts, causing her to tighten her grip on the phone as she brought it to her ear.

"Hey sis."

"Oh my god, HG!" Emma shrieked, elated to hear the voice of one of her dearest friends. "We haven't talked in *forever.*"

"Chillout Emma, we talk at least once a week."

"Good point," Emma uttered, pulling herself together. "Sorry, you caught me at a crazy time."

"I get it. I'm sure the past few months for you have been anything short of normal," HG added dryly. "I just called to know if you figured out what time you'll be flying into SeaTac. It's a long drive out there and I want to make sure we're on the same page."

"Yeah absolutely," Emma began, her voice faltering as she decided against further burdening her friend by sharing the news of her extension.

"Are you okay?" came HG after some silence.

"It's nothing, I went to see my advisor this morning—" Emma stopped herself again. "I'll fill you in when I'm back."

"Hm, okay. Just text me with the details of your flight. I'll see you this weekend."

Emma hung up and drew a long breath before contemplating the crossroads she found herself in as she stared into the bleary evening sky.

A few months ago, the idea of journeying to the concrete jungle for this internship was all Emma cared about. Her passion for art was still there, but it was supposed to be for one semester. No more, no less.

If she chose to return after the holiday, then surely she would also be committing to her dream career, while also bringing implications she was determined to keep on the backburner.

Living in New York was a big one. While it was never a dream of hers to spend the rest of her life on the West Coast, suggesting she was more inclined to settle this far east was just as presumptuous of an idea. On the other side of the coin, specifically, was leaving Seattle: her home, her friends, desired routine, and willingness to retire the memories as a past chapter of her life. Hunter was another. A boy she hoped would only be a distraction, was slowly winning her over. She knew there was no way she could come back and not see their relationship evolving.

Which brought her to the single obstacle preventing that from happening: Jack Douglas, who despite their good-natured inception, had become estranged due to a layered, unhealthy mixture of insecurity, doubt, and miscommunication. Baylee made a good point in suggesting Emma's decision to shut off contact with him was not the most effective approach in healing the wound. Emma hated Jack's tendency to be...overbearing at times. No. Most of the time. For too long, she had displaced her willingness to sort out her priorities. Now that they have begun to materialize, Emma hoped that some clarity would also come forth.

Love should be understanding and supportive. She felt Jack was selfish to expect her to turn down this internship. Never once did he express support in her reflecting on what she needed to do for *her*. And now, being here in the city – with the potential to capitalize on something she always wanted – Emma understood why Jack reacted the way he did when she told him. Whether it was fair for her to leave was irrelevant. He misconstrued what they were and forced what he wanted. But if he did not – and if he truly loved her – than the details matter none. He should be understanding, and willing to work with her through this dilemma.

She would take it one day at a time, preserve her options, and open her heart, hopeful that her conscience will aid her in making the right decision. Whatever that may be.

*****

Underneath his ever-existing cynicism for most people, Tommy genuinely believed there to be hope in the few like-minded individuals who shared his outlook on the universe. Particularly women, whom he concluded long ago to have a generally better, raw grasp on their feelings, whereas men seemed more troubled in sorting their own place of belonging at the expense of their obsessive emotions toward their respective partners.

He considered Jack as one of these men.

Tommy was aware of his pride. But Jack? That was a bit more complicated, especially when considering his naturally careless demeanor toward everyday struggles. However, in the presence of more strenuous predicaments – that was, issues that require rationale to resolve – Jack resorted to his own skewed justifications, many of which were the cause to Tommy's frustration that he would frequently acknowledge when he felt warranted.

Contrary to Jack's assurances, Tommy suspected his friend's willingness to obey his wishes fell short of his expectations. He could empathize with someone dealt with a bad hand. But not Jack, and especially not in the case he finds most detrimental to obtaining any degree of happiness. Never was a time in the past when Tommy was not in Jack's corner, readily prepared to console him for the range of troubles he helplessly endured. Growth is experienced by all, but at varying points in time. And time, unfortunately, has no concern for one's feelings. For Tommy, who even after exercising his own diligence on things important to *him*, discovered that he had fallen victim to a growing burden that was Jack's inability to manage on his own.

The realization came a week following Thanksgiving, when he learned he had failed his Calculus exam. He intended to dedicate more time to studying but fell short of doing so as a result of, once again, Jack.

"Are you fucking kidding me?"

"Forty-five percent?" Bennett observed Tommy's redmarked paper while their professor continued handing out tests. "That is very unlike you."

Tommy swiveled back and panned the classroom.

"Who are you looking for?"

"Jack, who else? You're the only two people I talk to in this class."

"Easy man, no need to get anal about it. Jack hasn't been here all week."

"What? How do you know that?"

"How do you *not* know? You're his roommate."

Their professor, Dr. Yore, cut them off by audibly clearing his throat.

"Please pay attention Tommy," Dr. Yore addressed, returning to his desk at the front of the classroom. "We are about to begin the lecture."

Tommy nodded and noticed the guy sitting on his other side staring back at him.

"Hey, your name is Todd, right?"

"Tom," Tommy corrected. "Dr. Yore just said it."

"I knew it started with a 't'," the guy said to his friend behind them before turning back to Tommy. "Do you know Alivia Caswell?"

Tommy nodded. He could not picture the face, but the name certainly rang a bell, as it just happened to be the same name as the girl he took home last weekend.

The guy's curious look was replaced with a rather frustrated one.

"Yeah, she's my girlfriend."

Tommy straightened up in his seat, quick to connect the dots.

"Oh shit, my bad brother. In my defense, she approached me."

Tommy expected a fist to his face. Instead, the guy shrugged and dipped his head in glum.

"It's okay man, I get it," he said. "I'm not upset. Well, I am, but not with you. She's just a hoe."

Tommy's eyes bulged, stunned by how personal this brief exchange had turned.

"I don't know her well enough to speak on whether she's a hoe," he uttered, choosing his words. "But I guess it's okay now that you two are no longer together."

The guy gave a confused frown.

"You *did* break up with her…" Tommy added.

The guy maintained an empty stare.

"…Because she cheated on you…with me. Tommy Beech. Me. Sitting next to you."

"No I didn't break up with her," the guy finally said. "I love her, bro."

"She cheated on you, *bro*. What does matter if you love her? You obviously shouldn't anymore."

"That's not how it works dude," the guy replied, shaking his head. "If you love someone, you forgive them and move on."

"You're insane."

The guy glanced at his friend behind them, the two chuckling at Tommy's expense. Which mildly annoyed him, as he could tell they were singling him out as the naïve one.

"Love is unconditional Tom."

"Okay mate," Tommy scoffed. "I wish you two godspeed in your unconditional love."

"Thanks, you're a good dude," the guy said, giving him a side hug.

Tommy looked over to Bennett, matching his shock at the interaction.

"Okay that's it, I'm done with today," he said as he began packing up.

"Where are you going?"

"Back to the apartment," Tommy answered, rising from his chair and starting for the exit.

Dr. Yore curiously inspected him edging out of the row.

"Where are you off to, Tommy?"

Tommy reached the door and turned back to Dr. Yore, readjusting his demeanor as he addressed his professor.

"Frankly, it's none of your business."

As if they were in grade school, a medley of *oohs* came from the students.

Tommy carried off though, having no care for his professor's reaction.

He bolted back to his apartment, repeatedly calling Jack on the way and barely managing to contain his frustration as it went to voicemail each time. Meanwhile, Jack was off his phone, busying himself with a show when Tommy arrived in the apartment. He circled around and stood between his friend and the tv.

"Hey, I've been calling," Tommy said.

Jack was slow to acknowledge Tommy, lifting his head before glancing back down to see the missed calls on his phone.

"Oh yeah, you have," Jack observed nonchalantly, setting his phone down and focusing back on the tv.

"Bennett told me you haven't been showing up to class."

Jack peered up at Tommy.

"You're just realizing that, huh? We always sit next to each other."

"Well I'm sorry for not paying attention to you in class. It's definitely all on me, right? It's not like I should be focusing on anything else. You're totally right."

Jack gave him a puzzled look.

"Not sure if that was an apology or not, but I forgive you either way."

Tommy reached for the remote on the table and shut off the TV.

Jack reacted immediately, jolting upwards and shooting Tommy a dismissive glare.

"What the hell, Tom?"

"Shut up for one second and listen to me," he demanded, tossing the remote on Jack's lap. "This is getting ridiculous. People go to jail. Big deal. And I know you are heartbroken, and your mind is probably somewhere in New York with Emma, but this needs to stop. You have shit to do here."

"You don't think I know that?"

"No, I don't think you do. You have been skipping class; you show up at the apartment in the middle of the night without letting me know where you have been; you don't talk to me or any of the other guys about *anything*…" Tommy took a breath and lowered his head. "You're just not yourself man."

"Wow, I didn't realize that we were a married couple."

At that, Tommy sighed. He knew this was his friend's best attempt at deflecting his genuine feelings, and usually he did not mind showing complacency, as he believed sympathy as an ineffective approach to resolution. Not that Jack could understand, as Tommy considered him to be already prone to confusing one's intentions. He wondered if it would be wise to keep following such precedent.

"Look Jack, I am not going to tell you to stop loving her, because I know that is an impossible request, at least right now. That said, if you are still determined to keep fighting for her, then you better not give up. Because once you do, that will be it. And the way you have let go of everything that *should* matter to you," he shook his head. "Well, let's just say that your choice to double-down on this hand is not the best bet you've wagered."

"You don't know what you are talking about. Not everything is about Emma." "Tell yourself that! Because for the life of me I can't tell you what else could explain this phase you're going through. And yes, I'm calling it a phase

because I hope that it is indeed temporary, and not some permanent shit you brought on yourself."
Jack sometimes questioned if Tommy found pleasure in lecturing others or if he did it strictly for the sake of hearing himself talk. Not to say he did not welcome it, as he regularly would at even the most inappropriate times. But for whatever reason that morning, he had grown tired of Tommy's rant.
"This is my problem Tommy, not yours," he relented. "I know that you mean well, but I don't want to hear it right now."
Tommy shook his head. "I'm sorry," he managed reluctantly, for he had acknowledged how intense his delivery was. He did not want to accept Jack's request, yet he understood how most people did not distinguish advice from instruction.
He left Jack alone and headed for the door, stopping halfway out.
"The boys and I are grabbing supper later…if you want to join."
Jack ignored him, waiting until he heard the door close before burying his face in his hands. He tried so hard not to think about the glaringly obvious issues spinning in his mind. He retreated to his bedroom in hopes that the change of location would suffice as a distraction, laying on his bed and allowing his vision to graze over the nightstand, where they fixated on a framed photo of him and Emma. They had their arms wrapped around each other like meerkats – not just out of affection, but because it was considerably freezing that afternoon, and they forgot their jackets. The irony was that the sun was clearly bright to make Jack squint noticeably back at the camera to avoid being blinded.
He then focused on Emma. She was not looking in the direction of the camera, but her happiness was seemingly obvious, as she had rested her chin on Jack's chest, peering up to him as she boasted the brightest smile.
A tear escaped Jack's eye and rolled down his cheek, dripping off his face and onto his hand. How could it have come to this? Two souls that were once so close that they could feel one another's heartbeat, somehow leading to this.
Yes, it was never a good call to label the outcome of a relationship as definitively over, but Jack feared it was true. He had changed since the last time they were together, and per Tommy's "advice," he felt the change as a negative one.
Jack's intermittent sadness was replaced with surging rage, like a sizzling fire rising in his stomach and bottling up in his throat. He picked up the frame and

threw it across the room, unflinching when it shattered against the wall. Indulged in wrath, he paced across the room and began driving his fists into the drywall, wincing from the pain striking through his arm at the first punch, and unsure if the loudening crack was from his potentially fractured knuckles, or the possible breakage of the wall. That did not stop him, nevertheless, causing him to become even more agitated as he swung again. And again. And again, like the wall was a literal punching bag, taking the needless battering from Jack until blood splattered off his hands and over his eyelids. He finally tired himself out, collapsing to the floor and burrowing his head between his knees as he wept uncontrollably.

*****

Tommy found Jack still on the floor later that night. The dry blood stained on the walls was more than enough for him to accurately assess what happened after he left.

"Jack," he said, lightly nudging him with his foot. He was still breathing, to Tommy's relief, but remained still on the floor.

"I guess we're doing this then," Tommy mumbled, taking off his jacket and digging his arms under Jack's back to lift him up. He let out a muted shriek after accidentally planting his foot on a hidden piece of broken glass, quickly regaining control of his friend and carrying him to the bed.

"Of fucking course," he muttered silently, gently placing Jack under the blanket and closing the door behind him before going to the bathroom to wash the speckles of dried blood on his fingers.

Tommy debated whether it was still worth respecting Jack's wish to not involve himself. He quickly reconsidered, producing his phone and scrolling through the contact list. Many think they know what is best for them, but Tommy learned early that the majority of these claims were riddled in self-doubt.

Tommy waited patiently on the line, when finally, after three rings, a voice came from the other end.

"Hello?"

"Harmony Goodwynn," Tommy said. "Long time no talk, sister."

"You know I prefer to go by 'HG' right?"

"Others' preferences are not really in my scope of tolerance."

HG moved on, impatient for Tommy's friendly ridicule. "Why are you calling me so late?"

"I'm sorry, but this is important. It's Jack. He has been going through this thing…it's a long story—"

"Are you talking about him breaking up with Emma?"

"Uh, yeah. Wait, who told you that they broke up?"

"There are a lot of rumors fluttering around."

Tommy did not question further, noting her longtime gift of being in the know of just about every piece of gossip in the world of drama.

"I talked to Emma earlier this week and she didn't confirm. And Jack, well, he's apparently M.I.A," HG added.

"Jack's not lost. Well, *physically,* he's not lost. As for mentally, that's another story."

"Is it appropriate for someone to joke about the mental health about their best friend?"

"Probably not, but definitely warranted," Tommy giggled to himself before growing more serious. "For real, though, I have a favor to ask."

"I'm listening."

"Jack's been hung up on Emma ever since she left this summer. I know you're good friends with both of them, so I'm not expecting you to take sides, if it ever comes to that, but—"

"Today, Tommy," HG cut in again. "Just tell me what you want me to do."

"I need you to talk to him."

"Pass."

"*Pass?* What do you mean?"

"I mean, it's not my business to get in the middle of it. If Emma broke up with him, that's her decision. I don't know what I can say to Jack to make him feel better."

"Stop saying that they broke up, Harmony. You know how indecisive they can both be," Tommy reasoned. "From what I gathered, Emma needed more of a break than anything."

Silence on the other end.

"Have you spoken to Emma about all of this?" Tommy added.

"I don't see the relevance in doing so. Shit like this happens all the time. Jack isn't the first person to go through heartbreak. 'Heartbreak' might even be a stretch when you take in account how short their relationship was."

"I would appreciate it if you told him that there is still hope and to not give up."

"*What?*"

Tommy sensed her defensive tone, leading him to wonder if her opinion on the topic was influenced by more than her similar outlook on relationships. For reasons he never considered, Tommy and his friends rarely invited the idea of a platonic girlfriend into their group. Whenever a girl was mentioned amongst them, it always followed with the implication that she is, or would be engaged intimately with one of them.

But when it comes to HG, Tommy would be remiss to deny that at least one of the boys generated feelings for her over the duration of their friendship. And for anyone that knew HG, the need for speculation was obvious.

HG was an amazing person, and her stunning beauty was overshadowed by an even more attractive personality. Even though they subliminally agreed to keep their acquaintance reduced to the friendzone, Tommy would, admittedly, occasionally wonder if he ever still had a shot with her on the marginal chance that he made a move. He had doubts, particularly based on how alike they were. For someone who loved himself more than he had ever loved anyone else, Tommy suspected that HG had a similar vision, if not a similar train of logic.

"Normally I would agree with you, Harmony, but this is Jack we are talking about. Except for his mom, you're the only other girl that has been in his life for as long as I can remember," he paused. "Maybe I'm crazy, but I think there is some sense to the idea that the message will be more effective if it came from you."

Tommy could feel HG's hesitancy from the other end of the line.

"Okay," she finally said.

"Really?"

"Yeah, really. But you'll be paying for my drive up to the city."

"Thank you Harm, I appreciate you."

"Jesus Tommy, give me better nicknames or don't do it at all."

Tommy hung up and crept back to Jack's bedroom for one last checkup, pleased to see his best friend snoring in bed where he left him. He moved on to his own room, soothed by the knowledge that he was no longer alone in the pursuit of Jack's inner peace.

XX

"Come on HG, can you please stop for one second so we can talk?"
Aiden is an asshole. So much of an asshole, that Harmony refused to
recognize his muted plea behind a percussive din of the car door.
His hands could have been glued to the vehicle by how desperately he leeched
on the window. But Harmony disregarded him and kept her eyes straight
ahead as she shifted in reverse. She noticed the car momentarily lift offside
and level out, watching from the corner of her eye as Aiden wailed and
collapsed to the pavement. Three years, and it was the first time seeing his
sensitive side. All it took was three thousand pounds of sophisticated German
engineering strategically applied on his left foot.
Either way, more than what she needed to conclude their time was well spent.
Freedom was newfound for Harmony, who relished a resonant high that
increased with every mile driven. The wind's brisk chill whipping over the
cracked windows whistled along to her wistful rendition of the song on the
radio, her voice nearly gone by the time she pulled up to her father's office.
She was received with a scornful glare from her younger sister sitting behind
the secretarial desk.
"You're late," Sally stated.
"Very observant of you," Harmony retorted cheerfully, circling around the
desk and sitting beside her.
Sally leaned closer to her, sniffing blatantly.
That's interesting."
"What are you doing?"
"Your voice sounds weird," she inquired, nose-crunched as she treated herself
to a sip from her Yeti. "But you don't smell like cigarettes."
Harmony's eyes widened.
"Are you crazy?"
"People have smoke breaks when they work. It's not weird."
"I think *you're* weird."
"You're lucky Dad isn't here to hear you say that. That was rude, you know."
"Again, very observant. Imagine how much better off you'd be if you used
that same concentration to something that actually mattered."

"Based on that overrated comeback, you are indirectly implying that you don't matter. To which, I wholeheartedly agree."

"Go choke on a kernel."

"Gladly. It's more respectable than your preference."

She peeked over to her father's office, the door ajar and lights off. *Perfect, he's not here.*

A cautionary measure the girls adopted shortly after their first day working for him.

"'Nice work Harmony," she muttered to herself, propping her feet atop the edge of the desk and her phone out. "You're doing such a great job."

Working for Russell Goodwynn was a winning scenario for Harmony. Even upon acknowledging the finite limit of time humans are given, she was confident that her father would still be able to run the whole operation on his own. Funnily enough, he had to for quite some time, until his largest clients relocated out of the city and still demanded his physical attendance during each of their ongoing trials.

The office accommodated only the partners, who felt the need to lease a smaller, discreet office centrally located from their homes. It also offered more hands-on experience for the girls, who Russell deemed competent enough to handle the work typically performed by paralegals. The eldest daughter Mira, in fact, was the first of the children to be employed, and has since grown into her role as a formidable associate. She even had her own office on the floor, for whenever she decided to pop in and spend a few hours cajoling with the partners before announcing her plans to put her upcoming "clarity" trip on the corporate card.

Harmony was on her phone when Sally slapped her feet on the desk. Before she could react, she saw the main door swing open and a man enter. He was about her age, and undeniably handsome.

"Hi, how can we help you?" Sally greeted.

"Hello," the man said, first meeting eyes with Harmony before focusing on her sister. "I'm a law student here in town. I know I'm a little late in the game, but the semester is almost over, and I was going around hoping to find a firm that would be interested in letting me intern for them."

"Oh cool! Um…" Sally turned to Harmony. "What do you think?"

At that, the man looked back at Harmony, giving her a kind smile.

Harmony rolled her eyes.

"None of the attorneys are in right now," she relayed.

"No problem. Do you know if they'll be—"

"Won't be back for the rest of the day."

"Oh, okay. Maybe I can come back tomorrow, or whenever one of them are back in the office?"

Sally decided to chime in, sensing her sister's unusual brashness.

"If you leave your contact information with us, we will pass it on and they will give you a call."

"Great! I would appreciate it."

Sally handed the man a notepad, shooting Harmony a scornful look when he was not paying attention.

"Thank you again," the man said, handing the notepad back to Sally. He glanced at Harmony again, smiling. "Have a good day."

She dismissed him with a compliant nod, leaving a rather awkward silence before he turned back to the door.

"Are you nuts? He was *so* cute," Sally said after the man left.

"Eh, too boring."

"Boring? Come on.

Daylight fizzled its end when the girls strolled out the office.

"I'll be late to dinner," she said to Sally.

"Going to see a boy?"

"Would you chill? I'm heading over to Anna's."

Sally giggled. "Is it normal to be on a first-name basis with your therapist?"

Harmony shrugged. "Considering I've debated making her my emergency contact, yeah I'd say so."

It may sound like a joke, but it could not have been a more real statement to Harmony. She became acquainted with her therapist shortly after they moved to Renton, initially as a method for her to cope with being so far from her dear friends. The scope of topics grew organically as time went on, and thanks to Dr. Anna Kays' irregularly casual demeanor, it evolved into someone oddly greater than a basic friendship.

"What's up Anna?"

"Harmony," Dr. Kays greeted wearingly. "You *do* know that I have a life after hours right?"

"This is a one-time exception."

"You said the last four times."

"Well, fifth time's the charm then," Harmony moved the binder from her designated chair and placed it on her therapist's desk. "I did it: I broke up with Aiden."

Dr. Kays nodded affectionally and relaxed in her seat. "Well don't keep me waiting. Spill the details."

As a result of her extreme emotional depth, Harmony was quick to embrace her unwavering determination in not settling with a partner until she was absolutely certain of an outcome suiting her dream expectation. She not only believed in the idea of a soulmate, but that the search for that person was well within her grasp if she chose to dedicate enough effort to find him. She acknowledged the mystery in love, and paid less mind to its inner workings, as she figured none of it mattered as long as her heart trumped the logic.

"So in addition to all the clearly negative actions on his part, you're saying that you have always felt this debilitating hope that he would change?"

"Sure, that's a nice way to put it," Harmony concurred. "It's like waiting for a train that will never come."

"Well, in this context, it seems to me that the train indeed arrived, but you did not approve of the destination of where it was taking you."

Harmony starting snapping. "Yes girl, keep preaching."

Dr. Kays shook her head amusingly. "I understand your sentiment though. What if you thought of this way: Aiden was a wet log of firewood."

"Excuse me?"

"Wood," Dr. Kays clarified. "Wet wood is harder to light. You feel that you have tried to light it many times, and each time the fire would eventually go out."

"Are you a big camper?"

"My husband and daughter love it, me not so much," she admitted. "The point I'm getting at is in this situation, one is presented with a few clear options. They can hold out and wait for the wood to dry, or they can find another log to light, to which I'll ask where you think you find yourself at this time—"

"And I would say in response that I'm done waiting, evidently, since I dumped him."

"In your current mindset, would you ever be open to trying to relight the log?"

"Absolutely not," Harmony shot back proudly. "After a while, I've been accepting of who people are inherently, ya know? Like when they say a cheater is always a cheater, there are things about each of us that will always be the way they are."

An expert manipulator of social situations, she found that such tactics should be acted on only if it was for the betterment of the people involved, rather than for the sake of her sole benefit. True love was not meant to be experienced by all; it takes someone with the ability to comprehend even the most unique dynamics that make up a partnership. A man seeking her love would be sure to find themselves abandoned at sea, drowning helplessly in the delusion he once believed to be sound.

Ironically, Harmony did not think it was wrong to entertain the queue of simpletons waiting for their opportunity to earn her heart. And boy did they come often. Matter of fact, the moment her first ex dumped her – on her birthday, of all days – Harmony proceeded to receive a bouquet of flowers from three random guys. Sure, they were kind gestures, but Harmony knew it was nowhere near enough to actually earn her undivided attention.

Passion was at the center of all of Harmony's endeavors. It was her foundation of measuring one's approach to situations, regardless of nature's severity. The more passion she saw in a person, the more inflated her attraction toward them.

"Good, that's good," Dr. Kays observed candidly. "I've mentioned this, but sometimes I think your quality of constant self-assurance makes you not needing therapy."

"You're probably right. I think I just like to hear myself talk about these things out loud to someone else."

"I understand. On that note," Dr. Kays transitioned. "Have you talked with your family and friends about this yet?"

"Not yet."

"Because of time, or something else?"

"Definitely the first."

Vulnerability – no matter its portrayal – was as green flag for Harmony, as she knew its crucial role in creating an ideal relationship; one that was safe, uncontrolled, and potentially forever lasting.

It was not limited to romanticism. She felt her wholesome family exemplified an emotionally harmonious dynamic amongst each other. Furthermore, Harmony appreciated the varied personalities amongst her friends. It was great when she found someone who opened a new realm – even the narrowest – of perspectives from what she considered normal. Like many, she retained a tight group of close friends: an "inner circle," comprised of only the most loyal, who despite their varied characteristics, shared an unconditional willingness to be there for Harmony upon her request. Years could pass, and they would still be there, with unflinching regard for each other's well-being. Emma Keva was a founding member of the group.

"I'm aware of how meaningful your friendship with Emma is. Hearing the opinions of someone so close to you, especially being non-familial, will continue to be an important source to resort to in times like this."

Her first memory of Emma was back in her elementary days. She came off strong and hardheaded, yet timid enough to mute a mime. It initially confused Harmony, who spent a large portion of their friendship dictating how anyone could portray an easy-going, passive handle on life, while pedaling vigorously toward such a uniquely personal ambition that they kept hidden from the world.

"Even your other friends – the 'boys' as you often put it – may offer a perspective that could help bring more insight into how you understand and cope with the situation. Are there any of them that you would trust with this level of vulnerability?"

Tommy was an option, but Harmony knew it was likely his insouciance showing more than his care for her feelings. The more ideal choice was, well, who else.

"I don't understand it either," she recalled him say in response to her unveiling of a potential new friend for him to meet. "That's how I feel about my buddies sometimes. When we're all hanging out, we can just be total idiots and act like there is no care in the world. But I know, deep down, that they are all so put-together and focused on their futures."

"I think you're like that too," Harmony contested delicately, flashing a warm smile.

"We'll agree to disagree on that," Jack sighed, pressing his finger on his lips in ponderation. "Anyway, what is your friend's name again?"

She remembered feeling incredibly ambivalent when he had asked her, like a metaphorical slap in the face at the fact that her crush's interest in another girl came even after he received a fairly apparent flirt. At the time, Harmony was just beginning to spend time with the older kids at her school. And given Emma's noticeably attractive quirks, she admittedly felt too insecure to even give a name after that, let alone an introduction to one of her best friends.

The only one of Jack's friends who knew about Emma was Tommy, which was unsurprising given his immense popularity with the rest of the student body. But between the drugs and parties he frequented leading up to graduation, he found little reason, if any, to spend even a moment with the innocent, nerdy girl who turned down a social invitation.

Shortly after the boys graduated, Harmony's father chose to open his own law practice down in Renton, leaving her to abruptly relocate out of the city and away from the social dynamic she had put immeasurable time and effort in structuring over the years. And since all the older kids were transitioning to a new life in college, she was once again left with Emma, who remained as close as ever despite the distance. She concluded that the possibility of Emma ever being incorporated into their friend group was slim to none.

So imagine her surprise, when three years later she received a call from an ecstatic Emma narrating her splendid night with a group of familiar Davison alumni. Specifically, her encounter with Jack Douglas.

"I expect there to be drama coming soon," Harmony said to herself, causing Dr. Kays to look up from her notepad.

"Drama that you cause?"

"Maybe, we'll just need to see."

"*You'll* need to see," Dr. Kays, corrected, motioning to the clock at her desk.

"We'll have to cut this short, because it is getting late, and you technically didn't schedule this appointment."

"Yeah my bad," Harmony gave a sheepish grin. "I appreciate you listening as always."

"Anytime, and don't worry this is off the books."

Harmony dabbed up her therapist and headed for the door, when she remembered something.

"And the third?"

Dr. Kays faced her. "What's that?"

"When you used the wet firewood analogy, you said in that situation one has a few options. You only gave two."

"Very astute of you," Dr. Kays noted. "The third option, and perhaps the most powerful, is to not use firewood at all. By doing so, you eventually come to realize it was never needed."

Harmony left on a positive note that evening, using her drive home for serious contemplation.

She knew how infatuated Emma felt for Jack at that moment. The last time she spoke so seriously about a boy was in high school, when she came over chattering on and on about some shady drug dealer who agreed to take her to prom. And while Harmony saw her friend's meeting with Jack as a dramatic step up, she was bothered by the fact that of all handsome richies in the Northwest, it *had* to be him.

The granular details of their relationship were unknown to her, but in truth, it mattered none. She clearly foresaw their eventual falling out, because she knew Jack better than most girls. He may try his best at being a good man and believe it with his heart. But he was just like every other guy, stricken with chauvinistic insecurity and further pressured by ever-evolving, progressive societal forces. Emma may have grown more comfortable with the uncomfortable, but regardless, Harmony knew such a drastic distinction between those two was incapable of a successful convergence.

So, she chose patience, and waited. Waited for the moment when one of them would take a lesson out of the Book of Loyalty and ask for her advice. Emma came closer than Jack ever did, but for months, Harmony was left on the outsides, in curious wonder as to if they were going to work out.

Alas, it was Tommy B who came to her. She regretted saying yes to his request. Clever bastard, waiting until late night when she was half asleep and capitalizing on partaking in the vast sphere of dramatic gossip that ultimately lured her in.

Unknown to Tommy, Harmony was already planning on making the trip to Seattle, as she had another request from a friend to tend to.

xxi

Traveling was stressful as-is. During the holidays though? Well, that was just unbearable.

Ninety minutes at JFK shuffling through security and to the gate. Over six grueling hours of flying. Another forty-five minutes to disembark and retrieve her luggage. And now, shuddering out at the pick-up zone while mentally tracking how long she could see her frosted breath fly from her mouth before evaporating into the misty air.

But when she saw the lights flashing from her ride, Emma knew it was worth the wait.

The passenger window rolled down, revealing beaming grins from HG and Morgan.

"You ready to go?" Morgan asked.

Emma joined them in the backseat, her aching body sinking in the soft, warm leather. Finally, she was home.

HG detoured through downtown Seattle, where Christmas had already arrived. Even in the late hour, the streets were brightened from the vivid decorations lining both sides of the avenue. Live music echoed from every corner, its sound blending beautifully with the swarms of spirited pedestrians intermingling below the constellation of lights wrapped around leafless trees.

"I missed this."

"It certainly missed you too," HG said.

They pulled up in front of Emma's house, where Morgan helped her with the bags.

"Are you coming in with us?" Morgan asked.

"I'm pretty tired, otherwise I would," HG groaned, turning to Emma. "I'll be at my dad's rental in the city. Let's get lunch while you're back and catch up?"

"I'd love that."

They watched HG drive off before going inside.

Emma's mother, Julia, was first to greet them, nearly tackling her daughter in excitement.

"My babygirl is back!"

"Hi mom," Emma bemoaned, using all the energy left in her fatigued state to reciprocate her mother's joy. Her extended family was present, forcing her to bid patience with their line of questioning before she could set her backpack down. The younger cousins were the main partakers, making Emma wonder if they had previously schemed a competition amongst themselves to see who could pester her the most with their overly broad inquiries.

"What is New York City like?"

"Is it big?"

"Do you have a boyfriend there?"

"Did you meet Mona Lisa?"

"Are there a lot of rats?"

"Did you get mugged?"

At last, Julia stepped in after seeing Emma's tolerance fading.

"Let's give her a moment to unpack and relax," she said, leaving Emma and Morgan to retreat upstairs.

"Personally, I think Josi asked the best question," Morgan giggled when they were finally alone in Emma's bedroom.

Emma perked up, curious to learn what Morgan was getting at.

"*'Do you have a boyfriend?'*" Morgan added, quoting Emma's cousin.

"You're still hilarious, Mo."

Morgan sat on Emma's bed to watch her unpack, permitting a handsbreadth of time before coming to the main course of her discussion items.

"Let's go out tonight. Remember Damon?"

"Your friend from Bishop?"

"He's having people over since everyone's back in town."

"Damon," Emma sighed apathetically. "Sounds like a high school reunion."

"That's the best part about winter break," Morgan countered. "It's like taking a trip down memory lane. Who knows the next time we will have another chance like this?"

"I guess so."

"So you're down?"

"Only for a little bit."

Emma recollected her late teenage years, and her frequent interactions with those from neighboring schools like Morgan. The idea of reconnecting with them drew little appeal, and contrary to Morgan's point, it had been nice not seeing them since they graduated.

Her resentment was only reinforced when they arrived, choking for air amid ear-rattling chatter from the rowdy party.

Damon was the loudest, jabbering on about how many rushing years he piled up over three short weeks starting for the Bulldogs. In his defense, he was known citywide for his exceptional career. If the expectation was not to pay respect to the hosts' grandstanding, Emma surely would have thrown herself off the roof by now. Not that it was a crazy option, considering there happened to be a thirty-foot wide, heated pool already brimmed with a hundred drunkards.

Despite her contempt for just about everyone there, Emma found the entire dynamic quite humorous, noting how unchanged the majority of them were from high school.

Morgan had temporarily escaped Emma's purview, leaving her to reluctantly engage with a couple idiotic guys desperate for female validation. She was all too accustomed with the situation, and hated that they were not in a bar, where she could actually monetize their horniness in the form of double vodka cranberries.

It only seemed like several minutes when Morgan returned, plainly wasted off shots as she gripped Emma's arm.

"Are you enjoying yourself?" Emma asked condescendingly.

Morgan was about to reply when a booming cheer came from across the room.

Emma's eyes gravitated to the front door, where she saw Tommy Beech enter rather dramatically and mouth something seemingly funny enough to cause the crowd to erupt in laughter.

Her heartbeat skipped at the sight of him, accurately guessing the next person to follow him through the door. And sure enough, there he was: Jack Douglas.

He sported a classic, plaid Burberry as he paced coolly past the crowd, trying to regroup with Tommy, who was busy circulating around.

Emma shot Morgan with a concerned glare.

"You didn't tell me that *he* would be here."

"Tommy?" Morgan's brows furrowed. "You know we're still talking, right?"

"Not him. *Jack.*"

"Oh," Morgan said blankly. "I didn't think it mattered."

"We're just not on the best terms, and with the internship news that's probably just going to make things worse."

Emma's phone rang.

"Give me a minute," she said to Morgan, plugging her other ear so she could block out the noise.

"Hey Emma, how are you enjoying your break?"

"Hunter," she began. "Sorry, you sort of caught me at a weird time to talk."

"Oh, my bad. No problem, I'll let you get back to it," he replied quickly. "I just wanted to hear your voice. I've been missing it already."

Even through the phone she tried concealing her blush, stealing a quick peek at Jack, who was fortunately preoccupied with some randoms.

"Call me whenever you're free. I hope I see you again." Hunter said, and hung up before she could respond.

Well shit, Emma thought, returning to Morgan.

"You won't believe who just called me."

Before she could say, Tommy suddenly appeared between them.

"Am I interrupting something here?" he interjected, boasting his ever-so charming grin.

"Hi Tommy."

"Seattle's treasures," he added, leaning closer to Morgan. "Tell me: how does it feel to be the two most beautiful gals in the city?"

Emma gave him a facetious eye roll as Morgan reddened.

"What a response," he jested, facing Emma. "Is HG with you?"

"Uh yeah, she was earlier," Emma replied, slightly confused by his question. "She actually picked me up from the airport."

"I see," Tommy uttered to himself. "She takes her time with things. I respect that."

She wanted to analyze further into his comment when Jack walked up to them. He met Emma's eyes, who instantly turned away.

"Hey Emma," he initiated.

"Jack," she replied dryly, growing self-conscious when bystanders gazed in their direction.

"How was New York?"

"It was great. I miss it already."

"That's good to hear," Jack grinned. "I'm happy that you're back. I really missed you."

Emma privately cringed at hearing that. Hunter had just said the same, and he was thousands of miles away. It was not hatred for Jack that made her reluctant to speak with him. Rather, it was how she anticipated the conversation to go. There was no chance she could skid by an eventless dialogue with him without the mention of her program extension. It did not matter that the decision was not made; she knew how Jack would react. And such a reaction was not ideal in their current scene.

"You're not one to come to parties like this," Emma said, changing the subject.

"You know how persuasive Tommy can be," Jack chuckled. "I never pegged you as someone to enjoy this scene either."

"Well, Morgan can also be pretty convincing when she wants to be."

An awkward pause split through the exchange until Jack spoke up.

"How was your semester? I'd love to hear more about it."

Emma sensed the tension in his tone.

"Amazing. The classes are great…my job is too. And all my friends there are incredible. I've been hounding them to come visit once I'm back in Seattle permanently."

"I'm glad it's going well," Jack muttered, snatching a bottle and two glasses from the nearby counter and handing one to Emma.

Truthfully, he was happy to see her. Just the sight of her radiating glow was enough to melt. But as he poured the vodka into their glasses, he could see the indifference in her face. Something was off.

"Let's toast," he announced. "To you being home. Finally."

Emma caught herself as she observed Jack's inattentive demeanor. Maybe it was just a façade. Regardless, she felt that it may be favorable to rip the bandage off while the opportunity was still good.

"Tentatively," she heard herself say, regretting it immediately.

"What?"

"I was waiting to tell you in person," she began, figuring her excuse would be good enough. "But I was offered an extension to my internship."

For a moment, Jack thought he was victimized to a twisted form of déjà vu. He studied Emma's nervous frown, knowing that giving the news brought as little enjoyment for her as it did hearing it. He chose to play along, suppressing his uprooted frustration and forcing a smile.

"That-that's awesome," Jack stammered, feeling his hands tremble as he tightened his clutch around his glass. "Are you going to take it?"

"I don't know yet," Emma admitted, oblivious to his surging temper. "I talked to a lot of people about it, and all of them have said that I should."

"Oh, I see, so you thought it was nice to tell everyone else before you tell me."

Emma pressed her lips.

"It's not like that at all," she defended. "Like I said, I was waiting to tell you in person."

"The same way you waited to tell me that you were leaving to New York last summer?"

"Jack—"

"It's okay Em. I get it, making big decisions is something you like to do on your own, without your boyfriend's input."

Emma did not like that.

"Not sure if 'boyfriend' is the right term to use when we haven't been acting like a couple these last few months, but okay."

"You're right. I mean, if I was *actually* your boyfriend, then you would have to explain why you have been cheating on me all this time."

"What are you talking about?"

"Please don't deny it, Tommy told me last month that you were telling Morgan all about how swooned you were from that guy you've been talking to."

"His name's Hunter, and we're just friends," Emma clarified. "I mean, yes, he's told me he likes me but—"

"Oh, he did? Did you tell him that you had a boyfriend. Or tell him who I am?"

"I did."

"I see, so it's okay if you use 'boyfriend' to describe me, but not the other way around when I do?"

Emma was annoyed by Jack's pettiness.

"Two very different circumstances, Jack." she rolled her eyes.

"I don't think so," Jack tested steadily. "I mean, are we not together anymore?"

"That's not what I said—"

"You implied it, though."

"Jesus, Jack, will you relax for a minute? I knew you were going to be like this."

"Be like what?"

"You're acting like the world is ending. It's not that big of a deal."

"After all this time in New York, I thought you'd change," Jack said, shaking his head. "You never took us seriously, did you? All you did was lead me on and play with me because you know I'll just keep coming back."

"Dude, you act like wining and dining a girl automatically means you've won their heart forever," she said, her patience relinquishing by the second. "Let's just table this conversation for the time being. You are being *way* too much right now."

She walked away and pinballed through the crowd to find Morgan now in the kitchen, sitting beside Tommy as she listened intently to whatever story he managed to captivate her with.

"Let's leave."

Morgan frowned. "What are you talking about, Emma? We just got here,"

"And I want to leave," she repeated more sternly.

Tommy noted Emma's discerned frown.

"What's going on, sugarplum?"

"Please Tommy, not now."

They were interrupted when Damon came back into play, hopping on the island and extending his reach to the chandelier above. In one swift motion, he kicked his feet up and swung over their heads, causing his audience to cheer wildly.

"What is going on right now?" Emma shouted, her voice subdued by the growing uproar.

Tommy only made the situation worse, as he begun to clap his hands in support of Damon's idiocy.

"That's that shit we like Damon!" he screamed.

Emma's eyes traveled across the excited faces as Damon hovered overhead. She retreated to the edge of the room, her mouth gaping as she watched Damon propel himself over the sea of heads and dive into the crowd like a rockstar in a mosh pit.

Jack had not realized what was going on – and just happened to be in the landing zone – feeling his drunkenly weak body thrust into the people in front of him as Damon rammed over his back.

"What the—?" he started to say until the wind was knocked out of him as he stumbled to the ground beside Damon. He quickly regained his stance and glared down at Damon.

"Are you crazy, dude?"

"Take it easy, Douglas," Damon muttered passively, still sulking in the moment of his deliriously outrageous feat.

Jack was already not in a good mood after speaking with Emma. Coupled with his rapid ingestion of alcohol, and now the unprompted tackle from an overly-testosteroned bum, he was near the verge of losing it completely.

"Go fuck yourself!"

He thought he had seen the worst of a bad temper, but Damon's was another beast. Unsurprisingly, given his athletic build and clear alpha-male vibes that he insisted to project *all* the time.

Damon stepped up to Jack when Tommy cut between them.

"Let's think a minute about we're doing here," he eased, causing Damon to get in Tommy's face while bystanders let out indistinct gasps in observance.

"I'm thinking about kicking your ass!"

Tommy was quick to waive Damon's threat, keeping his feet planted in front of him.

"Now Damon, that's not nice."

"Tom," Emma came forward, fearing the pummeling Tommy would undeniably get if he kept politicking.

Luckily, one of Damon's friends came to Tommy's aid, resting his hand on his shoulder.

"Come on man, keep it chill. Let's go smoke," he said.

"…Fine," Damon obeyed, raising his hands in the air as he looked back to Tommy and Jack. "I'll admit I got a little out of pocket there. That's my bad."

Damon's friends joined him as they started for the stairs, when Tommy called at him.

"Wait!"

Damon turned back to him and puffed his chest again.

"Could I smoke too?" Tommy asked.

Jack's eyes widened in bewilderment.

"Are you fucking serious?" Damon hissed back.

Tommy scanned around at everyone's frozen expressions, seemingly oblivious at how daring his request was to someone who was on the verge of kicking his ass.

"Yeah," he replied casually.

Damon walked back up to Tommy, and to everyone's surprise, smirked and wrapped his arm around him.

"Of course you can, Beech! Come on, get your ass up here."
"Sick," Tommy said, joining them with Morgan following close behind.
Jack and Emma remained there, utterly stunned as the crowd promptly
returned to their festivities.
"What just—"
"Tommy," Jack said flatly, cutting Emma off. "That's all you need to know."
They laughed, staring at each other as they quieted down. Even when they
were at their worst, Jack still found her beautiful. Upsetting her was never the
objective, and he was ashamed that his affection for her translated into their
argument earlier.
"I'm sorry for being an ass," he said.
"Me too," she smiled.
Jack was hesitant to keep speaking, as he dreaded the words he would say for
his own sake.
"You should go back to New York."
"Jack…"
"Hold on, let me finish. Please."
Emma nodded.
"I still want to be with you, and the idea of you leaving again sucks. But at the
same time, I know that this is something that makes you happy."
"Thank you for saying that Jack. But it's not just about whether I leave or
stay. It's more than that. The last few months, I just haven't felt the same. I
don't want to feel obligated to run anything by you, or anyone, for that matter,
on things that I think only involve me."
"I know, and I didn't mean to put you in that situation."
"And again – while I appreciate you telling me that – I still don't think that is
enough."
Jack lowered his head, knowing what was to come.
"You want to breakup?" he guessed.
"I don't know, Jack. That's such a hard question."
"Just tell me what you want, Em."
"I want time," she replied rather abruptly. "I need to figure all this shit out.
What I want, what I don't – it just feels like I never had the chance to know
because I've been too busy worrying about other things."
"And 'we' are one of those things?"
Emma gave an ashamed nod.

"Personally, I think that you are the one person I can spend the rest of my life with," Jack added. "No matter what happens, I truly believe that we will find each other down the road, and everything will work out the way it should. But…"

"…But?"

Jack grinned. "But, if it means letting you go so you can figure things out, like you said, then okay. I'll do it. However long it takes."

Emma hugged him. "Thank you Jack. I love you."

"I love you too."

Emma took a step back and adjusted her hair.

"I should probably get back to Morgan."

"Yeah, of course."

She left him and continued upstairs. He would feel much better for the rest of that night. Even though he did not know how Emma perceived them, the reassurance that they could be together again was enough for him to believe things would work out. If he believed it to be true, living life without her was not as difficult of a task. That is, as long as she eventually came back to him. There was, however, a glaringly outstanding issue that they did not clarify: the *actual* status of their relationship. A potentially dangerous item to leave open-ended, too.

Jack would be too nervous to bring it up again. He would end up being too late, too, with Emma's ultimate decision to return to New York approaching. And unfortunately for Jack, it just so happened that Emma's takeaway on their discussion was, well, not aligned with his own.

xxii

Logan despised studying. He acknowledged its necessity for academic success though, and discovered a tolerable compromise through audiobooks. All it took was four hours probing the internet for digital files of his textbooks that he had downloaded on his phone. Now instead of hunkering down in the library judging the masses of students frantic for superficial recognition, he could dedicate the time to something else he hated equally: exercising.

He kept a steady jog that late morning, controlling the rhythm in his breath while simultaneously taking mental notes of the monotone speaker lecturing him through headphones lodged in his ears. He rounded the street corner, slowing down at the sight of an assembly of cars parading the street ahead.

"Berg!" came a familiar voice, startling him as the man leapt two feet away in view.

"Ryder!" Logan greeted, embracing his former acquaintance. "It's been years dude. How has life been?"

"It's been great man. I'm truly thankful, let's leave it at that," Ryder grinned cheerfully, something Logan had grown used to from their time together. "What have you been up to lately?"

Logan held up his headphones for Ryder to see.

"College," he groaned. "I'm hanging in there though. It's wild, I once thought I'd be done with all this shit after high school."

"Apparently not. I'm happy for you Berg. It's not every day that I see one of my homies making it big in the world."

"I wouldn't go that far, but I appreciate it nevertheless."

And appreciative he was. Ryder was the first person Logan befriended when he begun selling. They were the same age in an environment staunched in provocation and combative masculinity, so it did not take much for them to grow close at the expense of their shared fear of engaging in the dangerous hustle. Baker often paired them when they hit the streets. Looking back on their adventures, Logan credited Ryder for his ability to endure through the horrific episodes. He was a brother, and one that would always be there for him, no matter what.

"Sorry for just showing up out of the blue like that," Ryder apologized, taking a step back. "I was chasing you for the last block waiting for you to stop at one of these lights."

"Don't sweat it, Ryder," Logan said, pocketing his headphones. "Let's catch up. It's been too long."

They continued across the street, exchanging a series of new stories since they had last connected. Logan found himself laughing at everything Ryder said, prompting him to remember his old friend's impressive ability to make even the most tragic things entertaining.

"How are you making money nowadays?"

Ryder shook his head.

"Still working for Baker," he groused, going out of his way to kick every rock they passed onto the street. "It's been better."

"How is he?"

"Different. A lot has changed since…you know…"

"Yeah, I can imagine…look—"

"You don't need to explain yourself Logan," Ryder assured. "We *both* know how difficult Baker could be."

Logan maintained his composure despite Ryder's skittish demeanor at the mention of his former employer. His falling out with Baker was nothing short of public news, which was a driving reason why he never reached out to Ryder. Silly of him, to believe that it would affect their friendship. Still, Logan feared his prior actions would someday warrant undesirable repercussions.

"So I take it he's still in town?"

"That's right, and not far from here actually," Ryder affirmed, glancing around him to make sure that they were alone before continuing. "If you want, I can take you to him."

Logan trembled at the invitation. Seeing Baker again was not a proposal he wanted to entertain. He was prepared to shut it down right then, but instead reasoned the benefits that could come if he made up with someone capable of destroying his chances of a better future. Also, never not a good time to make peace.

"Okay," Logan agreed. "Take me to him."

Ryder guided Logan down the avenue, where they trailed under a bustling highway, eventually reaching a quietening intersection on the outskirts of the city. The fine pavement abruptly broke into a loose gravel path. Logan felt as if they crossed over to another realm; one Seattle had consciously bordered off from the rest of the world. He had spent so long living amongst the wealthy, that he had forgotten about the harsh actuality of city life that tormented a significant portion of the region's inhabitants. Only minutes from downtown, and yet, the striking dissimilar scene was astonishing for Logan, uneasy about his presence in the hood.

The district sat on the edge of a small portion of the Sound. The picturesque image of massive edifices ceased to exist here, being replaced with the skeletal frames that was left of poorly sustained developments. The streets were desolate, free of any cars and pedestrians. Other than Ryder, the only movement Logan could detect sourced from the heavy wing that whistled past his ears before barreling in and out of the ransacked shops that lined the block. He lowered his gaze as they trudged on, grimacing at the unbearably foul scent of the littered sidewalk strewn with miscellaneous clumps of garbage.

"What happened here?"

Ryder sighed, disdain leaking in his reply as they maintained a steady pace. "Nothing."

They cut into an alley before sliding through barb-wire, where in front of them rested an abandoned apartment complex.

Logan stopped for a moment, slightly unsettled by the development, when he was struck by a wave of nostalgia.

He was just a kid when he found the complex. The first night, he had broken into one of the windows and sheltered in the corner of an empty room. He recalled the stench covering him when he emerged the following morning, hitching for any car willing to take him back to Mercer.

The building appeared untouched from how he left it. Its foundation was weak, and once appealing panels have now decayed from weathering over the years.

"It's been like this for as long as I can remember," Ryder said. "I guess things don't change much, eh?"

"Sometimes they never do."

The idea of reconnecting with Baker had started to settle for Logan. He was unafraid of confrontation; however he acknowledged his short temper and lack of consideration when following through on his impulsiveness. He was sure just the sight of Baker would stir some suppressed anger. Whether it was justified or not, he knew keeping it cordial was his best course of action. There would be no reason for unnecessary provocation – for Baker's sake, as well as his own.

They treaded lightly up the steps and into the building, Logan staying close to his old friend as they walked through the corridor. The walls were darkened by patches of dust and dirt, its layers thickening the farther they carried from the windows draped in tarnished sheets. A group of hoodlums greeted them once they reached an opening into what was once a small lobby, causing Logan to lower his head so he would not be recognized.

"This is Berg," Ryder introduced.

One of the men spoke up.

"*Logan* Berg?"

Logan gave a hesitant nod.

"Holy shit!" another man. "I know you – this is the guy that was locked up after some shit went down with Baker."

Logan immediately feared for his life but was instead presented with a series of friendly hollers from the men. Ryder grinned as he watched Logan dab up each of them before guiding him to the end of the lobby and into another hall. They slowed in front of a closed door, Ryder clasping tightly on the rusty doorknob and looking back at him.

"You want me to wait for you?" he asked.

"I'd appreciate it."

His heart raced when Ryder twisted the knob vigorously and pushed the door open. He overheard the door latch behind him, looking ahead into the dim room. The air was somehow musky and dry, obscured in an unknown haze that was only noticeable from a faint glint of sunlight leaking under the blackened curtains. Logan squinted to make out a silhouette sitting on the other end from where he stood. He squinted harder, realizing it was a person sitting alone behind a grand desk. His feet slowly carried him closer, eventually drawing to a halt at the desk as he stalled in the deafening silence. He scoured the little courage riddling in his bones to speak.

"Baker."

Baker lifted his head, glaring back at him. Even in the haze, Logan could tell Age was unwilling to treat his former associate so kindly since their last interaction: his once rubescent appearance now roughened into a pale, sandpapery complexion; his feeble arms could be mistaken for sandpaper, pimply and wrinkled in all the wrong areas, and joints of his frail bones bulging out of his body, almost as if they could pop through his mottled skin at any given moment.

"Berg," Baker began, the monotone drawl in his voice seeming to exhaust him. "How have you been kid?"

Logan reached for a chair and sat down.

"I think I should be the one asking you that," Logan chirped, managing a smile.

"Right," Baker chuckled, glowering down to his liverish skin. "Well, let's just say that I refused to obey the one rule that all drug dealers are supposed to follow."

Logan grew uneasy, watching Baker struggle as he pushed himself up in his seat.

"I know I did not ask you here, so I assume you came voluntarily," Baker speculated, his disarming tone catching Logan off guard. "What can I do for you?"

"It's been a long time, Baker," Logan stammered. "And I know that bringing it up may not be the best idea on my part, but I want to apologize—"

"You do not have to explain to me why you did it," Baker interrupted, reaching for a half-empty bottle of whiskey on his desk. "I understand."

"Do you?"
Baker produced two glasses from his drawer, proceeding to fill one and momentarily glance at Logan.
"I'm good…thanks."
Baker tilted his head understandably and placed down the bottle before continuing.
"You care about others, even when they do not care about you," Baker added.
"I saw the look on your face…you thought about it, did you not? Giving that boy away. I do not know the details of your friendship with him, but I imagine it could not have been the best."
His accuracy made Logan uneasy. Baker always was more intuitive than he gave off.
"I didn't know what to do," Logan replied. "I knew I wouldn't be able to live with myself if I gave him up. He didn't deserve it."
Baker leaned forward in his chair, still fixated on Logan.
"What about now?"
"What do you mean?"
"Your friend. Do you now think he deserved it?"
"I don't know," he admitted after thinking the question over.
Baker nodded sympathetically.
"I know you Logan, and because I know you, I have no doubt that you thought about my question in the past…" he leaned back in his chair. "…what confuses me, is that you still feel obligated to not accept what you believe to be true."
Logan turned away, embarrassed.
"I don't know what you want me to say," he muttered. "Some days, I don't even know what I'm doing. I mean yeah, I've turned a page, and in college, and I feel like I am supposed to think that everything is fine. But it's not—" he looked back at Baker. "Back when we worked together, I was still going through a lot of shit, don't get me wrong. But compared to my life now, it made sense…or, at least I thought it did."
"Explain."
Logan swallowed hard before continuing.
"Growing up, all I wanted was to get out. I didn't feel like I belonged in this world. It was like God put me here by mistake. And sure, I know He doesn't do that, and He put me through all of it for a reason, but…"
"But?"
"…But if that's the case, then I think it's fair for me to think that it was meant to be for something good, right? If not for me, then for someone I know. And as much as I can tell, I haven't done anything to help another person, even when I try to."

"What about your mother?" Baker suggested. "Who knows where she would be if it were not for you."

"I guess."

"And your friend? If you *did* betray him then, imagine where he would be now," Baker chuckled slightly. "I can assure you that you did a blessing by stopping me."

"Sometimes I think about getting back at him for selling me out," Logan countered. "But like I said, now that I'm finally out of the hole, I think it's best for me if I just let it be, and let the universe take care of him, ya know?"

"And how will you feel if your 'universe' does not do as you wish? What then?"

The question struck Logan into silence, causing Baker to go on.

"This is *your* life. It does not belong to anyone and no matter how hard some may try it never will. We all make choices, and there are consequences for them. It is not – nor should it be –our power to know how much it *could* affect our lives. We only have partial fault with everything we do. And because of that, you should not feel the blame for what has happened to you." He sat back in his seat. "I know I am the last person you ever thought would tell you this, but in an ironic way, I think it is more appropriate that it *is* me saying it."

"I understand. Thank you."

A knock came at the door.

"Looks like my guys are back from their runs," Baker signaled, looking back to Logan. "You are always welcome here Logan. These guys are your family, and they will have your back for anything you need."

Logan left Baker's room, seeing his associates straggled along the walls. They shared respectful nods and continued inside, leaving Logan to retrace his steps toward the exit where Ryder was waiting for him.

"How did it go?"

"Not bad…" Logan whisper lowly. "Not bad at all."

"I'm glad," Ryder said, peering at the sun above. "You should head back. I know you have a lot of shit to take care of nowadays."

"Yeah, uh…" Logan began, reaching for his headphones upon remembering he was in the middle of his run. "Let's stay in touch this time, all right? I don't want to go this long again without talking to you."

"Even if we did, what's the difference? You're my brother, Logan. Doesn't matter how much time passes, I'll be here."

Logan went in for a sincere hug and waved Ryder goodbye as he watched him skip up the stairs back into the complex. It was a solacing experience for him, feeling his lips slowly stretch across his face. He pushed the headphones into his ears and started off, jogging away from the world he had once knew.

The campus was in sight when Logan reached his run's end. Physically exhausted, he found a bench on the corner of the block and observed the procession of vehicles speeding past. His earbuds died, causing the societal humdrum – once muffled – to reverberate in full force, the rest of his senses following. It had been a while since he had last eaten, and a sweet aroma from across the street tantalized his nostrils, leading him to give in to the hunger and detour toward the bakery.

It was quieter when he entered the bakery. So quiet, that he could pick out every conversation from the few groups whispering amongst themselves. And of those voices, there came one he identified as more than familiar.

He swiveled around, where just ten feet from him, was Emma.

She was sitting with another girl he did not know, and judging from their hardened expressions, reckoned it was a serious discussion. He ignored the social cue, nevertheless, feeling his weakened legs carry him to their table. Emma's eyes widened when she saw him, jumping out of her chair and embracing him.

"Logan!"

"Sorry if I smell, I just finished a run." he apologized in fluster.

"You smell fine," she smiled, gesturing to the other girl. "This is my friend HG."

"Nice to meet you." HG jawed, not meeting his eyes.

Logan reciprocated with a nod before turning to Emma. "I thought you were in New York?"

"My internship finished up a couple weeks ago," Emma explained, exchanging a mysterious glance at HG before continuing. "I'm only back for the holidays."

"Only back for the holidays," Logan echoed, dissecting her reply. "Does that mean you're going leaving again?"

He was initially confused when Emma tensed at his question. But coupled with HG's dismissiveness towards him, he was quick to connect the dots.

"Anyways," Logan moved on. "I came in here to get something and saw you, so I figured I'd come say hi."

Emma's reaction to his question filled her with guilt, fully aware of the awkwardness it caused.

"Why don't you join us?"

"It's okay, I still have some studying to do," Logan said quickly, knowing that he would be getting high instead.

"I should actually get going," HG finally spoke up, eyeing Emma as she grabbed her bag. "I got errands to run."

She hugged Emma and paced through Logan without a word.

"She seems nice," Logan chuckled once she was gone.

"She really is."
He could feel her guard still up for some reason. His was too, admittedly, unsure how to deal with her complacency.
"It feels like forever since we've talked. How have you been?"
"Good. I mean, better," Logan nodded. "What about you? I didn't expect to see you for much longer."
"Why is that?"
"I don't know, I guess when you left, I figured you would stay. I definitely would have, if I were in your shoes."
"It's still tempting, trust me," Emma assented. "I thought I was being reckless when I did it. There were a lot of things on my mind, and I was worried I'd get cold feet and not go. But I don't regret leaving. Everything sort of fell into place after a couple days."
"You found clarity."
"In a way, yeah. But it wasn't because I didn't want to be here…it was more of figuring out why I felt the need to leave to begin with." She paused. "If I'm actually being honest with myself, I still don't know completely why I did it."
Logan nodded understandingly.
"I think it was good for you to leave, even if just for a few months. You seem different now, like I'm meeting you again for the first time."
He could still feel Emma's unease as he watched how she cradled her mug.
"You all right?" he asked.
"Yeah, sorry. I guess you can say that I am at a crossroads, of sorts. It's been weighing on me the last couple days."
"Well if you want to talk about it, just know that I'm the last person to judge."
Emma looked off, unwilling to meet his eyes.
"I was offered an extension to my internship."
"That's great! Are you going to take it?"
"I'm not sure yet."
Logan sighed, as he was able to see through her uneager reception of the idea.
"It's Jack, isn't it?"
At that, Emma faced him.
"Have you spoken to him?"
"No, but we both know he wasn't happy about you moving away. I imagine he reacted similarly to this news."
"'Similarly,' is an understatement."
"I don't see the issue here Emma. This is the opportunity that you've been waiting for. What's holding you back?"
"If I go back, I'm afraid I'll lose Jack in the process."
Logan empathized with her dilemma. It did not surprise him that Jack meant a lot to her. He was slightly bothered, however, that someone as intelligent as

her was not able to comprehend the irrelevance in his opinion for a matter like this.
"What do you think I should do?" Emma asked him.
"I don't think I'm the person to give advice on how to handle Jack."
"You actually might be my best bet," Emma retorted, coming to realize fate's choice of bringing Logan to her in that moment. "It can't be a coincidence that you and I ran into each other when I have this problem."
Logan scratched his head. Had he known the nature of this matter, he certainly would have abstained from asking.
"Come on Logan," Emma persisted. "I always thought of you to be reasonable. You were so supportive of my decision to go to New York, too. All I'm asking for is your input."
Logan hesitated, his memory flashing back to his first night in juvie. Unbeknownst to Emma, he had other priorities to tend to that night. It was a small portion of his life he knew he would never forget, and he would not have put it past Emma to forget it, either. It was then, when Logan had once believed Emma to have closed the door to their friendship, forever.
Yet, here she was, asking him for his advice on how to repair a broken relationship with another guy. A guy, who had once happened to be his best friend. Go figure.
He had no interest in entertaining Emma's request. He cared about her – more than he could admit. There were even instances when he wondered if he could have a chance of reviving their relationship had Jack not been a factor.
Nonetheless, he knew that if he ever did act out of spite, now would not be time. Emma was hurting, and consoling her was all that mattered.
"Why did you go to New York?" he asked.
"Come on, Logan—"
"Just play along," he implored. "Please."
He heard a drawling sigh from her end.
"I left to do what I love."
"How did Jack react?"
"He wasn't happy," she replied flatly. "Which obviously sucked. I hoped he would be supportive."
"Did he explain why he wasn't happy?"
"Yeah, he accused me of leaving him. Don't get me wrong, I totally understand where he was coming from, but he also couldn't see the bigger picture, you know? I didn't go to get away from him. Sure, he annoyed me with the nonstop calls just to check in on me. I get that he likes me a lot, but I didn't sign up for him to become obsessive."

Logan grew silent, pitying Jack as he listened to Emma. He did not consider him to behave obsessively, as Emma put it. Instead, he reasoned that Jack's actions were out of love.

Logan had also come to realize another glowering truth about his significance to Emma: he had none. The way she stressed over what Jack thought about her actions – how determined she was to also consider his feelings before her own – Logan knew she had never done it about him. Even if the affection she had for Jack was not defined as love, it was still miles ahead of whatever she felt toward him.

Logan was confident that Emma was mesmerized about what she and Jack could be, and not what they actually were. And he only knew this, because it is exactly how he perceived Emma back then. Logan would not tell her, figuring that revelation should be intended for her to discover on her own. If she had not already.

"It seems to me that you know everything you wanted to know on your own," Logan said, placing his hand on hers.

"I think you're right," Emma finally concurred.

"Hang in there, Emma," Logan said definitively before rising to his feet. He paused on his way out and turned to her to speak one last time.

"I'm always here if you need anything."

And with that, he left, concluding there was nothing more to add.

Perhaps Emma struck a good point about fate and its methods of bringing situations to light. There was a reason why he went on a run that day. Little did he know that such a decision would unknowingly result in the reacquaintance with people he had not seen in years. Especially Baker, who despite having been viewed by Logan as his fault for a period of his life full of turmoil and misery, had surprisingly transcended into almost a mentor of sorts. Logan had him to thank for much of his personal growth.

He also had regards for Emma, who even in her current state being so detached from his way of life, was still capable of influencing his decisions, which would ultimately impact how he shaped his future.

And yet, Logan did not feel compelled to bestow that satisfaction on her behalf. If anything, he was ambivalent of his own willingness to become susceptible to Emma's unintentional motives. A flaw he perceived it to be, and one that he longed to rid after witnessing the dreadful effects that could follow from it.

His entire life, Logan had welcomed interferences, and ultimately accepted them at his own expense. Although he understood that he was not to be fully blamed, he also knew that continuing to fall into the schemes would only warrant the cycle to repeat. Emma was a great person, and he wished her the best. But there were that demanded his attention. Commitments must be prioritized. And for the time being, he knew she could not be one of them.

Logan arrived outside of his building, taking in one last breath of the bristled air before skipping inside.

He did not ask for this life, and yet, he finally considered the idea of living it.

xxiii

Jack awoke having virtually no recollection of the previous night. How often he felt inclined to drink in stupor with the hope that it could solve his vexations were beyond his capability, or reason, to understand. In recent time, his nights typically consisted of spending a half hour alone at the bar milking a drink, privately assessing a litany of excuses he made up to justify his decision to down five more. Or, until a suitable prospect presented herself, in such case he was never not willing to engage.

He let out a subtle yelp when he tried to sit up, noticing the arms of a naked girl beside him tightly wrapped around his waist. She opened her eyes and brought a hand to his chest.

"Good afternoon," she smiled.

"Um, hello," Jack hesitated, gingerly sliding off the bed and reaching for his clothes balled up at his feet. A minute passed when he turned back to the girl, surprised to see her still staring.

"Is everything okay?" she asked.

"Yeah, I have to get going…" Jack paused. "I can get you a ride if you want."

"What about lunch? Last night you told me we could go somewhere."

"I did?"

"Yes," she replied sternly. "Right after you said that you wanted me to meet your parents."

"Oh yeah," Jack shrugged as he finished buttoning his shirt. "My bad, I forgot I have a meeting." A lie, but he would say anything if it got her to leave.

She inspected his standoffish mood. "Are you lying to me?"

"Of course not! Here, I'll call you when I'm done and we can meet up…" his voice trailed in astonishment at the blank of the girl's name. "…Nicole, right?"

"Elizabeth." She corrected, crossing her arms.

"Nicole Elizabeth?"

"No asshole, just Elizabeth."

Elizabeth jumped out of bed and got dressed quickly before storming out of the bedroom, where she was met with Tommy in the kitchen.

"Hey Nicole," he greeted, offering her a plate. "You want something to eat?"

Elizabeth stomped her foot in frustration and shot him a glare.

"It's Elizabeth!"

Tommy managed a dumbfounded smirk, placing the plate on the countertop. "There's sausage on the skillet," he added.

Elizabeth screamed and headed out the door, muttering an assortment of stifled remarks.

"What was that about?" he asked Jack when he entered moments later.

"Apparently her name is not Nicole."

"I could've sworn it was…"

"Me too."

"Hm, well," Tommy motioned to the stove. "There's sausage on the skillet."

"I'm good thanks. I need to go for a walk. Clear my head."

Tommy nodded and went about his business. A drunken night with a forgettable girl: situation was all too familiar for him to be surprised by Jack's desire for solitude.

The weather's influence on the mood of an individual is interestingly uncanny. It was particularly evident that morning, had he been awake before the brumal chill eventually warmed in the later hours. Snowflakes melted away into a shower of heavy droplets falling from the cinereal skies, with iridescent streaks goldening over Jack's sunglasses before climbing down from his polo to his loafers. When it rains, it pours. Oddly fitting for Jack, only in his case, it always pours.

He picked a bench on campus, catching himself in a confused state and observing his knuckles. They were nearly healed from his manic night, running his fingers over the newly formed scars before rising and slogging across the empty grounds.

Now that finals were over, he had a couple days to breathe before returning to the basic, studious routine next semester. And God, did he welcome the opportunity for relaxation. Or the privilege of knowing the meaning of the word.

Because instead of reaching a worry-free state of mind, his conscience was still fixated on Emma. Seeing her at Damon's party did not help. Sure, she bolstered growth, but it was growth from him. Leaving for New York on a claim to prioritize her future. How foolish was he to pray it would lead to her coming back to him? Clarity came in the opposite form, and despite his reluctance to accept their broken relationship, the reality had begun to settle, nevertheless.

He faulted his naivety expecting a serendipitous outcome from a drunk meet with a girl at a bar. It was not until he woke up that he once again forced himself to face what he believed never to be true. This was loneliness at its finest.

Stranger things have happened, he thought.

He relocated to the opening of the courtyard, briefly wiping the specks of water from his shades. His attention was redirected after he put them back on, when he saw a girl waiting at the crosswalk ahead. Her appearance was strikingly familiar, notably rings on her fingers as she pulled back her maroon hair that settled just above her hips. Jack left the bench and drew closer, overhearing her hum an indistinct tune as she readjusted the buds in her ears. Her tone was sweet, and melodic.

"Emma!" he called, immediately embarrassed to see a random face turn back to him.

"Who are you?"

"Sorry," Jack caught himself and took a step back. "I thought you were someone else."

The girl eased up.

"It's okay, mistakes happen," she replied with a hint of intrigue. "Who did you think I was? Who knows, maybe I know her."

Jack noticed the traffic light flashing.

"No it's fine. Thank you though."

The girl exchanged an understanding nod and strolled away.

HG was directly across the street and saw the entire interaction play out, letting out a soft chuckle as she passed the girl on the street, and toward Jack.

"Wow, you might just be the most down bad guy in Seattle right now."

Jack's jaw dropped when he saw her.

"What are you doing here?"

"'Hello to you too,'" HG retorted, hugging him. "I happened to be in the city and figured I'd come surprise you."

"Just randomly, without letting me know?"

"Well, Jack, it wouldn't have been a surprise if I told you beforehand, now would it?"

"No, I guess not," Jack muttered, his eyes still on the fake Emma in the distance.

"Did you get her name?" came HG.

"Nah, I just thought she was someone else," Jack scratched his head. "How long are you here for? Do you want to grab lunch or something?"

"I already ate—" she began to say, catching herself from revealing that she was with Emma earlier. "How about a walk? It's a beautiful day."

Sure, that's all I do nowadays."

"Hey, it's a nice hobby. Plus, it keeps me looking sexy."

They started off toward the city. HG may have been kidding about her looks, but Jack admitted its obvious truth. He kept stealing glimpses of her incredible physique, and admired how her straight brown hair naturally curled at the ends of her fair shoulders. Her eyes were bluer than the deepest pits of the ocean. And her smile? Well, it was bright enough to warrant a second pair of shades. Flower buds would bloom if she also had the sun's capability to generate insurmountable heat. Not to say that she was not hot, but the term would be more applicable to her appearance, rather than chemical makeup.

"Emma told me what happened with you two," HG said after a few minutes walking in silence. She was never one to drag on with pleasantries. "I'm sorry. I really thought that you two were going to work out."

Jack raised an eyebrow.

"You're saying it like it never will."

"Not at all! It's just – sometimes these things happen for a reason."

"Tommy would have a fit if he heard you say that."

"Please, I think everyone in the world knows about Tommy and his *opinions*," she groaned. "Look Jack, there are a lot of ways to show that you like someone, but you have to act on it. Love is best when it is shown."

"You make it sound easy."

"The complete opposite. Nothing in life is supposed to be, especially this."

Jack stopped walking and turned away from her.

"How do you want this situation with Emma to play out?"

"I don't know how to answer that HG. I just want to be in her thoughts."

"You're a true hopeless romantic," she smirked, causing Jack to blush helplessly.

"Do you think she will be happy if you got what you wanted?"

Jack frowned. "I don't understand your question…what's the point of wanting her if she doesn't want me?"

"My point exactly," HG said and pulled his arm to get him moving again. "Think about all the happy people in the world, and how many of them have no idea who you are. Sometimes, someone's happiness is *their own*, and it's kinda selfish to expect them to include yours."

Her advice was nowhere near what he wished to hear. Wishing happiness for someone who was unwilling to do the same? That was, as the Silent Generation say, crazy talk.

"I'm not saying that Emma doesn't want the same for you," HG added, reading Jack's discouraged expression. "But this comes back to you tuning into her feelings. Empathizing is one of the hardest things to do when you're involved in the situation. We tend to weigh in how it affects us."

Jack nodded glumly. They were not the best at keeping in contact, but HG's concern was enough for him to reminisce the peak of their friendship. She was his oldest girlfriend, and was always there for him, particularly when he required an ear from the opposite sex to give insight on his relationship drama. He had his boys, but there was only so much he could say before they tuned him out. Or worse, ridicule him for being too sensitive, as simps do. HG was never like that, and it was perhaps due to how often Jack would switch roles whenever she confided in her trials with the plethora of shitty guys who had taken advantage of her over the years. For most young girls, there is nothing worse than falling for the "fuckboi."

HG still sensed Jack's sadness and hugged him again.

"I'm here if you need anything."

Then something happened to Jack, who was initially puzzled when he broke away to stare into her consoling gaze. He knew this feeling, but never with her. It was almost uncomfortable for him, having always considered her pretty, but going so long seeing her as nothing more than a friend, he was usure how to acknowledge his sexual attraction surging in that moment. HG felt it too, managing a flirty smile before pulling away.

"I should get back," Jack cleared his throat, also his best impression in pretending nothing weird happened.

HG followed the gist, crossing her arms and eyeing toward the parking lot.

"Care to walk me back to my car?"

"Not at all."

It was another silent walk to HG's car where they exchanged their farewell. He waved her off when she entered her car, failing to notice the window roll down.

"Jack."

He turned back and they locked eyes, anticipating her to address the obvious. Instead, she shook her head and said, "Don't be a stranger, all right?"
With that, she turned off the lot and down the avenue.
Tommy was watching TV when Jack returned. He was still in a funk, apparently, given how many steps it took for him to reach the living area from the front door.
"You're back earlier than I expected," Tommy said when Jack threw himself face-down on the sofa. "How was your walk?"
"Not bad. I ran into HG."
"Harmony," Tommy exhaled, pretending to be surprised. "How is she doing?" "Good."
"Just good?"
"Yeah."
"That's it huh?"
"Yep."
"So, nothing happened?"
Jack sighed boorishly and sat up. Once Tommy started probing, there was no way to stop it.
"Something *did* happen," Jack confirmed and retold his interaction with HG. He was unsurprised to watch Tommy's arrogant, but stoic grin widen as he progressed further into the story. He returned to a lazed slouch when he finished, waiting patiently for Tommy's turn to speak.
"…okay?" Tommy monotoned.
Jack's face hardened in astonishment.
"That's it? No witty remark or philosophical anecdote?"
"Not really. You and Harm are good friends. Always have been. I figured you two would have hooked up by now."
"We didn't," Jack countered. "But like I said, there was definitely a—"
"Spark."
Jack sighed. "Yeah."
Tommy muted the TV and leaned forward.
"What do you want me to say here? That it would be a good idea to try things with HG when you're still in love with Emma?"
"It's not that I want to be with HG. That will just make things weird."
"True."

"But still, it made me think that maybe in order to get over Emma, I should actually explore a *serious* relationship with someone else."

"Did you forget the fact that you woke up with a girl earlier today? This is old news man, and we've talked about too many times. I don't think this is a matter of whether you should be with someone else, and it doesn't make sense to over-complicate your situation when you haven't yet resolved the one you're in."

"Wow," Jack said, chuckling. "I think for once, we're on the same page." Tommy mimicked his reaction as he directed his attention back to the television.

"Even if we're not, as long as the pages are in the same book, we'll be fine."

*****

Jack.

He was all Harmony could think about as she clutched the steering wheel. What was the cause of this sudden, surging attraction? Perhaps it was out of pity from listening to his desperate longing for Emma. Or was it out of envy, desiring a man to obsess over her in a similar way? *No, impossible,* she reasoned, knowing that she would have some self-resentment if it were true. And to that degree, she did not.

Maybe it was something deeper: an attraction her subconscious buried long ago when she friend-zoned Jack due to her unwillingness to entertain anyone but the best. She was uncomfortable with how flimsy her grasp on her inner thoughts were, and tried rejecting it entirely.

Damn you Tommy. If she had just denied his request to talk to Jack.

One thing was true: she needed advice. And who better to give it than from someone who had experienced Jack in a different light? Someone who could, to her earlier point, overcome the difficulty of empathizing with someone directly involved in the situation?

HG detoured from the path home, veering off the exit and toward Emma's. She was quick to be greeted when she rang the doorbell, forcing an intense smile when Emma answered.

"Sorry for dropping by without saying anything. I wanted to apologize for leaving earlier today like I did."

"No worries," Emma said, letting her in. "I had a great talk with my friend after you left."

"Logan, right?

Emma grinned. "I'm surprised you remember his name. It didn't seem like you cared about who he was."

"I don't, but that doesn't mean my memory is shitty."

Emma led them to her bedroom, where HG was stunned by muddles of garments strewn across the floor. She high stepped to the bed to avoid the clutter, mistakenly fumbling a neatly folded pile of sweaters.

"It must be a coincidence that you came over. I was going to call you," Emma began, closing the door behind them. "I talked to Logan about, well, much of what we discussed, and after spending more time thinking about it—"

"You're going back." HG finished

"Uh, yeah…how did you know?"

HG motioned to the messy wardrobe between them. "All the years I've been your friend, you've never been a slob."

"I'll take that as a compliment," Emma chuckled, plopping on the floor and proceeding to fold her clothes into one of the few suitcases. "I don't know why I was debating it for this long. Everyone told me that I should do it, including you."

"Jack too?"

Emma cocked her head.

"Jack…" she muttered. "That's still a whole other thing."

The tension in her tone was apparent for HG, who resisted the urge to delve into that particular rabbit hole of drama.

"Anyways, you're the only one who knows about this, so I would appreciate if we kept it between us." Emma added.

"Are you going to tell anyone else?"

"I will, but in my own time. There's so much I need to get done that delivering the news is the last of my priorities right now."

"I'm not trying to tell you what to do, but maybe you should think about letting others know sooner than later, like Morgan. Or Jack."

Emma looked at HG, now more quizzical in her long pause.

"Why are you bringing Jack up again? Did he say something to you?"

At that, HG retracted, figuring that disclosing her conversation with Jack would not be the best idea.

"Sorry, I'm just trying to gather the full reason behind why you're going back."

"I already told you at lunch."

"Did you though?" HG challenged, hoping that it would lead to Emma sharing details she may had intentionally kept secret.

Instead, Emma shook her head in mild annoyance.

"I don't see what you're getting at."

"Look Em, I didn't drive up just to have lunch with you."

Emma gasped. "So you *did* speak to Jack?"

"Tommy asked me to because he was worried about him. He said that he hasn't been the same since you left. And I'm not blaming you at all, but in his defense, you sorta left him hanging."

Emma lowered her head in shame.

"How is he?"

"Not great," HG said flatly. "And before you ask, I only told him what I knew: that you were back for the holidays, and you leaving again was up in the air." "Well that's the truth," Emma nodded. "He also gave me his blessing when I saw him at Damon's, so I don't understand why he's still acting like this."

"Perhaps it's because that's no longer the truth, Emma. If you don't tell him soon, he's going to think I deliberately lied to him. And if you wait for him to find out on his own, he'll probably take it out on me, and I don't want that."

"Jack's not like that. Besides, since when do you care what other people think about you?"

HG hesitated.

"Jack is different. I grew up with the guy. He's been one of my closest friends."

"Same goes for me, and I can recall many times when you've told me that you don't care about my opinion of you."

"Come on, I'm clearly kidding," HG rubbed her face before continuing.

"Let's be real here, I care about what you think of me, and the same goes for all my friends. I'll say stupid stuff I don't mean, but it's all in good love. You know that."

"Okay," Emma rolled her eyes. "So what should I do about Jack?"

"You have to tell him. The kid is deep in his feels and confused about if you like him. Don't forget he's a boy. He'll never admit it unless you bring it up."

"That's the problem! I don't even know how I feel about him. Yes, we've said we loved each other before all of this, but it's been so long since we even had a meaningful conversation."

"Who's fault is that?"

"Probably mine…maybe both of us. I don't know," she sighed, rattled. "My point is that you're assuming I know what I want, and I have *no idea*. I figured if I keep doing what I think is right that it will give me more clarity."

"Pretend that you're Jack for a minute," HG requested. "Imagine you called him up right now and told him. How do you think he would react?"

"He'd probably be upset," she guessed uncertainly before shaking her head. "Yeah, he would *definitely* be upset."

"I agree, but by telling him now, you would give him more time to find whatever closure he needs and move on."

Emma's phone went off from the nightstand before she should reply.

"A little late for a call, don't you think?" HG noted.

Emma nodded despondently as she grabbed her phone and retreated to the hallway for privacy.

"Hello?"

"Ms. Keva, this is Clarene Hanzel from the Ember House. Sorry for calling so late."

"Hi Dr. Hanzel, no worries, we're a few hours behind over here. What's up?"

"I was going through my calls to returning students and am checking in to see where you are in regard to deciding if you would like to come back this spring."

"That's perfect timing, I started packing tonight and was going to call you tomorrow seeing if the offer was still open. I'll gladly accept."

"That's terrific! I will put you down as a 'yes' then," Dr. Hanzel replied. "Fingers crossed that we don't get another disgruntled individual contesting our integrity."

"What?" Emma giggled faintly.

"The gentleman who asked me to rescind your offer."

"Wait, I don't get it," Emma processed. "You got a call from a someone who didn't want me to come? When did this happen?"

"Shortly before the beginning of last semester. I assumed you knew about it."

"Do you remember who it was? Did they give you a name?"

But Emma did not need to ask. She knew the truth, but she needed to hear it for herself.

She should have trusted her gut. From the moment he lied about who he was, she should have known he was not as perfect as he tried to come across. That said, never could she have imagined him to be capable of something this nefarious.

She recalled his demeanor at Damon's party. For him to look at her in the face and accuse of *anything*, knowing that he went behind her back to do something like this – she hated that it was true.

"Jack Douglas," Dr. Hanzel finally answered, still dainty in her tone. "I distinctly remember it because it sounded like the name of a main character in an action movie. I looked him up, but I was redirected to a bunch of pages about this man named Wayne Douglas—"

"Of the D-Group, I know," Emma finished, quick to connect the dots. "I guess that's how you knew I was from Seattle."

"I put the two together."

"Well, uh, I appreciate you calling," Emma relayed, her head spinning. "And thank you so much again for everything that you've done."

"You're welcome. Give me call if you have any questions. If I don't hear from you within the next week, I'll see you back in the city."

Emma hung up and returned to her bedroom to see HG against the wall.

"I heard what I could," HG addressed uneasily. "I assume it has to do with Jack?"

Emma's face hardened at the sound of his name.

"It has everything to do with him."

Typically, such a statement would captivate HG into spewing a spiral of questions. Instead, she made her way to the door.

"I'll get going so you can deal with all of this. Let me know if you need a ride to the airport."

"Thanks HG, and I can't do that to you again. I'll get an Uber."

"Oh, are you sure?"

"Yeah, I'll be okay," she managed a grin.

"Okay." HG relayed, defeated. She wanted to tell her about her feelings for Jack, but especially after how her mood changed from the unknown call, she wondered if she had missed her chance.

At the same time, Emma's resentment for Jack presented a potential sliver of hope. Perhaps there was no need to tell her, if it had no impact on the inevitable outcome of their relationship.

Emma stood in the front entryway as she watched HG get into her car and pull off the driveway. She closed the door and sighed, gracious to be alone again. It was only for a short minute, as her mother's voice came from the top of the stairwell.

"You're going back to New York?"

Emma looked up, initially startled to discover her mother had been home the entire time.

"You sound surprised."

"You're my daughter, Emmalyn. I know what you're going through, because I remember thinking I knew what was best for me when I was your age."

"Are you saying that I don't know what's best for me?"

"No, but you should run these things past your family first. Especially me."

"Right, like the same way I ran past the idea of me going to college last year, remember? You were *so* supportive of that."

Her sarcastic tone caused Julia to frown.

"I support you, Emma."

"The only thing you supported was Jack, who ironically, somehow centered himself in this entire situation even though it has nothing to do with him."

"Where is all this coming from?"

"Oh I'm sorry, did we suddenly forget about how many times you would discourage me from chasing my dreams over the last eleven years?"

"Emmalyn—"

"I love you Mom, but please, can we not do this right now?"

Julia sighed.

"I just want to make sure that this is truly what you want to do."

"That's not what this is about," Emma snapped back. "I think you're mad that I'm doing something different than what you wanted me to. You don't want me to stay because you care about my future. You want to control it."

"Listen to what you're saying – do you have any idea how ridiculous you sound? I'm your mother!"

"Reiterating that you're my mom doesn't change the fact that you disagree with my dream of being an artist."

"Photography is not a sustainable career."

"But being a good housewife is, right?"

Her mother's face scrunched up at that.

"Don't you dare throw that at me," she scorned. "You wouldn't even be here if it wasn't for what I did for you. I chose you over my career."

"So did Dad, but very convenient for you to leave him out of this."

"Your father and I were on the same page when we had you—"

"No, you weren't. Dad was always there for me even when he came home in the middle of the night after working all day. All you did was tell me to look pretty so you could marry me off to some bachelor, and now that I'm actually doing what I love – and proving you wrong, at the same time – you feel obligated to say whatever you need to convince me otherwise."

Emma immediately regretted her outburst. Generally, there was never an acknowledgement of defeat from either side. And although Emma always considered such an instance to bring her joy, it only filled her with guilt.

"You're right," Julia replied softly. "We shouldn't get into this. Go do what you think is right," she paused. "But just know that I love you, Emma. And I always will be here for you."

With that, Julia retreated to her room, leaving Emma alone once again. She took another deep breath, taking her time to calm down before proceeding back to her own room to finish packing. There was much to get done prior to her return East.

*****

Like most of her friends, Harmony was raised in a traditional, successful household. Her parents cared deeply for their daughters. Specifically their safety, having installed a home security system the day they moved in. Unknown to them, the girls had quickly identified a workaround to bypassing their enforcement for curfews.

Harmony loved her siblings deeply, but there are downsides to everything. One she encountered often was whenever she would sneak into the house, because no matter how many times she prayed the family would be sleeping during the late hours, not once had her younger sister met the expectation. Harmony scurried to the only source of light in the darkened home, fervently tapping the in the code and disarming the alarm.

"Where have you been?"

It took everything for Harmony to hold back her frightened scream, quick to turn to annoyance as she turned to Sally's silhouette at the base of the stairwell.

"Every time," she groaned. "It's almost like you want to be murdered."

Sally brought a finger to her lips, glancing at the closed door to the master bedroom at the top of the stairs.

"Shut up, they're sleeping. You'll get us both killed if you keep shouting."

"*They?*"

"Trial got over early. He took the first flight back."

Sally remained close behind when they moved to the kitchen. Harmony ran her hands over the wall until she felt the switch to turn on the light, shocked to see her older sister, Mira, waiting for them on the counter.

"Am I living a scene from Paranormal Activity or something?"

"My first boyfriend took me to see that," Mira muttered as she momentarily nodded on before shifting off the counter. "Nice to know that I'm not the only one getting old."

"What are you doing here? I thought you were in China?"

"Laos," Mira politely corrected. "It's much warmer there. I'll take you sometime."

"I thought you were asleep?" Sally gawked.

"You can't be sneakier than your elders," Mira scoffed. "That's just a fact."

"You're only two years older than me," HG defended.

"Yes, and four years older than you," Mira said, pointing at Sally. "That is also another fact."

Harmony rolled her eyes and carefully opened the fridge door.

"What did you go to the city for?"

"Had to run some errands."

Sally nudged Mira.

"That's code for 'sexing.'"

Harmony spun around and flicked Sally's forehead.

"I had to give Emma a ride from the airport," she added, returning to the fridge for the communal jar of pickles she nevertheless claimed as her own.

"But you were gone for days, so you obviously did more than that," Sally persisted, rubbing her temple. "And you *hate* driving."

"This is true," Mira chimed. "Remember when you got your first car but never wanted to drive? You demanded Mom to be your chauffer for a month."

Harmony regretted taking a large bite of the first pickle, her face scrunching instantly from the bitter juice seeping into her dry tongue.

"Oh my god," she squealed, bringing the jar to her eyes to check the expiration date.

"That's been in there for a hot second." Mira commented. "Pretty sure I made that same face when I tried them over Easter."

"And you're telling me *now?*"

Sally was still deconstructing Harmony's whereabouts when her eyes lit up. "You went for a boy, didn't you?"

"Would you stop talking if I said you were right?"

Sally and Mira exchanged pondering looks.

"Yes," they said simultaneously.

"Okay, I went for a boy," Harmony stated definitively, raising the jar above Sally's head. "Now go to bed or else I'll dump this on you."

Sally grinned and marched off.

"I win," they overheard her say as she disappeared up the stairs.

Mira waited patiently until Sally was out of sight before refocusing on HG. "You want to talk about it?"

"Not really."

"If you said 'no,' I would have left you alone," Mira explained. "But 'not really' implies that you may be reluctant but are still willing to share."

"You sound like Dad."

"Yeah, we have a lot in common. Aside from me also studying to be a lawyer, we also happen to be related. It's a crazy coincidence."

"Very funny," HG relented as she replaced the jar and closed the fridge. "Did you talk to Dad when he got back?"

"Not for long. He said he'll be sleeping in tomorrow," she tilted her head and sighed. "I don't know how he has the grit to keep doing this kind of work after so many years."

Also unlike Harmony's friends was the fact that their father was not Russell Goodwynn. Widely recognized in the legal field as "The Giver," Harmony's father was notorious for meeting the wishes requested from his clients. It mainly consisted of getting them off whatever crime, no matter how insidious. Fear came alive when he entered the courtroom. He could stir the sternest, and the few words he spoke outside of trail quaked even the most overly ambitious men who long vowed to put him in his place.

As the child of a strong-willed attorney, it was befitting that Harmony, and her sisters echoed such traits with maturation. Russell demanded control in everything he did, and believed it was necessary to project a skeptic outlook on any who took an interest in his family. For he was knowledgeable of how cruel people can be, not just through actions, but from the motives that drove their thoughts and intentions. Harmony prided herself in having the ability to detect and out-manipulate the manipulators. Inspired by her father, it was a skill she used responsibly, or, when it suited her.

"I'll leave you alone," Mira said, bringing Harmony back to present. "Find time to meddle with whatever is on your mind and get back to me."

"Thanks sis."

Harmony made a sandwich and took it to her bedroom. The news from Emma still lingered. She was partly excited, naturally, that her friend was making strides in her dreams. She was also secretly glad that such decision could leave Jack as an open option to pursue.

Nevertheless, Harmony had no intention of swelling an already dramatic situation. If only she knew how little her intentions mattered.

xxiv

"I'm freezing my balls off right now."

"Relax Saac, you have ten layers on."

"*Two* layers," Isaac corrected Tommy. "Three, if you count the jersey."

Jack ignored his friends, cursing himself for not bringing gloves as he rubbed his palms together while overlooking a stringy line of fans between him and the gates. It was uncommon to experience snowstorms this late in the season, and he hoped it would pass before the weekend. Had he checked the weather instead of fretting over Emma that morning, he would have dressed more appropriately.

Speaking of which, he eventually learned of Emma's decision to go back to New York, when he overheard Morgan telling Tommy on the phone once classes started up. And to his unsurprise, her friendship with this Hunter character – according to Morgan – was more than Emma had claimed. Yet, Jack expected the precedent to settle: overly delayed replies to his text, and rejoicing at each rare instance when her name would light up in his notifications.

But it was different this time, as it had been six weeks since he had heard from her.

Was it me? Did I say something I shouldn't have?

No. There was no way it was him. She would have told him.

But if that's the case, why hasn't she? What is she waiting for?

His desperation reached an all-time high since, each night brooding an array of possible things she could say that may excuse her abrupt halt in communication with him. He knew this was not a result of Emma's new relationship. There was a new motive at play, and it frustrated Jack that he had no way of figuring it out on his own. It is disheartening when a blossoming infatuation between two like-minded souls wither. It happens so often that it is arguably nonsensical when one believes their newfound love sustain beyond initial commitment, and is ignorantly selfish when assuming such a tragedy is applicable to unique cases. Regardless of aspiration, the ironic truth reveals no virtual difference in outcome. Self-pity is a poison for the weary, who are incapable of stomaching truly unfiltered melancholy. Jack did not want to fall deeper into despair and welcomed distractions of any kind to keep his mind at bay.

Lucky for him, there was not a better one than rival gameday with the boys.

"I'm with 'Saac," Bennett agreed, pulling up his hood. "How much longer do we have to wait?"

"It shouldn't be long," Jack reasoned, shielding his face from the blowing snow.

"Jack!"
He swiveled around and saw Molly rush up and embrace him. "It's crazy seeing you here! How are you?"
"Not bad," Jack replied, noting her friends behind exchanging whispers.
"Is that…?"
"Shh, I think so—"
"—It is."
Molly shot them a harrowing glare before returning to Jack.
"Sorry," she giggled. "I've talked to them about you."
Jack did not mind. He was used to the attention.
"You must be freezing." he continued, seeing that she was showing more skin than the brisk weather called for.
"I am, we took shots before coming here though, so fingers crossed it keeps us warm during the game," she glanced at the line. "Why are you in line with the rest of us?"
"What do you mean?"
"Well, you're Jack Douglas. You can do whatever you want."
"Including skip to the front?" Kevin interjected, seizing the first opportunity to make his presence known to Molly's attractive friends. "We've tried telling him, but he didn't listen."
Jack shrugged.
"I don't want to be that guy," he said. "But you girls should join us when we get in. We have good seats."
An attendant on the line overheard Jack's name and approached them before Molly could reply.
"Mr. Douglas!" she gleamed, motioning for security. "I've been looking for you. We were told you would be joining us this afternoon. Please wait here and we will take your group to your suite."
"Oh, we can wait in line, if that's easier—"
"Don't listen to Mr. Douglas," Tommy chimed. "He has the tendency to be modest at the worst times."
The attendant nodded and directed the security officers to guide them toward the front.
"You have a *suite*?" Molly gaped, linking arms with Jack on their way to the gate.
"Yeah, my family are huge Huskies fans."
They were escorted through a private entrance and proceeded up the stairwell to their suite. The air-conditioned room was simply exquisite: burnished countertops full of a variety of snacks and drinks; sporty art lined between plasma screens; and the most comfortable seats overlooking a glistening Union Bay.

Jack brought Molly to a window overlooking the stadium. Even though he could care less about sporting events, he could not argue a more phenomenal sight in University District than on college gameday.

The once barren space transformed overnight, packed fully with boisterous fans erupting with incredible energy. Blobs of the rival fans streaked across sections in green, their cries ultimately drowned in the dense sea of purple and gold. There was no doubt most of them commenced their festivities the night before, drinking and dancing into the sleepless morning before finding themselves recklessly pounding and swirling in the bleachers, their collective roar pulsating through the suite's enclosed, paneled glass. Beyond the field, a fleet of boats tailgated the event, waving their school colors pridefully in united anticipation of the biggest game of the year.

"It's so different seeing it from here," Molly awed. "I would go to every game if this was my view."

"It's all right," Jack replied, watching as his boys busied with Molly's friends on the other end of the room. "How was your winter break?"

"Great! I spent most of it with family, since all my friends went back home. What about you?"

Jack chuckled uneasily.

"Let's just say I'm glad it's over."

"Sounds like it wasn't so enjoyable. Did something happen?"

"Sort of," Jack paused. "I'm on a break with my…girlfriend."

"Oh, I'm sorry—"

"No, it's okay. I'm sorry, I shouldn't have said that…"

"Is she coming here?"

"No, she went back to New York for an internship," he explained, rubbing his head. "It's actually the primary reason we agreed to put things on hold."

Just then, Molly's expression changed, now looking more intrigued.

"Well she's missing out, if you ask me."

Jack saw Molly's smirk grow, causing him to grin back.

"Hey, sorry to interrupt," Tommy came up, turning to Jack. "Can I talk to you for a minute?"

Jack nodded and looked at Molly. "We'll be right back."

He followed Tommy out in the hall, closing the door behind him.

"What's up?"

"You brought girls."

"Yeah, they're Molly's friends. I don't know any of them but it's not like I was only going to invite her, you feel?"

He was confused by Tommy's hard stare.

"What is it man?"

"It was her," Tommy insinuated. "The girl you met at the Locks last summer, right?"
"Psychotic memory, but yes, it was her."
"That figures, you made the same face when I asked you then," Tommy said. "Why didn't you tell me?"
"I forgot to bring it up since it happened," Jack shrugged. "I didn't think it mattered at the time."
"Does Emma know?"
"No way," Jack shot back. "Not like she'd care anyway."
"I see," Tommy sighed. "What makes you say that?"
"She left *me*."
"So is this your way of getting back at her or something?"
"No, not at all!" Jack hesitated, pondering over the question again before moving on. "You said so yourself: maybe it is time to move on."
"And I stand by what I said. But still, I hope you know what you're doing."
"Thanks for your input Tom, but trust me, I'm fine."
Molly was speaking to Isaac by the tables when she saw Jack enter and find his seat, causing her to join him before he could settle in. Jack saw her coming right before noting an odd frown Isaac sent him once Molly had left.
"What was that about with Tommy?" she asked, sitting next to him.
"Nothing important, he just wanted to talk about some stuff." Jack relayed, praying he would not be pestered into delving further.
She scoffed at his response, leading Jack to examine her sudden irritable demeanor.
"Is everything good?" he asked.
"That was just a dismissive answer you gave me," she retorted, folding her arms.
"Um, sorry."
He was unsure what else to say to Molly. One thing was certain, she had already proven to be a suitable distraction from the ache Emma left in his heart.
He looked back at the bar where his friends were brewing up cocktails.
"What are you making over there?"
Bennett was already tipsy as he raised his glass for Jack to inspect.
"This is so fire," he rambled. "They even brought limes."
"Why don't you cook one up for me and my lady?" Jack invited.
Kevin beamed at his request, filling two more cocktails and bringing it to them.
Molly blankly studied the drink in front of her before looking at Jack.
"It's a little early to start drinking, don't you think?"

"Not when it's gameday," Jack mused, downing his glass and tossing it back to Kevin for a refill.

Molly followed his lead, nearly choking off the strong liquor.

"Whew!" she blurted, her giggle growing into profound laughter as they took turns ramming down shots of the boys' choosing.

Jack gradually lost grasp of his self-control shortly after. His surge of energy was apparent in his articulation, the words leaving his mouth faster than the flutter of a bird's wings.

It did not take long before he started to wonder how much alcohol he had ingested. The game clock winded down to halftime when he debated taking a break. But by then it was too late. His stomach felt it first, tightening up and constraining his legs to move freely. He let out a muted belch, shuddering at his foul breath.

Six shots later, he was staring down at an empty cup that Molly snatched to refill, not noticing his dissipating soberness.

"Excuse me," he droned, casually retreating to the bathroom across the hall from the suite, immediately overwhelmed with the rancid combination of beer, sweat, and shit that filled the narrow stall. He crouched before the toilet and took a series of deep breathes.

Oh God, he thought as he drove his fingers down his throat. The worst part of the rally would be coming soon: the puke.

Jack eventually finished, unfolding from the toilet and staggering out of the stall. He paused at his reflection in the mirror, proceeding to swash his reddened face until the pungent aroma of his vomit faded from inside his runny nose.

His boys were waiting for him outside the bathroom, Tommy's amused grin matching the others' as they pulled him in the huddle.

"That took you a while," he teased.

"I don't know what came over me," Jack muttered, taking one last sniffle before straightening up.

"Are you feeling better?" Bennett asked.

"Barely. Where's Molly?"

"She left with her friends," Kevin replied. "But she told us to tell you that she will text you later."

Jack's eyes widened.

"What do you mean she *left*?"

"They wanted to freshen up before going out tonight."

Jack peered at Kevin, noticing his hesitance to meet his eyes.

"What's up, Kev?"

"Nothing," he dismissed. "It's none of my business."

"Well I'm making it your business," Jack chuckled, curious at his friend's tension.

"It's about Molly…"

"All right, what about her? Is she okay?"

"Are *you*?" Bennett came in. "She's a terrible rebound, dude."

"I see you shared your two cents on the matter," Jack relented to Tommy, who gave a helpless shrug.

"We briefly touched on it."

Jack turned to Isaac.

"What about you Saac? You must have an opinion on it," he invited. "I noticed the face you gave me after talking to her. What was that about?"

"She's…cool," he muttered. "I support your choice."

"Come on, you don't seriously mean that," Tommy chided. "Let's have an open discussion here."

"What is there to discuss? It's not like I'm in love with her," Jack defended. "We're just friends."

"That's how it always starts," Kevin stated.

"That's not true."

"Well, it's a little bit true," Tommy agreed.

"I still don't understand what happened with Emma. You said she was the one."

"It's complicated…" Jack paused. "Besides, I think I have waited long to start talking to other girls. Shit happens, and you move on, right? Sometimes it's best to just accept that and go with the flow."

"I disagree," Kevin chided. "Remember Moriah? I only talked to her to get over Jaidyn. Everything was pretty great until I realized that she was not at all what I hoped she would be, so I cut her out of my life like a stage-four tumor."

"Jesus Kev!" Isaac exclaimed. "We're in public – let's choose our words a bit more carefully, eh?"

Jack rolled his eyes over his friends' groans.

"While I get your point, it's not the same," Jack relayed. "For one, Molly is not a rebound—"

"That's what you think," Kevin interjected.

"—And two," Jack continued, ignoring Kevin. "I may not now think that we'll be going anywhere, but who am I to say that it won't? For all we know, Molly may end up being the one for me – wouldn't that be something?"

"Okay dude," Bennett cut in. "I'm sorry. I don't mean to be an asshole, but I think we all have a shared responsibility to give advice when it is needed."

"I appreciate you all trying to look out for me, but you're wasting your time," Jack affirmed. "There is nothing going on here. Molly and I are just friends. I am not rushing into anything – you all have my word, okay?"
Jack panned across his boys' reluctant nods, relieved to have settled their concerns for the time being.
Like most gamedays, the real fun did not begin until later in the evening. It typically warranted an evening nap prior to parading into the night, but Jack's anticipation to reconvene with Molly caused him to continue without, taking the liberty to keep drinking until the sun finally set over University District. He was plastered when they arrived at the Den, where on cue, he spotted Molly in a booth with her girlfriends.
"Look who it is!" Molly exclaimed upon seeing the boys approach their table.
"Sorry about earlier," Jack apologized. "I guess I wasn't paying much attention to how much I drank at the game."
"Trust me, I wasn't that far behind you. That's why we decided to leave."
"That was smart of you," Tommy retorted from behind Jack, inconspicuously nudging him before turning to the bar. "How about we get a drink, boys?"
Molly finished her drink and slid out of the booth.
"Care if I join you?"
"Not at all" Jack took her hand and followed the boys to the bar. The bartender skipped the queue of awaiting payors and went straight to them.
"I'll have five Jack-Cokes and a…"
"Vodka-cranberry," Molly finished, giggling afterward.
"What's so funny?"
"Do you get that drink on purpose?"
"Yes actually," Jack mused. "It's makes for a great icebreaker with the ladies."
"Oh, I can *definitely* see that," Molly snickered, her nose scrunching at the potent smell of the alcohol pouring before them. "I still don't know how anyone can like that."
Jack clinked his glass with Molly's and tediously sipped at his drink.
"It's an acquired taste forsure," Tommy sniffled, cheersing with Jack. "Only real men drink whiskey."
"I bet" she motioned to Jack. "You drink like you're scared of it." Jack motioned to Kevin, lightly sipping at his drink. "Seems I'm not the only one."
They rejoined the girls, all of whom tittered hysterically when they successfully squeezed into the booth.

Jack was shouldered firmly between Molly and Tommy as he humorously reached for his glass on the table, ultimately giving up when he realized the impossibility of pulling his arm out from his side.
Tommy motioned to Jack's glass.
"Want me to get that for you?" he jokily offered.
"Could you actually?" Jack sniggered, opening his mouth as Tommy carefully tilted the cup down his throat. He choked on the whiskey, forcing himself to keep it in and groaning at its stiff taste.
Everyone laughed at their antics, and the attention he received instantly boosted his ego. He loved this role of his, interjecting into any and all subconversations without having to be fully invested in any particular one. Coupled with the increasingly festive atmosphere in the bar, Jack had momentarily abandoned all concern for Emma. The notion of reliving his worries through partying was generally ineffective in the past, but he was starting to see its upside then.
And Molly Brown: how could he have predicted that one short-lived interaction months ago could resort to their propinquity? He would be lying to himself if he denied ever fantasizing about them since their initial meet. Just her presence alone was enough to keep him stimulated and wanting more.
Two doubles later, and Jack accepted he was at the point of no return. He had reached past the optimal level of intoxication, which, given Jack's poor resilience to blacking out, made it a hard reality for him to swallow.
One minute, he was in the bathroom, looming over a nauseous Isaac straddling in front of the toilet seat. They were talking to each other, but what about, he had no idea; only that it somehow ended with a long, teary hug and several reassurances of their shared brotherly love.
Another minute, he tripped over random feet and slipped uneasily to the center of the dancefloor. It took a moment, but he had realized Molly was grinding on him, her hands softly grazing across his chest and up his neck as her head tilted back to the colorful strobes flickering overhead.
The next minute, he was outside of the Den, deliriously incoherent as he feverishly inhaled a joint he supposedly willed his way to chain-smoking with a throng of unfamiliar students. Bennett and Kevin were the only two he recognized, both of whom were too distracted engaging with the others to acknowledge him.
He closed his eyes to stop his head from spinning. The voices outside his head were too loud to listen. He needed to breathe.
"What are you looking for?" Molly's voice came.
He opened his eyes, suddenly managing to grasp his senses. He was back inside the Den, leaning on the bar, and facing Molly. Judging from her curious gaze, he reckoned they were in a deep talk of some kind.

"Do you mean, in a person?" he uttered, having no idea what the context was and hoping what he said would stick.

"In general."

"That's a hard one," Jack pondered. "I'm not sure if I know how to answer that anymore."

"I appreciate your honesty," she smiled. "I'd much rather accept that over a stupid lie that most assholes here would tell me just to get in my pants."

Jack busted out laughing. It was not just Molly's cheeky attitude that enticed him. It was also her quirks. Even the most subtle movements. He marveled at her dreamy eyes, his gaze dipping to her mouth as she ran her tongue over her lips as she spoke with a seductive, raspy voice. His fondness for this girl was growing, and while the liquor intake may be the cause, he could not resist noticing the sheer resonation to Emma. He wondered what she would think, if she knew he was with Molly now, and knew what he was thinking. What she would say if she was here…

It doesn't matter, he reminded himself. If Emma really did care, then she would not be in New York. Whether Molly was an episode or a season in his life did not matter. She was here, and Emma was not. A break is the same as a breakup. They were no longer together, and it was time to move on.

"Come on," Molly said, taking his hand and starting for the exit.

"Where are we going?"

"Your place."

Jack's head twisted to his friends, all of whom watched in astonishment – specifically Tommy, who met his eyes from over Morgan's shoulder.

Fuck, Tommy thought, knowing that his reaction was enough to cause Morgan to stop talking and turn in his direction.

"Is that Jack?" she asked, bewildered.

Tommy swiveled back to her.

"Jack? Where?"

"That *is* Jack, isn't it?"

"I'm going to get another drink," Tommy said, changing the subject. "Come on, I'll get you one."

He wrapped his arm around Morgan, sneaking one last glance at Jack as Molly dragged him out of the bar.

Jack's recollection was murky. He was walking, then in a car, then walking again, then tripped upstairs, then walking again, and somehow, was back in his apartment. The liquor had hit him again, this time harder. Molly was in no state to resist her objective to seduce him, and he was in no state to resist. There was little time for retrospection. Nevertheless, he knew it was not an overstatement to assume he would be taking another ride into a potential relationship – one he hoped to not ultimately regret.

*****

Jack woke up alone in his bed, the scent of espresso titillating his nostrils. He had the vaguest memory of how he ended up at his place. Not that it mattered, since he knew if he tried it would only result in self-humiliation, he was not yet ready to face. He opened his door to see Tommy on the phone as he waited for the coffee to finish brewing. Tommy nodded at Jack before proceeding to speak to the unknown person on the line.

"I totally understand where you are coming from," he consoled, shooting Jack a worrisome glare. "Don't worry, I will let him know. It'll all be fine – okay, okay I'll let you go. Say hi to Baylee for me."

Tommy hung up, tossing his phone aside and focusing on Jack.

"How are you feeling?"

"Fuck," Jack grimaced.

Tommy sighed and took the pot to fill a couple mugs. "Yeah, that's what I figured."

"What happened last night? How did we get home?"

"Sounds like you blacked out." Tommy noted, handing him a mug.

"Thanks," Jack murmured, carefully sipping as Tommy continued to stare. "What is it?"

"You don't remember what happened last night do you?"

"Well, you said it yourself, I blacked out."

"Right," Tommy snorted, arching back in his chair. "That was Emma on the phone."

"Actually? What did she want?"

Tommy walked into his bedroom. "You should call her yourself," he advised, closing the door behind him.

Jack fumbled for his phone, panicking at the low battery and plugging it in before dialing Emma's number.

"Hi Emma," he began, finding his words. "It's good to hear from you…"

"How are you Jack?" her voice came, the disdain in her tone more than apparent.

"It's been fun," he uttered. "I went to a football game yesterday. Can you believe it?"

"I can," she droned, slow to respond. "I wouldn't put it past you to do things you claim you'd never do."

"Okay…" Jack trailed.

"How about your night?"

"Oh," Jack paused. "The night was good…how was your night?"

"Really Jack?"

"…What?"

"Okay let's cut the shit," she scoffed. "Are you going to keep beating around the bush like you always do, or are you just going to tell me, for once, without me having to pry it out?"

Jack hesitated. He had not the faintest idea what Emma was referring to, but judging from her tone, it could not have been anything good.

"I'd love to tell you what you want to hear, but I got really drunk last night."

"Morgan told me what you did," she sighed. "Did you really think I wouldn't find out?"

"What are you—" Jack shut up, his memory suddenly flashing back to his psyche.

Molly.

The clear image of her on top of him appeared; his hands running across her naked body; the alluring sound of her moans amidst his moment of pleasure. He did not want to believe it. He *refused* to.

"Shit," he mumbled.

"Yeah," she said coolly. "*Shit.*"

"Emma, it's not at all what you think—"

"I tend to disagree," she spat back. "It sounds to me that you knew what you were doing last night."

"Why do you care Em?" Jack shouted back. "You broke up with me and went back to New York, *again*. That was *your* choice. And now you call me up thinking you can ridicule me for moving on?"

"What I said was that I needed time to figure things out," she replied calmly. "Which reminds me of something else I've been waiting to say."

"Oh fuck, what is it this time?" Jack shot back impatiently. "Are you going to tell me that we never should have been together now?"

"You tried to get my offer rescinded."

"What…" he uttered, belting up in stunned disbelief from what she had just said.

Emma expected his silence, continuing. "My advisor told me over winter break. Apparently after she said no, you went ahead and bribed her to change her mind."

More silence.

"All I wanted was for you to see my decision to come here as a good thing, for me, *and* for you. But for you to keep this from me, and still make me feel like absolute shit for being here—"

"Emma, please listen to me—"

"And then for you to fuck that girl, who according to Morgan, you've had eyes on since last summer – Tommy did his best to deny it, but he looked pretty stupid after I caught him lying. Honestly Jack, I don't even know what to say to you anymore."

Jack did not defend himself. He recalled how dismissive she was when he regrouped with them that day. At least he finally got confirmation that she did in fact see them together. Kicking him when he's already down. It was a smart move on her part.

"I never cheated on you," he finally said, sounding almost like it was a declaration. "And I wasn't thinking when I called your internship. I got caught up in the moment."

"That doesn't sound like an apology."

"You're right, it's not. I tried to make things better. I called you almost every day while you were in New York, and you ignored me. This is the longest we have spoken since you left last summer – and you expect me to bend over and take this shit from you?"

"Thank you for letting me see this side of you, Jack," Emma said dryly. "It must have been difficult for you to hide it from me all this time. I can only imagine how many other people don't really know the real you. But I finally do."

"Fuck off Em, I see right through what you're doing, trying to come across as perfect and paint me the villain."

"You said it, not me."

"You best get back to enjoying yourself in New York," he said definitively, and hung up the phone. "Fuck!"

He did not notice Tommy eavesdropping, standing at the doorway to his bedroom.

"I take it you remember now?" he asked.

"Shut up."

"We all make mistakes man," Tommy paused. "But you have to admit what you did was pretty fucked."

Jack slumped back in the chair. "It doesn't matter anyway. We're done, for good."

Tommy took a seat beside him on the couch.

"I'm sorry Jack," Tommy sympathized. "I know how much she meant to you."

Jack lowered his head. For some, the morning of a hookup is tokened as a significant period of reflection. It offers a chance of humility, and acceptance of misdeeds in hope that it would prompt a change in future actions.

All Jack could think about was how much he believed to have hurt Emma. But even so, he was curious if she found it upsetting, or simply chose to capitalize on the situation for the purpose of guilting his conscience. Given how they left things, he had no reason to resist his own doubts over whether she was truly capable of doing something so manipulative.

"Maybe it wasn't a mistake though," Jack finally said.

"Really?"

"Yeah. You know, it could be the first good thing I have done in a long time."

"That's interesting," Tommy chuckled. "Because if you ask me, I think what you're saying is fucking ridiculous."

"You're the one who told me to get over her," Jack recalled. "What I did last night proves that I am on the right track, right? Please don't tell me you are going back on your word now."

"What I said—" Tommy pointed out, raising a finger. "Is that you do what you think is right, which, *clearly,* you didn't."

"Who are you to say that?".

"When has someone consciously knew what they were doing when they were drunk?"

"Let me think about that."

"It was rhetorical," Tommy clarified. "Why do I have to explain that to you every time?"

Jack shrugged off Tommy's comment.

"I'm tired of sulking over someone who doesn't give a shit about me," he added. "I'm Jack fucking Douglas, for God's sake. What's ridiculous is that I cared so much about her. Do you know how easy it is for me to get bitches? I wasted so much time thinking she was the one."

"You're overreacting right now. There is no need to burn bridges."

"Sometimes there is a benefit to remaining as friends."

"Such as?"

Tommy hesitated, slow to respond.

"A runner does not know he has won until he crosses the finish line."

"For the thousandth time, you gotta stop with the metaphors."

"*Idioms,*" Tommy corrected. "But anyways, you can't deny that there is a good side to Emma. And from that good side, you learned a lot about yourself, including the qualities you like in a partner."

"You're absolutely right about that. Being with her made me realize that I should stay as far away from anyone remotely like her."

"Okay, you know that's not where I was going with it—"

"I appreciate you always trying to be there for me, Tommy. But you have to stop with this one. I can do this on my own."

Hearing him say that crushed Tommy. He shook his head in disappointment.

"I've said this before, and I'll say it again," he muttered. "I hope you know what you're doing."

For Jack, it was not a matter of sorting his feelings for Molly, or any girl in that regard. He was spiteful of Emma's hypocrisy.
Why should he continue to consider Emma's needs over his own? She did not care about him; her actions were evident of that. The ego began to settle, infecting his well-natured intentions and instead of clouding it with a thickening layer of complacent vanity he had tried so hard to push out of his conscience. After everything, he would be alone, left thinking about the one person he was trying to forget.

XXV

It was a challenge to focus that afternoon for Emma. Dr. Yuki was giving a routine lecture – an hour typically spent admiring her professor's eccentric takes on the profound impact ancient artistry had on contemporary culture – but it was different this time. No matter how intently she tried to listen, Emma struggled to concentrate, scribbling recklessly in her notebook without any coherent takeaway on the material. Her mind was preoccupied on one thing. Or rather, one person.

Jack Douglas.

She had hoped coming back to New York would bring clarity. And surely, one way or the other, it did, especially after a testy argument with him earlier that morning.

The incessant calls and texts were bothersome, and being on the opposite end of the continent made her contemplate the upside in maintaining a relationship that did not bring happiness. A breakup would be easier to cope with then, but only under the presumption that Jack gave up his obsession with her. To her surprise, he not only moved on, but rather quickly, and even had the gall to defend his actions. She recalled gawking at her phone, dumbfounded by the subtle drone emitting from the dropped call. He was wrong about what he did, but Emma blamed herself for letting her emotions take over the call, and secretly owned up to mishandling a breakup that, well, should not have escalated as much as it did. It was surely more spite over maturity that willed his actions, but it happened. The time for healing had commenced, and with it, the end of Emma and Jack.

You have figured out everything you wanted to know on your own.

Emma's clench around her pen slowly eased up, and she relaxed with a long exhale.

Thank you, Logan.

Dr. Yuki's back was turned when Emma snuck her phone out to see a text from Hunter.

Dinner tonight?

what do you have in mind this time?

It's a surprise. I can meet you at your place in a couple hours?

it's a date

"Ms. Keva?"
Emma looked up, dreading the sight of Dr. Yuki's pointing directly at her.
"What was that?"
"What was your impression of this passage?"
"Um…" Emma began, her voice faltering as she side-eyed Baylee sitting next to her. *Say something you idiot,* she read from her constricting stare.
"Someone who…believes to be incapable of love is not yet…equipped for partnership…" she ignored her wish to stop talking and kept going.
"…because that person first must acknowledge love unto themselves."
Emma hesitated when a sharp silence filled the room.
"Brilliant," Dr. Yuki finally said, directing her attention back to the class.
"Everyone should take a page out of Ms. Keva's insight. She understands the speaker's lyrical explanation and its resonation throughout the novel," she turned back to Emma. "Gold star once again."
The scattered applause from the students caused Emma to grin uneasily. *That was a close one.*
"That was an impressive rebound you had in class!" Baylee cheered on their walk back home.
"You think so?"
"Absolutely. Had Dr. Yuki asked anyone else, they'd find themselves on the Throne of Shame."
Emma giggled. "Is that a real thing?"
"Hopefully soon. I've been a strong advocate for its implementation, but the dean hasn't gotten back to me yet."
They reached their building, where Baylee stopped and turned around.
"I'll see you later tonight."
"Wait, you're not coming up?"
"I have supper with the Damsels' Design Club. This week's discussion: 'Coping with Your Client's Conundrums.'"
"You know, your frequent use of alliteration is inspiring. Why didn't you go into writing?"
"Have you ever heard of money? It makes your pockets happy."
Emma laughed again and bidded Baylee farewell before continuing inside.

She mulled over Baylee's comical reply – also debating its intention given its coincidental example of a hypophora – when she was taken aback at the sight of Hunter behind the kitchen counter in her apartment.

Hunter's eyes beaded eagerly out of his head when he saw her.

"Keva!"

Emma welcomed his embrace, distracted at the assortment of foods spread on the counter.

"What's all this?"

"I thought that we could switch it up a bit tonight," he explained. "I'm making enough for the three of us."

"How sweet of you," she smiled, setting down her backpack in the living room. "Unfortunately, Baylee won't be joining us. She's having dinner with this club she founded. Looks like it'll just be us tonight."

Hunter's head dipped in disappointment.

"Well damn," he frowned. "I was really looking forward to finally meeting her. I even came here early to take note of what you both eat to make sure that it was suited with my meal."

"I'm glad you brought that up," Emma pointed out, approaching him. "How did you get in here? I don't remember giving you a spare key."

"It was unlocked," Hunter said confusedly as he nodded to the door. "I figured you left it open for me since you knew I was coming over."

Emma glanced back at the door, failing to recall ever leaving the apartment without locking it.

Baylee, she thought. *Typical Midwesterner with her lack of security.*

"Are you hungry?" Hunter asked, moving on.

"Starving," Emma emphasized.

"Kick your feet up and relax, it'll be ready in a little bit."

Emma did not have an opinion on gender roles, but seeing Hunter dressed in a decorated apron as he meticulously pieced their entrees together was arguably one of the most attractive things she had ever seen. She could see the care in every step, demonstrating elegance as he drained pasta, sliced fruit, sauteed vegetables, and seasoned the cubed meats. She pretended to be on her phone but could not help herself when she hovered over him and watched him work diligently.

The dining table was adjacent to the kitchen, and beside the window where they had a view of the city lights. She took a seat and quietly observed Hunter bring the plates and glassware forward before finding a chair across from her. She was about to dig in, when he extended his hands for her to hold.

"What are you doing?"

"Well, we have to say grace, right?"

Emma's face tightened. "You pray before you eat? I've never seen you do that before?"

"We've always eaten in public," he reasoned. "I get self-conscious about it because I don't want to make anyone feel uncomfortable…oh shit, am I doing it to you now?"

"No," she giggled. "I wasn't judging, just curious. I like it."

She was not religious, but she went ahead with it anyway, taking his hands and closing her eyes as Hunter recited a prayer.

"Amen," they spoke in unison.

Emma took her first bite, immediately tasting the spiciness and instantly reaching for the water. But before she drank, the heat ceased, and her buds were greeted with a pleasant, sweet zing.

"What do you think?" Hunter asked.

"This is amazing," she muttered. "Where did you learn to cook?"

Hunter gave a perplexed smirk.

"Right," she added sillily. "I forgot that your parents are big restaurateurs."

"My parents want me to learn every inch of the business," he said after he finished chewing. "They think by doing so I'll make a better manager when I take over."

"Makes sense."

She took another bite and met Hunter's eyes, suddenly flashing back to a strangely similar experience shared with Jack on their first date at the *Crepuscolo.* The image of his warm smile fleeting as soon as it appeared. Just then, she felt her eyes swell up.

"Is something wrong?" Hunter asked, catching Emma's grimace.

"No, I'm sorry," she blubbered, wiping the tears. "I got into a fight with Jack this morning, and I guess I'm still not over it."

"I'm sorry, I didn't know," Hunter consoled. "For what it's worth, it's understandable that it's still on your mind…being that the wound is still fresh?"

Emma sniveled and took a drink of water.

"You know—" Hunter began to say, when Emma cut him off.

"Please, Hunter. Don't."

"Pardon?"

"You're probably thinking this is the perfect time to swing in and have your shot. I know what you're going to say," she continued. "'Don't cry, Emma; You're worth so much more; he's a fool to treat you as such.'"

"You know, you have the tendency to be a bit presumptuous," Hunter chuckled.

"It helps that my presumptions tend to be accurate most of the time."

"I don't doubt it," he set his fork down and linked his hands together.

Emma waited as Hunter mulled momentarily, clearly hesitant to bring up whatever was on his mind.

"I need to be honest with you, and since you brought it up, I still think now is the perfect time."

"Perfect time for what?"

"I'm in love with you Emma."

The words hit her like a truck, and faster than she could comprehend.

"Hunter—"

"Hold on, it's my turn to finish."

Emma stopped talking and let him continue.

"I tried to keep it to myself, but as you can see, I can't help but try to make it obvious," he added, motioning to the food. "Now that I have gotten that off my chest, let's set that aside for the time being. I don't know Jack, but from what I know about you, my guess is that aside from all your drama with him, he's a good guy, and whatever he may have said, he deserves another chance."

"Are you serious?" Emma asked, bewildered.

"I am."

"It's not what he said, but what he *did,* " she corrected. "There are no second chances."

Hunter raised his head, trying to meet her eyes.

"Another girl?"

She nodded, sniffling through her muffled breaths.

"I'm sorry," his voice faltered. "My last girlfriend cheated on me, so I can try to relate."

"Someone cheated on *you?* That's a joke, right? You have to be kidding."

"Is it that hard to believe?"

"Well, kind of. I mean, look at you – you're the total package."

"I appreciate that, although I'm sure you are also saying that for other reasons."

"Other reasons?"

"Not to be crass, but it's not the first time I've heard that…can't help but think this has to do with it," he lamented as he pulled out his wallet thickened in bills.

"Well, look who's being presumptuous now," she scorned sarcastically.

Hunter burst out laughing before skidding his chair closer to her.

"I like being your friend," he paused before continuing. "But as I said before you left in December: whenever you are ready, I would like to be something more."

Emma blushed. For someone who had everything, he behaved as though he was still undeserving. She admired this side of him: blessed in privilege yet riddled in humility. It was all too familiar.

"A friend," Emma laughed. "I don't even know what that means anymore."

She felt Hunter's hand on her chin, gently bringing her face up to his.

"It means that I care about you and will do everything I can to make sure you are happy."

"Kinda cringe," Emma deflected, secretly loving his cheesy move. "If I didn't know any better, I would assume that's the boyfriend side of you talking, not a friend."

He smirked. "Same difference, right?"

Emma was unsure what came over her at that moment, as she pushed her lips against his. She brimmed in delight when he kissed her back, running his hand over her head and caressing her cheek.

She pushed his chair back and settled on his lap, kissing him more intensely as he wrapped his arms around her back.

And naturally, Constraint faded, and Lust took over.

*****

Oh no, Emma. Here she was again.

After Jack, she promised herself to keep better check on her impulsiveness. She despised casual hookups and the feeling of post-regret, but neither of those were felt with Hunter. Admittedly, she considered the decision to jump his bones as inevitable at this point. Somehow, someway, it signified a good first step toward moving on from Jack.

Baylee was already up and about in the living room when Emma strolled out of her bedroom.

"Baylee!" Emma shrieked, instantly returning to a normal pitch. "I figured you would be in class by now?"

"Got canceled," Baylee retorted, smirking. "Who's the boy?"

"What boy?"

"The one hiding in your room right now."

"Don't be ridiculous, there's no one else here."
Emma palmed her face when a half-naked Hunter emerged from her bedroom.
"Hey Em, is there an extra towel around here I can borrow—" he trailed off when he saw Baylee, comically rubbing his eyes before looking again to confirm.
Well shit, Emma thought.
"Well hey there," Baylee mused, finding pleasure in his startled expression. "You must be Hunter."
"You know who I am?"
"Emma has talked a *lot* about you."
"This is Baylee, and she is just saying that—"
"No, it's true," Baylee affirmed.
"Nice to finally meet you Baylee. I actually had a meal prepared for us last night."
"Cute! But I think we can all agree it is probably best that I wasn't here this time around, huh?"
Hunter chuckled nervously and looked at Emma.
"They're under the sink," she said to him, patting him on the back as he strode to the bathroom. She looked back at Baylee, her smile wider.
"It's not what it looks like," she began, finding it difficult believe herself as the words slid out of her mouth.
"I think it is *exactly* what it looks like," Baylee countered.
Emma was embarrassed, lowering her head and resting her hands on her waist.
"How did you know?"
"I came home late last night and heard you two going to work," she revealed, moving toward the wall and tapping for dramatic effect. "They're pretty thin, if you haven't noticed. Next time, you should turn on some music to offset the thumping."
"Thanks for the advice," Emma muttered, joining Baylee as they prepared a pot of coffee.
"So, how was it?"
"Baylee!"
"Oh come on, you know I'm not the judging type."
Emma sighed in reluctance.
"It was good, okay? Are you happy?"
They were interrupted again by Hunter, noticeably hurrying out the bathroom and grabbing his shoes.
"Leaving so soon?" Baylee asked.

"I promised my dad I'd check in on a couple properties," he explained, fixating on Emma. "Maybe I can pick you two up in a few hours and we can all get lunch?"
"We'd love to."
Emma glanced quizzically at Baylee before going to Hunter.
"Perfect," he grinned, and he kissed Emma's sweaty forehead.
Baylee waited until he left before throwing her hands up.
"Oh my God, he's gorgeous," she blurted.
"Take it easy, Bay; we're just friends."
"Well, he shouldn't be. What's the holdup here, is it Jack?"
"A little bit," Emma shrugged. "It's just too soon."
"Let's be real for one second: it is hard – dare I say almost impossible – to find a guy that checks all the boxes in this day and age. True or false?"
"I don't want to play this game—"
"*True* or *false?*"
"True," Emma mumbled.
"You and Jack are officially done, after he stupidly cheated on you. True or false?"
"In addition to being a complete asshole."
"I'll take that as a 'true,'" Baylee noted. "Lastly, you are in New York City, a place where you have not once, not twice, but seventeen times declared that you would make it a priority to find yourself and grow into the person you have always aspired to be. True or false?"
"You've been counting how many times I've said that?"
"Emma!"
"Okay true, yes, you're right," Emma agreed. "Geez, I shit on Jack a lot, but I gotta sympathize with him since I now know what it's like to have my own Tommy."
"I don't know Tommy, but the context makes me think he's almost as smart as me," Baylee noted. "All I am saying is that Hunter is the perfect chance to really get after all those objectives. It's fate."
"Don't you think that's a bit of a stretch? I didn't come here for a relationship. I came here for my career."
Baylee settled back in her seat. "Why do you have the impression that you only have to choose one of those things? For all you know, one may be needed in order to get the other."
"I don't regret what I did last night," Emma admitted. "But I'm still trying to figure out what this means moving forward."
"Jack," Baylee echoed, shaking her head. "The guy that you just broke up because he, quote-on-quote 'cheated' you, but not really, since you two were silly enough to never put an official label on what you two ever were?"

Emma listened to the deliberately condescending question, and then playing it over in her head again before responding.

"Now when you say it like that I feel really stupid."

"Sorry, that wasn't my intention," Baylee said. "But now that you've finally thought about it, let me ask you this: what do you have to gain from feeling guilty about something where *you* are the only one to have the impression of it being measured as right or wrong?"

"If I'm following your question accurately, I would say it relies to my own moral interpretation of the matter."

"Sure, and most would agree with you if you were *actually* in a healthy, stable relationship with Jack," Baylee added. "Which, based on how you have talked about it since we met, leads me to believe that was never the case."

Emma tried to take Baylee's rationalization to heart, eating the silence as Baylee opened the fridge.

"Well would you look at that, it's time for another food run" she announced. "Care to join me?"

Emma lifted her gaze at Baylee, her eyes lighting up.

"I would love to."

It would only take the short walk to the grocery store for Emma to come to the realization of how right her decision was to return to the east coast. She could cope with being away from family. She was comfortable with the distance between her dear friends. She was fine with spending time away from home.

Home.

She used to stew over what that word meant. It was always a place for her, even after she left it for the first time. The idea extended beyond the street address, or the neighborhood, or the mountains and ocean. Acknowledging her hesitance to go back to a place lingered with drama and problems, she discovered it was a state of mind.

And Jack? Their situation was an enigma in and out of itself. Part of her hoped that seeing him again last month would ultimately lead to them getting back together. But now?

No. No more.

It was over. Not just for now. Forever.

Emma envisioned her life with Hunter. It was surprisingly easy. What's more, is that she knew she had already made the decision.

And alas, she was prepared to live it.

Part IV: The Decision

xxvi

Jack considered himself as pretty easygoing. As long as others in company were satisfied, he could roll with the punches and find splendor in nearly any activity. And while there were few he loathed, they all beat going to the mall. The shopping aspect did not bother him as much as the mindless stroll through a store comprised of smaller stores – the majority filled with overpriced products – and often associated with an aimless objective to purchase anything that sparks even the most minute desire to possess. Not something he would view as *fun*.

It happened to be Molly's preferred pastime, and one she frequently wrangled Jack into. Strike one.

He immediately regretted joining the pointless spree, privately judging passing pedestrians who determined their time was not wasted bouncing between stores with baseless value in basic merchandise. What made it worse, was Molly not being the first girl who successfully dragged him into this hellhole. He had been here *many* times, and due to his willingness to submit for others' satisfaction, found that it also caused his wallet to be thousands of dollars lighter. Tommy's persistent urge for him to meditate regularly was paying off, apparently, seeing that his temperament was still largely kept in check up until now.

It was strangely comforting to admit, but it made Jack reflect on how little he thought about his wealth when he was with Emma. She was his only ex that opened his eyes to another side of himself, a side that did not elevate material wealth over appreciation of his identity. Despite the other concerning flags, he admired her for the inattention she gave the elephant, no matter what room they were in. Before her, the two were essentially indistinguishable. He tried not overindulging, at least when he was sober. Now with Emma gone came an increased strain to denounce how much money influenced, well, everything. In contrast, Molly's demand for attention was recurrent, as was her acknowledgement of Jack's wealth.

They had already visited four stores over the first hour, and in addition to the burn in his checking account was an equally bothersome sensation in his arms from carrying all of Molly's purchases.

"I'm having such a good time," she said, skimming across the displays before glancing over at Jack's clenched expression. "Are you going to get anything?"

"No."

"What? Don't you like shopping?"

"Not really. Besides, I've been getting my stuff online lately. It's more convenient."

"Oh, come on! You sound so boring," she critiqued, quick to disregard him upon glossing over a leather handbag behind the paneled glass.

"No way," she uttered. "One of my friends has the same exact purse! I've always wanted one for myself."

Jack gazed emptily at the purse, unimpressed.

"You want to get the same purse that your friend has?"

"Yes silly. Then we can match when we go out."

"Of course," he sighed. "Silly me."

"I'm going to get it," she decided, entering the store.

Fuck me, he mouthed before following her in.

Molly grabbed the purse and posed with it before a wall mirror.

"How much is it?" Jack asked.

She gave him a confused grin. "Does it matter? You're like a billionaire."

Jack gaped at her, bewildered by her response.

She proceeded to one of the workers, the bag over her shoulder.

"Excuse me, I would like to buy this."

"That's a great choice," the employee replied. "Are you still browsing or would you like to check out?"

"Yes!" Jack interjected. "That would be nice, thank you."

"But Jack, we just got here. What if I want more?"

"I think we have enough," he asserted, turning back to the employee. "That will be all, thank you."

The worker awkwardly nodded before leading them to the checkout counter. The price tag did not bother Jack. It was never the issue. The problem was how he was to benefit from all of this, for at the end of the day, he was nothing more than an expensive mule following around a lowly girl turned queen overnight. Sure, the sex was a plus, but if that was the only upside to being with Molly, then he may as well go into pimping, where he could at least get passive income on top of it.

Jack expected an earful on the drive back. But to his surprise, Molly appeared completely fine.

"I'm starving! What should we eat?" she trilled.

"I told my boys I would get dinner with them later. Bennett said that he has big news for us," Jack said. "Are you cool with that?'

Molly dismissively bit the inside of her cheek. "Sure. As long as it's a nice place."

Too hard to please. Strike two.

Jack kept quiet for the rest of the drive as they headed to a local sports bar outside the city. They arrived just in time, Jack scoping his friends in a booth with an ideal view of one of the TVs.

"Jacky boy!" Bennett hollered. "Not late, that's a first! The game is just starting."

Jack gently wrapped his arm around Molly's waist as they made their way to the table.

"You all remember Molly?" he introduced as they sat down.

"You came with us to the game a while back!" Kevin recalled. "What are you thinking messing around with this little bitch here?"

"Easy Kev," Jack muttered.

"We actually just done shopping," Molly replied, her light reaction to Kevin's profanity taking Jack by surprise.

"Shopping, huh? That's the last thing I'd imagine Jack doing in his spare time," Tommy chortled.

"It was really nice," Jack fibbed, causing his friends to giggle from sensing the obvious insincerity in his tone.

"What's so funny?" Molly asked, trying to get in on the joke.

Jack tensed at his friends' goofiness, suspecting they already had a decent intake of beers. He hoped they maintain enough self-control to not say anything stupid.

"How about a drink?" he offered, changing the subject as he fished out his credit card from his wallet and handed it to Kevin, casually whispering to him, "Nothing too expensive, okay?"

"I see!" Kevin rejoiced, jumping out of his chair and darting for the bar.

Jack then turned to Bennett. "So, care to share the news that couldn't wait?"

Bennett's eyes flashed, rising out of his chair and folding his hands as he patiently waited for Kevin to return with the drinks.

"Okay boys, before I tell you, I want to let you all know that I absolutely love each and every one of you. You are all the reason—"

"Can you just tell us?" Kevin interrupted.

Bennett tilted his head, mildly irritated.

"Can't I just take a moment to show my appreciation for you all?"

"I'm hungry Benny," Isaac droned.

"Fine, fine." Bennett threw his hands in the air. "I'm going to on vacation with Naylah's family next weekend."

The boys stared blankly at him.

"What?"

"That's the news?" Tommy jeered. "Haven't you two been dating for a while, now?"

"No, you don't understand. This is *the* weekend."

"You're going to propose to her?"
"Not yet, but I will be asking for their blessing to marry her," Bennett clarified.
"Oh."
A moment of silence.
"I didn't know people still did that," Isaac finally said.
"I think it was a thing people did back in the day, when society was more into traditions and stuff," Tommy added.
"We still have traditions Tom." Jack said.
"But asking for the parents' blessing? That had to be going on back when women didn't have equal rights like they do now."
"Well, I wouldn't say women are exactly equal to us yet," Bennett countered.
"I hope we can get there though."
"Bro, they're essentially equal."
"'Essentially' isn't the same as 'exactly'."
"*Essentially,* they are," Tommy cackled.
Bennett groaned under the sneers from the other boys. "You're all a bunch of misogynists."
"Oh my god, don't give us that shit," Kevin playfully chuckled. "You're not joking about it because you're the only one with a girlfriend."
"Apparently not," Isaac chirped, gesturing to Jack and Molly across from them. "Jack, are you planning on asking Molly's father for a blessing down the road?"
Jack swallowed hard, hating that the attention had shifted onto them. But before he could respond, Molly spoke up.
"My dad is dead," she uttered pensively.
Jack remained still at the sight of his friends, all of whom were embarrassingly horrified.
All of them, except Tommy, of course, who notoriously defaults to making jokes whenever he is nervous.
"On the bright side…" Jack heard Tommy say.
Don't, Tommy. Fucking don't.
But even he knew that in that moment, when Tommy begins something, he always finishes.
"…You won't have to worry about her dad saying no."
Jack's head fell in his palms.
"What the hell does that mean?" Molly snapped back at Tommy.
"Oh shit," Kevin grumbled, nudging an uncomfortable Bennett.
Tommy immediately knew he was on the other side of the line with Molly saying that. No point in trying to defuse something with total guarantee to

detonate. The clock was already ticking, and all he could do was expedite the boom.

"It was just a joke."

"A little tasteless," Bennett murmured, stealing glances from Tommy and Molly. "But a joke, nevertheless."

"You're an asshole," Molly shouted, glaring at Tommy. "No wonder why you're still single."

"I deserved that," Tommy retorted. "Could you chill now? No one likes the person who takes everything too seriously."

"Did you just tell me to chill?"

"Tommy—" Jack started.

"Yes, I did."

Molly turned to Jack, stricken in disbelief.

"Your friend is being an asshole. Aren't you going to do something about it?"

Jack blankly stared back at Molly before shifting his gaze at Tommy.

"You know, I think we should head out."

"Don't do that, you haven't even ordered yet!" Isaac chimed.

"No it's okay, we're going to go," Jack decided, slowly backing out of his chair.

Molly clutched his arm and pulled him back to his seat.

"Wait Jack, I want you to do something about Tom. Right now."

Jack looked back at Tommy's subtle, menacing smirk. Anything he could say to him could not resort to reconciliation. It was already problematic having to deal with one stubborn bitch. Now he had two, both within punching distance – probably not the best time to double down and pick sides.

Bennett thankfully stepped in. "I love how quickly we just brushed past my news."

"Congratulations Bennett. We're happy for you," Jack assented.

"Are you kidding me?" Molly scoffed, leaving her seat and storming out of the bar.

The boys exchanged apathetic murmurs as Jack glared at Tommy.

"Why did you have to go there?"

"Molly sucks, man."

Bennett once again drew in his friends' attention upon releasing a deeply prolonged sigh.

"And I don't understand what more you want from us," Tommy directed at Bennett.

"Since it's not already obvious for you guys, I was hoping for some advice on how to go about it."

"You don't need our advice," Isaac soothed. "Everyone loves you. Just be yourself."

"No, don't do that," Kevin chimed. "You have an effeminate quality that
could turn them off."
"*What?*" Bennett gasped, baffled. He looked over to the others.
"Kevin's just saying that to piss me off, right? He's not being serious?"
He was met with antsy shrugs.
"It's not a crime to be effeminate," Tommy noted. "Besides, it could bode
well that you don't come off as a piece of shit."
"I'm not a piece of shit!" Bennett snapped back.
"I know, that's exactly what I'm saying."
He swiveled back to see Jack had remained stoically fixated on him, causing
the initial tension from his reply to resurge over the ongoing conversation that
he hoped would have backburned his actions.
"Look man, I'm not sorry for what I said. I can't pretend to be nice to
someone that I don't respect."
"Well you can, but you're choosing not to."
"Are we talking about Molly again?" Bennett peeped.
Tommy ignored his question, still on Jack. "You're trying to act mad because
Molly is, but you don't actually care."
Jack had known how difficult it was to shatter Tommy's stubborn rationale.
And with Molly waiting outside, he did not have time, nor patience to chip
away at it.
"I'm going to go."
"Let us know in the morning if you two are still together!" Isaac hollered as
Jack paced off. Knowing Molly's radical temperament, however, he would be
lucky to make it through the night.

*****

It has been said that the line between love and hate is bizarrely thin. It likely
stems from the false theory explaining polarities in emotions, that spend less
attention to the quality of the feeling, rather than the degree of weight applied
drawing the reaction. Women – having a natural edge over men with their
rapport in their feelings – can experience a variety of 'different' emotions
over the course of a single day. An insane concept for Jack to dwell on, but
upon seeing Molly thrusting wildly on top of him just minutes after soaking in
hysterical screams about her dead dad, he wondered otherwise.
It felt nice, but he still struggled to pay attention to her against his wandering
line of thought.
"You like my pussy daddy?"

Never had he given himself enough time to identify his kinks, but after hearing those words leave Molly's lips, Jack was quick to scratch off dirty talk from the list.
"Excuse me?" he said, stopping abruptly mid-thrust.
"No keep going, I'm getting close."
Jack pulled out and rolled away, turned off by her disregard.
Molly came back to earth and opened her eyes.
"What's your problem?"
"I'm not comfortable with that stuff when I'm having sex."
"Please tell me you're not being serious?"
Jack shrugged. "I've never done it before."
Molly scoffed and turned her back to him. "You're so weird."
"You don't think that it's weird to refer to me as your 'daddy?' How do you expect me to react to that?"
"It's not supposed to be taken literally Jack," Molly snapped back. "It's just a flirty expression."
"I didn't find it flirty."
"Whatever," she murmured, leaving the bed and getting dressed.
"What are you doing?"
"I want you to go," Molly said, refusing to make eye contact.
"Wait, can we talk about it?"
Molly held the door open for Jack as he hastily reached for his clothes and threw them on. "I don't see what there is to talk about."
"You're kicking me out in the middle of the night," Jack contested. "Clearly, there is something that you're upset about."
Molly reached for Jack's jacket on the floor and carelessly tossed it at his feet.
"I just don't understand how you are so insecure," she pressed, frustrated.
"You have so much talk about how cool you are, but you can't deal with this. You're a pussy."
Jack's jaw fell. "So I'm a pussy for not wanting to hear you talk about yours?"
"It's not just the sex Jack. You can just get so finicky about everything. Like today at the mall—"
"Oh right, at the mall, of course. You mean where you spent thousands of dollars – my money – like I was some walking ATM machine."
"You offered!"
"Because I was trying to be a nice guy! What about you? What kind of person deliberately uses someone else like that?"
"Oh right, like you're not using me for anything?"
Jack was confused by the question. "What are you even talking about?"

"Oh I don't know Jack, how about the fact that you put me on as a laughingstock around your friends?"
"No one was laughing at you. Everyone knows Tommy is an asshole sometimes. It's just who he is—"
"*See,* right there," Molly interrupted. "You accept things that you can change, like who your friends are. Bennett seemed to be the most normal, and even he was sorta weird."
"You *do* realize I grew up with them right? They've been my friends for as long as I can remember. I'm not going to stop hanging out with them because you disapprove."
"I bet you wouldn't say that if I was your ex."
Jack's face tightened.
"What does Emma have to do with this?"
"I see you remember her name."
"Obviously I remember her name. She's not a stranger."
"You made that pretty fucking clear."
"Where are you going with this?"
"Are you still in love with her?"
Jack hesitated, for in that moment, he was forced to face the question he had asked himself every day since she left.
"No." he lied, doing his best to sound genuine.
"Mhm, okay," she replied dryly, storming out of the bedroom. Jack was close behind, watching as she swung the front door open and looked back at him.
"You're still kicking me out?"
"We're not going to work out if you don't fix yourself first. I don't care if you want to be stupid with your friends, or cry about how much you miss your girlfriend. But do it on your own time. I'm not going to put up with this if I don't have to."
Jack could not believe what he was hearing. It was too preposterous to be gaslighting. He hoped even Molly could see the irony.
Nevertheless, he walked past her and out the door.
"So is this it?" he asked.
Molly rolled her eyes.
"Call me after you have your shit figured out."
"Wait—"
Molly held the door ajar for his last words.
"I assume you're just going to keep all the things I bought you today and not return them like a decent human being?"
He felt the slam from the door under his soles. He looked up and down the hallway of the complex, hoping no one had overheard. It would not have been a good look in the eyes of a spectator, and God only knows the

lengths Molly would go to capitalize on beaming a spotlight to further embarrass him.

It likely does not need to be said, but still: strike three.

Arguments are nothing more than verbal tornadoes: overly common to the point that its cause is certainly dissectible, although so spontaneous that even the whiff of insurgence could be enough to admit defeat and cower amid unstoppable obliteration. There is no premeditated counter upon initiation, and winning is rarely, if ever an option due to the inability to control time, which also happens to be the most uncontrollable of variables. Even if one was gifted with Nostradamus' foresight, all they could do was prepare for the inevitable.

And by the time one partner revisits the aftermath – mentally shrouded in melancholy with a new purpose to resurrect the goodness they once shared with their lover – concludes the reality of their situation, and even the attempt to correct such actions could open a Pandora's box of unwanted repercussions. The past is the past, and no matter how long the list of "lessons" are that they force themselves to "learn," the ultimate recourse to move on is the same. Dysfunction welcomes chaos. And in case there are still those who refuse to admit it, Jack has proven to others, if not already yet to himself, that he epitomizes the term.

It was Friday, and the Fremont community was far more enthusiastic than their common humdrum. He considered staying out to partake in the nightlife, before he remembered the last time he found himself out there without Molly. Tommy had driven, and their unawareness of how badly placed they were until the end of the evening when their car was thirty seconds away from being doused in paint. According to the police report the family lawyer returned to the Beech's, there was also discussion of including rainbow-colored lettering across the hood, reading, *FASCIST*.

Another memory from a singular page out of the book of Tommy's Trials. Fortunately for Jack, his beamer was only touched by the full moon gleaming overhead. And even more so, Tommy had coincidentally invited him to join on another excursion on their familiar, preferred grounds.

*****

Harmony was blown away by the sheer number of drunkards shoveling through her when she entered the Den. She scanned the club and spotted the boys almost instantly, encircled in a booth adjacent to the dancefloor on the other end of the venue. Jack was the first to see her, middled between his friends when he approached the table.

"Look who it is!" he exclaimed, causing the rest of them to roar raucously as Harmony squeezed beside Tommy on the end.

"You drove all the way up here to hang out with us?" Bennett asked.

"Pretty much, although I debated turning around halfway through the trip."

"Well, we're happy you're here," Jack added, to which she automatically chose to read deeper, assuming that it was his roundabout acknowledgement of the mutual emotions they shared their last time together. Upon overhearing his falling out with Molly earlier that night, only a pea-sized brain could misconstrue the tension mounting. Harmony hoped that even in Jack's murkiest state, the rationalization behind her commitment to trek up to see him was clear.

"Eyes up, gents," Isaac announced, nudging Tommy and Kevin beside him. Harmony did not need to follow along, as she understood the guys too well.

"Holy Mose, she is marvelous," Tommy remarked as they watched the girls pass their table.

Jack was the only one who did not notice, as he downed the little vodka left in his cup. Harmony tried to make eye contact, hoping that his disregard was intentional on her behalf.

"Fuck them," he said and shook his cup in Bennett's face. "They're just a bunch of Molly's. Stupid bitches who think they can control the world through their toxicity and good looks."

"Poetic, yet insulting," Kevin noted. For a moment, that was enough to ease the group's acknowledgement of Jack's negative attitude. But Jack doubled down on his insistence to make his mood the anecdote of the night, shaking his cup in front of Bennett still, this time vigorous enough for the watered down cubes to rattle above the deafening 808s.

Harmony was appalled when Bennett's focus returned to the cup, eyeing it in quiet poise.

"Is that for me?" he asked Jack.

"It's your turn to get a round."

Bennett shrugged and left the table, returning quicky with a platter of mixed drinks. Jack was first to claim his share as he was hoarding two cups in his grasps.

"Take it slow man," Bennett cautioned. "The night just started."

Harmony had seen them all drunk before, and generally having been more sober than the rest never failed to make her uncomfortable. But the source of her unease was not the same this time around, largely due to Jack's uncharacteristic manner. Even when he was most inebriated, she knew he could still control himself. Something about him was off, and though their destination of choice warranted his desire to indulge, Harmony knew this extreme version of Jack had everything to do with Emma.

Jack drained his drink in minutes, once again raising the cups above his head for the gang to see. This was another side of Jack. And one Harmony was quick to hate.

Tommy could tell, observing her reaction and motioning himself to the edge of the booth.

"I think it's my turn to get a round," he uttered, tapping Harmony's arm. "Wanna join?"

She took the hint and followed him to the bar.

"Six Jack cokes," he said to the bartender as he put all his weight on the bar and turned to her. "So, who's the next guy in your lineup?"

As she pondered the question, he caught her eyes quickly drift over to their table. He did not need to ask, as he was certain it was Jack she was looking at.

"No one," she replied flatly.

"Your face tells a different answer."

Harmony resisted the urge to break her world-class poker face, shrugging carelessly as she thanked the bartender for their drinks.

"You can tell me. That's what friends are for," Tommy insisted.

"Are you asking me because you're trying to change that?"

Tommy reacted opposite to what she expected, giggling to himself as he pulled a couple bills from his wallet.

"I'll stop you right there and confidently say that *this* would never work," he said, gesturing to both of them.

"I never said that I wanted it."

"In that case, there's no point in having the conversation," Tommy said, grabbing his drink and starting back to the booth.

Harmony grabbed his arm and pulled him back.

"Out of curiosity, why do you think we would never work out?"

Tommy turned back to her. "We're too alike, and only in the bad ways."

"Okay, fuck you. I can get more guys than you can girls."

"You're probably right," he winked. "But you saying that proves my point exactly."

HG sighed, coming to understand Tommy's argument. Only she would react to such a statement by glorifying her own self. And apparently, so would he.

"We would be a power couple forsure," Harmony laughed. "But you're right, there would definitely be more negatives than positives if that ever happened."

"What won't happen doesn't matter. Besides, I heard there was electricity in the air the last time you were with Jack."

"That's not the saying," Harmony rolled her eyes. "Also, who told you that? Was it Jack? Because nothing happened, if that's what you are getting at."

"Playing dumb," he observed. "That's so unlike you, Goodwynn."

"I'm serious, nothing happened."
"Maybe not physically, but we both know there was some heat simmering from that magical crotch of yours."
"Jesus Tommy, how many times do I have to tell you: *that is not how you are supposed to speak to women.*"
Tommy shrugged her off. "You're a bro at this point."
"Besides, I don't even know anymore about Jack," she added. "Maybe I thought I was crushing on him that night, but after seeing him now—"
"You mean, seeing who he *really* is?"
"I wouldn't put it like that. I've known him since we were kids. He has never been like this before."
"I've also known him since we were kids. And believe me, there is a side to all of us that we don't want anyone to know."
"Are we still talking about Jack here?"
She watched Tommy's grin mischievously. "Perhaps we should both stick to finding people with less ambition."
"Is that a compliment?"
"It's whatever you want it to be," Tommy said, slurping up the watered-down whiskey from his empty cup and shaking it in her face. "Gender equality. You're next up to buy."
HG glowered down at her cup, still filled to the brim.
"We haven't even sat down yet!"
"You're the one who wanted to keep talking about this. Chop chop girl, let's go."
Harmony obeyed grudgingly, spinning around to the bar and running into a familiar face.
He was alone, and appeared distressed as he returned a glare.
"Aiden?" she spluttered. "What are you doing here?"
"Who is this guy?" Tommy whispered.
"I'm her ex," Aiden replied bitterly.
"I see," Tommy nodded, extending his free hand for a shake. "Tommy Beech. I'm her friend."
Aiden refused to shake his hand and focused on Harmony. "So, you dump me for this queer?"
"Take it easy," Tommy warned.
"Are you two fucking?" he shouted at them, still directed at Harmony.
Tommy lowered his hand, having concluded that this dude was unworthy of his time or respect.
Oh no, Harmony bit her lip and grabbed Tommy's arm as he leaned closer to Aiden, fearing whatever he would say would be nothing short of provocative.

"It's crazy you ask," Tommy whispered to Aiden. "Because we were *literally* just exploring the idea before you showed up."

At that, Aiden shoved Tommy, causing him to stagger back and nearly fall over if it was not for Harmony catching him.

"Tom! Are you okay?"

Tommy regained his stance and shook himself out of her grasp, angry at the sight of the spilled drink on his shirt.

"You must hate your life," Tommy persisted. "What was your objective coming here and starting this shit?"

"This is none of your business," Aiden warned. "I have the right to talk to her."

"No, you don't." Tommy argued.

Aiden did not wait a second longer, hurdling toward Tommy and wrestling him against the bar. They were even in their efforts to bring the other down, at least at first. Harmony was nervous for Tommy, who had not measured the degree of rage Aiden could achieve if he was poked enough.

A crowd generated around them within seconds, hollering in Tommy's favor. Aiden pressed his left forearm hard on Tommy's chest, forcing space and proceeding to throw his right fist to his chin. Only two knuckles landed, but it was enough to change the pace of the altercation. Because out of nowhere, Tommy reached for Aiden's fallen wrist and pulled it down below his hips, while placing his other hand behind Aiden's head.

Harmony watched as he drove Aiden's face into the tray of drinks on the bar, the sound of the shattered glass muting her shriek. Security rushed in, a pair of officers seizing Tommy and pulling him back toward Harmony as she circled around them and knelt beside Aiden, now whimpering on the booze-soaked floors.

"Oh, give me a break!" Tommy shouted, his feet grounded as he resisted the officers.

Her contempt for him remained, yet the sight of Aiden's stolid expression earned him a sliver of sympathy. She twisted back to Tommy, baffled at how quickly the commotion had settled. He was now free from the guards' hold and casually tossing bills on the bar, proceeding to shake an assortment of hands, like he had just finished a speech.

Harmony had little time to comprehend what was happening when the guards came forward, nearly stomping on her hand when they reached for Aiden and dragged him toward the exit.

A fight is one thing. But inflicting more harm on the other person, and buying immunity without any consideration for the context behind the matter?

Harmony could not believe what she had just witnessed, let alone find the will in her to applaud Tommy, who was now pompously cajoling with those who witnessed his unforeseen victory.

This was a mistake, Harmony thought. *I shouldn't be here.*

She buried her face within the growing crowd and fled out of the bar, momentarily catching her breath in the cool ocean air.

She once believed her distaste for Seattle was because of the city as a whole. But in times like these, when submerged in a cycle of self-denial, she understood that it was from her discontent of the people; specifically, the ones who resonated with her memory of growing up there. Her friends, whom she believed would be there for her through thick and thin, and subliminally reassure her that any internal feelings were misguided. They were the problem.

Perhaps she was cursed, to find herself on the barren downtown streets: a beautiful woman in her early twenties, filled with strong-willed ambition, seeking nothing else than love and respect from someone who cared enough to accept her for who she was. How hard she had tried to make it known for those she loved the most. And yet, it seemed to be that time was not the only constant in this natural world. For as long as there are others who call it home, there too will be wickedness that they inevitably bring.

"Is something wrong?" came a voice.

Her mind was rounding the finish line when the question registered, lifting her head and seeing a concerned man staring back.

"Yeah, I'm okay."

"Just checking," he said. "You look paler than from the last time I saw you."

Harmony glazed over his face again, this time recognizing his sullen grin.

"I remember you," Harmony started. "I met you when I was having lunch with Emma—"

"Emma Keva, right," he finished. "My name is –"

"Logan Berg."

"You remember my name?"

"You sound surprised."

"I am, a little bit," Logan chuckled. "I have a reputation of leaving negative impressions on people."

Harmony cracked a smile.

"Even if that were the case, you would still be remembered, wouldn't you?"

"I guess that's true," Logan replied meekly, scratching his head. "What are you doing out here alone?"

Harmony glimpsed at the club behind her, impartial as to whether she should divulge.

"It's too crowded in there," she began, instantly giving in. "One of my friends got into a bit of an altercation."

Logan let out a genuine laugh.

"I feel that. I got myself into one not too long ago."

Harmony's eyes widened. "A bar fight?"

She noticed his awkward reflex when he said it, as if it inadvertently slipped out.

"It was more a scuffle…" he added, swallowing hard. "But yeah, it's never easy trying to reason with unreasonable people."

"You're describing most of my friends," Harmony spoke, pointing at Tommy through the windows. "I love them, but that doesn't mean they don't get on my nerves."

She realized he was no longer smiling, his lips thinly pressed with a cold stare.

"That's him," Logan uttered.

"You know Tommy?"

"Very well," he added. "We grew up together."

His tone was transparently aloof, leading Harmony to question the nature of their acquaintance.

"If I didn't know any better, I'd say your time growing up with them didn't end well."

He maintained a cool expression, prompting her to dwell on her assumption of the nature behind Logan's paranoia. She was puzzled, to say the least, and even with the pieces she had already gathered, it was telling how much more she needed to obtain the complete the finished picture of Logan's mysterious dynamic with the rest of the boys. No way it was as simple as a sigma's intolerance with testosteroney alphas.

"We don't have to go inside," she offered. "Come on, let's go somewhere."

"Really? You're down to just ditch your friends like that?"

"Trust me, it's not my first time," she exhaled, linking her arm around his and dragging him away from the bar.

It was odd to her, how comfortable she felt around someone that anyone would perceive as a stranger. Even if he had no familiarity with the boys, his impressionable innocence would have been grounds enough for her to trust the guy. There was a subtle danger in him she detected, but it felt that it was out of protection for her, and never inflicted toward her.

They were undoubtedly in a merge of their own, strolling several blocks and engaged in light chatter. Harmony did not prefer it but also became aware quickly of the effort needed to get deeper substance out of him. He was incredibly shy, as she noted the delayed pauses he had after asking him a question. Perhaps his silence came from fear or insecurity – unlike an emission of malice that she expected from her actual friends. Logan was too authentic to be pretending. Same went for his affection toward her, which she noticed almost immediately and could not help but blush at how nervous he was to speak to her, regardless of how disarming she made herself.

A couple hours had passed when Harmony recognized the Den's neon sign hovering over them.

"And here we are," he acknowledged, peeking at the colorful blobs circling beyond the tinted windows of the bar.

"You want to go inside?"

"Not exactly," Logan replied gently, slow to unlink their arms. "This is where I leave you tonight, so you can meet back up with your friends."

Before she could speak, he added, "I know that you have ditched them before. But since they none of them have contacted you since you left, they must still be in there. And if this progresses, it's probably best if I don't steal you from them the same night officially meeting you."

Harmony smirked.

"If what progresses, may I ask?"

She ogled Logan, awaiting him to finally utter the words she was certain to leave his mouth.

"I like you," Logan muttered.

It sounded exactly as she imagined. Timid, yet determined. Sure, the brevity of their encounter may not be enough for many to have a strong degree of certainty. But Harmony had been in this situation countless times from the other end. And now that she was on the receiving end, it was ironically clear why she had been let down so many times as a result of falling too hard too quickly.

"Are you the kind of person to ask to kiss me?"

"What? No!" Logan stammered, shriveling up. "I mean, I guess it depends on if the moment is right."

"And if the moment is right?"

Logan picked up the hint, leaning closer and pulling her hair behind her left lobe. He placed a gentle kiss on her lips, immediately taken aback at her welcoming reaction, as she wrapped her arms around his waist.

They stared into one another's eyes for what seemed like an eternity, before Logan started inching backwards.

Like clockwork, the Den's doors busted open, vomiting out a horde of sweat-stenched students. And as Logan assumed, there were the boys, stumbling out and letting out a unified shock at the sight of Harmony staring back at them.

"Holy shit," Kevin exhaled, out of breath. "You're alive!"

"So are you," Harmony retorted, acknowledging all of the boys and leading them away from the dense crowd.

"Where have you been?" Tommy asked her, in a clearly drunker state than when she left them.

Harmony hesitated, noticing a sobering Jack nearing to hear her reply.

"I…went for a walk," Harmony tried, shifting awkwardly in her stance. Thankfully, Tommy was hammered, blinding him from any scrutiny of her physical uneasiness.

Jack spoke next.

"Come on, let's get out of here," he announced to the group, seemingly having total disregard in Harmony's whereabouts. They reached Jack and Tommy's apartment, where they had all agreed to stay for the night. Including Harmony, who had mentioned earlier the ludicrous idea of driving home at a distasteful time.

Tommy offered his bed, knowing full well she'd be gone first thing in the morning so that he could sloth back under his comforter for an already anticipated second-half of his slumber, commonly referred to as "sleeping in." Unbeknownst to them, though, was Harmony's agenda the next day.

*****

Seeing HG in the latter half of the morning baffled Jack, who if asked last night, would have bet the entirety of his fortune that she would be long gone and pulling up to her driveway in Renton.

Yet, there she was in his kitchen with Tommy, and judging from the spright in her arm waves, he knew Tommy was entrapped in a tangent on the latest drama in her life. Common, and frankly expected from her.

Jack crept into the bathroom without her noticing, taking his sweet time and emerging a half hour later, where Tommy was now alone where he left him.

"How was that?" Jack asked.

Tommy sighed exhaustingly. "Not terrible, she just left."

"Are you two…"

"God no. The other guys were here before you got up, but they were just smart enough to find excuses to leave."

"So she's driving back home now?"

"I guess so."

"You didn't ask?"

"I did not," Tommy admitted, turning back to the espresso machine. "I try not to delve into other people's lives."

"What do you mean, you delve into mine all the time!"

"Count yourself lucky then!"

"Fair enough," Jack paused, moving into the living room and checking the time on his phone. "Don't you think it was weird that she was still here?"

"A little bit," he agreed, joining him on the couch and turning on the television. "Maybe she just wanted to sleep in. People's habits change all the time."

"Come on man. It's HG, she'll never change."

"Good point," Tommy acknowledged, giving a mild shrug. "Who knows, maybe she's got a sneaky link that she wanted to see before she left?"

"Damn, you think so?"

"Well, she *did* dip from the bar midway through the night and randomly appear outside when we left," Tommy reasoned. "It's not the craziest idea that she met someone during that time."

"Don't you think she would have told you that?"

"Perhaps, but maybe not if it was with someone we knew, which would explain why she would keep it to herself," Tommy added, becoming more intrigued with Jack's line of questioning. "Imagine if she was talking to someone we didn't fuck with, like that guy Paul from our Global Policy course last semester."

"Oh God," Jack gasped, cringing at the image of that pimpled-faced menace slobbering over HG's face. "I think I'd prefer it if it was a woman."

"You think she's curious?"

"I mean, I wouldn't put it past her. She's always been more of a 'guy's girl,' anyway. Have you ever heard her talk about handing out with *only* girls before, when a dude was never present?"

"Come on though, that's probably just because girls are able to see through her fakeness, whereas guys don't care as much since she's hot and can take our shit."

Jack returned to the kitchen to treat himself to a glass of juice. He opened the fridge and let out a sigh at the empty shelves.

"Guess it's time to go grocery shopping," he called out to Tommy.

"I can't," Tommy exhaled. "I told Morgan I'd hang with her this afternoon."

"No worries, I'll take care of it this time."

Tommy tilted his head back to look at Jack.

"You a dog for that."

He was in and out of the supermarket, leisurely loading bags in his car when he was blinded asudden by a glint coming from the light traffic. He let his eyes pan around until they locked on the source of the glare: a leather handbag, embossed in sparkling diamonds. Jack tracked the thin strap, stunned to see the strikingly familiar face of its owner.

HG?

He failed to get a definitive look, given that she was on the opposite side of the street pacing briskly alongside other pedestrians. He jumped in his car and turned onto the avenue to follow her, for once not minding the traffic's sluggish pace as he kept sight of her ahead.

It was peculiar seeing her this time and day. Maybe shopping was one of her errands, too. *But if so, would she not have mentioned it to Tommy?* Unless she did, but Tommy left that detail out.

Jack's overthinking was stopped shortly when he noticed her make a sharp right into what appeared to be a pub.

Since when do people who don't like football have drinks on a Sunday morning?

The events were steadily adding up, and it only intrigued his curiosity more. Perhaps this was the same feeling the stalkers felt.

He was disappointed when the congestion let up, leaving him to cease his investigation and proceed home. He made a single trip with the groceries, eagerly shouldering up the stairs to the apartment to share the juicy news with Tommy.

But when he had arrived, he was already gone.

*****

Harmony knew she had spent far too long retelling her dramatic escapades with the boys. She thought it was quite unusual how long she spoke without being cut short. Granted, it was nowhere near the first time she had been criticized for her recollection of redundant anecdotes that, simply, boast no interest from anyone hearing them.

Well, apparently not everyone.

Logan Berg was sure to enjoy every minute, which largely factored into her lack of anxiety that afternoon on her way to meet with him for lunch before the inevitable departure home. They initially planned for the same café where Emma brokered the introductions, but instead resorted to a pub nearby, due to Logan's disrelish of large crowds.

Logan was alone at the bar when she entered. He seemed very content, naturally suiting the loner aura he gave off.

"Am I interrupting?" she greeted.

She noted Logan's almost surprised grin when he saw her, as he rubbed his hands nervously on his legs.

"Hi!" he stammered, pulling up a barstool for her to sit. Truthfully, he was not expecting her to actually come. He had a poor telling of when someone liked him, and even though Harmony's reciprocated interest was, well, transparent, it still was not yet enough for Logan to settle his own self-doubt that anything of this sort could possibly work in his favor.

"Do you want something to drink?" he asked.

"Yes please. No liquor though, I have to drive home after this."

"That's totally fine, this place doesn't serve liquor for another several hours," Logan signaled the bartender. "Did you find your friends okay after I left you?"

"I did. They were absolutely trashed and going on about your guys' typical 'locker room talk.'"

"Oh yeah, that's certainly something we all do," Logan muttered, hoping she would hear the sarcasm in his tone.

The bartender returned with a drink for Harmony, who engulfed half of the tall glass before jumping in yet another lengthy prattle on the rest of her night.

It did not bother Logan, who considered himself more of a listener anyways. He waited until she found a break in her endless narrative before he spoke up.

"Is this awkward for you? I know that you've thought about my history with the guys. And well, while I don't think it is super important to get into it now, I want to make sure that you feel comfortable being around me."

Harmony burst out laughing, taking a moment to regain her breath.

"You're such a boy," she joked. "Trust me, I don't care about your relationship with them. Guys are different than girls: you get into silly arguments, fight for a bit, and then get over it like it never happened."

"I hope you're right about that last part. Sorry, I tend to overthink a lot," Logan lowered his head. "This is sort of my first *"first"* date, if that makes sense."

"Is that what this is, a date?"

Harmony was charmed by the timid frown on Logan's paled face. Before he could give a response, she added, "I'm just messing with you."

"Thank God," Logan relaxed. "As I was saying though, I know I am right, and *no*, I do not feel awkward about it," she went on. "I've been out of touch with them for so long, that I feel almost like my own person, if that makes sense. Whatever you went through with them has no effect on this," she assured.

The fact that she found him remotely appealing shocked Logan, who was certain that the reaction he gave after seeing Tommy at the Den would have spurred enough awkwardness to dissolve any possibility of them working out. He knew she noticed, and although he was glad that she was not the initiate the topic, also made him somewhat uneasy with what else she chose to keep close to heart.

There was no doubt in his feelings for Harmony, but regardless of how hard he may have fallen, the prospect of them reaching a unified relationship would be nearly impossible with Jack and Tommy in the way. They would never permit it, had they ever caught wind of their relationship. And given her close friendship with those boys, such a confrontation would be unpreventable.

As for Harmony, Logan would be the only thing on her mind for the rest of the evening. Driving back to Renton; reconnecting with her sisters over dinner (including during their ever-so predicable spat that would ultimately cut their time short); as she laid in bed that evening, rummaging through the events of her day, and long after she was fast asleep. It did not alarm her. Why would it? He had reciprocated his feelings – transparently too, if it should reinforce her contentment of this fresh dynamic they had formed.

Frankly, Harmony knew it was too good to be true.

xxvii

Creativity was one of Tommy's fortes. He viewed the ability more as an art: not only capable of mastery through repetition and time, but obviously enhanced when coupled with intrepid confidence. It was usually more effective on *first* dates, though, which he learned the hard way after noticing Morgan's failure to reciprocate the appreciation.

Yes, Morgan. Emma's friend and onetime roommate. Tommy felt that still entertaining her was a result of his procrastination to revisit their relationship status. After all, he engaged with her initially because he figured it would benefit Jack, who at the time, was engrossed with Emma when they first met. But following Emma's move east, Tommy underestimated any possibility that he and Morgan would progress. He did not show the best initiative to see her, but neither did she. They hooked up, but only when his horniness trumped rationale, which usually occurred over periodic instances when they ran into each other in public. The underlying intention was gone with Emma, and what was worse for Tommy, is that he suspected them of fizzling as time dragged on. Never once did he expect Morgan's interest in him to grow with Emma's absence. Not that it bothered him, as he was typically inclined to spend time with anyone. But he knew Morgan – at least in this current time – envisioned a deeper relationship, the total opposite to what he wanted. Especially with his everlasting promise to the one who got away.

Nevertheless, he capitalized on the beautiful weather that day and brought Morgan to Myrtle Edwards Park, spending some hours strolling beside a lapping shoreline as he awed at the massive ships tediously slugging atop the glistening Sound. His place of choosing was delicately planned, as the natural scenery leveled his intolerance of Morgan's tendency to rant. While he loved conversation, it bored him when the degree of intellect mismatched his own. He paid little attention to the speckles of sand crawling over his goatskin soles, deliberately nearing the shore where the tide was just high enough to steep his ankles in the waters. He admired the movement of the water, wishing that he could imitate its nature. Formless, and liberated. Free from any restriction or constraint.

He was busy breathing in the salty aroma from the ocean when Morgan's voice pierced through his conscience.

"Hello Tommy, are you there?"

He swiveled around to see her distressed glare.

"Sorry, I haven't had my coffee yet today," he replied, hoping it would make for a sufficient excuse in deterring her frustration.

Morgan's eyes lit up.

"That's such a good idea!"

They continued down the path, eventually reaching the end of the block before crossing back into the city. It was too late in the day for caffeine, but Morgan unexpectantly calling his bluff forced him to comply with the sizzling latte before him.

He took his first sip when Morgan, quite abruptly, said, "You know, Jack can be such an asshole."

Tommy nearly choked on his coffee. Had he not been used to Morgan's unfiltered declarations, he certainly would have challenged her remark. Instead, he sipped and listened to her drawl on further.

"Do you not have anything to say?" she added after a couple minutes of criticism.

"No," he replied, knowing full well that escalating situations with strong personalities proved to be a losing battle, every time.

"Well, what's your take on it?"

He blinked rapidly. "On what?"

"Jack and Molly," Morgan clarified. "The nerve for him to drop Emma and hook up with such a slut absolutely blows my mind. What was he thinking?"

"I was not aware of Molly's...slutness."

Morgan squinted in annoyance.

"Tom!"

"I'm not going to speak ill of Jack," he shrugged. "He's one of my best friends."

"Why does it matter? Don't you still think what he did was wrong?"

"I guess, but my reason for disproving his actions isn't exactly aligned with yours."

"Okay, then what's your reason?"

"I'd rather not say," he said flatly as he took another sip of his coffee.

"*Excuse* me?"

Tommy peeked up to see Morgan's hardened expression.

"Jack and Emma have both been through a lot," he added disarmingly.

"Maybe it's best if we leave the drama for them to sort out."

"There wouldn't have been any drama if it wasn't for Jack!"

Tommy's patience thinned with each syllable emitting from Morgan. His self-praised ability to empathize with the concerns of others were rarely acted on. He reasoned it did more harm than good, and that the best approach to consoling someone was not to appeal to their emotions but supplement their worries with a logical solution.

"Stop making this about us, because it isn't," he said coolly to Morgan. "They are responsible for the situation that they are in, and *I personally* don't think that this conversation is going to fix anything. If you have an idea on how to help them, I am all ears. But if you are just going to bitch about it, then you can do that on your own."

Morgan stared at him, astonishingly agape.

"What has gotten into you lately? You defending him like this – what, is there another girl *you're* not telling me about?"

The question stirred his already present displeasure, causing him to let out an irking sigh.

"What a wild accusation…" he mumbled, immediately sensing an opportunity to sever from her. "In fact, there is another girl Morgan, and since we're on the topic, I *love* her."

Morgan shot up from her seat and snatched her coffee. Tommy's alarm bells rang, already anticipating her reaction. He planted his feet on the floor and pushed his stool to the right of the table, just missing the cup Morgan had hurled toward him.

Multiple heads in the café caught the aftermath of the incident, swiveling in their direction and having subtle gasps as the spilled cup leaked coffee across the hardwood floors.

Tommy looked back at Morgan, shaking his head.

"That's going to stick, you know."

Morgan furiously stormed out of the café, promptly giving Tommy the finger from outside the windows.

Tommy waited there, still feeling a couple pairs of eyes on him. He was not sure what to do next.

This must be how Jack always feels, Tommy contemplated, easily dismissing Morgan's absence as he reached into his wallet and slapped a hundred on the table.

He solaced in deep thought as he left the café and approached the end of the block. Over a single breadth, he examined mere glimpses of drivers' distinguishable, facial expressions as they sped past him down the avenue. It was too beautiful a day to be upset, let alone sulk for a girl he, truthfully, did not regard to be anything more than a fling.

Jack was busy flipping through movies to watch when Tommy returned to their apartment.

"I thought you were sleeping over at Morgan's tonight?"

"Yeah…" Tommy exhaled as he propped his feet atop the coffee table. "It's not going to work out with her."

"I'm sorry man. That's hard," he lowered the volume "What happened?"
"She said something I didn't like."
"Okay…" Jack paused, waiting for Tommy to continue.
"It's not important anymore. I knew it was only a matter of time."
"I understand. That's how I felt after my fight with Molly."
"What about?"
Tommy shook his head once Jack finished retelling the night. "I don't get why she was so upset…who even likes dirty talk?"
"That's what I'm saying!" Jack agreed. "What's worse is that I spent a fortune at the mall the same day just so she wouldn't be in a bitchy mood."
"Love can't be bought Jack, you know that."
Jack rolled his eyes. "Even so, it doesn't hurt to flex it."
"Maybe it does," Tommy relayed, crossing his legs. "You're worrying about whether money is enough to get a girl when there are things far more important. What about your family and friends? What about school?"
Jack flared his nostrils and clenched his head, fighting the stress away one deep breath at a time.
"I know Tom," he finally said. "I'll admit it has been hard to focus lately, not that I need to tell you that. I don't know, maybe I just need to clear my head and take a trip or something," he flashed Tommy with a cautious scorn. "And by trip, I *do not* mean with drugs."
Tommy brought a finger to his lips in stoic ponderance before flashing a grin. "I have an idea."

*****

"What's the point of this again?"
"I told you," Tommy replied coolly. "It's to channel energy in search for your inner peace."
"What is my inner peace?"
"Theoretically, it will be your acknowledgement and acceptance of understanding your state of consciousness and its relationship with any discord that influences it," he paused. "Realistically, though, it's just your respective truth."
"So like an epiphany?"

"Sure. Now hush. You told me you were struggling to find love because you were unable to define it yourself. This is my idea to helping you find out, but we can't do it if you keep talking."

If Tommy was a scientist, then love was his most treasured experiment. He shared Jack's desire for consumption, but failed to see it in its abstract, for he believed the path was riddled in hypocrisy. An abstract problem warrants an abstract solution.

What compelled the sailor to navigate into the treacherous storm, or the hunter to draw his weapon before the malevolent mammoth? Was it hope? Rage? Ambition? Fear? The intense desire to seek the truth tormented Tommy, who dedicated his life to revealing even the most undesirable answers. While such truths would not be absolute, they would be *his*. And if they were his, that was all that mattered.

He could conceptualize meditation, but Jack was not a practitioner. He was at odds with tranquility, and resistant to let go. The park was relatively sparse, and even after finding a quieter field away from the crowd, everything was a distraction from freeing his consciousness; the grass tickling his thighs; the aromatic kisses from the blooming blossoms; hearing the pensive edge in his own breath.

Time to time, he risked a peek to Tommy, noticing his gradual recession into a wooded posture, resembling an extension of the still earth around them.

Why can't I be like that?

He yearned the chance to break away from reality, even if for a moment. And the more he sat there…perhaps it was not the evergreens in their synchronized dance, or the flitting frolic of nearby wildlife that could trigger this state of mind. Hell, the thought of Emma brought more peace to his mind.

Emma.

He did not require mediation when he was with her. The adamance to keep her engrained in his thoughts was surely enough to replace this "inner peace" Tommy flaunts. Emma left a hole in his heart, and maybe only she was capable of filling it, as she was the one who pulled it out in the first place.

Tommy's nose scrunched.

"I can feel your confliction from here," he spoke, the words tearing through the static air. "Acknowledge what is troubling you and face it."

The timing of his statement was already unsettling for Jack, let alone the fact that Emma was on his mind when he said it.

"No offense man, but this isn't working," he sighed, rising to his feet. "I'm not trying to harsh on your way of things, but it's not for me."

"You're wrong."

Jack blinked hard. "What?"

Tommy opened his eyes and peered up at him.

"Do you actually love Emma, or are you doing everything in your power to prove your delusions?"

"That doesn't make sense. I was with Molly."

"Right, and how did that go for you?"

"What's that supposed to mean?" Jack's chest warmed.

"You're trying to cut Emma out of your life with these blithe misgivings. Instead, you should understand why you feel so connected to her. Whatever it is, is also likely the source of your confliction. Nothing will ever come to fruition if you stay on this imaginary course, and if you double down on it, it will cause you to spiral."

"For once, can you please use simple English?"

"*You* are the problem. Emma, your parents, me, Kevin, Bennett, Isaac – *everyone you care about* – you use us all as distractions from confronting your own shit," Tommy said, arching his brow. "Is that clear enough for you?"

"Damn. You must have been thinking of this for some time now," Jack muttered, sensing the mild frustration in his already demanding tone.

"I know you," Tommy eased up. "Arguably better than you know yourself."

"How do you figure?"

"When have you ever regretted my advice?"

"That's not fair, I don't make most of my decisions without first running it by someone."

"Exactly," Tommy noted. "The fact that you feel the need to get someone else's insight implies that you are unwilling to trust yourself wholeheartedly."

"Okay," Jack assented, coming around to his friend's reasoning. "Why do *you* think that is the case?"

"I'm still trying to figure that out," Tommy admitted. "But what's more important is that you can always trust me and everyone else who cares about you. We'll always have your back."

"I appreciate it. Really, I do." Jack paused. "But I still don't see how sitting here and thinking is going to help. I've done that. I *keep* doing it."

"Thinking is just the start. The whole point of this is to give you a chance to learn. If we were unable to find peace in our own thoughts and actions, then we are also unable to find comfort with living in the present."

Jack sat back down beside Tommy, tilting his head back to watch the sky.

"Think you'll go back to Molly?"

"Not sure yet," Jack mumbled. "What about Morgan?"

"I don't think so, especially after the pickle I put myself in with her," Tommy scratched his head. "Relationships. Who needs them?"

"Both of us, apparently."

They burst into laughter.

"Holy shit man," Jack exhaled as his laugh died down. "It's all terrible…"

"Terrible, eh?"

"You have no idea dude. I honestly don't know why I am wasting my time with her."

"There must be something about her you like, otherwise you wouldn't be in this situation."

"I guess. Don't get me wrong, she's super smart and self-assured…"

"And hot."

"Oh, *obviously*," Jack exhaled. "It's shitty to say, but I knew from the start that she wasn't the 'one'."

"She's your rebound – there's nothing wrong with that. We all do it."

"That's true, but to me, it's still wrong because I was aware going into it. I don't know Tom, I don't feel anything when I'm with her. Maybe I did at first, but not recently."

Tommy studied Jack's frown, pleased to see his friend slowly drawing closer to a potential revelation.

"Keep going."

"It's Emma," Jack continued. "I know you probably think I'm just in my feels. I know the other boys do. But nothing has been the same since I met her…and since she left…"

Tommy gathered his thoughts as he stared at the clouds grouping overhead.

"Sometimes we end up hurting the ones we love the most," he began. "It's not a bad thing to put someone else's needs before your own. But there is always an instance when it can be too much. And when that happens, you can risk hurting yourself in the process. I know this because I'm a victim of it as well."

"Are you talking about me and Emma?"

"You seek acknowledgement. You envy it, because you feel as if you never lived up to it. If you asked me, I think that's why you bonded with Emma in the first place: because you shared a mutual understanding of what that felt like. But how you each demonstrated it was not balanced, and it caused you to act conversely by disregarding her feelings at the expense of your own."

"You're getting deep again, Tommy. Just tell me what you are trying to say."

Jack was stunned when Tommy flicked his head.

"Hey! What was that for?"

"Did it hurt?"

"I mean, a little…" Jack admitted, rubbing his forehead.

"You asked for it," Tommy said calmly. "She noticed you stopped trying, and she gave up. That pain you are feeling right now –" he tapped Jack on his head. "—isn't even comparable to how she must have felt after what you did with Molly. You spent so long moping about her leaving and didn't once consider the pain she must have also felt when she left. And instead of inviting her to discuss it with you, you overwhelmed her with your own feelings and intentions."

"Okay, I get it, but what does she expect me to do? I couldn't sit and wait until she was ready to be with me again…*if* she wanted to be with me, for that matter."

Tommy nodded, his eyes returning to the sky.

"Are you going to say something?" Jack pressed.

"I think you know what I am going to say."

He was right. Jack knew exactly what he would say. He knew, because he thought it himself. And even when he decided it to be his own truth, still happened to stumble back into questioning it.

"Say it anyway. I want to hear it."

Tommy sighed, bringing his eyes to Jack.

"If you are unwilling to travel down this road, consider changing course. Maybe it is time to finally move on from Emma."

The words stung more than his reluctance to do it. He had reached an uncomfortable dynamic with the girl he loved. Although he believed the thread was still intact – even if by a single thread – it was not by equal forces of same strength. If it was not Emma growing tired of pulling weight, it was Jack pulling too much. He thought that being with Molly would help him loosen his grasp on Emma, but it did not work. He was not ready to sever the connection, not yet. For if he did, the relationship would be lost, and if put back together, will be too impaired to return to its original perfection. Maybe there was no longer a chance, as many times as he prayed there was.

"I once told you that I will do whatever I can to help find your wife," Tommy said. "Whatever happens between us, I promise that it will happen. I love you brother."

"I love you too Tommy," Jack said, pivoting to face him and crossing his legs. "Shall we get back to it?"

Tommy managed a heartful smile, joining him in a meditative posture and closing his eyes.

Friendships are commonly formed from a foundation of shared beliefs or interests. But they are sustained through sacrifice, and decisions promoting collective triumph. There is a certain degree as to–

"Oh! By the way, I have something to tell you!"

"…And that is?"

"I saw HG when I was shopping."

"Not the craziest thing," Tommy breathed, his eyes still shut. "Probably getting a diet coke for the ride back. You know how much she loves her diet coke."

"She wasn't in the market," Jack clarified. "She went into a pub around there, next to the café where they have those sick fogs."
At that, Tommy puckered his brow.
"She didn't have any grocery bags?"
"No, except her purse if you count that," Jack added, noticing a twitch in Tommy's lip. "Why, is that important?"
Tommy caught himself. "No," he lied. "I just can't focus with you talking."
"Sorry, sorry, I'll get back to it."
Tommy snuck a peek at Jack as he resumed meditating. Seattle was his city, and he knew it well, particularly the area Jack described where he saw HG. It was a shopping hub; in other words, HG's heaven. It did not make sense to ever find her anywhere else, that is, if her purpose was to shop. He tried to remember the events from the night before, when he had gotten into an altercation with her ex. Her sudden departure was not worth mulling over at the time, but he did think it was odd when she reappeared outside of the bar at the end of the night.
She left somewhere, and regardless of whether she returned that night or not, he knew her well enough to expect such details to be shared that morning. The fact that she intentionally refrained from telling him was enough to intrigue his suspicion.
Where could she have gone that she wouldn't tell us?
He contemplated it for a moment before asking himself another question. *If not where, who was she with that she wouldn't tell us?*
It would have to be someone HG feared to reveal, which meant Tommy had to not only have known the person, but openly resent them. Said person must also frequent the pub Jack saw her enter, and there just so happened to be one person, specifically, that came to mind. A farfetched assumption, possibly, but Tommy always examined all scenarios, despite its degree of incredulity.
Another time, he said to himself.
Anyway, getting back on track: there is a certain degree as to when these factors can impact the nature of a relationship, and although it may be circumstantially based on surrounding incidents of an individual's overall experience, time prevailed as the only independent variable capable of preserving its prominence. Tommy may not have been an expert in bridging strong friendships, let alone over a short span of time. Perhaps it was his tenacity that expedited his status with Jack, disregarding their contesting philosophies. Or perhaps, it was their undeniable chemistry to blend a healthy balance of sapience and sarcasm, intermixing into fertile conversations, each riddled with engaging insight into their personal views that toppled over their mutual interest to escape reality. Never was there a discussion – unless through puerile motives – when Tommy played as a technique to appeal to

those he cared about. And unsurprisingly for Jack and his simpler mentality, he was a sucker for it.

That said, there were a lot of things about Tommy that peeved Jack. He could illustrate his occasional, brash arrogance. And his repetitive tirades over what he believed to be right could sometimes come across as a heap of rubbish. While they certainly differed over aspects of their general outlooks, Jack knew he would always appreciate his friend's willingness to exceed expectations in being there for him.

Jack joined Tommy as he drifted into contemplation, feeling a sense of achievement. He knew Tommy had his best interests in mind. He was thankful that Tommy was a scapegoat for his own insecurities, aiding in combating the internal struggles that meddle with his life on a daily basis. Tommy was a lot of things, but selfish was not one of them, as Jack knew that his happiness ranked as one of his friend's most important objectives. All he wanted for Jack was to accept who he was, trusting that what he identified as flaws were strengths that he could use toward growing into the strong-willed man he is meant to be. Jack knew – from the depths of his heart – that Tommy will always be there for him, and he would never risk any chance of putting him in any jeopardy. Not after last time.

xxviii

Midnight. Logan would usually be idling along in his apartment, drifting off steadily into blurred slumber after inhaling one last dab into oblivion.

But things were different now, with Harmony laying by his side, who too had been antsy to escape her boring evenings now that her ex was finally out of the picture. It may not be her topmost priority, but she was reminded of how much she missed intimacy the deeper she snuggled in his arms. Manipulating men to fall under her spellbound hold of infatuation was a specialty, but for the first time, Harmony's intentions were not quixotic, rather mutually acknowledged from Logan, who willingly permitted such feelings to conquer his mind.

He lifted his head slowly to notice Harmony staring intently at a wad of cash on his desk that was peppered in remnants of what she correctly assumed was cocaine. It was not the first time she had been exposed to hints of his past life, and it would have been more difficult to keep it hidden on Logan's part, if he tried.

Transparent honesty usually occurs following the couple's honeymoon phase, and while Logan preferred some details to remain a secret, he knew deep down that everything would eventually be shared with her.

Women, unfortunately, have exceptional memory, and a propensity to revisit such sensitive topics at the most unideal times. And based on her unusually quietness that night, he knew there was no way around sharing everything with her then.

"You want to know how I started selling," Logan guessed, regretting his choice to initiate the conversation.

"Sorry," Harmony began, acknowledging the awkwardness in her sudden silence. "We don't need to talk about it now."

"No it's okay, I'm ready to tell you." He took deep breath and continued. "I didn't have the best relationship with my dad growing up. We got into a lot of arguments, and almost every time we fought, he kicked me out of the house and said I couldn't come back until I learned my lesson. I was rarely gone for long, a day or two max, or just whenever I could come back and he'd be too hammered to know I was there."

"Where would you go?"

"There was a run-down hotel in the city. I never had money for a room, but I always went there and begged the manager to give me one just for the night. They always had an empty room, and after I explained my situation with him, he was nice enough to let me stay there whenever it happened.

"I did that for years. When I was fifteen, I got into a *big* fight with my dad. When he kicked me out that time, I took a bus into the city, as usual, and went to the hotel. But this time, they didn't have an open room."

As he spoke, Logan's remembrance of the night came back to him in full vision.

It begun to rain when he left the hotel after being told there was no space for him. It was night, and his stomach ached as he shuddered uncontrollably from the freezing rain pelting his bare skin. He had no direction or idea as to what he should do.

"For a second I was lost. I just wanted to go back home, back to my bed. But I didn't have enough change to afford another ride back."

"What did you do?"

"I waited on a bench for the next bus to Mercer. I figured I could convince the driver to take me, even though I didn't have money…it was while I was waiting, when I met him…"

"Who?"

"How're you doing?" the boy greeted. "I'm Ryder."

"Logan."

Ryder inspected Logan and took off his jacket before sliding it across the bench.

"Here, I have an extra at home."

"I'm good, but thanks."

"Are you sure?" Ryder smirked. "Because I've seen you here before."

"What'd you just say?"

"It's not hard to see someone in a shitty spot when you've been through it yourself," Ryder raised his hands comically. "I can help. It's not the best option, but it's probably better than what you got going on."

"Leave me alone man."

Ryder shrugged and rose to his feet.

"You can keep the jacket," he insisted. "Let me know if you change your mind. I'm sure I'll see you around."

Logan grimaced after a noticeably brisk gust had swept through him. He was unsure how much longer he could stay out here without freezing to death.

"Wait." Logan uttered.

Ryder stopped and turned, grinning. "Well come on then!"

Logan followed him toward the edge of the city. He did not remember much of Ryder's relentless chatter, only that it was enough to realize how little they had in common when they eventually arrived at an abandoned apartment complex.

"Here we are!"

"This is your home?" Logan asked, perplexed.

"It's not as bad as it looks."
Logan watched as Ryder picked up a rock and loft it at the door.
"A safety precaution," he added. "It's a good way to weed out the feds."
A minute later, the door opened, and a man emerged on the steps.
"We were about to send a search party," the man said. "Where have you been?"
"My bad, I got caught up with stuff," he began, motioning to Logan. "This is Logan. I want to introduce him to Baker."
"We've been through this Ryder. We can't be accepting every person you find off the streets."
"Come on Primo, we're from the streets too. I'm vouching for him."
Primo folded his arms and focused on Logan. "You better not be up to anything stupid."
"He won't," Ryder said and turned to Logan. "Come on, I promise everything will be fine."
Logan forced a smile and remained close when they entered the complex.
"Well, did you do anything stupid?" Harmony asked.
"You could say that. It took a long time to accept, but the mistake was not meeting Baker," Logan shook his head. "It was choosing to stay."
"You were just a kid though. It's not your fault."
"Yes, it is. When I went home that day, I could have left it all. But I didn't," he sighed. "I worked for Baker until I was arrested my senior year. A lot of things happened over the few months after I got out of juvie, including losing touch with Ryder. But I know he will always be there if I need him."
Harmony tightened her hold on across his chest.
"I will be too."
He lowered his head to meet her eyes and kissed her forehead.
Some may view Harmony's swift dive into the deep end as a red flag, but not Logan, who thanks to his parents, had witnessed the drastic difference a relationship can seem according to those on the outside, versus the individuals involved. The certainty of Harmony's affection for him was undoubtedly clear, and he had already worked so much on his own fear of attachment to reject his ego's claim that this situation was just another tactic to suppress his longing for a partner.
Harmony reached for her ringing phone, sighing when she saw Tommy's name.
"Speak of the devil," she said, setting the phone down to let it ring. "I'll call him later."
"What do you think he wants?"
"Probably something to do with Jack. He loves looping me into their drama."
Logan wanted to leave it at that, but he could not help himself.

"How long can we keep this up? You know, without you telling them about us?"

"You keep asking me that. Why?"

It may have been directed as a question, but he knew just as well as Harmony that she had the psychic ability to read his thoughts. She was waiting for the truth here.

And he told her. He told her everything.

Harmony was sitting up in bed now, covering her mouth in total shock.

"If all that is true, then why haven't you done anything about it?"

"It happened so long ago. And if we're real here, it's not like Tommy would get in trouble for any of the shit he does."

"He ratted you out!"

"But he didn't necessarily lie," Logan countered. "Even if, by some miracle I was able to prove that he was involved, he'd find a way out of it. And I am not going to ruin my chances of ever living a good life because I was so petty to turn him in."

Harmony looked at him, bewildered.

"You sound like you're scared of him."

"You'd be smart if you were too."

"Logan, this is ridiculous. Sure he can be mildly sociopathic sometimes, But he's not a bad person. He can hate you for the rest of his life, but he will never act on it."

"How can you say that when you know him as well as you do?"

"That is exactly the reason why I am saying it," Harmony assured. "Why don't you just talk to him?"

"I've tried. Many times," Logan sighed. "But that's not what I'm getting at. My point, is that my life has been a living hell ever since."

"Based on everything you told me, he's not the only one to blame for that…"

"What, you're saying that if I hadn't met him, my situation would still be like this?"

"Essentially. Look, your dad wasn't a good role model, and you pushed your mom away to go and deal drugs."

"My mom chose my dad over me. She didn't do anything after the cops took me away."

"But what could she have done? You committed a crime!"

Logan stopped defending himself.

"You're right," he admitted. "I know I can't throw the blame around. And I don't want to, really, I don't," he paused. "But it is *very* hard not to when every time I try to do better, Tommy gets in the way."

Harmony nodded understandingly.

"And Jack?"

"What about him?"
"Well, have you ever thought about how he feels about the entire situation between you and Tommy?"
"He doesn't know."
"You never told him?"
"Tommy threatened me not to. There's no way Jack would trust him if he ever knew the truth."
"Once again, it comes back to Tommy," Harmony echoed, her comprehension finally marinating to Logan's point.
They then looked at each other, mutually helpless for not coming up with a proper remedy for the issue.
It was easy for Harmony to empathize with Logan. No one in their right mind would have the gall to pick a fight with Tommy. Unless of course, it was someone who knew him well.
"Let me talk to him."
Fear overtook Logan's face. What better way for Tommy to reach his breaking point than to reveal a secret he had tried to suppress, let alone have it come from one of his best friends, of whom is to also be romantically involved under his nose?
"Don't do that," he said flatly. "I'll figure it out. Everything will be fine."
He eased up when he saw her frown.
"Thank you for listening to me," he added, pulling her back to his chest. "It means more than you know."
Harmony gradually tightened her hold around his shoulder. "Of course."
They laid there silently for a few more minutes.
"This is nice," Logan said.
"Oh please, do tell."
"I'm just expressing how much better my life has been since I met you."
"Spoken like a true romantic."
"I'm serious!" he replied playfully, bringing her face to his. "I hope I don't scare you when I tell you this, but I love you."
Harmony tilted her in dismay. The complete opposite reaction he wished for.
"I know that you know that you love me, but I want to know that you love me."
"I don't understand what you are saying to me."
"I'm *saying* you need to show me how much you care about me."
His eyes widened. "So, you somehow expect me to know when you need approval of my feelings for you?"
"I don't *need* anything from anyone," she tested. "But yes, it's very easy if you actually care about them."
"Did you get that straight out of Vogue?"

"Women's Health, actually."
Harmony was nearly dressed when Logan had awoken the next morning.
"Early shift?" he guessed, rubbing his eyes.
"I wish. My sister is studying for the SATs, and I promised to have lunch and help her study," Harmony check her phone. "Which, if I'm doing the math right, is in four hours."
"Damn, sounds like she's in good hands."
She leaned over and kissed him.
"What about you?"
Logan scratched his head, thinking about their conversation last night.
"I'll probably head up to my mom's house. Hopefully I'll catch her before she leaves for work."
"I'm proud of you," she smiled endearingly, grabbing her keys from the nightstand. "Well, if I get done with Sally early, maybe I can come back here afterwards and we can get dinner or something?"
Logan grabbed he back and kissed her again.
"That would be fantastic."
"Sweet. I'll text you."

*****

Logan feet were planted in the driveway's center, staring back at his home. Even after all this time, Logan could see the subtle details in its appearance: cracked shingles on his bedroom window from one poorly executed attempt to sneak out (his last of many); the faded oil stain lining out of the garage door (likely from the bedraggled pickup his father never fixed despite countless promises); the yellowish lawn receding to dried dirt lining the edge of the driveway. It was a place he consciously avoided, and the memories he associated with it. Logan tried the front door, unsurprised to hear the subtle click of it lock. Instinctually, he stretched his arm above the light fixture and ran his fingers around until he felt the spare key cradled between the shoddy brick.
"Mom?" he announced when he entered the house, slightly relieved at the absence of a response. She must have left for work already, which gave time for him to peruse without interruption.
Wes's recliner was still in the living room, the thin sheet of dust leading Logan to wonder how long it had been since it was used last. There was a time when he thought the disappearance of his father would bring relief to the severe pain he was forced to bear with as a child. Nevertheless, recent events proved otherwise.

"Get off of him!"
The sultry tone in Tommy's voice had startled Logan, prompting him to cower
behind the mass students spectating the altercation.
He had known that inviting himself to the Douglas' private dinner party was a
bad idea, in addition to his decision to show up at the same bar afterwards
that prompted the unnecessarily inevitable scuffle with Jack. He had watched
helplessly as Jack defended himself before the cops took him away.
All he had wanted was an opportunity to tell Jack the truth. A surprisingly
difficult feat, even under what he presumed to be normal circumstances. He
could not help but despise his former friends. Had they known what he was
going through – what he had to go through – perhaps they would be more
sympathetic.

Logan went on to his bedroom. Or at least, what *was* his bedroom growing up.
Other than the stack of boxes in the corner near the ajar closet, the contents
remained well-kept, and in the same place as he remembered. Its familiarity
did not bring any nostalgic condolence, however, as it only reminded him of
how much worse he had it.
He was only a teenager when he was arrested for the first time, and while
much of the details are faint, there were two things he did remember: the date,
Saturday April 21st, and letting down the girl of his dreams.

Sitting there was anything short of pleasurable. He felt powerless, growing
sore from the sturdy, uncomfortable frame of the cot as he needlessly fumbled
with the threads stringing out from his tarnished jacket after being thrown to
the ground by the cops earlier that evening. After three hours sitting in the
holding cell, a sympathetic officer finally lent Logan's phone back to him,
where he was saddened to see numerous missed calls from his date. He was
young, and although he did not have a firm grasp of love, nor what it was like
to give and receive it, Logan was sure that his handling of the opportunity
that night was far from acceptable. He spent the rest of that night thinking
about Emma, wondering what she would say, had she learned the excuse for
his absence. It would be years later until he would speak to her again. And
little did he know that when that time came, that she would not have forgotten
about him. Not only for the things he did wrong, but things he somehow
managed to do right.

Being sequestered in juvenile detention was undoubtedly one that he longed to
forget. Assigning six months locked away was a horrific proposition to most;
and for Logan, it was nearly unbearable. He recounted the few occasions that
his mother would visit him, each time having been unaccompanied by his

father, who, as his mother put it: "would be tempted to kill him the next time he saw him."
Wes' animosity did not bother Logan. Hating someone for afflicting pain on their wellbeing was nothing unfamiliar for him to grasp. Wes had done it toward him for as long as he can remember. If anything, Logan considered it just that the pain was finally reciprocated. Even if it was only for a few short minutes.

He remembered the day when he had learned of his early release. The muted footsteps growing louder toward his cell; the screech from the cell gate sliding open; the unsettling fear that had leached off to every fiber of his weakened muscles as he was brought before the Sheriff.
"Don't worry Mr. Berg. I come with good news," the officer soothed.
Logan had never listened more intently to words spoken to him than in that moment. The satisfaction percolating across his widening grin was merely a start once he had discovered the apparent success of one anonymous benefactor who pled in favor of his case.

Logan left his bedroom, eyeing the hanging frames lined through the hall. His mother had a knack for retaining even the menial events of their lives through photographs. One frame caught Logan's attention, specifically a photo of him draped in his gown with a teary Adriana embracing him. Maybe graduating high school marked a proud memory for most kids. But it was not for Logan.

Wes disappeared when Logan left juvie. Through the same benefactor, he was given the chance to finish high school and graduate with his diploma over the summer. And by some miracle, he was accepted to attend college that same fall.
"I don't understand," Logan had said in disbelief as he skimmed pensively over the acceptance letter. "I didn't even apply."
"Frankly, I don't either," his probation officer replied, resting his hand on Logan's shoulder. "I do not know who this person is, or why they keep helping you, but if there is one piece of advice I can give you, it's this: take the help when offered."
Logan had never forgotten the advice.

He passed the master room, catching the warm, comforting scent of his mother. Their memories were his most vivid, and treasured. Distancing himself from her the last few years remains one of his biggest regrets. Something led him to the garage, where in on the opposite end was Wes' shop. Since it was the one place in the house his father frequented, he tried to avoid it at all costs. The only times he trespassed was to steal a six-pack, or when he would go out to admire the motorbike his father had spent countless hours rebuilding. His mother always said it was intended to be a gift for one of his eighteen birthdays. All of which came and went, and the bike was still there, partly put together. Logan was nearing the front door once again, when a buried memory stopped him and led him to the garage.

He ran his hand over the handlebar, imagining how joyous it would feel to ride it far away from this place. It was never the bike he wanted. It was the chance to rid himself of everything he hated. Including himself.

He startled himself when he had unintentionally stepped on a loose bulb, ignoring the loud crack and reaching for the broom. As he dumped the shards, his eyes took him to a gray case on the top shelf of his father's workstation. It had been years since he opened the case, and wondered if it was ever returned after his arrest that night.

Logan picked up the case carefully and rested on the table in front of him, scoffing when he saw the pistol inside.

The sight of the gun angered him. In a way it worsened the impact of his actions, as well as the hardships he endured. for in some way if he had known it was here all along, he would not have had to endure the trial of hardships from Wes.

At the same time, there was another concern separate from home.

Tommy Beech.

Even with Wes out of the picture, Logan's remained conflicted with Tommy. He wanted revenge, but knew doing so could have adverse effects. The semester had just began, and he needed to focus on his academics. For an actual moment, he even considered forgiving Tommy. Perhaps doing so would result in finding the peace he desperately longed for. Unfortunately, Tommy was not only attending the same university, but sought after him before Logan could make his decision.

It happened on the second day of their freshman year, when he approached him between classes.

"Logan Berg! Now that is a name I never thought I would ever say again."

"Tommy," Logan acknowledged, his thoughts falling short in the time when he had asked for it most.

"What are you doing here?"

"What does it look like? I'm a student here."

"Wow, now that is surprising. I gotta say, I figured you would have given up on life by now. I mean, I can't imagine how hard it must have been for you these last few months…where did your parents end up sending you off to?"

Logan remained composed in the face of Tommy's arrogant remark.

"You know damn well that it was not my parents," Logan spat back. "Don't pretend like you had nothing to do with it."
"I warned you," Tommy clarified. "I told you not to get yourself involved with that shit, and you didn't listen. And then when I gave you a chance, you tried crossing me. I saw it in your face…" Tommy faltered, panning around to make sure no one was around. "Don't be upset that I was smart enough to do it before you. If you are going to direct frustration on anyone, I suggest looking in the mirror."
Logan kept his fueling wrath in check.
Tommy gave Logan a hard stare in anticipation of a response, before concluding that he had the last say.
"It's good to see you again, man. Happy you chose to be a Husky," Tommy said, his sarcastic tone leaking out of his voice.
Logan stood motionless as Tommy patted his shoulder and strutted away.

The incident was fresh in mind after describing it to Harmony last night. He remembered everything: the fear in Tommy's eyes. The evil in Baker's. The blood broiling in his veins. His index finger wrapped around the gun's trigger. The earsplitting ring that immediately followed. The scent of sulfur filling his dry nostrils. The recoil reverberating over his whitened knuckles and up his arm as his entire body jerking back to the pavement. The endless ruptures of windows shattering as he rolled under his car. The series of curses he spewed as he shielded his face with his scabrous arm. The sheer panic striking through his heart when the tires burst from the spewing bullets raining over him. The sensation from the truck crushing his spine as he uttered what he had believed to be his last breath.
He had imagined dying there on the spot, finally relieving himself of the pain he was reluctant to continue enduring. But it was not until being blinded by a brightening flash when Logan realized he had survived the shootout, wincing in pain as he glowered down at his blistered hands while the paramedics rolled him away from the scene. Blue and red lights flickered out from the corner of his blurry gaze.

"Get some rest, Mr. Berg," the detective stated when he threw him in the backseat of the patrol car. "We have a lot to talk about."

It came full circle for Logan, who knew as much as he tried, he could not forgive Tommy. He may not have been the sole cause of his turmoil in the beginning, but he was now. And even after all these years, he knew his torturous ways were still in effect.

*****

He stopped at the pub on his way home, figuring he would rather purge his negative thoughts in alcohol and not bring it to his home. First twenty minutes were peaceful. What followed, not so much.
"Isn't this a surprise?"
Tommy appeared behind him, lacking every ounce of tact in his sarcastic tone has he seated himself beside Logan.
"What are you doing here?" Logan asked, slow to acknowledge him.
"Oh just walking around the neighborhood."
"You don't live anywhere near here," Logan corrected. "Are you stalking me now?"
"Goodness, you can be so defensive."
Logan scoffed and proceeded to drink the last of his beer.
"I'm leaving."
"Oh come on, don't be like that!" Tommy insisted, signaling to the bartender. "Two whiskey cokes, please."
"I don't drink liquor anymore," Logan said flatly, motioning to his empty beer glass.
"Well, you are today."
The two sat in silence as the bartender returned with their drinks.
"Anything else I can get for you guys?" she asked.
"Good question," Tommy replied. He noticed Logan shift in his seat. Whether it was out of hesitancy or rage, he could care less. They were equally leveled, yet Tommy always considered himself to have the upper hand in every situation.
"Actually," Tommy added as the bartender walked away. "We're going to have a bit of fun. How about you come back in ten minutes with the same order? After that, we'll continue to have the same until you have to throw us out of here for being too drunk."
The bartender stared blankly at Tommy.
"Are you asking me to serve you until you get drunk?"
"That's your job, isn't it?" Tommy mused, flashing an ever-charming smile.
She returned a flirty grin and continued off.
"I see you still haven't changed," Logan muttered.
Tommy held up his glass to toast Logan.

"Change is relative," Tommy stated, this time more serious, as he waited for Logan to reciprocate.

Logan saw through Tommy's facade. This was nothing short of a sinister game he was playing. He was not worried, however, as he had grown to understand the rules from when they were children. As much as he would refuse to admit it, perception meant everything to Tommy. It was not for the sake of his own gratification, but solely so that he could rebound in a manner where he would still come out on top of a possible confrontation. Logan knew he was accurate in Tommy's estimation of how the sequences would play out. He would nominate himself as the house, willingly deal the cards in hopes that his subjects would blindly fall for his deceit, only to betray their hopes and collect the winnings for himself. That was just who Tommy was.

As a result, Logan played along, clinking his glass against Tommy's, and taking a sip.

Tommy maintained his calculated stare at Tommy as he tasted the starch whiskey.

"You look like you have something on your mind," he began.

"Do you see the irony in what you are doing, Tommy?"

"Enlighten me," Tommy tested behind the confused frown he painted across his face.

"You detest victimization, yet you sit there, trying to scheme a situation where you try to come out on top by pretending to be one."

"Wow, very insightful," Tommy mocked, draining half of his glass. "I also noticed that you picked up some big words since the last time we spoke. I have to say, congratulations."

Logan scoffed and took another drink, not once choosing to look in Tommy's direction.

Tommy, on the other hand, was quick to realize that his initial tactic to rile him up was unsuccessful. Although indirect ridicule typically worked, he could sense there was something bigger on his mind that kept him tense. He did not care for him in the slightest, but in truth, he was taken aback by how insignificant his presence mattered to Logan in that moment. And whether it was due to a hidden, sliver of compassion he felt for him, or more likely his internal pride, Tommy was compelled to have the issue revealed at all costs.

"How was the rest of your Thanksgiving?" Tommy probed.

At that, Logan finally faced him, making sure to keeping a cool head.

"Why do you do it?"

"Do what?"

"Intentionally try to get under my skin, when it has no benefit for you."

"But you see, it does," Tommy raised a finger. "Because you and I have a history, Logan. Granted it is not a happy one, but it is a history nevertheless."

"So we're at odds with each other. Big deal. I don't see why you feel like you have a part in tormenting my life, when you have been clear about not wanting to be a part of it, to begin with."

"'At odds,' what a tactful phrase to use for our particular situation," Tommy noted before continuing. "And for the record, I don't think that what I am doing is torment at all. You're a rebellious dog that keeps biting, and you're just upset that I bite back."

Logan took another drink.

"This is about Jack, then?"

"You said it, not me."

"You apparently have a problem with me talking to him."

"And you know exactly why that is the case, Berg."

"So why don't you explain to me why that is? Because to me, it seems like you are too afraid to admit it to yourself."

There's nothing I have to admit," Tommy said flatly.

"Really?" Logan shot back, his brows furrowing. "You don't think it is important for him to know about what you did to me—"

"You put both of us in that situation," Tommy interjected. "The moment you can accept that truth is when I will consider backing off."

He finished his glass, and like clockwork, the bartender returned with two fresh whiskeys for them.

Logan waited for Tommy to take another light swig from the second glass.

"Let me say this clearly so even a dumbfuck like you could understand," Tommy began. "Jack is capable of only handling one thing on his plate at a time. Unfortunately for you, his plate has been pretty full lately…arguably for the last year. What *you* are proposing is essentially dropping more shit on his plate, which, as his best friend, I feel obligated to prevent from happening."

"You're preventing it because you are at the center of the shit," Logan snapped back.

Tommy raised his hands as if he was surrendering.

"You want to clear the air with him? I'm cool with that, I really am. I am and will always be an advocate for the truth."

Tommy leaned closer to Logan so that only he could hear.

"But if – and I mean *if* – you choose to do it, I will make sure that the words that come out from your mouth are only that - the truth."

Logan felt the blood heating up in his chest. He was over Tommy's attempt at belittling him, but he also acknowledged that this was the farthest the two have progressed on this topic. He was not going to ruin his chances at a compromise by blowing up.

"You talk a lot about how much you love the truth, but all you have done is lie," Logan said. "You lied to me, to Jack, to the cops…" he paused, stopping himself from mentioning HG. "Everything you have done has always been for yourself."

At that, Tommy's expression drastically changed. His face tensed, and the noticeable flicker in his eyes froze into a dark glare.

"I guess that makes two of us," Tommy said. He emptied the rest of his drink and shoveled cash out of his wallet.

"Leaving already?" Logan asked.

"I have plans with people I *actually* care about," Tommy said as he slapped the money on the counter for the bartender to see. "There's only so much time I can stand being here with you."

Logan remained in his stool as Tommy rose to his feet.

"You're a psychopath," Logan said lastly.

Tommy's back was turned when he said, causing him to dip back toward Logan, giving him a dead stare just inches from his face.

"No. I am an extreme example of someone who lives based on his own terms," he said, keeping his voice to an ominous whisper. "I expect you to understand it better than anyone."

"I promise, you're going to cross the line one of these times," Logan tested unflinchingly. "And I'm not going to hold back."

Tommy momentarily eased off, nodding to himself before quickly returning a fist to Logan's nose.

The strike took Logan by complete surprise, the force pushing him off the stool as he slammed to the floor.

"You didn't see anything," Tommy immediately directed to the frightened bartender, compensating the incident with another hundred he added to the cash on the counter.

Logan capped his hands over his face and groaned in pain, his eyes still on Tommy as he watched him crouch above him.

"What happens when a dog doesn't learn after so many kicks?" Tommy sneered.

The question made Logan's skin crawl. For the first time in his life, he was legitimately terrified of Tommy.

Tommy then broke out in hysterical laughter, patting Logan's shoulder.

"Have a good one, buddy," he mused, and with one last glare, he walked out of the bar.

Especially after literally saving his life, he was perplexed as to how Tommy had not once reciprocated any graciousness. Telling him would not work; Tommy was just as stubborn as him, if not more so. Although Logan considered himself to be a bad person, he was still convinced that there was a sliver of good in him. After all, what else could prompt him to risk his own life for someone else, especially if that someone also happened to vehemently resent him? To Tommy's point, he may have contemplated betrayal. But he chose against it, and for Logan, that was more than enough evidence of any rectitude in his heart.

Logan was slow to rise to the bar, exchanging a defeated look at the bartender.

"I'll call the cops if he comes back," she said to Logan.

"No need," Logan replied calmly, feeling for the gun hidden in his waistline, and turning to walk out.

He hated Tommy more than he hated himself. And yet, he had hoped to reach a peaceful compromise with him. Upon witnessing his brash interaction, however, Logan had come to a renewed conclusion. One that he had made long ago.

The line had been crossed. Logan vowed to never go back on his promise. Now, he was even more adamant to stick to his word.

xxix

They were coming up on two hours of studying. It would have felt quicker, had it not been for Sally's intermittent complaints after every other practice question.

"This is ridiculous. I've never had lower than an A in a class. There was the one B in Calculus, but that doesn't count," she sighed. "I don't see why I have to now take a longer exam – why can't they just look at my report cards over the last ten years?"

Her sister's unique blend of arrogance and naivety made Harmony smirk.

"It's stupid, I know," she nodded sympathetically. "But if you don't do well, it will affect which colleges you can get into."

"Someone needs to change this process."

"Hey, when you make a name for yourself, you can be the one to change the game," Harmony countered, tapping on the booklet. "But first, you're going to have to play by the rules."

Sally sighed annoyingly and resumed reviewing her notecards.

Mira emerged from the hallway and joined them, looming over Sally to inspect her notes.

"Has anyone ever said that you have good handwriting?"

"Every boy in my class."

Mira looked at Harmony, widening her eyes.

"Wow, who knew men would get cleverer in their flirts?"

Harmony chuckled, tapping the booklet to recapture Sally's attention.

"This is impossible!" Sally groaned.

"Let's take a break. But I really think we should finish this section today."

"Ugh, fine."

Sally hopped on her phone and trailed off to her room, leaving Mira to take her place.

"You're a good sister for helping Sally."

"As if I had a choice! Mom and Dad forced me."

Harmony slouched and pulled out her phone to check if she had any notifications from Logan. She frowned, seeing that he had still not replied to her text.

"Expecting a call?" Mira asked, noticing her sister glued to her phone.

"Oh, no—"

"Come on Harmony. You can tell me if it's a boy. We're sisters, after all.

Harmony rolled her eyes, giving in.

"Do you remember Jack Douglas?"

Mira snuck a sly smile.

"Let me stop you right there. It's not him, it's his friend. Logan Berg."
Mira's smile grew wider.
"Same boy from your last time in the city? Seems like there was truth to
Sally's accusation, huh?"
"A little bit," Harmony admitted. "We haven't even been talking for that long,
but we got close so quickly. I'm actually supposed to drive up to the city
tonight to see him, but he hasn't texted me back."
"Maybe he's busy."
"He always replies immediately," Harmony countered. "Not even kidding,
like moments after I text him."
"Did you two get into a fight?"
"The opposite, actually," Harmony said, briefly walking Mira through the
nature of their deep talk. "Maybe I said something he didn't like last night,
but he seemed fine in the morning and agreed to let me know if I can see him
again. I'm not sure why he isn't answering."
"Something probably came up," Mira reasoned. "But if he likes you – which
you've made clear he does – then he will respond. Don't worry about it."
Harmony took her sister's advice and put her phone away. Whatever came up
for Logan, she figured it was likely for a good reason.

*****

The vibe on campus was apparent in its seniors, shifting between a collective
mental burnout from their studies, and the urge to clinch onto every bit of
sanity while they grinded through the penultimate semester.
Jack could feel the dullness transmit through the rest of Seattle, noticing the
city's unusually quiet atmosphere that particular evening as he paced into the
bar to meet his friends.
He spotted Tommy and Isaac sitting inside, already unwinding with a bottle of
bourbon as they prepared for the stressful – and inevitable – period of finals
right around the corner.
"What's going on guys," he greeted, scanning the relatively empty bar.
"Where's Benny and Kev?"
"They went home."
"Which translates to: Kevin wanted to get high, and Bennett wanted to watch
him get high," Isaac added humorously.
Jack chuckled lightly.
"How long have you all been here?"

"A *while*."
Only one more round after this, Jack reminded himself, content that he had gotten this far in his academic career.
Sure, his ability to completely move on from his past relationships (primarily Emma) still lurked in his mind, but he was thankful for his friends, who without them may have made his predicament more difficult to stomach the last few months.
Especially Issac, who always found a way to positively distract Jack from the most serious matters. There was never a dull moment with the kid, and everyone lucky enough to know him acknowledged his glowing presence and inviting gift of wit galore. It was the one trait Jack treasured most about him.
 "Hilarious, if you ask me," Tommy choked as he downed the last of his boiling whiskey. "I'm cooked and I can still tell this whiskey is shit. This place sucks."
"I thought there'd be more people here," Saac said, observing the few stragglers thinly sparsed across the bar.
"I'm down to go somewhere else," Jack grimaced at the sight of the bottle. "I think I drank enough this week to last the rest of the month, if I'm being honest."
"You can't say that minutes after walking into the bar," 'Saac commented, finishing what was left in his glass. "Just have one and we can all head back. I don't know about you two, but I would also like to see Kevin baked out of his mind."
Jack halfheartedly agreed and settled in for a couple of beers over the next hour. The head start 'Saac and Tommy had on him was clear, as they each slugged down three more doubles in the same allotted time.
Before long, they trio were stumbling out of the bar, hollering raucously at the civilians passing by that were not actually there.
Jack was distracted by the sizing puddles of rainwater when he bumped into Tommy.
"Did you forget how to walk buddy?" he joked, before realizing that his friends were no longer moving. He followed their stare, where directly ahead of them stood an obscure silhouette middling in the alley. Jack took a long squint at the shadowy figure approaching them, recognizing the familiar face as it crept under the streetlight.
"I was wondering how long you guys would be in there."
"Logan," Jack acknowledged. "What are you doing here?"
"We need to talk, Jack."
"When are you going to realize we want nothing to do with you?" Tommy interjected.
Logan blinked at Tommy, keeping his cool.

"You don't seem to be comfortable having me talk to Jack, Tommy…care to tell us why?"
Jack glanced at Tommy, noting his sudden change of expression.
Tommy motioned toward Logan, abruptly shoving him.
"Get the fuck out of here!"
Logan stumbled back, immediately reaching for his handgun tucked away under his shirt and pointing it at them.
The boys all backed up, alarmed.
"Don't shoot!" Isaac shrieked.
"What the *fuck* is your problem?" Jack cried, instinctively raising his hands above his head.
"Since Tom's not going to let me talk to you, we'll have to do it this way," Logan eased. "Do you guys remember the last time we all hung out?" he fixated on Jack. "We were just kids. We didn't care about anything." he took a step closer. "We definitely didn't know what we would become. And yet, you thought that leaving me to fend for myself was the right choice. After everything that I went through…" his voice faltered, shouting through the tears. "Dealing with my shitty dad, going to juvie, being alone the entire time…you left me when I needed you boys the most. Why? Because I'm such a disease. Is that right?"
Jack froze, unable to utter any response.
"I knew though," Logan continued. "I saw it all along. I knew *exactly* how everything was going to happen to us. And you know what I realized Jack?"
"Not really." Tommy cut in.
"I realized that it wasn't you at all," he continued, still to Jack. "You were always so kind, and fair. There wasn't a bad bone in your body. You always felt so misunderstood; like you had to pretend someone you weren't just to get by. I did the same thing for a long time."
"Logan, whatever it is you're thinking about doing with that, it would be in your best interest if you didn't," Tommy added, shuffling closer to Jack and Isaac.
"Tommy," Logan said, peering at him. "It was always you."
"Is that right?"
"You are the reason for all of this. Jack and I were best friends, and you hated that. *You* took advantage of him, and still control him for your own gain."
"What are you talking about? No I don't."
"You do! What other reason could it be to rid me out of your lives? You knew I threatened your friendship with him."
"Are you kidding me?"
Logan aimed his gun at Tommy. "Fuck you. You know it's true. Admit it."
"What is going on?" Jack muttered. "Tommy, what is he talking about?"

"Tell him," Logan insisted, his voice growing louder. "Tell him what you did to me!"

Tommy stared at Logan, unaffected by the gun in his face. His face hardened, growing darker, and more menacing.

"You're right," Tommy revealed. "I saw you for what you are: a disease. I hated it, and I knew that someone like you would only take Jack – *my* best friend – down an irreversible path. I wasn't going to let that happen," he glanced at Jack. "And I still won't."

"What makes you better than me Tommy, huh?" Logan snarled, cocking his gun. "What gave you the right?"

"What right?" Jack interjected. "What did you do, Tommy?"

Logan stepped closer Tommy.

"You tell him now, or I swear to God I will."

"Watch yourself Logan," Tommy warned.

"He framed me!" Logan seethed, shifting his body to face him.

Jack glanced at Tommy.

"You *framed* him?" he asked.

"It wasn't like that," Tommy lamented, peering back at Logan. "He's not telling you the whole story."

"What's the whole story?"

"It's not important. All you need to know is that I did everything for us, Jack – for *you*."

Jack gaped at Tommy.

"I'd be happy to tell him everything," Logan shouted. "It's time that he finally knows the truth."

"Stop," Jack stuttered. "Please just stop all of this. I need time to think."

Unfortunately, time was not on Jack's side, as at that moment, he watched Tommy fling a rock toward Logan, striking the side of his head as the trigger went off.

Tommy then lunged toward Logan and tackled him to the ground, instinctively hammering at his sides. They wrestled, exchanging clumsy blows until Logan pressed his feet on Tommy's stomach and kicked him off. Tommy turned over and flinched at the sight of the barrel of the gun aimed directly at his head. The air grew mute, clouding his consciousness.

Logan hesitated, rubbing his finger on the trigger.

"Isaac!" came Jack, causing them to turn and see him crouching beside Isaac's motionless body.

The gravity of Tommy's concern for Isaac settled quickly as he scurried over to Jack and Isaac.

Bewildered, Logan rose to his feet and watched the boys screaming incoherently. He tucked the gun and scampered out of the alley.

Tommy caught a glimpse of Logan at the end of the alley as Jack panicked. "Fucking help me!"
Tommy tore off his sweater and placed it on Isaac's wound before pulling Jack's hands to hold it in place.
"Keep the pressure here," he instructed.
Jack did as told, feeling the warm blood seep between his fingers as he pushed down.
"You're all right buddy," Tommy stammered, pulling out his phone.
Jack disregarded Tommy's conversation with the operator, meeting Isaac's eyes.
"Don't let me die here," Isaac winced, tightening his clench around Jack's hands. "Please, don't let me die here."
"You're gonna be fine," Jack assured, looking back at Tommy on the phone. "Will you hurry up?"
"I'm fucking trying!" Tommy shouted back, doing his best to stay composed on the line.
He hung up and returned to the boys. "Ambulance is on the way," he announced, tending to a shaking Isaac. "Try to relax man. Talk to me, just keep talking to me."
Isaac shuddered, his complexion paling and only uttering sounds.
"Lift his head, we need to keep it elevated."
Jack gently grabbed Isaac's head and rested it on his lap as Tommy kept the sweater on his wound.
Isaac's pupils dilated and started to roll upward.
"Don't do that," Tommy demanded. "Come on man, stay with us."
"What are we going to do?" Jack stammered.
"Just shut up and keep his head still," Tommy ordered, the panic growing in his tone. "Jesus, keep your fucking eyes open Issac! You'll be okay, just stay awake!"
Isaac squinted hard, taking one final look at his friends before drawing his last breath.
"Fuck," Tommy cried. "This can't be happening…fuck!"
Seconds followed. Then minutes.
Jack's mind was racing, observing his blood-painted hands caressing Isaac's head. He entered a shock. His eyes were wide open, but everything he saw did not register. Not the paramedics arriving, nor the ambulance ride to the hospital.
Everything was white. He heard only voices.
"The Bensons are with the doctor now. They should be out in just a moment."
An unfamiliar one.
"Thank you." Tommy's voice.

Tommy.

The nurse left behind the swinging doors when Jack returned to his senses. He looked over at Tommy beside him, clearly distressed as he palmed his face.

"I want to know what happened."

"Trust me Jack, it's best if you don't know—"

"I wasn't asking!" Jack fumed. "I'm done doing what you think is best for me."

Tommy was about to insist, but he could see his friend on edge. Fighting this could only make things worse.

"Okay…"

He hoped it would never reach this point; that it could have been buried with him at the end of his life. Alas, here he was, pulling together every ounce of humility as he recounted the night.

The truth will set you free. That is what they say, anyway. Surely, time as a variable may dictate the truth's impact, but it is fair to reason one's willingness to be honest is unwavering to the result.

Tommy expected to feel accordingly – like a weight was lifted off his shoulders. But seeing Jack's sullen expression when he finished his recount, he knew he had scarred his trust.

They were silent for a while longer, other than intermittent sniffling caused by a bleachy scent wafting into them every time someone walked through the swinging doors to the emergency room.

"I'm sorry I never told you," Tommy finally said. "I thought I was protecting us by not telling you."

Jack hesitated, lifting his head to meet Tommy's eyes.

"Protect us from what?"

"Remember the talk you had with Emma at the cabin? When we got home, you told me what you said to her: that your biggest fear is never being accepted for who you are. You said our wealth distracts people from seeing who we really are, and they will pretend to like you so they can use you."

Jack nodded in agreement. "That was a little different. I dated Emma."

"It doesn't matter Jack. Logan is one of those people. I will never forget the face he gave me. He *considered* selling me out to his dealer because of money," he paused. "If you were there that night, I know he would have the same thought, because he doesn't cares about himself more than anyone else. That guy is a leech, and he latched onto all of us."

"How could he take advantage of us, though? Did you think he would try stealing our money or something?"

"Even if he didn't before, who's to say he wouldn't if the price was right?" Tommy shrugged. "And in your case, we both know it's much higher than mine."

"You still lied to fuck him over."

"I did it to save us," Tommy corrected. "Are you even listening to what I'm saying?"

Jack rubbed his head to process.

"If that's how you feel, why did you go with him to begin with?"

"That was a mistake," Tommy admitted. "I liked the idea of having a little bit of cash, as dumb as that sounds…" he faltered, turning to Jack. "More money, more problems, right?"

"That's not funny."

"Sorry…"

Jack fell silent, still trying to wrap his mind around everything Tommy said. His best friend – so brilliant and loyal – to have such a dark secret? Even if it was in his favor, it was difficult to stomach how far he or Logan were capable of going to betray each other. He forced himself to sympathize to Tommy's logic. Yes, he was young, and more naïve. But should that justify his premeditative move to ruin someone's life?

He was angry with Tommy, but he did not resent him for what he did. Logan certainly had a history of dragging them into his shit, the same way Jack knew he did with his friends.

"Jack, I really am sorry. I know I may have acted irrationally, but I assumed that it would work, and that we would be rid of him forever."

The doors to the waiting room suddenly swung open, and their friends and family poured in. Jack rose to his feet and gave Tommy a disappointed frown. "I appreciate that you were looking out for me, but you failed." Jack muttered quickly. "Isaac is dead, and it's both our fault."

Their parents prevented Tommy from speaking further on the matter. Not that there was anything more he could say. Jack was right, and he knew the time would come when he could rationalize his choice to not divulge the truth. Until then, he would burden himself for not handling it better.

Now was the time to mourn.

*****

There is a joyous feeling when one is liked. Euphoric bliss is complemented with a tinge of anxious contemplation, as one wonders whether the path chosen with their potential significant other would truly shape into a boundless companionship, ridden of smoke and toxicity, and instead bumbling in a seamless rush of happiness magically bestowed upon one another like a creek babbling back into action after hibernating from its former icy state.

Emma knew when she had reached the Merge with Hunter and was relieved when he agreed to skip straight to their Decision to be together.

It was the farthest she had progressed with a partner, and frankly, she could not anticipate what more could come. That is, until the day she found him waiting for her in the kitchen when she got back from work. She expected the usual: preparing a meal and spending the evening cuddled on the couch retelling their day. Sometimes with Baylee, sometimes without. It was simple, sure, but it was enough for Emma. She was happy.

That afternoon however, the counter was polished clean, and the dining table was not set.

"I have a fun surprise for us tonight," Hunter greeted.

"Another surprise, huh?"

"I hope it's not getting old."

"I don't think it ever will," she smiled, kissing him.

Hunter reached for his backpack and headed for the door.

"I'll be back in an hour to pick you up," he announced. "Wear something nice."

Emma shrugged it off. *Another fancy dinner. Yes please.*

Hunter returned as scheduled, ogling when she stepped out of the bathroom, freshly dressed.

"Damn, now this is something *I* know will never get old."

Emma blushed. "Are you going to tell me what the surprise is now?"

"Soon," he smiled, reaching for her hand. "Ready to go?"

Nothing stood out to Emma about the drive, as she listened intently to Hunter's narration of his day. Her phone vibrated under her leg, and she stole a peek to see a text from Jack.

I wanted to let you know that Isaac passed away. I'm here if you want to talk.

She let out a gasp causing Hunter to stop his oration.

"Everything good?"

"Yes," she stammered, stashing her phone away and doing best to behave normally. "Keep going."

They arrived outside of what looked like a museum; its tall windows tinted behind vast pillars that stretched across a wide staircase. Hunter handed the valet his keys and opened the door for Emma, gently taking her hand and escorting her toward the building.

"What is this?"

"Every year, my family throws this charity banquet," he explained and gave her a wink. "This is the first time I'll be attending with a guest."

"*This* is the surprise?"

"Yeah. Is that okay?"

"Of course," she uttered hesitantly, having no idea what to expect. One thing was for sure though: Hunter's parents were inside, and they were likely awaiting to meet the person Hunter had probably preached about since they started talking.

"You'll love it, trust me," he insisted.

Emma paced uneasily into the room, aweing at the heap of celebrities she recognized instantly as Hunter pulled her deeper into the crowd.

It was like a scene out of a movie. Everyone acted in perfect pretense, with their suits and dresses; the elegance in their flowery language; even their nonchalant demeanor, tediously sipping from their sparkling cocktails. She overheard resonances of the orchestra stringing triumphantly, dullening the raucous conversations between the attendees to insulated murmurs.

They stopped in front of a table, where Emma acknowledged an older couple gently speaking before lifting their gaze at her.

"Mom, Dad: this is Emma," Hunter introduced.

"Hello Emma, I'm Patricia, and this is Roger," Hunter's mother greeted.

"It's very nice to meet you both."

Roger tapped the table. "Come sit! We were just about to order another round," he leaned to his wife. "Right honey?"

"It's his fourth tonight," Patricia said affably to Hunter before fixating on Emma. "Why don't you tell us about yourself dear?"

Emma took a moment to muse over the question.

"I'm originally from Seattle and am here temporarily for this student-work opportunity in the city."

"The Ember House," Hunter politely added.

"Their reputation is laughable," Roger chimed in while simultaneously snapping at a waiter.

Patricia ignored him focused on Emma. "That's exciting. Do you like it so far?"

"Have you had the opportunity to meet Hakim Pestrotto?" Roger interjected.

"I don't believe I have," Emma shook her head. "Does he go there too?"

Roger and Patricia shared a dainty laugh, causing Emma to glance at Hunter, who gave a reassuring nod.

"Dr. Pestrotto is the superintendent at Ember. We were in the same graduation class from our Yale days," Roger clarified, biting his lip as if it was a secret. "Believe it or not, he does not know the first thing about art. He dreamed about working on Wall Street. We called him 'Pest' because it was one of the many annoying things he talked about. He found the most creative ways to insert it into conversations. Shame he stopped pursuing it. He always had a hard living up to his promises."

"That's very interesting," Emma replied. "I've heard stories about him from other people there. From what I understand, he's something of a genius."

Roger snickered. "Debatable, but then again, he was smart enough to find an industry more suited to his…eccentricity."

Emma shifted in her seat as she wondered if there was an underlying implication to his remark. Hunter reacted with a deep laugh, leading her to assume it tied to an inside joke the family shared toward those were did not think similarly. Or as he put it, *eccentric.*

Her usual peachy cheeks turned red as she looked down at her heels, silently acknowledging how painful they were to wear even when she was not standing in them. She did not feel like she belonged here, with this type of people. To make it worse, she was growing anxious at the idea of them realizing the same.

"I'm going to use the restroom," Emma whispered to Hunter before exchanging a kind smile to his parents.

She paced quickly into the bathroom and locked herself in a stall before collecting her breath, when she was immediately interrupted by her phone ringing.

"HG?" she answered.

"Hi, sorry I don't know why I'm calling," came HG's voice from the other end. "I just wanted to see how you were doing, since we haven't talked in a while."

Emma suspected if this had to do with Isaac. Another topic she had yet to process.

"I've been good…how are you?"

"I'm okay," HG replied, the uncertainty in her tone apparent for her to detect.
"Is there something you want to talk about?"
"Nah, just boy shit. You know, the usual."
Emma chuckled, relieved to hear the nature of the call was lighter than she anticipated. "Is it Aiden again?"
"No, someone new."
"Thank God, that guy was never right for you anyway."
"You're telling me." Slight pause. "How are things with your boytoy? Hunter, right?"
"Yeah," Emma assented, softening her voice at the mention of his name.
"We're actually having dinner with his parents as we speak."
"First time meeting them?"
"Yep."
"Yikes, sounds like you have more drama going on right now than I do," HG laughed. "I'll let you go."
"Wait," Emma paused. "Are you sure everything is okay?"
"Yeah, why do you ask?"
"Well, it's not like you to randomly call unless something is going on…" her voice trailed. She wanted to bring up Isaac, but did not know if it was her place to deliver the news. And there was only so much time before Hunter would begin to worry of her whereabouts.
Hesitation on the other end.
"I'm good," HG finally said, still uncertain. "We'll talk soon, okay?"
"…Okay. I love you Harmony."
"Love you too."
Emma hung up and stared blankly at the wall. She took another minute to collect her thoughts and left the restroom, where she bumped into an older gentleman busy on his phone.
"Pardon me miss," he started before pausing when he saw her face. "I can't believe it…Emma?"
Emma peered up at the man's tender smile, almost like he recognized her.
"Sorry, how do you know my name?"
"You're Bruce and Julia's child."
The remark left her frazzled, leaving the man to add, "You may have been too young to remember, but I was a good friend of your father's…" he paused. "Your mom never mentioned me?"

Emma studied his curious expression, and before she could ask for his name, a younger suit passed and patted him on the back, saying, "Marshy! Nice to see you out and about. I hope your wife is recovering well."

"Thank you," he replied, his focus off Emma temporarily to shake the man's hand before turning to face her again. "Incoming associate. I feel bad about how long it takes me to know their names."

Marshy. The name registered in Emma's memory, and it was not long before she connected it to her parents – notably, the day they moved to Mercer. She recalled that same name leaving the mouth of both her parents on several occasions.

"You're Marshall Carrington," she finally said. "You gave your house for us to live in."

Marshall smiled. "So you do remember me?"

"To be honest I'm just piecing everything together right now. Forgive me if I start going crazy, today has been overwhelming."

"I forget my own daughters' birthdays sometimes, and they're twins. Believe me, we have all been there," he laughed. "I knew Bruce for a long time. He got me out of a jam some time ago. When he was diagnosed, I wanted to pay him back anyway I could—"

"So you let us stay at your house," she finished. "You paid for my tuition at Davidson. You're literally the reason that everything worked out well for me."

"I wouldn't go that far," he replied. "If there was one thing Bruce made clear to me, it was that you were a survivor like him."

Emma embraced him, paying no care to the tears soiling his dress shirt.

"I have so many questions," she uttered. "What are you doing here?"

"My wife and I moved here to be closer to the kids, they're both in residence upstate," he explained. "Now that I'm semi-retired, I have more time on my hands."

"Semi-retired?"

"Roger sometimes doesn't trust the younger attorneys for counsel, so he loops me in every now and again."

Just then, Hunter appeared from behind Marshall.

"Mr. Carrington, I see you've met Emma," he said.

"Yes, it is indeed a small world we live in," Marshall breathed, still looking at Emma. "I was on my way out, but I'll have one of my associates give you my contact before you leave here tonight. I'm happy to tell you anything you'd like to know."

"Thank you for everything."

Marshall nodded respectfully and shared one last shake with Hunter before leaving them.

Hunter relaxed at Emma. "So, you know my dad's lawyer?"

"In a crazy way that I promise we will talk about later," she asserted. "And I'm sorry for walking out like that. I guess I'm not feeling so well."

"You *guess*?" Hunter smirked. "Is everything all right?"

"Yeah," she replied dismissively.

Hunter studied her frown. "What's going on Em? Did I do something wrong?"

"No, you didn't!" she assured, wrapping her arms around his waist in hopes that it would soothe his concerns. "I'm just getting self-conscious about being here."

"What do you mean?"

"Well, when you said that you had a surprise, I assumed that we would be going to another fancy restaurant, or something along those lines like we have usually done every time we go out," she admitted.

Hunter nodded understandingly.

"You weren't expecting to meet my parents."

Emma grinned sheepishly. "Amongst other people."

Hunter's demeanor shifted, mirroring Emma's awkwardness as he stepped away from her embrace and crossed his arms.

"I don't see the big deal, personally."

"The *big deal*, Hunter, is that we haven't been going out for that long, which, let me just say, I think we should have discussed a little more than just sleeping together and calling it good."

"Why?"

"Because this is all going to be over soon. I'm leaving at the end of the semester, remember?" Emma could feel herself growing hysterical now, feeling the reality rushing back to what she mistakened for a dream. "…I don't know, it just seemed a bit premature. Don't you agree?"

"I thought that you would have a good time," Hunter mused. "No need to be snappy."

The word rattled in Emma's ears. She had not been called that, let alone heard the term since a conversation with the most important man in her life.

Emma recalled running into her room and throwing herself under the covers as she wept uncontrollably.

There came a soft knock at her door.

"Leave me alone Mom," she had cried.

"When has your mother ever knocked before coming in?"

Emma popped her head out of the blanket, seeing her father peeking through. "Dad!"

Bruce entered and sat on the bed beside her.

"What's wrong, Snappy?"

"Boys."

"Boys," he repeated. "We're a funny bunch, aren't we?"

He snuggled beside his daughter, resting the bottom of his chin on the top of her head.

Emma loved her father more than anything in the world. He was her rock, who was always there to help her through the most difficult times.

"Do you want to tell me his name?"

"Logan," she muttered between sniffles. "He said he would take me to prom, but I haven't heard from him at all. And then when I went, he wasn't even there."

"I'm sure he had a good reason," Bruce soothed. "He'd really be a fool to miss the chance to be with you, you know."

Emma giggled at her father's relentless need for wittiness.

"Tell me more about this boy. Is he a good kid?"

"My friends always say he gets into trouble. I think he was suspended once for cheating," she shook her head. "But I don't care. He's super nice to me, and I think that is what matters."

"I agree, but have you ever thought about what kind of person he is when he is not around you?"

"Why does that matter?"

"I don't know this boy, so I won't go into it too much," Bruce began. "But you just told me that he got in trouble for cheating in school. People who cheat do not do it for themselves, but for others as a way to validate who they are."

"I get it," Emma muttered reluctantly at her father's truth. "If he cares more about what other people think about him, then he will become someone different than who he really is."

"You're on the right track, sweetheart," Bruce said, chuckling at her insightful, yet naïve comment. "He is still young, as are you, and all of your friends. You are all just beginning to learn more about why it is important to need each other. At the same time, you are starting to see why caring *too* much about what others think about you could not be the greatest idea."

Emma buried her face in a pillow.

"He told me he likes me though!" she pouted.

Bruce reduced his voice to a consoling whisper.

"We can like a lot of things, but a person has to love themself before they can love someone else," he took his daughter's hand. "Your mom and I tried our best to teach you that, and personally, I think you know I'm right. Not everyone is taught the same lessons growing up, and I would challenge you to imagine Logan being one of those people."
Emma played the question over again in her head. Her father was always right about things.
"Bruce, your taxi is here!" Julia called from downstairs.
Bruce rose from the bed and started toward the door.
"I have to go," he sighed, looking back at his daughter. "I'll be back before you can recite the alphabet backwards."
He rose from the bed and started toward the door.
"*Backwards?* Can I at least write it down and read it that way?"
"Well, that would be cheating, now wouldn't it?" Bruce playfully chirped.
"What do we always say about cheaters?"
Emma rolled her eyes, reciting one of his many overly used liners.
"Cheaters are the dumbest smart people."
Bruce nodded approvingly.
"That's right, Emmalyn. Do you want to be a dumb, smart person?"
"Come on, Dad. I think I have already proven that I am the smartest, smart person to have ever walked the earth."
"Well, clearly not smart enough to know that your Logan friend was going to play hooky on prom night. Who, I should add, is also known to cheat, am I right?" Bruce slapped his thigh and let out a bellowing laugh.
"Dad!"
"Too soon, I get it," he said apologetically and ran back to kiss her head. "I love you babygirl."
"I love you too, dad."
With that, Bruce left her room. Emma sat quietly in her bed, listening intently as she overheard the front door open and close. Complaining about boys. Had she known that it would be her last time seeing her father, perhaps she would have picked a less superficial topic to discuss with him.
"Emma?"
Emma snapped back, looking back at his perplexed expression.
"What happened?"
"You sort of zoned out there for a minute…was it because I called you 'snappy'?" Hunter said hesitantly. "I didn't mean to upset you, I was just messing around."
Emma stared hard at him, now realizing his age was the only distinction between a spitting resemblance of his father.

Roger Graham. What a guy, right? She was quick to judge him, and her distaste escalated upon noting how his traits contrasted with her own late father. His snobbish cynicism could have been a mechanism displayed only to people he felt were below him. Given his stature, however, there were few who could justify not being so.

"Do you remember on our 'first' date, when you took me to the theater after dinner? Your friend was playing in it."

"Not sure why you still don't admit it was our first date, but yes, of course I do," Hunter replied lightheartedly, although confused now by the change of topic.

"You told me that there are times when you need to behave differently for the sake of making others happy…do you remember that?"

Hunter nodded at her question.

"What are you getting at, Em?"

"It's because of your dad, isn't it?"

Hunter scanned to make sure no one was around to overhear.

"How about we talk about this later?"

"I'm right, aren't I?"

Hunter took Emma's hand and guided her away from the crowd.

"Look Emma, I'm sure I don't have to tell you that we were raised in very different worlds. And when you are a part of the one I'm in, there will always be some truths that you are forced to accept."

"Are you defending your dad right now?

"Don't think of it as me defending him, rather me trying to paint the reality of my situation."

"No offense Hunter, but I think the world would agree with me when I say that your 'reality' is vastly better than any of us will ever have."

"Respectfully Emma, you will never have an idea of just how hard it actually is."

"Oh, that's so cliché of you to say."

"Well isn't life one big cliché?"

"Touche," Emma murmured. "But if you can also see the kind of person your dad is, why do you put up with it? I think my dad was the greatest man I've ever met, and sure, I'm biased when I say it, but I can't imagine what kind of person I would have turned out to be if—"

"If you were raised by my dad? So you're implying that I am like him?"

"The opposite, actually. That's what astounds me, Hunter," Emma said, bringing her hand up to Hunter's cheek. "You are one of the kindest, generous, most patient guys I have ever met."

Hunter lowered his head into her hand.

"I was lucky to find out what kind of person he was before it was too late," he said.

"This obviously means a lot to you," Emma observed. "Why have you never shared this with me until now?"

"Emma, you said it yourself. My reality is better than most people will ever have it. From the outside looking, I'm incapable of experiencing struggle of any kind."

"But you just said that it is harder than it looks."

"Regardless, we both know that no one would bat an eye if I claimed otherwise. That's just the way of the world," he placed his hand on Emma's. "I know better than anyone how crass my dad can be and had to put up with it my entire life. He may not have treated me the way a parent should treat their child. He may have been an abusive, intolerant asshole who wasn't there for me or my mother emotionally. But that said, he stuck around. He's still here, Emma. He cared more about his money than he did about us, sure, but with that money he still put food on the table, and clothes on my back. I wouldn't be who I am today if it wasn't for him, and I love who I am, even if he couldn't care less. Because of that, I feel like I owe it to both my parents to make them proud in any way they see fit," he smirked. "Although between you and me, I'm pretty sure my mom was behind the scenes directing him to do all of that. She's so much cooler."

Emma realized she had begun crying. She wiped her tears away and laughed at Hunter's joke.

"Trust me, I *definitely* got that vibe about Patricia."

Since she met him a year ago, Emma had always known that Hunter was unlike every other boy she met. He was a stranger then, but now, was one of her best friends. She tried wondering what it was exactly about him that drew her in.

But thanks to this chaotic night – and oddly familiar vernacular – she finally understood he was like her father. She was only a child when Bruce explained the secret of a successful relationship, and as a result, she was miles ahead of her friends when it came to knowing what to look for in a soulmate.

A person has to love themself before they can love someone else.

She knew it for years, and still wasted the majority of it entertaining other boys. Including Jack, who although she admits to believe him being the one in the past, was aware of the lingering doubt in her heart that she was ultimately wrong. Her long for romance got the best for her then, and she was afraid it would get the best of her again with Hunter.

Alas, she was not afraid anymore, as she knew in her heart that this time, it was right.

XXX

Dr. Skinner was shuffling through papers when Tommy entered his office. "Hi Tommy, thanks for stopping by," he motioned to one the chairs in front of his desk. "Please sit down."
Tommy obeyed, not realizing the chair had wheels when he slumped into it. He swiveled around and knocked into a bookshelf before planting his feet to keep him from moving.
"What's up, professor?"
Dr. Skinner stared blankly at him.
"Tommy, I want to extend my condolences for your friend. He was not one of my students, but it is always hard to hear when anyone at our university goes through a tragedy like his," he took off his glasses. "With that said, you chose to return to class as soon as you did, and as a result, we need to talk about your recent performance."
Tommy gave a quizzical frown. "I don't understand. Am I doing something wrong?"
"It is not a matter of what you are doing, but what you are *not* doing," Dr. Skinner corrected. "You are not showing up on time; half your assignments are incomplete or overdue; you have been entirely unfocused to my lectures; even your demeanor toward the other students has been *concerning*, to say the least."
Tommy leaned back and lowered his head in acknowledgment. He knew he had not been the same since Isaac and was aware of how it impacted his daily routine. The details of Isaac's death were suppressed, but it did not stop the public from coming up with their own theories. It was difficult for Tommy at first, overhearing strangers whisper their most bizarre tales. The only reasonable story was a hit and run, to which Isaac happened to be one of the unlucky bystanders. Tommy did not confirm nor deny, but he did not mind the plausibility. The only trace of Tommy's involvement that night was through Jack's 911 call, to which he was fortunately not name-dropped. Understandably for some of the most powerful families in the Pacific Northwest, this was not the kind of news they wanted out there.
It was important for them to carry on like normal, because the more dramatic their behavior, the more likely it could draw someone's curiosity to

investigate. As such, the objective was clear for Tommy: *keep your mouth shut and do what you are told.*

And that is what he did to Dr. Skinner.

"I'm sorry, I will do better."

Dr. Skinner nodded. "For most students, I usually advise they meet with one of our counselors for these…matters," he paused. "But given our rapport – and my understanding of your resentment for therapeutic outlets – I offer my time if you would ever want to talk about it. And of course, whatever you say, will remain between us."

"I appreciate everything you have done for me all these years professor, but talking about it won't solve anything."

Dr. Skinner nodded slowly.

"I understand. Let me know if you change your mind. In the meantime—" he held up a poorly graded paper for Tommy to see. "—I cannot have you continue with this in my class. This is the first and last time we will speak about it. Am I clear?"

"Crystal," Tommy affirmed, pointing to the paper. "Is there any way I could have another shot at that?"

A faint smirk ran across Dr. Skinner's face, prompting him to hand the paper over to Tommy.

"Have it back to me by the end of the week."

Tommy was rarely criticized for his performance, so such an ultimatum from his advisor failed to spark any self-doubt. Time and time again, he had proven to achieve far more than a well-graded essay over the span of a week.

He will pass this class, and graduate skid-free. But to do so, he knew that he must first prioritize the lingering tasks in his mind.

Tommy thanked Dr. Skinner and left the office, stopping in the bathroom to change into a more formal outfit for his next appointment.

He was reluctant to attend the memorial. Part of his reason to believe he had no business being there was directly tied to his inability to save Isaac that night. He blamed himself, naturally, and dreaded the truth ever surfacing as he scanned the hundreds of people who came to pay respect.

He would much rather be invisible than hide behind a mask of disbelief. Even Jack – who to Tommy's surprise, kept a cool composure for the public – refused to engage with the line of family friends walking past their pew. Each time Tommy would look over to Isaac's parents speaking with the priest before the altar.

Keep your mouth shut and do what you are told, he reminded himself, agreeing that accidentally oversharing would only create more complications. The boys regrouped after the service, choosing a spot on the opposite end of the parking lot away from the rest of the crowd. Jack was last to enter the huddle, acknowledging anyone who looked in his direction. Including HG, who he caught staring back while she waited for her parents to finish speaking with the Bensons.

"That was nice of them to come," he heard Kevin say.

Jack faced the boys. "Should we tell her?"

"No," Tommy said flatly. "Better if we keep it between us."

Jack nodded and looked back to the parking lot, where a pair of suited gentlemen caught his eye.

"Why do you think they're here?"

"Looking for answers, I bet," Bennett reasoned.

Although he was relaxed, Tommy could sense the nervous tension swelling amongst them, almost seeming to increase as the seconds drawled on. Even the menial aspects of the boys' changing dynamic was noticeable to him, noting the momentary pauses in their conversation; the lack of enthusiasm in their demeanor had disappeared altogether. Unsurprising, given the role once belonged to Isaac. Now in his absence, Tommy felt it was appropriate to credit their late friend for his impact on the group and see that it never be replaced.

Tommy watched the detectives closely. They kept their heads low, almost as if they had shared an attempt to keep their identity a secret amongst the mourners. He shuddered when the intercepted the Bensons and pulled them out of the procession. Seconds later, the foursome all turned toward the boys.

"Shit, they're talking to Isaac's parents," Jack added.

"As they should. Don't worry boys. As long as we keep our cool, we're fine."

The detectives exchanged handshakes with the Bensons and began to make their way to the boys

"This is it, we're going to prison."

"Keep your mouth shut," Tommy reminded them, his eyes glued to the detectives nearing them. "Let me do the talking."

"We need to tell them what happened Tom."

"No we don't, and we *won't*. They're fishing for information, which means that they'll be throwing shit at us until something sticks. If they single us out, remember the story."

"Good afternoon boys," one of the officers greeted as he pulled out a notepad. "My name is Thomas Nestle and this is Marcus Hill. We are detectives assigned to this case. Do you all have a couple minutes for a few questions regarding your friend?"

Before Tommy could speak, Jack said, "Sorry, but I'm a little confused. What's the point of this?"
He could feel Tommy's glare behind his shades.
"We have reason to believe that there was prejudicial motive behind the incident," Detective Hill explained. "Isaac's parents gave us permission to disclose this to you, and since a couple of your names were listed on the report, we just want to make sure everything lines up."
Tommy anticipated this would happen, but not as suddenly as it came. He was nervous to shut it down all together, as it feared it would cause the detectives to grow suspicion. As such, he decided to play along.
"We're happy to answer any questions you have," Tommy removed his shades. "That said, I don't find it appropriate that you are asking us here, at his funeral."
"On behalf of myself and my partner, we apologize and share our condolences for your loss," Detective Nestle prefaced. "But if this incident evolves into a motivated homicide, then we do not have much time to investigate."
Tommy gulped, fearing there was no way to get out of this.
As if God heard his silent prayer, his parents appeared from behind the cops.
"Is there something I can help you with?" Harrison chimed.
"Mr. Beech!" one of the detectives exclaimed, taken aback. "How are you this morning?"
"What I want to know is why you are speaking to my son and his friends without first relaying your concerns to us?"
Tommy let out a quiet sigh., *Bless you Dad.*
"While that may be true, it is still our job to find the person responsible for this incident."
As if they had coordinated their approach, Jack's parents emerged from the crowd and joined the circle.
"Is everything okay here?" Wayne said, his tone commanding the group's attention and piercing through the detective's quivering gasp.
Anita and Maria were behind him, circling around to the boys.
"Bennett, Kevin, your parents asked for you," Maria spoke gently. "Give us a few minutes, will you?"
Bennett and Kevin caught the hint in her vague request, pacing off and leaving Jack and Tommy with the adults.
"Hold on, we would like to question those two," Detective Hill muttered.
"You will be speaking to us now," Wayne said, gesturing to Harrison beside him.
"Respectfully sir, all of your children are no longer minors. And given the information from the report, they were present the night of the victim's death.

Any information they share with us will go a long way in figuring out what exactly happened."

Harrison shook his head in disgust.

"Is this how you handle your investigations now? Targeting innocent children?"

"…No, sir."

"If you read the report in its entirety, you would know that the boys were at a bar together before departing separately," Wayne added. "There is nothing on file that alludes to your suspicion that they were all still together at the time of the incident."

"We are not accusing your children of anything, Mr. Douglas," Detective Hill assured. "But frankly, we can't rule anything out."

"You are overstepping," Harrison replied flatly. "To my knowledge, they were already questioned at the hospital on the night of the incident, correct? What additional information are you hoping to learn from them?"

"This is a delicate matter, Mr. Beech. Perhaps we should control the level of our voices."

"You will not tell me how I should conduct myself. Moving forward, you will focus on the suspect still out there. Any questions you have for our children, you direct them to me at this time, now, and never again afterwards."

"Do you need anything from me Harry?" Wayne asked.

"No, you should head downtown. I got it from here."

Wayne patted Harrison's shoulder and signaled their wives.

"Come on boys," Anita said to Jack and Tommy. "Let's go find your friends."

They followed their mothers' lead, pacing slowly out of the circle.

"Jack," Wayne called out to his son.

Jack spun around to his father, nearing his vehicle.

"Have your friends drop you off at my office when you get back to the city," he ordered. "I'll give you a ride from there."

Jack nodded silently, resuming to join his mother in the crowd.

The boys later reunited back inside the chapel, all mentally drained from the encore of sympathetic wishes from the family friends. They sat beside one another; their heads drooped as if they were in collective prayer.

"That was scary," Jack mumbled.

"Do you think they know?" Bennett whispered to Kevin, glancing back.

"Hard to say," Jack muttered. "Our parents said they'd take care of it."

Tommy was still focused on the officers outside the church, feeling his chest warming up as they entered their car and drove away.

"They aren't going to do anything," he said darkly. "This is my problem to reconcile."

Jack's brow raised. "What are you talking about?"

"I'm going after him."

"*What*?"

"Logan," Tommy clarified. "He can't get away with this."

"And what do you expect to do, Tom?" Bennett pressed. "You gonna kill him?"

"I didn't say that."

"You didn't deny it either!"

"I'm with Benny, Tom," Kevin chimed in. "You're not thinking this through."

"I don't think you guys are!" Tommy spat back. "He *killed* Saac. Am I the only one here who thinks he should be punished for what he did?"

"You'd only be asking for trouble doing something like this," Bennett pleaded.

Tommy faced Jack, pointing at him.

"This is the reason why I did it," he said, waving his finger. "I tried protecting *all* of you from him and this still happened."

"Jack, what is he talking about?" Kevin asked, visibly confused.

Jack disregarded the question, fully engrossed in Tommy's rant. The proposition was wildly irrational, even for him, but he had a point with Logan. He was dangerous. Indeed, there was no guarantee that he would stop meddling in their lives, and sending a clear message was a logical method to put an end to their feud once and for all. Tommy's anger began to transcend into him. Nevertheless, he knew Tommy was not thinking straight. Revenge could not be the answer, nor should it ever be.

"Everyone is probably heading for the reception," Kevin changed the subject, checking his watch. "Are we ready to go?"

"Give me a couple minutes," Tommy said. "I'll meet you guys at the car."

Jack stole one last glimpse of Tommy rising from the pew as the followed the rest of the boys out the chapel.

Tommy embraced the cooler air now that everyone was no longer inside the vacant chapel, strolling to the bottom of the altar. He let out a deep sigh as his eyes glossed over the coffin. Alas, he was finally alone to think about the loss of his dear friend.

Everything happens for a reason. Jack told him the day they successfully fled the bear attack. For Tommy, it was also the day he arrived at Death's door. Or so he thought…

Everything happens for a reason.

Despite his veneration for Aristotle, Tommy disagreed with the ancient philosopher's depiction. He accepted the notion of his inability to accurately explain every piece of misfortune that made a person's reality. Where he drew the line, was abiding to the suggestion that such misfortunes were impossible to analyze in search for absolute truth. Deciphering what was real between fake came easy to him. The challenge laid deep inside the psyche of the deluded, seemingly bogged down under layers of profound ignorance.

He vowed not to be like them. Amid a vast ocean of deception, Tommy believed the shard of truth existed, floating against the winding current. His choice to dive in was not an act of courage. It was not spurred from fear, or anger, or confusion. Rather, it was the relentless curiosity that drove Tommy deeper in the bottomless abyss,

Sure, one could argue that Tommy was perhaps the victim of his own skewed form of delusion. He did not care, though, for he would always insist otherwise.

Isaac was gone, and a scapegoat was needed. A viable response could be taken literally, which in this case, would fall on Logan Berg, who to Tommy's knowledge, had vanished from the scene, his exact location inexplicably unknown. That said, there was the option of taking a non-literal approach to the question.

If God existed, then it would be the result of His ultimate decision. For indeed, He was capable of all things. Good and bad, right and wrong, fair and unfair; it did not matter to the Almighty, whose ability to foresee even the most miniscule components of humanity transcended beyond the social constructs fabricated by humanity itself.

There was still truth to be sought, for even an all-knowing God was restricted to His own compass. If it was a game, for instance, then the game could not be sinister, but benevolent. Not indecent, but just. Not hateful, but loving. Perhaps this was the work of Satan, who was adamant to project his wickedness over the lost souls of the world. Conversely, even an action made by the Dark Prince could have been anticipated by God's glowing supremacy. And if Tommy's analysis was correct, then it not only would have been a questionable move from his Father, but one that he made with the intention of challenging Tommy's skulking emotions.

Tommy closed his eyes, recounting the vivid image of Isaac earlier that night. His inflexible, lifeless body sinking into the icy mound. His clothes tarnished, reveling slivers of his milk-white skin. He wished the horrific picture to leave his memory, shuddering at the water kissing his blistered palms, washing off the blood still stained across his rubbery fingers.

He opened his eyes, shuddering. The image was too unbearable to recount. Regardless of who was at fault, Tommy was determined to ensure someone would suffer the blame. Revealing Logan as the suspect would not be enough for Tommy, who was concerned that doing so would only further complicate the situation. Besides, Logan would be sure to bounce back. He did it before. Not again. Not ever.

Tommy's eyes drifted from the coffin to the massive crucifix suspended above.

"This is mine to reconcile," Tommy said.

He apologized to his Savior, for they both knew that Tommy had already made his decision to meddle with his demons.

*****

One week ago, Harmony imagined her next time in Seattle would be waking up next to the man she was quickly falling in love with.

Here she was a week later, with her parents to celebrate the life of her hometown friend, after his sudden, mysterious death.

She debated going to begin with, having felt out of touch with her city friends ever since she moved all those years ago. Sure, there were the occasional calls and hangouts, but there had always been a hidden boundary separating her from the internal dynamic of her friends, including the detail behind unforeseen events.

Taking the funeral for example: Harmony would have had no idea he died, had it not been for a social media post she saw a couple days after with information on the upcoming memorial. Apparently even a death in the friend group was not enough for such "friends" to let her know.

Jack did not appear to be in the mood for her when they caught eyes after the service. Harmony reckoned his dismissiveness was purely because he needed time for himself to cope. But how difficult would it have been to come up and say hi? Or a quick text acknowledging the respect she still had to show up? Instead, he gave her a nod of recognition from across the crowd. Perhaps the most inconspicuous of ways to treat a member of a friend group when they had both lost someone they cared about deeply.

Harmony remained quiet in the backseat, letting the drone of the car overpower her thoughts.

Her mother, Laura, swiveled from the passenger seat and placed her hand on Harmony's knee.

"How are you doing sweetie?"

"I'm okay. Thank you for coming with me," she met her father Sam's eyes in the rearview mirror. "Both of you."

"Of course. It is unfortunate that it was under…tragic circumstances," Sam glanced at his wife before returning to his daughter. "We know you are still processing all this, but we are here if you want to talk about it."

She felt ashamed. Everyone, including her parents, assumed her distress was obviously because of Isaac, but it was not.

It was entirely on Logan, and how through all of this, he was nowhere to be found or heard from. Every ten minutes, she would stare at her texts with him, praying to see the bubbles pop up in the message box. It never showed.
She chose to stay out of the drama as much as she could. And when she offered her help, it was strictly on behalf of the requests from others. Thanks to Logan, she saw a new light of truth in her friends. For whatever reason she chose, they were too toxic for her to bear. Nothing would improve in her personal life if she kept putting their needs before their own. What is worse, is her inner need to keep going back to them, even when she knew their willingness to return the favor was, to put it simply, unlikely.
Emma and Logan were only people from her hometown who were different in that aspect. The first was unfortunately across the country, and the other…well, she did not know what he was up to.
Where is Logan?

*****

Logan knew he should have left town that same night. In his mind, it was the smartest thing to do. Get out before people started pointing fingers. Fingers, that would undoubtedly be directing at him.
It was not just his self-hatred that convinced him to stay, but the guilt he had for hurting someone who was undeserving of his wrath. He always liked Isaac. Everyone did. All he was trying to do was get his point across to Jack. He never had any intention of involving Isaac, let alone pulling the trigger.
The least Logan could do at this point is pay his respects. He knew he would be unwelcome at the funeral, nor would it have been smart to show his face given that the other boys would certainly be there.
He was perched atop a building a couple blocks away overlooking the chapel. Out of sight, but with a clear view of the procession where he could dip unnoticed. The boys were easily to pick out, given their decision to group away from the crowd. Even from here, watching them made him nervous.
He lowered his head to see an incoming call from HG, which he let ring. He looked back to the parking lot, watching two men in suits speaking with the boys. He was knowledgeable enough to know feds when he saw them and dipped under the ledge. He was distracted by another notification from HG, which he ignored again. He liked her more than he was willing to admit but knew he would be a fool to reply to her. The less she knew, the safer they both were.
Logan watched cars drive off the chapel lot before retreating down the fire escape and into the alley. It was much louder from behind the drove off the chapel lot before retreating down the fire escape.

Ryder was waiting for him in the alley, pacing slowly to not startle him.
"Long time no see," he greeted, observing the stairwell. "What were you
doing up there?"
"I was on the roof."
"Okay, not weird at all. Is everything okay?"
"No," Logan replied flatly, panning around in case anyone was nearby to hear
them. "I need your help. I fucked up, and you're the only person I trust."
"What happened?"
"We don't have time for that."
"Look, whatever you're going to ask of me, I imagine it's not an easy request.
I need a little context."
Logan crouched against the wall and buried his face in his hands.
"Isaac…it was an accident."
Ryder did not know Isaac, nor did he need to. Logan's state of dismay was all
he needed to assume the severity of his so-called "fuck up."
"Okay, stop talking. You're probably right, the less I know the better."
"I didn't mean to—"
"Shut the fuck up," Ryder pulled him up. "Stop talking, you understand?"
Logan was nearing a panic attack, his breath pumping harder each second as
Ryder did his best to hold him still.
"Relax Logan," Ryder eased. "Just tell me what you need. Anything."
"I need to get out of town. I can't come back here again."
"I got you man. I can put you up somewhere south of here as soon as tonight."
"No man, now."
"I have to talk to Baker first. We have a guy that takes care of this kind of
stuff," he explained. "Trust me, it would be a miracle if we can manage to do
it as soon as I'm telling you."
Logan slowed his breath, forcing himself to calm down.
"Okay," he finally said. "What should I do in the meantime?"
"Now you listen to me," Ryder said. "You're going to get a hold of yourself
and go back to your place. Pack lightly, and *only* the things you need."
"Okay."
"Once you're done, wait for me to text you. It will come from a blocked
number, that's how you know it's me. I'll tell you where to meet from there."
"Okay, okay I got it."
"You understand?"
"Yes."

Ryder rubbed his eyes, breathing deeply.

"I guess this is goodbye for a while," he mumbled.

"Thank you, Ryder."

"Don't thank me yet," he said. "There's a lot to do. But first, get this out of your mind, and focus on what I told you. One thing at a time."

Logan jolted back to his apartment, not taking a second of rest and proceeding to stuff his backpack with every piece of clothing within arm's reach.

Only the things you need.

Not the most challenging instruction, since he was not the possessive type. The spiking adrenaline cinched his ability to choose items with sentiment. Time was the biggest concern, and he had to disregard all potential distractions. Including HG, making her presence known through the mix of calls and texts that Logan stuffed in the backpack with his gun.

The doorbell sounded off, causing Logan to freeze and stare at the door.

"Who is it?"

"It's your mom. Open the door."

Logan's face flushed. He hoped things would have improved when he returned home from his release from juvie. As joyous as he was then, the verity of his optimism was shortsighted, fleeting from the moment he stepped out the patrol car. He imagined his parents in the driveway inviting him back with open arms. But everything worsened, having fallen back into the dreadful dynamic with his father. While he loved his mother and sought to protect her, he knew his presence under the same roof would only put her in more danger. So he left, concluding that it was the best option in assurance of her safety, as well we his.

He had not seen his mother since Wes vanished all those years ago, and when she periodically reached out for a reunion, he turned her down with one of his several excuses. But now? He actually had an excuse, and arguably enough to reject an invitation.

Nevertheless, he checked the peephole and nervously opening the door, when he was met with a warm embrace from his mother.

"I missed you," Adriana wept.

"I missed you too," he stammered. "What are you doing here?"

"I was in the area and thought I'd stop by. Is that okay?"

Truthfully, it could not have been a worse time. But the last thing he wanted was to reveal the horror of his current situation.

"Sure," he replied, playing his cool as he let her in.

Adriana was slow to enter his apartment, chuckling at the crazed mess of clothes strewn across the floor.

"You were always a slob."

Logan remained still by the door. "I was looking for something…"

Adriana spent another minute inspecting his room, occasionally smiling at a remnant from his childhood.

"We have a security system, you know," she began. "I wanted to come see you the same day after you left the house, but I couldn't summon up the courage."

"I'm sorry I didn't tell you. Things happened so quickly—" he paused. "College has taken up a lot of my time, and I knew I couldn't move too far away in case you needed me."

"Well, I knew you were *around,* but I assumed you'd be on campus," she smiled. "How were you able to afford all of this?"

Logan tensed, reluctant to share the details. In truth, he did not know the source himself. Better to not over-complicate the conversation when there were more necessary things to tend to.

"I saw a picture of your friend Isaac on the news. I'm sorry."

Logan lowered his head, reluctant to meet his mother's eyes. She put her hand on his shoulder.

"Do you want to talk about it?"

"No," he said, pulling his hand away.

Adriana straightened up, slightly embarrassed by her son's despondence.

"I'm sure you have a lot on your plate, so I'll make it quick. I just wanted to apologize, about everything."

Logan peeked up to see her weeping now. He took her hands in his grasp and met her eyes.

"I forgive you."

She managed a sheepish nod.

His phone vibrated from inside his backpack. He fished for it and read the text.

Ravenna Park. At the Spring. 20 minutes.

"I have to go."

"Wait, where are you going?"

"I'm sorry Mom, I can't—"

"Are you coming back?"

At that, Logan looked back at his mother.

"No…go home Mom. I'll call you later."

Logan did not wait a moment longer and sprinted out of his apartment, leaving his mother and her indistinct cries behind the closed door.

The park was empty when he got there. He found a bench and waited here, glancing at his phone to check the time.

He was a few minutes early. His job was done. All he could do now was wait. He sat in silence, paying no mind to the muted car horns a block away.

A faint echo of church bells rang on the other end of the block, plummeting him into another trail of deep reflection.

Isaac.

The thought of him ate away at Logan's already mangled conscience.

He remained on the bench long after the ringing fizzled, waiting until dark clouds loomed to move on.

I should not be here, he thought to himself, forcing himself to remain composed despite his mind frantically mulling over his own brooding self-judgements

He wondered if he should have done something different, if it would have changed the outcome. Going in, he had no actual intention of harming Jack, or any of the other boys, for the matter. He loved them. They were his friends. They *were* his friends.

He debated apologizing at first, but after contemplating how such a confrontation could potentially unfold, he decided against it. He even went as far as considering leaving town – if not permanently – then at least until the tension settled down.

At the end of the day, Logan figured it would not change anything. He made a choice to be there that night, to approach the boys the way he did. There was no way to revert the actions he made, and he feared any sort of reconciliation would ultimately blow up in his face. As it always had. As it always will.

Logan was not aware of what struck him, wincing as his legs gave out from under him.

He did not ask for this life. Yet, he would be forced to suffer from it.

*****

Jack was nervous, exchanging glances with Bennett and Kevin as he trembled in the backseat. A heightened sense of uncertainty filled the car as Tommy drove them deeper into the blackened night. His cool demeanor disturbed Jack, particularly due to his impromptu request for them to obey his outrageous request to tag along, without providing much context regarding

their destination. The haste in getting there was also worrisome. But
nevertheless, Jack trusted Tommy beyond any reasonable doubt.
They exited off the highway, turning onto a desolate street near the water's
edge. A sliver of familiarity waded into Jack, as his attention gravitated to the
orange clouds reflecting off the illumination from the cityscape in the
distance. Tommy kept them on course for several minutes before finally
pulling into the lot of a colossal structure resting at the bank of the sea.
Jack stepped out of the car, gaping at the warehouse towering over them. He
immediately recognized his first time seeing it months ago, on his errand run
with Tommy.
"What are we doing here, Tom?"
Tommy started toward the warehouse, his friends following close.
"My dad owns it. It was leased out to a startup from the Bay Area," he
explained as he forcibly unshackled the chains bordering the doors.
"That's pretty sweet," Kevin said. "We should throw a party here sometime."
"Maybe," he replied flatly. "We have other things to take care of first." Jack
was the last to enter the pitch-black room, where he was met with a blistering
draft. He continued aimlessly before accidentally walking into a halted
Tommy.
"I don't like this man," Jack whispered nervously.
Tommy took hold of Jack's wrist before he could fidget for the light on his
phone.
"Don't," Tommy warned, his grip on Jack tightening.
"You're scaring me, man."
Jack's screen lit up, dimly illuminating Tommy's maniacal stare.
"You know I'll never do anything to hurt you," Tommy assured, turning to
the other boys. "Or any of you, for that matter. I need you all to trust me
here."
He guided them into another room. The air was drier, yet Jack's hands were
noticeably clammy from the nervous sweat. Tommy waited until they were all
inside before closing the door behind them, rattling the door to ensure it was
locked.
He switched on the lights, the bright rays temporarily blinding Jack. He made
out a shadow across the room as he rubbed his eyes to adjust to the light. But
when he looked again, he discovered that it was Logan sitting in a chair. He
leaned closer, realizing that he was strapped to the seat, with a thick cord tied
across his gaping mouth.
Logan let out a painful, terrifying shriek at the sight of the boys.

Jack locked eyes with Logan, pulling away the boys in a circle where they were just out of earshot.

"What did you *do*?" he scolded Tommy, his voice a feverish whisper. "This is evil Tom. Revenge is not the answer for this."

"Exactly what I said I would," Tommy shrugged, matching his tone. "And this isn't revenge. It's retribution."

"You can't be serious, Tommy. This is fucked," Bennett said.

Tommy scowled in his direction.

"I'll tell you what's fucked," Tommy snapped back, reaching for Logan's unzipped backpack behind the chair. "He was *literally* going to make a run for it, because he knew he fucked up. And you all were going to let him get away with it," he turned back to Logan. "And to that I say fuck no. As you can see, I am here deciding to take care of it myself."

"I was very clear that I wanted nothing to do with this," Jack relented.

"Good thing I'm not asking you to do anything."

"Then why did you bring us here?"

Tommy glanced behind him to Logan.

"I figured you all needed closure," he answered.

"Not sure if what you are doing is the right way for us to get closure," Kevin countered, shaking his head. "Plus you've officially made us accessories, so thanks for that."

Jack left the huddle and slowly approached Logan. He was disturbed, examining the blackened swells under Logan's eyes as he helplessly flinched with every step he drew closer. Jack had longed for the moment to confront Logan, anticipating his feelings would be clouded in rage. However, upon seeing the fear in his rival's eyes, he could not help but sympathize with his pain.

"I want to talk to him," Jack said, turning to Tommy. "Get rid of the gag."

"Are you kidding—"

"Tom!" Jack screamed.

Tommy reluctantly obeyed, circling around Logan and loosening the gag from around Logan's face.

Logan immediately lowered his head, choking and spitting out whatever fluid was left in his dried mouth.

Jack squatted in front of the chair, his eyes levelled with Logan.

"Look at me Logan," Jack said, keeping his voice low.

Logan's head was still drooped, struggling to catch his breath.

"Logan," Jack repeated.

At last, Logan lifted his head, staring back at him. He slowly opened his mouth, moving his lips as if he was trying to say something.

"It…It was—"

"What?" Jack pressed.

"Isaac," Logan grimaced, his voice trailing. "It was a mistake. I'm sorry."

"That's not going to cut it, Logan."

"Don't be like Tommy. Please," he pleaded, glancing at the rest of the boys, all of whom returned a dismissive glare. "How many times do I have to say it?"

"You clearly knew that it would resort for the worse. Otherwise, you wouldn't have brought the gun to begin with."

Logan turned to Jack, knowing he would have no chance of getting through to Tommy.

"Please Jack," he pleaded. "What do you want me to say, huh? I obviously did not want anything bad to happen…I was just angry…" his eyes swelled with tears. "Please…I just needed to let you know how I felt – "

"Felt about what?"

"The night I was arrested…do you still not realize how much that changed my life afterward?"

Jack peeked back at Tommy before returning to Logan.

"Tommy ruined my life," Logan continued. "I should have had the chance to defend myself, but Tommy took it all away from me. He threw me under the bus for something he was also a part of…" tears swelled in his eyes, averting his attention to Tommy. "I mean, fuck Tom! We were only kids! What gave you the right to do what you did?"

"We've been through this," Tommy replied calmly. "If you think I am going to sympathize with the shit hand you were dealt – especially after Isaac – you are out of your mind."

Logan focused back on Jack.

"I was there at the Locks," he began. "I spoke with Emma."

"I know," Jack's face tightened.

"You want to know what she said to me? She told me that she was not surprised that you and I were so close…she compared me to Tommy. Which, I gotta say, really pissed me off at that moment. I spent so long contemplating why she thought that. I mean, me and Tommy? It just didn't make any sense. But then I figured it out. And I have to say, she could not have been more right…I now understand why we both liked her so much."

"What do you mean?" Jack pressed.

"Emma had flaws of her own, but one thing I will admit is her ability to see through people. She understood who I was, the same way she understood you. Her decision to leave you was not out of spite. She did it *for* you."

"You don't know anything about what we went through," Jack shot back, growing more irritated. "You can pretend like you do, but we both know you are full of shit."

"I don't care if you believe me or not. I'm just telling you what I know to be true."

Jack rose to his feet and turned away. He paused for a moment before swiveling back at him.

There Logan was: a childhood friend of Jack's who was undoubtedly responsible for the undeniable pain that rotten in all their hearts. He had ridden him of one of his brothers, as may as well partially for his falling out with the girl he loved more than anything. Yet, amidst his wrenched expression, Jack could not help but sympathize with the man. Jack liked to think he was smart enough to see through people, and although he was skeptical of Logan, the truth seeped through his cries. He faced Tommy, still unflinching at Logan's agony.

"I don't know about this, Tommy," Jack uttered.

Tommy ignored him, creeping closer to Logan.

"What do we get out of this?" Jack continued. "I already can't live with myself after Isaac. What if we are only making things worse?"

Jack could see the lack of sympathy in Tommy's eyes.

"Remember why we are here boys," Tommy said. "This is for Isaac, and what this fuck did to him."

Tommy reached into Logan's pack, slowly pulling out the handgun.

"I remember the last time I held this…don't you Logan?"

"Come on man," Logan trembled. "Think about what you are doing here. This isn't you."

Tommy waved the gun at the boys. "Any takers here?"

He met Jack's reluctant gaze, extending the gun for him to take.

"I won't do this," Jack asserted, taking the gun and placing it on the floor a few feet from where Logan sat.

"What do you mean you won't? He's a killer, Jack!"

"And I'll also be one if I go through with this," Jack reasoned. "We aren't murderers. Logan knows he made a mistake. He's changed."

"You think he's changed? Is that right?" Tommy bellowed.

Logan remained silent and watched them bicker, doing his best to keep his fidgeting subtle as he successfully broke through the binding around his wrists without alarming anyone.

Jack focused on Logan's narrowing eyes. He could read his fearful expression, pivoting to Tommy before turning back one last time.

"I'm sorry Jack," Logan uttered, "But you should have listened to Tommy."

At that moment, Logan dove for the gun and pointed it at Tommy.

"Logan!" Jack screamed.

Without hesitation, Logan shut his eyes and squeezed the trigger.

It all happened so quickly for Jack, who turned away from him, bracing in fright.
A muted click, followed by a long passing moment is all it amounted to.
Logan peeked an eye to see Tommy menacingly smirking back at him.
"What?" Logan gasped.
"Figured you'd know me better by now," he stepped closer to Logan. "Jack obviously wouldn't have it in him to kill you, and I *did* anticipate the possibility of you freeing yourself in the time that I left you here."
Logan was stunned, hastily inspecting the unloaded gun.
"For the record, I never had any intention of killing you either," Tommy added, quickly snatching the gun from Logan and tossing it aside, startling the other boys as it skidded ten feet upon slapping the floor.
"I don't understand…" Logan's voice trailed off.
"I guess I'm a sucker for the dramatic effect," Tommy gave a short chuckle before returning to his glare. "It is not up to us to justify what happens to you. I'm leaving that up to the cops," he glanced over to the other boys.
"Who, by the way, should be pleased to hear we got the perp and will stop their investigation."
"Are you fucking kidding me?" Jack raged. "This was all a charade you decided to pull?"
Tommy shrugged. "I can't hurt him – least I can do is put a little fear in him before he's taken away."
His plan was apparently successful, but it did not take long for the terror in Logan to settle, promptly scampering away from the boys. He reached the exit, swinging the door open and retreating into the dark otherside.
"Wait, Logan!" Jack called out, feeling his legs move after him. He ignored his friends' hollers and sprinted after Logan, his sight eclipsed by the lack of light in the other room. His heart was pounding, failing to slow down despite having no idea of his whereabouts. He could barely make out Logan's receding footsteps in respect to his own, suddenly noticing a blinding rectangle appearing directly ahead of him.
Jack was met with a brisk chill as he rushed out of the building, panning for Logan, who was nowhere to be seen. His boys joined him shortly after, letting out intermittent pants as they circled around him.
"Where did he go?" Bennett asked.
"This is fucked," Jack stated, turning back to Tommy. "Are you happy now, Tom? Is this what you wanted?"
"He couldn't have gone far," Tommy indicated, his eyes adjusting to the lightless avenue.
"Guys!" Kevin shouted, pointing across the street, where Jack made out a shrinking silhouette shifting up an invisible hill.

They all darted towards Logan, keeping close to each other as they stumbled through a back alley of the desolate neighborhood. Purpose overcame Jack, finding it easier to lift one foot after the next as they picked up the pace. He tried controlling his laboring breath, growing more determined as they neared the enlarging shadow. It did not take long before he could detect Logan's back, his arms flaying wildly into the blackness.

Logan twisted back, his yelps growing louder at the sight of his former brothers drawing closer. He was no longer looking ahead of him as he plodded into the dimly lit street.

But Jack was. He noticed the pair of lights increasing in size, emerging from the left and barreling toward Logan. He was certain about its result. There was no doubt in his mind. And it unfolded exactly as he imagined. It was a series of events that he would never forget; one that he would share with his best friends as one of the most traumatic occurrences he had ever experienced. He tried warning him, but he knew he was too late.

Logan was exhausted when he finally came to a stop. The horrified look on Jack's face – his arms stretched out to grab him – would be the last thing he ever saw in his life.

The deafening squeal of the semi was not enough to alert him for his undesirable fate. Nor was the assortment of cries that he heard from the boys. And for yet another time, Jack's already wrecked heart broke a little more.

Logan was already dead when the truck struck him, his lifeless body flying down the road and cracking onto the pavement as he rolled another twenty yards before hammering the side of a traffic pole.

Earsplitting silence.

It was only thirty seconds, but it could have been an eternity. Not that Jack was able to tell the difference. He collapsed to his fours, unbothered by the frozen ground smacking against his knees. He opened his mouth, unable to find his voice amidst his overpowering screams.

Green. Yellow. Red. The dim hue had no effect on Logan's blood-steeped clothes – what was left of it, for that matter. A stream of carmine pooled out of his icy corpse, with indistinct pieces of his apparel peppered around him, similar to the flakes of a withering tree bark.

"Fuck, fuck, fuck!" Bennett screamed.

Tommy started toward the street, Jack snatching his friend's arm.

"What are you doing?"

"We can't leave him here, someone will find him."

Jack was going to argue until the rest of the boys followed Tommy's lead to Logan's body.

"You two get the legs, and Jack and I will get his arms," Tommy instructed to Kevin and Bennett.

"Where are we taking him?" Kevin wearily asked, nearly vomiting at the sight of the twisted body before them.

"Where he won't be found," Tommy replied, gesturing to the shore downhill from the road. "Down over there."

Jack reluctantly participated, sharing the weight on one end of Logan's body. The foursome trotted quickly one hundred yards to the shore.

"Do we just throw him in?"

"Not yet," Tommy muttered through an exhale. He ordered his friends to temporarily drop him on the muddy sand before hurrying back to the hill.

Jack watched as Tommy inspected the ground, occasionally picking up a large rock before corralling them back over to the group.

"Here," Tommy continued. "Stuff these anyplace you can. We need to make the body sink in case the tide tries to pull him back to shore."

"This is fucked," Bennett said.

Tommy faced him, Jack believing to see a mild panic in his eyes.

"We didn't kill him," he stated as he produced a lighter from his pocket. "We are not at fault for this."

"We are now that we're trying to get rid of the evidence!"

"If they find his body, we are the first people the cops would suspect. Do you not understand that? Did you forget that we were questioned at Saac's *funeral*?"

"Then we could just say we had nothing to do with it."

"I'm not going to take that chance."

"But you'll take this one? I don't get it—"

"Bennett!" Tommy exploded. The tone in his voice made Jack's skin crawl; he had never heard his best friend emit such wrath.

Bennett caved and took a couple rocks from Tommy's arms, the rest of the boys following his lead.

Jack completed his role, staring sightlessly into the night as Tommy finished the task and rolled Logan's body deeper into the calming tides. The water was near his chest when he left the body and rejoined his friends on the shore.

"Good riddance," he said bitterly, the tone piercing through the numb air.

Jack kept his eyes low, knowing Tommy's comment was directed at him.

It was then, at that moment, when Jack truly saw what Tommy B was capable of. Underneath his loving loyalty, was a ruthless young man, cruel and apathetic in his pursuit for revenge. To Jack's surprise, it did not startle him, nor make him resent Tommy. He was oddly content to finally understand how he had always felt. Logan's intentions were always there, but he was indeed a threat to Jack's livelihood. Tommy knew what he was capable of, arguably before Logan knew himself. And after all these years, Tommy would end up being right.

He finally raised his head, seeing that all his boys were staring back at him. "You're my brothers," he uttered.

They all reciprocated his sincerity, placing their hands on each other's shoulders and lowering their heads.

Jack did not need affirmation, for he understood perfectly. What transpired that night was to die with Logan. This was their pact. An unspoken covenant, and one that they guaranteed would bind them together for the rest of their lives.

xxxi

Emma tensed in her seat and glanced at the clock illuminated on the dashboard.

"I hope we're not too late."

"Don't worry, we're almost there," Jack assured, reaching over to rest his hand on her thigh. "Are you comfortable? I can turn up the music if you want."

"I'm okay, thanks," Emma replied uneasily. "If I'm being honest, I can't stop thinking about what I'm going to do if we don't make it in time."

"We will, Em."

"Do you promise?"

Jack chuckled. He had become more comfortable with the question.

"I'll tell you what: if we don't make it, I promise that tomorrow, we can do *whatever* you want," he shook his head. "We can even go to Chihuly if you want."

"Don't act like I won't hold you to that."

Emma braced as Jack briefly slowed and reeled around the corner, when she was momentarily blinded by the glimmering neon beaming back at her.

"Thank *God!*" she screamed in delight.

She darted out of the car before Jack had time to put it in park, hurrying to the window at the front of the building. Even amid the sweltering heatwave sustaining through the evening, he admired how she appreciated the little things. Specifically in this case, the friendly grin on the young worker as he placed the fragile cone in her hands. Emma did not waste a second after as she lapped away at the ice cream as it melted down the cone and over her fingers.

Jack smirked, having only caught the end of Emma's rather messy consumption.

"Was it everything you wished for and more?" he mused.

Emma was on her last bite of the cone when she acknowledged him.

"If you must know, it was, in a word: *exquisite.*"

"I'm glad," he laughed. "Because I forgot to mention on the way here that they don't close for another half hour."

Emma gave him a playful shove.

"You asshole! Are you kidding?"

"I'm sorry," he laughed harder. "Though, you have to admit it that it was pretty hilarious how nervous you were that we weren't going to make it."

Emma turned away from him, smirking.

"Come on," Jack started, offering his hand. "There's something I want to show you before I take you home."

Emma held his hand and followed him back to the car.

Half of their attention was on the world passing outside. A beautiful sight: above the remarkable scape of the city were gray clouds so rich in fluff, branching through the sky like spires of a mountain range. The moon was full, yet only visible through the rays penetrating through the masked haze resting atop the calming waters.

She overheard Jack chuckle.

"What's so funny?"

"Nothing, it's just that you're acting like you've never been here before."

"I don't think I have, to tell you the truth."

"Actually? I feel like all the locals know this place. How is that possible?"

"Come on Jack, you know me. I didn't spend my childhood exploring the city like you. My parents would have never let me do this sort of stuff."

"By "stuff," you mean going on a night drive?" Jack pressed kindly. "It's gotta be the most popular pastime for city folk."

They reeled into an empty lot, a quarter mile from a deadstop overlooking the narrowing lake separating them from downtown. The clouds had passed, revealing a luminous moon penetrating through the tinted windshield.

"I can never get tired of this," Emma gasped, her distraction shifting to the song playing as she gestured to the screen between them. "What is this song?"

"*Midnight Rider?*" Jack answered. "It's a classic. There are a lot of versions, but Alman's original is hands-down the best."

"Jack Douglas, and his hidden passion for music."

"*Good* music, babe. There's a big difference. Imagine if someone had a passion for art and they liked…" he pursed his lips in contemplation. "Who's a bad artist?"

"Music, like art, is all about perspective. Even if I said one was bad, it would be my opinion, not a fact."

"Interesting," Jack hummed, taking her hand again. "Here's a fact for you: we're meant to be together."

"Are you sure that's not an opinion?"

"Oh absolutely. Unless you tell me I'm wrong," he leaned toward her. "Am I wrong, Emma?"

"You're hilarious," she blushed. "Next you're going to say you love me."

"Wouldn't be the craziest statement. You can break my heart and I'd thank you."

"Don't say that," she countered. "You're putting negative energy in the universe by suggesting that to even be a possibility."

"You tell me that anything is possible if you believe it to be true," Jack's brows furrowed. "Or maybe it was Tommy B who said that."

"I think that's from the Bible."

"Bible…," he trailed in thought. "Never heard of him. Cool name though."
Emma hated herself for laughing at that. Jack was in prime wit, shooting one-liners off no matter how cheesy. He knew they would stick.
They were peak-Merge. His secrets were all out there, and she still stayed. It was now, finally, that he accepted his hopeless romanticism, and all of its strings. After all, he was prepared to do anything for her. He would drop out of college, as she was more than enough to keep him enlightened. He would throw away his fortune, as she was all he desired to feel worthy. He would go as far as sacrifice his own life, as she was his purpose for being alive.
"I'm happy I met you Jack."
"Me too. I already know I'm always going to remember you."
"*Really?* Keep going."
"You can be on the other side of the world, and I will still always think about you."
"Be careful what you wish for," she giggled. "Life has a weird way of throwing curveballs at us every once in a while."
"Well, it's a good thing that I was the best batter in my little league team," Jack retorted.
They fell silent at the sound of Emma's phone ringing from her back pocket.
"That's probably my mom," she relayed. "Sorry, I promised her earlier today that I would call her back."
"We all have parents, I understand," Jack said gently. "Come on, I'll drive you home."

*****

Jack jolted upwards at the screech from the jet's wheels smacking the pavement. He must have startled his mother, who rested her hand on his arm.
"We're here," Anita said calmly.
Jack nodded and leaned over to see his father glance back at him and give a stoic wink.
He struggled to remember the last time he joined his parents on one of their ventures. They only dragged him along as a child when the babysitter was unavailable.
Needless to say, he figured the invitation was a gesture of sympathy as a result of Isaac's passing two months ago. Jack did not mind, as he agreed a trip abroad was not a bad suggestion to get his mind off the tragic reality back in Seattle. This was an unprecedented phase for him. One that Wayne and Anita were hopeful to pass in due time.
They were off the plane and in a private car shortly after they arrived, where they were taken into the heart of the city.

Wayne insisted that this would be a quick trip, with an even quicker turnaround to get on their early morning flight.

Jack followed his parents as they sifted through the jostling crowd. He may have been in the Old world, but it felt so New to him, taking time to awe at the mountainous edifices, walled in platinum as they soared past the thickened fog draping across the landscape. Despite the city's modern amenities, it was still compelled to cling to its historical brilliance, charmed by noble splendor. That said, there were few aspects to the city that certainly resembled his home in Seattle: most notably the gloomy weather, which Jack easily shrugged off as he pulled over his hood, peering up at the light drizzle falling out of the granite sky.

They stopped in a tavern, where Jack's parents treated him to an afternoon cocktail.

"We have errands to tend to," Wayne announced, glancing at his watch. "Why don't you take the time to explore, and we can meet back at the hotel tonight?"

Jack nodded, unsurprised at his father's urgency to get back to work.

"Do you need anything before we go?"

"No, I'm okay."

"You know you can call me for anything okay?"

"Don't worry mom," Jack insisted. "I'll be fine."

"Okay," she hesitated. "Let me know if you are coming back late. If you want to sleep in, we will arrange a car for you to the airport for whenever you wake up."

"Sounds good."

"Call us if you need anything," Anita added, giving him a hug before she left with Wayne.

Jack glanced at the bartender, raising his empty glass.

"I'll have a stout this time, please."

He settled on the barstool, taking notice of the city's rhythmic beat outside. It was a heart, pulsating life into its inhabitants bustling through its arterial avenues and alleys. Even though it was his first time being there, he felt as if he belonged, inhaling the salty air that reminded him of home.

The bartender returned with his drink, to which Jack naturally overpaid.

"Cheers," the bartender remarked and paced off.

"But you're not drinking anything," Jack muttered, recognizing he was already out of earshot.

"You'll get used to our quirks," came a voice from behind him.
Jack spun around to see a girl standing awfully close to him. Her high
cheekbones were prominent as she smiled back at him; her hazel, beady eyes
striking him into silent admiration. She had on a black rib-knit turtleneck and
jeans, which she wore under a camel overcoat.
"Thanks for the tip," he uttered. "This is my first time here."
"Gee, I wonder what it was that gave it away," she retorted, shaking his hand.
"I'm Leah."
"Jack."
"Nice to meet you Jack. Where are you from?"
"Seattle," he replied. "It's in America."
"I know," she giggled. "What brings you here?"
"Nothing important, honestly," he admitted. "I'm here with my parents on
business, so I'm just chilling until they get done."
"And you thought *this* place was the best choice?"
"Was I not supposed to choose here?"
"Pardon, I assumed your people didn't come to places like this. You all
usually like to stick to touristy areas."
"I prefer a more authentic experience."
"Well in that case, I'm here with my mates over at that table. Why don't you
join us?"
"Really?"
"Of course," she beamed. "I wouldn't be doing my due diligence as a local if I
didn't extend an offer."
"I see."
She took his hand and led him deeper into the tavern. He noted her confident
demeanor contrasting her petite figure, and admired how seamlessly they
weaved through the busy pub.
They reached Leah's table, where he was greeted by her friends, all of whom
were also neatly pleated in lusterless, yet elegant attire.
"The daft cow returns!" one exclaimed.
"Shush Timothy!" Leah snapped, gesturing to Jack. "Everyone, this is Jack.
He is an American, so be nice."
Jack initially regretted getting himself into this, but was instantly taken aback
by how readily they welcomed him as if he was one of their own,
incorporating him into their enthusiastic banter as the drinks flowed through
the evening.
He learned that they were students at the university just up the road, all of
whom had just finished the semester and were adamant in celebrating
appropriately.

Jack could not take his attention off of Leah, whose timid posture surprised him given her initial assertive nature.

The conversation eventually came to a lull after a few hours, prompting one of her friends to speak up.

"Let's go somewhere else," he suggested, finishing what was left in his drink. "I happen to not work tomorrow and would love to get sloshed tonight."

The group concurred with a series of interesting lingo.

Jesus, they're just like my friends.

Leah leaned to Jack.

"What are your plans after this?" she whispered.

"Good question," Jack paused, pulling out his phone to discover a series of missed calls from his parents. He had no idea where the time had gone.

"I should probably head back to my hotel, actually," he mumbled as he quickly shot his mother a text. "My parents are probably wondering where I am."

Her hand tightened around his arm. "Where is your hotel?"

He pulled up the address on his phone for her to see.

"Oh that perfect, my house is on the way. I'll walk with you."

"Sure," he agreed. "That'd be great."

Her eyes lit up at his response, turning back to her friends.

"Jack and I are going to head out – I'll probably meet you all wherever you choose to go," she announced.

Jack said his farewells to Leah's friends before grabbing her coat and following her out the tavern.

It had since snowed from earlier in the day, the scent duskier with visibly sweeping flakes racing across the desolate cobblestone. He did not view it as dreary, but wondrously vivid, removing his hood to take in the icy, rejuvenating atmosphere.

"Shall we?"

"We shall," she smirked as she threw on her coat.

Leah sprinkled interesting anecdotes as they leisured down the avenue, trailing away from downtown. They arrived at a park near the outskirts of the city, blanketed in fresh snow that glistened from the full moon creeping out of the clouds.

"I take this path every morning on the way to class," Leah mentioned.

From a distance, Jack made out a large group of children in the center of the courtyard, soaked in spirited cheer as they repeatedly burrowed in and sprouted out of the fluffy ice.

"I see those kids don't seem to mind the cold," he chuckled.

"They are always out here," Leah said unamusingly.

"Really?"

Leah nodded. "There is an orphanage not far from here. The administration gives them time to be with each other outside because it helps them improve their social skills," she paused. "You know, since they are unable to experience it like us."

Jack adjusted his expression, watching Leah commiserate over the kids in the field.

"I love seeing them," she continued. "Seeing how happy they are, even though they have no reason to be…it helps remind me why I am here…why all of us are here."

"Why do you think that is?" Jack asked.

She turned to him. "To learn from each other, and love everyone unconditionally."

Jack silently nodded.

"At least I think so," she sighed, turning back to the field. "My mom used to always tell me that love is a combination of holding on and letting go. Once you are able to do that, then it becomes unconditional."

Jack entered his own state of contemplation.

"How do you do it?" he started. "Love, unconditionally?"

"There isn't really a right answer," she explained. "For me, however, I think it means to love freely. It isn't about how you feel about someone, or something, but how you want to make them feel."

"What is the difference?"

"One is selfish, and the other is selfless," she explained. "Love is not what you get; it is what you give."

"I see."

She looked back at him. "Have you ever been in love, Jack?"

The question swirled in his head, the image of Emma immediately appearing in his mind. He recalled meeting her for the first time: the surprise in her face after spilling his drink; her effortless beauty, from her fetchingly dimpled smile, to her stunningly unique personality; her quirky giggle after a cheesy remark; her glowing intellect, and ability to see the truth even in the face of deception; the comfort she brought him in response to his own insecurities. It was at that moment, when Jack realized his skewed definition of love. He found it in her, because he sought the feeling that she gave him. There were no instance when he reciprocated it. He was taking, and not giving.

"I thought I did," he admitted, lowering his eyes. "I don't know anymore."

He was caught off guard when she kissed him, her smooth hands circling around his waist as she firmly pressed her lips against his. He kissed her back – only for a second – before pulling away.

"I'm sorry," Jack apologized. "I can't…I'm sorry."

"Why?" Leah blinked. "Oh my god, please do not tell me you have a girlfriend—"

"Not anymore," Jack assured. "I guess I'm not totally over her yet."

"I understand," she nodded. "What's her name?"

"Emma." Even saying her name was hard for him.

"May I ask what happened between you two?"

Truthfully, Jack wasn't prepared to share anything about him and Emma, but he figured that it could be better with Leah, whose judgement would likely mean nothing to him considering they barely knew each other.

"We went to school together," he explained. "She moved away for an internship. We tried to keep it going long distance, and then it all sort of fizzled out."

"An internship," Leah stated. "That means she'll come back, right?"

"Eventually, yes. But I don't think it will ever be the same anymore."

"Why is that?"

"There isn't one specific thing, I guess. We've had a *lot* of ups and downs," he explained. "Let's just say she is trying to find her purpose in life…just like me. And I guess we both need space to do that."

"Do you think that you are keeping her from doing so?"

"I wouldn't say that, necessarily," Jack shrugged. "But now that I'm thinking about it, I can't see how I was helping, either."

He noticed Leah purse her lips, assuming she was uncomfortable with his venting.

"I'm sorry if I just made everything awkward."

"You didn't," she chuckled. "It is always nice to get stuff like this off your chest."

"I guess so," he agreed. "To be honest, I haven't spoken to anyone about this, even my best friend," he paused. "And I tell him *everything.*"

"Really? Why did you tell me?"

Jack studied Leah's wide eyes.

"I don't know," he admitted. "I don't want to get over her, but I think it's natural for everyone to feel that way right after it ends. Maybe it's time for me to get over her," he pondered for a moment. "What do you think?"

"I don't know if I should be allowed to weigh in here," she replied flatly. "I don't know Emma, and I literally just met you today."

"Fair point."

"But if I *had* to give any advice, it would be that whatever you decide to you, just make sure that it is what you want, and not what you think is expected."

The two stood there, motionless in the quiet darkness.

"Now come on," Leah grinned, taking Jack's hand. "Let's get out of here."

"Are you not going to join your friends?"

"Nah, I'm pretty tired, and also have an early morning," she replied. "The least you can do is walk me home."

They exchanged a quick smile before leaving the courtyard.

On his walk to the hotel, his phone suddenly erupted with a series of delayed texts. He checked to see they were from his group chat with the boys.

Anyone tryna smoke? Kevin had asked.

Already pulling up, from Tommy.

He read through the rest of the texts, trying to imagine the conversation played out in person. It was heartwarming to learn of their apparent siesta, as it indicated a healing dynamic.

Jack slept in. Rightfully so, given his long night of reflection. Thankfully so, as he initially imagined this trip would be nothing more than a waste of time. He skipped through the airport, frequently glancing at the time. There was no rush for the flight – they were not going to leave without him.

His parents were waiting at the gate when Jack came rushing up.

"There he is," she relayed to Wayne, dropping her bags and rushing to her son.

"Sorry we could not spend the day with you yesterday," she embraced him. "Did you do anything fun?"

"Yeah," Jack replied, joining them in line. "I actually made some friends. Also just had some time for myself to clear my head, and think about everything…" he trailed off in reflection before returning to his mother. "I'd like to make a trip back here soon."

"That is great to hear!" she beamed. "I'm sure your father would love to have you join him next time."

"Of course. It's good to see you son."

"You too, dad."

They boarded the plane, finding their seats and buckling in. Jack pulled out his headphones from his backpack and plugged in for the flight, setting his queue to shuffle. It was only appropriate that *Midnight Rider* happened to be the first song.

He smiled when he heard it, easing back in his seat as the lights dimmed, his body relaxing to the growing vibration from the airline's drone. It had taken a very long time for him to realize that Emma was the source of his renewed anxiety.

He used to feel the strained ache in his heart. He used to yearn for wanting to know how his life would unfold. He used to envision her in those fantasies. Seated beside her. Seeing her, as she sees him. Holding her, as she holds him.

Loving her, as she loves him. When it ended, he hoped it was merely the beginning. That if it was really meant to be, then it eventually will.
Maybe it's time to get over her. Those words from Leah still rang in his ears. How could he have let himself get here, in this predicament? What was so special about Emma that prompted him to abandon all means of reason? He was puzzled at how he allowed one person to have such a dramatic influence on his well-being. He had spent so long trying to understand Emma. Someone who fought for esteemed recognition, only to be disappointed by her own misguiding. She was not the cause of his own delusion, nor a product of the internal pain that corrupted his psyche. He loved her, and believed she would fall head over heels by his kind, chivalrous acts, always willing to do anything for her, no matter the inconvenience. He loved her, yet realized that it may not have been equally reciprocated, finding himself treading through his own fear of losing her, when it should have brought him peace. He loved her, permitting his inornate desire for her to be meaninglessly subjugated for her own benefit – because he forced himself to imagine that it was necessary to make her his. He loved her, refusing to resort to the blinding truth, and choosing to follow his heart, in hopes that it would cure his desperate reach for companionship.
He did all he could – at least, everything that he thought he should.
He loved her, and wanted the world for her…even if it meant withdrawing from his own wishes.
He was surprisingly relaxed, his desperate cling to Emma seeming to melt away as he prepared for the journey home.

Part V: Wholehearted Love

xxxii

After a prolonged season plagued in darkness, Spring finally returned to Emerald City. A thick veil of grey receding to oblivion in place of the awakening sun, flaring in renewed prominence after months in deep slumber. It was not long before natural progression took course, the once deciduous earth rejuvenated in a blossoming marvel from the soothing warmth. Even the scent of the air changed, refreshed with an aroma sweet enough to stimulate one's appetite. Glimmering tides were at a never-ending dance with the salty breeze, its choreography aimless, and lacking restraint as it toppled and crashed against the shore. The atmosphere appeared to transcend through the city's inhabitants, who carried about their lives in more animated fashion. Including Jack, who rejoiced the change of course as he awakened from Sleep's hold and rolled out of bed and onto the rubber mat directly in front of the panoramic windows overlooking the Seattle skyline.
Molly peeked into the bedroom.
"I'm heading to work," she whispered and placed a kiss on his head. "There's breakfast on the terrace."
"Thank you," Jack smiled, his eyes still closed.
Of all the developmental transitions he had undergone in the last four years, Jack's renewed partnership with Molly turned out to be the greatest godsend. She had crept back, and to his surprise, became closer than he imagined. Now proven in both their maturity, tolerance, and love – everything Jack sought for in a companion.
He had dreamed about another girl before, but Molly was his reality. It may have taken a few sleepless nights to accept, but he knew there was no way to revert the actions of his past. The disregard for his jealousy, misery, and angst dissipated with time. All there was left to do was move on.
"Remember, I have teacher-parent conferences this afternoon, so I won't be home until late," she added. "I could bring some takeout--?"
"No worries," Jack politely interjected. "Bennett texted last night asking to meet up with the boys for a drink. I'll grab supper then."
Sounds good," she smiled, heading for the door before pausing and turning back. "Don't forget to wear your mask."
Right, Jack thought to himself. *How could I ever forget?*
He waited until he overheard the door click before sitting up and stretching. He basked in the early sunlight and enjoyed his breakfast before returning inside to get dressed. The morning routine was embedded at this point; even the most minor decisions like what he would wear, where he lunched, his mode of transportation; all eager muses, instead of nerving deliberations.
Jack entered the elevator and scanned his keycard before pressing the

bottommost button on the panel. He stopped once the way down and was greeted by a beautiful woman who exchanged a kind smile.

"Morning Jack," she greeted, eyeing the panel. "Going to the lobby?"

"Hi Jamie, I'm all set but thanks."

"I always wondered why I never see you anywhere else in the building except for in here," she inspected his keycard. "What level does that take you?"

"The garage."

"But what about these five buttons right above it?"

"Yeah, this one is essentially the same. It's just—"

"Ah, okay I get it," she cut in. "It's the private level for the rich tenants."

"Way of the world, I guess," Jack murmured. "In my defense, I didn't ask for it."

They rode in silence until they reached the lobby. Jamie walked out once the doors opened up, turning back to him and smiling again.

"Have a good one."

"Yeah, you too," Jack returned nicely, albeit dismissively.

He took a deep breath when the doors closed again, gathering himself as the descended underground.

Jack reached his stop and left the elevator, inspecting the double line of luxury vehicles before him. The private garage was significantly smaller than the other levels. But the net worth of its contents were, clearly, significantly pricier.

And if it matters, also happened to belong to the owners of the building itself. Perks of being the heir to the Douglas empire, is that there are always things that never really change.

Jack ultimately chose his personal favorite, a sleek Jaguar in the far back of the lot.

The rest of his undergraduate career was underwhelming. Especially after Isaac, it was difficult to spend a lot of time with anyone outside of his core group. There were advantages to growing more reclusive. His grades dramatically improved, including his current studies for his master's program. It was easier to prioritize the things that mattered to him. The reputation everyone hailed on him his whole life was now a minute annoyance he chose to ignore. And the expectations he felt necessary to meet on other's accord, no longer accompanied with incredulous self-hatred.

Jack parked in his reserved spot on campus and started for his first class, when he was suddenly taken ahold by a pair of suits.

"Mr. Douglas, if you could come with us please," one said.

Sure, he may have said please, but the hard grasp on his shoulder could have said otherwise. Jack kept his cool, his eyes scrambling around at the other students observing the interaction.

"I should probably get to class actually," Jack muttered.

"We notified your professor. Don't worry, this shouldn't take long."

Jack reluctantly obeyed and followed the suits back to their vehicle. They drove off campus and back toward downtown, with not one word uttered along the way.

Jack sat rather comfortably in his seat, wedged between the two suits in the back as the driver toggled with the radio. He paused momentarily upon hearing a reporter speaking about a business merger of some kind. The volume was low, however one word caught Jack's attention.

"…Douglas…"

Jack leaned forward and noticed the driver scoff at the mention of his father's name in the news.

"I just want to make it very clear that I am in no way affiliated with my dad," Jack said. "What he does is his business."

He swiveled to the suits beside him, noticing their perplexed expressions.

"Like, I'm only saying that if this is one of those kidnapping situations."

At that, the three suits burst out in laughter.

"Take it easy, Mr. Douglas! We work for your father," one revealed. "We were given orders to bring you in as soon as possible."

Jack's jaw dropped in hysteria.

"Are you serious?" he exclaimed, nudging the man. "What the hell dude, I thought I was going to die!"

"You have your friend to blame for that," the driver added. "Thomas, I believe his name is? He caught us as we were leaving the building and paid us to do it this way."

Jack shook his head and chuckled. "Why was Tommy there?"

The driver met Jack's confused gaze through the mirror, his hardened, yet kind eyes looking back at him.

"Did you not just hear the news?"

Jack shrugged and left it at that, noticing that they had arrived at the building. Wayne was in his office, in his usual position, his head looming over an assortment of unevenly stacked papers strewn across the desk.

"You know there are some things Tommy says that you shouldn't listen to, right Dad?"

"He preferred you have a dramatic entrance," Wayne sighed, pushing the papers aside. "How are your classes?"

"They're good! It's sort of funny how easier it seems since it's only two more years instead of four."

"I'm glad to hear it," Wayne smiled. "Because I spoke to your dean, and you will be fast-tracked to graduating early."
"Wait, what?"
"Believe me, it was not that hard to convince him given your exceptional grades."
"But, why?" Jack asked, stunned. "I don't understand."
"Our firm is going through an interesting transition," Wayne began, folding his arms. "We are opening a second headquarters in Arlington. I'm sure you have been keeping up with our firm in the news."
"Not really."
"Well, your mother and I have been speaking about it for some time now, and between our jobs, we already have limited time for each other, and the opening of this new branch would only further strain our availability if I were to dedicate my time toward it…"
"I see."
"I proposed to the Board that we should lean on our younger generation of workers to take the reigns there while us older folk hold own the fort here," he pointed at Jack. "And I want you to lead the team."
"Are you serious?"
"I am," he insisted. "The time has come for you to step up, Jack."
Jack was shocked. Astonished was a better term, as he struggled to formulate a reaction into words. At this pace, there was no way he imagined himself taking over his family's enterprise. It was guaranteed, yes, but he assumed it would not be for much later in his life, especially after his personal decision to put his graduate studies on hold for his own personal peace of mind.
Yet there his father was, explaining to him that the time had come to pull on his coat and join the business. As ecstatic as he was for the opportunity, he could not help but creep toward his long-absent abyss of anxiety. It was all happening so quickly.
"And don't worry," Wayne added. "I spoke with Harry, and we agreed that Thomas will be joining you there on the general counsel. I swear that boy is a walking encyclopedia; given his knack for public policy, I'm sure he would enjoy his time in D.C."
"Dad, I don't know," Jack stuttered. "I mean, thank you so much for thinking of me for this, but I don't know if I'm cut out for it, if I'm being totally honest. I have no experience in anything like this."
"You already know everything about the business, and more importantly, you are my son. You knew that this day was coming."
"Not like this!" Jack exclaimed. "Come on Dad, I didn't agree to be sent across the country. My life is in Seattle. What happened to me staying here? Or me even having a say in all this?"

"We can discuss the details later, Jack, but things change," Wayne said coolly. "I shouldn't need to tell you that."

Jack slumped in one of the chairs and took a deep breath.

"We are holding interviews over the next couple weeks for the team. I want you to sit in on all the meetings. Figured it would be appropriate, since you will be in charge of the new hires."

"Of course," Jack nodded. "Just share your calendar and I'll make it work."

"Acting like a boss already! See, it's not that hard."

Jack was halfway out the door before Wayne called for him again.

"Be sure to tell Thomas that I would like you two to start coming into the office twice a week for now to learn the ropes. I'll get you a couple offices next to each other."

"Okay. Anything else?"

"Actually yes," Wayne recalled. "There is one fellow that we will be speaking with in a couple days. He applied to be our Head of Finance Operations. I would appreciate it if you greeted him at the airport and brought him here."

"Seriously?"

"It'll be a kind gesture to have you there," Wayne reasoned. "Think of it as a 'personal touch.'"

"I gotta say Dad, you're really changing things up around here. I like it."

"You were just saying that I should not always listen to what Thomas says."

Jack chuckled and bid his father farewell. Things were changing swiftly, and if he played his cards right, it would be for the better.

Tommy was waiting for Jack outside the bar later that afternoon.

"Where's Molly?"

"Conferences," Jack replied. "She probably wouldn't want to be with the boys anyway."

"Fair point," Tommy nodded. "Hey! I heard you got dragged off campus this morning. What was that about?"

"Very funny Tommy," Jack said as he pulled out his mask.

"What are you doing?"

"We're going inside."

"So?"

"Let's not do this again, just put yours on."

Tommy put forth no effort in concealing his distaste in shielding his face from a speculative disease, let alone being told what to do. Even so, he reluctantly snatched the wrinkled mask from his jacket and followed him inside.

Bennett and Kevin were already there, waving them over at a booth deep in the back of the bar.

"Boys," Tommy greeted, turning to Bennett. "Okay. We're here, Bennett. Are you happy?"

"I am, actually. I'm very happy."

"*Very* happy, huh? You going to tell us why now?"

Bennett took a breath and rubbed his hands like he was heating them up.

"All right boys," Bennett began. "I have a *huge* announcement to make."

"You love making announcements," Kevin chided.

"Trust me, this one is a biggie."

The boys straightened up in their seats.

"The wedding date is officially official!" he exclaimed. "Naylah and I are finally getting married!"

The air muted around Jack when the words left Bennett's mouth, hearing it gradually dissipate into a muffled drone as Tommy jumped up to embrace him. The quieted limbo was temporary as Jack struggled to seek a proper reaction to the news. Of course, he was happy for Bennett. Nevertheless, he could not resist the urge to compare it to his current love situation. There was a time in his life when he dreamt of delivering similar news to his friends. Ironic, considering that was when he was single; now with a partner of his own, the hypothetical had yet to reenter his psyche.

"Did you catch that, Jack?" he heard Bennett ask, pulling him back to the conversation.

"What?"

"The new date is this fall. November 11ᵗʰ, to be specific."

"About time," Kevin stated flatly. "Haven't you two been engaged for a while now?"

"Hence, my use of *finally,* Kevin. As you all know, we had everything set but our first choice for a venue opened up last minute, so we had to do a complete restart with reservations, vendors, etcetera. And it's way too much money to start from scratch, so we're adapting," Bennett explained. "Which reminds me, you will all get an email from us this week with all the new details."

"You're not even going to make new invitations?"

"*Waste of money*, Kev."

"Why didn't you tell us sooner?" Tommy asked. "We could've covered whatever you needed."

Bennett shrugged. "Because I'm not a beggar. But if you want to be a bro, then you can fund the honeymoon. We still haven't given that much thought."

The boys laughed together at him as Tommy proceeded to give a toast. "Time is a driving influence on the progression of love between two souls. Sometimes, time will allow two to progress rapidly, and while other times can creep rather slowly, almost like honey—" Tommy gave Bennett a snide grin. "We all know which category our boy Benny falls into."

Kevin chuckled.

"Anyway," Tommy resumed, raising his glass. "Cheers to Bennett and Naylah: a pair of loving souls we all aspire to be one day."

As Jack aged, he slowly grew aware of how much more he found himself reflecting on the past. He did not experience a closeness to his spirit, or however Tommy phrased on their recent meditation session. He did, however, become more adept at resisting the urge to overthink, as he was now guided by the rationale that reverting to how he was would only lead him to misery. His dependence on Tommy, for example, had decreased; at least enough for him to no longer constantly ask for his advice. It started shortly after Logan's death, who even though was the cause of losing Isaac, was a pinnacle moment for Jack to acknowledge that he was indeed lost. But everyone was, which made him reckon it better to trust himself than others.

Even sitting there, watching his childhood friends recount their collective progress in finding themselves, Jack knew there was still so much more to see; so much more to do; and most importantly, so much more to learn. All he could do was mentally prepare for the trivial journey that was sure to come.

*****

"Thanks again for coming with me," Jack said to Tommy when they reached the terminal.

"Of course," he replied, fumbling the name card for their guest. "Besides, it's the least I could do after your dad hired me. Which by the way, I'll have to fly to D.C. in a couple days to check out the new office."

"I thought it was your idea?"

"It was," Tommy confirmed, shrugging. "Doesn't mean that he was ecstatic to entertain it."

"You're something else."

On the opposite end of the terminal, Emma adjusted her backpack and regained her breath as she watched the stream of travelers stepping off the gate.

Alas, Hunter emerged from the doors, instantly spotting her across the walkway.

"You were quick to get off the plane," he commented, handing her a pair of headphones. "You left these in your seat."

"Oh, thanks," she said sheepishly. "The turbulence made me anxious. I had to get off as soon as I could."

"Well, I appreciate you sucking it up for me."

"Are you kidding? I'd never pass down the chance to visit home," she grinned. "You'll finally get to meet my cousins too."

"I can't wait," he returned a smile. "I must say, I never thought I would be so excited to be coming to the West Coast. Thank God it's just for an interview, though, I'm so nervous right now."

Emma echoed his anxiety. If someone asked her where she would be four years ago, she was likely to say here, in her hometown. She surprised everyone, including herself, when she ultimately decided to stay in New York. Returning to Seattle after all these years – perhaps her imagination was about to come to fruition.

They strolled over to baggage claim and picked a spot in front of the carousel. She may have been too close, because a woman hurried to reclaim her luggage, nudging through her in the process.

Hunter's eyes bulged at the disrespect from the woman, but Emma waved it off, too overcome with nostalgia to let it bother her. After all, there was once a time when Seattle was all she knew. Including the inhabitants and their cold nature, which at this point, strangely posed a charm of its own.

They reached the escalators and descended to the exit, where they were presented with a line of chauffeurs.

"Keep an eye out for my name," Hunter said eagerly.

She reeled him in for a kiss, feeling his excitement transcend into her. It was the moment she broke away and settled her gaze back to the chauffeurs when her heart dropped.

She saw him.

And he saw her. The one who got away.

Emma Keva.

Jack used to dream of the day that he would see Emma again, recalling the countless hours he spent missing her. It reached a point where he concluded such thoughts as a distant memory. A memory, that he had since grown from. Time, however, is a funny concept. It had eternalized Jack's drought, pressuring him to choose between his yearning for Emma's deluge, or drifting to another source of refreshment. He chose the latter, and consequently suffered for the better portion of the years he went without speaking to her.

All the work he had put into this disconnect suddenly rushed back. She was finally here, and coupled with her arrival, was the resumption of Time itself. Jack froze. At first, he could not believe it. Maybe his vision was playing tricks on him. There was no way...
There she stood, dazzled in a stylish black jumpsuit and woven sandals. His eyes panned across her body, noting every distinct change from the last time he saw her. Her auburn hair glistened from the natural light, stretching over her rounded ears, slim shoulders, resting just above her hips; the ring that once curled around her nose was now gone, bringing more attention to the dimples in her cheeks, growing more pronounced as she widened her lips to reveal the most brilliant smile ever bestowed on a person. And her eyes…radiant as ever, with speckles of hazel dusting over a pigment so grey it reminded Jack of the dense thunderclouds that commonly thickened over the city coast. Subtle, but piercing. Intimidating, but beautiful.
He was overcome with a powerful feeling. It could have been the classic case of infatuation, but he did not care. Seeing her there, staring back at him – it was more than he could have ever wished for. His affection for her was so transparently clear that it may as well have been visually detectable. She was different. She had always been different. He knew then, and he still knew now.

Tommy and Hunter's words were muted hums in Jack's ears. He was still locked in on Emma, watching her fill his sight as she approached him.
"Jack! I don't believe this!" Emma beamed, throwing her arms around him. She assumed he had been working out, finding it necessary to get on her toes as she wrapped her hands across his broad shoulders. Even with him wearing a suit, she felt his defined muscles protruding against her palms.
She never imagined seeing Jack again. He became nothing more but a distant memory, seeming to evaporate upon Hunter's introduction, who last time she checked, was now embroiled in her life. Especially given the circumstances, the eagerness she felt for him surprised even herself. If anything, seeing Jack again gave the opportunity to obtain closure after so long riddling over whether she had made the right decision.
Jack remained still when she embraced him, his nostrils immediately sweetened from the smell of her hair brushing over his face. He continued his fixation on her as she pulled away and greeted Tommy, hugging him and sharing a few seconds of small talk before turning back to him.
Hunter turned to him and shook his hand.
"Hunter Graham, nice to meet you,"
"Jack Douglas. Welcome to Seattle, Hunter."

"Happy to be here," Hunter grinned, leaning closer. "Although I gotta say, I just saw a random woman push my girlfriend aside at baggage claim. I'm hoping it's not normally like that here."
Jack could not help but laugh.
"They don't call it the Seattle Freeze for nothing."
"Oh God, now I'm getting even more nervous," Hunter replied. "It'll still be early by the time we check into the hotel…maybe we can all meet up later for a tour of the city?"
"What an awesome idea," Tommy added, coming to Jack's side. "I have the *perfect* spot to take us."
Emma rolled her eyes jovially, having a good guess to Tommy's choice. "You don't mean…"
"Oh, you bet I do," Tommy retorted, turning to Hunter. "We refer to it as the Locks at Ballard. You're going to love it."
Jack noticed Hunter massage his shoulder, likely from hauling luggage for the better part of the morning.
"Come on, we'll show you to the car," Jack invited, helping Hunter with his bags.
He hated to admit it, but their time at Ballard was exquisite. Jack intentionally kept the conversation light, doing his best not to speak to Emma one-on-one, which left him to focus more on Hunter. Who, as much as he tried not to, ended up really liking. It was spirit-crushing to spend the afternoon without ever acknowledging the glowing elephant, Emma. But Tommy and Hunter were engaged enough to keep the discussion rolling off-topic.
One thing he noted with Emma was her infatuation for Hunter. She ogled every time she spoke, and refused to take her eyes off him. What was worse, was that it did not appear to be out of pettiness, or with the intention of making him jealous. She seemed happier with him than she ever did with Jack. He was happy to see her happy, but at the same time, it made him furious when he considered the implication.
He wrestled with the reality long after their afternoon together, dismayed when he returned home to Molly.
"Hey babe, how was your day?"
"Not bad," Jack began, choosing his words. "I ran into Emma at the airport. She's with the guy who were hiring for the D.C. job."
"Emma…like your ex, Emma?"
"That's the one."
"Wow," Molly's head tilted. "What a small world."
"Yeah, Jack agreed, rubbing his eyes. "Anyway, I got a big day tomorrow. It's going to suck giving six back-to-back interviews."

"Emma's boyfriend, do you think he'll get it?"

"I think so," Jack admitted. "He's qualified and has a lot of potential. Exactly what we are looking for."

Molly walked up to him and brought her hands to his face.

"You look exhausted. Come here," she soothed, wrapping her arms around him.

Jack welcomed Molly's embrace, breathing deep and closing his eyes.

Jack did not lie to himself anymore. Seeing Emma again was a treat. He had imagined where he would be long after his break with her. He thought that she would have returned to him, falling back into his arms, pained by the fact that she had gone so long without him. He hoped that she was playing someone else today; that what was once a predicament would be an anecdote, she planned to tell their kids. He did not want to be just a memory, but also her future.

He understood the everlasting essence of Time, and Its refusal to stop at his convenience. Even then, he feared the notion that he would have to move on, and one day – someday – he could reflect on his decision to understand that it was for the best.

Jack may have been surprised seeing her again after all this time, but never once did he imagine feeling the same emotions he once felt the first time he met her. It was then, that Jack realized he had fallen short of his reassuring premonition: a relationship did not follow a linear pattern, but one that was cyclical.

This was Jack's new reality, burdened by his own infatuation for someone who he knew was undeserving of it.

xxxiii

If you love something, let it go. If it comes back to you, it is yours forever. If it does not, then it was never meant to be.

Given its universal familiarity, the adage warrants further analyzation from a radical analytic like Tommy Beech.

What does it mean for something to be unconditional? Must it be timeless, lacking emotion, or have meaning? If perhaps there was emotion or meaning, what constituting principles are deemed worthy of acknowledgement?

Under the assumption that the unconditionality was describing something like *love*, in this case: it not only filters under the emotion and meaning, but encapsulates it, as what is love if it not emotional, or meaningful?

To that point: what does it mean to be in love? Like the adage, the word "love" is tossed around so often nowadays that it warrants the possibility of being wholly misunderstood through the lens of modern society.

Is it intended to be sought for, with the hopes of being found? Is it inherently a part of every person, subjective to their own interpretation? Can it be formulated, replicated, or mimicked? Does it require assessment, or experimentation? Is there a methodological approach to determining an innate feeling that has blessed humanity since the inception of their existence?

Is it truly a blessing? Or a curse?

The cyclical thinking made Tommy's head hurt, who for years refused to entertain a moment so perfect to occur in his life.

But first, an explanatory flashback from earlier that day…

Tommy had dreamed of his long-awaited return to the nation's capital. He left on a disappointing note, having little contact with much of his freshly acquainted colleagues over the years since an unprompted end to their internship. Things would be different, he was sure, having spent much of the private flight glossing over his drunken memories with people he considered to be his distant family.

He commuted downtown directly from the airport, bypassing the heavy traffic and arriving outside of the office building, where he was greeted by a suited gentleman.

"Mr. Beech, my name is Daniel Rodriguez," he greeted. "One of our associates mentioned that you two worked together your last time in Washington, so I guess I should say 'welcome back' to the swamp."

"Pleasure," Tommy gleamed, swinging his Burberry satchel over his shoulder.

"The car service will take your belongings directly to your hotel. We appreciate it again that you made time to meet the team before your first day here."

"It's not a problem," Tommy waved off. "What is the name of the associate?"
"Chance Conaway," David replied. "He will be your Policy Director, so the two of you will be working closely.
"Terrific," Tommy chuckled, recalling his fellow former intern very well. If only 'Saac was here to witness the reunion.
He followed Daniel inside the building, doing his best to take in his surroundings while also listening to David's endless chatter on irrelevant information about the office.
"Wayne told me that you have been with the Douglas Group for some odd months now?"
"Yeah," Tommy confirmed. "We're family friends so it was an easy transition."
"What were you doing before?"
"Did some work for a few startups. It was fun, but I always knew working adjacent to the government was something I wanted to end up in."
"Well, you picked the perfect role," David grinned. "While we are strictly in the corporate field, our new branch into the government and policy arena has been an outstanding task that we are just now beginning to grow."
They went upstairs and into the conference room, where a table full of more suits waited patiently for Tommy's arrival. David closed the door behind Tommy, who immediately locked eyes with his friend, Chance.
Chance took the liberty to rise from his chair and embrace Tommy.
"Good to see ya, brother," Chance greeted.
"You too, man. Looking forward to working together."
Tommy resumed his introduction, controlling his hesitancy to look at Chance. While he was an exceptional networker, he credited Isaac for his familiarity with these people. It was true with them, and also with his friends back home. When Bennett asked for Tommy's toast on the night he announced his wedding date with Naylah, Tommy was secretly bemused, given how infrequently he kept in touch since Isaac's death. Not to say their friendship was ever shaken, however the dynamic was forever changed.
The same was sure to be expected from Chance; a kind intellect, who despite not being closely involved in Tommy's personal life, was sure to anticipate a reunion of sorts.
To Tommy's expectation, it came almost immediately after leaving with him for lunch that afternoon.
"How's Isaac? I hoped that he would be here too."
"Isaac," Tommy hesitated, reluctant to face the reality of the matter. "He passed away a few years ago. Hit and run."
"Oh my god, I'm sorry," Chance lamented, lowering his head as he paused in respect. "He was an awesome guy."

"Yeah, he was," Tommy nodded, moving on. "So how is it working here? Give me the tea."

"It's been great," Chance replied, eagerly welcoming the question. "Much of the other interns are still here working in different roles in the city; I stay in contact with all of them."

Tommy chuckled.

"Any that actually liked me all those years ago?"

Chance's eyes widened.

"Actually, the timing could not be more perfect," he resumed. "We've been taking advantage of our free time since we're not in session. I'm sure I could reel in a solid group to meet for drinks tonight, if you're available?"

"Efficient as always," Tommy commented. "Yeah, I'll make the time. Just let me know where and when."

Tommy attended a lot of camps growing up. Regardless of its extracurricular theme, whether it be for church or sports, he learned firsthand how valuable the friendships he made with those people – despite living so far away – remained so close to him over the years.

He viewed the phenomenon psychologically. In a situation when two people meet in such an environment, there is a mutual understanding that their time is limited. As such, there are two common approaches that the individuals are met with: keep the relationship civil; or indulge with the objective of expediting the "friendship process" so once they are forced to part ways, they have already built a solid foundation of what would eventually be a lasting friendship.

Tommy applied this reasoning to this particular friend group he had worked with in the short time he spent with them. It was odd, given that the majority of time was spent working, yet the nature of their likeness for one another had very little to do with it. He looked forward to reconnecting with them, and knew that the moment they were together again, it would be as if they were never apart.

Chance guided him through the bar, peering over the many heads to find their group. Tommy was too busy engrossed in the decorated interior, taking note of the gleaming lights suspended over an array of granite tabletops situated in the formation of a star.

"I don't remember this place."

"That's because it didn't exist last time you were here," Chance explained as they walked deeper into the bar. "It was opened up from a Member who retired a couple years ago…" he motioned to the tables. "…as you can see, he has a fascination for the American flag."

"I was thinking astronomy, but your guess makes more sense."

Chance pointed to some familiar faces nearby, waving eagerly and grabbing Tommy's attention.

"This is going to be so fun!" he exclaimed.

Reminiscing about the past may not have been one of his preferred pastimes, however this was different. It had been years since he had spoken to them in person. It was a cause for celebration, as he acknowledged the incredible feats each of them achieved since their time as lowly interns.

"If it isn't Nature Boy," one of them, Joseph, chirped when they approached the table.

"Here I am thinking that nickname wouldn't stick. Not due to the fact that I indeed love nature, but like you, come from a city where I can name ten things off the top of my head that are more important than trees and rocks," Tommy snickered coyly.

"Such as?"

"Correcting people who are wrong is the first that comes to mind," Tommy instantly shot back.

Joseph laughed as Kayla spoke up.

"We're more than happy to use any of the others," she gleamed.

"Hey, I could do the same here. Watch this," Tommy began, pointing at Joseph. "'Close-minded," he looked back at Kayla. "Hot, but needlessly flirty."

"Those are adjectives," Finley jumped in. "Joe's name for you was a pronoun. Get it right."

"Thanks Fin, I know I can always count on you to put me in my place whenever I try to leave it," Tommy acknowledged.

"Anytime buddy."

Chance got between them, knowing full well the banter would continue if he did nothing.

"Let's get some drinks. I'll get the first round," he insisted.

Tommy gave Chance a nod for his success in gathering enough of the gang to make it a notable night. The only thing that would have made it better was Tommy's secret hope of seeing one person in particular.

And in that moment – as if God answered his prayers – she appeared.

Her elegant formal wear, perfectly combed hair, and absence of rings on her hands took some quick adjustment for him to get used to. But it did not fool Tommy. Even with this matured appearance, he knew deep down was the beautiful, like-minded soul he once fell in love with.

"Zoe," he uttered, incapable of formulating a better greeting.

She returned a piercing stare as her mouth stretched from ear to ear.

"Tommy B."

Tommy's heart jumped. Lo and behold, the time had finally come when he was reunited with his soulmate.

They went back and forth for hours, exchanging stories of their time apart. He loved listening to Zoe's narration of her tumultuous journey. From her younger brother graduating high school; taking a job in wealth management at her dream company; traveling outside of the country for the first time; losing her beloved black beauty and her grandparents over the course of four months; disastrous dates with a range of eccentric men (excluding the gas-station working skater boy that somehow managed to keep her loyalty for over a year); her return to work after the pandemic. There were many lows that balanced the highs, of course, but her drive to persevere was a breath of fresh air for him.

After hours of drinking, the reunion naturally came to an end. Tommy led the group out of the bar, bidding farewell to each of his friends. From the corner of his eye, he saw Zoe waiting at the curb.

She held up her phone as he approached her.

"I'm just waiting for my cab to get here."

"Cool, I'll wait with you," Tommy offered. "The city can be a dangerous place, you know."

"I appreciate it," she laughed.

"Did you have a fun night?"

"I did! It's crazy, I live here too and rarely see those guys…"

"We're busy with life. Happens to the best of us."

"Talking about yourself now?"

"Both of us actually."

Zoe rolled her eyes playfully.

"How long are you here for?"

"Just for today, I fly out in the morning," Tommy replied. "I wish I could've had more time with you."

"Me too."

Tommy looked away for a moment, suddenly remembering Bennett's wedding.

"A couple of my best friends is getting married this fall," Tommy blurted, immediately choosing to double down and keep talking. "I want to bring you, as my date."

Zoe chuckled.

"That's very bold of you."

"How is that bold?"

"I don't know, maybe because the same night we reconnect after *years* of not speaking, you invite me to your best friend's wedding in a few months?"

"Fair point," Tommy replied, pursing his lips. "What can I say? I like you. And I always have, regardless of our lack of communication. I don't think any of that matters, if I'm being completely honest. What matters is that I'm here now," Tommy smiled. "Signed, sealed, and delivered. Just for you."

"Stevie Wonder. Very nice," Zoe remarked. "I understand you saying this back then, when we were together. But how can you say it now?"

"I presume you're quizzing me here, so I'll entertain it with my best, impromptu argument," Tommy began. "We are perfect for each other. When we first met, I knew that we both wanted two conflicting things."

"Go on."

"We wanted to be with each other, because we had acknowledged how much we mirrored one another from an intellectual level. Most importantly, we wanted to be free, and that was the only reason we parted ways."

"Well, our internship was also cut short, if you recall correctly."

"Come on, we both know that if either of us really wanted to, we would've followed the other back home," Tommy countered. "The reason why we didn't was because of—"

"—Freedom."

"Yes, freedom. You wanted to be free from any limitations so you could chase what you believed to be most important. And for both our cases, that was reaching the ambitions we put in place for ourselves. The *same* ambitions that drew us together in the first place. Once we have achieved our dreams, we would come back to each other."

"What makes you think I'm done enjoying my freedom?"

"You're still standing here talking to me, aren't you?"

Zoe could not help but smile.

"I knew you were different when I met you, Tom," she said. "And for the record: yes, I was quizzing you, and you passed with flying colors."

"I love you Zoe," Tommy said, taking her hand. "Come with me to the wedding."

Zoe kissed him before having been distracted at the sight of the cab approaching.

"This is me."

Tommy reluctantly opened the door for her after giving her one last kiss. Zoe entered the car and rolled down the window, looking at him. Tommy could see tell she was hiding her reciprocated excitement behind her retort. A glaringly poor effort in his opinion.

"Text me the details," she smiled.

Tommy waved at the cab driving away, which happens to be a perfect segue into the current time.

His ability to focus was like a pubescent boy's first time at an Italian beach. But the immense wonder was unfortunately mixed with his fear at the uncertainty of his feelings. It gave him a headache, causing him to overanalyze the source of his confusion.
He stopped himself from delving more into the matter, reflecting on the fact that his hope for being with Zoe again was left on a positive note. He checked his watch and proceeded to walk back to his hotel. Anticipation was useful, but not always.
For the time being, he would only focus on preparing for his trip back West.

xxxiv

For anyone who had ever gets anxious about the future, it may be helpful to consider Emma Keva as a case example for when it may be best to trust the universe.

Five years ago, she journeyed to the concrete jungle in pursuit of her passion. Through perseverance and charm, she subsequently willed the opportunity for an extension at the Ember House, graduated while simultaneously working parttime in admissions and start her photography career. Hunter's support came in handy when he happily offered to fund their trips across the globe. This went on for years, and she loved it.

Hunter would be busy with meetings all morning, giving her the desired time to soak in the city she missed so dearly. Most of the day was spent in the public library. She loved its concept, believing books were commonly overlooked – and often undervalued – in a society so adamant in resorting to their own prudence, rather than literally taking a page from another perspective that would likely expand their knowledge in virtually any predicament encountered.

By the end of the morning, she was downtown, treating herself to street meat across one of Seattle's renowned parks. Even the nature scene bested New York, where in comparison, defaulted to only having a single (yet enormous) park in the heart of Manhattan.

She thanked the attendant and turned back to throw away the saran paper when a familiar voice echoed from the curb.

"Emma!"

She was still adjusting to Jack's new look: his hair cut short, and dressed more formally, mirroring a stereotypical image of a Wall Street broker.

"What are you up to?"

"Just out and about. I'm waiting for Hunter to get off. The interview process is very time-consuming," Emma returned, awkwardly smiling. "Well, I guess I shouldn't have to tell you, since it's your firm he's trying to work for."

"Right," Jack echoed a similar awkwardness, straightening his posture. "Trust me, he'll get the job. We don't wine and dine just everyone, you know."

"Is that in reference for your prospective applicants, or everyone you take a liking into getting to know more?"

"Perhaps both," Jack responded, clearly understanding her insinuation to their aged relationship. He checked his watch, remembering he had a meeting at the office in an hour.

"I was going to grab a quite bite before heading back to work. Are you hungry?"

Emma looked down at the corndog she just bought before tossing it into the trash.

"I could eat."

"Great, plus you can tell me all about New York. I have all the time in the world," Jack checked his watch. "Well not really, but as much as we can cover in forty-five minutes."

Emma chuckled at the remembrance of his charm. And boy, did she tell him everything.

It was odd at first. The last time they had a lengthy exchange, she slammed him for his dishonesty. She believed in second chances, by principle, but refused to permit exceptions since then. Jack was the first person to earn the exception to her exception, which he not only broke but somehow managed to keep wanting more of him. For a reason she was incapable of determining herself, there was something about the kid that compelled her to still believe that he was worth more than he projected to be.

She assumed he would initiate the revisitation of their conversation years ago. But he did not. Instead, his temperament was kind, and controlled. He laughed at her jokes, and replied with friendly, platonic conversation and tact. It came off too genuine to be suspected as fake, leaving her to secretly wonder if the plausibility of an ulterior motive was truly nonexistent.

They finished their lunch when Jack checked his watch again and pulled out his wallet.

"Oh, I can—"

"Emma, I can pay the tab and *not* have it be a date," Jack chuckled, throwing a hundred on the table.

Emma blushed and thanked him before following him out of the café.

"I'm sure I'll see you around soon," he said. "You were invited to Bennett and Naylah's wedding, right?"

"Yeah, I remember getting an email about that. What's the deal there?"

"It's a whole thing. Long story short, they pushed it back and it's at a new venue," Jack paused. "Are you going?"

"Yeah, if we're not still here by then, I'll try to make sure we come back."

"Let me know. If you do come, we can take care of the flights."

"We?"

Jack gestured to his suit. "Company funds."

"Yes, of course," Emma swallowed. "It was nice seeing you Jack. And thank you for...well, everything."
"Good seeing you too Em."
She hugged him again and watched him leisure off.

*****

Jack thought he handled his encounter with Emma well. But the truth for him was beyond clear: he was lovesick. Again.
Emma was the same as he remembered her. Strong. Capable. Understanding. Free.
He fell in love with her because she is everything he is not. Independent, and free from pain and insecurity. Those who are helpless are naturally drawn to this out of love, but infatuation, and their own subliminal yearning for self-gratification. Leeching onto something so powerful can lead to a skewed scope of reality, clouded by confusion, frustration, and pride. Acceptance is always unprecedented because precedent first requires clarity. And clarity is always based on the perception of the individual.
He was with Molly, and frankly, he loved her. What they had was great, and Jack had accepted that he would take her into his autumn years. And yet, from the time he left her on the streetside, not a minute went by that he did not think of Emma.
He started daydreaming again, the same way he did when he first met her. Still lucid, but the image of Molly was becoming mixed with Emma's. He had improved over the years by controlling such thoughts, but in that moment, it had reverted. Could this truly be love? Was it always?
He missed everything about her. Her eyes, smile, and contagious laugh. Her figure, style, demeanor. Her confidence, ambitions, vision. Her kindness, humility, and warm, but bright dynamic with everyone she came across with. Her.
He hated having to go back to work after their lunch, trudging into his office and kicking off his shoes as he slumped on the couch situated across his desk.
"Heyoo," Tommy announced as he barged into Jack's office. "The reps from PanCorp are waiting for us in the conference room."
"I'll be there in a minute," Jack lamented, sighing deeply.
Tommy hesitated, noticing his friend's despair. He slid in the office and closed the door behind him.
"Are you okay? You seem a little off."

Jack's gaze drifted off the monitor and onto Tommy's concerned expression.
"I'm fine, Tom."
"You don't seem fine," Tommy objected, circling around the sofa until he was standing directly above him.
Jack sat upright, opening his arms.
"See?" he said, his eyes widening. "I'm good."
Tommy inspected Jack's expression.
"You should know by now that you are going to have to try harder than that if you want me to believe you," Tommy pressed, shaking his head.
Jack did not want to reveal his concerns to Tommy. Time and time again, the two have wrestled with his petty feelings over girls.
"Don't worry, I'll take care of it," Tommy reassured, taking one last look at his friend before closing the door.
Jack reluctantly left his office for the conference room but was distracted at the sight of his father through the windowed walls.
It was not uncommon for Wayne Douglas to already be in the office. Jack frequented his father's office regularly when he was younger. He remembered the oddity of the empty floors, minus the handful of overachievers desperate for recognition in one of the most cutthroat office environments in the Northwest.
He had no idea what to expect entering his father's office, noting his calmer than usual demeanor as he inspected the world pass from his panoramic view sixty floors overhead.
"Good morning, Jack," Wayne greeted.
"Hey, are you busy for non-work stuff?"
"Never for you, son. What's on your mind?"
"How did you know when you were in love?"
"Have we discussed this before?"
"Probably," Jack assented. "Doesn't hurt to remind me."
Wayne face creased as he contemplated Jack's question.
"I didn't," he replied flatly.
Jack squinted as if there was a layer of truth hidden behind his father's blank expression.
"What do you mean?"
"Love is not the same for everyone," Wayne began. "When I met your mother, I did not if I was in love or not. What I did know, however, was that I knew I could go another day without wishing she was with me, by my side."
Jack took in the words. Emma came back into mind. Whether his love for her was true or not, he wanted her to be by his side for the rest of his time.

But it was appearing it to not be an option. And it would kill him to have to be given a reminder if he was to move across the country and work with her boyfriend. Sure, she would still be in his life, but not the way he wanted.

"I don't want to go DC," Jack said to his father.

"Why not?"

"I appreciate the offer, Dad, but it's just not meant for me. Tommy will be fine handling things over there. Especially if we bring on Hunter."

"Well, I would say I'm disappointed," Wayne began. "But I am proud that you know what is important for you in your life. I'll talk to my team."

"Thanks dad."

"Anytime, Jack."

Jack started for the door when he was called back by his father.

"Did you see this yet?"

Jack spun around to see Wayne holding up the newspaper.

"I don't read the papers," Jack said jokingly. "What am I, sixty years old?"

"It's about your friend, Logan Berg."

He forbade the name from his vocabulary in recent years. Never did he expect to hear them spoken again, let alone from the lips of Wayne Douglas.

"I see," Jack replied, doing his best to hide any emotion. "How is he doing?"

"He's dead."

Shit. This is it, Jack thought. *This is the end.*

"Wait…what?"

"Logan Berg," he repeated. "I was told that he went missing a while back, but I assumed he chose to run away. Which I understand, given his unfortunate circumstances…it says here that his body was found just north of the city, near the bank…" his voice faltered. "Have you heard from him at all?"

"Uh, no, I haven't," Jack stuttered, trying his hardest to remain calm before his father.

"I'm sorry about Logan. I know he was a good friend of yours."

"It's all right," Jack droned, ignoring how quickly his hands clammed up in his pockets. "We drifted apart over the years."

"Oh, you did? I was unaware," Wayne paused. "I knew there was friction between you two after he moved back home from his trip—"

"You mean, when he went to juvie," Jack interjected.

"Yes," Wayne affirmed solemnly. "But despite the choices he made in his life, he was still your best friend."

"A lot has changed since then," Jack said. "He wasn't the person any of us thought he was."

"Explain."

"He was troubled, Dad. All he did was bring me down."

"Surely you don't believe that?"

"I do," Jack affirmed sternly.

Wayne sensed the subtle anger in his son's tone.

"Hmm, I am sorry to hear," Wayne murmured, bringing his finger to his mouth to reflect as he looked out the window, overseeing the subtle movement of the city fifty floors below.

"I always thought he was a good kid, you know. Egregiously misunderstood, but still good at heart. I did what I could to help him."

Jack's brows furrowed; his face flushed as he shot his father with a quizzical expression.

"What do you mean when you said that you *helped* him?"

Wayne took a deep breath.

"I never told you how I've come to found this company," he started. "How I became who I am today."

"Yeah you have," Jack replied, sighing. "You came up with the idea in college with your roommate. And then after your graduated and had the business up and running for a few years, he found a girl and moved away to start a family."

"Yes, that is partially true," Wayne noted. "But there was a lot that your mother and I shielded from you, to which I want to apologize for doing so *now* before I tell you what actually happened."

Jack's eyes widened, utterly clueless as to where his father was going with this.

"Your mother and I were overjoyed when we had you. At the time, I knew that having a child would force us to adapt in more ways than one. She wanted what every good mother wanted for her child: a peaceful, safe environment to raise you. We were well prepared, you see, so such a request should never have been a problem."

"And yes, at this time, it was shortly after we graduated. Your mother's parents hated me in the beginning. They said I was too ambitious, and it would ultimately interfere with my commitment to having a wife, and a family. But Anita – God bless her – she believed in me, and supported me through everything. She convinced her parents to cover my costs to get this company started. More than half of her inheritance. I felt guilty for the longest time, Jack, because I did not deserve it. And I hated the fact that the person I loved the most felt the need to relinquish her dreams for my benefit. I never felt love like that before, and to this day, for her to unconditionally celebrate my achievements like they are her own…I prayed that more of her traits carry into you.

"My roommate, Wes, he was a good man. I met him through your mother. They actually grew up together and dated for a little bit in high school."

"Seriously?"

"Yes, and before you ask: no, nothing happened between them. I trusted him like he was my brother. He was genuinely a good man…but, he had flaws, like all of us. During college, he met another girl. They were in love for a couple years and broke up by the time we graduated. The heartbreak changed him, Jack, and for the worse. He developed a drinking problem, took pills, would disappear for days at a time…and I'm sure it affected life at home with his wife. It troubled me as a friend, but also as his business partner. There were many times I was tempted to push him out, because his reputation was damaging to our business, and to my family."

"What happened?"

"It was like this for years. Our company was making great strides. He offered to travel east to source investments from connections he had. The next time I saw or heard from him was about the time you were graduating high school. I read in the papers that he was murdered outside of the hotel he stayed in in New York. Drug violence."

"I'm sorry, Dad. I had no idea."

"No, I'm sorry," Wayne apologized, continuing. "Because the reason I brought this up, is because that same day, I received a call from his wife, concerned for her son who had been getting into trouble a lot. He was the same age as you. I felt guilty, because I saw the signs. I knew my best friend was in trouble, and I disregarded it, because I valued myself and my family more. And as a result, my best friend was killed, and a child was fatherless.

"The son's mother was a housewife and relied solely on my friend to support them financially. So, I offered to help raise him in that regard."

"What are you saying, that you funded this kid's life?"

"Essentially," Wayne confirmed. At first, I wanted to take him into the family, but your mother and I agreed that it would likely make things more complicated for you. So instead, I supported him from a distance. I opened a trust and hired an attorney to monitor the child's life. I had to make sure that he would live a happy life because of my negligence for his father's wellbeing. I gave him the freedom we are all entitled to, but he still struggled. He was involved with an unpleasant crowd and was on the verge of expulsion; and I was there to bail him from the legal trouble he was constantly getting into. Because I made a promise to his mother."

As the words left his father's mouth, Jack had finally understood the final destination of the conversation.

"Your partner was Logan's dad," Jack mumbled to himself.

"Yes."

It all started to make sense. Going over to Logan's house when they were kids, and always seeing him home alone; the absence of details behind all of his frequent "trips" or "camps" that would take him out of the picture for weeks or months at a time. Even his surprising appearance at the same college, when he knew that he would have had no chance of acceptance had it not been for a longshot miracle.

Alas, it was Wayne Douglas. The hidden hero of a child's trialed success.

"I don't understand, Dad. Why are you telling me this now?"

"It was a mistake on my part. I was not much older than you are now, Jack. Please understand, that I truly believed keeping this private would be best for all of us."

"It sounds like you were embarrassed if anyone found out of your fuckup," Jack tested. "You knew what kind of person he was going to become because you were the one who put him on that path…" Jack faltered off, overwhelmed in confusion. "And you kept us close. Literally, right next door growing up. You sent him to the same school as I did. You knew the shit he was getting into when we were younger, and you still kept us close. Why?"

"Because I need you to understand the importance of never giving up on the people you love and trust. You were a child at the time. There was nothing you could have done to help him, but I did."

Jack sat back in his chair, still in disbelief.

"Again, I am sorry for not telling you," Wayne reiterated. "But in regard to Logan, I did what I thought was right, and I do not regret it."

"No, I'm sorry," Jack finally said, doing everything in his power to let his empathy table the frustration. "I love you for doing what you thought was right…" he paused. "But I have to ask: you could have helped Logan with *everything* in his life, but why did you keep him so close to mine?"

Wayne interlocked his fingers and drew a deepening sigh.

"In this world, there are two types of men: weak, and strong," he said. "The weak man cowers in the face of uncertainty, whereas the strong man charges courageously into the unknown."

"And then there is the smart man," Jack said, memorizing the saying preached to him since he was a child. "The smart man is both weak and strong, for he knows when to yield, and when to stand firm."

Wayne smirked.

"The smart man, unlike the weak and strong men, is the only one who understands what it means to carry the weight of both sides of his actions. And it is something that only he can carry alone."

Jack nodded, smiling. "I understand, Dad."

"I was younger than you are now when Harry told me that."

"Like father, like son, apparently."

"Apparently so."

Jack controlled his feelings; but even so, he could not believe what he was hearing. For the better part of his life, he had resented Logan for reasons he believed to be just. Considering him to be "good at heart" as his dad put was the last way he would describe his perception of his longtime rival.

Jack trusted no one more than Wayne Douglas. Coupled with the unconscious bias of being his son, he regarded his father as having knowledge on par with other brilliant minds. Even from the sense of understanding people, Jack considered him to be the epitome of an empath.

All said, he found it nearly impossible to accept what Wayne was saying now. He wished he had known of his father's perception of Logan before his death. Maybe, just maybe, it could have ended differently.

Jack darted out of his Wayne's office and to the elevator, maintaining his composure until the doors closed before suddenly bending over to catch his breath.

Holy fuck, he thought, catching his breath through the deep, prolonged gasps he emitted as he reached his floor. He overhead the ding from the elevator, prompting him to straighten up and fake a smile as he leisurely strode across the floor. On the way to his office, he spotted Tommy returning to his desk. Jack slowed his pace and waved his hands to Tommy, who after a few moments, noticed the commotion outside his glass room and acknowledged his friend with a subtle nod.

My office, Jack silently mouthed, continuing to his office. He temporarily forgot that there were wheels on the bottom of his desk chair, slumping on the cushion and letting out a mute shriek as he rolled back into the wall behind him.

I need to calm down, he said to himself, distracting his mind with every other thought other than the conversation with Wayne in fear that he was risking a panic attack right there in the office.

He buried his head in his hands, demanding his pulsating heart to simmer.

Jack overheard the playful tone in Tommy's voice as he entered his office.

"Is this how it's going to be, you ordering me into your office when you need something done?"

Jack sat up, having no effort in displaying his confused expression.

"What's going on?" Tommy asked, matching Jack's mood.

"My dad asked about Logan," he revealed, trembling in his seat.

Tommy managed a fixed expression.

"So?"

"What if someone starts digging in about what happened?"

"That won't happen."

Jack straightened up in his chair, taking a deep breath.

"How did the PanCorp meeting go?"

"Not bad, considering the one person they needed to speak to was unavailable," Tommy shrugged. "Good thing they're headquartered a block away. I'll make sure to schedule a time for later this week."

"Sounds good."

Jack waited until Tommy left his office before swiveling around to face the window. Maybe Tommy was right. The chance of someone going out of their way to investigate Logan's whereabouts were small, and even if they did, it would take someone with knowledge of their history to even consider them as potential suspects.

*****

Across town, Harmony was busying away in an effort to spend underbudget as she admired how well a mannequin wore a sparkling red dress.

I don't need this, she said to Temptation, who had a clear one-up at that moment. It did not bother Harmony, as they had recently settled on a sufficient thinking relationship. Mundane life and its incessant demands had dominated Harmony's last few years, and as a result, she forced herself to cut off any controllable elements that only dragged her down.

A positive note is that she had found more peace in her life. The last instance of severe overwhelm was around the time when Isaac died. She forced many adjustments: with her family, Logan, and her Seattle friends. On the latter, she stopped keeping a pulse on the endless drama the group always appeared to fabricate. Perhaps Logan ghosting her was the final straw…she never quite pondered too deeply on that matter. What she did know, was that the anxiety she experienced was not worth enduring, especially when it was on people who clearly did not care as much about her as she did them.

Emma was the only one who remained close, and that was partially a reason why she changed her mind to attend Bennett and Naylah's wedding. The last time she spoke to her at length was the same day she learned of Isaac's death. Part of her wished that she brought it up on their call, but Emma *did* sound stressed with having to sit through an evening with her boyfriend's parents. She was pleased to learn that they had remained together over the years, and was more excited at the chance to reconnect with her in a few short months. As for Logan, her wish to hear from him came and went. It was difficult for her to accept that he was just another chapter in her life, especially after all they had been through under such a short span. But like with everything in life, things heal over time.

She scoffed at the price tag on the dress and turned around, accidentally bumping into a man passing by.

"I'm sorry!" she shrieked.

"You're okay, that was all me," the man politely responded. "You'd be surprised how many times this happens to me. I'm such a clutz."

"Better than being an addict," Harmony started, quickly realizing how bad that sounded. "To shopping!"

The man grinned, allowing her to notice how the particular cuteness in his smile.

He looked over to the dress behind the glass.

"That dress looks familiar," he murmured.

"Oh, were you thinking about getting it for yourself?" Harmony teased.

"Very funny," the man chuckled. "I'm pretty I know a boutique around has this exact dress. And for much cheaper."

"No way?"

"Yeah, you'll just go a few blocks in that direction."

"Can you show me?" Harmony asked abruptly. Usually, she'd be smarter than to trust a random person she met on the corner. But it was midday, with many people around, and she was armed with her bear spray.

Plus, there was something about this man that intrigued her. Not necessarily in a romantic sense, but more juvenile; almost as if he was easily threatened. The man hesitated at her question, as if she touched on a sensitive topic.

"Um, yeah, I can do that," he said. "I guess it would take ten minutes out of my day…are you sure?"

"I am," Harmony insisted, reaching out to shake his hand. "I'm Harmony, by the way."

"Ryder," he replied.

Ryder took her to the boutique, where he motioned to the identical dress on display.

"This is the same one, right?"

"Looks like it," Harmony confirmed, checking the price label at the bottom of the case. "And you are correct: it is *far* cheaper."

"Glad I could help."

"Thank you! I never would have thought about coming to this area for something like this."

"Is there something wrong with this area?"

Harmony caught herself, taking a step back.

"Oh no! I didn't mean it like that—"

"It's okay, I was just messing with you," Ryder retorted. "And I completely understand. I reckon this dress was secondhand, but they play it off like it's new. They wouldn't be the only store that does that here."

"I take it you're from here?"

"Born and raised," Ryder revealed, pointing across the street. "Right there, actually."

Harmony followed his direction to see an oddly familiar apartment complex. It appeared abandoned, with a rusty fence bordering it away from the mundane society that chose to disregard its existence.

Harmony frowned momentarily as she observed the building.

"You said your name is Ryder?"

"Yeah," he replied, his eyes on the complex. I don't live there anymore. Sometimes I miss it though. It was home for me and a lot of people who were just trying to find their way in life.

Harmony gasped, having connected the reason for its familiarity.

"This is going to be an absolutely crazy question, but by chance, do you know someone named Logan?"

Ryder's brows raised.

"Logan Berg?"

"Oh my god, this is insane," Harmony gasped. "What a small world."

"Yeah, I knew Logan well. We went way back…" he turned back to the complex before facing Harmony again. "You thought of Logan when I showed you…wait I'm sorry, how do you know him?"

"We used to talk years ago," Harmony explained. "That was, until he ghosted me randomly."

"He *ghosted* you?"

Harmony noticed him growing uncomfortable. Yeah, but it made sense. We were very different people. I don't even live in the city, but we had mutual friends; that's how I first met him…" she paused. "I guess the 'mutual friends' weren't so fond of him when he first got together, but oh well. Old history."

Ryder pursed his lips, choosing his words carefully.

"How long ago was this?"

"Like I said, it's been a few years. I think four, to be exact."

Ryder's eyes widened as he drew closer to her.

"Are you being serious right now?" he asked, his voice much lower now.

Harmony was confused by his sudden demeanor.

"What's wrong?"

Ryder glanced to his left, then right. He circled around her so his back was to the boutique, and subtly motioned for her to come closer.

"I haven't heard from him around the same time," he began, keeping his voice to a whisper. "Next time I even hear his name was this morning, when I read that they found his body in the ocean in the morning. It's all over the news."

"What are you talking about?"

"Look, I'm telling you. They haven't done an autopsy yet, but I know for a fact that it was him. They're already suspecting it was foul play, but I know there was. He was murdered."

"You're freaking me out right now."

"I'm sorry, I don't mean to," Ryder apologized, giving her space. "But the fact that we both have not heard from him at the same time, and then to find him not only dead, but washed up on a shore outside of the city? Is that not a little coincidental?"

"Maybe," Harmony echoed. "How do you know Logan?"

"Let's just say we didn't meet under positive circumstances," Ryder said. "We were both very lost, doing stupid shit. But he cleaned up his act. Not long before that, I ran into him again and brought him back here to meet our old gang. I was shocked when he told me he was in college. I really thought he turned his life around."

Harmony knew little about Logan's past life. The most that he was willing to share anyway.

"Do you know anyone who would have done this?"

"No idea. We never had a falling out or anything. It just fizzled out after he got out of juvie. And then after we re-connected, it was the simple

pleasantries as you do with old friends—" he paused. "—but the last time I saw him, he was talking about some trouble that he had gotten in to. He asked me for help to get out of the city."
Harmony was beginning to understand what type of person Ryder was; specifically, why Logan would turn to him for help in a dismal situation.
"What kind of trouble?"
"He just said he fucked up," Ryder said, pondering about the question. "He also mentioned a name…Isaac, I think it was."
"*Issac?*"
"Yeah, that's all I know."
Harmony stopped herself from divulging.
"Thank you for telling me," she took a breath.
"You seem like you really cared about him."
"I think I loved him."
Ryder nodded sympathetically.
"I'm always here if you want to talk about it," Ryder consoled. "But I hoped this brings you some closure. It definitely did for me."
He was taken aback when she hugged him.
"Thank you, Ryder."
Ryder smiled again and started inching back.
"You're welcome. Here, I'll give you my number," he said. "Maybe we can get a coffee sometime."
"I'd love that," Harmony said, taking out her phone.
"Stay out of trouble, okay?" he said playfully, and walked away.
There were questions that had to be asked.
And Harmony knew exactly who to direct them to.

XXXV

The probability of two people remaining in love is never definite. But the marriage of Bennett and Naylah was always believed to be an inevitable eventuality, and exception, to Jack. They were perfect for each other, and the day would come that he and his best friends would stand there beside him as they witnessed their ceremonial promises of eternal love.

And speaking of love, it is rare for expectations to accurately come to fruition. Yet it was materializing right before Jack's eyes: Emma specifically, was reintroduced in his life, and despite his doubt, they picked up right where they left off…at least from the perspective of friends, anyway. Circumstances change, yes – admittedly more than Jack wished for – but he had also changed. All former judgements ceased to exist for so long that even if they were to resurface, his confidence in combating it rationally was certain. It was meant to be different this time around. Jack could feel it in his heart.

The party was already underway when he and Molly arrived. It was oddly overwhelming to see so many familiar faces. Neighbors, friends from grade school and college; and of course, the extended family meandering the field like a swarm of bees. Staged in the center was a mini symphony, its string section melodizing a charmful tune that caused singing birds to circulate in splendor delight. Everyone dressed uniquely different from each other yet maintained an ocean-inspired color scheme enforced by Naylah's OCD.

The venue was entirely outdoors, overlooking western Seattle. At the edge of the cliff was a small chapel, its rustic origins protruding despite thorough renovations to keep it erected. There were no clouds or haze that afternoon, permitting a snow-capped Mount Rainier to bolster prominently across the bay.

"Jack!" came Tommy, accompanied by a beautiful woman Jack had not seen before. "There is someone I want you to meet."

"So this must be the one who got away," Jack greeted, motioning to his girlfriend. "This is Molly."

Zoe and Molly and got into it instantly as Tommy wrapped his arm around Jack.

"I love when worlds collide," he muttered. "Isn't she beautiful?"

"She certainly is. I can't believe I'm finally meeting your perfect match.

"Things take time. I always knew she was worth the wait."
Jack nodded silently, wishing he felt the same for his own counterpart.
"We'll be right back!" Zoe told them before pacing off with Molly toward the snack spread.
"Seems like they're hitting it off better than we did when we first met…"
Tommy paused. "I would pay to see it."
"Inappropriate, Tom."
"Don't act like you weren't thinking it."
"Why would I be thinking it?"
"Because it's hot."
"Take it easy!" Jack started, but eventually shrugged. "Okay fine, it sounds kinda nice."
Kevin joined them "Look at your pretty ladies!"
"Look at you!" Jack retorted, patting his perfectly tailored suit. "You clean up well brother."
"Thanks, I had to pay extra to remove the brand labels."
"Why would you do that? Now no one will know what it is."
"Exactly. Also, guess what?"
"You're gay?" Tommy chuckled.
"Very funny — remember when I told you a couple months ago that my grandma is moving back to London? Well, I'll be joining her there."
Jack shook his head, confused.
"Wait, you're *leaving*?"
"That's right! At least for a couple months, but we'll see what happens. My boss agreed that I can take a sabbatical, so I may as well get some traveling in."
"That's awesome Kev…" Tommy started. "But this is so sudden. I mean, what's the rush? Things are just beginning to change for the better here."
"I'm not sure I follow," Kevin put a finger to his mouth. "Last I checked, Bennett is getting married. Jack will be soon—" he placed his hand on Jack's shoulder when he noticed his eyes widen "—and you're leaving for DC! If all my boys are starting new chapters, it only makes sense for me to do the same."
"Damn, if that isn't the fairest argument you've given," Tommy mused.
"Let's make sure to have a going-away dinner or something."

"Dinner to celebrate," Jack groused. "We really *are* getting older."

His eyes carried past Kevin's shoulder, where he spotted HG standing amidst a group of former classmates. Jack waited until she looked in his direction to wave.

HG returned a look of disgust and returned to her conversation.

It confused Jack, but before he could think about addressing it, he was interrupted by Zoe's voice.

"Oh my god, look at your dress!" she exclaimed.

The boys spun around to see Emma and Hunter circling with Molly and Zoe.

"And the worlds continue to collide," Tommy whispered to Jack.

Jack sighed and reluctantly followed Tommy and Kevin into the huddle.

"You must be Molly," Emma began, shaking her hand. "I'm Emma."

"Wow, you're very pretty!" Molly cheered rather condescendingly, turning to Jack. "Better not cheat on me with this one, huh?"

Jack let out an uneasy laugh, wrapping his arm around Molly's waist and looking at Emma's perplexed gaze. "She's a funny one."

Tommy turned to Hunter.

"Today is all about our friends, but I'd be remiss if I didn't 'informally' congratulate you on getting the position."

"Thanks man," Hunter replied, annoying Jack slightly at the idea of his best friend becoming chummy with him.

"You two are working together?" Molly asked.

"You know that Mols," Jack whispered to her. "We talked about it, remember?"

Hunter, oblivious to Jack's comment, replied happily.

"That's right! We leave for DC in a couple weeks," he added, glancing at Emma beside him. "We'll have to throw a party of some sort before we go though. Of course, you're all invited."

"*Another* party!" Kevin cut in, inspecting Hunter. "Do you like to travel?"

"I do," Hunter affirmed, reaching out to shake Kevin's hand. "I'm Hunter, by the way."

"Oh I know who you are, *trust me*."

"Um, okay," Hunter chuckled, glancing at his watch. "We should probably find our seats," he said to Emma before turning back to the group. "It was nice seeing you all again."

"We'll come with you," Tommy initiated, gently taking Zoe's hand and turning to Kevin. "Come sit with us."

"So I can fifth wheel? No thank you," Kevin snapped, pointing toward the chapel. "I'll be joining the single moms over there."

Molly waited until everyone strolled off before focusing on Jack.

"Who is she to you again?"

"Which one?"

"Don't play with me," she tested. "Emma. Who else?"

"A good friend of mine. We dated for a bit." Jack said, his smile faint. Molly turned back to watch their friends join the crowd as they all made their way toward the chapel.

"It was more than that, wasn't it?" Molly pressed.

What is it with girls and their ability to read my mind, Jack thought.

"Yes," he admitted. "I was in love with her."

Molly took it better than he expected, shrugging it off.

"Gold star for knowing when someone isn't right for you," she relented disdainfully, checking her phone. "Oh! Jasmine is having a movie night tonight with the girls. Do you care if I don't make the reception?"

"Not at all. You should go," Jack agreed, secretly relieved that he did not need to deal with her for long.

They found their seats beside Tommy, who gave Jack a quizzical look by the tension he felt emitting off them.

Later, Jack mouthed.

It was Harmony's first time stag at a wedding. Not a fun scenario when all her friends had dates. She was surprised to receive an invite in the first place, but at the same time, there were a *lot* of people she never imagined would make the cut; like their high school football coach, who – to attend the wedding for a former student who never played the sport – struck her as odd. In retrospect, she was relieved not to bring a plus one. Doing so certainly would have distracted her from the true motive for coming. She was there to investigate. Before inevitably confronting Jack and Tommy about Logan, Harmony knew that she first had to be armed with the facts. Additionally, if the truth about her friends was darker than she hoped, making it a public spectacle seemed more fitting, particularly because it would be the last place the boys would expect to be called out on something they may, or may not be keeping secret. The bad news, was that there was no good time to confront them. They were with their girlfriends (a surprise to see in Tommy's case), and even appeared on good terms with Emma and her boyfriend.

She picked a seat near the back of the chapel, avoiding eye contact as she watched Kevin, Tommy, and his girlfriend walk past her toward the front pew.

"Are these seats taken?" Emma asked.

Harmony jumped out of the pew and embraced her.

"I'm so happy to see you! How have you been?"

"Oh just peachy," she replied, motioning to her boyfriend beside her. "Hunter, this is *literally* one of my best friends, Harmony."

"Nice to meet you," he smiled, shaking her hand. He subtly pointed toward Tommy and Kevin in front. "More childhood friends, I presume?"

"Something like that," Harmony affirmed, making room for them to sit. Hunter glanced at his phone as Emma sat beside Harmony.

"Sorry, it's my mom. I have to step out for a minute," he said to them. "I'll leave you two to catch up."

Emma gave him a heartfelt smile and focused back on Harmony.

"He's great," she assented.

"I'm sure he is," Harmony agreed sincerely. "He's hot too."

"*Right?*"

Harmony giggled, going on. "How have you been, being back here? Do you miss it at all?"

"Yes and no," Emma admitted. "Seeing the family has been great, but you know how there's just some other things that come with visiting home that you wish you wouldn't have to deal with."

"I hear that, only in my case, it's every time I come here."

"What about you? Are you still in touch with that guy you were talking to after Aiden?"

Harmony shook her head.

"Nah, a lot has happened since then," Harmony disregarded. "Also, since I never told you, it was Logan."

Harmony hoped her casual name drop would lead to a casual reaction. Emma Keva did not catch it accordingly.

"*Logan Berg?*" she gasped. "No way, are you serious?"

"Hope I wasn't overstepping or anything."

Emma laughed.

"Oh my god Harmony, no, not at all. I'm just shocked that you two ended up talking in general. I remember introducing you two all those years ago, but like, it never occurred to me that he'd become more than that."

"We didn't, until we kinda did. It's a long story, I'll tell you about it another time. It was *very* short-lived."

"Did he ghost you like he did to me at prom?" Emma chuckled. "I swear, he was always a gentle soul. I wonder what he's up to nowadays."

Harmony raised a brow.

"You didn't hear? He died a while back."

Emma frowned, horrified at the news.

"What do you mean he died?"

"*Murdered,* actually," Harmony corrected herself. "I just learned myself recently when I ran into one of his friends."

"Murdered," Emma repeated, still in shock. "When did this happen?"

"Four years ago."

Emma glanced past Harmony to see Jack and Molly entering the chapel.

"That was the same time Isaac died," Emma recounted. "Poor Jack, having to lose two of his best friends so close to each other. I regret not reaching out after he told me."

Harmony's brows furrowed.

"Wait, Jack told you about Isaac?"

"Yeah, it was the same night you called me when I met Hunter's parents…" Emma revealed. "I figured that was what you wanted to talk about when you called. By the way, sorry for not following up with you about that."

Harmony nodded slowly, recalling Ryder's narrative about Logan being in trouble.

"Must be a crazy coincidence. And for the record, I was just calling to check up." Harmony clarified, clever enough to know that keeping Emma at bay from the truth would only protect her from the truth.

There were dots, and lines were starting to draw themselves. If Harmony's suspicions were right, this revelation would become more sinister than she ever imagined.

"Anyways…sorry for dropping all this on you right now." Harmony added.

"Don't apologize. Thank you for telling me," Emma said. "Logan and Isaac were both amazing guys."

"Yeah, they were."

Hunter returned to the pew and sat beside Emma.

"I'm back," he addressed, looking at Harmony. "Did you give Emma enough time to shit on me? I promise I don't sweat as much as she claims.

Emma eyed Harmony, who gave a sheepish laugh.

"Only good things," Harmony affirmed, glancing at Emma once Hunter looked away.

Jack was relieved when he watched Molly storm off after the ceremony, his eyes settling on Tommy, who gave a perplexed frown.

Embarrassed, Jack retreated outside from the reception, breathing in the crisp air that wafted across his face as he trailed to the end of the compound. He sheltered himself under a massive willow tree, picking incessantly at the trimmed lawn as gazed back at the illuminated tent across the field.

He could not help but feel selfish while he sat there overhearing the indistinct cheers of the reception. Bennett had just gotten married, but rather than take the day to celebrate his friend's joyous occasion, he still found himself submerged in his own wave of misery.

Jack wept, proceeding to droop his head between his knees and tightening his eyelids to prevent any tears from escaping.

A few minutes passed before he heard footsteps approaching him.

"Something must have went down with Molly," came Tommy's voice. "I'd ask if you two were okay, but I think we both know the answer…"

Jack kept his face down.

"I told her about Emma," he said faintly.

"What about Emma?"

"That I loved her."

"I see; how did she take it?"

"Very well…like *incredibly* well," Jack replied. "She's heading out to meet up with her friends for some 'girls' night'".

"Hmm, wildly inappropriate of her to skip the rest of the reception when it just started, but okay."

Tommy's concern grew upon noticing Jack's lack of reaction to his joke.

"Are you sure that's all on your mind?"

Jack lifted his head to look at Tommy's concerned expression.

"I'm still in love with her, Tom."

Tommy slowly nodded, processing Jack's revelation.

"You still love her, after all these years?"

Jack subtly nodded through his sniffles.

Tommy squatted beside Jack, his gaze drifting at the tent ahead of them. He was frankly stunned at Jack's miserable state, as he could not recall the last time he had seen him this down in the dumps after going back to Molly.

"I don't know what is wrong with me. Why do I feel this way?"

"Because it sucks when we love someone who doesn't love us back," Tommy answered, shaking his head. "I shouldn't have told you to forget about her."

"What?"

"It wasn't my place to say it, and I'm sorry."

"Give me a break Tom," Jack chuckled. "This was my choice, not yours."

"Still…I can't help but feel responsible for swaying your decision."

"Your intentions were where they needed to be," Jack assured. "'Live with no regrets:' isn't that what you always say?"

"I didn't actually coin the phrase myself," Tommy clarified. "But yeah." Jack went on.

"I did not know how I felt myself until I saw her again at the airport. Who would have thought that I'd still be hung up over her after all this time? I mean, so much has happened since we broke up. We have been through *so much,* Tommy…so why do I still feel like she belongs with me?"

Tommy was slow to respond as she pondered Jack's question.

"You never got closure," he guessed.

"I never got closure," Jack repeated, letting the words sink in.

It made sense.

"Fuck, I need to get my mind off of this."

"What are you doing later?"

"Nothing. Molly is having a girls' night, remember?"

"Well she shouldn't be the only having fun," Tommy retorted. "What do you say we have a boys' night, just like the good old days? I'm down to leave right now frankly."

"What about Zoe?"

"She left already, has some emergency meeting or something with one of her clients. I'll see her later tonight." he waved off. "Money shit. You know how it is."

"I don't…but sure," Jack chuckled. "I'm gonna stick around here to say goodbye to the couple and then I'll meet you back at your place?"
"Thank god you suggested that, because I already bid them adieu, and I did not want to go back in there and face all my exes again."
"Okay Tom. You still keep your spare key in the same place?"
"Absolutely. I'll see you soon."

*****

He swelled with curiosity at the sight of an oddly familiar car parked outside of Tommy's house. It was soon confirmed, when he unmistakenly overheard her voice wailing incoherently from behind the door.
Jack entered slowly, first meeting HG's eyes. She was standing in the center of the living area, facing a slouched Tommy on the sofa.
"Hey HG," Jack hesitated.
"You seem nervous."
"No, I just wasn't expecting you to be here," he admitted. "Why didn't you call?"
"So apparently you're both on the same page," she said, turning back at Tommy.
Tommy rose from the sofa and walked past her and toward Jack, shooting him a cautious glare without her knowing.
"HG is freaking out about some stuff," he muttered dismissively.
"What about?"
HG rubbed her temple and sat down.
"Stay away from me," she warned when he tried to sit beside her.
"What's going on HG?"
"I was with Logan. We were together. Did you know?"
Jack froze. He did not expect that name to come out of her mouth. He did, however, have an accurate guess on what was to follow.
"This is news to me," Tommy commented, still relaxed.
"A couple months ago, I ran into this guy who told me that Logan had died years ago. I won't get into the details—"
"No please do!" Tommy contested arrogantly.
"—Apparently, Logan came to this friend asking to get out of the city. Said that he was in trouble. It was the same week that Isaac died."

"You don't need to remind me about 'Saac," Jack said. "I'll never forget about losing one of my best friends."

"That's interesting," Harmony replied with a stony glare. "Because I spoke to Emma today, and she said that you were the one who told her that Isaac died."

"Yeah, that's right."

"Interestingly enough, when I was talking to Logan's friend, he told me Logan was trying to leave the city because he had gotten himself in trouble. He even mentioned Isaac's name," Harmony went on. "This also happened to be the same night I did not hear back from Logan after we made plans to see each other."

Jack froze. He knew if he looked at Tommy that HG's suspicions would grow. He needed to keep it together.

"How did you know Isaac died that night? Were you with him?"

"We both were," Tommy confirmed.

"And so was Logan," Harmony asserted.

"I don't know what makes you think that?"

"This is ridiculous," Tommy interjected Jack. "Where are you going with this, Harm?"

"Look, let's grow the fuck up here. I know what you two did. And I am giving you the chance now to tell me the truth."

Jack met Tommy's discerning glare.

"I don't know what you're talking about," Jack relented.

"Logan," HG stated. "You killed him."

Dead silence.

"What the fuck are you saying? Do you hear how crazy you sound?" Tommy stepped in.

"I'm not crazy," Harmony contested. "I put it all together. After all these years, I thought he just ghosted me. But then after what Ryder told me—"

"Ryder, Logan's friend," Tommy pointed out. "Probably another lowlife drug addict that shouldn't be trusted."

"Of course you would say that," Harmony shouted at Tommy. "You were the one who pushed him out in the first place. You're the reason he was arrested that night—" she looked at Jack. "You know about what happened, don't you?"

"Harmony, you need to relax. Please," Jack said gently. "There is a lot that you don't know."

"I know *everything*," she shot back. "Before he died, he told me all about your falling out with him; he told me about when it started; and he told me that it was all Tommy's fault as to why you stopped being friends with him."

"And because of an isolated night when we were kids, you seriously think that a decade later, we would kill him?" Tommy tested.

"Yes, especially since he was the one who killed Isaac!"

Jack's nose scrunched in reaction to her comment, forcing himself to accept that Harmony knew the secret he had feared anyone ever finding out.

Realizing that Jack was nearing a loss, Tommy chose to jump in.

"All of that is irrelevant," he said. "You made a mistake being with him to begin with. He's a pathological liar, and a dangerous person."

"So as a result you kill him?"

"We didn't kill him Harmony," Jack defended, bringing his hands to his chest. "Look at us: do you *seriously* think that we're capable of doing something like that."

HG paused, controlling her breath.

"Honestly, no Jack. I know that you aren't," she faced Tommy. "*You*, now that's another story. I bet it was your idea."

Tommy shook his head, growing impatient at her hysterical line of questioning.

"I think it's time for you to go and reflect on how crazy you sound right now." "I know what you're doing. You're trying to insult my intelligence. Well I promise you I'm not crazy, and I know exactly where my head is. You can't keep this a secret forever." Tommy shrugged, becoming cockier in his demeanor.

"You can keep interrogating us, but it's not true. And *even* if it was – how do you explain the fact that we are in no way tied to the incident? And that there is absolutely no evidence backing up what you are accusing us, other than your own delusion and the words from some random guy who knew him? For all we know, he was just another druggie that crossed paths with him. You know that Logan was a drug dealer right?"

"Discredit him all you want," HG said. "I knew him better than you ever did. And whether you want to admit it or not, I know the two of you just well," she crossed her arms, now more confident. "You're misunderstanding this conversation. I'm not here to interrogate you; I am here to enlighten you."

"Meaning?" Jack asked.

"Meaning," HG countered. "That I am giving you the chance to come forth and turn yourself in."

"You're crazy."

"Fuck you, stop calling me crazy!" HG screamed. "I promise I will do whatever it takes to make sure you get what you deserve for this."

Tommy slowly rose from the chair.

"Have you forgotten who I am – who *we* are, for that matter?"

HG gulped, keeping her demeanor stern.

"No, I haven't," she admitted. "And I may not know the details, but I *do* know that this had to be more you than anyone else. You are a horrible influence on Jack and all your other friends, and that they would take my side if you tried anything."

"Tried anything? Jesus HG, Jack just said that we're incapable of killing someone, and you're still behaving under the assumption that we did it. What do you expect us to do here?"

"No, I said that *Jack* was incapable of killing Logan. Not you," she cautioned. "You have had Jack under your finger since you were kids. You love controlling people, especially those you care about. If you were never in the picture, not only would Logan still be alive today, but I'm sure he would be Jack's best friend. And I think you're scared for something like that happening."

Jack listened intently to Harmony. It made him think about how he felt when he saw Tommy speaking with Hunter earlier that day. Was it possible that someone like Tommy – riddled with individualism and a tinge of nihilistic undertones – be capable of caring so much about others, that he would be so manipulative?

"And what about you?" she shot at Tommy? "Does your girlfriend know who you *actually* are? I'm sure she'd be interested to find out."

"Careful now," Tommy tested, his expression growing darker.

"I'm not scared of you Tom," she assented. "That was Logan's mistake for falling for your stupid threats on ruining his life."

Reconnecting with Zoe forced Tommy to come to the realization of his toxicity toward not only his own relationships, but those he cared for. He had vowed to never serve as the catalyst for another's demise anymore.

Of course, with this instance as an exception.

Tommy remained collected, fixating on Harmony.

"I was not threatening you…but just so we are clear here, I am now," he began. "From this point on, whatever you believe, you will keep it to yourself and never tell anyone—" he slowly approached her, keeping a safe distance. "Do not challenge me."

His chilling tone alarmed Harmony. She gulped, controlling her fear from who was once one of her closest friends. She turned to Jack.

"Do you have anything to say?"

Jack scanned both their expressions. He did not agree with Tommy's approach, but it was already said and done. And he was not prepared to go against him. Not now.

"What happened, happened Harmony," Jack finally said. "We never had this conversation, and as long as you respect that, everything will be fine."

His heart sank at the sight of tears filling her eyes. He could tell she felt endangered, and while he would never hurt her, at the same time, he had no control over Tommy's actions.

Harmony wept and stormed away, briefly stopping at the door to turn to them one last time.

"I will never forgive either of you, and I will never speak to either of you ever again."

The boys remained silent after she left.

It would be the last time Jack seen or spoke to Harmony. He would wish her well, and hoped that one day they could reconnect under better circumstances. As Tommy once stated, there are consequences to our actions. Consequences that, unfortunately, are irreversible and can only be accepted.

xxxvi

"You have a week to consider the offer," Wayne said, sliding the paper across the desk. "But I wanted to make sure you have a physical copy in addition to the one HR should have sent you this morning."

"It's no problem at all," Hunter relayed, skimming through the document and signing his name on the dotted line. "I've never been a fan of such formalities."

Wayne smirked. "I believe we can all agree on that part."

By everyone, Wayne was referring to Jack and Tommy standing behind him, both of whom flashed Hunter respectful nods.

"That said, I hope your swift review of legalese does not lead to any errors once the work actually begins," Tommy added teasingly.

Hunter handed the letter back to Wayne and looked to Tommy.

"That's why I'll have you, right?"

They all laughed. Except Jack.

"Welcome aboard," Wayne congratulated, shaking Hunter's hand. "We'll send you the details on travel and your first day. In the meantime, take a deep breath, enjoy this moment, and best of luck when you get to D.C."

Jack took the liberty to escort Hunter toward the exit.

"You must be relieved," Jack remarked when they left the building.

"I am," Hunter signed agreeably. "Though, it was all worth the wait though. My parents were already upset when I told them I didn't want to stay in New York and take over the business, so I'm pumped to actually know I'll be taken care of."

"As are we," Jack tapped his watch, figuring it was a polite way to signal he did not want to engage anymore. "Anyway, I'm taking off early. I know you have that meeting with IT in a bit. Let me know if you have questions about their presentation."

"I appreciate it. You're coming to the Blue Mud Tavern, right?"

"Blue *Moon*," Jack corrected. Ever since he was of age, it was a popular spot for Jack and his friends whenever they wanted post-work beverages. The place and its memories meant a lot to him, so the idea of an outsider casually mistaking the name was mildly annoying.

Hunter had been pleasant since his arrival, but now with his departure near, Jack's attempt in faking the nice guy act was dwindling quickly. Certainly his relationship with Emma was the start, but there had been so much change he did not want to accept. Isaac and Logan were gone. A married Bennett was busier now; Kevin was taking his sabbatical; and his best friend Tommy was moving. Which surely, given the fact he will be working closely with Hunter, caused Jack to worry if he would be eventually forgotten. The remaining facets he clung onto were not enough for him to tolerate, let alone accept. He admittedly dreaded this day, and was still unable to face the potential of his new reality. Alone, and forced to embark independently.

"Of course, wouldn't miss it," Jack replied apathetically. "I have to go up to my parents' for some things, so I may be a little late."

"On Mercer Island?"

"Yeah, how did you know that?"

"Emma gave me the whole rundown of all of her friends. She said you all grew up within a two-mile radius of each other."

Jack nodded blankly. "It's strange how accurate that is."

"This is a perfect coincidence! I have a huge favor to ask—" Hunter went on., producing his phone. "Emma ordered a cake for the party tonight, and we put down her mother's address for the delivery. Some stuff came up for her job and she can't pick it up, and because of this meeting, I won't have time to get it myself. Could you swing by and grab it while you're out there?"

Jack hesitated. "Can't you call them and change the address?"

Hunter shook his head helplessly.

"Bakery closed when I tried calling over lunch," he explained, now pleading. "Please Jack, I don't care much for cake, but I'm sure you know her better than I do. She'll be disappointed to know that everything didn't come together after all the effort she put in to make it happen."

In Jack's opinion, asking the ex of one's girlfriend to do something for the sake of said girlfriend was a bold move. But he could not deny the ingenuity in Hunter's tone. This request was not a power move: it was a respectful, and arguably desperate ask to someone he was eager to build a friendship with. Above all, the fact that it directly involved Emma's feelings was more than enough to persuade Jack to help.

Jack forced a smile. "Yeah, I'll grab it for you."

"Thank you! Again, I really appreciate this man," Hunter thanked him, checking his watch. "I should get back to it, but I'll text you her address before you head up there."

"No need, I know where it is," Jack politely dismissed. "Childhood friends, you know?"

"Right," Hunter chuckled. "See you tonight!"

It was not uncommon for Anita to be home whenever Jack bid a visit. Especially since the start of the new decade, she preferred to shield herself from any chance of infection. Jack simultaneously found it necessary to frequent trips to see his mother (not so much his father, as he interacted him almost daily), as he knew how easy it became with increased responsibilities in life and work to excuse himself from dedicating time to things he cared most about.

Anita overheard Jack enter the home later that afternoon, emerging from the top of the staircase to see him shuffling through his on the coffee table.

"Hi honey, why didn't you call?" she greeted, making her way downstairs.

"Hey Mom," Jack greeted, holding up his mail. "I can't stay for long. I just dropped by for this."

"You should always have enough time for your mother," Anita reminded, hugging him. "How are you?"

"Good. Dad's been keeping me busy," he said dully. "But it's been good."

Anita frowned at her son's fixed expression.

"Just 'good?' Are you sure everything is fine?" she placed her son's hand on hers, revealing her wedding ring. "How is my beautiful Molly? Have you been thinking about putting one of these on her finger anytime soon?"

"Whoa Mom, take it easy. There's no rush for that."

"I'm not saying there is, but at the same time, I would love to finally be able to take care of your kids when you two are off working."

"You're talking about *kids* now? I still have a little more growing up to do."

Anita chuckled and shook her head.

"I knew we should've had another child," she teased. "Only increases my chance of having grandchildren."

"You'll get your grandkids. The day will come don't worry," Jack soothed comically. "You haven't been talking to Mols behind my back about this, right?"

"Of course not!" Anita winked. "But if I was, could you blame me?"

"I guess not," Jack admitted. "She's great, though. We had a bit of a thing a couple weeks ago when we were at Bennett's wedding, ironically, but it wasn't about getting married." He paused. "It wasn't even a 'thing.' Sorry, I don't know why I phrased it that way."

"What was it about?"

"Emma," he admitted, feeling the urge to suddenly rush his words. "She's been back for a bit before she goes off to Washington, D.C…I'm actually going to see her later at a party tonight."

"That's wonderful, good for her. Why is she going to D.C.?"

"Her boyfriend," Jack added. "He's working with us now. Well, with Tommy."

"Ah, I keep forgetting Tommy's moving. This is starting to make sense now."

"What makes sense?"

"Well, we both know how much you liked Emma," Anita stated. "I'm sure there may still be some residual feelings for her, and I can only imagine how Molly reacted to that."

Jack shrugged, not denying the truth in his mother's diagnosis.

"She has a boyfriend, and I have Molly. That's just the way it has to be."

At that, Anita shook her head in disagreement and gestured to the sofa.

"Sit down, Jack."

Jack reluctantly obeyed.

"I know you have to go, so I'll be quick: as your mother, you know that I will always do everything I can to see you happy. And part of my job as your mother, is making sure you understand what I am about to say:"

Jack nodded as Anita continued.

"Your Dad and I did not teach you to accept things not working out your way if they are in your control. If you still like Emma, you should tell her."

"I love you Mom, but that's insane," Jack said, almost smirking at how astonishing his mother's advice was. "It's been years since we were *anything*, and I'm still having to deal with the fact that what we did have was not that serious, to begin with."

"You shouldn't care how your relationship with her was perceived," she corrected, placing her finger on his chest. "What matters is how it was perceived by *you*. I love Molly and think she is terrific for you. But your reason for being with her should not be because you were not able to be with the girl you initially wanted. If it is, then fine, it's your life. But your father has always told you to explore all your choices before making a decision – in this case, it includes you telling Emma how you still feel about her. After that, and *only* after that, when you know the full scope of your situation, then you should reflect and move on from there."

"You're right," Jack relented. "I just don't know how I should go about that."

"That's for you to figure out," Anita said. "But you have us and your friends to help get you through this," she smiled. "And everything else, for that matter."

Jack stood up and hugged Anita. He did not think it at first, but it was exactly what he needed to hear then.

He left his mother and drove to the Keva household, slow to approach the door when it opened before he could knock.

"Hey Mrs. Keva. Not sure if you remember me: I'm Jack—"

"Douglas, of course I remember you! Look at you, all grown up," she waved him inside. "I have to say, I think it is *hilarious* that you lied about who you were the first time you came over."

"What—" Jack stopped himself, as he completely forgot the stunt he pulled back when he and Tommy stopped over to pick up Emma and Morgan all that time ago.

"I wasn't thinking clearly then, and it was a challenge to find your face off a Google search," she continued. "It's okay dear, Emma explained why you did it."

"Yeah, I'm sorry about that," Jack muttered. "I regret doing that for as long as I did."

"It's all in the past, don't worry about it," she tapped his shoulder. "Hunter told me you would be stopping by for the cake. I have it in the fridge."

Jack followed her through the entryway, instantly glossing over the multiple frames hanging on the wall to his left. One picture caught his attention: Emma in a maroon gown holding a diploma, centered between Hunter and two adults, to which he reckoned were his parents.

"She sent me that when she graduated," he heard Julia say.

"You didn't fly out there for it?"

Julia shrugged.

"She didn't tell me."

They continued to the kitchen, where the potent scent of the brewing tea made him let out an unconscious sigh.

"Would you like some?" she asked, noting his fatigued posture as he leaned on the counter.

"Yes please," Jack replied politely. "Thank you."

Emma's mother poured tea into a mug and handed it to Jack, his muscles relaxing as he lightly sipped.

"What have you been up to all these years?" she asked as she grabbed the cake from inside the fridge.

"Not much. I finished school and have been working for my dad," he paused. "Hunter is working with us, as I'm sure you know."

"I figured that was the case," she giggled, gesturing to the cake between them. "We didn't get too into it when they stopped here a couple weeks ago, but I got to meet Hunter." She paused, almost like she had not formulated a conclusion on her feelings toward him until that moment. "Have you been in touch with them?"

While he did not show it, Jack thought it was an awkward question. It sounded a bit more investigative than curious. They may have lived in the same neighborhood, but Jack's interactions with her were brief – and short-lived – when he was dating Emma a half-decade ago. He recalled the few times Emma would actually reveal the details of her relationship with her mother. One piece he did vividly recall, interestingly enough, was Emma's resentment toward her when she was much younger. He knew that her father's passing also contributed to the strained dynamic in the house. And based on the lack of information Julia knew about Emma's current situation, he assumed the dynamic remained unchanged.

"I haven't been in touch with Emma for a long time," Jack relayed, hoping his remark would sooth Julia's disappointment. "Emma and I didn't have the most positive breakup, as I'm sure you know. If I'm being real here, I think the only reason we're communicating again is because Hunter is working for my dad."

Julia gave a helpless smirk.

"Actually, before they visited, I was under the impression that you two were still together."

"Did she not tell you?"

"She doesn't tell me anything, frankly."

Julia's willingness to be as transparent as she was in that moment was somewhat odd for Jack. It was growing more obvious that she had been waiting for an opportunity to vent, and while he was unwilling to get too deep into it, Jack recognized the feeling all too well to refuse being there for someone in distress.

"It's not my business – and I know I just said that I haven't spoken to Emma in years prior to recently – but between you and me, I know that Emma really loves you," Jack affirmed.

Julia giggled.

"Jack, you're a sweet boy and I know what you are trying to do. I am aware of how…poorly…I treated Emma. I called her every day after she left again to New York, and I know why she never answered. It took me a long time to realize, but I know that I was living my life through her, and not once gave her an opportunity to chase her own dreams."

"I'm sorry…"

"No, it's okay," Julia waved off. "I'm sure you know about how she lost her dad – my husband – when she was younger. It has been different ever since. I didn't cope well, and I took it out on her," a tear left her eye. "It sucks, but it is something I have to live with."

He was reluctant to engage further, but felt his lips move before he could stop himself.

"Bruce, right? She always kept much of it to herself. I figured I'd just give her time until she was ready, but the opportunity never came."

Julia nodded. "We moved here from the city. My husband oversaw Investigations for the SPD. He was loved by everybody, always did the right thing and by far and away the humblest man I've ever known. Emma was closer to him than to me growing up, and he was the sole reason we came here."

"Totally okay if you do not want to, but may I ask how?"

"He got swept up in the politics of his job…he never told me all the details, but I'm sure he did it to protect us."

"I'm sure you're right," Jack agreed. "And again, it's not my business, but as someone from her generation, I can tell you firsthand that whatever you two went through, she will forgive you, and still love you," Jack reiterated. "You know how we can be when we're kids. We think we know what is best for us and it takes time to grow up and realize that everything that our parents have done for us was for the better."
"She is free to live her life however she wants," Julia stated. "Even if that means never rebuilding something with me, I will always be proud of her."
At that, Jack's brows furrowed.
"She's your daughter, and essentially a grown woman. and she doesn't even have the maturity to make up with you. How can you be proud of that?"
"Because she found herself, on her own," Julia clarified. "And, embarrassingly it was something I could never do. I wasn't strong enough."
Jack's thoughts were swirling on the drive back into the city. Two interactions, although distinct in theme, consistent in their degree of wisdom. Mothers know best, including when they did not all along.
Listening to the message was easy; the issue for Jack was knowing how to apply it in his particular situation. Jack had long accepted his knack for hopeless romanticism. After all, there was a time that he was prepared to do just about anything for Emma. He could have dropped out of school, and she was more than enough to keep him enlightened. He would throw away his material fortune, knowing that she was all he needed to feel worthy. He would go as far to sacrifice his own life, because she was his purpose for being alive. *There was a time*, Jack thought. The reality, however, was whether that time had truly faded, or appears to be faded as a result of his suppression on the probability of it never happening.
There was only one way he could find out for himself.

*****

Jack was the last to arrive that night, hearing the party already underway from the parking lot. Molly gave him last-minute notice that she would not attend, leaving him to dedicate he better half of the evening piecing his approach to Emma, visualizing it as a climactic moment where he would finally get closure on his desire to be with her. And by closure, he meant a successful acquisition.
He entered the Blue Moon, immediately spotting Emma and Hunter in the center entertaining their guests.
She met his eyes and rushed up in excitement.
"Jack! You're literally my hero," she greeted.

He was initially perplexed by her introduction, but then watched her look
down at the cake he forgot was cradled in his palms.
"Sorry I'm late," he apologized, suppressing the urge to bring up his
conversation with Anita. Or Julia, for that matter.
Hunter joined Emma, flashing a wide smile at Jack.
"Thanks again for this man," he said, taking the cake. "We have shots waiting
for you!"
Jack joined them, eager to see that his boys were also waiting around the table
as they all overlooked a few platters of glasses.
"Took you long enough," Zoe remarked when Jack shouldered beside her and
Tommy.
Jack exchanged a stunned look at Tommy.
"I told you we're the same person," Tommy joked.
Jack took a shot with the group. One after the next, with brief interactions
with the next person he had to reconnect with. Time passed, and each time he
choked down another shot, he would notice Emma in his purview. Each time,
he hoped that she would be the next one he would speak to; but as the drinks
frequented, so did the temptation to approach her. *Okay, come on,* Jack
thought. *How am I going to do this?*
As if the universe heard him, Emma walked right up to him.
"Hey, do you have a minute?" she asked.
Jack's eyes widened. He glanced over her shoulder to see his boys waving for
him to come over at him. He signaled them to wait as he refocused on Emma.
"Yeah, absolutely."
They retreated away from the endless holler and fracas, and situated
themselves on the curb directly in front of the bar. He was delighted to be
alone with her again. Just her presence was enough for him to reminisce their
time together all those years ago. It was if she never left.
He remained silent as he watched her take a deep breath, seeming to collect
herself as she turned to face him.
"I know we haven't had a lot of time to catch up since I came back here…"
"We had lunch," Jack uttered, feeling dumb for interrupting. "Sorry, yes I
agree."
"Yes, thank you again for that!" she grinned, returning to a serious expression
as she continued. "Anyway, since I'm moving again I just felt that not would
be a perfect chance for us to reset, you know?"
This is it, Jack thought, astonished that he did not need to do anything for this
moment as he mentally prepared himself to hear the words he had longed for.
"I just want to apologize for everything," she said sincerely. "And I hope that
me being here with Hunter isn't awkward for you."
"Why would it be awkward?"

"Well, I know that we haven't been in touch for a few years since we broke up. And – speaking for myself – felt a little weird when I met Molly," she explained. "Where is she, by the way? I wanted to hang with her more."
"Couldn't make it. She didn't give me a reason either," Jack chuckled. "She does that sometimes."
"She seems great. I'm happy for you."
Jack tilted his head, slightly annoyed by the direction Emma was taking in the conversation. Nevertheless, he went along with it.
"Are you excited to move to D.C.?"
"Not really. It all happened pretty quickly," Emma admitted. "Hunter was originally planning on work for his parents – that's a whole other story – but when he found this job, we didn't have a lot of time to talk about it. We sort of just went with it. Carpe diem, right?"
"Would you have wanted to stay in New York?"
Emma pondered the question.
"If I'm being honest, I would have come back here," she revealed. "I didn't realize how much I missed Seattle. Looking back on it, I think I just wanted to explore the possibility of living my life someplace else. But after doing that, I don't know…it just makes me miss home and my friends," she met his eyes.
"You know what I mean?"
"So that's why you went to New York in the first place?"
"I mean, there were many reasons," Emma shrugged "We certainly discussed that at length."
Jack squinted at her nonchalant handling of his tone.
"Was I one of those reasons?"
"What do you mean?" she asked confusingly.
"Not trying to dredge up the past," Jack began. "But from what I understand, you left for New York when we were dating. You waited to tell me, and then left. And now you're dating Hunter – which is fine – but when he asks to move, you didn't fight it or do what you wanted," Jack paused, finding his words. "I guess I'm confused as to why you made an exception for him but not for me when I asked you to stay, especially since this is where you wanted to be."
"Well, it was different back then Jack," Emma explained. "For one, I wouldn't have even known Seattle is where I wanted to end up if I didn't first leave for New York. Does that make sense?"
"But in doing so, you told me that we couldn't be together."
"Sorry, but I don't see how that's relevant," Emma politely disagreed. "I went to New York for work."
"I get that Em, but you can't deny that by leaving, I had to force myself to move on. And while you ghosted me while you were there, you find someone

else and are clearly more willing to do whatever he wants. All I'm asking is whether I was also a reason as to why you left. I think you owe me that explanation."

"Jack, I already told you. I didn't—"

"If that's the case, then please make me understand!" Jack interrupted, a bit louder this time. "You said you didn't want a relationship, and then you come back here with *him*. How do you think that is supposed to make me feel?"

Emma paused and took another deep breath.

"Are we just unable to be happy for each other, Jack?"

Wanting the best for someone who was unwilling to consider the feelings of others? Jack believed such concept to be anomalous.

The liquor took over Jack in that moment. He abruptly leaned in, pressing his lips against Emma's. He missed the sensation, sharing his breath with hers. It felt like home.

He jolted backwards, realizing that Emma had pushed him away.

"Jack! What are you doing?"

"I'm sorry," Jack froze, immediately embarrassed. "I didn't mean to, I just—"

"

"I'm with Hunter. And *you're* with Molly. You can't be doing that."

"You're right, I'm sorry," Jack pleaded.

Emma ran her hands through her hair, exasperated. "Look, I care about you a lot. And I want you to still be in my life. But it can't be like that. Not anymore…"

She turned away from him, placing her hand on her lips as she started back for the back.

"You still mean a lot to me," she added. "If anything, I have you to thank for everything that has happened to me all these years. I grew so much. I learned a lot about myself, including what is right for me. I will never forget what you did for me…"

She proceeded back to the bar, resting her hand on the handle to recollect herself.

Jack was ashamed. He had never acted so irrationally. He just wanted to show how much she still meant to him. He jumped to his feet.

"Why do we have to do this though? Who cares that we're both in relationships? Why does that have to stop us from being together? Because it clearly didn't when you starting talking to Hunter."

"So now you're asking me to cheat?" Emma released her hand from the door handle, facing him. "The same way you did to me?"

"That's not what I'm saying," he scoffed. "And that's not exactly true."

Emma rolled her eyes.

"My dad told me that the only way a person is capable of loving others is by deciding to love themselves first. Do you understand why that is the case?" Jack did not answer, sensing the rhetoric in her question.

"My dad also always said that cheaters are the dumbest, smart people," she added. "He believed an honest person was disciplined; that they loved themselves so much that they did not need the approval of others. Many think that people cheat for their own benefit, but the reality is that they do it because they are afraid of what others will think of them if they fail."

"What are you implying?"

"I don't know how I could make it any clearer," Emma said. "Come on Jack, let's be honest. We never really knew each other to begin with."

"I don't know how you can say that," he said. "I fall in love with you every time I see you."

"Please Jack, you sound like you're living out of a movie. If that was really the case, we wouldn't be in this situation right now."

"You were the one who left me," Jack tested, upset with Emma's dismissive tone. "That was your choice."

"It's been four years, Jack." Emma reasoned. "A lot has changed since then. We've both changed."

"Right, right," Jack chided, angry that her repetitive remarks. "We certainly did change, didn't we? Seems like you really figured out what you wanted, huh?"

"What did you expect me to do, Jack? Put my whole love life on hold for you? What did you expect me to do?"

"I tried doing that for you!"

"I didn't ask you to!"

"I loved you Emma!" Jack screamed. "And I still do! I did everything in my power to get over you – and you're acting like it all never happened."

"That's enough Jack! I'm tired of having to go through the same drama with you. It never ends."

"You have no idea what I've been through these last few years."

"I don't want to know. You clearly have a lot on your mind, and think that dragging me into your problems will help you get over it. You can't keep doing it anymore. I'm sorry."

Emma shook her head and turned away, holding back the tears building up in her glossy eyes.

Jack retracted, carefully tracing his words. He lowered his head, falling victim to his mind tracing through all his rotting pains. Emma. Isaac. Logan. He had been through so much loss. He had spent so long bottling his past, all of which he could not help but blame himself for.

He went back inside the bar, where through the crowd, he could see Emma speaking to Hunter. He could not make out what she was saying, but from observing her hysterical demeanor, assumed that she was relaying everything that had just happened to Logan. Per his assumption, Hunter suddenly glanced at Jack, promptly storming towards him.

Jack froze, fearing the worst as Hunter neared him.

"What the hell is going on, Jack?" he howled, getting in his face.

"I need to talk to Emma," Jack said.

"You'll be talking to me!"

Jack peeked past Hunter's grimace, meeting Emma's eyes as she speculated from a distance.

"This isn't worth my time," Jack uttered brashly.

Jack tried slipping past, only to be crossed by Hunter, who immediately brought his hand up to Jack's chest. He took hold of Jack's shirt collar and shoved him. Jack stumbled back, digging his fingers between Hunter's tight hold as he was pinned to the wall behind him.

"Chill man," Jack eased, trying to keep his cool.

"Don't tell me to chill, you little shit," Hunter hissed. "You kissed my girlfriend! Where do you get off?"

"I can explain," Jack pleaded, peering over Hunter's shoulder at Emma now rushing up to them.

"Hunter!" she cried out, closing in behind him. "Stop this before someone gets hurt."

"Let me handle this Em.

"You're not thinking straight," she continued, refusing to look at Jack as she focused intently on Hunter. "Let's just get out of here."

Jack winced as Hunter pressed him firmer into the wall, overhearing the paneled wood behind him subtly cracking against his body.

"You obviously don't know who I am," Jack said, smirking to save face. "If you were smart, you'd listen to her."

Hunter pressed his arm harder against Jack's throat, leading him to choke for the air fleeting quickly from his mouth.

Jack finally had enough of Hunter. He jammed his knee into Hunter's gut, breaking away from his hold as he watched him stagger back before folding over a table. Jack disregarded the deafening crash of the clattering utensils on the hardwood, lunging swiftly onto him, one hand on his chest to pin him down, while he used the other to violently strike. Hunter was only down for a moment, and quick to demonstrate his superior physical strength as he pushed Jack off of him and kicked at his ribs. Jack rolled to Hunter's other side, reaching for a knife that had fallen of the table and rising to his feet in a readied stance.

Hunter flinched at the knife in Jack's hand, causing him to remain on the floor has Jack slowly neared him.

"You plan on using that?" Hunter tested.

Jack glared down on him, squeezing his tight clench around the knife. Hunter may have thought he called his bluff. Unbeknownst to him, Jack was not in his usual headspace that would prompt him to react civilly. He was angry. More than angry. He was furious.

Jack hovered over Hunter, secretly finding pleasure at the sound of his weak whimpers. His satisfaction was instantly replace with regret when Emma suddenly appeared in his gaze, kneeling beside Hunter and holding his head up as she lightly spoke to him.

"Emma," Jack tried, his voice diminishing to a whisper.

He watched Emma's head lift slowly, tears trickling down her face.

"I don't know who you are anymore."

Jack swallowed hard, letting her words sink and wrestling his own sanity as he fled out the bar.

Tommy was close behind when he saw Jack plopped on the curb outside. His face was buried in his hands, and his rage was apparent through coarse breaths.

"Well, you got your closure Jack. Are you happy?"

Jack remained silent, causing Tommy to shake his head and crouch beside him. He believed he understood Jack at an intimate level. Closure signals the finalization of the reading, but Jack's habit of putting the book down without permitting an analytical assessment of the passage was his own demise. It was not a pretty sight, and one Tommy was more than familiar with. Such a degree of emotional instability proved more harmful for oneself than others, and it terrified Tommy that Jack had yet to realize who was truly responsible for the self-affliction.

And for the first time, Tommy's patience with Jack had neared its breaking point.

"Something was different about you when you came back from London. I saw it in your eyes," Tommy began. "You were enlightened, like you had an epiphany of some kind, about what was important to you."

Still no response.

"Look, I've said it before man and I'll say it again: sometimes there are things in life that leaves us misunderstood. And sometimes, it's better if they stay that way."

At that, Jack raised his head and met Tommy's eyes.

"You really think so?"

"I do."

Jack shook his head disdainfully. "So what about you?"

"Excuse me?"

"Why must it stay misunderstood? What is your motive in all this?"

Tommy's face scrunched. "I don't understand—"

"You've been here through all of it, always saying I should keep trying to get Emma, and then saying I should give up on her…but why? So you can have her for yourself? Is that your angle?"

"Dude, I'm dating Zoe. I didn't think I had to say this, but my heart has been with her since before you met Emma," Tommy relented. "My angle is that you are my best friend. My *brother*. I would do anything for you." He rose to his feet. "As a matter of fact, I *have* done everything for you. When I saw you ruining your future, I stepped in and helped you solve every one of your problems. And even as you continue to fuck things up for yourself, I stay by your side. That's what friends do."

"See, you say you will always have my back, and that everything you've done was for me, but you've only made my life worse," Jack tested. "After everything with Logan, you expect me to trust your intentions are as pure as you say?"

"I never said my intentions were pure, nor that I don't make mistakes. Besides, I already explained to you why—"

"Saac is fucking dead because of you!"

Tommy fell silent at the feeling of his blood boiling as he glowered down at him.

"You know, I always hoped you would change," Tommy spoke slowly, his frown hardening. "But all I see is a troubled piece of shit who has dug himself deeper in a hold he may never get out of."

"Fuck you Tommy."

Yeah," Tommy scoffed, pacing toward the lot. "Fuck me."

He stopped after a few steps. "No," he muttered, turning back to Jack. "I'm not going to let it end like this."

Jack was caught by surprise by Tommy grabbed his arms and pulled him to his feet.

"I'm done with being the sympathetic nice guy, Jack."

Jack flinched as his face connected with Tommy's face, instinctively throwing his hands up and clutching his friend's shoulders as he pulled him back into the ground. Tommy maintained his stance before crippling over the hidden curb, grunting in pain and slamming Jack into the sidewalk before scrambling away. He saw Jack was not done, bracing for his tackle, shoving him back, and throwing another fist squarely at Jack's nose.

Jack yelped angrily, suppressing the ache as he kicked his feet off the ground and hurled his weight on Tommy again, this time missing him entirely and rolling on the street.

"Are you kidding me?" Tommy shouted as he hovered over him. "I'm fucking done Jack!"

Jack remained face down on the pavement and controlled his breath. He overhead Tommy's footsteps receding in the distance before sitting up and cursing himself. Defeated, he sluggishly carried himself back to his car and drove away, praying the space away would heal his regrets.

Molly entered the apartment later that night when she saw Jack's silhouette on the balcony. She slid the door open and watched in silence as he kept his focus toward the city lights.

"Jack?" she called, wrapping her arm around his shoulder. "I just got off the phone with Zoe. She told me what happened tonight," she said gently. "Do you want to talk about it?"

Jack did not respond. Instead, he fell into her lap and begun to weep. His cries intensified with every breath, to the point when Molly required both hands to control him. She ran her hand over his head, patient for him to calm down. Eventually, Jack would, as she understood this was not a matter to justify or defend. It was an opportunity to acknowledge his wrongdoing, and hope for forgiveness.

Regardless of whether it happened, Jack knew only Time will tell. Until then, all he could do was exercise patience the way he knew best: a break from reality.

*****

It was a quiet drive into the Washington wilderness.
She was not used to long periods of silence, yet Molly knew there was much
for Jack to process. She recalled the multiple stories Jack had narrated of his
time at this cabin. Sometimes with family, or friends, but largely on his own.
It was his preferred destination for contemplation. The best way he could sort
through the mud and return with a clearer outlook on whatever issue troubled
him at the time. As such, she knew his reluctance to talk was not out of
indifference, but necessity for his own growth.
A melodious sequence of cheeps trilled Jack's ears when they left the car,
causing him to stare intently at the mountains in the distance. Molly was
grabbing their bags out of the trunk when she caught him in limbo, smirking
lightly and observing his still posture before reaching forward to wrap her
arms around his waist.
"Go on, I can take care of this," she offered. "I'll stay awake until you get
back."
Jack kissed her and started toward a path beyond the estate. It was not long
before he began to reminisce about a beauty he would never grow tired of.
Including the single instance when he and Tommy feared for their lives, there
still existed a limitless wonder between the trees; the same trees that watched
him age each time he passed on the way to his destination.
As he anticipated, the forest eventually opened up, clearing way to the
seemingly endless valley. He paused, briefly, admiring the moon overhead as
it casted on the eternally snow-capped mountains below. Even from where he
stood, Jack noticed the subtle glimmer of the recent snowfall, blanketing
virtually every inch of the treetops; except for the valley, which had melted
prior to his arrival. It was a spectacular sight. So peaceful, and enchanting.
Jack took a step forward. Then another, until he reached the center of the
field. He fell on his back, feeling the slight tickle of the cool grass on his bare
skin as the back of his head touched the soil beneath him. He drew his
attention to the sky, where right before his eyes, a star shot across. Within
seconds, he inhaled in utter awe as the black night was replaced with a
celestial mural of flickering lights.
The movement of an asteroid is reasonably predictable, at least initially. But
even amidst a thickening darkness, the directional path of the massively dense
rock can be affected by external forces, both gravitational and non-
gravitational, a few of which some may argue are supernatural in nature.
It is not uncommon for two asteroids to pass in orbit, which, depending on
their respective speeds, could be quicker than the blink of the human eye.
There is a heap of technology supporting the illustration of this phenomenon,

yet, there are still instances where what was forecasted initially, ends up falling short of expectation.

So imagine rationalizing the reason that a pair of lovers, who, despite experiencing an unprecedented obstruction that thwarts them away from one another, floating in space, still compelled to believe they are ultimately bound to reunite at a later time. Is it an argument based out of logic, or hope? Is there even a difference?

Guess Shakespeare was right when he described Romeo and Juliet's love as star-crossed.

Jack always knew love was more than an emotion, reasoning that it had to be expressed through his actions. He accepted love as putting Emma's wellbeing before his; overwhelming the negative aspects with deluded justifications to remain by her side; drawing it back in when he began to feel it flee; overcoming the disappointment with desire; minding the gaps in a puzzle and filling it with his own pieces, not caring if they fit in the end; whipping out favors at the expense of his ego, because a display of affection seemed more important; crashing and burning, yet emerging from the flames dust-free; disregarding the imperfections of a seemingly perfect being, shifting his own understanding of what is right and wrong into what *should* be right and wrong according to her welfare; succeeding the highs, mediums, and lows, and surrendering his relevance for her; losing his way and never risking an attempt for self-love, because at the moment, a sliver of admiration blinded his urge to find himself once again; throwing out all the rules, because he learned love to be unobstructed. And if it is indeed supposed to be unobstructed, then it would be wrong to impose restrictions, because it risked negative repercussions, impacts of which he feared were unprecedented.

Regardless of how hard he tried, nothing would change. Regardless of how much he pushed, it remained grounded in its own kind, and there was no sort like it. Regardless of what he did, it did not matter. And if none of his attempts in love mattered, then love did not matter, either.

And in his period of Jack's intense contemplation, she appeared: the woman who would steal his 'I love yous' from the rest of the world, forever.

It was then that Jack finally understood; a vision so clarifying as it swept through his psyche. It was so pronounced, so definitive, and for the first time in his life he was able to see beyond his own denial. Through a multitude of trials with girls, it always seemed to be the subjective differences that colluded with his perception, rather the objective reality that he subliminally acknowledged, but refused to accept. It was never a matter of whether it felt right or wrong because of her, but why he already knew that it was not right, in which case the ultimate problem revolving around his own insecurity. His father was right; Tommy B was right; Emma was right. His entire life, Jack leaned on money as his recourse, believing anything was acquirable through it. The argument was apparent, but the truth – contrarian to his understanding – could be identified from his own experience.

Through the exchange of flimsy greens, he discovered happiness; he bargained for time; he sought for purpose; improved his health; created friendships; inspired confidence; formulated trust and loyalty; brewed positivity; earned respect; avoided pain; revealed truths; infused wisdom. Love however, well love was different.

Because alas, he finally concluded that being in love has nothing to do with justifying his own concerns on how *he* feels, or how *she* feels, but how *they* feel. It was a mutual partnership, equal in its existence and intentions. There was no ownership, and it was effortless. Love should not be confined, but boundless. And if it is boundless, then all that is accompanied should also be – its absurdity, intricacy, instability, linked with its naturality, pleasure, and brilliance – all part of a continuous cycle of trial and error, mutual exchanges, venturing down a road always ventured, and impossibly eternal.

The English dictionary was invented with the objective to define words, but even the dictionary lacks clarity on aspects beyond the language, including experiences. For Jack, it was impossible to choose a term to define Emma. Rational or irrational; it was semantical at the presence of the absolute truth. Achieving perfection is theoretically impossible, but she was the closest thing to perfection. And someone closest to perfection is unable to understand what it means to be far from it. Jack believed it had nothing to do with timing, circumstances, or excuses. It simply came down to love, and the ability to love unconditionally. Because when it is unconditional, it is timeless, and free of any restriction. Cognitive, emotional, passionate, courageous, wonderful. And most importantly, sustainable. An unshaken permanence.

In that moment, Jack accepted his own limitations to compromise; that his decisions based on intense fascination had corrupted his perception.

He will never find someone like her because there was truly no one like her. Opinionated, likely so, but it did not matter to him as long as he knew it, and surely it will be so, and there was nothing he could do to change it.

She deserved everything, including freedom from burden. She is the best thing to have happened to Jack, because she is the best thing to have happened, ever. She is his reason to live, even if she was not with him. She was his soulmate, even if he was not.

Jack smiled, closing his eyes and awaiting Sleep to reaccompany him one last time.

Time did not end; it simply passed. He had no knowledge of how long, only that when he had reopened his eyes, he was staring head on at a jaw the size of his head. The musty scent of the creature's breath huffed into his nose. He felt the urge to scream, but he did not. Instead, he embraced the bear's presence, his breath powerlessly calm, and controlled. It was oddly comforting: two animals, alone in nature, having no inclination of surrendering to instinct.

As quickly as Jack could comprehend the potential danger in his situation, the bear lifted its head and turned away. He sat up and watched it saunter back toward the woods, squinting to make out a litter of cubs following close behind.

I understand, Jack thought, rising to his feet and making his way back to the cabin.

Molly was nearly asleep when Jack entered the bedroom later that night. She pulled the blanket up for him to join her in bed. "Feeling better?" she asked.

Jack placed his hands on Molly's face and brought her close.

"I love you."

Molly smiled and kissed him.

"It's about time."

They chuckled and kissed again more intimately. Before they both knew it, passion took course, leaving Jack to imagine the consequences of his decisions that night.

Only this time, he knew it would not be a repercussion. It would be a blessing. Jack was no longer afraid of his shield shattering. No longer did he question the thoughts in his head.

Because truly, he believed he found the oasis to his desert; the light to his shadow; the cure to his cancer; the blessing to his curse. Perfection, in its most imperfect state. She was her, and he was him.

And he loved her.

POSTLUDE

It was raining when they arrived at the restaurant. Jack instinctively took his suit jacket off and wrapped it around Molly before strolling through the parking lot. An ambrosial scent wafted through Molly when they reached the door, causing her to nearly faint in verve.

"I was looking forward to this all week!"

Jack kept the door ajar for Molly to enter, smirking privately at her choice of words. Time had passed from the last time they chose the *Crepuscolo,* but he considered it fitting for the occasion.

The host recognized Jack immediately, frisking for a couple menus and approaching them.

"Mr. Douglas, it is great to see you!" she greeted, nodding for nearby staff to grab their coats. "Your table is this way."

Jack took Molly's hand and guided her deeper into the restaurant and to their seats. He sat down, allowing his eyes to carry over men on nearby tables. It was easy to spot the first timers, with their anxious tight lips and minimal eye contact toward their partners. Their collective hope in moving past the Merge was apparent. Love was still blind to them, and it relieved Jack when he recognized the difference in his demeanor.

"Your server will be with you shortly."

Jack gave a thankful nod and focused on the menu while Molly linked her hands, trying to take her mind off the rumbling in her stomach.

"When is everyone coming?"

"The limo should have picked them up by now," he replied, checking his watch. "We can get a starter while we wait."

"No that's okay. It's not that," she muttered skittishly. "I'm just worried if I forgot something for the sitter."

"I'll be sure to tip her well when we get back. Don't worry, it will never beat our first weekend away—"

"I was just thinking about that," pouted Molly, rubbing her head.

"Mols, everything will be fine. We'll have a fun night and be home with her in no time."

Molly calmed down. "You're right, thank you. It's weird now with a baby. You know I love Lily—"

"As do I."

"Yes," she paused, grinning slightly from his remark. "But I feel guilty whenever we go out without her. That said, it is *so* nice to have a break from it all."

"I agree. Our friends are lucky for not having kids yet. They have no idea what's coming when they do."

The waiter arrived with a couple bottles of wine, pouring them into the unattended glasses, one at a time.

"Compliments from the couple over there," the waiter added.
Jack tracked the waiter's direction to his longtime colleague, Steven Dumphreys, holding up a glass with his wife, Natalia.
Jack raised his glass toward them, whispering to Molly, "I swear those people are regulars."
Molly giggled and followed his lead, holding up the glass for them to see.
"This reminds me," she began, returning to Jack. "I know we said a book club was the move, but I talked to Naylah, and she suggested we could change it a weekly movie night."
"Oh come on, we haven't even given it a try."
"I know, but Bennett thought it was a good idea too! We agreed that it would be easier to pick a movie than take time out of the week to read to a certain chapter of a book. We all just have a lot going on."
Jack gave a defeated whimper, causing Molly to laugh.
"Come on Jack, let's not pretend that you don't think it is a better idea."
"It is," he groaned. "But you know why I brought it up in the first place."
"I know, you hate reading but think it will be a positive look for Lily. I told Naylah the whole backstory."
"And what did she say?"
"Well…she said, and I quote 'If Jack wants to involve us in something he is doing for Josie, then he should also consider if it is something we all can enjoy.'"
"Damn, that sounds like her." Jack folded his arms. "Okay fine, I guess we can pick informational movies then."
"I think that is a great compromise."
"But when Naylah gets here, I'm going to have a word with her about going over my head on this matter!"
Molly shook her head endearingly, as she expected nothing less from her husband.
"*Whose* head are you going over?"
Jack looked up and saw Naylah return with an enigmatic grin.
"Naylah!" Jack gulped, so alarmed he shot out of his chair and bowed awkwardly. "It's great to see you again!"
Bennett appeared behind her and circled around the table.
"Good catch," he embraced Jack. "If only you saw her coming ten seconds before."
Jack shouldered off a laugh as he watched the rest of the party arrive. Tommy and Zoe were next. Then Kevin. At last, Hunter came into view, accompanied with the beautiful woman. Always so elegant, in her indigo-sparkled dress and diamond earrings and French braid, pacing gracefully toward the group exchanging greetings with Molly.

Jack sat down first, feeling his lips stretch across his face. Such a reunion of best friends was rare nowadays. It was a blessing to find a weekend when they can all coordinate something like this. He was blessed. Truly.

He waited until everyone finished pleasantries before addressing them.

"I appreciate you all coming," Jack started. "Before I get into it: Tommy B, would you do us the honor of giving a toast?"

"But I didn't plan for one," he countered.

"When do you ever? You shoot them off like fireworks."

Zoe nudged him. "Jack has a good point. You literally toasted on the flight here."

Tommy rolled his eyes. "Only two rows did it, though."

"We were one of those two rows," Hunter added.

"Ugh fine," Tommy rolled his eyes and reached for the merlot before him. "If everyone could please raise your glass—"

"Do we need to drink this?" Kevin cut in. "I don't know if this is keto-friendly."

Tommy looked dumbfounded. "I have so many questions."

"No Kev, you don't need to. And Tom, we *definitely* will," Jack stepped in, signaling for him to continue.

Tommy cleared his throat. "As I was saying, if everyone could please raise your glass…"

As they listened to Tommy, Jack glanced over to Emma, who was already looking back at him. Even under the dim lamps, he noticed a glimmer from Emma's ring finger. He quickly averted his gaze, almost like he saw something he should not have. There was hesitance. But for the first time, instead of bringing sorrow, it brought him joy.

And when he refocused on Emma, she gave him an endearing smile. And he smiled back.

THE END